Littleton Community Center
1950 W. Littleton Blvd.
Littleton, CO 80120
794-9216

Also by J. R. Salamanca

The Lost Country
Lilith
A Sea Change
Embarkation

SOUTHERN LIGHT

SOUTHERN
LIGHT

a novel by

J. R. Salamanca

Alfred A. Knopf   New York   1986

Author's Acknowledgment

I would like to thank
the John Simon Guggenheim Memorial Foundation,
the National Endowment for the Arts, and
the Special Research Assignment program of the
University of Maryland for the generous aid and
encouragement they have given me over the years
I have been working on this book.

THIS IS A BORZOI BOOK
PUBLISHED BY ALFRED A. KNOPF, INC.

Copyright © 1986 by J. R. Salamanca
All rights reserved under International and Pan-American Copyright
Conventions. Published in the United States by Alfred A. Knopf, Inc.,
New York, and simultaneously in Canada by Random House
of Canada Limited, Toronto. Distributed by
Random House, Inc., New York.

Grateful acknowledgment is made to
Harcourt Brace Jovanovich, Inc., and Faber and Faber Ltd.
for permission to reprint an excerpt from "Little Gidding"
by T. S. Eliot. Reprinted from *Four Quartets* by permission of
Harcourt Brace Jovanovich, Inc. Copyright 1943 by T. S. Eliot; renewed
1971 by Esme Valerie Eliot. Reprinted from *Collected Poems 1909–1962*
by T. S. Eliot by permission of Faber and Faber Ltd., London.

Library of Congress Cataloging-in-Publication Data
Salamanca, J. R.
Southern light.
I. Title.
PS3569.A458S6   1986   813'.54   85-19825
ISBN 0-394-48252-2

Manufactured in the United States of America
FIRST EDITION

For Bill and Jane McClure

"Has my friend Giovanni any disease of body or heart, that he is so inquisitive about physicians?" said the professor, with a smile. "But as for Rappaccini, it is said of him . . . that he cares infinitely more for science than for mankind. His patients are interesting to him only as subjects for some new experiment. He would sacrifice human life, his own among the rest, or whatever else was dearest to him, for the sake of adding so much as a grain of mustard seed to the great heap of his accumulated knowledge."

"Methinks he is an awful man indeed," remarked Guasconti . . . "And yet, worshipful professor, is it not a noble spirit? Are there many men capable of so spiritual a love of science? . . . I know not how dearly this physician may love his art; but surely there is one object more dear to him. He has a daughter . . ."

Nathaniel Hawthorne, "Rappaccini's Daughter"

Thou still unravished bride of quietness,
Thou foster child of silence and slow time . . .

Heard melodies are sweet, but those unheard
Are sweeter; therefore, ye soft pipes, play on;
Not to the sensual ear, but, more endeared,
Pipe to the spirit ditties of no tone . . .

Bold Lover, never, never canst thou kiss,
Though winning near the goal—yet, do not grieve;
She cannot fade, though thou hast not thy bliss,
Forever wilt thou love, and she be fair! . . .

Thou, silent form, dost tease us out of thought
As doth eternity: Cold Pastoral!
When old age shall this generation waste,
Thou shalt remain, in midst of other woe
Than ours, a friend to man, to whom thou say'st,
"Beauty is truth, truth beauty,"—that is all
Ye know on earth, and all ye need to know.

> *John Keats, "Ode on a Grecian Urn"*

SOUTHERN LIGHT

Solomons Island is a tendril of land two miles long and half a mile wide that curls with a strangely languid and voluptuous look of tension, like a finger arched in ecstasy or death, into the estuary of the Patuxent River. To someone walking early in its river meadows, that ecstatic configuration of the island is not visible, but can almost be divined from the intensity with which objects are infused by its atmosphere. Scoured by the salt wind and the sunlight, things look as they must have looked in the Cenozoic dawn, when they stood in their primal, fervid shapeliness to astound whatever witness was abroad in that morning of the world. If you look along the horizon, you can see the roofs of the nineteenth-century wooden houses serrating it like teeth, spare and bright, the tips of their white dormers bared in desire or rage or their lifelong pangs of hunger. Those of the old abandoned houses on the Point stand tottering like tombstones, mumbling their epitaphs to heaven, or with their rows of ragged chimneys groping at the sky like knuckled fingers from a pit. They are falling into ruin, their porch rails sagging under clumps of honeysuckle, their bleached clapboards burning with a gray luster, like clamshell, in the sun. They are built so close together that when one of the sheds in a backyard collapses, it falls up against the fence of the next house, and they stand staggering together for a minute—a few years or a decade—until that ravenous honeysuckle swallows them up and they tumble down in a great, blossomy mound, plangent with the moan of bees, like plainsong. There are not many of those old houses at the Point, and I don't know why they are abandoned or unoccupied, perhaps because of the winter wind that sweeps across the river from the open bay. I don't know why, but it suits me entirely; I am an old man and have become jealous of this island's treasures: its solitude, its silence, its immaculate austerity.

In the center of the island there is a slight rise in the ground, and another tooth—a decaying, solitary one—gnaws the sky: the square tower of the stone church, which was built in 1869. It is blasted by wind and light, which have weathered the fieldstone tower to the look of old bone. There are a pair of weeping willows in the churchyard, very often rapturously astream in the wind, but which, on a hot, calm day, hang there for a moment in a gust of sudden awful inanition, like the stillness between two beats of one's heart.

Up at the north end of the street—I say "the street" because there is only one street in the village, and the village occupies the island almost entirely—there is a small crab-packing plant that backs onto the harbor, where you can see the masts of the crab boats tilting above the tin roof, and a little maritime museum with a huge whitewashed ship's anchor standing askew in front of it, one of the great tines sunken into the grass of the front yard. Then there are a couple of marine supply stores and a restaurant whose back doors open onto a planked deck above the harbor water so that people from the marina can moor their boats to the pilings and step directly into the big wire-screened back dining room. I eat there occasionally in the fall and spring, when it is not so crowded with summer people and the weather is cool. It's a fine place to sit on a September evening with a mess of crabs and a bottle of wine in front of you and watch the slick swollen sides of the harbor waves catch the red light from the western sun, and the white fishing boats nodding at their lines when a yacht glides through, and the gulls sweeping and mewling around the sandbar at the harbor mouth. If you are lucky you'll see the osprey coming home to roost in her stickly nest on top of the steel tower that supports the channel light. When it starts to get dark a girl named Dolly with eyes as big as marigolds comes and lights the brass storm lanterns on the tables. You can see the beacon start to blink out at Plum Point and the lights come on in the bait shanties along the shore and the red and green running lights from the last fishing boats coming in from the bay with their motors throbbing in the dusk.

There used to be an oyster-canning plant here, years ago, but it didn't survive the Depression; all that's left of it now are half a dozen rotting stumps of pilings that sway back and forth among the marsh grass at the north end of the harbor when the boats go by. Boys tie up to them sometimes to net for peeler crabs among the rushes. They sit there in the sun in battered rowboats and you hear the handles of their crab nets thumping against the gunwales and their voices coming muffled through the reeds like the muttered conversations of the dead. There's a prow and part of a wheelhouse of a sunken oyster boat sticking up there among the cattails and the blades of mallow grass, where a bird will sit for hours, sunken in reverie or stealth, staring out across the harbor. At low tide there is a foot of brown slime showing on the exposed grass stems and a smell steams up from there that will daze a man, an ancient salty fetor that casts distraction in the air like myrrh. But before the tide comes in again, the slime on the grass stems is baked dry by the sun and glows like brown velvet, inviting you to wade there among the reeds and stroke them with your fingers. I have done that on a summer afternoon, plashing through the warm shallow water, my trouser legs soaked to the knees, my hands stained with the dusky pollen which I wear home like gauntlets.

Fifty yards down the street there's a public pier with a lunch shack at the end of it where you can rent day sailers or rowboats fitted with outboards. It runs out a hundred feet into the river, and walking up the street on a summer night you can hear the current suckling at the piles and see the shadowy rowboats tugging at their painters like restless, moonstruck mares. I go up and walk through the church meadow on fine nights, to the river shore. There is not much in this world to equal the experience of swinging down that slope through the wet grass, ringing with crickets, on a warm night, to where the Patuxent lies spread out before you, vast and darkly shining. The place is almost too beautiful; for an old man, certainly. There are too many evenings of my life to count when I was not here, when the place lay vacant of my presence under these same stars, unknown to me, and when, if it had been known, it would have gone unclaimed, like the people I can never call back now to share it with me. I find that regret, by some unpleasant process of pollution, can contaminate the very beauty that begets it. There are evenings I have spent on that bank with the dark current of my memory sliding through my mind aglitter with its ugly luminosities, its moments of spurious triumph, its vanities and trophies, all of its misshapen brilliances, as the dark stream at my feet has seemed then to slide between its shores, soiled with bent, convulsive moons and rabid stars. The town is better seen by sunlight.

A bit further down the street there's a grocery store that used to be the Dorsey house until the thirties. It has a front porch whose pine floorboards are worn smoothly hollow between the ridges of the yellow veins of sap, as bright as topaz; they set out produce there in the sunshine: crates of melons and sacks of chicken feed and ice-cream freezers with price tags tied to them that flutter in the wind. A new broom with a clean handle and fresh tight-bound golden broom straw is a lovely thing. I buy my groceries there, as a bachelor or a widower buys, a little at a time, enough for one day: a stick of butter, a lamb chop, a pint of milk, three eggs. I detest the thought of someone having to clean out a refrigerator full of moldy cheese and sour milk and rotting lettuce after I am dead. I like to buy a single tomato—a small, firm one—and hold it against my cheek to relish its coolness while I walk down the street past the bend at Hargison's motor shop to where I live. The fruit will often be warm —which is equally agreeable—by the time I arrive at my cottage down there at Embarkation Point, and I will have walked half the two-mile length of Solomons Island. This street is not dusty, like the streets of inland towns, but sprinkled with sand from the river beaches, fine sand of a very pale gold that drifts across the pavement in the wind and makes clean tawny ridges in the cracks and runnels of the asphalt. This constant presence of sand, and the water everywhere in sight, and the purity of the air, blown over long stretches of bay and salty marshland, create a sense of cleanliness in Solomons Island that continually surprises one. I wake to that surprise every morning and dwell in it all day. The wood of the houses, whether white as porcelain or bleached to glimmering gray, is clean as fish bone in the sand. Even the rotting timber of the old houses or the nodding piles rots cleanly; it seems to be burning with a slow invisible flame that consumes it cleanly and utterly, it dissolves into the air—into time, perhaps—the way a lump of salt dissolves in water.

In one of the abandoned backyards next to my house there's a bleached and tattered pair of old jeans flying from a wire clothesline. God knows who left them there, or how long ago, but on a windy day they flap and snarl proudly, tugging out the rusty line like a bowstring, crackling with something that sounds to me like indignation. But on a still, hot day they seem to yield, they hang there ragged and motionless in the sunlight, and you can almost hear the faded stitches bursting, the rotted seams splitting with a sigh as they are sundered into rags. It's the light that does that, I think, as much as wind or time. It is my prayer to be pried cleanly apart like that, with no ache of unreadiness or unwillingness, with no pain or putrefaction, only a gradual merciful abrasion by wind and light and silence until I am honed away entirely. The thought came to me watching a boatman polishing a turnbuckle out on the pier, burnishing it with a rag until I thought he would wear the steel away, until there was almost nothing left of it but the gleam, the scintillation. I get up before dawn every morning and stand in my dooryard looking across the garden and the beaten silver of the estuary to the open bay in the distance, and in those moments I feel swept, almost devoured, by the great voracious cleanliness that reigns here at this end of the world.

I say it is the end of the world because it is the end of the highway, a fact that provides the place with its second blessing: solitude. There is no through traffic and few tourists here on Solomons Island. Thirsty people, people out after beer or jukebox music or the movies—even the largest part of the swimmers and day fishermen—are absorbed by the roadhouses and beaches and drive-ins that they find plentifully enough throughout the two counties that separate this place from Washington. Anyone you see at Solomons Island is either lost, or desperate, or dying—as I am—or indigenous to the place. You can tell the natives easily enough; they speak and move very slowly, with a calm, almost crocodilian sense of the vanity of those functions, or perhaps of their futility—although they don't seem like people stunned by futility to me. There is too much of a kind of curious ambition in that indolence of theirs, a kind of avarice, not for yachts or jewelry or sports cars, but for something even more expensive; for luxuries greater than any the marina people know. They have pale light-bleached eyes—clean eyes—and a clean, grave way of touching things, cup handles or boathooks or cucumbers, that has no worldly cupidity in it, no haste, none of the agitation with which you see stray folk from

Washington snatch up a pack of cigarettes from the counter or plunge through a purse for a credit card. They seem to be satiated, soaked in light until they are illumined inside, and nearly still. I think they must have silent veins, and hearts that barely beat at all, that blaze in their rinds of light like candy apples. I wasn't here a week before I realized that mine had been beating many times too fast for years.

Route 2 ends here at the island. It makes a loop around Embarkation Point, enclosing the abandoned cottages and the ruined backyards, rejoins itself beyond Hargison's, and then winds back between the tobacco fields and pine woods and country towns to Annapolis and Washington. From the Point you can look across the estuary, which is a mile wide here, and see the shore of St. Marys County with the boat sheds and shadowed cottages among the trees, but there is no way to get there, except by boat, or if you drive back to Dorseyville and then thirty miles west to Hunterstown, where the first bridge crosses the Patuxent. The western shore of the island is swept by that river, then here, at Embarkation Point, the fingertip curls inward to enclose the harbor, which is divided at the entrance by a sandbar where the steel tower stands that holds the warning beacon. It's a small, quiet harbor, lined with boat sheds, rickety piers that heave gently in the backwash when a boat goes by, the roof of the seafood restaurant rising above its docking platform, a chandlery, converted from a Victorian house with gingerbread gables and surmounted by a sign smoking in the sun that says: PREPARE HERE FOR YOUR VOYAGE. Beyond are the ice-and-bait shacks, the tin roof of the crab-packing plant, the rotting stumps, the hot, slumbering marsh grass, and the drowned hulls. The right branch of the harbor is narrower and dwindles to a creek that rambles up into the mainland between low wooded hills whose shores are rimmed with narrow yellow beaches where I have seen deer come to drink and herons tread, peering avidly into the warm, brown, shallow water. The inlet leads back to the marina, which is new and bright and has a very different look from the rest of Solomons Island. Fortunately—in my opinion—it is almost hidden between the hills at the far end of the inlet. You see only a slice of the clubhouse with a pennant flying over it and over the neat, symmetrical slips of fresh, darkly oiled timber that reeks of creosote. There is a constant, distant tinkle and glitter from that end of the harbor, from the white hulls of the sailing yachts, and the aluminum masts and bright steel shrouds and spars and steering helms. The yachts, whatever one may think of the marina, are a fine sight coming up through the channel with their tall masts advancing steadily and the light from the water sparkling on their polished hulls, riding evenly through the quiet water toward the harbor mouth, skirting the sandbar and the steel beacon tower, loosening their wings with a great walloping rustle of sailcloth as they bear by the piers of Duncan's boatyard at the entrance, then heeling over with tense snarling sails as they strike the wind-riven choppy water of the estuary and lunge out toward the bay. I don't know how far a love of wind and water will go to unite people, but far enough, I suppose, to make brothers of a kind between the marina people and the Solomons Islanders, if money didn't go farther to divide them. At any rate, I have an interloper's gratitude that we don't see much of them; they have their own marine supply store and a dining room in their clubhouse and a trio of musicians, I understand, that plays for them on weekends, so there is little reason for them to come into the village. I have snipped out the appendices and tied the tubes of a good many hundred of them in my lifetime, and yet, as they were strangers to me then, they are even more so now. They come from the same suburban banlieues that I have lived in for a large part of my life—Bethesda, Chevy Chase, Potomac—they know the same quiet streets and tennis courts and swimming pools, and yet I feel that I scarcely understand their speech. What is new to me is the regret I feel at their strangeness—or my own—which it may be too late ever to redeem, and the very novel glamour that they have for me, something I never felt before. I feel a curious diffidence in their presence —a very odd sensation indeed—almost the disabling shyness of a young man in the presence of a girl he longs to court but whom his sense of unworthiness, or provinciality, or shame, forbids him to approach. It seems that the more foreign they grow to me—or I to them—the more infatuated I become with them; and yet I know that I can never speak to them again until I learn the language of these spellbound islanders. What I see most clearly in them now, and for the first time in my life, is their beauty. They are truly handsome people. And while I realize that the ability to perceive human beings as very shapely objects is something short of insight, to a man in my spiritual circumstances it might almost be considered revelation.

What one does not appreciate until he sees an object in full illumination, as he does here, is how devoutly things are shaped, how sovereign form is in this disintegrating world. Here, in the light of a summer noon, objects—a rusty ship's bolt in the sand, a broken binnacle, a wooden pot buoy bobbing in the tide—seem brimming with the poetry of their forms, like bells ringing with a rhyme of their own being. I thought once that if a man were to perfect his vision, he would be able to see the naked essences of things, the innocent heart of substance, devoid of all significance, passionless as snow. But I am beginning to believe that nudity does not exist in matter; matter is clothed in intention when it is created, and it is the clothing of intention, just as man-made objects are. I don't know whether things are nothing more than the wrought ambition to be the things they are, or to be the things they might be, and have been. Whether they are the spoken history of their whole passionate progression, from primeval fire to gas, to molten rock, to gems of anthracite or opal, to oyster shells and poets—a genealogy of desires reaching back to the very birth of matter—or if they are a hymn of contentment in themselves, in their present comeliness; or of their aspiration to be something other, some more intricate, more artful utterance of their passion to exist. Whatever they may be, they are not silent; they are speech itself, often so eloquent that they seem to me like prophecy.

There are days of piercing lucidity on the island when things cry with portent, they are emblems, insignia, like the designs of heraldry. The oriole that sings outside my kitchen window in the crab tree might be stitched on the sky behind it as on a blue banner billowing over minarets. That bar sinister of sunlight that slants across the door of Sylvie's house emblazons it with some dire, lustrous legend of her lineage that sometimes makes me shield my eyes when I approach it with my basket of pears or tulip bulbs or a string of fresh-caught rock.

I have an oyster shell on my mantel shaped like an escutcheon that I take down every day and ponder on. I set it beside me on the porch step in the morning light, or on the kitchen table, to study while I eat my lunch. It is wonderfully beautiful, both its inner surface and its outer, one made for repelling and destroying life—ridged, hard, horny, scarifying—and one for cradling and preserving it—opalescent, cupped tenderly as a mother's palm against her child's cheek, smooth as moist membrane or magnolia petal. There is a great deal to be learned from it; everything, perhaps; although I doubt I have the wit to comprehend it. I have spent many years of my life examining the creatures of this world, under a microscope and with a meticulousness for which I was once celebrated, but from the point of view of a doctor and always motivated by my interest in pathology. I am moved by a different spirit now; one whose futility, and perhaps immodesty, I very much suspect. My eyes have been too long adjusted to the dark, and the light in this place is too strong to allow unblemished vision, or even altogether unblemished sanity, at times. At times, I have been virtually demented by it.

There are daylong storms of light that lash the village and the fields until everything—stones and trees and animals and men—is drenched, dumb-founded, beaten by torrents of light into a kind of reverent subjection. The horses in the river meadow stand like brazen statuary, light riveting along their loins and flanks, as if fetched fresh from a foundry. The lizards on the fieldstones close their tiny jeweled eyes and nod, steeped in the ambrosial light that scalds their hearts like brandy. Snakes slide in coils of platinum through the meadow grass. Along the creek, the deer stand shivering, their bones fused with delight. Birds sit stupefied on the pilings and sunken hulls and telephone wires or flutter drunkenly in the hot sand of the street. The peaches swim in golden aureoles, the ivory magnolias blaze frigidly, frozen in ingots of light among the leaves like flowers in a paperweight. Wineberries twinkle like garnets in the hedges, persimmons hang palpitating, jellied in light like congealed, inextinguishable hearts. The earth is scarified by livid gusts of light that leave it lacerated, oozing drops of bright geranium and cardinals and tanagers, plump, tremulous, scarlet gouts that well up, glistering, like blood behind a scalpel stroke. I am not speaking of heat only, because often the air is cool, with the wind blowing from the estuary, but still that searing light teems from the sky in gales that blister the paint from the white walls and flay the shadows from the stones and the flesh from the carcasses of gulls in the sand of the beaches, sluicing off the roofs in glittering sheets that set the spouts aglow and thaw the iron palings in front of the post office as if they had been thrust into a blast furnace. At noon the town seems to crumple under glaciers of light, to tremble in pyres of light that clamber at the cringing, withered flags, the tin roof of the cannery, fuming, curling at its edges, the zinc mailboxes down the street, swollen and seething like bubbles in a cauldron. The shops and houses convulse with a weird evanescence, almost on the point of disappearance, of evaporation, as if seen through an imperfect pane like the sheet of silica in my kerosene heater or the gnarled glass of my parlor windows. The rooftops are decked with capering gelid plumes, flying like pennants from their eaves. The church tower quakes, the spires of the wind vanes pulsate limply, the flagstaffs shudder like snagged twigs shuddering along a riverbank in swollen torrents, in rivers of ravaging light that flood over them.

There are times when I thirst for darkness, as a man lost in the desert thirsts for water. I feel almost desperate for refuge from the merciless midsummer light that spouts in endless paroxysms out of the inexhaustible geysers of the stars. It is slung like wheat seed from the spinning carousels of the galaxies, a blazing grain or ghostly burning sperm that saturates the earth and pullulates in every crevice of it, between the stones, in the delicate webs of moss, in the seething scum of marshes, in the bright, wildly impregnated eyes of animals and the fallow red loam of their hearts. One is not equal to such light. The eye is vitiated by it and sees only chimera, as wavering and illusory as the church spire quaking in the sun; or the thing seen is disfigured by the light that beats against it, twisted into wracked and quivering shapes by the brilliance of that illumination. At times I despair of seeing truly in this place, or understanding with the clarity I had imagined. What I thought to be the products of my moments of vision or acuity may be only feverish aberrancies, somehow humbled by the unearthly candor of the light, or defiled by the earthly perplexity of my gaze.

The oyster shell on my mantelpiece, however, will survive my troubled meditation as the stars survive the troubled eyes of Galileo. I shall never understand it as well as Sylvie, who brought it to me on my birthday, saying, "I would like to give you the whole world," and took it out of the pocket of her wet storm suit and put it in my hand. She has done so: a little world of hidden shining, wrought by a blind creature out of its own excretions, the sweat and slime of its own darkling struggle to invent a home.

My days begin in the eastern dooryard, watching the sunrise over the bay and the estuary, unshaven still—so as not to lose a spoonful of the silvery bounty with which my garden brims—leaning against the doorframe or, if the dew has dried, sitting on the wooden steps that lead down among the beds of portulaca which look as if they held the ruins of a rainbow. The crushed oyster shell is overlaid with a delicate, meandering filigree, the glistening inscriptions of the snails who all night long have scrawled their lore along the path. I watch the flight of a gull or an echelon of geese across the dazzling water of the estuary, the mist below the trees on the St. Marys shore, an early fishing boat sliding out soundlessly across the harbor to the bay, cleaving the virgin water into glassy mounds that glide toward the shore, where they will ripple the wrack of twigs and cork crumbs and slime-coated bottles and tipple the stranded clamshells like little empty coracles. I smoke a pipe and wander through the garden for a quarter of an hour, pausing to pluck a dead leaf from a geranium, or a Japanese beetle, sparkling like an emerald, from a rose. Then I go back through the narrow hall that divides my cottage, still illumined halfway down its length by the low morning light, to the kitchen, where I take down a cardboard matchbox from the shelf above the range, slide open its drawer, fumblingly pluck out a blue-tipped wooden match, strike it on the side, and light the gas flame to boil a pan of water, the sound of each of these operations dropping like an offering into the tray of silence of the kitchen, like a coin into a salver: the rasp of the match head on the patch of brown emery, the click of the turning knob, the gasp of the liberated gas, the soft flutter of the ignited flame, then the sudden animated splash and mewl of water as I turn the faucet handle to fill a pan, the leaden tinkle as I set it on the grill, and the faint tumult as my morning egg tumbles gently in the boiling water. I sit at the table rejoicing in the blue-and-white-striped china of my crockery, the clean smell of my oilcloth table cover, the tigerlike sheen of the worn and polished pine floorboards, the windowpane which begins to blur like frost with morning light, the smell of apples and cinnamon and bread. I love this clean, cool, silent house with its bare rooms and bone-white walls on which the southern windows cast slanted plaques of light that slide, daylong, towards the corners, where they are folded up at evening, like fans, in strips of golden damask. I found the house empty and have bought only a few pieces of stern Duncan Phyfe–style furniture to place against the chalk-white walls and a large oval rag rug to cover the parlor floor in front of the white-painted brick mantel, above which I have hung a print of Blake's "Isaac Newton," the house's only ornament, being the single piece of conscious art which I find inexhaustible. (The oyster shell on the mantel I don't consider an ornament; it is essential to the house, its principle, perhaps the model of it.) The dining room is furnished with a round, dark-mahogany table and four cane-seated ladder-back chairs which I doubt very much will ever be occupied, but which fulfill the dignity of the room. In my bedroom there is a stalwart bed with posts like hewn hydrants and a plain oak chest of drawers; on top of it I have set a huge stoneware basin and pitcher; they have a massive feminine voluptuosity which I like to lie in bed and contemplate, the breastlike, hiplike curves of a gleaming Rubensian giantess, their dimpled glaze chipped here and there to reveal a ragged glimpse of her abdominal gloom. The second bedroom I have converted to a very elemental study; there is a chest, a chair, and a towering secretary, in which I keep the pages of this journal and where I sit every morning to set down another portion of this account of my existence. The window faces south and the room is illumined by the pale, champagne-colored morning light which lies tenderly across my shoulder as I write, burning with soft orange flames in the old mahogany and trembling in the pool of jet inside my coffee cup. There is a Cape jasmine bush outside the window, whose shadow moves very slowly across the floor until eventually it will clasp my shoulder coolly and extinguish the dark flames in the polished wood. It is sweet to sit here, writing timelessly, in this sunny, silent room. I don't know how long I write, or between what hours exactly, since I have no watch or clock; my life is measured only by fluctuations of light and dark, by the passage of shadows. When my cup is empty and the flames have died, I will shuffle the sheets together, set them in the bottom drawer, rise stiffly, stand for a moment, lost in the bewildering lane between two worlds, then leave the room, go down the length of the narrow hall, which is now wrapped in pearl-dim shadow, toward the blazing portal of the open door and out into the bath of light beyond. It is morning for me, whatever the hour.

I will have taken down my Panama hat as I pass the hat tree in the hall, and with my brains defended by its almost weightless weft of straw I walk down the gravel lane behind the backs of the close-pressed houses, half of them deserted, past the honeysuckle-laden fences with amber-and-onyx bees raining through them, bouncing like beads from a burst necklace. I unlatch Sylvie's back gate and walk up the path to her kitchen to see what she will need from the grocery store, finding her as often as not still sitting at the table with a bowl of milk, untouched for hours, in front of her, her fingers straying over its rim, or over a spray of quince blossom or a stone. She will touch the tips of the quince thorns with her fingers or press the stone against her temple while she recites her necessities to me, most of which I must prompt her in: a bag of sugar, a cantaloupe, a loaf of bread, occasionally a quixotic item which I do not comment on: a lump of beeswax, a horn-handled knife of any kind I can find, or perhaps a bag of marbles. With her list tucked into my hatband—I lose things, I find, increasingly—I walk the remaining length of the lane, the gravel crunching under my feet like frost, to where it joins the street below Hargison's outboard-motor shop, then through the haze that lies above the hot asphalt toward the grocery store, splashed with the sun dance from the harbor water to my right and the river to my left. If I pass any of the townspeople—Norm Hargison, filling an outboard-motor tank from the gasoline pump outside his shop, or Louellen Parks, sweeping a carpet draped across her porch railing, or Harvey Weems, scraping the hull of a cradled trawler in his cluttered boatyard —I will lift my hand and drop it, and they will return the gesture silently, their eyes revolving to meet mine through the warm veils of air with a habitual economy of movement, with as little rotation of the head as possible, like those of the dozing dog I pass, outside the post office. The cool dimness of the grocery store is delicious after the long walk up the hot street. I am leisurely about my purchases, which are fetched and set with patience, one after another, on the counter in front of me by William Dorsey or his wife, both of them as lean and wrinkled at the throat and grave as lizards. Sometimes I eat a peach or a slice of watermelon from the cooler before I set foot again into the burning street. They will stand behind the counter and watch condolently, making no overtures, however; nodding and murmuring peaceful, compassionate replies to my observations, nearly all of which, for some reason, take on the tone of grievances before these taciturn people. " 'Deed it will rain," they say. "And time." "You oughten sit plums in the sun. You git prunes that way." "Yes, indeed. Shad is sweet, but bony." They are old in every instance of calamity, from shad bones in the throat and blighted plums to drowned sons. They are not stirred by my sufferings, but seem to hear them distantly, with rue, almost in reverie, as one hears the tinkle of cowbells across an evening pasture. Their sorrows are encysted inside of them and do not pain them any longer. I am fascinated by these people. There is something I have to learn from them. When I first came to the island I used to see their son, whose name was Alton, when I came into the grocery store. He would be sitting on a crate or keg at the back, among the bolts of linen and garden tools and sacks of fertilizer, watching the commerce in the store with a kind of stunned attention, his big black-nailed fingers twined together in his lap, his eyes like pebbles in a stream. I don't know how old he was, not more than twenty-one or -two, certainly too young for such absolute frugality of speech; he never spoke at all, not to me, at any rate. He would nod to my greeting and drop his eyes hastily; they swept downward to his loose-laced fingers with an opaline flash, almost as pale as milk. I heard him say once to his father, holding open the screen door of the porch and turning back before he stepped out into the sun, "Be back." They are the only words I ever heard him speak. I would see him sometimes at noon, shuffling down the sandy street between the silent houses, a bottle of whiskey sparkling on his hip, or wandering between the pilings underneath the docks along the harbor shore, poking at the matted seaweed with a stick. He got drunk one night and fell off the end of the town pier into the river—or leapt, perhaps, his mind riven by an especially poignant shaft of moonlight—disappearing as soundlessly as he had lived. I think of him often, floating somewhere toward the sea in his bloated, baggy trousers, his white eyes swollen with the universe, that fatal sliver of moonlight lodged in his brain. I have often wondered if he said "Be back" to anyone as he set abroad that evening.

On my way back to the Point I stop at the post office to see if there is any mail for Sylvie (that there will be any for me I have stopped believing long ago). I fear this faded building; like the grocery store, it is converted from a dwelling and has the same sand-ground, foot-worn floors, the same wry, desiccate smell of old wood, and the same high ceilings of embossed tin, their garlands painted over with successive coats of tarnished paint until they look like blunted, sea-worn cameos in a sunken hall. I set my bag of groceries on the ledge in front of the grilled window while I wait for Mr. Becker to shuffle through a sheaf of envelopes with his stiff, almost transparent hands, peering through lenses so thick that they turn his eyes into gigantic burnished bulbs, monstrous as a dragonfly's. There is something awful in this ancient man. He lifts his head and fixes me with his vast eyes. "Nothing," he says, terribly.

It is noon, I judge from the midday silence and the absolute angle of the sun, when I go back out into the white street, and animals have fled for shelter from the light. The dogs have wriggled under the floors of porches, where they settle, sighing, in the cool sand. Chickens stand puffed and huddled in the shade of maples. Clumps of sparrows nod with stupor in the jasmine bushes. Even the shadows have been driven back into the stones, which lie shorn, radiant in their poverty, like skulls. The posts, too, are stripped of their dark pennants, which at sunrise fly as far as eternity, lapping at it with their shredded tips, as they do at sunset, in another wind. Shadow, in its endless pilgrimage, fascinates me: I think how it flows out of the stones in the moment after midday, reaching for the infinity where it arrives at sunset and in which it roams all night, slinking back from its debauchery at dawn into the stone, where it sleeps for the measureless instant of the noon. I pause to rest for a moment, setting down my bag of groceries in the road and mopping my forehead with a pocket handkerchief. I am tired, and perhaps mad; a mad dog *and* an Englishman, I decide, nodding to invisible jurors of my plight.

Sylvie is wandering through her house when I return, touching things: the walls, the tips of the fireplace tongs, the glass panes of the windows; I watch her for a moment through the kitchen door. "Carl?" she calls out, when she hears me setting her parcels on the table; and when I enter the parlor, where she is standing with her palm against the windowpane, "This is south. It's warm. Those over there are cool. That's north." She points across the room, smiling at her ingenuity.

"That's right."

"Do you know, I never used to know north from south—or right from left —before. I'm learning things."

"How do you tell right from left?" I ask.

"Because I've decided one goes with south, and one with north. Do you know which?"

I consider for a moment, and say, "South is left?"

"No. You've got it backwards."

"I should think south was sinister, and north was dexter," I say.

"For you, maybe. Not me." She turns back to the window and lays her cheek against it above her spread hand, saying in a moment, "Did you have enough money?"

"Yes. The change is on the table. I've got you a fine cantaloupe and some cottage cheese. They're in the icebox."

"Thank you, Carl." There is a pause, filled with trembling reticence, like a glass of wine on a window ledge.

"There wasn't any mail," I say.

"Oh. Thank you." The wine is stilled.

"They tell me at the store it's going to rain." There is another pause, of a different order, which prompts me to invite her to lunch.

"No, thank you, Carl. I've got to have a bath and a nap. I didn't sleep last night. There was so much thunder." She turns to face me, her hair smoldering against the sunlit pane, and holds out her arms to me. I go to her across the room and take her shoulders in my hands. Their rounded curves are cool through the soft cardigan she wears. Her flesh is always cool, like apples. She lies against my breast, her arms encircling me loosely, and I reel with the sweetness of her embrace. I lay my open hand against her hair, pressing her head to mine.

"There's a Vivaldi concert on WGMS at four, remember. Don't sleep too long."

"I won't. Thank you, love."

I think of her, straying about that sunny house, as I walk back down the lane toward my own, and quell the disorder in my breast with difficulty. A yacht passes through the lips of the harbor past the Point, bearing a group of pleasure-seekers who cling to the shrouds and lean far out above the windward rail, exulting. I stand and watch them with delight, and with strange gratitude. How beautiful they are: caryatids, marble chefs d'oeuvre—and how different in their beauty from the woman I have just visited. Sylvie is certainly not one of them, although she comes from outside the island, as they do. Nor do I feel toward her as I do toward the island people (none of them, except, perhaps, that grocer's drowned, drifting son), although she may in fact be more an islander than any of them; perhaps she always was. I felt that about her even when she first came here, last winter; yet she never fraternized with them. She never solicited their friendship, or their aid or sympathy, not even after she went blind. They offered it, of course. Ladies from the village came—and men, too, standing hat in hand at her kitchen door—offering to cut her firewood or cook her meals or sit with her for an hour, and discovered that their ministrations were not needed. Their apple pies and garden squash and bowls of blueberries were accepted gracefully, and marveled over, her fingers rippling over them to test their warmth or weight or size—but only standing, in the kitchen. There were no invitations to a cup of coffee in the parlor, to an hour of conversation, to share a confusion or despair which so far as they could see did not exist. As a matter of fact, they were more distressed than she. She was cool and smiling as a tearoom hostess, solicitous of their evident discomfort, their embarrassed silences, their sense of blundering trespass upon her orderly kitchen, the quiet tenor of her life. It was made courteously apparent that she was competent to find her own way about the house, to learn to cook and sew and make her bed; but they understood another thing: that she wished to take her first faltering steps into the dark world on whose threshold she stood with no consolation or companionship or escort, in utter, solemn loneliness, as one is born. They left feeling they had intruded upon something almost ceremonial. Something they respected, out of their own profundity. There is a true hauteur about Sylvie, now more than ever, which is not pride at all—she is one of the humblest people I have ever known—and which must be wounding, I suppose, to those who love her, and yet without which they would probably not love her at all. I think the islanders understand that, because they share it to a more modest degree: that strangely fortunate air, that eminence of spirit, such as one feels in consecrated people, nuns or poets, which is not conferred by birth or circumstance, but by their intensity, the brilliance and intransigence of their passions. Her kinship with them—which doesn't need to be solicited, and cannot be—she may have felt instinctively, and taken comfort in, or refuge; although they seem improper words for anything Sylvie would require. But I do think she is comfortable here, as comfortable as she is apt to be anywhere on earth. I think she is grateful for the silence of these people, their imperturbability, their calm movements, their recognition of her solitude, and I think she understands, on her part, that patient greed I sense in them for some sort of unearthly bounty. So she is alone, among her kindred; although she is different from them, in degree, if not in kind, paler, freer, more illustrious.

Even before she went blind, I would see her straying solitarily along the shore, gathering the stones with which she built those monuments of hers, those cairns she used to pile up on the beaches. If I passed her on the road or hailed her from the bluffs, she would barely acknowledge my greeting, with a nod or murmur or a startled glance from the windy beach. She used to go out at dawn sometimes and set up her easel on the river shore to paint those pictures—I don't know what to call her pictures: infernal; they were that. And yet they were supremely, harrowingly beautiful. Everything in them—trees, rocks, buildings, blazing animals and men—was fused with light, pulsing, coalescing in a blinding igneous mass of matter that made me recoil from the canvas the first time I ever looked at one. She used to bring them home and burn them. Coming down the lane one winter evening, I saw her prop one of them against the back of an iron garden chair and pour kerosene over it and light it. I had met her only a short time before—one troubled week before, in fact—and I don't think any other circumstance would have given me the courage, or the temerity, to reproach her as I did. Although I was already plentifully aware of her beauty, no other woman except Molly—in a very different moment—has ever seemed so alluring to me as she did then. There was something almost bitterly bewitching about the way she stood to watch the fire devour the withering, crumpling canvas, a white pall flooding over it from the roots of the flames, like the pall that flooded her enchanted face as she watched, her knuckles pressed against her belly, her upper lip held bitten white between her teeth. I felt an indignation I could not account for.

"What are you doing?" I said. "Good heavens!" She looked up, startled. Her eyes were very blue then. Celestially, almost inhumanly blue, I realized.

"I'm burning it. Can't you see that?"

"Well, that seems very foolish to me. I thought it was beautiful."

"Did you? You can't know very much about art."

I said contritely, "No, I don't, I'm afraid. But still, it seems a pity to do all that work for nothing."

"Not a pity. Vanity," she said. She stood watching the flames devour the painting almost as if they were a part of its own fiery composition, as if it had burst into reality and consumed itself, collapsing into a wrinkled pane of ash that fell apart and drifted down from the iron chair in lightly fluttering flakes. When the flame had died she crouched down beside the chair and sifted the ash in a spellbound way between her fingers.

"At least I can make it true," she said, "if I couldn't make it beautiful. Look at it now. Now it's true. Now it's honest ash." She ground a handful of the gray ash between her fingers and blew it from her hand, watching it drift in the palest of clouds across the yard, casting the faintest of shadows on the light snow. "Don't you think that's wonderful? No brush, no paint, no anxious fiddling. It's much easier than making something beautiful. All you need is flame." She looked up at me intently, as if demanding confirmation.

"I suppose it's a kind of truth," I said. "If you prefer it. I think I'd rather have had the painting."

"You're a generous man. Or a foolish one."

"Foolish, I suppose." I could think of absolutely nothing else to say. After a moment, I turned and nodded with foolish irrelevance down the lane. "There are fox tracks in the snow back there. Did you know there were foxes on the island?"

She scowled as if struggling to comprehend, but too sunken in pursuit of her own thought to make the effort it required; then her eyes grew slowly, wearily resigned to my civility. She stood up, raising her hands and dusting them against her breast.

"I want to thank you for being so kind the other evening," she said. "When my furnace went out."

"It was a pleasure. Truly."

"I'm not really rude. I mean I don't try to be." She dropped her head. "I've got to go in now. I left a pan of water boiling on the stove."

I nodded and murmured, "Good evening," in a chastened way.

"You mean good morning." She looked about in sudden confusion at the sky and the long shadows on the snow. "Good God, it is. My pan will be burnt." I watched her stride across the yard into her kitchen, sucking a fingertip which she had burned, apparently, in the flame. The screen door banged behind her with a bewildering clap, like a gunshot, or the sound of a branch breaking suddenly in a silent forest, or of ice splitting across a frozen river. I closed my eyes with the pain of it.

I had been at Solomons Island for six months when Sylvie came. She arrived two days after New Year's, at the beginning of a stormy January whose gales and cold winds kept me indoors a great deal of the time, and I was not aware of her presence until one afternoon on my way back from the market I saw that the shutters had been folded back from the windows of the Potter cottage, two doors down the lane from my own. Only the fact that this new neighbor had arrived in winter reassured me; I hadn't come to Solomons for company, and I had been on the island long enough, and was sufficiently in the spell of its solitary beauty, to resent the intrusion of "outsiders" and "summer people," as I had come to think of them already, particularly at such close quarters. But frivolous, boisterous, or inquisitive people were not apt to arrive at a lonely, windswept place like Solomons in the middle of winter, or to give such convincing evidence of the gravity of their nature and intentions as to have a gigantic concrete reproduction of what looked like a Grecian urn set up outside their kitchen doorway within three days of their arrival. I asked about her at the grocery store and was told that she was a Miss Linthicum, who came from Port Federation, not thirty miles up the highway, and that she had taken a year's lease on the Potter place. I was for some reason set at ease by the strangeness of those facts, as I was by William Dorsey's solemn, unsolicited assurance that "she won't bother you none, I'll guarantee you that."

A few days later, standing at my back door one evening to toss bread crumbs to the sparrows, I smelled the smoke of a fruitwood fire in the air from her chimney, and took a profound and inexplicable comfort in the experience. Her kitchen windows cast a glow out through the misty air that touched the tips of her picket fences and breathed a warm rime on the sodden honeysuckle; I liked to see it when I tramped back through the rain from a march along the blustery shore. It lent an eloquent tincture to my bleak corner of the island that I was chastened to discover I appreciated; a kind of lustrous emanation that seemed to be not only of the kerosene lamps behind the misty panes, but of her unknown spirit, in quiet conflagration there within. The conclusion that I had been lonely—for how long or to what degree, I did not dwell on—was oddly embarrassing to make, but I could not disguise my gratitude for her presence there, unobtrusive, delicate, fragrantly pervasive as the smoke of burning applewood from her hearth. I was suffused by it for days, without once setting eyes on her. I don't mean that I gave her a great deal of conscious thought; I was glad enough *not* to know her, and yet to sense her comforting but unprovocative humanity. As I read my Ruskin or worked out my chess problems in the evenings, it added to my serenity to know, without having to ruminate on the fact, that she was there, not more than a hundred yards away, smiling or sighing secretly, or knitting perhaps, or staring into her firelight, or humming while she stirred a bowl of batter in the kitchen. I liked her all the more, and was all the more drawn to consider her, by reason of the fact that I did *not* know her, that I was not burdened by any unsettling, and unavoidable, relationship. I admired her sense of privacy and her evident respect for my own, and was cheered to find, in the course of several days, that she made no garrulous, plaintive, coarse, importunate, or otherwise disconcerting overtures toward me, and yet did me the strangely splendid courtesy of existing. It seemed to me at the time an almost ideal situation: to be able to gratify whatever instinct it is that calls for the proximity of other human souls without being subjected to the so often suffocating, contentious, or banal reality of their acquaintance.

I was confirmed in the belief the first time I *did* see her, on a cold windy morning about two weeks after her arrival. She was beating with a broom handle a shabby carpet that was draped across the railing of her kitchen stoop. There was low, gray, fast-moving cloud boiling across the sky, almost at the treetops, and the light on the earth was scabrous and mottled, as if filtered through soiled parchment. She had on a dark unbuttoned cardigan that flapped wildly, and her turbulent chestnut-colored hair billowed and streamed like a wind-struck treetop as she swung the broom handle savagely. I was prepared to nod and touch the brim of my hat as I passed her backyard fence, but she did not look up. I went on down the lane, taken aback by the intensity of her appearance and by the peculiarly brutal sound of her blows, thudding against the carpet, that pursued me in the wind, like that of a body being clubbed repeatedly and viciously.

The winter of her arrival was a long and bitter one, but I took delight in it, rejoicing in the respite from the summer-long deluge of light with an almost festive feeling of relief. I had begun already to respond to the alternations of the earth's moods in a way I never had before, insulated as I had been from them for almost forty years in laboratories and lecture halls and operating rooms. There was an almost metabolic rhythm about the earth, an almost organic, systolic and diastolic flux, as if it were a living thing. As a doctor, I suppose, I found a particular fascination in the discovery. I liked walking abroad in bad weather, scouring the barren river beaches and the rain-pitted, stuccoed yellow sandspits of the estuary, watching the dark, choppy, harbor water splash against the bulkheads and the boats lurching feverishly at their lines, or standing with my hat clutched to my head on the windy bluffs below the church-field meadow to watch with watering eyes an osprey struggling through the gale. I would often come home wet and exhausted but full of a wonderful exuberance, an almost hilarious feeling of pleasure that would keep me smiling while I peeled off my sodden clothes and made a cup of tea in my bathrobe and carried it up, steaming, to the shower, to sip while I stood and let the hot water splash like an elixir over my numb shoulder blades.

When she had been on the island for only a few days I began to see Sylvie occasionally when I was out on such walks—sometimes no more than the top of her head, prowling through the tall dune grass on the long sandbar of the cable crossing, or sitting huddled, with her knees clasped to her chin, at the end of the vacant pier, or clambering over the rocks of the breakwater at the harbor mouth with the agility and unconcern of a child or an animal. She would stand like a shorebird for half an hour, her hands plunged into the pockets of her pea jacket, staring out at the pitching current of the estuary. Her favorite occupation seemed to be gathering rocks and piling them up into cairns on the stony beaches. She would lug huge ones for as much as fifty yards, clutching them to her belly and staggering with the weight of them as she stumbled across the pebbles to the site of her monument. One day I was bold enough, or jubilant enough, to hail her from the bluffs, but I realized from her look of startled dismay that it was an act of trespass upon her privacy, that I was guilty of the offense for her own innocence of which I had been silently congratulating her. Humbled, I turned and hurried on. Afterwards I was more circumspect, but although I did not speak or wave to her again—until I came to know her much better—it gave me pleasure to see her in the course of a lonely ramble. Even if our paths did not cross, I relished the feeling that she was very likely abroad at the same time as myself, sharing the same vast gray sky, the same cold virginal air, and perhaps the same jubilation. The thought of claiming this strange girl as a fellow reveler, or fellow communicant, gave me, already, an odd sense of distinction.

I might never have laid any claim on her at all, but for the blessed fierceness of that winter's weather.

Her furnace broke down on a bitter evening in the second week of January. It had snowed earlier in the day, a fine granulated snow that whispered for an hour against the windowpanes and whitened the folds of the frozen soil in my garden. Then the clouds had blown raggedly apart and there was one of those magnificent scarlet winter sunsets with everything scrawled black against it, naked branches and housetops and duck blinds in the marshes, a scene of such stark splendor that I stood at my kitchen window for half an hour to watch it fade into twilight, a vast wash of tender rose across the horizon that left me feeling almost abject at the beauty of the world I had walked on for longer than most men live, and scarcely been aware of. The sky was nearly dark—and the kettle of water I had set on the stove for my tea had just recalled me to reality with a terrifying shriek—when I saw Sylvie's body, outlined with a fragility clean of any touch of pathos, against the rose glow at the end of the lane, moving along the fence toward my back gate. She stopped and looked out at the dying flush that was withdrawing across the water of the estuary, standing quite still until the water and the darkling floes were sunken in shadow; then she opened the gate and came down the walk to my back door. I heard the rasp of her boot soles on the blade of my shoe scraper and opened the door before she had time to knock. She stood looking at me in level-eyed surprise.

"I saw you through the window," I said. "I was watching the sunset. Come in."

She stepped inside the door and closed it behind her. She had the collar of her pea jacket turned up and a knitted watch cap pulled down over her forehead almost to her eyebrows, but even with so little of it revealed, I felt confused by her beauty; I had never seen her so close before. The kettle screamed on the stove and sent a plume of steam into the air. I plucked it up and stood foolishly with it in my hands, the jet still burning.

"I don't think I've ever seen the sky more beautiful," I said. "I was in something like a trance."

— "I can see that."

"I'm making a cup of tea. Can I offer you one?"

"No, thank you. I was just wondering if I could use your telephone. I'm having trouble with my furnace, and I don't have one. I'm sorry to trouble you."

"No trouble at all. It's right there on the wall. Please help yourself."

"I've got to call the appliance man in Prince Frederick. I'm afraid it's a toll call. Can I ask for the charge and pay you for it?"

"If you have the change," I said. "But please don't worry about it. I'm happy to oblige."

"Thank you. I wouldn't bother you, but I've run out of firewood, and I'm freezing to death down there." She went around the table to the wall phone, tugging off her gloves and stuffing them into the pocket of her jacket.

"Are you sure you won't have a cup of tea?" I said. "You must be pretty well chilled."

"No, thanks. I won't stay. I'm hoping he can tell me something to do before he gets here." She took a piece of paper out of her pocket and dialed the number that was written on it. I switched off the gas and poured the boiling water into the teapot that stood waiting on the table, jiggling the silver tea ball by its chain and breathing in the aromatic fumes, while Sylvie spoke with growing irritation to someone who appeared to be the serviceman's wife. It was Sunday, and he had gone bowling, the woman explained, and wouldn't be home until very late.

"Well, isn't there *someone* who can take care of it?" Sylvie said. "I mean, it's an emergency. I'm freezing to death." The nearest other person capable, it seemed, was in Upper Marlboro, sixty miles away.

"Oh, Lord. Well, can you get in *touch* with him? Can't you call him at the bowling alley or something? Or tell me the name of it, and I'll try to get him myself." After an exasperated pause she said, "I see. Well, just a minute," then covered the mouthpiece with her hand and turned to me. "Would it be a terrible imposition to have him call back here? She says he'll call within half an hour."

"Not at all."

"Well, do that, then," she said into the telephone. "But please try and make it within half an hour. I'm at a neighbor's, and I don't want to inconvenience him." She hung up the phone and leaned impatiently against the doorjamb, turning her head to look out into the living room.

"God, what a bore. Life is mostly a matter of getting things repaired. I thought I'd escaped that here."

"I think you'd better have that cup of tea," I said. "Sit down and thaw out for a minute. There's nothing like a cup of tea to pull you together."

"All right, I will. Thank you."

She came to the table, peeling off her cap so that her hair fell thickly about her face. While I took down another cup and saucer from the cabinet and poured the tea, she drew a chair out and sat down, propping her elbows on the table and lacing her fingers before her face.

"You have one of my favorite pictures over your mantel," she said.

"Really? Isn't that remarkable. It's mine, too." I set cream and sugar on the table and sat down across from her. "It's the only painting I have, actually. It seems to be the only one I need."

"Well, with sunsets like we had tonight, one doesn't need very many." She poured a dollop of milk into her tea and stirred it. "I'm Sylvia Linthicum. I've taken the cottage just down the lane there, with the red shutters, I guess you knew that."

"Yes, I've seen you out walking occasionally," I said. "I'm very pleased to meet you. I'm Carl Ransome. I hope you're comfortable down there."

"Yes, it's comfortable enough. When the damned furnace is working."

"It's a pity you've had that trouble. Of course, it always happens on the coldest day of the year."

"Yes." She sipped her tea, then licked her lips and blinked. "That's good tea. Better than I make."

"It is good, isn't it? It's English—Earl Grey. I get it sent down from Washington. It's my one vice, that tea."

"You're not English, are you?"

"No, but I've been there to conferences and things. It's where I got the habit." I sipped at my tea, using the moment to observe the restive vigor with which her long unmanicured fingers gripped the teacup, disdaining its handle. "A friend—a professor of mine—gave me that painting as a present when I finished my residency, and the fact is, I hardly looked at it for the next twenty-odd years, until I retired." I smiled, moved by the unexpected felicity of her company and no doubt by the sea-water blue of her eyes to confess, "As a matter of fact, I'm beginning to think I never looked at anything very much, except tumors, lesions, things of that sort."

"You're a doctor."

"Yes."

"Is that why you like it, being a scientist?"

"I really don't know. It may be one of the reasons. Although they keep changing. I keep finding different things in it entirely."

"Do you write?" she asked suddenly.

"Write? No, why? Well, I keep a journal, but it could hardly be called writing."

"So many doctors have become fine writers. That's always interested me."

"Have they? Who, for example?"

"Well, all the way from Sir Thomas Browne to William Carlos Williams. And in between you have people like Brecht, and Maugham, and Chekhov, and André Breton. And Keats, especially."

"Keats was a doctor? I didn't know that."

"Well, he was apprenticed to a surgeon, and he was a medical student at Child's Hospital in London. Would you have known that from reading him?"

"It certainly never occurred to me when I was reading the 'Ode on a Grecian Urn.' But that's probably all I've read of him. I'm afraid I haven't read much of anybody at all. Are you a student of literature?"

"Yes. I teach it." She lifted her cup and buried her nose in it, her fingers encircling the rim. "This smells good. Like Ceylon, or India, or somewhere. Fragrant forests with sunlight in them. It's so clean, isn't it, tea?"

"Yes."

"My mother made iced tea all the time, in the summer. We drank gallons of it." She set her cup down and said restlessly, "I'm sorry about this, honestly. It's an awful imposition, making you sit here and wait for that damned phone to ring."

"Not at all."

"I don't think the damned man is going to call at all. His wife will ring up in a minute and say his truck has broken down or something. He's not going to drive all the way down here on a night like this. I'm not sure I blame him."

"Well, don't let it bother you," I said. "I'm enjoying it, really. You're the first visitor I've had since I've been here."

"Do you get bored here?"

"No, not at all. I'm quite content. But it's very pleasant to be able to talk to someone for a change. I couldn't be happier that you dropped by."

"I'd be furious, I think, if you had."

"Not if you hadn't had a proper visit with anyone for six months. I didn't quite realize it, I guess, until you arrived, but I've missed that."

"You've been here six months? And you're still quite content?"

"Yes, more all the time. It's very beautiful, don't you think?"

"Yes. But I don't suppose I see it quite the way that you do. I was born here on the bay. I've lived here all my life."

"I envy you. The strangest thing is, I've lived a good part of my life in Washington—I went to medical school there—and I've never really seen it at all. Oh, I don't mean literally; I had a glimpse of it occasionally from the Bay

Bridge, a lot of pretty little toy boats and a patch of blue, like a picture postcard. But I never felt the reality of it, I mean. I had no idea how beautiful it was."

Sylvie did not answer, but the gravity of her eyes encouraged me to continue. "I don't know what I was looking for when I came to this place. I drove down here one afternoon just after my wife died. I just got in the car, and started driving, anywhere at all. It's very likely that I'd still be going, if the road hadn't brought me here. But then I came over the culvert there—by the Texaco station, you know?—and got my first look at the place, the masts and the cannery and the sand in the street, and the water everywhere—and I knew quite literally and absolutely that the road ended here; that there was nothing beyond. That whatever remained for me to do, I had to do here. It was really a remarkable sensation; I don't know if you've ever had one like it."

"Do you mean permanently?" Sylvie said.

"I think so, yes." I looked around the kitchen at the white walls, the stern ladder-back chairs, the string of scarlet onions against the plaster. "I can't imagine being anywhere else. Not at the moment, anyway."

Sylvie did then a small but remarkable thing that marked her genuine advent into my existence. I think there are such events, by which people make emotional recognition of each other, and after which they are never truly independent of each other again. Until that moment I had been perfectly content with the impersonality of our acquaintance; I could very happily have lived out the rest of my life without exchanging another word of conversation with her; if I had felt the need of discourse, anyone of her approximate intelligence and sensibility would have served just as well. In a year, I would have forgotten her name; in two, I would not have recognized her in the street. But at that moment she picked up the teapot, lifted the lid, glanced inside to see how much it contained, and then filled both our empty cups in a charmingly unselfconscious and familiar way, as if she were a dweller in the house, an old friend or relation. She did it very naturally, without presumption, and with a suggestion of affection, of concern about my necessities—and a companionable assurance in supplying her own—that I found as intimate and endearing as a caress.

"The second cup is always better," I said. "It's had time to steep a bit."

"Yes."

I stirred my tea and sipped it, whatever guilt I may have felt at my loquacity dissolved in the warm glow of confidence cast by her gesture.

"Do you know one of the things I like best? The age of the place, the sense of the continuity of things. That's something so profound that you wonder how you ever got along without it. Or you do if you've lived most of your life in a suburban neighborhood. Row after row of split-level ramblers, and automobiles seldom more than three years old parked down both sides of the street. Now, I look out my window every morning and see this old brown pool, littered with the bones of fish that swam in it a million years ago. Do you know the Calvert Cliffs?"

She nodded.

"Well, of course you do; much better than I do, I'm sure. But I drove up there one day, a couple of weeks ago, and looked at them. Eighty feet high, they must be, in places; a solid mountain of fossils; layer after layer of skeletons and shells and petrified teeth of creatures who lived before there was a man on earth. It gives you a sense of your own relative importance, of where you fit into the history of the world. You see yourself, and your whole generation, your whole century, as just another layer of chalk in that cliff. You wonder what they'll find in that one."

She had lowered her eyes to the cup which she held broodingly between her palms.

"Teeth," she said, and swirled the tea in her cup, as if she might discover one, even there. "It's full of teeth, that bay. They seem to be the things that last longest."

The phone rang, very loudly and apocryphally, it seemed to me.

"There's your man," I said.

"I hope so. More likely, it's his wife, with a sad tale."

She was right; after a brief, agitated discussion, she banged the phone onto the cradle and stood scowling. "It's just what I thought. He's in a tournament or something, and won't be in till after midnight. She doesn't have any idea when. I suppose I'll have to drive up to Marlboro."

"Why don't you stay here?" I said. "I've got a spare bedroom upstairs. There's no point in your going all that way, and then back again in the morning, when it's sitting empty."

"All right, thank you. I will," she said with no hesitation whatever. "If you promise you won't let it disturb you. Just go on with whatever it is you usually do. I'll go up and go to bed."

"Well, you can't go to bed yet; it's barely dark. Have you eaten?"

"No."

"Well, look here, I've got a pot of oyster stew on the stove there that I was just going to heat up. Why don't you have a bowl with me?"

"I don't think I can refuse that," she said. "If you're sure you've got enough."

"There's quarts of it. And they're fine fat oysters; I just got them this morning at Captain Jack's. I make rather good oyster stew." I rose and went to the stove to light the gas.

"You're being very kind to me."

"The pleasure is mine, entirely. You can't go down there and cook in a cold kitchen all by yourself."

"I hope to God the pipes don't freeze. I'll be flooded in the morning, on top of everything else."

"I don't think so. There'll be a bit of heat left in the house, and it takes colder weather than this to freeze pipes. Why don't you take your coat off and relax? This won't be a minute."

She did as I suggested, hanging her coat on the back of her chair, then came and stood beside me at the stove to look into the pot that I was stirring.

"It smells wonderful."

"Good. You'll sleep better with a bellyful of this."

"I hope so," she said, in a tone of simple, chronic affliction that made me glance at her involuntarily.

"Maybe you'd like a book to take up. I'm afraid I don't have much to offer you, but Ruskin—or Pritkin's *Elements of Ophthalmology*. That should put you to sleep all right."

"I don't want to read," she said. "I don't intend to read a book for the next six months. Maybe ever."

"You're not teaching now?"

"No. I'm on sabbatical until the fall." She raked her hair back restlessly. "Shall I set the table?"

"All right, good. I think you'll find everything up there in the cupboard. The cutlery is in that drawer by the sink."

She opened the cupboard door and began taking down china and setting it on the table. It tinkled poignantly. When the stew was hot, I brought the pot to the table and ladled our bowls full; then a loaf of rye bread and a dish of butter; then a bottle of white wine from the window cabinet where I kept it to cool. When I offered to fill her glass she said, "Thank you, but I don't drink."

"I think it's quite good wine."

"I'm sure it is, but I don't drink anything at all."

"Isn't that strange," I said. "And I'm just beginning to."

We settled down to the oyster stew and ate for a moment in silence. Sylvie raised her eyes to mine and nodded in a congratulatory way.

"It's really marvelous."

Outside, a wind had begun to rise, as it does after a day of winter rain, and I could hear the fire thorn branches scratching at the kitchen walls. Once, the house had had a wood stove in the kitchen; the hole where the stovepipe had entered the chimney was covered with a painted metal plate, and now, when the wind rose, you could hear it singing in the old flues with a strange fluting sound. With the peppery stew and the cold dry wine and the good coarse bread, I felt voluptuously at ease in the warm kitchen. Sylvie ate with her eyes downcast, earnestly and silently, like a hungry child. I enjoyed watching her; I enjoyed her silences, the meditative pauses between her occasional gently voiced questions and observations:

"Your house seems to be humming to itself."

"It does; I've often thought that. Mozart, I think. Sometimes I can pick out a whole bar or two of *The Magic Flute*. Perhaps I imagine it."

"Mine moans," she said. "It's as if every nail in it ached."

"Maybe it's older," I said. "I think I've heard that the Potter place was one of the first built down here."

She listened thoughtfully for a moment, then smiled at me and said, " 'There is music in the island.' "

"What is that from?" I asked.

"The Tempest."

"Oh, yes. I don't know that play. I regret not knowing literature."

"But you're reading Ruskin."

"Oh, well, I've just begun. Ruskin interests me because of the change he went through in his middle life. It must have taken something very like a revelation to move a man out of the realm of aesthetics entirely into a preoccupation with poverty, with the problems of working people, with political economy. It's almost as if he was reborn, in the middle of his life, through an awakened social consciousness. That interests me very much."

"Yes. He had his 'unconversion,' as he called it, just after looking at the paintings of Veronese in the Uffizi gallery. He went almost immediately after into a cathedral and heard this vapid sermon delivered to a bunch of benighted, impoverished peasants. That's when he lost his faith; or gained it. In a cathedral. People dispute the point."

"I haven't read that yet," I said.

"It's in *The Stones of Venice*, I think. It's a very great passage." She nibbled at a chunk of bread and added, as if to herself, "And then, of course, he went mad."

Later, after studying the piece of Woolworth's cutlery in her hand for a moment, she asked gently, "Do you rent this place furnished?"

"No, I bought it."

"Oh."

And a moment later, as if completing a sentence that had lain in suspended turmoil in her mind since the beginning of our supper: "I feel like a terrible fraud, not working on an academic project of some kind, which of course is what you're supposed to do when you're on sabbatical. But I think it would be even more of a fraud, almost, if I did."

I considered that for a moment before framing what I thought was an appropriately reassuring reply: "I don't think one is necessarily idle simply because he isn't following a plan of action, or turning out a certain amount of regular work. I haven't touched a scalpel, or taken a pulse, or examined a specimen for months; and yet I never felt more active in my life. I think I learn more here in the course of a day than I learned in months of medical school. Or perhaps I'm learning the meaning of what I studied there."

She scowled at this suggestion, almost as if offended by my offer of reassurance, and made an impatient, constricted movement of her head, so that I felt obliged to add, almost in apology, "A vacation is a very necessary institution, after all. A person has to pause occasionally, to learn the meaning of what he's been professing for so long."

She sat bleakly, crumbling a piece of bread between her fingers. "Or doing?"

"Or doing, yes."

"There are things one does by way of professing," she said in a moment, "and there are—the other things one does. Don't you make any distinction between them?"

I thought uneasily about her question for a moment. "Or fails to do."

"Or fails to do. It comes to much the same thing." She swept together with her palms the little mound of crumbs she had deposited on the tablecloth and began to sprinkle them into what remained of her stew. She seemed to choose her words with almost painful caution. "There is something that speaks in one that has nothing to do with what one professes. That almost cries against it. That you could say, perhaps, creates the need for a profession. I wonder how many are created like that, in fear or plight?" She lifted her hands and licked crumbs from her palms in a strangely animal way, with the tip of her tongue, then raised her eyes to mine. "People of your profession—doctors—have always fascinated me. You're so ambiguous. You seem to me to be inscrutable. Are you a research doctor, or a practitioner?"

"I've done some of both," I said. "But I'm a researcher, mostly, I suppose. Almost entirely."

"Yes. A scientist. So it could be said of you that your life has been devoted to the search for truth. And yet the popular conception of a doctor is of a man dedicated to the easing of suffering. To comfort. I think comfort and truth are very different things. I'm not sure at all that they're compatible. I'd be very interested to know if you think so."

I took refuge in a mouthful of stewed oysters, and after lingeringly devouring them, suggested humbly, "I suppose it's possible for a man to be moved by a passion for both. We like to believe so. For comfort's sake."

She broke into a low purring chuckle, catlike and mirthless, of appreciation, then said, "You called it a vacation, being here. Which means a respite, an intermission, being free from duty or service, a periodic private bacchanal. But there's another word for it: a holiday, which means quite the opposite: a holy day. Which implies that one's *life* has been a bacchanal, and that this is a period of abstinence, or redemption, of solemn meditation on God or virtue, or whatever. Now, which of us, do you suppose, is embarked on which?"

"Well, there's no doubt that you've made today a *vacation,* for me," I said. "Not quite a bacchanal, perhaps, but very festive, certainly."

"I'd call it a bacchanal," she said, "considering the amount of oyster stew I've eaten. Maybe I'd better atone by doing the dishes."

"If you like. I'm feeling very unregenerate myself. I'll have another glass of wine and offer instructions."

I did so, lounging back in my chair with uncustomary indolence and sipping at the brisk delicate Soave that sparkled in my glass, less intoxicated by it, I think, than by her presence, her restless energy and beauty, the brilliance and earnestness of her speech, the swift change of her moods from impatience to girlish gaiety, and the startling depthless blue of her eyes, which gave the impression, not of looking into her spirit, but outward, through panes of amethyst, into illimitable distances. I watched her wash and dry the few dishes we had used, and replace them in the cabinet, bemused again by the syncopated, chiming music of her labor, which with the splashing of water in the sink and the fluting of the wind in the chimney made in the kitchen a romantic fugue that delighted and gently plagued me, like a tune one struggles to recall. I asked if she would like to play a game of chess before she went to bed. "I'll bring in a couple of logs," I said, "and we can play by firelight. I generally do that, in the evenings."

She seemed pleased by the suggestion. We went into the parlor and sat in front of the fireplace in the amber light that billowed over the walls, brooded over by a naked giant crouched among lichenous, lunar rocks, with a scroll unrolled before him, his godlike eyes alight with the ardor of his scrutiny. I play chess badly enough at the best of times; after two glasses of wine, my challenge to Sylvie had been ridiculous; and yet I won. Not because I played well, or she badly, but because her flashes of brilliance were fitful and brief; she obviously had no concern for winning; her interest was in creating patterns on the board and studying them for the pleasure she took in their complexity, rather than in relation to any eventual "victory." When they were consummated, or dissolved, her attention lapsed; she fell into scowling or vacant-eyed abstraction, staring into the firelight or about the shadowy room or raising her head to study for long moments the naked dreamer above us with absolute absorption, with a look of intent so like his own that it seemed almost as if they were locked in the same dream, both held in the same rapture of inquiry, their eyes and hands frozen and illumined by some mutual icy passion, so that I had the sudden startling impression that they were brother and sister, or lovers, cruelly divided by a picture frame, by the impassable boundary between their two worlds of life and art. Once, after waiting several minutes for her to move, and seeing that she was still lost in her engrossment with the picture, I lit my pipe and sat back in my chair; and we fell into a threefold trance of fascination: Newton with his arcane formulae, Sylvie with Newton, and I with her.

"I'm sorry," she said, becoming suddenly aware of my attendance on her. "Is it my move?"

"It doesn't matter. Enjoy the painting."

"What you said about it is true," she said. "It does change. It's changed since the last time I looked at it, almost unbelievably."

"Or perhaps you have, like me."

"Yes." She tossed her head as if oppressed by the enigma, and dropped her eyes to the board. After regarding it disconsolately for a moment, she plucked up her king and held him clenched in her hand, looking down at his tiny crowned head protruding from her encircling knuckle like that of a captured Lilliputian.

"How has it changed for you?" she asked.

"Oh, in many ways, as I say. One is that I used to think of him as a hero, as I think Blake meant him to be, and certainly my professor did, when he gave the painting to me—" One of the chief blessings of a pipe is that a reliable one goes out almost constantly, giving one almost endless opportunities for discretion; I took advantage of one such at the moment, striking a match and puffing away with exaggerated vigor.

"And now?" Sylvie said, relentlessly.

"Well, now I see him differently. Would you say that Blake was a moral man?"

"One of the most so who ever lived."

"Yes. And yet this hero of his, this creature he has made, seems to me now almost like a savage. A kind of intellectual savage. I'm horrified to think of him in love. Do you know what I mostly think of now, when I look at that painting? Of *Mrs.* Newton. Was there one?"

"I have no idea," Sylvie said.

"I think about her a good deal. I wonder whether she liked ocean bathing, or turnips, or babies, or would have if she existed. That would never have occurred to me as a young man." We sat in silence for a few minutes, listening to the peaceful rustling of the embers. "And for you?" I asked.

"What seems to matter to me almost entirely now is the source of light in it. Where does it come from? Not the sun, because it's night. The sky is quite dark, and there seems to be no moon. And there is no artificial source of light; he has no lantern, and there is no fire burning, but he is flooded with light which seems to come from somewhere forward of him, and quite low, almost on a level with his hands. But it's impossible to tell, because there are no shadows, which is perhaps the strangest thing of all. Only the hint of a shadow, under his forefinger on the scroll. Yet the legs of the calipers, which ought to cast corresponding shadows on the paper, cast none. There is also the barest suggestion of a shadow behind his right heel, but it dwindles away without ever conforming to the remainder of his leg; and the rest of his body casts no shadow whatever on the rocks. I thought once that it did, because there is what might be considered a shadow running upward behind him on the stone. But I see now that it's a fissure in the rock; it's too long and narrow and irregular to be the shadow of his body; and besides, there are other, almost identical fissures running closely parallel to it in the stone. Nothing will account for that lack of shadow, or that uncanny light. It seems to be inward, to have no outward source; as if his body were self-luminous; or his mind; irradiating that strange gnarled corner of the universe where he's crouching. Or perhaps it comes from the scroll, from the diagrams he's drawing there. Or from the thing he seeks, from some luminous ore he's about to mine, some jewel, or some ghostly heart he's on the point of laying bare."

I had fallen into a spell under the incantatory power of her description, following with my eyes the details of the painting as she examined them, appreciating more than ever its magical ambiguities.

"I see now why you paint," I said. "You think like a painter, it seems to me. You certainly talk like one. I think you're one of those people who mostly live and understand through their eyes." She stood up from her chair, looking down for a moment into the fire; then sat with her toes touching the hearth, clutching her knees in the crook of her elbows, baring her face to the flames with narrowed flickering eyes, like a sun-drenched cat.

"I've only begun to realize how totally I've always been governed by the sun," she said. "When I was a little girl I lived in a house on a cliff, here on the Western Shore. I spent my days roaming along a little strip of beach that runs for miles, from South River to Cove Point, very near that place you went the other day. It lies at the foot of the cliffs, and because it's on the Western Shore it's always in full sunlight in the morning, but later in the day, as the sun moves westward, the shadow of the cliffs begins to fall across it. In the summer, when the sun is high in the sky, that doesn't happen until evening, until almost six o'clock. But in the spring, in late March or April, the beach is in total shadow by a little after noon. I always knew that; no one ever commented on it; it was simply one of those facts of existence that you understand almost from birth; and although I never consciously considered it, the knowledge of it regulated all my days: the time I got up in the morning —because I was always up and abroad long before breakfast, even in the winter

—the kind and number of things I would embark on, the distance I would dare to travel from the house, the clothes I wore, the amount of food I ate, my feelings about everything. I made some kind of instinctual calibration between the sun and the tides; I knew—always, I think; I can't remember ever first becoming aware of it—that there was an interval of almost exactly twelve and a half hours between like tides; that if the tide were high at noon it would be low at a quarter past six in the evening, and high again at half past noon the following day, so that if I went far beyond a certain promontory where the cliffs jutted out almost into the bay about a mile beyond our house, I would not be able to get back after twelve o'clock without wading through the water around the promontory. Even on cloudy days, when the light was dispersed, when there was no shadow to align one's life by, and the sun was not visible, I knew its position in the sky almost at any hour, by some sort of temporal or solar wisdom. I made a continuous circling curtsy to it all day long on my little jackstraw legs, like a flower on its stem. I think if I had any idea at all of God's actual location in the universe, his place of residence, it was in the sun. Perhaps he was the sun itself, for me. I knew that God was hot and golden, not cold, like the god my people worshipped. I loved the afflictions that he laid on me —such scalding sweet afflictions, like love wounds: the boiling amber resin that oozed out of the pier planks on a summer day and blistered my lips with its succulence of pine and made my fingers and the soles of my feet sticky with a reeking mucid gum, like sperm. And the blazing noonday sand that I would race across, yelping with agony, to sit and nurse my feet at the water's edge, shivering, with a hornet sting of pleasure in my heart. And the glorious tender ache of sunburn that swathed my thighs and shoulders when I lay in bed at night, like the breath of some bright succubus. And the dawn light, reaching across the water with little ladyfingers to touch my lips and throat and eyelids where I sat dreaming on the pier. I would take off the cotton halter that I wore and let the silver fingers of light slip over my girl's breasts, oh, a pain so exquisite, my breasts were like mounds of warm beeswax, white hives swarming with newborn, sun-stirred bees. I used to walk barefoot in the hot September days under the persimmon trees along the bluffs and among the rotting apples in the orchard, sinking to my ankles in the glorious mire, reveling in its slippery brandy-dark corruption. My feet and hands and mouth smelled of apples, and wild persimmons, and resin and sea mist and the musk of honeysuckle, and my sun-smirched hair, of light; do you know that hot, innocent smell of summer children? My brows and eyelashes were bleached with sunlight, like the tawny dust of butterflies' wings, and my whole body tinseled with an incandescent down. Oh, I shone with lust, with adoration! My marrow slid through my bones like syrup, my heart seethed with a kind of sweet pollution, like a peach simmering in the sunlight, I was aflame with my infatuation for the sun. I think

I wanted in some way to be betrothed to him, the sun. He had sullied me, from my brindled hair to my soiled feet, with his brazen hands, and I needed to solemnize my abasement, to proclaim myself, in some splendid ceremony of obeisance, as his bride, his queen, his child concubine.

"One day we had visitors, a family from Baltimore who were distant cousins of my mother. There were a boy and girl, much younger than myself—I was twelve then—grave, awkward city children of eight and seven, who knew nothing of the bay or of the country. Aaron was in bed with the flu, and it was left to me to entertain them. It was June, one of those first summery days when the earth and air are sultry, but the water is still cold and there is cold in the cloud shadow that races across the earth. I decided to take them for a long walk up the beach; it would seem a natural enough thing to do. I went in to tell Aaron, who was lying in bed staring out the window at the pigeon loft."

"I'm going to take them up the beach," I said. He did not answer. "I'm not going to take Jamed. We're going quite a ways, and he'll get too tired." He coughed with a wracked sound, pressing his fist against his breast.

"Does it hurt, Aaron?" I said. He closed his eyes, shaking his head. "I got you some sherbet this morning at Offutt's. It's in the icebox. Would you like a bowl of sherbet?"

"No."

"It's pineapple. You like that, don't you?"

He shook his head. The shadow of a flying dove flickered across his face.

"Where you going?" he said.

"Up to where that log is. You know, where we were the other day." He turned toward me and stared feverishly into my eyes. "I'll bring you your knife back," I said. "I know right where it's at."

Three days before, this had happened: we had wandered up the beach together to a log, half buried in the sand, that had tumbled down from the eroded cliffs above. Aaron had a knife that he had bought two days before at Offutt's, a country store not far from our house. It was the first knife he had ever owned, and he was very proud of it; he had bought it with the money he had saved from mowing lawns and selling sweet corn from the garden at a stand he had set up at the edge of the highway. He had dreamed of owning the knife all summer long. A humpbacked Barlow hunting knife with a staghorn handle. It had a sinister look; I hated it, and I hated the way he looked at it in a glass display case every time we went into the store, an avid, almost amorous look that was very private, that excluded me entirely. It came from some feeling that I was not supposed to share, that I was never invited to share as I had always been invited to share his discoveries of shells or shark's teeth or a trove of wineberries. There was something that I recognized as valedictory about that look.

We sat on the log and watched a gang of gulls harrying the carcass of a dead fish in the sand. The air was cool and restless. Aaron took out his new knife and began cutting into the pale silvery trunk of the stranded log. It was very sharp and I could see the slivers of fresh-sliced wood sprinkle down as he whittled. It looked to me as though he were cutting letters into the wood, or the beginnings of what might have been a letter: a straight vertical line, and then a connecting slanted line, what might have been an M or N or W.

"What are you writing?" I asked.

"It's none of your business," he said.

"How come you're so stuck-up?" I said. "You act like you were a king or something, just because you got that stupid knife."

"You're just jealous," Aaron said. "Why don't you mind your own business? You're not supposed to be watching what I'm doing, anyway."

His disdain filled me with a fury unlike anything I had ever felt before. I stood trembling with the chill of it, feeling an awful desire to maim or slaughter something. I struck his arm suddenly, knocking the knife into the sand; then, before he had time to move or recover from his astonishment, I snatched it up and ran away from him across the beach. He leapt up from the log and raced after me, stumbling in the sand. As he was getting to his feet I flung the knife as far as I could hurl it, up the cliff, seeing a puff of dust where it struck the dry clay, thirty feet above the beach. Then I turned and ran along the hard sand at the water's edge toward the house. When I had run twenty yards or so he had caught up with me and seized me by the arm, jerking me down into the sand.

"You give me that knife," he said in a shrill whisper. He twisted my wrist until I shrieked. I had never seen him do anything so violent before—and I don't think I ever did again.

"I don't have it! I threw it away. It's back there in the sand."

"You're lying," he said savagely. "You give it here, Sylvie, or you're going to be sorry!"

"I don't have it. Honest, Aaron. It's back there by the log."

He pried apart the fingers of my hands to see that they were empty, and then flung me away from him and ran back to the log. I got up and raced away along the beach to the house. When I got home, I stayed in the kitchen, close to Momma, terrified to face him alone. I knew he wouldn't say anything in front of her about what I had done. I knew he understood that our quarrel had nothing to do with the world of adult scruples—even of reasonable behavior —and that he couldn't honorably appeal to her for justice. Aaron was always like that: honorable in everything—God, is he not honorable!—and his honor fell on me like a curse as often as like a blessing. I knew he wouldn't strike me or punish me physically, once his anger had abated, because he was never physically violent. If I had thought that he would, I wouldn't have run for shelter to Momma's presence; I would gratefully, delightedly, perhaps, have delivered myself to his wrath. But he would *say* something to me: something far more terrible than a reproach. One of those awful, devastatingly innocent, excruciatingly humble offers of reconciliation that he muttered when he was injured or offended, as if in apology for having, by his mysterious vulnerability, provoked his persecutor to whatever outrage had been worked upon him. Something that would have given no such redemption, no such expiation, as a bruise or blow. Something that, in Momma's presence, he would forbear to say, to spare us both the shame of being called as witness to my atrocity, of seeing it held up to scorn and judgment, its commission acknowledged by the world of adult righteousness. Sometimes he would not speak, even, but only look at his tormentor with his sad, astonished eyes, not so much aggrieved at being the victim of malevolence as dismayed by the mysterious evidence of its existence in the world; and in me, especially. I don't know if you've ever known anyone like that, who could make innocence an affront, a constant, lifelong threat to one's comfort and convenience and desire. And *innocently* do so! Not knowingly; not in any consciously self-righteous, or self-congratulatory way. But in the way we are reproached by flowers, so that we sometimes crush them with our feet, in indignation, I think, as much as inadvertence; the way a violet or an oriole can awaken resentment in us at its beauty and fragility, can make us aware of our own vileness, and the grossness of the whole world which surrounds it. Maybe you never felt such a passion, but people do, you know. Herod did. All Rome did. *I* did, too, sometimes; and then I would be doubly cursed: by the fact that my ignobility was confirmed by my anger at what his innocence implied in me. Oh, my God—innocence! Sometimes I think it's all we really have to fear. Eve didn't do her work well in paradise; why didn't she exterminate it utterly? Why does it linger on in this world, like the scent of a lost garden, defiling everything we do? Why are dogs and dung beetles allowed to keep it still, rutting and ravaging blamelessly, while we blaspheme with every breath we draw, our every deed an indecency?

Aaron didn't come home until almost dinnertime, and I could see that he had not found the knife. He was pale and silent and went to his room immediately, without speaking to either of us. He punished me—*unknowingly*, of course—in the subtlest, most intolerable way of all: by doing nothing. Neither by words, nor wounded forlorn looks, nor by conspicuously avoiding me, but by a kind of humbly private, destitute air, like that of bereaved people whose only comfort is in solitude. He seemed hardly to be aware of me, certainly not as the author of his affliction. He even spoke to me with a kind of abstracted, formal courtesy when, at last overcome with guilt and penitence, I went into his room to tell him dinner was ready.

"I don't think I can eat anything, Sylvie," he said. "Tell Momma I don't feel very good. I'm going to go to bed."

Of course: he had compounded my sentence by becoming ill! I was agonized by those words; now I had sent my brother into some terrible physical decline, possibly to death, by my wickedness! I was damned. Within an hour he was panting feverishly in bed, and I was standing horrified at the door, watching Momma bathe his face with wet towels. And yet—this was perhaps the most appalling thing of all—along with my awful, nauseating guilt, I felt a far more awful, calm, imperturbable sense of confirmation in my belief in some elemental baseness that was abroad in the world, that used me, as it used everything, as its agency.

I lay awake all night, listening to his labored breathing and restless tossing in the bed, waiting to hear his final cry of expiration. Jamed, who shared the bed with him, had been moved out to the living-room sofa, and Aaron's door had been left open so that Momma could attend to him if there was anything he needed. I had begged her to let me take care of him, but she was afraid I'd catch his illness, and refused. I would say that I went through purgatory that night, except that what I did the next day, when our visitors arrived, disproves any such contention.

When I told him I would bring his knife back from our walk up the beach, he closed his eyes and lay without moving or speaking for a long time.

"You're not going to die, whatever you feel like. Whatever you think," I said. "Whenever people get sick, there's a reason for it. You'll find out that's true, Aaron. Just don't worry, O.K.?"

He might have nodded; I told myself he did; there was an almost imperceptible drooping of his head. I went out and told the children, who were waiting at the door, that I was ready.

"Now don't you children get wet down there," their mother told them fiercely. "I don't want you coming back here soaking wet, getting pneumonia. You hear me? Marge? Paul?" They nodded dumbly. "And you do what Sylvie tells you, you hear me?"

"Yes, ma'am," they said together. Marge, Paul! Those are terrible names, I thought; I wanted to slight them in some way. But they were.beautiful children; they looked almost like twins, although the boy was a year younger than his sister; dark-eyed, suave-looking Mediterranean faces, with chestnut hair that curled in shorn, uplifted waves around their ears and napes.

I led them down the cliff to the hotel and then down the steep flight of wooden stairs that descended to the beach. It was one o'clock; the tide would be full in an hour or less. The beach was dwindling rapidly in width. I began to lead them along the shore toward the place where I had flung Aaron's knife up the cliff. They pattered obediently beside me, clutching the keepsakes that I found for them along the water's edge: sprigs of coral and sand-polished lozenges of bright-colored glass. We passed the promontory where the beach narrowed; it was scarcely more than a yard wide now in the incoming tide. The sand lay in full sunlight, sending up a shimmering veil of heat beyond which the world lay subtly agued and deformed, the trees warped with a soft arthritic frenzy, the cliffs pulsating as if shaken by some paroxysm in the earth, a freighter quaking on the horizon. I led the children to the log, half buried in the sand, where Aaron and I had quarreled. We sat and watched the distant freighter quavering in the pall of heat.

"Now you watch and see if you can see a sailboat," I said. "The first one that does will win a prize."

"What prize?" the boy asked.

"That's a surprise. A real fine surprise."

While they waited, I went and climbed the cliffs behind them to where I had flung Aaron's knife. The climb was steep and dangerous and would have terrified me on an ordinary day, but I felt no fear at all. I was breathless and exalted. I felt a kind of cool perfection flowering in me, like the opening of white, dire blossoms, that blooming of audacity that blows the cold scent of heroism through one's heart like a gale. The loose layers of calcified shells crumbled under the weight of my hands and feet, and I slid and scrambled, often nearly falling backward down the cliff. The children had turned to watch me, standing up and staring with excitement. I saw the sun directly overhead above the cliff, with nothing between me and it but the translucent steps of air. I climbed toward it to where Aaron's knife lay in the clay, stretching out my hand as if I might touch that blazing grail that spilled its scalding oil over me, anointing my reckless hands, my shining hair, my bright, arrant expedition. The bone shaft of Aaron's knife burned my fingers when I closed them over it. I put it in my mouth, holding it between my teeth while I worked my way back down to the beach, dropping the last five feet into the sand. The children stood in awe of me as I walked back to the log, brushing the crumbled shell dust from my knees and skirt.

"We have to go now," I said. "It's getting late. Did anybody see a sailboat?" They shook their heads.

"We was watching you," the little boy said.

"Well, we have to go. Maybe I'll give you a prize anyway, if we get back in half an hour. I'll give you a piece of bubble gum if we do."

They followed silently while I led them back along the water's edge until we came to the promontory; then the little girl clutched at my skirt in fear

when she saw that the water now lapped at the wall of the cliff. The beach
had disappeared entirely.

"Look at what happened!" the little boy cried. "There ain't no way to get
back."

"The tide came in," I said.

"Are we going to drown?" the little girl said, and lifted her crumpled fingers
to her mouth in terror.

"No. We'll have to wade, is all. It's not too deep."

"But we'll get wet," the little boy said. "Momma'll skin us."

"You'll have to take your clothes off," I said. They stared furtively at the
sand in sudden shame.

"I ain't taking my clothes off," the little boy said.

"You'll have to," I said, "or your mother will whip you. And you'll catch
pneumonia and die, in wet clothes. Remember, your mother said to do what
I told you."

"Couldn't you carry us?"

"No, you're too heavy. Then we'd both fall down and get wet. Come on,
now, we've got to hurry. It's getting higher all the time. Remember, you get
a piece of bubble gum if we get back in half an hour."

They began to undress slowly, in fumbling desperation, torn between
shame and fear and a kind of spectral excitement, watching each other furtively
as they stepped out of their clothes and underpants and then stood naked,
trying to shield their genitals with their crumpled clothes.

"Ain't you going to do it too?" the boy said.

"No, I don't have to. I'm tall enough so I can wade without getting my
dress wet." I raised my skirt and tucked it into my underpants. "I'll carry your
clothes. Then if you fall, you won't get them wet. Come on, now." I took their
clothes and herded them out into the shallow water. They gasped at its cold
and hugged themselves, sucking their bellies in with shock, the boy sobbing
with humiliation. I watched his little genitals, tight and blue with cold, jiggling
as he stumbled over the shells of the coarse bottom. Their hard round buttocks
and white thighs were marbled with blue and glistened wetly as they splashed
through the icy water. I came behind them, holding their bunched clothes
above my head, the water reaching just to the line of my tugged-up underpants.
When we had rounded the promontory and waded back to shore, I made them
stand naked while I flapped at their bodies with the boy's shirt to dry them.
I watched his eyes glimmer over his sister's body, lingering on the plump bare
cleft between her thighs, and the girl's eyes, bolder than his, clinging to his
tight little testicles and the tenderly jutting blue bud of his penis. They stood
in a kind of shivering, strengthless abasement while I dressed them, making

no further move to disguise their nudity, and as we walked back toward the shop there was a hushed, servile intimacy about them.

"Come on, let's run. We got to get warm," I said; and I raced ahead of them toward the shop in a sudden feverish exultation, feeling the weight of Aaron's knife in the pocket of my skirt, thumping painfully against my groin.

I took them to the shop and bought them bubble gum from the penny vending machine inside the office, letting them drop the coins into the slot and turn the handle themselves. They were dumbly grateful, and reanimated, running up the path ahead of me to the house and shouting out our adventures to their mother in a burst of vitality they had shown nothing like before.

"Well, my land!" she cried. "You sure do sound like you had a good time!"

"We went way up yonder on the beach," the little girl shouted. "And we seen a freight boat, and Sylvie give me a ruby jewel she found, and she climbed the cliff, and we got bubble gum!" They said nothing of their chief adventure. From moment to moment their glances clashed in brilliant soft confusion, like butterflies jostling one another in flight.

In a moment I went into Aaron's room. He lay without moving, with his eyes closed, but I knew he wasn't asleep; that he was waiting. I sat down beside his bed and watched him for a moment, seeing his eyelids tremble.

"Are you asleep, Aaron?" I said. He shook his head faintly. "You look better. You don't look as hot." He didn't move or speak. "I got your knife," I said. I took it out of my pocket and laid it on the sheet. He opened his eyes to look at it, but did not move his hand. "I had a time getting it. It was way up there." He did not move or speak. "So you'll get well real quick now. Now you got your knife, and all."

I wanted him to rejoice, to seize the knife with delight, to acknowledge the peril I had been through for his sake, to bless my intrepidity. But his face was sallow and still and his hand did not move on the sheet. He stared into my eyes for a moment, blinking hotly.

"You better get out of here," he said in a hoarse, parched voice, as if his throat ached. "You might catch this."

"O.K., Aaron," I said. "You better sleep some now. Aren't you glad you got your knife back?"

He closed his eyes, his head sinking back deeply into the pillow, as if into the surface of the sea.

She sat huddled in front of the fire, which had fallen low, casting a red glare over her still, haggard face. I leaned forward to turn the lamp up in the darkened room, and then checked myself, feeling something imprudent in the act. We sat in silence, watching the tongues of blue flame caper along the crumpled, incandescent logs, making a soft guttural sound of ire. I felt perturbed by the strangeness of her story, and yet distinguished at having been chosen to bear witness to it; because she did not so much relate it to me as re-create, or commemorate, it in my presence. It was more, I understood, than an act of simple impulsive confidence; like so much that Sylvie did, it was almost ceremonial in its gravity and intensity, and I had a sense of eminence at having been admitted into this mystery of her childhood and her existence.

"Shall I get another log?" I asked in a moment.

"No, I'd rather watch it die, wouldn't you? It's a beautiful fire. And then I'll go to bed." She turned her face to me. "Aaron is my brother."

"Yes, I understood that. And Jamed, too?"

"Yes." She looked back into the fire. Studying her head, limned with its brimming nebula against the firelight in front of me, I had a gathering sense of sorrow that crept over me like nausea. I closed my eyes, feeling faint with it. "Have you any children?" she asked.

"I have a daughter. Who would be very nearly your age, I should think. Maybe a little older." I laced my fingers together and clasped my hands between my thighs so that I should not act upon the impulse I felt to touch her hair. "They're in California, I believe. Or they were at Christmastime. She's married to an Air Force officer."

She sat attentively, but I was too weary with the weight of the sadness that I felt to say more; and she did not question me any further. We watched the fire die, the flames dwindling away, the logs slumping and breaking into crimson coals in the black hearth. I rose and drew the fire screen closed and put the chessmen away while Sylvie gathered our cups and saucers and took them to the kitchen. I leaned against the doorframe to watch her rinse and dry them, and then I led her up the narrow stairs to the spare bedroom across the hall from my own. She smiled in admiration, apparently, of the stark simplicity of the primitive furniture against the white walls, for she said, "It looks like a house in Greece, or Spain. I like that. It's a very pleasant house."

"Yes, it is. I'm very comfortable here."

She went across the room to the window and stood looking out.

"The sky is clearing. You can see the stars."

"You can lie in bed and watch them," I said. "I do that often. But if you want to sleep late in the morning, you'd better draw the blind, because you get the sun quite early. By seven, it'll be lying across your pillow."

"I won't mind that at all."

"Good night, then," I said. "I hope you sleep well."

"Thank you, Carl."

I did not sleep well at all. I lay watching the last thin rags of cloud stream, tattering to shreds, across the bright barbs of Orion, which lay like a cruel bramble in the sky. The cold front was coming through behind the snow, and

I could hear the fire thorn creaking in the wind and the bell buoy at the harbor mouth tolling across the black water, hour on hour, inconsolably, as much a knell for something lost forever, it seemed to me, as a peal of warning to souls at sea in the dark tossing wastes beyond my garden fence. That I had given refuge to one of them, at least, if only for this night, I took solace in.

In the morning she was gone, leaving her bed made and a note for me, weighted down with a stack of quarters, on the kitchen table:

Carl:

Thank you for everything (including the cup of coffee which I filched this morning). I got the repairman, and he's coming down at ten, so I'll have heat. The quarters are for my calls.

Love, Sylvie

The day after Sylvie's visit was one of cold and blazing tumult. There was a sky of royal-purple brilliance and a ceaseless icy wind that set the marsh grass raving and the fire thorn scrabbling against the house like claws. I went out into the garden while my tea was brewing to stake the rose trees that were yawing badly by the fences, and came in with my knuckles blue and my ears and cheeks on fire. The water of the estuary was pitching like a cauldron, the current running against the west wind so that the wave tips were blown into a streaming spray, the buoys heaving in a kind of heavy anguish, the naked willows lashing like the hair of Medusas on the shore. I drank several cups of tea and allowed myself an extra English muffin, sitting at the kitchen table and looking out of the window at the pale furor in which the earth was seized, sharing its agitation, apparently, to the extent that I didn't feel at all disposed to perform my usual morning ritual of filling a page or two of my journal.

I went outside to bring in a fresh supply of logs from the woodpile, and since I was already dressed in jacket and mittens, walked down the lane a few paces toward Sylvie's house in time to see a red service van departing from her gate. Satisfied that she would not freeze to death, I retreated to my own backyard, carried in an armload of firewood, and built a fresh fire in the grate, which was still warm from last night's embers. It was too cold to venture out, even as far as to the post office—which, in any case, would have yielded me little—and I lacked the initiative or sense of calm to read or work a chess problem. I sat in front of my new-laid fire, stirring it restlessly with a poker and feeling mysteriously ill at ease until a wholly unexpected resolution formed itself in my mind. It was one for which I have no explanation at all. Why at that moment I should feel the impulse to excavate the least glorious souvenir of a life whose most illustrious one I had little reason to cherish is a mystery, the first of many which Sylvie's advent wrought in my existence.

After my wife's death and my decision to retire and to sell the house on whose steps I had stood to watch her borne away in her final, wordless solitude, I had flung everything in the way of records or mementos of my entire life into a footlocker I had bought expressly for the purpose—everything with the exception of Sir Isaac Newton, my medical bag, and the few books that lined my shelves. Anything that would not fit into the locker I had sold or—since my daughter expressed no more interest in it than she had in possession of the house itself—had given, quixotically, to a charity called the Purple Heart. Every other relic of my passage through this world reposed, untouched for eight months—some of it for as much as thirty years—in the windy attic of my cottage: photographs, diaries, receipted bills for goods and services, programs of official functions, correspondence I had once considered worthy of salvation, notes, memos, certificates, awards—a kind of midden heap of my existence—with no attempt whatever to classify, expurgate, or arrange it. Much of the stuff was my wife's and daughter's, abandoned on their respective (and almost equally taciturn) departures from the house, to be swept up, along with everything else that had a remotely memorial look about it, and tossed into the locker, which owed the voluminousness of its contents not to any reverence of mine for the memories it preserved but, on the contrary, to my reluctance to examine it with the attention necessary to set it in any kind of order. The few critical records, documents, and affidavits necessary to the settlement of my estate—my birth certificate, will, insurance policies, the titles to the cottage and my car—I had months before gathered together and deposited in a safe-deposit box. Why I had kept the rest of that trunkful of sad memorabilia I don't know. I am not a sentimental man, nor one, God knows, who has very much to expect of nostalgia; and yet perhaps I cherished the hope that somewhere among those shards and sweepings of my existence there might exist some souvenir of genuine grace or virtue on my part, some emblem of an act of generosity or kindness that I had forgotten I had ever performed, a relic of some moment of unrecognized, involuntary love. It is not very probable, however. It is far more likely that I was simply unable to dispose of it; that it was for some reason indispensable to me. Perhaps I felt the serenity I enjoyed in that house to be contraband, and my sojourn in it, fugitive. Perhaps I realized that I could never live there in a true and solvent peace until I had resolved the threat to my tranquillity from that teeming heap of testimony overhead.

I don't mean that I wanted merely to set it in order. A concern for order was not the impulse that led me, finally, up the rickety collapsible ladder to the attic to unlock and tug open the dusty cover of the trunk where those remnants of my stay on earth had lain in waiting for so long. Poetry, perhaps; not order—although "poetry" is not a word I use with comfort. "Order," on the other hand, is one I use with far less assurance than I would have fifty years ago. Order promises us refuge from chaos, respite from confusion, which is to say, I suppose, perfection, or the earthly imitation of it; whereas poetry, as I understand it, makes no such promises: it curses us as often as it blesses us, blasphemes as wantonly as it praises, and is very apt to leave us in bewilderment or woe in exchange for a moment's rhapsody. Which is why I suggest that it may have been an interest in something much more like poetry than order that led me, quaking, up the shaky attic stairs. An interest that was inspired, I think, in some involuted way, by Sylvie's hushed, incantatory monologue of the night before.

As I listened to her in the storm-beset house by the fabulous, soft fire, images had formed themselves in my mind; none of them with any great felicity and one of them with such an excruciating and insistent clarity that I could not rest until I had looked at it again: the image of a pair of little girls sitting at the seaside in the light of a lost and haunted summer afternoon. One of them was only three years old, dressed in a tight blue bathing suit—picked out for her with evident indifference—that clung glutinously to the rolls of flesh of her infantile body. She clutched a tin shovel loosely in her fat, limp hand and sat with a look of wan, impassive vulnerability before the glittering, flat, implacable sea that stretched behind her. The other was considerably older, nine or ten, a child with a face of mythical delicacy, with curls of shredded amber and dark blue eyes of sibylline serenity which were raised toward the man who sat beside her, reading, in a beach chair under a striped umbrella, his feet and elbows withdrawn fastidiously into its shade. Beside him, on the sand, there was an open notebook and an unsheathed fountain pen; and on his face the shadow of a frown, the barest token of an unpleasant consternation that had diverted his attention from the text. Somewhere in the depths of my jumbled locker there was the photograph of such a scene set in a small silver frame, and I was moved by the very strange desire to hold it in my hands.

Much of the contents, as I had anticipated, was my wife's and daughter's, not my own; emblems and trophies of their secret triumphs and passions and ordeals that until that hour I had scarcely been aware of, all flung indiscriminately into their coffinlike depository before which I sat in growing discomposure on a stack of ancient telephone directories while I shuffled and delved amongst them. It took a long time—freighted hours—and a great deal of very desultory, very obdurate rummaging to find the photograph, buried deep among such eloquent distractions as these: a faded crepe-paper party hat bearing the legend *Happy Birthday Daddy* in a childish crayoned scrawl around its crown; a paperweight in the shape of the Washington Monument, agonizing in its banality; a cheap little jewel box with its lid crudely embossed with a replica of the Arc de Triomphe, which I remembered quite suddenly having bought—perfunctorily, impatiently counting out the coins—in a tobacco shop in Paris, where, in the course of a medical convention, I had stopped to buy a packet of my favorite tobacco and remembered suddenly that I had forgotten to buy a present for my wife. Or this: a stack of thirty-five anniversary cards, all signed with my name and bearing the brief message *Much Love.* And a weighty, clothbound photograph album, which only the blessed knowledge that the picture I was seeking was mounted in a silver frame relieved me of the necessity of exploring. A thesis, bound in marbled fiberboard, containing something like 150 pages of typewritten script and bearing a title label on its cover which read:

SYPHILIS

A Brief History

With a Summary of the Chief Theories of Its
Origin, Symptomology, and Epidemiology

by

Carl August Ransome

Presented in Partial Fulfillment of the
Requirements of a Bachelor of Science Degree

George Washington University
April 1932

And, perhaps most devastating, most chastening of all, a handsome morocco-leather portfolio bearing my monogram in gold leaf and bulging with awards, degrees, diplomas, certificates of merit, fellowship announcements, letters of commendation, and citations in their dismaying dozens, to the uppermost of which I had attached, with fulsome concern for its survival, a further note of homage from my wife, one whose ambiguity had evidently gone unappreciated at the time: *Carl: I thought you might need something to preserve your honors in. Love on your birthday, Molly.*

All, indeed, is vanity. The locker reeked of it, a sickening smell of spurious, exhausted ardor, like the smell from a laundry hamper of stale perfume on a strumpet's underclothes. I was so oppressed by it that I nearly abandoned my search for the photograph, sitting for a moment with my head bowed in mortification. It must have been a very powerful impulse that gave me the will to pursue it; but I did so, my fingers touching at almost the next moment the oval silver frame I sought. In another moment I had unearthed it, dusted the pane with my cuff, and looked out again onto that silent, sun-drowned beach.

I was astonished at the fidelity with which I had borne its details in my mind for over thirty years.

There was the flat, bright, baleful sea; there was my plump, defenseless daughter, set haplessly between its and my own dire indifference; there was her exquisite, elfin playmate, her eyes lifted with their forever undecipherable look of temerity or tenderness or contempt; there was the studious, slightly distracted man, sequestered in shadow; there, like a cudgel on the sand, lay Molly's cumbrous shadow, bowed over the box camera whose cheap glass eye had seen without deception the sinister, shameful paralysis of our lives and had burned this instant of it onto the scrap of paper I held now in my hands. And there, too, startling me again with its hallucinatory clarity, was a distant, frozen cry of lamentation, pealing endlessly across the sand.

Nature is remorseless. As if I didn't hold sufficient evidence of it in my hand, in the next moment I was offered appalling confirmation of the fact. Because—as if that lost cry still rang through the world—I raised my eyes involuntarily to the attic's gable window through whose quartered panes of Victorian stained glass I was made to bear witness to one of those travesties of nature that nothing on this side of sanity can explain: some livid wintry reflection of the summer tragedy that photograph commemorated. Down there in the water of the raging estuary, a boy in a capsized launch was struggling in frenzy to survive. He seemed to be clutching with one hand a line that was wound around his chest under his armpits, flailing desperately with the other at the churning water of the swamped cockpit. At the apex of each of his frantic strokes something glittered in his hand like a knife blade flashing in the sun; but it was difficult to make out his actions with any clarity because of the distance and confusion, the turmoil of his thrashing arms, the streaming spindrift thrown up by the waves smashing against the upturned hull, and the pall of mist that hung over everything like an aureole. The boy looked no larger than a tin soldier gone terribly amok, and only the fact that he had had the foresight to put on a rubber wet suit before setting out—to tend his crab pots, most likely, as they did all winter long, or simply to savor a reckless boyish challenge of the storm—lent any hope at all to his wild exertions in the icy water; I could see the black sleeves glittering on his arms. God help you now, I thought.

I could not believe for several moments that the scene below me was a genuine part of the reality of that bright tormented day, and not a fantasy of mine, created as I had only just re-created in my mind with bitter clarity the earlier disaster of a long-spent holiday. Framed by the attic window and blotched with its bleeding hues of red, blue, green, and scabrous yellow, it looked startlingly like any of the ancient color photographs I had myself occasionally taken (invariably blurred, as this one was, by the strange palsy that afflicted me whenever I was assigned to memorialize some moment of our lives). I could not move—I could scarcely breathe—for several seconds, groping my way toward belief in its reality. When I had done so, in a blaze of recognition that stung like the splash of acid in my mind, I made my way across the attic floor—hobbling like a routed beggar after having sat for so long— down the lurching stairs, across the kitchen, and out onto the garden walk with a speed that no one would have believed possible in a man of sixty-four. I left the gate flung open behind me, running down the lane to Sylvie's house and up the backyard path to her kitchen door, scattering oyster shells like hail. I pounded only once before opening it, and stood panting on the threshold with the brass knob in my hand. She was baking bread, standing over a mound of fresh, sweet-smelling dough, her hands covered with flour to the wrists. She looked up with a startled frown.

"There's a boy drowning in the channel," I said hoarsely, gulping breath between the phrases. "Run down to Hargison's and tell them to get a boat out. They'll have to hurry, he'll be dead in five minutes. I've got to go back for my bag."

"Where is he?" Sylvie said.

"By the second buoy. Just to landward of it. In a launch. It may have gone down by the time they get there, but I think he's got a life ring." She swept her hands across her apron and snatched her pea jacket from a chair. "Tell them to bring him straight in to the Point; it's too far to the pier."

She laid her hand on my arm. "You take it easy," she said. "You've got time to get there before the boat."

"Yes. Hurry, now."

"All right." She passed me in the doorway and fled up the walk through her back gate, plunging her arms into her jacket sleeves as she ran. I closed the door and followed after her at a lumbering trot now, as far as the lane, then back down my own garden path and through the kitchen to the hall, where I took my medical bag down from the closet shelf. I plucked the afghan from the sofa as I went through the parlor and in a moment was outside again, trotting down the lane toward the Point, peering with burning eyes through the cold wind out across the stormy water of the harbor. From the level of the ground it was impossible to see anything except, occasionally, the tip of the heaving harbor buoy as it rose and fell among the streaming crests; whether the launch had sunk or was hidden by the tossing waves I could not tell. But I could see that there was already a group of people—four of them—standing on the small beach by the drum of the launching cable peering seaward, the one woman's skirt snapping in the wind; and others running along the dark planks of the harbor bulwarks to the Point. Looking back toward Hargison's pier, inside the harbor, I saw that Norm was already setting out. He stood clutching the helm of his lurching Boston Whaler while his son, clinging to the pulpit rail with one hand, reached up to catch the line that Sylvie tossed down to him from the pier. I heard the coughing roar of the huge outboards suddenly thrown into full throttle and stood for a moment, panting, to watch the launch gain speed and plow out through the churning water toward the open estuary, its hull bouncing wildly as it smacked into the heavy waves, the two men in their glittering yellow foul-weather jackets clinging to the helm and rails, spray flying over them like driven snow. I stood long enough to regain my breath, then trotted down between the backs of the last houses on the lane and across the clay road to the small-boat hoist to join the group of watchers on the beach. I knew only one of them to speak to: Turk Edwards, a withered man who sometimes peddled vegetables along the lane in summer; but all of them turned to nod and murmur greetings to me, as I did to them; we were gathered instantly into the strange fraternal intimacy of participants in tragedy.

"Howdy, Doctor," Mr. Edwards said. "He be lucky to have you here. If he lucky enough to git back."

"Who is it?" I asked.

"Jeff Daniels, down there at the five-and-dime."

"You reckon that boy's got a chance?" the woman asked.

"He might," I said. "He's got a wet suit on. I saw him from the attic."

"If he don't drown."

"What you reckon that fool was doing out there?" another man said.

"Damn if I know. He's a wild one."

We heard the thumping of car springs and turned to see a battered yellow pickup truck come bouncing down the clay road from the village, a cloud of carmine dust billowing madly from under it. It slid sideways to a stop, and before the springs had ceased to lurch, the door on the driver's side had opened and a woman in a red plaid lumber jacket, much too big for her, had leapt out and was running down the beach to join us.

"Miz Daniels," a man said.

"Tom Daniels's up to Poole," another said. "I know that."

She came and stood beside us, her feet, in shabby blue bedroom slippers, dug wide apart into the spray-wet stones to brace her against the wind, her skirt blown back between her thighs, giving her a carven look of statuary which her face accorded with; the features bleakly engraved, almost haughty in their stern composure. There were murmurs of greeting to her.

"Miz Daniels."

"Cora."

"Ma'am."

The woman in the group moved to stand next to her, putting her arm

around her waist. "This Dr. Ransome, Cora," she said. "He come right down."
Mrs. Daniels turned to me with eyes as cold as stones.

"You a doctor?" she said.

"Yes."

We watched the skiff smack out into the channel, scattering spray, the two
men bouncing like riders galloping. Jim Hargison raised up to his full height
in the bow and turned to face his father, pointing seaward. We followed the
direction of his arm and saw for an instant, rising in the purple sea, a sliver
of upreared hull and the boy flung across or clinging to it, his arms and
shoulders shining in their wet black rubber sleeves.

"Yonder he is!" Turk Edwards cried. "Lord God, they nigh got him!" He
turned to smite me on the shoulders, howling in triumph. "Look a yonder, Miz
Daniels. That boy's all right."

"They'll git him sure enough!"

"If that skiff don't go down. She got flotation, Cora?"

"I do believe so," Mrs. Daniels said. "I do believe I heard Tom say she did."

"Hell, that thing'll stay up till Judgment Day. They'll git that boy."

Others had joined us on the beach, running along the seawall from the
harbor. Sylvie was among them. She came and stood beside me, and I said to
her, "He's still afloat. They're nearly to him now."

Watching, we saw the Whaler pass the surging buoy, then slow to half its
speed, the bow slumping suddenly in the water. Jim Hargison stooped to lift
a yellow life ring, then stood and leaned forward in the pulpit, holding the ring
raised, clutching the rails against his chest. The skiff swung in a wide circle
to starboard, and we saw clearly for a moment, in a rising swell of the dark,
foam-marbled water, the foundered launch, sunken to its gunwales, rising
peaceably to the swell. The boy's slender body rolled loosely in the swamped
cockpit. He did not seem to be aware of the circling launch, or of anything.
I felt hope guttering in my heart like a flame in a draft.

"Why doesn't he move?" Sylvie said. "Why doesn't he *move?*"

I shook my head, afraid to utter any word of doubt. The whaler slowed
further, to a trolling speed, and began to edge toward the foundered launch,
pitching crazily in the beam-on seas. Jim Hargison had dropped the life ring,
and we saw him now coiling a line about his waist.

"He's got to board her," a man said. "Jeff ain't going to catch no ring."

We saw Jim edge back amidships in the skiff to where the lifelines dropped,
leaving the gunwales clear. He stepped up onto the gunwale, clutching a
stanchion, and waved directions to his father, his figure lurching hectically
against the sky like a statue tottering, one arm upraised. His father plied the
clutch from forward to reverse and back, following Jim's directions, maneuver-
ing delicately. When they had come abreast of the wallowing hull, the son

crouched low in the whaler, almost out of our sight, clinging to the rails with one hand and leaning far out above the swamped boat, working frantically with his free arm; he seemed to be trying to make fast to her. His father put the engines into neutral and, leaving the helm, made his way forward, lurching against the rails and stanchions, to assist him. Then, together, laboriously, perilously, staggering for balance in the pitching skiff, they tugged the boy's body, limp and all too evidently unconscious, across the gunwale and aboard the Whaler.

"They got him!" Turk Edwards shouted. "By God, they got him!" There were cries of triumph from the crowd, and they turned to Mrs. Daniels to reassure her:

"They got him, Cora."

"They'll have him here in a minute now, Miz Daniels. He be fine."

I turned to Sylvie and was astonished to see her rigidly shuddering like a windswept staff, her face clutched in her hands, her eyes gone bleak with horror. I touched her on the shoulder and she started.

"Are you all right?"

She turned her face to me, sallow through its rouge of windburn, and said harshly, "Yes." Then, when her eyes had swept over me, "What about you? Why didn't you wear your coat? You're freezing."

"There wasn't time."

"Well, put this on." She tugged off her jacket and draped it around my shoulders. "I'll go back and get yours. Where is it?"

"Back of the kitchen door. You might bring another blanket while you're there, from off my bed. And some brandy, from the shelf above the sink."

"All right." As she turned to go, I reached out to touch her arm, detaining her.

"And you'd better call the ambulance."

"The ambulance? You haven't done that?"

"No. The Prince Frederick Rescue Squad." I turned back to the beach and heard the scramble of her departing feet across the stones. The launch was making, at full throttle now, for the Point, splitting the seas into two high-flung foaming fountains at her bow. Two of the men ran down the beach and out onto the stone jetty beside the boat launch. I followed, making my way across the wet stone cautiously, hugging my bag against my ribs and swaying in the wind. Thomas Dorsey accompanied me, clutching my elbow in his huge brown hand to steady me. The others came behind, the boy's mother measuring her steps with solemn patience.

We watched as Norm Hargison cut the motors of the launch and edged up to the leeward side of the jetty, wallowing in the pitching water. He tossed up a line to Thomas Dorsey, who held the bow of the Whaler to the wall while the others, crouching and kneeling on the stones, reached down to take hold of the boy's loosely dangling arms and haul him up onto the parapet, his head lolling, his legs thumping strengthlessly against the wall. I folded the afghan and laid it on the stone.

"Lay him on that. On his back." When they had done so, I took Sylvie's jacket from my shoulders and covered his legs with it. Another man peeled off his woolen mackinaw and handed it to me. I laid it across the boy's torso and knelt beside him. There was evidently no respiration and his color was very bad; the marbled blue of anoxia. I ran down the zipper of his snorkel suit to the waist, opened my bag, took out the stethoscope and put it to his chest. There was no heartbeat. I doubled my fist and pounded it, with a brutal thump, onto his chest, above the heart. I heard his mother grunt, almost like an echo of the sound, then sigh heavily. I repeated the blow, then reapplied the stethoscope. The heart was beating now, a faint, uncertain, weary rustle, like the footsteps of a lost child in a forest. I looked up at his mother and nodded. She nodded back to me, a single, eloquent declination of her head.

I put my thumb in the boy's mouth and, grasping his chin with my fingers, pulled his jaw open and forward. Then, lying on the jetty beside him with my arm encircling his head, my face above his own, I pinched his nostrils closed with the fingers of my free hand and pressed my lips tightly against his. They were as cold as the stone we lay on, but no kiss I could remember had ever stirred such ghostly agitation in my breast. I blew my breath into his mouth until his chest had risen, then drew my lips away, releasing his jaw for a moment to press gently on his swollen stomach. There was a trickle of watery saliva from his mouth. I turned his head to the side to let it flow, then pressed my mouth to his again. There was a taste of the sea; cold, salt, abysmal. Again I blew into his mouth, feeling the gradual inflation of his chest beneath my arm, and again released him. We fell into a contrapuntal rhythm, his breast rising with hesitant inspiration as my own sank in exhaustion; then we reversed, exchanging between us in our strange, musical intercourse the breath of life and the cold miasmal air of his drowned lungs.

I had completed perhaps twenty cycles when the group on the jetty parted to let Sylvie stand above us. She held the blanket, the brandy bottle, and my jacket.

"How is it going?" she said. I nodded. "Put this on. You'll have pneumonia."

"Just hang it on my shoulders. And put the blanket over him." She did so, kneeling beside the boy's body. "Now put the stethoscope on his chest. I don't want to stop this." I raised up slightly to let her take the auscultation disk that dangled at my breast and place it on the boy's chest. "A little higher. There." I listened for a moment; the heartbeat was weakening, and there was a systolic flutter that I did not like the sound of. "Do you know how to fill a syringe?"

"No."

"Mr. Dorsey," I said. "Do you think you could do this for a minute or two?"

"I reckon."

I rose to my knees to let him take my place, and watched for a moment to see that he maintained the proper rhythm. I took my syringe and an ampoule of epinephrine from the bag and loaded the syringe. I flushed it, then zipped open the right sleeve of the boy's wet suit, lifted and bound his arm above the elbow with a rubber tube, searched until I found a vein, and injected the solution into it. I handed the syringe to Sylvie, unfastened the tubing from his arm, and set the auscultation disk back on the boy's chest. There was an almost immediate strengthening of the beat and a noticeable fading of the fibrillation. I listened for a moment to make sure it was sustained, then took out my flashlight, lifted his eyelids, and illumined his pupils. There was good light reaction in both eyes. I nodded again to Mrs. Daniels and heard the heavy exhalation of relief through her nostrils.

"Thank you, Mr. Dorsey," I said. "I'll take over now."

I lay down again beside the boy and resumed the grave, languorous exchange of breath between our bodies; there was a sound of assuagement, a silken sibilance, like the wind in leaves. I must have continued, without effort or fatigue, for a quarter of an hour, falling into a kind of trance in which I remembered the stir of curtains in a summer breeze in a quiet room, the shadow of leaves dappling the sunlight on the ceiling, and a fragrance of mimosa from the window; until at last I felt a stir of animation in the body I held enfolded in my arms, a quickening, a warming of the lips, a gently reborn cadence in the breast. I drew back to watch his face, and saw the eyelids quiver, then open wide, and the astonished eyes stare for a moment without moving, as blue as lapis lazuli, into the stream of sunlight on the jetty. They blinked, as if brimming with its benison, and brightened with a tincture of weird gaiety.

His mother dropped to her knees beside him in an instant, a burst of her coarse laughter ringing in the wind like a pang.

"Why, you Jeff!" she cried. "You boy. You no-'count thing!"

She crouched above him, their arms encircling each other, rocking in a strange hilarity. I got to my feet, cramped from the cold stone, and raised my legs to bend my knees, after a moment touching her on the shoulder. She nodded and stood up. I took the brandy bottle from Sylvie, unscrewing the cap and pouring a thimbleful of brandy into it.

"You just lie there, Jeff," I said to the boy. "We're going to help you get your breath good. If your mother will pretend she doesn't see, we're going to give you a little shot of brandy." He grinned faintly. I watched for a minute, until his breathing became more deep and regular, then crouched beside him and raised his head, holding it in the bend of my elbow.

"Try a sip of this," I said. "It's pretty hot, now."

He parted and pursed his lips as I tilted the capful of brandy between them, closing his eyes and shuddering as he swallowed it. "That good?" He shook his head, grinning. "You feel cold?"

He nodded and whispered, "Little."

"Well, the ambulance'll be here in a minute, to take you to the hospital. You're going to rest up there tonight." He nodded and closed his eyes again.

I laid his head back on the afghan and stood up, so exhausted suddenly that I had to brace my legs to keep from staggering. Mrs. Daniels took off her mackinaw, folded it, and then knelt to remove my jacket from her son's breast and replace it with her own. She stood and held the jacket for me while I put my arms into its sleeves. I buttoned it and looked down at the boy, my legs faltering.

"Just let him rest there until the ambulance comes." I took my pipe out of my pocket and tried to fill it from the pouch which I held in my trembling fingers. Crumbs of tobacco fell and whirled away like shreds of gold.

"Would you like me to do that?" Sylvie asked. I nodded. While she filled the pipe I stood looking up into the sky and saw a white bird soaring into the gale high above the harbor; it lifted him up and up, like the ecstatic rising of a violin, through crystalline sheer heights of shining air, higher and higher yet, his outspread wings shivering with exaltation, to some bright pinnacle where for a moment he hung, nailed like a white rose on the noon.

"Look at that bird," I said.

"It's one of his doves." She put the pipe in my hand and I heard the ambulance bearing down on us through a cloud of roseate dust, its siren ringing like a paean through the windy shining precipices where the white bird hung enshrined, pealing to every quarter of the world the wild tidings of salvation.

The next morning I drove up to Prince Frederick to the County General Hospital to check on Jeff's condition, stopping in the village to pick up his mother, as I had arranged. She sat very stiffly beside me on the front seat of the car, wearing a hat of a kind I had not seen for thirty years, which she raised her hand to touch repeatedly, as if assuring herself of its reality. She took a Blue Cross Health Insurance card out of her purse and gave it to me to look at.

"Is that that card you said I'd need?" she asked. She had not had it with her when her son had been admitted, and I had had to vouch for him.

"Yes, fine."

"I never did use it before. We only got it two years ago, when my husband went to work in the Navy base, across the river."

"I see. Well, if we decide he can come home today, you'll have to have it."

"Does it pay for you, too, Doctor?"

"Well, there won't be any fee, as far as I'm concerned. I'm retired, you see. It isn't as if I were in active practice."

She put the card back into her purse and said after a moment, "We have a vegetable garden. We sell produce in the summer; I reckon you've seen our stand by the road. I'd be proud if you'd come up and pick out anything you might need. It's up back of the house. You just come up and take anything you like, anytime at all."

"Thank you very much," I said.

"We get some fine corn and spaghetti squash. Tomatoes, peas. You just help yourself."

"I'll look forward to that," I said. "I enjoy fresh vegetables very much."

Even when our conversation had died and we sat watching the countryside sweep silently past in the bright winter morning, I felt at ease with the woman. I had been out of the village only once since I had first arrived there, six months before, and the world north of the island looked strangely alien and glamorous to me, like one's first view of a foreign countryside from the boat train after debarkation. The gaunt tobacco barns, silver in the sunlight, and the great stacks of fresh-milled timber in the lumberyards along the road, and the stark, ruptured cliffs of the quarries all had the fabulous and stirring quality of a new world, never seen before.

Jeff was in very good condition indeed; he might have just returned from a holiday. I signed his discharge papers in the ward office, and after his mother had attended to the bill, drove them back the thirty miles to Solomons. His chief concern was for his boat, which had been righted and towed in to the harbor by the Coast Guard on the afternoon of his rescue. He wanted to go down to the pier and flush out his engine as soon as he got home, before the salt water could damage the cylinders.

"You leave that to your daddy," his mother said. "That'll keep for another day."

I agreed that he should rest and keep warm for another day at least, as much for her sake as for his. He was shyly obedient, dropping his head and murmuring, "Yes, sir," whenever I addressed him. I left them at the end of their walk, drove home and parked my car in the wooden clapboard shed at the end of my backyard, and walked for an hour along the river shore before I went in to lunch. The wind was blowing still, but far more gently and warmly than the day before, casting a silver stipple over the swampy shallows and setting the bronze marsh grass merrily astir. I watched a winsome little shorebird, a curlew or a piper, patter daintily along the sand, pausing to nip at sand fleas in the bubbling flats. The sky and earth were peaceful; there were soft, clear-edged clouds languidly adrift, their shadows roaming gently as cattle on the hills and casting monstrous bruises on the water. I felt idle, contented, as submissive to the marvels of that lovely, indolent hour—the silvery water, the curlews, the steady southeast breeze—as the great white clouds themselves, and swept by gratitude at the comeliness and clemency of the world.

I went back to the house and made myself a corned beef sandwich, munching it with the mindless pleasure of a cow as I looked out at the sparkling water of the estuary. When I had cleared the table I went up to the attic and put back into the locker the things I had left scattered on the floor about it in my hasty departure of the day before—all but the bound manuscript of the treatise on syphilis, which I clasped under my arm and carried back down the rickety ladder to the kitchen. When I had brewed a pot of tea I carried it into the parlor on my tray, settled into the lounge chair under the southeast window with a cup beside me, opened the faded fiberboard cover, and began to read:

PART ONE. HISTORY.

The disease known as syphilis has a fascination about it which is unmatched by any other affliction of mankind. Its protean and incredibly complex effects are of course a worthy challenge to intelligence and imagination, as they are to scientific method; the suffering it produces calls forth, as nothing else can, compassion, the desire to serve one's fellow man; and the struggle to understand and conquer it has evoked dedication and heroism almost unrivaled in the annals of medicine, or indeed of any science. But there is more than this to be said.

The disease has haunted the thought and history of mankind immemorially, like no other thing. In one form or another it has swept every corner of the earth, leaving behind graves and mutilated bodies and ravaged minds too many to be counted, and a sense of dread that is never quelled. It is the Great Darkness. Not only the darkness that dwells beyond the campfire or the comfortable living room, or the farthest stars, but within them, too. It is among us here. It is within the gay and swirling salons, the congregations of worshippers, the theaters, the marketplaces; all are teeming with it. One out of every eight people whom you meet on your path through life will be afflicted with it; it is everywhere, wherever human beings join their bodies in desire. And so long as they do so, it is inescapable.

There is a famous passage in Deuteronomy which could be a very accurate clinical description of the three stages of this disease: "The Lord will smite thee with the botch of Egypt, and with the emerods, and with the scab, and the itch, whereof thou canst not be healed. The Lord shall smite thee with madness and blindness, and astonishment of heart: And thou shalt grope at noonday, as the blind gropeth in darkness."

There are many such passages in the Bible. David, in Psalms, tells us, "My wounds stink and are corrupt because of my foolishness . . . for my loins are filled with a loathsome disease; and there is no soundness in my flesh." In Exodus, the Second Commandment says in part, "for I the Lord thy God am a jealous God, visiting the iniquity of the fathers upon the children unto the third and fourth generation of them that hate me." In Jeremiah, we read, "In those days they shall say no more; the fathers have eaten a sour grape, and the children's teeth are set on edge." And in Numbers there is what is almost certainly a description of a macerated syphilitic stillborn child: "Let her not be as one dead, of whom the flesh is half consumed when he cometh out of his mother's womb."

Some authorities have interpreted these passages as references to leprosy, but the interpretation is very difficult to support, because leprosy is not transmitted either sexually or congenitally, as these descriptions imply. As a matter of fact, syphilis is one of the few known communicable diseases which can be passed from one generation to another.

There are many other allusions from antiquity. In 460 B.C., Hippocrates, the father of medicine, described genital lesions which followed sexual exposure. In the first century A.D., the Roman physician Celsus described hard and soft genital sores. The treatment of non-traumatic aneurysm of the aorta—one of the most common lesions of tertiary syphilis —was mentioned by Greek and other writers hundreds of years before the time of Columbus.

I introduce Columbus because one school of theory—largely European, as one might expect—asserts that syphilis had its origin in the New World, that it was acquired from the Indians and carried home to Europe by Columbus on his return to Spain. There is much historical evidence for the fact that in the spring of 1495 a violent plague, which most contemporary records attribute to syphilis, broke out among the troops of the army of Charles VIII, who had crossed the Alps into Italy and was besieging Naples. The proponents of this Columbian or New World theory maintain that it was spread by sailors from Columbus's crew, some of whom, along with mercenaries from all parts of Europe, had joined Charles's army. There is, in fact, no proof that any of his sailors had done so; the plague, however, was enough to break up the army of 32,000 soldiers, who scattered in a disorganized retreat. And shortly thereafter, a terrible, continent-wide epidemic broke out in Europe, killing numberless thousands. So severe was it that authorities banished infected persons from cities on pain of death. When consulted for advice, astrologers and physicians produced potions and devices almost as numerous as the victims, none of which, apparently, had any very beneficial effect. Throughout Europe there was dispersed anew that ancient sense of horror which permeates so much of the Bible, and of human history. Italians called the pestilence the Spanish or French disease; the French called it the Italian disease; the English called it the French disease; the Spaniards called it the disease of Hispaniola, or Haiti. Syphilis always comes from the Outer Darkness, never from one's own neighborhood.

Opponents of the Columbian Theory, however (those who propose the pre-Columbian or Old World theory), insist that, given our present knowledge of the epidemiology of syphilis, it would be ridiculous to assume that so small a number of men—if they had indeed joined Charles's army—could have infected the whole of Europe, and that if the disease had been introduced by Columbus and his sailors, it would certainly have been mentioned—as it was not—in the detailed chronicles of his voyage. In fact, Columbus noted in his journal that there was no sickness of any kind on his ship except that of an old man who was "troubled with the gravel." (On the other hand, this sometimes equivocal navigator also reported to Isabella that his voyage took only thirty-three days, whereas it in fact took seventy-one; it is not inconceivable that he may have adjusted other facts to his advantage.) One Old World theorist, Sudhoff, goes so far as to refute entirely the story of the terrible epidemic in the French army before Naples, referring to the reports of Marino Sanuto, the Venetian ambassador to Naples, which have been published in full. He adds that the story of the American origin of syphilis did not develop until almost a generation after the discovery of this continent, and that it was first published in 1518, as an advertisement of the therapeutic value of guaiac, introduced from Santo Domingo. He asserts that there was syphilis in Spain before Columbus's voyage, and that it was quite possible that some of his sailors carried it to the New World and back again. The view is supported by many other Old World theorists, who point out that bones showing the gummatous lesions of tertiary syphilis are found in European and Near Eastern skeletons dating from centuries before Columbus's voyages. And although the curious name of the disease has its origin in a poem by the Italian physician Hieronymus Fracastorius, in which he describes a swineherd named Syphilus as suffering from its symptoms, a poem which was not written until 1530, this, the Old World theorists contend, was no more than a rechristening, by Europeans, of the same disease that they had in ancient times called leprosy; a rechristening that relieved them of the responsibility for it, and thereby their consciences. Their own lovemaking was pure, their own desires impeccable; they were guilty of no iniquities that would be passed down through the generations. As explanation for the sudden and unprecedented virulence of the fifteenth- and sixteenth-century epidemics, Old World adherents offer the further fact that in 1490 and 1505 there were Papal bulls issued which abolished leper houses, allowing thousands of their inmates to wander freely about Europe, carrying with them leprosy and many other diseases that went by that name. If Matthew of Paris can be believed, these leper houses, shortly before their abolition, numbered around 19,000. It is very possible that this liberation of "lepers," many of whom may actually have been syphilitics, accounted in large part for the sudden epidemics.

Proponents of the New World theory reply that many of these freed "lepers," even if in fact syphilitic, would have progressed to non-infectious latent stages of the disease by the time of their release. They add that many pre-Columbian New World bones exhibit lesions indistinguishable from those of ancient European or Asian skeletons, and that, in any case, both or either may have been caused by arthritis deformans rather than syphilis. Dr. William Brown has noted that a physician named Diza de Isla, who was practicing in Barcelona when Columbus's first expedition returned in 1493, wrote that syphilis was unknown prior to that date, and that it was introduced by the men of Columbus's vessels on their return from Hispaniola. Diza stated that he had treated several of these men for a disease which he called "bubas." The term "buba," however, was in use long before the discovery of America, and meant a scab, a wound, or small tumor; which I take as evidence that some disease of that symptomology had previously existed in Europe.

Whatever it may be or has been called—bubas, leprosy, morbus gallicus, mal franzoso, mal français, grosse vérole, pox, yaws, pinta, syphilis— the disease has scourged the world and darkened man's imagination, and his hope, and his thoughts of love, from the beginning.

At this point I closed the notebook and laid it on the tray beside my chair, looking out the window at the cool bright day whose grace had waned dishearteningly since I had sat down to read. I regretted the impulse that had led me to compromise that charm by bringing the treatise down with me from the attic. I don't know what I had expected to discover in it; when I had taken it from the trunk I had remembered with piercing clarity a chilly rented room in Washington on a winter morning forty-two years before where I had sedulously composed it as a sort of covenant, a declaration of commitment to the study I would devote my life to; perhaps I had hoped to find among its pages some reassuring conception of myself as a youthful visionary, a little overzealous, perhaps, but an ordained—and genuine—servant of mankind. But nothing in its perturbed and oddly urgent language furnished me with any such conviction. There seemed to me something very close to counterfeit in its grandly pietistic phrases: ". . . calls forth, as nothing else can, compassion, the desire to serve one's fellow man . . ."; ". . . has evoked dedication and heroism almost unrivaled in the annals of medicine . . ." I closed my eyes wearily. And yet there *had* been such a sense of dedication, of adventure, of mystery; there *must* have been. Perhaps it was just that I wrote very badly. But why could I not feel the palest vestige of that mystery again, reading its youthful testimony—however inept it might be? With my eyes closed, fumbling through my pockets for my pipe in a kind of desperation, I tried to rekindle it in myself, like an aging voluptuary trying to rekindle the passions of his youthful flesh. But the only genuine mystery I could recover from that buried winter afternoon was not the mystery of my consecration to the service of mankind, but the runelike, delicate, spoked footprints of a sparrow in the fresh snow on my windowsill.

In a little while, clutching my pipe bowl in my hand like the butt of a revolver, I fell asleep and was ferried out across dark waters toward a depthless maelstrom whose uproar reached me as a horrifying rumor through the rank mist. I was delivered from catastrophe by the sound of Sylvie knocking at my door. She stood on the top step with a loaf of warm, fresh-baked bread wrapped in a tea towel, its fragrance sweetening the evening air.

"This is real bread," she said. "Whole-grain wheat. You were eating that store-bought junk the other night."

"Come in," I said. "What a wonderful surprise. It smells like manna."

"I bake twice a week. I'll bring you a loaf whenever I do. You can't go on eating that manufactured poison."

"Then you'll have to let me pay you," I said. "That's very expensive charity."

"You can buy me a bag of flour now and then."

"Fair enough. I'm going to have a slice of this while it's still warm. Will you join me?"

"No, but I'll have a cup of tea," she said.

"Good. Let me have your jacket." I took it from her and hung it on the back of the door. She wandered to the window and examined my pothos and philodendron plants while I put a kettle of water on the stove and sliced and buttered the warm bread.

"How is your patient?"

"He's fine. Back home. I drove up this morning and discharged him. They're indestructible at that age."

"I suppose it was the suit that saved him."

"Yes. Still, anyone over thirty would have been dead of exposure, three times over."

"It's a wonder you're not," Sylvie said. "How do you feel?"

"A little stiff in the knees, but very well otherwise."

"You look a little pale," she said. "I hope I'm not upsetting your afternoon."

"No. As a matter of fact, you rescued me from a pretty terrible situation."

"What was that?"

"A dream. A particularly ugly one. I was about to be engulfed."

"You have bad dreams?"

"Occasionally."

She leaned against the windowsill, her arms folded, watching me across the kitchen. "Is there anything I can do?" she asked in a moment.

"Well, yes, if you don't mind. I left the tea tray in the parlor. You can bring it in, if you like."

"All right." She went out into the parlor while I set the buttered bread, the cups and saucers, and the teapot on the table. While I poured the tea she came back into the kitchen with the tray, set the sugar bowl and creamer on the table, and picked up the manuscript, which lay where I had dropped it beside my empty cup.

"What's this?" she said.

"A very badly written thesis on syphilis. It's what put me to sleep."

"Can I look at it?"

"You'll find it very depressing," I said, "being a lover of literature, particularly."

She sat down at the table, opened the notebook, and began to read, sipping at her tea.

"This is absolutely the finest bread I ever tasted," I said.

"I'm glad you like it. I love to bake bread. I think it's the sanest thing a person can do."

"I not only have a source of homemade bread now, but a lifetime supply of fresh vegetables. Mrs. Daniels said I was to come up and keep myself supplied from their garden whenever I liked. They grow everything, apparently."

She murmured and frowned in concentration, her eyes roving brilliantly along the lines. I munched my slice of bread, taking advantage of her absorption to study her face carefully for the first time. She had a type of beauty which is common in the women of Appalachia and the southern Atlantic states, an exquisite English beauty, like that of a Doulton shepherdess, but transplanted and translated, gone slightly barbaric after generations in the laurel hells of the southern mountains and the pine barrens of the Tidewater; very delicate lips and nostrils and a sweetly modeled chin with an air of bitterness about them; a high, queenly forehead, hollowed at the temples, and fine, fierce eyes set under thin, tall, ireful brows and very prominent milk-white vaults of bone, smooth as the swept curve of a seashell; eyes like hot blue pearls under a canopy of nacre. She reminded me of the heroines of the Elizabethan ballads which, with her own ancestors, had been borne across transforming leagues of sea; Barbara Allen or Lady Greensleeves, but sturdier, surer-footed, with nimbler, more skillful hands, hands gone brown with mountain bane, as her eyes had darkened with the woe of exile; she enchanted me.

It was late evening. The sun was very low across the water, and I watched the blown ribbons of shadow from the branches of the fire thorn bush outside the window fluttering avidly across her eyes. The cheap electric clock on the shelf above the sink purred hoarsely with a soft, agonized sound, like the long-drawn death rattle of some endlessly expiring thing. I watched the room darken, little hectic jewels of light sprinkling the cut-glass canisters on the shelf beside the clock. I was moved almost to tears by the beauty of her face in its ardent, royal solitude of thought, with those lascivious shadows lapping at her eyes.

"You'll go blind," I said, and moved to light the lantern.

"Don't light it." She looked up, closing the book and laying it on the table. "It's so lovely in this room. I want to take your book home and finish it. May I?"

"I thought you weren't going to read a book all summer. Or ever, perhaps."

"I'll make an exception. This will be the last one I ever read. Yours."

"I would hate to think so," I said. "If I had written it with that thought in mind it would be very different."

"It's fascinating. Is that your specialty? Syphilis?"

"Yes."

"I would never have guessed it. Yesterday you were behaving very much like an old-fashioned country G.P." I shrugged. "What was that you were saying about Mrs. Daniels?"

"She has offered me a lifetime supply of fresh vegetables."

"You'll be very healthy. You'll live to be a hundred, with nothing but fresh vegetables and homemade bread."

"I will indeed," I said. "I think I'm going to have another slice right now." I began to cut the bread carefully, the still-warm dough clinging to the knife blade. I was aware of her eyes resting studiously upon me.

"Carl," she said. "Why didn't you call the ambulance?"

"I didn't think of it, I guess. Things were rather rushed, if you remember."

"It would have been here by the time they got him to the jetty. With the respirator, oxygen, everything."

"Yes, I suppose it would." I buttered the bread carefully, trying not to crumble its soft, warm flesh. "I wanted to do it myself, I suppose."

"That was quite a gamble."

"It didn't seem so at the time. But I suppose it was." I bit into the bread and munched busily. Our eyes met, and after a moment she smiled sweetly. "Will you tell me something?" I asked. "I mean, as a literary critic?"

"I'm not a literary critic," she said. "And, after all, I've barely begun it."

"Have you read enough to say whether there was any—passion—in it?"

"Why don't you let me read the whole thing, before I have anything to say about it?" She dropped her eyes to the cover of the manuscript and read the lettering. "Nineteen thirty-two. How old were you?"

"Twenty-two. I was just about to enter medical school."

"And you'd already decided to become a—what do you call it?"

"Syphilologist? Well, communicable diseases was my field, actually; of course one doesn't begin to specialize until he's graduated, got his M.D. and begun a fellowship. Still, I suppose that thesis was a sort of declaration of intent. I think I was always fascinated by syphilis, from the time I was a boy. 'Obsessed' is a better word, I suppose."

"Why?"

"I don't know. Oh, I suppose I have an idea. One can't help having an idea about the things that 'frame one's destiny,' to use a very much too splendid phrase." I dusted my hands over my plate and wiped my greasy fingers with a napkin. "They hardly make for teatime conversation."

Sylvie peeked into her cup, lifted and drained it, and set it down. "Well, I've finished my tea. If you feel like talking about it."

I stared steadily for some time at the croaking clock on the shelf, the quaking of whose entrails seemed to furnish my thoughts with a mordant obbligato. "I think it must have had something to do with the terror I've felt of blindness all my life. Ever since I was a boy. I can remember that when I was no more than five or six, the sight of the pale glazed eyes of dead fish, lying in the chipped ice of a market stall, filled me with a sense of dread that turned me cold: that extinguished brilliance, round and perfect, staring in fixed, perpetual astonishment. I used to touch them with my fingertips sometimes, in a kind of thrilled horror.

"When I was a boy we used to spend our summers at a house in Maine, an old cottage on a salt pond near Blue Hill. It had a cellar with an earthen floor and a trapdoor that led to it from the yard. One very bright summer day I was playing in the yard, swinging in a tire that was tied by a rope to an apple tree, when my mother called out to me from the kitchen window to fetch a basket of apples from the cellar. I lifted the trapdoor by its iron ring and went down the stone steps out of the brilliant sunlight, letting the door fall shut behind me. I found myself suddenly blind in the cool darkness underground. I stood there paralyzed with fear and, at the same time, a kind of exaltation.

I felt myself enfolded by the dank, deeply comforting earthen scent, the musty, subterranean seclusion, the dark odor of roots and tulip bulbs drying on their wire screens, the mold-encrusted stone. After a time the shapes of beams and barrels and shadowy baskets of fruit were reborn slowly as my eyes were reconciled to the dark. I never forgot that moment, the curious glamour of it.

"Once, reading in a school biology textbook about a species of blind fish that lives in the pools of underground caverns, I remember feeling a kind of grief, so abject that it was almost recognition, almost a personal subjection to the plight of this creature that had never in its life, or for hundreds of thousands of years in the life of its species, beheld anything; that had lost even the racial memory of what it means to see while still carrying in its head the useless, withered organs of the most precious of all faculties. I was forever reading about blindness. I exhausted the encyclopedia's lore on the subject. I shared and suffered the degradation of bats, moles, earthworms, and all the creatures of the bottommost ocean depths. I dreamt of myself as one of those pale, groping things, moving among them with wavering, bleached, slime-coated tentacles, lost to light forever, sunken in sunless dreams of what the world must be. When I was twelve, I read a story by H. G. Wells entitled 'The Country of the Blind,' and I was sick for a week with the revulsion it woke in me.

"There was a blind man who used to wander through the streets of the little suburban town outside of Washington where I lived. He carried a white stick held out tremulously in front of him like a wand, tapping at curbs and lampposts and mailboxes. I thought of him as a magician, an evil but infinitely powerful wizard, laying spells on everything that his pale staff touched or singled out for damnation. The sound of the metal ferrule of that cane, tapping along the sidewalks, used to haunt my sleep. Someday he would point it at me, I felt sure of it. He would seek me out and jab that awful white wand at me, and I would feel my heart wither in its black spell, and my eyes would darken forever. Sometimes, walking home from school in the early afternoons, I'd see him coming toward me down the sidewalk. He walked slowly, but very erect, with his head held high, like a blind soldier. It was a terrible walk: resolute, unhurried, the cane held out in front of him, touching things. He seemed to be in implacable pursuit of sinners, of the doomed—myself mysteriously among them. I would shrink back into a doorway, feeling a thrill of terror sweep over me like a caress.

"One day when I was walking home with a schoolmate, he turned the corner suddenly in front of us and came toward us, tapping the stone in that weird, predatory way. My friend clutched my arm and dragged me back against a shopwindow. We stood there with our backs pressed to the pane, watching him pass. 'You know who that is?' my friend whispered. 'No.' 'That's old Rim Frailey. My daddy went to school with him. You know what he's got?' 'No.'

'He's got syphilis. That's the worst thing you can get. My daddy told me to never let him breathe on me. If he does, you can get it too.'

"I'd never heard the word before. It was the foulest word I'd ever heard. It had an evil, sibilant sound, like a serpent hissing. It echoed in my head for days. At night it shrilled through terrible dreams I had of a filthy, blank-eyed wizard stalking me through endless, labyrinthine streets, thrusting out a pale viper that struck at me repeatedly, spitting the awful word like a curse.

"I became obsessed with it. In the next month or so I ransacked the school and town libraries, searching out every desolate fact that I could learn about it. I went through dictionaries, encyclopedias, and medical textbooks (when I could gain surreptitious access to them in reference rooms), studying its hideous symptoms and history and etiology. Nothing else I've ever suffered on this earth equals the shock of my discovery that it was transmitted through the act of love. It was the sovereign revelation of my life. Why would God punish human passion in this monstrous way? It was evident that he detested it. Sex was abominable in his sight. It could not be dismissed as irony, as one of life's random, mindless incongruities. God's wrath spoke through this horrible disease. It was a divine execration of man's vilely imperfect love. The fact demanded reverence as well as horror. Such a manifest expression of God's loathing of our base desires could not be ignored. I can remember forcing myself, as a religious duty, to stare at a colored photograph of a chancre in a medical textbook, telling myself that this hideous flower of evil was just as compelling evidence of his existence as a rose. (The thought didn't occur to me that a rose is a peculiarly voluptuous genital organ, created for the explicit purpose of seduction and sexual intercourse.)

"I was twelve then. Four years later, in my final year of high school, another friend persuaded me to accompany him one night on a graduation celebration along the Block, in Baltimore. I guess you know the Block. I had ten dollars, donated by my father as a reward for the unsullied column of A's I had accumulated on my report card. (I was an outstanding scholar, if an unreliable theologian.) My friend had managed to get the addresses of several speakeasies along that tawdry street, to which its easy virtue gave us access, in spite of our ages. We moved from one to another of them—ten dollars went a lot further in those days—and for the first and last time in my life, I got very drunk. I've begun to drink a little now, as you saw the other evening, but I don't think you'll ever see me drunk. Even then, I wasn't drunk enough to yield to my friend's attempts to persuade me to join him in a visit to a brothel with whose address he had also been provided. My memory of those terrible texts and noisome illustrations was far too strong for that. I stood downstairs in the doorway of a deserted bakery while above me, at the top of a flight of moldy stairs, he made what I'd come to think of, in the language of my research, as 'the beast with two backs.' He came down half an hour later, flushed with achievement, and mocked me all the way home for my pusillanimity, giving me extravagant descriptions of the beauty and ardor of his hostess and his own heroic prowess. Two weeks later my humiliation was redeemed, not very joyfully. He took me to his house, very pale, his face gone bleak with fear, led me upstairs to his bedroom, locked the door, took down his trousers, and begged me to refute the diagnosis he himself had made of the great copper-colored ulcer that was the flower of his lechery.

"It may not surprise you to learn that my interest in the opposite sex languished considerably, and for some time. It would certainly not surprise anyone who had ever joined the Army and been required to watch the indoctrination films on venereal disease which I myself have helped to prepare. I became even more studious, even more dedicated to the life of scholarship, to reason, method, discipline, prudence, self-restraint, and all the virtues celebrated by my teachers, ministers, parents, scoutmasters, and a brace of maiden aunts, who rewarded them with such tribute as a leatherbound Bible, an Eagle Scout insigne, a bicycle, a set of encyclopedias, and, eventually, a scholarship to George Washington University, all of which I eminently deserved.

"But I'm not naïve enough to credit all of my youthful accomplishments, or all that I became, to the series of misfortunes I've been describing to you. Perhaps I found in those events the auguries I wished to find. Perhaps I used them to justify obsessions and compunctions that dismayed me in myself. Maybe we're all too eager to ascribe our faults and failings to our experience. Perhaps all experience is innocent; we make of it what we will. If we search diligently enough, we can find very convenient proof in it for the validity of our fears and incapacities. Let me tell you a very strange thing: I can remember hearing a wolf howl on two separate occasions, in northern Maine, when I was a boy. But I can't remember, ever, hearing birdsong in that place." I took a sip of tea, which had turned quite cold.

"Do you think you would have been a syphilologist in any case," Sylvie said, "no matter what experience you might have had?"

"I think it's very likely. I don't know. I know I heard wolves howl, and I feared them. No one ever told me that they gambol like puppies, too, and chase their tails, and die of grief sometimes." She frowned at me across the table, her eyes falling to a troubled contemplation of her teacup. "The fact is," I said, "that I can remember the very moment I decided to make the study of syphilis my life's work. It's one I can't forget."

"It sounds like quite an awful moment," she said.

"It was. I don't think you want to hear about it."

"I do." I saw that she meant this.

"All right. You have yourself to blame. It was the first time I ever saw a case of it. With my own eyes, I mean—not a photograph. And apart from that brief glimpse I had of my friend's primary ulcer. In my third year of medical school a group of us were taken to the clinic to see a patient in the advanced stages of a mucocutaneous tertiary form of the disease. She was a Puerto Rican woman, in her middle thirties. I can even remember her name: Clara Mundo; an odd sort of name that means 'Clear World,' or 'Bright World,' or something of that sort. She was wearing one of those cheap rings with a magnifying glass stone that you can slide a picture behind, and there was a photograph inside it of a dog's face. A dog with a huge white spot around one eye. A grotesque thing. I suppose that dog was the thing she loved most, I don't know. Or the only thing that loved her any longer. This woman had massive gummatous lesions of the face. There was extensive caries of the facial bones, the nasal septum, and perforation of the hard and soft palates. Most of her nose had been eaten away, and the center of her face, from eyes to lips, was laid open in a gaping septic cavity. It was such an unholy deformity that I couldn't sleep for days after seeing it. I can remember, much less clearly, the first time I ever saw an abdomen laid open by a scalpel, or an active carcinoma, but this experience was very different from those. I really can't describe it adequately. Looking at that woman's ruined face, I felt a kind of ancient, total horror, so great that it seemed impossible for any one person to conceive of, or to bear. I seemed to be looking at all disease, all filth, all evil, and what I felt was something like the cumulative outrage and anguish of an entire race, through all the centuries of its history. Something a little less horrible might have turned me away from the practice of medicine entirely, but I could never turn away from such a sight as that. I could never pretend it didn't exist, or that I hadn't seen it. It seemed to me that from that moment on I would have to measure every instant of grace or ease or beauty, every pleasure or joy that I ever experienced in my life, by that sight, that awful, irrefutable reality. That was the moment I decided—or was condemned, perhaps—to study it, to stare at it forever, until I understood it.

"Not long after, we went to the clinic again one day for an exercise in diagnosis. The patients we examined were presenting themselves for treatment for the first time. One of them was a tall, rather faded-looking but still vigorous man in his early fifties. He complained of a sore throat, nasal congestion, and a general sense of feverish fatigue. We examined him carefully, and afterwards were questioned by our instructor, a senior physician named Loughran, a man of considerable reputation as a diagnostician. The consensus of opinion was a pharyngeal bronchitis with no involvement of the lungs, a simple respiratory complaint. I agreed with this, but I had an additional diagnosis to make, one I was so eager to announce that I delivered it with a good deal of boldness and assurance. I became famous for that, later. When Dr. Loughran asked if I concurred with the general verdict, I said, 'Yes. But I think there's more the matter with him than that.' 'You do,' he said. He was a very forbidding man. 'Yes. I think the patient has syphilis. I'd say that within three years he'll probably be blind.' I was reassured to see the eminent man smile and tug at his eyebrows, a gesture I'd learned that he reserved for his very rare approval of a student's judgment. 'Can you tell us why?' I was eager to. I had noticed, on shining my flashlight into the man's eyes, a subtle but unmistakable deficiency in the light reflex of his pupils, together with a slight sectoral reduction of the pleats of his irises. They were drawn out somewhat too tightly, like the pleats of a paper lantern that has been stretched beyond its intended shape, causing the irises, which were a caramel brown in color, to lose the brilliant shimmer of those of a healthy eye. There was no inflammation, and the condition might well have been overlooked by an inexperienced observer. I was inexperienced enough, but my lifelong preoccupation with sight and blindness led me always to make a particularly scrupulous examination of the eyes. It was rewarded now. 'There is light-near dissociation of the pupillary reflex,' I said. 'And also a partial reduction of the iritic pleats. This seems to me to be an example of the Argyll-Robertson syndrome. I think the patient is exhibiting the early symptoms of tertiary syphilis. I would predict an onset of tabes dorsalis or paresis.' 'Well, that's a little dramatic, Ransome,' he said. 'And maybe a little overconfident. But the opinion is basically sound. Neurosyphilis is certainly indicated, and every effort should be made to confirm it. Have you been reading Dutemps, by any chance?' I had; in fact, the language I'd used to describe the symptoms was borrowed almost verbatim from the famous monograph. It was an old text, and not one assigned to us, but my zeal had led me into its pages. 'It's a remarkable monograph,' Dr. Loughran said. 'Especially when one considers the date of its publication: 1906. I'm pleased to see that you've profited by it. Suppose we get Mr. Corvo back in here. Let's see how you proceed with him.'

"The patient was brought back into the examination room. Waiting outside, he'd grown nervous and distressed. His face was pale and he asked for a glass of water. I gave him one, and asked him to roll up his sleeve. Dr. Loughran stood by, frowning studiously. 'Mr. Corvo, you have a bronchitis,' I told the man. 'It's not serious. We'll give you some medicine for it, and if you stay in bed for a couple of days you ought to feel much better. But we'd like to make some additional tests.' 'What sort of tests?' the man asked anxiously. He was an uneducated man, a mechanic, and seemed to be unpleasantly awed by the preparations I was making. I tightened a rubber tube around his forearm, swabbed the inner arm with alcohol, and took a syringe out of the sterile cabinet.

" 'Well, we're going to take a little of your blood and have a look at it,'

I said. 'If this bothers you, just look away.' His pallor deepened and his jaw muscles knotted as the needle went into his vein and the blood welled up into the glass cylinder of the syringe. I withdrew it and set the filled scarlet cylinder in a test rack. 'Now, we're going to ask you to come back in two days, and we'll take some more. Then we may need to extract some spinal fluid. It's a very simple procedure. Can you arrange that?' 'Why do you have to do all this?' he said. 'I don't have anything but a cold. A touch of bronchitis. I don't see why you have to do all this.' 'We think you may have more than just a cold,' I said. 'What? What do you think I've got?' 'Well, it's possible that you have a disease called syphilis. We want to make sure, so you can be treated for it if necessary.'

"It's a long time since that happened; forty years. But I don't think I ever really saw, until years later, what my eyes registered at the time. It's as if a photographic print had been developing in a tank of chemicals, very slowly, all those years, its details emerging by incredibly minute stages until it was sharp and clear at last, and I could understand what I had seen, the verity of the image withheld until that moment. What I saw was terror, an august, immeasurable terror that transfigured the man's face. He was suddenly made larger, nobler, vast with it, distended almost beyond human dimensions, like Oedipus. A kind of supernatural afflatus possessed him, and those telltale eyes of his were crowded for a moment with all the furor of a nebula. I think the only observance I paid him at the time was to press a sterile swab against the puncture in his vein. I should have knelt to him."

Sylvie did not reply immediately. Neither of us spoke for some time.

The room was quite dark now; only a roseate afterglow tinting the clouded ceiling. We sat facing each other in identical positions, our elbows on the table, our fingers laced together, our joined hands supporting our chins, so that for an instant I was able to beguile myself with the fantasy that I was confronting my own image in a mirror, seeing fleetingly an authentic version of myself that I had never seen before: young, feminine, beautiful, impassioned, and possessed of enough grace to say, as she did then, "Well, we all see through a glass, darkly. You don't need to be ashamed of it forever, Carl. I think I would trust such eyes to see for me."

I n the middle of March there was a week of unnaturally fine weather. The warm bright days brought the willows into early bud and their beaded branches swung like rosaries in the breeze. The soil of my garden split and swelled almost overnight with hyacinth and jonquil buds that here and there thrust through the moist lips of the cleft earth the tip of a tiny, pale green tongue, as if tasting the honey of the spring light that lay in sweet fathoms in the huge hive of the sky.

I did not see much of Sylvie; she was up and out at dawn, and abroad all day, as I often was. I would see her thrusting through the dune grass with her paint box and easel and a square of canvas board clutched under her arm; or standing waist-deep in the waving grass before her easel, her hair glowing like a great soft mallow flower; or wading in the shallow water along the edge of the sandbar by the cable crossing, her bunched skirt clutched in front of her with one hand, the other outstretched for balance as she picked her way among the shell banks in the sand. She never failed, however, to bring me a loaf of fresh-baked bread on Wednesday mornings. If I was out, or upstairs in my study, she would leave it on the kitchen table wrapped in a tea towel, sometimes with a sprig of budding pussy willow or a stalk of forsythia that had broken into yellow blossom.

One day she came into the kitchen when I was sitting at the table with my morning cup of tea listening to a symphony of Bruckner that was playing, very loudly, on the radio in my parlor. She stood at the door for a minute, listening, and shuddered.

"I'm afraid it's very loud," I said. "I've gotten a little deaf. Let me switch it off, and we can have a cup of tea."

"No. For God's sake, don't switch it off for me," she said. "I just can't stand symphony. It's such damned noisy stuff." Before I could detain her, she had turned and gone.

A few days later, on my way to the grocery store, I saw her outside the post office with what looked like a manuscript in her hand. If it was a letter, it was a very long one, because it was composed of fifteen or twenty sheets of typewritten paper. She held them clutched loosely in one hand that hung against her hip. Her head was raised to stare out across the broad glittering water of the river bend with an idle, almost weary look of feeling. When she heard my steps in the street she turned her head toward me without seeming to recognize me until I spoke to her:

"I want to thank you for the bread. It was delicious."

"Oh. You're welcome."

She raised her hand to comb her hair from her eyes with her fingertips and then stooped to thrust the sheaf of pages among the parcels in the network market bag that lay at her feet.

"And the forsythia. It's in full bloom now. It lights the whole room up."

"I'll bring you another loaf tomorrow."

"Will you stop and have lunch with me?"

"All right."

"I'm just on my way to market," I said. "I see you've been already."

"Yes."

"I'll see you tomorrow, then." She nodded and turned down the road toward the Point, walking in her yare and thrusting way, like a boat in a fresh breeze.

She came at noon the next day with a loaf of fresh bread which we ate for lunch. She seemed impatient and distraught. The weather was warm enough to open the windows, and there was a sweet smell of grass from the yard. Sylvie carried her cup to the window and stood looking out.

"Your crab apple is coming into blossom," she said.

"Yes. You must take a spray of it home." She said nothing, staring out into the yard without hearing. "Have you been walking already?" I said.

"No. I slept as if I were dead. It's awful to sleep like that." She came back to the table and stood plucking crumbs from her plate and nibbling them. "I'm going home next week, for Easter."

"That will be nice," I said. "You don't have far to go, do you?"

"No. Momma thinks it's very odd, my staying down here. But I think she's finally beginning to realize that I can't stand to be there for more than a few days at a time. She doesn't fuss about it anymore. I go home for all the holidays, and her birthday, and Jamed's."

"Does Aaron come home, too?"

"When he's not too damn busy. I must say he's pretty good about it, usually. We always have to have an Easter egg hunt for Jamed. He couldn't stand to miss that."

"For Jamed?" I said.

"Yes." She looked up in answer to the confusion that must have been evident in my voice. "Jamed is retarded. The world stopped for him when he was nine years old. We have a birthday party for him every year, with nine candles on the cake. That's a ritual my father inaugurated." She began to cut a slice of bread, watching with frowning fascination as the blade sheared off the tottering white slab. It fell backwards like a collapsing headstone, and she stared at it with chagrin. "Would you like another slice of bread?"

"I think I would, thank you. You're a marvelous baker."

She dropped the slice of bread onto my plate and watched me butter it. "At least, he's coming for *my* birthday this year. For once. He'd better. I'll kill him if he doesn't."

"You sound very determined."

"It's the halfway point of my existence. I'll be thirty-five. Half my life is gone." She looked at me across the table in a kind of surly disbelief of her own words.

"I wish I could say that I still had half of mine to *live*," I said.

"He promised," she said, as if she had not heard me. "He swore he would. I made him swear it: that he'd spend the noonday of my life with me. I'll kill him if he doesn't."

"When is your birthday?" I asked.

"The twenty-second of June."

"That's the summer solstice, isn't it?"

"Yes. I had a lover once who said he could always remember it because I came floating in on the flood tide of the world like a frangipani blossom out of tropic seas." Her voice glinted with a mockery that I understood was more of herself than of the author of the phrase.

"He must have been a poet," I said.

"He was." She picked up the bread knife and touched the ball of her thumb to the edge of the blade, closing her eyes while she tested its sharpness. "Can you imagine saying a thing like that about me? Of course he was very young. Or he seemed very young." She frowned suddenly, lowering the knife to the table. "Actually, he was older than most of the students, because he was in Vietnam. He may even have been older than I was. I don't really know how old he was. Isn't that odd?" She turned her head and stared out of the window. "He seemed almost like Jamed sometimes. As if he were still a child, in a strange, spellbound way. As if his life had been arrested in some moment of experience it had never been able to surmount. He had that wide-eyed, inno-cent, faintly astonished look sometimes when he was thinking. Aaron sponsors some children like that. What are they called? They're usually very beautiful, but almost mindless."

"Autistic?"

"Yes, that's it. He had a beautiful face, but that devastated look, as if something in him had gone soft and rotten. There was a center of pain in him, a kind of pulpy, mutilated core, like a bruised fruit. A windfall apple or a persimmon that has been beaten against the branches in a spring storm. They get ripe too early and they're soft and brown inside." She turned her head sharply from the window and looked into my eyes as if replying to an accusa-tion. "I didn't want to meet him, God knows. Not then; it was far too late. Although I'd longed all my life for a poet's love. It was all I'd ever really sought. And I'd sought it very—industriously—to put it in the pleasantest possible way. But not then. Not when my life was beginning to assume form and order of some kind. And not when there was someone else involved, someone I had an enormous obligation to; as there was. I don't think the circumstances could have been less propitious." She came back to the table and sat down across from me. "Shall I tell you about it?"

"Yes."

It was an April afternoon and raining a little. There was a gray warm sky and elm blossoms and cherry petals falling everywhere around the campus, littering the grass and pavement like confetti. The world looked like a dance floor after a ball.

I teach at the University of Maryland; I don't know if I ever told you that. There is a path that goes down the hill from Tydings Hall across the common and through an old brick viaduct that's crusted with moss and lichen. He was standing in the arched passage under the viaduct, sheltering from the rain, and I came running through the quickening drops to share the shelter with him. We stood and watched it fall, our hair shining.

"Do you think it will last?" I said.

"I don't think so," he said. "It's too nice to last."

He could say a thing like that without making it sound nimble, cunningly suitable. Nor mournful. It's important that I make you understand the nature of this boy; and very difficult, with only myself as witness. You simply must hear people speak, to appreciate them truly. A tone of voice can be just as illustrative of nobility as a single-handed assault on a barricade. Or of folly, or bravura. And since I'm telling you this at all, I'd like it to be absolutely true, in everything. For example: I love the smell of certain exotic colognes and after-shave lotions that men wear. Now, that's appalling, I know, but it's true. I see them advertised on television and I'm appalled. But if a man stands near me on a bus wearing one of them—or under a viaduct in a spring rain—I can be ravished by it. I'm sure you find that hilarious. If I said he smelled of leather or wet tweed or tobacco, I would have a much more respectable claim on your attention. Or of gunpowder—God knows, I *could* say *that*—and we would both be more comfortable. The trouble is, he didn't smell of any of those things, but of something called Parliament Cologne, which Aaron used to do the TV spiel for. This poet did. Now, it's true; and in your opinion, the beginning of either a maudlin or a comic tale. You feel entitled to smile. I want you to bear that in mind.

He made that modestly intense remark that showed his pleasure in the situation, and I was flattered. I think you may have guessed that I'm not ordinarily flattered by men's overtures. Also, I was somewhat astonished by his looks, because he certainly didn't look like the kind of man who would douse himself in Parliament Cologne. He was wearing the old Army fatigue uniform that he never took off—I never saw him in anything else. It was faded and frayed and there were dark green patches on the breast and sleeves where he'd ripped off the insignia. He was very tall and had a look of hard physical strength that wasn't matched at all by that soft ruinous intensity of his face. He had dark attentive green eyes that clung to you almost importunately when he spoke, as if he were begging you not to misunderstand him, and large, rather livid lips with tiny freckles sprinkled around them, and long, dark red hair through which the tips of his ears protruded honestly. I don't like small, close-set ears at all; they give a man a simian look. I loved his face the minute I saw it and I suppose I loved him, too, as much as I ever could, and yet there was something about him that made me ache with apprehension, even then. It was that wounded quality, I suppose; it seemed to suffuse all of him, everything he did and said. All his words and expressions and gestures—even his silences—seemed to be tainted by some hectic, afflicted energy that animated them. This is a terrible thing to say, but I had the feeling, sometimes, that he fed on his own wound; that it was still open, bleeding, inside of him, and he drank the blood of it as his chief nourishment. Do you know that a lot of the Vietnam veterans went off into the woods when they got back and lived in there like animals or mountain men? Hundreds of them. There are still some of them in there, in Washington State and Oregon and Michigan, who can never live in society again, who've been turned into wolves or hermits. I had the feeling that that might have happened to Nils, and that it might still happen, almost anytime, if it weren't for me. And yet he was so wonderfully intelligent and sensitive and gentle, and he reminded me so much of Aaron, and of Jamed, too, in that childlike, spellbound way of his.

Well, there we were, under the arch of that culvert, with the rain coming down on the quince hedges and the willow oaks outside, and I could feel him watching me so steadily and hungrily that I began to fear he had been waiting for me there, that he had waylaid me. After all, I went that way three times a week after my six o'clock class, and he might have known that and skillfully arranged this meeting with me. There is nothing I distrust so much as skill, skill in conversation, in relationships, in composing the circumstances of one's life—such as this one—skill in anything. That calculated quality, that blights things, takes the bloom from them: peaches in a bowl; those still lifes arranged with a kind of skillful, blasphemous vapidity on a table in a studio. Some of the most endearing lines in literature to me are from Cortázar's *Hopscotch:* "People who need lines on their writing paper, or who squeeze a tube of toothpaste from the bottom up. People who think nothing is true unless there are programs and ushers." When he shifted his eyes away from me for a minute, I watched him watching the rain beyond the arch and the shining roofs of wet automobiles moving above the top of the gray stone wall that divides the campus from the avenue. He seemed to regard them artlessly enough, a bright mist gilding his hair and eyebrows, and I felt a kind of fearful rejoicing. I realized that I had been awaiting such an encounter for years, and had feared that it might be arranged. That *I* might arrange it, even, in desperation. He turned his eyes back to me and said, "I just came out of your lecture. I really enjoyed it."

"You *did?* Well, I hope you didn't find it incomprehensible. I tend to get intense about the Romantics."

It was not unusual that I had failed to recognize him, if he was one of my students, because it was a freshman survey course, in which there were something like two hundred people registered; but, on the other hand, by the last month of the semester I have usually learned their faces, certainly one like his. But of course many are often absent, and with so many students, there is no time to allow discussion, to associate tones of voice, intelligences, with faces.

"I don't belong in it. I mean, I'm not registered. I just sneaked in to hear you lecture because I heard you were great."

That, again, could be skill; but when such a thing does happen, it usually is not. And of course, nothing is more flattering. With so much flattery, and the rain, and the cool air around our throats and faces—and, of course, that cologne—I was growing demented. Then there was that arched, crumbling refuge that we shared, like a little private cathedral, a passage between two worlds.

"It wasn't incomprehensible," he said. "But some of it was difficult. For me. What you said about Keats, for example. I never heard that said before."

"I hope not," I said. "I don't like to say anything in a lecture that you can just read in a book. That's someone else's opinion, memorized."

"No." He backed against the wall, bracing his shoulders just below the curve of the arch, looking out into the rainy air with a scowl which I thought enchanting, like a child pausing halfway to the store, trying to remember what it has been sent to buy. "You disagree with him? At least with the 'Grecian Urn'?"

"I don't know whether I do or not." I looked at my feet, which were enormous, then leaned against the opposite wall to face him. We were established there, it seemed, with the vault of dark moist air between. "I would rather believe that poem than anything in the world. I think it's important for everyone to decide whether or not he disagrees with it. I think belief in it, or not, is almost what divides the world into its two selves." He looked toward me, waiting, with his attentive eyes. "Which are not really liberal and conservative, or Republican and Democrat, or the young and the old, or bohemians and bourgeoisie, or even idealists and materialists. But those who believe in truth and those who believe in beauty, as different things. Or those who believe in truth as beauty brought to such perfection that it no longer answers its old definition. It has changed in kind, not only in degree. Keats denies that, or evades it, or at least appears apprehensive of it. The poem is an expression of that apprehension. His infinity is a frozen finite world. It is simply a suspension of time, not an extension of time into eternity. He says beauty is truth and truth is beauty, and that is all we know *on earth.* It may be all we know in heaven, but it is certainly not all we know on earth. Or all we need to know." He leaned against the wall, thinking, speechless at this extravagance. "We need to know, for example," I said, abandoning my argument in sudden desperate frivolity, "what time it *is,* exactly. Whether they will have run out of the special at the Italian Gardens. Whether my friend is waiting."

"Oh. You're going to have dinner with someone."

"If it stops raining. I hate to sit through dinner soaking wet."

"I was about to invite you to have dinner with me," he said, regarding me with great serenity, with great hospitable eyes. "Here, I mean. I have some sandwiches with me, and some wine. In a bottle."

Where would he have wine but in a bottle? I thought. What is the matter with this boy? I'll kick him if he's being disingenuous. I will not be deceived like that.

"I mean I put it in a fruit jar," he said. "So there isn't any question about my drinking it on campus. It looks like grape juice or borscht or something." He pointed to the canvas shoulder bag that lay on the path at his feet. "I have a tuna fish sandwich. And some Twinkies. I don't know if you like them."

"I never had one," I said, captivated by the prospect and by the gravity of the offer. And Ronnie there, in the Italian Gardens, under that dreadful picture of Vesuvius, waiting for the eruption, the lakes of molten lava to enfold him. "But I think a woman would be a fool to pass up a Twinky. And it doesn't look as if it's going to stop."

"Oh, good. Wonderful." He knelt down quickly to unbuckle his bag with a kind of festive haste, chattering away. "I made this wine myself, believe it or not. I learned to make wine from my grandfather. I hope you like it. You don't think your friend will worry?"

"He hasn't stopped worrying for forty years," I said. "But he'll go ahead and eat, I'm sure of that. And after all, our relationship is based largely on the fact that everything in life is very tentative."

This odd, delightful boy arose, unwrapping a tuna fish sandwich, which he held out to me with sudden shyness. I took one of the neatly divided halves and began to eat, watching him hold the other and study it with concern, scowling; absorbed, apparently, in my last remark.

"Do you think that's a good basis for a relationship?" he asked.

I nodded, mumbling through my tuna fish, "Umm." We leaned against the opposite walls and ate, hearing the splash of raindrops on the asphalt and the whisper of the rain-rinsed grass.

"I think I have to disagree with you," he said in a moment, having swallowed, with charming difficulty, a mouthful of his sandwich. "Or maybe not disagree, but just understand you better. There's a story by Borges called 'The Secret Miracle.' Do you know it?"

I nodded.

"Well, it seems to me that in every work of art there are two time systems to consider. That of the principal, the protagonist, the actor, the observed; and that of the observer, the audience, the rest of the world. In Borges's story, when the playwright, Hladik, is standing before the firing squad waiting to be executed, and the soldiers fire, and the bullet speeds toward his heart, time continues for him; it is not arrested. There is an eternity before the bullet reaches him, an eternity teeming with incident, with thought, with visions and revisions of his play; he is able to complete his drama in his mind. But it is only to Hladik that time proceeds phenomenally, in this way; not to the others, the soldiers. For them, time is frozen, and when it resumes, they will be aware of no such vast hiatus as that which Hladik has experienced. They stand with their rifles at their shoulders, smoke curling motionlessly from the barrels. The bullet is suspended in midair, its shadow hangs motionless on the stones. But for them, the observers, and us, the audience, and all the rest of the natural world, that frozen instant is not an eternity. It is only a moment, empty of incident, except perhaps for a fleeting sensation of remorse or awe or vicious joy. In the splintered second between their squeezing of the triggers and the entrance of the bullet into Hladik's heart, nothing happens to them at all. Only for Hladik, the poet, the man caught in a creative trance, is time deformed, extended endlessly to accommodate his desire.

"In the 'Grecian Urn' there are also two time systems; that of the lovers and celebrants on the urn—the priests leading the heifers to the sacrifice, the minstrels playing their pipes—and that of the world which observes them, frozen there. The world goes on changing, aging. Keats says, 'When old age shall this generation waste, / Thou shalt remain, in midst of other woe / Than ours—' For the lovers, the minstrels, the priests, that frozen moment is empty of incident. Nothing occurs for them between the instant they were captured there by the artist and the moment, thousands of years later, when Keats first sees them. Their passions are not slaked or altered, the kiss is not yet taken, their bodies are still virgin, the heartbeats that gathered in them in that wild moment have not yet exploded. But for the observers, centuries have passed. Generations have died and new ones have been born. Other woes have come into the world and will continue to do so, endlessly. It seems to me that the situation is the opposite of Borges's, in which it is the time of the principal that is extended to infinity, not of the observers.

"Now, this is what I want to understand: Is it the frozen passion of the lovers on the urn that you call truth, and the endlessly proceeding, uninter-rupted, incompleted passions of the world which watches them what you call beauty? Or is it the opposite? Is it Borges's poet who is merely beautiful, and the soldiers who are true?"

I said humbly, "Perhaps the poem is greater than I knew. You make me think of it differently."

"It is certainly different from 'The Secret Miracle,'" he said. "What happens in that story is much the same as what happens in Bierce's 'An Occurrence at Owl Creek Bridge.' And in a lot of modern fiction: in Heming-way's 'A Clean, Well-Lighted Place,' and Marquez's *One Hundred Years of Solitude*, and in much of Doris Lessing's fiction; 'To Room 19,' for example, or 'A Room,' or 'Each Other,' which is the strangest one of all. Because in that story, the lovers—who happen to be brother and sister—willfully, frenziedly conspire to eternalize their passion. They refuse to arrive at orgasm with each other. They are locked in a terrible, lifelong embrace, at the very brink of ecstasy, which they eternally postpone. When they are with others, of course, time resumes for them."

He turned his eyes from the open archway onto me; the beautiful languor of his features, stilled by thought, was erased by the sudden reanimation, the thousand tiny reborn tensions and convulsions of seeing something real again; if I am real.

"Do you know that story?" he asked. "I think it's terrible."

I breathed deeply, testing my reality. Everything the inspired air caressed —my nostrils, the shining walls of my throat, my billowing lungs—seemed real enough; too real; cruelly sensitive. "I never read it," I said. "But she is an exceptional writer."

"Yes." He unscrewed the cap of the fruit jar and held the wine toward me. I shook my head.

"I don't drink."

"Not ever?"

"No. Thank you."

"Why?" he asked intently.

"I don't like to be intoxicated. I can't afford it."

"You don't think so well, so clearly—is that what you mean?"

"Yes."

"But do you need to think all the time?"

"Oh, yes. I'm a girl who needs her wits about her, every minute."

"Why?"

"I don't know. Well, all right, I do. Because other people have other things to protect them. Their dignity, or tact, or cunning. Or their grace. I have only my intelligence."

"You have your beauty."

"I don't know that beauty ever protected anything from pillage," I said. "That's why flowers get plucked, and girls get raped, and temples torn down by barbarians. Anyway—even if one really had it—beauty is an accident of nature."

"So is intelligence."

"Intelligence is a faculty. It has to be used, if one wants to preserve it. You have to work to be intelligent. You have to think. It takes will, character. To be beautiful, one only has to stand and glow. It's no particular credit to one."

He listened, nodding soberly, and said, "Well, you made the right decision, I think. Choosing to be a teacher, rather than a beauty queen." Then he made a little snort of consternation and added, "That doesn't sound much like a compliment, does it? But it was meant to be." I chuckled in foolish, fervent acknowledgment of it, feeling more than a little desperate myself. "I mean, I could see that you really love it, teaching. You were so absolutely rapt, giving that lecture. I was, too, listening to you."

"Thank you. I do, yes."

"I feel like that, too. Ideas are the only real music for me. I suppose it's what other people feel listening to Mozart or Bach." He smiled at me in a clear, merry way. "I suppose *that's* wine for you: ideas. That's how you get intoxicated." He swirled the bottle in his hand, peering into it; then raised his head and smiled again, with the same clarity. " 'The true, the blushful Hippocrene,' " he said. " 'Beaded bubbles winking at the brim.' " We laughed together. "Do you think Keats was drunk when he wrote 'Ode to a Nightingale'? And had fuzzy vision, maybe? And mistook his beautiful companion for someone else? Someone more beautiful? For his true love?"

I closed my eyes tightly, numbed by his grace, feeling blind. Poor Beauty, I thought, to be confounded by such a misconception. To live a counterfeit existence, in lifelong peril of having her simple comeliness revealed for what it was; aging, as her illustrious rival never would; pressing wine upon her addled lovers in fear that her spurious resemblance would be discovered. Fearing sobriety in men. Corrupting their intelligence. Impostor, dissembler. It is a terrible thing, I thought, to be unworthy of love, and wantonly ambitious for it. I sighed with these thoughts, as might well be expected.

"You look upset," he said. "I hope I'm not responsible for that."

"No, I'm just chilly." I gathered my jacket across my shoulders. "It's getting cold."

"It is, a little." He turned his eyes back to the open arch. The willows on the campus had grown purple with evening and beyond the gray wall there were now headlights spraying through the mist along the avenue. "I'm sorry we didn't have any sunlight. But we have water, which is the second treasure of the world." There were dark pools glimmering in the flooded grass. I saw his eyes move downward to them, resembling the pools themselves in their somber aqueous luster. "I think, sometimes, how bright this planet must be, seen from space. There is so much water on it. Two-thirds of its surface lying there like a great curved mirror, reflecting light. The other planets have none. If there is anyone out there watching us, they must say, 'God, how bright that planet is! How brilliant life must be there!' Not today, though."

Oh, more today than most, I thought, turning my collar up; I had decided some time ago that I must flee.

"Do you have to leave?" he said.

"Yes. There's still time to join my friend for coffee, I think. He's just down at the Italian Gardens."

"Can I walk with you?"

"You can *run* with me," I said. "If you're going that way."

"Good. Can you wait just a minute? I'm going to take my shoes off." He stooped down, pulled the bows of the big Army boots he wore and shucked them off, hobbling about on one foot at a time. He tied the laces together and stood up, swinging them happily. "Why don't you try it?"

"I'd get cold feet."

"Well. Are you ready?"

And off we went, running down the campus, I on the asphalt of the path, he through the sodden grass beside it, yelping in two tones, one of consternation, one of exultation, like a terrier and a Dane in uneasy celebration. At the wall, I paused for a minute to catch my breath; the Italian Gardens, and Vesuvius, and Ronnie—now up to his chin in ashes, stirring tea—were only a few doors away down the rainy street.

"Well, thank you for the lunch," I said. "And for—everything."

"Could I come in and meet him?" he asked. "Your friend?"

"Well—we have some things to talk about that are—well, personal, I guess."

"Oh. It's that sort of a relationship." Even this he managed to make sound innocent. "I mean, long-standing."

"Yes. I live with him."

"Oh." He stood wriggling his toes in the wet grass, regarding them ruefully. "But you haven't told me what you think. About the Keats."

"Oh, I need a lot more time to decide. Years, maybe. I'll let you know, when I do. Somehow."

"But you don't know my name."

"No. What is it?"

"Nils Larsen."

"Is that Swedish?"

"Danish. You won't forget to let me know?"

"No."

He smiled. "Shall I leave you the book? I can drop it at your office."

"What book?"

"The Lessing book. It's called *A Man and Two Women*. You said you hadn't read it."

"Oh. Not just now. Thank you. I'm so busy, I haven't time to read anything at the moment. I'm doing two Honors papers this term."

He stood for a moment, holding my eyes with his, and raised his hand, as if to touch my face.

"Please. Please!" I said.

"What is it?"

"I have to go now. Goodbye."

"Goodbye."

He turned and strode away across the grass into the mist below the chapel, planting his feet with strong delicious squelching sounds in the puddles of wine-dark water. I stood watching shamelessly until the evening mist had separated us again—this Dane, this vintner, with that warm ichor flooding between his toes, and myself, looking after him, bruised and defamed, with a splendid heelprint stamped upon my heart.

When I came into the Italian Gardens, I had to lean for a moment against the rim of the weakly gurgling Roman fountain before I was able to stand upright and shake the mist from my lapels and search along the stucco walls for Ronnie. He wasn't yet incinerated, after all, only a little dusty and tattered-looking, which was customary.

It's very easy, and ignoble, to parody people like Ronnie, which is the last thing I want to do. How do you go about describing a man, without being patronizing about it, who recommends himself to you as a paramour chiefly by reason of his incapacity either to inspire or experience romantic passion of any very great order? Such men abound, of course, and the fact that women marry them by the thousands must be a testament to their merit as well as to our cunning. But it's difficult to describe them with as much enthusiasm as that with which we marry them. The fact is that he reminded me of one of those people you see being interviewed on television who has just been eyewitness to a disaster of some sort—the collapse of a wall or a gas explosion in a subway—someone who happened to be passing by, who is unscathed by the event (although there's a good bit of dust or ash on his lapels), and who has a decided look of gratification both at the distinction of having witnessed something so exciting and of being asked to provide—which he does very well —a reliable, concise, and articulate account of what occurred. That was very much Ronnie's relationship to life; he was a good and earnest witness of it, and gave the impression of being lightly sprinkled with the residue of other people's passions and disasters; and, occasionally, of experiencing a very moving regret at not being involved as a principal, at not feeling the pain of the injured man being borne out of the ruins, or the anguish of the bereaved wife, or the terror of the victim trapped beneath the rubble. I think he even used literature largely as a refuge from life, rather than as a fierce and passionate exploration of it. Although that's not quite true, or fair; because he wanted me to love him, and he loved me, I think, or wanted to, apparently with no conception whatever of what it would mean to love, or be loved by, such a creature as I am. I think he wanted my love almost as an academic honor of some kind; as if, by formally announcing it, I would confer an advanced degree on him, Doctor of Life or something, that would entitle him to wear a slightly more colorful robe at graduation exercises. How bitter that sounds, how unjust. But the fact is that he did love regalia, ritual, emblems, rather than the realities they stood for; roles, of every imposing kind. Sometimes he would assume, with almost comical theatricality, the convention of the man lost nobly in nostalgia; in the rustle of Emily Dickinson's skirts, the perfume of her faded handkerchiefs, or the ring and glitter of Stendhal, or haunted Chekhovian afternoons. Whether that was a compensation for the poverty of his life, or an evasion of its splendid, possible confusions, I don't know, yet. But I think it was the quality in him for which I had the very least respect, however endearing it may have been, because it seemed to me a forfeiture of life and feeling, a kind of renegade and charming quaintness which wins easy amusement and approval by defaulting on far greater faculties that he might have exercised.

I say all these things with a great deal of compunction, because the fact is that I was in a very equivocal relationship with Ronnie. You may not think it would be any particular comfort or credit to a woman to be the object of such a humble passion as I have made his out to be; but believe me, at the point in my life at which I met him, the modesty of his emotions suited me exactly. If I had thought he would ever feel any grand, consuming passion for me, I would never have agreed to become his mistress. I have never wanted to be confronted by such passions in men I didn't love, and couldn't love. I've always been honest in that; I've never pretended sentiments or devotions I didn't feel, and could never learn to feel. I was perfectly contented to be warmed by the kind of low-grade fever that life produced in Ronnie—or did, when I first met him. That may sound brutal to you, or callous at least. But I'd like you to believe that I had a very great affection and respect for him, from the first, and till the last. I never wanted to hurt him in any way. I never wanted him to be tormented by unseemly and impossible ambitions toward my soul—my pink and yellow soul with the deckled edges—and I was careful to make no promises, ever, that would encourage him in that.

I don't mean that what we shared, what we were able to exchange, was not of great importance to me, as well as to him; it was probably of even greater importance to me. It was certainly not wine, but it was bread and water. I had drunk a good deal of wine already in my life—cheap wine, vin du pays, not the grandes marques—and had been very drunk for the greater part of it. What I needed when I met Ronnie was a long spell of sobriety, of good and simple food, of calm and order and time to do my work. I had—I have still, God knows —a great deal of thinking to do in this world, a great deal of understanding to achieve. Not from more experience—I had had a full enough measure of experience for the time—but from the contemplation of it; my own and other people's; that which I found in works of art as well as in my own life; that of the knightly visitors to this world in whose testaments I found, grain by grain and drop by shining drop, its truth distilled, spectral as the shifting stars in sapphires. Yeats said once, "All that is personal soon rots. It must be packed in ice or salt." I thought, then, that I had few real companions in this world but men and women like him, most of them long dead, some few unknown living, hived away above the wild streets making beautiful radiant things, shapes of translucent salt and ice, where I could find those crystalline essences, those pale attars, which are what we really live on in this world. What I wanted then was to emulate those people, those dead or sequestered friends of mine; I wanted to discover and pack in the ice and salt of art the truth of my mad, unknown life, and so save it from decay. And that was what he gave me the opportunity to do, in exchange for the daily crust of bread and glass of water which was all that I could promise him. It wasn't a bad exchange, I thought. We dined simply and well on one another's wares, and, I thought, with mutual respect and good will and civilized appreciation of each other.

But as I lived with him, and began to know him better, and to understand the dimensions of his possibilities, to take pride in him as a friend and highly valued human being, I began to long to see those possibilities fulfilled. I longed to see his spirit grow out of its stifled, fearful provinciality, as I began to realize that it could. I hated his self-deprecation, his self-parody as an arid, fastidious scholar, his circumspection about life and feeling, the wasting of his good and generous heart. Oh, it was a very equivocal situation for me! Because, although I longed to see him become more spontaneous, more daring, more easily masculine, more assured in his sexuality, prouder, freer, gayer; although I longed to see him take delight and comfort in the love that he deserved, I didn't want to be the woman that he loved. And as he did change slowly, as those possibilities were gradually fulfilled, as I saw him grow more greatly himself, more capable of love, I both rejoiced in it and felt an infinite regret and apprehension, knowing that I never could return it. Knowing I was the source of it, and would be the only chosen object of it, and that I could destroy it, and very likely would, unless I constantly forbade it to evolve. What does a woman do in such a dilemma? I would gladly have gone out and procured women for him, if I had thought that he could love them, but he was interested in no one but me. Sometimes I would become indignant for his sake, at the injustice of his situation, and rage against his patience, his tolerance of me. Why does he waste himself on such a woman? I would think. What kind of a creature can she be, to withhold her heart and spirit from such an interesting, intelligent, kind, good, gentle man? She ought to be horsewhipped. And it would startle me to remember that the creature I was speaking of was myself.

I should have left him earlier, God knows. But I took such pride and pleasure in seeing him evolve from a dusty bystander of life toward the possibility of becoming a great-hearted, gallant participant in it, and I was so contented and productive, so grateful for the refuge and comfort of his presence, that I couldn't. My chief regret, always, was that my contentment was, in itself, whether he was aware of it or not, an indignity to him; it seemed to say: I want no more than you are able to provide; you are made to the measure of my much-bridled need. It was not a reproach to him at all—which I pray he understood—but a deprecation of him, nonetheless, an unhandsome measure of my forbearance, whose vastness I think he must sometimes have suspected. Only the suspicion of it would have been enough to weary a man, to help account for that look of dilapidation that sat upon him, even in the relentlessly undergraduate clothing he put on—those corduroy jackets with their leather buttons and suede elbow patches, those flared jeans, that needlepoint vest he wore to parties. And in spite of his boyish face and his physique, which was still fit enough, at forty-two, to play a fierce game of tennis.

Do you know, I can't really remember the first time I met him. He was one of those people you meet at a G.S.A. spring mix and forget immediately; whom you pass the next day in the hall and say "Hi" to, trying to remember where it was you met him. I must have spoken to him on half a dozen occasions —faculty meetings, committee meetings, Christmas parties—back as far as '65, because that was the year he came into the department from Wayne State, but I don't remember them at all. Then he went away for a year to teach in the University College program in London, and I forgot all about him until he sent me a card at Christmas with a picture of Shakespeare's boyhood home in Stratford on it. The first clear memory I have of him was after he came back, in the spring semester of '67. I can remember *that* year all right, because it was the year that Poppa died. I was still working on my dissertation—it took me five years to get my Ph.D. because I was working part-time, teaching as a grad assistant and doing research at the Folger. Somewhere around the end of February there was a department meeting to discuss the case of a young professor who was due for tenure, and had been denied it—or so some people thought—because of his participation in the campus protests. Ron got up and made a speech in his defense that I thought was marvelous. It wasn't what you'd call impassioned, but it was sincere, articulate, and principled without being either hysterical or grandiose, which was in happy contrast to the kind of rhetoric we were beginning to hear on the campus in those days. I liked him for his speech, and for his offer to petition the administration on behalf of the professor concerned, and I stopped after the meeting to tell him so. We talked for a few minutes, walking down the corridor. He seemed flustered by my approval and a little bit uneasy about his role as champion, which I liked even more. After that he used to wave to me in the cafeteria occasionally whenever our lunch periods coincided, and once he came over with a bowl of vegetable soup and a sandwich on his tray and asked if he could join me. I said yes— I had almost finished my lunch and was about to leave, but once we started talking I stayed for quite a while, because I found that I enjoyed it. We talked about the war and the campus protests—we had National Guard troops on the campus in those days, and there'd been some rock-throwing and tear-gas incidents. Then we got onto John Skelton, who was the man I was doing my dissertation on, and he told me an interesting story about Wolsey's wrath on the publication of *Speke, Parrot* that I used, later, in my Ph.D. defense with considerable effect. Ron was a Modernist scholar, actually, but he knew quite a lot about Elizabethan literature. He knew quite a lot about literature of every period, and he understood and loved it; I could see that immediately. He asked if he could take me to a movie the next week and I said yes, because there was an old Bergman film playing—*Summer with Monika*—that we'd both missed the first time around and were anxious to see. After that we went out quite a lot together, to movies and concerts and once in a while to dinner, but that was as far as it went. You know I never went to bed with him? And he never asked me to, which was pretty remarkable, when you consider the kind of scene I was up to my neck in at the time. I appreciated that, and I liked it. He was a male friend, and I realized that I'd never had one before and that it was a nice kind of relationship. I wanted it to go on like that. I think Ron did, too; then. I think he realized that if it went any further it was likely to go up in fumes and furor, the way all my escapades with men seemed to end, and he didn't want that to happen any more than I did. We had a good time together. It should have stayed like that forever; I wish to God it had. I knew I could always call him up, almost any hour of the night or day, if I wanted to meet him down at the Italian Gardens and have a couple of beers and just talk to somebody for an hour or two. That's a really comfortable feeling to have about a man. I'd never experienced it before, except with Aaron. I was starting to pull myself together for a few months.

Then, just after my birthday, Poppa died—or vanished, or whatever the hell he did—and I went all to pieces for a while. When Momma called me up and told me what had happened, I lay down and slept for thirty-six hours. I think I'd still be lying there if I hadn't had a date with Ron. He came around and started pounding at the door to find out where I was and woke me up. I told him what had happened and he offered to drive me home, down to Port Federation. They were having a memorial service for Poppa and Aaron was coming down from New York. So we went down there, and he met Momma and Jamed and Aaron. Aaron didn't like him very much, which didn't surprise me at all because Aaron never liked anyone I dated. But Ron thought Aaron was wonderful, and Momma and Jamed, too.

I got pretty strange after that, for quite a while. It seemed to me that the foundation had crumbled away under everything, and I didn't much care what happened to me, or what I did. I was really very wild for a couple of months; I even scared myself. I don't know how I managed to finish my dissertation, but I did. I got my Ph.D. in July, at the end of the summer session, and also an appointment as assistant professor, beginning with the fall semester. I decided to stop seeing Ron because it didn't seem fair to him, to be sleeping with half a dozen different people and just using him as a sort of anchor, or confidant or something, like an aunt or girlfriend or an older sister. It seemed derogatory to him, and undignified; although I think he was pretty well aware of what was going on. He was very worried about me. He called me up every couple of days and asked if I wouldn't like to have a beer or go to a concert or something, but I said no, I didn't want to see anybody for a while. The man was so damned virtuous that it embarrassed me; it enraged me, as a matter of fact. I finally told him to just leave me alone, that I'd get in touch with him if I wanted to see him again. I guess that hurt him; it must have; but anyway he was sensible enough not to impose himself on me anymore.

I didn't see him again until the first week of September, on a Sunday morning, in a drugstore at the corner of University Boulevard. Ron was standing at the cashier's desk waiting to pay for a copy of the New York *Times* when I came in, very bloody-minded, with my teeth unbrushed and one of my earrings missing, to buy a cup of coffee and a chocolate doughnut. We said good morning, and although I didn't find it possible to produce a smile at the moment, he came and sat down on the stool beside me at the counter after he'd bought his newspaper.

"That won't do you any good," he said, nodding at the doughnut. I told him to mind his own damned business.

He got up to go, and in immediate remorse, I said, "I'm sorry. Sit down, Ron. It's just that I've had a bad night. I've had a bad couple of months, as a matter of fact."

"What's all this?" he said. "Haven't you just got your Ph.D.? And an assistant professorship?"

"Yes. But I've lost one of my earrings, and my hair is a mess, and this is the most awful doughnut I ever ate." I took another bite of it, and a sip of coffee, and added, "I want to thank you for the story about Wolsey. I used it in my examination and it made quite a hit with Threlkeld. I don't know if I ever thanked you."

"That's O.K. Glad to have been of service. I don't think I've had a chance to congratulate you yet. How's it going?"

"O.K., I guess. I love teaching. I really do."

"I know you do. I'll bet you're good at it."

"I don't know. I don't think I'm much good at anything."

"Hey," he said gently, and then sat staring at the counter for a while. I thought he was going to leave, because he was starting to get distinctly fidgety on his stool, but after a few minutes he pulled himself together and with what seemed to be a heroic effort, said, "I was wondering what you had planned for the day."

"I'm going to get into a hot tub of water," I said, "and sit there for an hour. By which time I will have decided whether or not to slit my wrists. If I decide not to, I'll probably get out and do the crossword puzzle."

"Well, look, I've got a better suggestion, I think. I was going to go down to Georgetown and take a trip on the canal barge, out to Dalecarlia. I wonder if you'd like to go along." When I didn't reply immediately he went on quickly, "I've got the *Times*, so you can do the puzzle on the barge, if you like. It's a beautiful day, and it ought to be lovely on the canal. You don't have to say a word, if you don't feel like it."

It was really a very nice invitation. I don't think anything else in the world could have been quite so appealing to me in the circumstances. I had a very genuine feeling of succor, as if the man had been sent with the suggestion on his lips direct from heaven.

"I think I'm going to take you up on that," I said. "If you think you can stand me. I have a filthy hangover, and yesterday's clothes on, and fur on my teeth, and I haven't had a shower. I'll leave it up to you."

"I think I can manage," he said. "I like dirty girls." Oh, Ronnie.

So we went out and got into his battered 1947 MG and drove down to Georgetown in the late-summer sunlight. It was beautiful in the barge on the canal, just as he had promised. The mules plodded peacefully ahead of us along the towpath, the scalloped fringes of the striped canopy twittered over us in the breeze, birds chirruped in the great green clouds of foliage along the banks, little yellow butterflies flittered through the sunlight, and down below us the water of the Potomac glinted between the gray trunks of the beeches. I sat there feeling like a lady in a Corot painting—which was pretty incredible, considering my condition—feeling every minute cleaner, prettier, daintier, more virginal, more lovingly conceived by some bearded, merry-eyed master in a velvet jacket. Every few miles we would pass through a lock with stone walls and a gate of huge old silvery timbers. The canal banks widened at these spots to enclose a spill pond where ducks glided smilingly past in the sunlight wagging their tails contentedly, and at every lock there was a stone house set back from the bank, where the lockkeeper and his family had lived, a century and a half ago. I thought about those lives as I was towed through the shadow of their dwellings in my dirty blouse; and after a while I fell asleep to the gentle clopping of hooves and the far-off murmur of the river. I woke when the barge stopped at the Dalecarlia lock, and we had half an hour to spend while the mules were unhitched and harnessed to the other end of the barge for the journey back. We decided to explore the lockhouse that stood on the bank above the wall of the canal. It was a beautiful old house, made of brown Maryland sandstone, a gaunt, two-storied building with a solemn chastity of line, utterly naked of ornament except for the weathered, gray, square beam ends glimmering beneath the eaves like rows of inlaid stark escutcheons of the spare, taciturn people who had lived their lives there. It stood abandoned in the sunlight, enclosing within its walls all that remained of the richest harvest of its land, a great warm, fragrant bale of silence, of sweet, aboriginal American solitude. When we pushed open the heavy old weather-beaten door and stepped inside, I breathed that undefiled, unguent air like an elixir, and went and stood with my forehead pressed against the rough moist wall, feeling it, cool and curative, against my brow, like the healing stones its inhabitants had used to draw the fever out of them.

Afterwards, we went and found a sunny mound to sit on in a grassy patch of forest between the canal and the river. Ronnie recited me some Latin verses which Skelton (remembering in the nick of time that he was a clergyman and a Poet Laureate) appended to one of his lewdest, wildest, most rambunctious poems, verses saying that he denounced dirty, drunken, and loquacious women and trusted they would take his warning to heart. I laughed and said, "Well, I have. You can't say I'm loquacious."

"That's better," Ronnie said. "You know, the most extraordinary thing happened just now, on the barge."

"What?"

"You fell asleep, and you cried in your sleep. I never saw anyone do that before."

"It isn't possible," I said.

"I didn't think so, either, but there they were: two great fat tears, oozing out from under your eyelids."

"Well, it's no wonder," I said. "I lead such a god-awful messy life. But I have no one but myself to blame, so I don't have any right to your sympathy."

"It isn't something you have to earn the right to," he said. "Anyway, I don't have anything else to do with it. I mean no one else to spend it on, particularly."

"Well, I appreciate it. But I hope it doesn't go any further than that," I said. "I don't think I could stand anything more stirring than sympathy this morning. Or ever, very possibly."

"You're feeling pretty lousy, aren't you?"

"I was. I'm much better now." Then, for a variety of reasons—to disburden him of any illusions he might have about me, or any designs upon me, perhaps to gain some meager measure of absolution, to claim proper title to this clean, bright day, and out of simple weariness of spirit; and also, I suppose, of sheer, chronic perversity—I said, "Do you know where I'd just come from, when I met you this morning?"

"No."

"From Dallas Counselman's apartment. Do you know who he is?"

"Oh, the grad student? The big red-headed one, with the very tight jeans?"

"That's the one. I spent the night up there. And about three o'clock this morning I found that he was screwing me on the living-room floor, and that contrary to my expectations I didn't like it at all. That it simply wasn't going to work. It's a discovery I've made before—I mean, with other people—but never quite like this. Never so absolutely, so—well, appallingly. And so, when I realized that it was happening again, I got fed up. More than fed up, actually. And I did something really awful, that I'm ashamed of; which is why I feel this way; why I'm being such an awful bore.

"It wasn't him that I was fed up with, particularly; because after all I was just as responsible for the situation as he was. But it wasn't myself, either. I didn't know what it was, at the moment; I was too bogged down in my indignation to really understand the source of it. But, on the other hand, he *was* making a god-awful to-do about things—you could practically hear drum-rolls and trumpets. He was more graceless than most, and so a natural victim, I suppose. And as I lay there, with him on top of me, giving me this—treatment; I don't know what else to call it, exactly, because he was working away very much like a chiropractor—I felt the sense of outrage growing, welling up in me, becoming quite unbearable. I can only compare it to what a person must feel when he's told that he's suffering from a loathsome, incurable disease; and I knew that I had to do something to express it, to relieve myself of it. I saw my purse lying on the coffee table within arm's reach, and I remembered that inside of it there was a pack of peanuts I'd bought in the snack bar the afternoon before. So I stretched out my arm and felt inside the purse and found it. He was far too busy to be distracted by anything I was doing; I think he may even have considered my wriggling around the convulsions of ecstasy or something. So I fished out this cellophane package and bit off a corner of it with my teeth and poured a generous helping of peanuts into my mouth and began to crunch away on them. He went on huffing and puffing for a minute, completely unaware; then, gradually, he began to slow down in his labors. You could see that something was coming through to him; he was beginning to register this very strange, horrendous crunching sound, right beside his ear. He held his breath and listened for a minute, very still, like a man listening to something stalking him in a dark forest, and then he said, very slowly, incredulously, 'Just what in the *hell* are you doing?'

" 'I'm eating peanuts,' I said.

"He reared up on his elbows as if he'd discovered he was lying in a bed of red ants and glared down at me with a look of repulsion such as I have never seen before.

" 'That is the most disgusting thing I ever heard of in my life,' he said. 'You are probably the most revolting female in this entire world.' "

Ronnie began to laugh in an uproarious and yet apologetic way, as if he were not sure at all that it was the proper response to my story, and yet was unable to contain it. He rocked about on the grass like a buoy wallowing in a high sea, flushed and strangulated.

"I know you don't think it's funny," he said. "But it really is, you know. Honestly, Sylvie. Especially if you know the man. Oh, my God, it's very funny!"

"I suppose I'll think so, someday," I said.

"You will, I'm sure of it. You'll live at least that long. What happened then?"

"So then he got up, looking rather splendid, really, in his rage—it was his best moment of the whole affair—and snatched up his clothes from the floor, and said, 'Now get the hell out of my apartment, you bitch.' Then he went into the bathroom and slammed the door behind him. So I got up and put my clothes on and went down and walked over to the campus and let myself into the English building with my key and lay down on the sofa in the faculty lounge until nine o'clock, when I came over to the drugstore and met you. I didn't sleep, though. I lay there thinking about what had happened and growing more desolate and ashamed every minute, as I began to realize what a terrible thing I'd done.

"Because it was. It was an act of desecration, of profanity, no less. It really was. I began to realize that, very slowly. I had vilified something very much more than a vainglorious graduate student; because however grotesque or pitiful his performance had been, however marred by vanity or the exercise of

power, however merely mimetic—merely human—it was, it was still an imitation of the act of love. It was no doubt the best that he could do. And how
much better can most of mankind do? How many of us are much more perfect
in our lovemaking? I began to realize that I had defamed all of our poor
desperate attempts at adoration; my own, too. And I was so ashamed that I
think if I hadn't felt I must redeem that act of sacrilege in some way, I would
have died. I would have gone out on the highway and flung myself in front
of the first truck that came by.

"As it was, I decided on a chocolate doughnut, which was perhaps punish-
ment enough."

"That, and me?" Ronnie said.

I laid my hand on his arm and said, "No, not you. You made everything
much better. I don't know what I would have done without this lovely trip,
and you to talk to. I think you were sent straight from heaven."

"Funny, my mother thought that, too." He smiled at me, a little too
ruefully for my entire comfort, and yet with a certain reassuring equanimity,
in the manner of a man who has lived long enough and humbly enough to learn
that what we all dine on, eventually, are the leavings of the lords.

The barge had been made ready by this time, and we strolled back to it
and sat down on the wooden benches with the other passengers and began our
journey back. The sun had lowered in the sky, and came in under the fringe
of the canvas canopy, falling on my arm, where it rested on the iron bench rail,
with a sweet, deep warmth. I felt peaceful enough, restored enough in spirit,
to work the Sunday crossword puzzle, delighted to find that my ingenuity, at
least, my faculty for solving the puzzling little contrivances of entertainers, was
unimpaired; that I was, apparently, still capable of diversion.

It was growing into evening—one of those long-shadowed, molten summer
evenings—when we got back to Georgetown, and the streets with their sleepy
Sunday hush between the little brick houses were so invitingly peaceful that
we strolled along them under the sycamores for a while before we went back
to the car. When we got into it, we sat in a vacant-minded trance of contentment for several minutes, which I broke by inquiring wonderingly, pacifically,
as if considering the atrocities of some totally unknown delinquent I had read
about in the morning newspaper, "Why do people do things like that, do you
suppose?"

"I can't give you the answer to that," he said. "But I'll tell you what I can
give you. A good plain meal of steak and potatoes, and time to think about
it, and a hot shower, and possibly a ride home, if you tell me where you want
to go."

"I can't think of anything else to ask for in the world," I said.

"I'm afraid I haven't got any wine, but we can stop and get some."

"Don't, for God's sake. I must have drunk a gallon of it last night. I've had enough cheap wine to last me a lifetime."

"Whatever you say."

"And let me make the salad. It's a specialty of mine."

"You've got a deal," he said.

So we went back to his apartment and after I'd had my shower and brushed my teeth with the spare toothbrush which he miraculously produced, we made a wonderful meal and ate it on his balcony, on the top floor of the apartment building, which stood on the very summit of College Park Hill, looking down breathtakingly over the great soft purple swath of Greenbelt Park, and far off in the misty summer evening, Washington, with the gilded dome of the Cathedral glinting in the dusk and the lights beginning to twinkle along Constitution Avenue. He put Strauss's *Death and Transfiguration* on the stereo and we sat and listened to it in the dark through the sliding doors, watching the purple martins sweep through the candlelight from the balconies. When the music stopped, we could hear their wings whispering in the warm air. A heavy dew began to fall, and our clothes grew damp and chilly, so we went inside and had coffee by the light of a brass ship's lantern. Then we did the dishes, and afterwards sat on the rug and played a game of chess. I watched him frowning over a move, and said, "Ronnie, would you mind if I stayed here tonight? I don't feel like going home just yet."

"Stay as long as you like," he said.

I thought about that for a while before I replied, "I might take you up on that if I were sure it didn't make you think that I might fall in love with you. The last thing I want to do is hurt or humiliate anybody else, ever."

"I'm not asking you anything," he said.

"I'm trying to write a book, you see, and I'm not having much luck at it, because my life is such a bloody mess. I need to be quiet, and do some serious thinking, and eat fairly regularly, and get a certain amount of sleep, and try and figure out just what in the hell I'm doing in this world. I'd like to build one of those stone houses we saw today." He went on frowning at the chessboard, pinching together the center of his lower lip. I waited for him to speak, but he didn't say anything. "And the fact is, I haven't met anybody in ages who kept a spare toothbrush. You have no idea how reassuring that is."

"Well, look, it's your move," he said.

So I moved in with him, the very next day, and started to write my book.

Sylvie separated her clasped hands and laid them on the table, paired like a freshly opened seashell. She sat regarding her pink, nude palms with a fortune-teller's murky eyes, as if seeking in the patterns of their lines a translation of the manuscript they had written.

"When you showed me your book the other day, and asked me if I found any passion in it, I ached for you," she said. "God, how often, with what fear and trembling, I've searched the sentences of my own with just that question in my mind." She sat still for a long time. "I don't know if I can tell you about my book. Except that it was, for a long time, the only genuine passion of my life. And the only genuine hope."

"You don't write anymore?" I said, after another long moment in which the electric clock went on murmuring hoarsely of extinction.

"No. I discovered, like Aaron, that I'm not an artist. Not a literary artist, at any rate."

"But you paint now."

"Not that, either. I'm an amateur of the arts. I teach them. I don't know to whom. Myself, most likely." She shook her head distressfully. "I'm neither innocent enough, nor wise enough, to be an artist. But I thought, then, that I could be wise enough, at least. If I were given a year, to discover wisdom. A year of calm and dignity, a year of reprieve from myself. And Ronnie gave me that reprieve. I hope he understands how grateful I am. Even if I couldn't do what I wanted with it. I hope he understands how heroic, now, his patience seems to me."

On that day, for example, when I came into the restaurant after meeting that boy and saw him raise his hand to me and smile from his table, I felt what I think all women feel after infidelity: such a wave of tenderness for him, such a gratitude for his birdlike gravity and consternation and length of neck, for the pride and diligence with which he bore me—flapping back unfailingly from his humble forays on the world—wisps of straw, unraveled string, pinchbeck earrings, every sort of fascinating oddment to set on the coffee table and beguile me with. I felt dim—not with treachery, since I didn't believe that any existed on my part—but with appreciation for his generosity in simply being there, in providing me with shelter, as the shadow of even the meanest, most ragged tree gives shelter from the light.

I sat down across the table from him and smoothed my hair.

"You all right?" he asked.

"Yes. Just out of breath. I ran down through the rain."

"You get held up?"

"Yes. A student stopped me after class and had to talk. You know how they are."

"I thought you might. I went ahead and ate. Hope you don't mind. I've got my seminar at seven." He stretched out his arm, popping his wristwatch from his cuff and blinking at it.

"God, no. I'll have a cup of coffee with you. What's that, lasagna?"

"Um. Good."

I broke a chunk of bread from the loaf in his basket and wiped the orange-colored sauce from his plate, munching the stained bread mechanically.

"Want some?"

"No, just coffee. Maybe a dish of spumone."

"My God, you've got to eat, Sylvie."

"I had lunch late."

"You're going to get something terrible. Beriberi, or pellagra, or whatever it is."

"I've had them all. All diseases. I'm immune."

"All but love." He said this grinning at me in his good, funny, connubial way, but with the faintest thrill of lament in it, the faintest squeal of destitution, like a violin string being tuned, unskillfully, in a distant room. It was unfair of him, of course, because however lightly said, it was importunate, and plaintive. It was outside of our agreement, which he understood. And yet, once in a great while, quite involuntarily, he said something of that kind—perhaps once every six weeks, which was as often as I could bear—and I closed my eyes in grief at his servility.

"Too hot?" he said. "I sprinkled Tabasco on it. Sorry."

"No. It's not too hot." I shivered. "I think I may have caught a chill."

He frowned. "You're wet. Hair's wet. Clothes, too, I'll bet." He leaned across the table, clasping the sleeve of my jacket with reproachful fingers—really fine fingers, I thought, turning my head to look at them. "God, you're soaked. You better go home and have a hot shower. Don't sit here in those clothes." He withdrew his hand and I reached for it, drawing it back into the light of the little globular yellow candle that flickered on the table, to examine it more closely.

"You have nice hands," I said. "You ought to make something, Ronnie."

"Never seen them before?" He smiled genially. It was certainly no rebuke, but I accepted it as such, thinking how often, how obliviously, I had beheld them, in earnest, sedulous application of the instructions in Ulf and Helga Somebody's *Manual of Married Love,* "Applying Gentle Friction to the Areolas."

Well, you might think that a situation like that was an opportunity for charity that a woman as interested in redemption as I was would have seized upon. It was; but, you see, I don't believe in charity. I think it humiliates its recipients. I think it admits artifice into relationships between people, a kind of benevolent dissembling, to ease the pain of the disparities between them, the aching evidence of their differences in wealth, whether that wealth is monetary or spiritual or intellectual. Inevitably, an act of charity puts people farther apart than ever, it separates them by another millimeter, another measure of kindly subterfuge, another small tear of pity in the seas between them—pity, which is after all an admission of that already unfathomable gulf. I don't mean that we shouldn't feel pity—that would be impossible and inhuman in this kind of a world—but I mean that we shouldn't constantly be translating it into feckless and demoralizing acts of charity that degrade both the giver and the recipient. Because they do. If you want proof of it, you only need to meet my brother Aaron. My God, he's been an object lesson to me all my life. There's nothing he couldn't have done if he hadn't demoralized himself with pity, blighted his pride and initiative and will, let every little waif and wastrel who came mooning by suck the energy and ambition out of him, and finally destroy his talent. That was the worst sin of all—to let his talent wither and die like that. I'll tell you a little of his history sometime, and you'll see how a human being can be a victim of pity. I had no intention of letting it happen to me, of betraying my own work by draining my energy and independence that way, or of humiliating Ronnie by any sentimental acts of charity, by encouraging him in a false and fatuous hope of my ever loving him. It's dishonest to do that, and seditious of everything that really matters in this world. It would have killed him eventually, when he discovered the truth about me, or would have left him, at best, with a life of rubbishy, elegiac gloom, bowed like a beggar under the weight of even more pity, self-pity, which is the most demeaning kind of all. God knows, that was the last thing I wanted to do to him. There are too many cripples of that kind limping around this world already.

Well, I thought about all that, sitting there across the table from him in that awful restaurant—and you ought to remember that we were surrounded by an imitation Roman fountain, a picture of Vesuvius, another one of a vine-clad loggia looking down over an appallingly picturesque rendition of the Dolomites, platters of cannelloni and lasagna on every side, and half a bottle of cheap Chianti. That was the worst thing of all, I think: that cheap Chianti bottle with its machine-plaited straw and plastic-coated cap, pitifully confronting me; me, who had just refused a draft of the true, the blushful Hippocrene.

"Ronnie," I said. "We've had eighteen months together, and I think now—"

"Yes?"

I was still holding his hand in mine, admiring it, if you remember; and now, instead of releasing and depositing it on the table, as I should have done, I tightened the clasp of my fingers about his own—I *clenched* them, even—and closed my eyes in a weary, voluptuous way, and murmured, "And I think they've been the best months of my life. I've never told you that before, and I should have."

Out of pity, do you think? Oh, perhaps, to some degree; but even more shamefully, even more shabbily, out of fear, I think, and cunning. Fear for my own puny soul, fear of that wilderness outside the Italian Gardens, where Vikings prowled, white-footed, through the grass; and cunning, because it was, in a sense, quite true, if not at all in the way that he believed. I took craven comfort in the fact that although I was deceiving him by letting him misunderstand me, I was not "lying." You may not think that was such a monstrous act, but I do. I think it made me, for the first time in my life, a whore. On what other basis do so many women deceive and defraud men, hold them in lifelong empty, contemptuous bondage? Make a mockery of life and love?

And deceived he very evidently was, because he wriggled his hand free and then laid it on top of mine in a tender and possessive way that made me flinch, his eyes and heart too full, for the moment, to say more.

What infamies occur in restaurants! How little time it takes for moral universes to collapse! I was shocked, astonished, at myself. But even as I sat in witness to this calumny I had wrought on life and feeling, I consoled myself by thinking: It will be redeemed. It must be redeemed. I will go home and write it in my book, and the truth of this event will be revealed and preserved in all its purity; because the truth of the most unclean event is pure. Even though I have lied in life (with a drowsy smile, which is the way it often happens), I will go home and set the scriptural essence of it in the book which is the truth of my existence. Even if no one ever reads it—especially if no one ever reads it—it will lie and glow forever in shining letters on yellowing sheets of paper, like a jewel in a forgotten casket. It will not be lost in the fume of lies and treacheries which bore it and in which it struggles to be recognized. Somewhere in the world the truth of my existence will abide until it is resumed by time, as has that of all my dear companions. That is very brave language, but an ugly piece of truth to carry home to an echoing apartment.

Do you understand what my book meant to me? It *was* me. Now that it is gone, destroyed not quite timely enough—all but one dreadful, soiled page of it—I don't know who this is, quite, speaking to you; some ghost, something whining and tapping at the pane with rotten fingers, some gallows child.

"All truth," I said to myself in the shower, "does not shine, apparently. Some of it is as sordid-looking as lasagna." I stood there limply, as if hanged, my head and arms dangling, my neck bowed loosely, broken, in the hot rain, breathing the ascending steam, remembering what were almost his last words: "By the way, I did make something once. A birdcage, out of matchsticks. I wish you could have seen it, Sylvie. My mother said it was beautiful."

Sylvie was gone from the island for three days over the Easter weekend, and she left the lights on in her parlor. I don't know why; I'm certain it wasn't for my reassurance, although it had that effect, when I woke up in the middle of the night and went down to the kitchen to make a cup of tea and smoke a pipe of tobacco. I often do this, but not with the peculiarly disembodied feeling I had that night. I went out into the garden in my bathrobe and wandered among the moonlit shrubs. I could hear the tide lapping at the hulls in the boatyard slips and the halyards tapping. I clipped off with my thumbnail a white peony that hung broken-necked, its stem bitten by a squirrel. My hands glowed with a pearled, translucent pallor like the flesh of a dying patient. Looking down the lane, I saw the square illuminated panes of her windows shining above the hedges and the sight did more to restore my faith in my actual presence there in the soft spring night than the bulge of my hot pipe bowl in my fist.

In the daytime I was restless, feeling bereft of the possibility that she would drop by for tea, or that I would see her wading on the sandbar or sunning herself on the rocks of the breakwater. One afternoon I found a particularly fine piece of driftwood on the river shore, bleached like ivory and smoothly convoluted to suggest a plunging sea gull. I took it to her house and went in the back door and set it on the kitchen table, then sat for half an hour in the cool stillness of the room. A vine of some kind had begun to grow up the base of the Grecian urn in her dooryard. I went to the post office to see if there was mail for her, and found it closed. A yellow dog lay in the sand beside the road. I felt a desire to touch the beast. I crouched in the sand beside him, studying his sleek, shapely muzzle and his arched, very definite eyebrows.

"How do you feel?" I said. He opened one eye and, after regarding me for a moment, winked. Sweet scoundrel, I thought; dozing in the sun, nosing into garbage, galloping after squirrels, shamelessly licking your genitals in public, lounging genially around the edges of the busy, orderly world. One day, I thought, he would paw over the rubble of that world with the same candidly scurrilous interest he took now in its offal. I had never before in my life given philosophical consideration to a dog; if I had, I think it would have been with very different conclusions.

They were fine April days, unavailing in their beauty. Boat owners had begun to spend days at the island, hauling and bottom-painting their hulls and outfitting their vessels for the summer sailing season. There was a constant whine of electric sanders and drills and the thumping of hammers from Hargison's boatyard. Men stood dusty and bare-waisted under the cradles, reaching up to scrape and paint the slime-tarnished hulls, or swung, singing, in bosun's chairs over the blue water while they rigged their masts. Sometimes they brought their wives or sweethearts and worked together with them, silently, arduously, in quiet conjugal contentment. I would sit as inconspicuously as possible on the breakwater like a voyeur, watching them for hours.

One afternoon when I came back to the house there was a man waiting for me in the yard, sitting on the chopping block beside my woodpile with his shoulders hunched and his hands doubled in the pockets of his woolen jacket, which was buttoned to the throat although the weather was very mild. He was a man of fifty or fifty-five with a dark, weather-roughened face and thick white eyebrows above his pale blue eyes. I recognized him as a man who sold firewood around the island, although I didn't know his name. I had seen him driving a battered pickup truck loaded with rows of split red oak logs. He stood up as I came down the lane and waited at the back steps, holding out his hand to me as I came across the yard.

"Good afternoon," I said. "I'm Carl Ransome."

"Yes, sir. How'd you do, Dr. Ransome, sir. I'm Virgil Bishop. I seen your car was in, so I reckoned you'd be back before too long."

"I walked down to the harbor, it's such a fine day."

"Indeed it is."

"You want to sell me some wood, Mr. Bishop?"

"No, sir, that's not what I come for, though I'd be happy to bring you a load." He spoke with effort, his voice hoarse and constricted. His eyebrows clenched with pain as he ground out the words. "Got a real bad throat."

"I can hear that."

"Folks generally go up to Doc Hance, up to Prince Frederick, but he's closed of a weekend."

"You'd better come in and let me have a look at it."

"I'd be real obliged. Feels like a piece of raw meat."

I went up the steps and held the screen door open for him. He knocked the sawdust off his boots before he entered the kitchen.

"Sit down," I said. "I'll get my bag."

"Thank you."

I went out into the hall and took my bag down from the closet shelf. When I came back into the kitchen he sat huddled at the table with his hands in his jacket pockets.

"You look cold," I said.

"Yes, sir. Got a bad chill."

"How long has this been going on?"

"Come down night before last. Got to feeling hot and cold, and felt like I'd swallowed a bucket of Drano."

"Let's have a look at that throat. Turn around there so I get the light from the window."

He turned his face to the light and opened his mouth, leaning his head back in the chair. I shined my flashlight into his mouth and held his tongue down with a depressor. The back of the throat, palate, and uvula were the deep scarlet of streptococcus infection and there was the typical capillary distension of the soft tissue. "Say 'Ah.' " The discoloration and distension ran deep down the back of the throat wall and there were mucus patches forming. "Well, it looks like you've got a strep throat," I said. "A real jim-dandy. We'd better see what your temperature is."

I shook down my thermometer and put it under his tongue. "Keep that under there for a minute or two. I'm going to write you a prescription for penicillin. Have you ever taken it by mouth?" He shook his head. "Well, some people, it upsets their stomachs. We'll see. You've got to take it on an empty stomach for best results. You start off with two of the tablets and then cut down to one every four hours. It'll be on the bottle." He nodded. "Let's have a look at that now." I took the thermometer out of his mouth and read it. He had a temperature of 103 degrees. "You've got a pretty good little fever. You must be feeling pretty low."

"I wouldn't want to go duck hunting, I can tell you."

"No, I bet you wouldn't. Do you have somebody can go up to Prince Frederick and get this filled?"

"My boy kin go. He's home."

"That's good. You'd better get in bed and stay there. You take the medicine and you'll feel a lot better in a day or two. But you get up and start cutting wood and you're liable to come down with pneumonia. You understand?"

"Yes, sir."

I handed him the prescription and he studied it, frowning hesitantly.

"I'll drop by tomorrow and see how you feel," I said. "Where do you live?"

"Just back of Harbor Island Marina. Got a sign in the yard says 'Wood for Sale.' "

"I know where it is," I said. "You better get in bed and drink all the fluid you can hold. Quarts of it."

"Yes, sir. I can't afford to be sick. Miss a day's work, it costs me." He folded the prescription and put it in his jacket pocket. "How much would that be, Dr. Ransome, sir?"

"There isn't any charge," I said. "I'm retired. I do this to keep from rusting out."

"I'm obliged." He stood up and went to the screen door, holding it open for a minute before he went down the steps. "I'll bring you up a cord of oak, next week. It's good wood. Been down a year."

"You don't need to do that," I said. "That's worth more than a call, even if I were still in business."

"Good day to you, sir." He went down the steps and across the yard to the gate, turning to close and latch it carefully before he went down the lane toward the village.

When he had gone I went down to the dune grasses by the river shore where Sylvie often stood to paint and trampled out a bower among the tall, dense reeds, then peeled off my shirt and lay for an hour in the delicious warmth of the afternoon sun, protected from the wind by the shimmering, softly seething curtains of wheatlike grass. I had never before sunbathed in my life. I have a particularly sensitive skin and have had a lifelong fear of melanoma. No one could have made me believe the tingling, blood-brightening thrill of being nearly naked out of doors. I sank into a roseate waking dream, watching its images flow through my mind like flowers on a sparkling, sunlit stream.

On the Tuesday after Easter, I saw Sylvie's car parked in the lane behind her house, but she did not come up to visit me, and I didn't see her anywhere abroad on the island for the next three days. By Saturday, I had become concerned, and on my way to the market I went in through her gate and knocked at her kitchen door. There was no answer. I knocked again, and when there was still no reply, I opened the door and went into the kitchen. A kerosene lantern, its chimney blackened and its wick reduced to a charred stubble, was burning faintly on the table amid a litter of soiled plates and crumpled paper napkins. I blew it out and went into the parlor, calling out her name. I had never been inside her parlor before—nor even seen it, since it joined the kitchen by a narrow hallway that shut it off from view—and I was dispirited and indignant at the sight of it. She had rented the house furnished and it was equipped with the maimed and cast-off furniture that inevitably finds its way into beach cottages: staggering, spindle-legged chairs and cheap Victorian tallboys, their drawers gone too awry to close entirely, and lumpily upholstered overstuffed monstrosities covered with worn, tobacco-colored figured plush. On one of these, a huge misshapen sofa, Sylvie lay covered partially with her pea jacket, one arm dangling to the floor, where an overturned bottle lay at the edge of a dark stain in the worn carpet. The room reeked of the sweet, heavy smell of rum. She had evidently been painting before falling asleep, because her easel stood beside the sofa with a tall barstool in front of it and on the floor at its feet a palette, an open paint box with a litter of tubes and soiled rags, and a glass of turpentine with brush handles sticking out of it. I took her by the shoulder and shook her gently, very much relieved to see her stir and murmur.

"Are you all right?" I said.

"Mmm. Carl?"

"Yes. I just thought I'd look in. I hadn't heard from you."

She opened her eyes and blinked at me in silence for several seconds. "What time is it?"

"About noon."

"What day is it?"

"Saturday."

"God. I suppose I'd better get up, then."

"Shall I make you some breakfast?"

"Oh, I just want some fruit. Are you going to the store?"

"Yes."

"You might bring me a cantaloupe, if you can find a ripe one. Or some apples."

"All right."

"I like the Granny Smith apples. Those green ones."

"I'll see if they have any."

"Thank you." She closed her eyes, sighed, and huddled down again into the sofa's ruptured depths. I walked to the door, then turned and looked back at the canvas that stood in the easel. It was apparently finished, or very nearly so, and the most representational of any of her painting I have ever seen, although as furiously brilliant as any of them. It showed a span of open beach stretching off infinitely into the distance, arched over by a depthless cobalt sky and bordered by a sea of burning blue, along the edge of which, through the incandescent sand, a lion loped toward me with a naked girl astride him, her thighs clasped about his mighty torso. She sat upright, supple and white as peeled birch, her copper-colored hair blowing lightly out behind her, one hand tangled in the mane of his great head, which was slunken forward in easy, powerful leisure as he strode, his eyes blazing like topaz in the sun.

This lion pursued me to the grocery store and back; I heard the fearful whispering thump of his huge feet on the sandy asphalt of the road behind me as I walked, and the impatient raking of his talons at the wooden panel of the screen door as I nervously made my purchases, and then again the heavy padding of his paws and the rhythmic panting of his breath in the hot silent street as I walked back, with growing haste, toward the Point. But when I looked back from Sylvie's kitchen door, he had melted into the sunlight, leaving only a faint, hot, tawny fetor, a fading leonine spoor in the hushed lane.

Whether he had mysteriously returned to his habitat in the painting I never learned, because the easel was taken down when I went back into the parlor, the jar of brushes and the rum bottle removed, and Sylvie had gone from the sofa. I went back into the kitchen, rinsed and peeled the apples I had bought, and sliced and spooned out the seeds from the cantaloupe. I could hear water running in the pipes and the faint splashing of a shower in an upstairs bathroom. In a moment I heard the opening of a door on the landing above and Sylvie's bare footsteps pattering down the stairs.

"Carl, are you here?" she called, and in a moment appeared in the kitchen doorway, stark naked, scrubbing her hair with a towel. I was breathless at the girlish pathos of her body and the ache of nostalgia it sent surging through me. Her breasts, like apples below her deeply cleft collarbones, and her lean hips, their blades protruding on either side of her flat belly like a little girl's, made me remember with dizzying poignancy Elizabeth pattering out of the shower after her swim at the neighborhood pool on a summer afternoon.

"I'm fixing the melon," I said.

"Good. I've got to get some soda or something. I've got a deadly hangover." She went across the kitchen to the cabinet and poked about on the shelf until she found a box of soda, the towel slung carelessly across her shoulder. "I think there's some Swiss cheese in the box. Make yourself a sandwich. I'll be down in a minute." She went back across the kitchen with the total unselfconsciousness of a child in the presence of her father or an older brother, and out the door into the parlor. I sliced the apples, set the table, and heated a kettle of water before she reappeared, wrapped in a white chenille robe, still fluffing her damp hair with the towel.

"I got you the apples," I said. "And I've made some tea."

"God, you're a good man. Have you made yourself a sandwich?"

"No, I'll have one of the apples. I got a dozen. They looked very good."

She dropped the towel on the back of her chair and sat down across from me, her hair hanging in limp strands about her face. She looked very young and smelled superbly of clean damp hair and dry, freshly laundered cotton.

"Did you have a good trip?" I asked.

"No." She took a slice of apple from the saucer and began to munch it hungrily. I did the same, reveling in its crisp juicy sweetness, in the smell of sunlight on the oilcloth table cover, the fragrance of the fresh-sliced melon and of her hair and clothing. She stared out of the window while she ate, her eyebrows constricted angrily.

"It's good to have you back," I said.

"It's good to be back. I'd have come up to see you, but I got drunk instead."

"I thought you didn't drink," I said.

"I don't, ordinarily. But about once every five years, I fall off the wagon; and when I do, I do a pretty thorough job of it."

I ate a piece of apple and asked, "Is your mother well?"

"Yes. She's getting older, of course, but not so much. Not as fast as I am. She loves to have someone there to fuss at, Aaron about his drinking, or me about not eating."

"How was Aaron?"

"He didn't come. The bastard. He sent me a letter instead." She licked juice from her fingers bitterly.

"Was he sick?"

"No. He claims he's busy. I don't believe it. You can get down here from New York in four hours, if you want to."

"And how was Jamed?"

"Oh, he was in a stew of course, because Aaron didn't show up. 'Where's Aaron? Where's Aaron?' My God, he must have asked me a hundred times. Of course, he did have the grace to send him a toy, so that helped. If he doesn't come down for my birthday, I'll kill him. I will." She began to spear slices of melon from the saucer with a fork, then murmured, with a full mouth, "Lord, that's luscious."

"They had it in the freezer. It's a good one, isn't it?" She nodded. "Are you feeling better?"

"Mm. I needed some food, I guess." She scowled. "I've been asleep since Thursday night. I sleep too much. I have something called narcolepsy, Aaron says. Is there such a thing?"

"Yes."

"What does it mean, exactly?"

"Well, it means that some people, when things get a bit overwhelming, simply fall asleep."

"As an escape, you mean?"

"I suppose so."

"My God, he's a good one to talk! He's been asleep for the last twenty years. What a nerve!" She spit a melon seed into her fist savagely. "He sits up there in his pad on Madison Avenue and entertains all the chicks, I suppose, swilling martinis all night long and spending the whole damned day burbling away about Preparation H or Parliament Cologne." She speared and munched another slice of melon, her anger apparently transposing slowly into sadness while she ate. She licked her lips and said, "You didn't have any brothers or sisters, did you?"

"No."

"Weren't you lonely?"

"No."

"You sound indignant about it."

"No. I'm just very sure of it. It's an emotion I never knew, until much later. I was too busy to be lonely."

"With what?"

"Learning things. I was always learning things. I had insect collections, chemistry sets, books. Then later, of course, I was studying. Medical students don't have time to be lonely. And I had less time than most."

"Why less than most?"

"I suppose I was more zealous than most. I did nothing but read, attend lectures, do ward duty and lab work. I don't think I had half a dozen hours to myself all week, and I wouldn't have known what to do with them if I had. I loved studying, and routine, and solitude."

"You're a strange man, you know that?" Sylvie said.

"Yes."

I very carefully began to peel another apple. She watched me for a moment and then added gently, "Still, I suppose there's something comforting about that kind of life."

"Yes. It's very much like being in the Army. You don't have to cultivate any social skill or imagination; there are no moral decisions to be made; there's no tangle of personal relationships to deal with. You have only to exercise a single faculty, and you have the peace of mind to do it in."

"It sounds something like narcolepsy," Sylvie said.

"I suppose it is, although I would have denied it at the time. My life seemed very rich to me. In spite of the fact that I lived in a room that measured eight by twelve feet and barely accommodated a bed, a bureau, and a bookcase. I left it at eight o'clock in the morning and usually didn't return to it until eight o'clock at night. The rest of my time was spent in laboratories, wards, operating theaters, libraries, the hospital cafeteria."

"How long did that go on?"

"For seven years."

"My God."

"Medical school, internship, and residency. I had no interest in anything else. I suppose my single non-professional activity in all that time was an occasional game of chess with a fellow student and a week of camping every summer in the mountains. Even then, I had textbooks with me, and spent my evenings reading them. In those seven years I don't think I read two works of fiction, or visited an art gallery, or attended a dance recital, or a concert, or the theater. I might have seen half a dozen motion pictures, of which I remember two."

"You were not a lover of the arts," Sylvie said, smiling.

"No. I disliked art intensely. All but music, of which I've always been fond. Some of it; not very much. I had records of the baroque masters that I played almost continuously on a little mechanical phonograph while I studied: Bach and Mozart, particularly, and also Vivaldi and Scarlatti, and some of Verdi, oddly enough. Music I understood immediately, the first time I ever heard it; it seemed very pure to me, almost crystalline, like the finest scientific prose. It has an inner logic and exactitude that I couldn't find in any of the other arts. I had always read widely, even as a boy, but never for aesthetic pleasure, or for vicarious adventure or romance. At an age when most boys are devouring the books of Zane Grey or Edgar Rice Burroughs, I was poring over the old American Encyclopedia in my father's library. Language, as a medium for spinning out the improbable adventures of insubstantial people in nonexistent times and places, seemed to me an inexplicable exercise in irrelevance. But as an instrument for probing between the cells and tissues and basic particles of reality, for naming, categorizing, describing with absolute precision, discovering and communicating to one's fellows the truth of the world we inhabit, it had for me the gleaming splendor of a cabinet of surgical instruments, each word as clean and fine-edged and meticulously designed for its function as a scalpel. I was stirred, as I was stirred by a Bach partita, by the glittering impeccable formality of medical prose. It couldn't be quarreled with; it cast a brilliance from the page like ice in sunlight. Writing of that kind was not designed—as it seemed to me the arts in general *were* designed—to obfuscate, to glorify some meager scrap of truth or some fatuous commonplace with florid, ostentatious images and colorful ambiguities, to gratify the romantic appetite for sweetmeats, to please the plump, epicurean mind. It was designed, on the contrary, to clarify, to denude, to pare away the ambiguities and deceptions, to unclothe the naked splendor of things. I would happily have traded the whole of Keats for a page of Pritkin's *Elements of Ophthalmology;* although it is, of course, a very difficult work to quote from."

"I don't know it," Sylvie said wryly.

"I don't suppose you do. But I loved reading books like that. By lamplight in my tiny room on winter evenings, or by lantern light, in the mountains, on long hot summer nights. Study was life itself to me. The only adventure I longed for was to explore the teeming world of unseen, unknown life around me, the secret universes pulsing on a slide under my microscope in a drop of saliva or pond water. I wanted to discover and understand what no man had ever known before: their unknown ways and relationships, the thrilling, pale, primordial laws of which they were the revelation and in which they flowed and whirled, like leaves in an invisible wind.

"I don't think it's possible to make anyone who hasn't felt it himself understand such a passion. It yields to nothing, and subsumes everything: food, physical exuberance, sexuality, art, war; time itself. That's the strangest thing of all: the way time is deformed, or held in astonishing abeyance, when the mind is functioning at its fullest, most fervent power. I've spent a whole day performing a laboratory experiment, step by beautiful, perfectly conceived step, which allowed no error or equivocation, feeling myself every moment closer to its radiant, absolute conclusion, held in a timeless trance of joy. I would be willing, as a scientist, to wager that time was actually, effectively altered for me, as if I had taken part in a space flight at incalculable velocities. At the end of such a day, no day had passed; I was no hungrier or wearier or older than I would have been in five minutes of ordinary terrestrial time. In such a trance there is no diminution or erosion of the spirit; patience is not involved, because there is no frustration or confusion, no sense whatever of adversity; there is only a noble, grave exfoliation, like the opening of a rose to light. A flower appears in midair, where no flower was, each stage of its unfolding so indivisibly connected with the last that no elapse of time can possibly occur between them; they are one inseparable event. I don't know quite how to explain that sensation, but consider this: if a motion picture is taken of an event at only eight frames per second, a very jerky and disconnected action is seen when the film is projected on a screen. If a greater number of pictures per second—twenty-four, for example—is taken, we see what we call 'natural' action when the film is projected. Things appear to transpire at their accustomed, terrestrial rate. An even greater number of pictures per second— thirty-two or sixty-four—produces what we call 'slow motion'; the action is greatly decelerated, far more of the intermediate steps in the event are seen than ordinary diurnal time permits us to behold, there is a vastly greater effect of fusion between them. Suppose an infinite number of pictures were taken of the same event. Motion would disappear entirely. With an infinite number of steps between each attitude, no change would be discernible at all; we should see everything. No alteration of attitude would be possible. We should, forever, witness one indissoluble, interminable event. I have had the dream, sometimes, when performing an experiment, that it would be the final one: the ultimate and primordial, frozen, only act; that I would become an immortal, immeasurably joyful witness to the one, infinite gesture which is the universe.

"Well, of course, when there is mental activity of that kind going on, distraction from it is less a blessing than a curse. The seven years of my medical apprenticeship passed like an hour, and I needed no more diversion from them than I would have in an hour's passing."

Sylvie sat with her head declined, in a kind of deferential silence. When I had paused for some time, she looked up at me and smiled gently. "I was known as Sticky Fingers," I said, somewhat abruptly. "I don't know why, exactly. I think as a kind of mocking tribute to my tenacity. I was never known to drop a scalpel, or to surrender a textbook willingly. Other students, just as good as I was, found time for recreation and romance. There were flirtations and parties and casual, good-natured fellowship in the wards and dormitories and the cafeteria, but they had little charm for me. I had no gift for bonhomie, and I had a fear of romantic relationships that I suppose was the consequence of the boyhood experiences I told you about the other day. I worked with the nurses comfortably enough, and some of them I admired for their skill and intelligence, but the thought of going to bed with one of them, or even of kissing or embracing her, would have sent a chill through me, if it had occurred to me at all. The fact is, it almost never did."

"But you must have married quite young, to have a daughter my age," Sylvie said. "You're not so terribly old as that. There must have been some romance somewhere along the line."

"Well, perhaps there was one, before I married," I said. "Although it hardly deserves the name. It doesn't deserve it at all, in fact. But there was a particularly aggressive nurse, during my internship, whom I dated for a while. Three times, to be exact. Or who dated me, to be even more accurate about it. I think my legendary asceticism must have been a challenge to her. She was the kind of woman who could be provoked by a challenge; she had very great initiative."

She was a Norwegian girl named Karen, tall and very good-looking, I realize now, and spectacularly clean. Nurses are, of course; but this woman was almost supernaturally so. She had gray Scandinavian eyes, frosty, determined eyes, and very pale blond hair of an icy brilliance. When she walked, her uniform crackled and glittered like a glacier. I was reassured by her cleanliness, I suppose, and overwhelmed by her initiative—to the extent of escorting her, twice, to the motion pictures. At her suggestion, you can be sure. As a matter of fact, my reason for remembering the two films I mentioned was chiefly the fact that I saw them in her company; and because of the indignation and unrest they produced in me. She was an O.R. nurse in the surgical ward, where I spent three months of my internship, and assisted me in several operations. One day, after I had helped the chief surgeon remove a ruptured spleen, she congratulated me on my performance afterwards in the wardroom, and I returned the compliment, sincerely enough, because I was impressed with her skill. It was evident that we were mutually gratified.

We worked together in surgery for six weeks or more, with growing appreciation of each other's capacities. Sometimes, when our off-duty hours coincided, we would have lunch together in the cafeteria, and on those occasions my conversation grew as nearly animated as any I'd ever had with a woman before. It wasn't that I was interested in her romantically at all; my discourse would have been just as spirited if it had been addressed to a man. It was the fact of our intense common interest in medicine, and our mutual acknowledgment of each other as peers in our profession.

One evening a young oriental girl was brought into the emergency room who had shot herself after a lovers' quarrel. I think she was Malayan or Burmese; she was very beautiful. I remember her face vividly. It had the delicacy of feature of many oriental women, with wonderfully gentle, tilted eyes that were disturbingly serene, almost victorious. She was wearing a pale blue silk dress that was stained in the strangely exact, recognizable pattern of a flower by her blood, as if it were decorated with a silk-screen print: there was a great scarlet poinsettia blossoming across its bodice. I felt almost as if it were a desecration to slice through it, as I had to, with a pair of scissors, to examine her wound. All the time I was doing so she held Karen's hand and spoke to her, softly, with great effort, but patiently and distinctly, as if she were reciting a credo.

"Do you know what Siriyat did?" she said.

"No," Karen said, patting her hand. "But you mustn't upset yourself."

"He made another lady pregnant. He is not true to me. That is why I shoot me. If he come to see me, I want you to tell him that I told you. I want him to know that there is some person in the world who knows what he did."

I heard this with an unaccountable bitterness, a kind of rancor that made me say to her sharply, "You must not say any more. You must not speak. We are trying to save your life."

Her eyes wandered to mine and after studying them for a moment, she said, as if in disbelief, or denial of my ability, "You can't do that."

I knew she was right. She was obviously in a critical condition. The bullet had deflected from the second right intercostal rib, shattering it and driving several jagged splinters into the pericardium, two of which had punctured the right ventricular wall. I knew as soon as we had placed her on the operating table and opened the wound that she would die. There had been almost constant hemorrhage, lobar edemia—which is a flooding of the thoracic cavity with seral fluid—rapidly weakening pulse, and finally, complete systemic collapse. The prognosis had been hopeless from the beginning, and while I had no responsibility in the case—a senior heart surgeon named Palmerton performed the operation, I was only his assistant—it was the first time that a patient had died under my hand on the table, and I was shaken by the experience. It was a strange emotion, I think more of anger or indignation than grief or guilt. But although I did not hold myself responsible for her death, I knew, even then, that I would never forget her last words, or the harshness with which I had spoken to her. Or the unpleasant sense of shame in my hands when they touched her body, as if what they were doing to her were less a surgical operation than a violation of some kind, almost a defloration.

Afterwards, Karen and I left the hospital together and stopped at a nearby delicatessen to restore our spirits as best we could with a bottle of Danish ale that she insisted on paying for. The delicatessen was old, unclean, and, except for ourselves, totally unpatronized. The proprietor was a frail little Jewish man wearing a yarmulke, who nodded and smiled at me quite unexpectedly and inappropriately whenever he caught my eye. The beer was the first I had drunk since my unhappy evening as a schoolboy in Baltimore, and the taste of it was far more bitter even than I remembered. I sipped it joylessly and had very little to say.

"You don't want to feel any guilt about it," Karen said. "No one could have saved her. The pericardium was like a sieve."

"It isn't guilt," I said. "It's the knowledge of one's limitations. That's what's agonizing. No one permits a patient to die willfully or maliciously. It's just knowing how damned stupid and imperfect we are. If there had been some way to deal with that edema, for example. It seems to me that with all the work that's been done in lumbar tuberculosis and pneumonia, there ought to be a technique developed by this time. What do you think of Palmerton as a surgeon?"

"He's one of the best two or three in the city."

"Have you worked with him before?"

"Yes. Several times."

"A simple pleural pump, for example. Why couldn't something of that kind be used?" I let my eyes wander unguardedly for a moment, and the little Jewish man beamed and nodded disconcertingly at me.

"Did you notice what beautiful hands Miss Pitting had?" Karen said.

"Pitting? Was that her name?" I stared for a moment at the old electric clock on the wall and saw with irrational displeasure that it was three hours slow. "That damned clock is slow," I said. "Or stopped." I looked across the room and the little Jewish man nodded a diabolically merry confirmation. I lowered my eyes to my mug and listened to the faint suspiring lament of the ale froth.

"You're beginning to look a little ragged," Karen said. "You'd better start getting more sleep, or you're going to collapse."

"Oh, yes. With all I've got to learn, and the amount of time I've got to learn it in."

"I don't say it out of sentimentality, but because to break your health down is stupid. You say you can't stand stupidity."

"I can't. It seems to me the nearest thing to sin there is. It's what Miss Pitting died of. Hers and ours."

"I think she died of love," Karen said. She put her hand on my arm. "Listen, we both have the day off tomorrow. Why don't we go and see a movie? There's a very good one at the Trans-Lux."

"I don't go to the movies," I said.

"You mean never?"

"Almost never. They bore me."

"This one won't bore you, I'm certain. You need a change, Carl, you really do." I grimaced and shook my head. "Listen, if we were to get one of those fifty-thousand-dollar fluoroscopes in the O.R., or an artificial kidney, or any other fine, complicated machine, would you deliberately abuse it until it broke down? It's just as stupid to break down and ruin a very fine, very complicated, irreplaceable doctor of medicine. You'll have to admit that."

I found it difficult to contradict the logic of her argument, and the fact is, I was exhausted and depressed to a degree that I had never felt before, or believed possible.

"What is this film about?" I asked.

"Paradise. I think you could use a little visit to paradise, after today."

"Where do they locate paradise?"

"In a hidden valley in Tibet, where no one ever dies. People live to be thousands of years old."

"I don't know that paradise is synonymous with immortality."

"I thought you did. Isn't that what you're trying to make the world into? A place where Miss Pitting would never have to die?"

"If a woman feels inclined to kill herself over lost love, nothing on earth can save her," I said. "Not all the physicians who have ever lived. She would be just as miserable tomorrow morning."

"Not in Shangri-La," Karen said. "When they have love problems there —a triangle or something—it's solved by the person who loves least very gracefully bowing out and leaving the field clear to his rival."

"Well, that sounds intelligent to me," I said. "Maybe it is paradise, after all. How do you know so much about this film?"

"I've seen it."

"And you want to see it again? My God, what for?"

"I loved it," Karen said.

"But you've already seen it. My God, what a waste of time."

"Why? I suppose you'd consider it ridiculous to buy a picture and hang it on the wall, because once having seen it, you'd find it absurd to go on looking at it day after day. According to that theory, no one would ever listen to the same music twice, or kiss the same person more than once."

"The world would probably be a great deal better off if they didn't," I said.

"It would be totally uninhabited," Karen said. "I'll come by your place at one o'clock tomorrow. And I'll pay your way."

"Why?"

"Because I make more money than you do."

"You're a very logical person," I said. "And I'm just drunk enough to accept you. This is the first beer I've had in eleven years."

"You don't drink beer, either?"

"I don't know why any intelligent person would, on any regular basis. It's one of the surest ways to break down a fine machine, as you put it. Did you know that a single martini destroys approximately fifty thousand brain cells?"

"Well, we'd better get out of here while I'm still able to tie my own shoes."

We parted in front of the restaurant, and she touched my arm and said, "Now, I warn you, I'll be around at your place at one o'clock tomorrow. That will give you time to get a good night's sleep. God knows you need it, Carl."

She was right; but in spite of my exhaustion, I spent one of the most monstrously restless nights of my life, slipping in and out of dreams such as that in which a company of masked, robed, silent figures, myself among them, stood with the stealth of sorcerers above a starlit table on which there lay a shuddering, slender girl, plucking from her gaping thorax clusters of dripping grapes, bruised, glistening plums, and lengths of writhing ivy whose bloodied leaves flickered like the scales of great, dark, sunken carp, tumbling in death through deep purple water. Her pale lips moved constantly, emitting a ceaseless bitter susurration which I bent down to hear, and was horrified to recognize as an obscenely insidious recitation of the rosary; it hissed through her cracked lips as if whispered by vipers from a ruined cistern. I woke from and sank into these vile dreams fitfully until at last I heard the staccato reveille of Karen's knuckles rapping at my door. I called out that I would be ready in a minute, and without making any more preparation to meet the day than dashing cold water in my face and dressing hastily, I opened my door and found her leaning against the stair rail in the hall, impatiently plucking at her fingernails.

"You haven't shaved," she said.

"No. I overslept. I stayed up late last night, studying."

"God, there's no way to deal with you, at all. Have you eaten?"

"No."

"No. You'll be having ulcers next. Well, we'll be late if we stop for lunch, but you've got to have some food. Suppose we pick up some apples and cheese and hard rolls, and nibble at them in the theater? We'll have a movie picnic."

"That's all right with me."

While she made these purchases in a neighborhood grocery, I followed idly along the aisles, watching her sidelong with a kind of perturbation I had never experienced in her company before and which it took me some time to account for: she was not wearing her uniform. I had never before seen her except in that formidably starched, glacial garment with her hair pinned back severely under her nurse's cap. Dressed as she was now, in a light blue suit and sweater, high-heeled shoes and silk stockings, with a string of pearls about her neck and her blond hair hanging free, she produced in me a feeling of strangeness and profound unease. She was also wearing perfume, which struck me as frivolous and unbecoming in a professional woman. As we walked to the theater through the sunlight of a fine summer afternoon, I began to regret having agreed to exchange it for the artificial delights of the celluloid paradise we were to inhabit for the next hour and a half.

I regretted it even more after our sojourn there; I spent an afternoon which rivaled the night before in discomfort. Not only was there Karen, in her disturbing proximity, her elbow touching mine, her scent of Muguet des Bois flooding inescapably over me, but there was Shangri-La, the only possible refuge, which spread its shameless fantasy before us, its green and fragrant valleys, its idyllic villages, its gentle, graceful people who, indeed, did not die, and whose chief preoccupation, apparently, for all eternity, was love. One of them, who in her nymphlike slender beauty reminded me distressingly of the girl I had watched die on the operating table the afternoon before, stripped off her clothing at one point and plunged naked into a forest pool. I had never before seen a naked woman under anything but clinical circumstances, and I was very much upset by the experience.

I expressed this feeling, and my general discontent with what I considered the outrageous romanticism of the film, to Karen later, on a park bench, as we finished the last of our provisions in Lafayette Square.

"How can people peddle that kind of rubbish," I asked, "in a world where people are dying of hunger and disease and physical abuse? What possible purpose does it serve, in a world like this?"

"Well, they're dying of hunger for romance, too," Karen said. "It gives them comfort. Which, after all, is what we do, isn't it? It helps to keep alive their vision of paradise."

"Paradise?" I said. "Where people stroll around all day with nothing on their minds but making love? It's not my idea of paradise."

Karen munched an apple, smiling at me in what I recognized suddenly as a very provocative imitation of one of the original inhabitants of that place.

"Don't you realize," she said, "that when you have *freed* them from disease and hunger and physical abuse, when you have turned *this* world into a paradise, one of their chief occupations will very likely be to meditate on love all day. Anyone who's interested in perfection ought to give a certain amount of thought to love." She munched her apple with very white teeth, seeming to study the effect of the suggestion on me.

"It's a good thing I won't be around when that state is achieved," I said. "I'd be out of work. It sounds like hell to me."

She laughed, but I could share her appreciation of my own joke only to the extent of an uncertain smile; I was not particularly reassured by the intimation that in paradise it was I who should be the idle one, the interloper, and those whom in this world we consider wanton, or indigent, or infantile, who would be most at home there.

Three weeks later she got me to the movies again, this time in celebration of a much happier event. I wouldn't have believed it possible except for the fact that I had recently applied for a fellowship in communicable diseases at my hospital, and had been accepted. In my exhilaration, I yielded to her invitation to a dinner of Scandinavian smorgasbord and, for reasons which will never be known to me, a film called *The Informer*, which concerned the Black and Tan Rebellion in Ireland and the betrayal of one of his compatriots to the English by an ignorant Irish roustabout for what I believe was the sum of ten pounds. I had never before seen a moral dilemma presented in aesthetic terms, and the experience was equally as unsettling to me as the nudity and indolence of Shangri-La.

I suppose, in those days, I had deliberately limited my consideration of disease to simple mechanical failure in the universe: bodily malfunctions, disruptions of physical and chemical processes, skeletal, muscular, or glandular; whatever could be corrected by the application of scientific method. The fact that there might be moral disorders, spiritual infections, or deranged passions raging abroad that could cause far greater damage was to me beyond the range of prudent consideration, since it was beyond the capacity of medicine to repair —and evidently of philosophy or religion, which, as I understood it, had been designed for the purpose. Both of these institutions, after all, considerably antedated medicine; yet as far as I could make out, there had been little perceptible improvement in human conduct since the time of Adam. Psychiatry I simply considered misconceived. It dismayed me that a branch of my own profession should have devoted itself, however indirectly, to the correction of maladies that were manifestly incorrigible. Had there been, since Freud, any appreciable decline in man's moral confusions? Did not people commit suicide in ever greater numbers? Were not neurosis, crime, alcoholism, drug addiction, promiscuity, sexual perversities of every kind constantly increasing? It was difficult to understand how men who prided themselves on logic and the use of the deductive principle could devote centuries of meditation to such afflictions and the possibility of cures for them; they might as well waste their time lamenting the fact that man had relatively poor hearing, or a very ineffective olfactory sense, or vastly impractical visceral suspension and vascular systems. Religious men, with only inspiration to depend upon, had much more wisely concluded that man was a morally imperfectible creature whose spiritual confusions were the result—or evidence—of his own wickedness and, like his physical limitations, the burden of mortality. Those confusions might be forgiven but hardly rectified, on this side of the grave. Any definition of humanity must include them, and it was no part of a prudent physician's purpose to redesign the universe. His only concern should be to restore to working order what, in its design, had fallen into disrepair or dysfunction. Drama, I decided after my two unhappy introductions to it at Karen's hands, added, to futility, offense, since it imposed upon the morbid and immodest speculations of philosophy the voluptuous ambiguities of art. It attempted to wring beauty out of everything—a tragic glamour from catastrophe, and from the simple mechanical process of procreation, rhapsody.

I had, in fact, a great distrust of art in general, as I had of the beauty it aspired to embody and perpetuate. Both of them were tenuous and delusive, not to say fantastical. They were the products of illusion, misconception, or privation. What was beautiful, or artful, to one man, or one creature, was abhorrent to another. A rose was generally considered beautiful because its scent and color and conformation were pleasing to many men, and to some insects, such as the bee or butterfly, which feasted on its nectar. But to the dung beetle, excrement was far more alluring. That deluded creature burrowed into a mound of fecal matter with an enthusiasm equal to that of the butterfly plundering the rose. Braque was venerated by one man and deplored by another, who admired Titian or Velázquez. I distrusted all of them, and the beauty that men believed themselves to have discovered in them. "Beauty is in the eye of the beholder," I had heard often enough, and I had heard nothing sounder on the subject. It reflected only the infirmities and idiosyncrasies of that beholding eye. It had no laws or substance or invariable principles. It could, in fact, be said not to exist at all. The beauty that men found in things, they invented, and invested in them out of a wistful, passionate desire for delight, for comfort, for assurance that the world was not a place of hunger, violence, and death, but of delectable, exquisite things; a desire to make a heaven of a dunghill. Certainly they did not invent it out of a love of truth. It was, in fact, like the act of its invention, a disservice to truth, a lawless and ignoble evasion of reality.

There was something about the aesthetic impulse, I decided, that implied desperation, deprivation, fear. But was this not equally true of the scientific or philosophic impulse? Did they both not imply just as desperate a desire for reassurance that there was order in the universe? I thought not; magnificently not. A scientist, perhaps even a philosopher of sufficient skill and integrity, would relentlessly pursue and recognize and publish a truth he had surmised, in spite of any personal repugnance he felt for it, out of his respect for it as truth. I recalled a story I had heard, that Darwin, when he had completed *The Descent of Man,* postponed the publication of it for a long time, out of the personal antipathy he felt for his own theory, and his apprehension about the havoc it would wreak among the ranks of Christian believers (an apprehension, as it turned out, that was justified). Yet he published it, in keeping with his faith that truth, eventually, will redeem whatever discomfort or dismay or disillusion it may work in the heart of man. Whether he would have done so in the face of the threat of torture—as Galileo failed to do—we could never know. A love of truth had limits, apparently, even in the most consecrated man. And yet, even if it were temporarily suppressed by fear, it was not born of fear, or insecurity, or illusion, as beauty was.

And yet when I considered the subject of beauty at all—which was much less often than I've made it appear—I was troubled by the fact that it manifestly did exist, and that it played an indispensable role in the functioning of the universe. If dung were not disposed of by the beetle or by other organisms equally enthusiastic about its charms, we should shortly have a world of dung. If such refuse of history as the bodies of dead dinosaurs were not devoured by vultures and delirious maggots, they would still be lying about the world, and in growingly unmanageable quantities. If roses were not ravishing and women beautiful, they would soon cease to exist, since nothing would find them sufficiently attractive to assist in fertilizing them. This, after all, was not an evasion of reality, but a fundamental principle of it. Then, too, as I told you once, I found something undeniably beautiful about the scientific method, about the elegance and precision of a perfectly conceived and executed experiment. Chastened by this paradox, I undertook the erection of a metaphysic of sorts, which it might amuse you to hear. It was a makeshift structure, built hastily and perfunctorily and with a certain sense of umbrage, but no more so, I suspect, than those that most men build to meet the doubts of their dark hours or to serve as justification for their errors, petty chicaneries, and more conspicuous departures from grace.

Perhaps, I reasoned, there were two principal faculties in man, the aesthetic and the rational. The first, and incalculably the more primitive, he shared with bees, dung beetles, maggots, and virtually every other form of animate life. Unless kept in balance by the second, it was what addicted him to beauty, that fabrication of the senses which, although it kept in motion the machinery of life by such wiles as leading bees to honey, often went seriously amok and led moths to flame and lemmings to the sea and poets on drunken, dire quests and men from diligence and duty into luxury and license, and very often into battle —insanely, artfully deceived by anthems and banners and the beauty of a Helen's face. This beauty was not only the object of the aesthetic faculty, but its invention; which was to say that those deranged by it manufactured their own enchantment—cast spells upon themselves—out of the dread of truth.

Not so the man of reason. Far from dreading truth, he worshipped it. The faculty of reason gratified not merely the senses, but some noble appetite as yet either unawakened or very rudimentary in the sensual man. Nor did the man of science suffer from an excess of that appetite, as the aesthete suffered

from the excessive love of beauty. Such a thing was by definition impossible.
No reasonable man would allow himself an unreasonable addiction to the truth.
If such a thing as an unreasonably reasonable man existed, no example of the
prodigy was known to me. His was not only a nobler but a more comprehensive
faculty, since it included the aesthetic, but transcended it. He was aware of
beauty and suitably appreciative of it, but immune to its deceptions and
derangements, rendered invulnerable, by his reason, to all excess.

As I say, this was a somewhat shaky metaphysical structure, and one of very
limited accommodations, which left the philosopher homeless. I was not much
troubled by this, as I considered the philosopher little more than a beggar at
the door of other disciplines. Unlike the artist, he made nothing; and unlike
the scientist, discovered nothing. He was a mountebank, or at best a wandering
entertainer, who earned his supper by juggling the inventions of the artist and
the discoveries of the scientist—that true and intrepid explorer of the universe
—in a kind of backyard exhibition of agility or virtuosity. His knuckles bore
no scars of the chisel—either from breaking the stubborn stone of reality to
mine its ore of truth or from shaping it into the torso of the Venus de Milo.
If he performed very well he might be allowed to spend the night in the
woodshed or the barn, but he could hardly expect to be granted permanent
residence in my Mansion of Ideas. That that ramshackle edifice was itself a
product of his uncertain practice, which probably gave him a greater claim to
occupancy than anyone, was an irony I hardly paused to consider.

Where the saint, or mystic, or religious man fitted into this scheme of
things, I was not sure. His claim for admission rested on neither aesthetics nor
dialectics nor experiment, but on faith, or as he sometimes chose to call it,
divine revelation. He was apparently just as skeptical of truth as he was of
beauty, and judging by his treatment of such people as Galileo and Erasmus,
just as stern in dealing with the adherents of either, unless they could be bribed
or threatened into his service. He would acknowledge, utilize, even celebrate,
the work of either or both if they were sufficiently tractable and so long as they
supported his own view of things, but he was not above anathematizing,
excommunicating, torturing, or even burning them alive if they were stub-
bornly heretical in their conclusions. His abhorrence of the squalid charms of
a Commedia dell' Arte I could heartily concur with, but his proscription of the
work of a Darwin or a Kepler made me uneasy, to say the very least. And that
I shared, in a vague, uncomfortable, and furtive way, his belief in the existence
of a Supreme Being, and without any sense whatever of the exaltation he found
in that belief, made me equally uneasy. Perhaps, I decided, God was the
invention of the pious man as beauty was the invention of the aesthete; and
just as the superior faculties of the scientist enabled him to invent and enjoy
—temperately—the delights of beauty, they enabled him also to conceive of

God and to enjoy—judiciously—the pleasures of piety. In fact, he was often a spirited amateur of the arts, as he was of religious matters. Einstein himself, who was said to perform passably on the violin and to hold lively opinions on the subject of theology, was living proof of it.

It would be difficult not to congratulate oneself on this portrait of the scientist: a man of superior sensibility who might dine austerely on the bread of truth, but had a palate fine enough to sip appreciatively from the cup of beauty and divinity—much as a gentleman might finish off a meal with a glass of after-dinner liqueur. I was especially pleased to have discovered the truth that he not only surpassed the aesthete and the mystic in the fearless rigor of his thought but equaled them in his powers of invention. But whether or not it was piety that led me to invent the god of syphilis, I was not quite strict enough in my reasoning to inquire.

I preferred not to consider the subject at all. In spite of all my theorizing and in spite of congratulating myself on my receptivity to beauty, it was still an oddly unnerving phenomenon to me. I could not reconcile the thought that it beguiled and inflamed, that it reduced men to apostasy. *I* might share the faith of the righteous man, but I was not at all sure that the artist or the aesthete did. However prolific it might be, art was the great dissembler, the great subverter of Order. It was an unwarranted, vain, and unpleasantly vulgar complaint against what its practitioners were pleased to consider the poor workmanship of the Creator.

That I should have been exposed to two such tasteless demonstrations of discontent by Karen in a single month did not gratify me at all; and her attitude toward my discomfiture I took as cavalier. It seemed to produce a kind of bemused affection in her, grand and gay, which I found patronizing as well as ominous. It occurred to me that she might be husband-hunting, and consider that my lack of worldliness or of romantic predilection made me, for the present, more available, and for the future, less disposed to delinquency. Or that she might be trying to "widen my horizons," "improve my sensibility," or some such rubbish, to shape me into a more desirable candidate for matrimony. I was very well satisfied with my horizons as they were; what lay beyond them seemed threatening to the energy and zeal and industry that they enclosed like a garden fence: nudity, indolence, moral miasmas, Renoir's buxom, rose-petal maidens, Sisley's shimmering meadows, Keats's bubbling flasks of wine and purple-stainéd mouths, Debussy's haunted, moonlit ruins, and the dirty, strife-torn streets of Dublin, where hungry, desperate men sold their comrades for a pocketful of coins and passage to America. I had quite enough to do without subjecting myself to such demoralizing luxuries or gratuitous agonies as those.

A week later, however, I was subjected to one even more outrageous. By a stratagem whose subtlety I suppose I have chosen to forget, she got me to the ballet, and inflicted on me the scene of the seduction of a very Miss Pitting–like nymph by a muscular young satyr with shaggy flanks and a pair of plastic horns. After twenty minutes of this travesty, of the rapturous intertwining of their pale, moon-washed flesh and sinuous arms and their astounding vaults of ecstasy, I crumpled my program in my fist and said, "Let's get out of here. I really can't stand this thing."

"But the first act isn't even over."

"Good God, how much more is there? Please, Karen. I've got a much better idea."

I rose and stumbled past the knees of a row of indignant votaries of beauty while she plunged after me, murmuring mortified apologies. Outside the theater, her fury broke on me.

"I've never been so embarrassed in my life!" she said. "Honestly, you're impossible. And I paid ten dollars for those tickets."

"Listen, if you want art," I said, "just come with me. We're going to have some of the real thing. Bach."

She followed me in bitter silence to the corner delicatessen, where, in penance, I purchased a pack of beer and one of ginger ale; then accompanied me, with what I failed to recognize as an ominously rapid dissipation of her rage, to my tiny room on the second floor of a shabby residential hotel on Seventh Street. I put a record on my portable phonograph, and with Karen seated on the bed and myself on my single, wobbly, straight-backed chair, with a bottle of beer and of ginger ale, respectively, clutched in our hands, we listened to Dame Myra Hess's ravishing rendition of *The Well-Tempered Clavier*. Although it was a very hot August night, I kept the window closed to shut out the sound of traffic from the street below, and both of us were sweating profusely. She was wearing a linen suit and looked extremely uncomfortable.

"Why don't you take off your jacket?" I said. "You must be very warm."

"All right." She set down her bottle of beer and stood up immediately, turning her back to me for assistance in removing it. As I took hold of the collar and my fingers touched her shoulders, I felt a sudden paralyzing flood of confusion at the apparently deliberate ambiguity of my own mindless suggestion, and of dismay at her wantonly complaisant interpretation of it. I held the jacket while she slipped her arms out of it, and after standing very indecisively for a moment with lowered eyes, hung it, with much fumbling, on the back of the chair.

"Would you like me to take off anything else?" she asked.

"No. I think you should be more comfortable now."

"Comfort is something we can never get too much of in this world," she said; and sitting down on the bed, removed her shoes, watching me with a look of roguish determination all the while. I sat down in the chair, laced my fingers, and tried desperately to restore my attention to the music. Out of the corner of my eyes I saw that she was peeling off her stockings.

"I'm getting more comfortable every minute," she said.

I thought of replying that I wished I could say the same, but the abject sound of the statement shamed me into silence. I smiled in a sickly way, and nodded. With her stockings removed, rolled up into little springy balls and tucked into her shoes, she stood up and began to unbutton the waist of her skirt. I found that my teeth were grinding in despair. A thick, dark, treacly substance seemed to be pulsing heavily in my veins. I closed my eyes, feeling the senseless, sickening revulsion one feels on stepping on a snake. I stood up suddenly.

"I'll go down and get some cigarettes," I said.

"Cigarettes? I didn't know you smoked."

"I do, occasionally." I plunged toward the door, but she put out her hand to block me.

"What's the matter with you?" she said.

"Nothing at all."

"Could it be that you're—offended?"

"I didn't mean at all what you thought," I said. "I would never have suggested such a thing. I don't think it's—decent."

"Decent?"

"No." I forced myself to look into her eyes, watching a serpentine brilliance develop in them, as if a breath of cold wind had blown across some rapidly jelling substance.

"You don't think love is decent?"

"I'm not in love with you. I should think you'd realize that."

She lowered her hand from the doorjamb and folded her fingers meticulously into her palm. "Oh, yes, I realize that, *Doctor,*" she said, her voice lifting with a deliberate, almost lighthearted sound of irony in emphasizing the word, "with me, or anyone. Although I doubt that's your biggest problem at the moment. Well, you'd better go and do your little errand."

"Yes. What kind of cigarettes would you like?"

I took hold of the doorknob and stood for a moment in craven pretense of concern about her preferences. She smiled at me bitterly. "I won't be a minute," I said and, lowering my head in humiliation, went plummeting down the stairs and out onto the railed stoop of the old row house. I placed my hand against the brick wall of the building and leaned there for a moment, weak with shame, and with a vicious resentment that sprayed along my nerves like acid. A little girl with her dirty cotton dress tucked into her panties was skipping rope on the sidewalk just beside the three steps that led down from the stoop. She was damp with sweat in the sweltering air of the summer evening; it ran down her throat and legs, making darker-edged rivulets of grime on the chocolate-colored skin. She was counting in a coarse whisper, as if toward the moment of some unspeakable event. "Sixty-two, sixty-three, sixty-fo', sixty-fi'—" The humid air, enfolding almost tangibly the noise of traffic from the street, pressed against my head like the clamorous fumes of an inferno. The little girl lowered her jump rope and approached me with the cautious, predatory glare of a sea gull reconnoitering a picnic on a beach.

"Mistah, you gimme fi' cint f' popsicle?" she said in a harsh, arrogant voice. There was something dreadful, witchlike, about the child; she held her hard little hand toward me like a claw. I put my hand into my pocket and separated a quarter from the clutch of coins I found there, bringing it out and holding it in my palm for her to see.

"Here's a quarter," I said. "If you can find it, you can have it." I drew back my hand and flung the coin out across the street, above the tops of the moving automobiles, to the opposite sidewalk. She did not hesitate a moment, but turned and plunged in pursuit of it like a retriever hound, dashing recklessly into the stream of moving cars. I stood and watched with savage fascination, my breath suspended. She was very nearly struck by a fast-moving dark sedan which came to a lurching stop, its brakes shrieking, as she raced across its path. The driver, a middle-aged man whose hat was toppled from his head by the abruptness of his halt, shouted reproaches to her through the window. She turned and spit at him.

I never saw whether or not she retrieved the coin; I strode to the corner delicatessen in a lunging stalk and, complying with my strangely obstinate fiction that Karen was patiently, starved for nicotine, awaiting my return (much mollified, her skirt smoothed out, her hands clasped penitently in her lap), I bought a pack of cigarettes and carried them back, with the same fulsome urgency, to my room. She was gone, of course; but the phonograph was still playing, scattering the cool fugal complexities of Bach into the room like the chips of shattered stars. I sat and listened to the music to its end, thinking how exact, how absolute its crystalline lucidities were in the dreamlike chaos of emotion about me. When it had finished, I carried the bottles—all but two of them still full—to the window and dropped them, one after another, onto the concrete pavement of the areaway, three floors below. They burst with heavy, liquid explosive sounds that reverberated up through the brick vault like cannon shots; twelve of them—a salute, I thought; although in celebration or commemoration of what, it was very difficult to say.

Well, of course, that was the end of my affair, if it could be called such, with Karen. Strangely enough, the remainder of my association with her was neither as painful nor as embarrassing as I expected. The fact is, I was relieved to feel no further social or romantic obligations to the woman whatever. She was, of course, noticeably—to me, at any rate—cool and formal in her manner; but prudent enough not to express anything that could be interpreted as the rancor of a wronged woman in the operating room, the ward office, or the presence, generally, of other members of the staff. As a matter of fact, I think she managed to make it very subtly understood that it was she who was discouraging any interest of a romantic kind I might have had in her. She was certainly capable of such subtlety; it would have served her pride; and any faculty that would have served her in any way, she would have put to use. Fortunately, she left the hospital within six weeks to go into private practice, and I never saw her again.

It was about one o'clock now. The sun was westering and fell obliquely through the kitchen window, casting a parallelogram of light across the oilcloth on Sylvie's table, in which the kitchenware—the salt cellar and pitcher and crockery—stood with a look of dramatic solidity and unity, as if placed on display, inviting admiration for their uniqueness. One of Sylvie's hands, superbly gilt, lay in the light, idly rotating a fork on the tabletop between her thumb and second fingertip. Her chin supported by the heel of her other palm, she gazed down thoughtfully at this activity, murmuring in a moment, "Did you ever think of her with regret, afterwards?"

"Not until now," I said.

"I gather she wasn't very much like your wife."

"Nothing in the world. They couldn't have been more different."

"Was it long after this that you married?"

"No. Six months, at most. I was still an intern."

We sat silently for some time, and I saw that we had entirely devoured the dish of sliced apple and melon. There was a little pool of juice in the saucer and, on another dish, a remaining sliver of Swiss cheese, which Sylvie lifted by its edge and nibbled daintily, like a raccoon. "God, we're all such fools," she said. "You, too, I guess. All of us."

"Yes."

She finished the cheese, rubbed her fingertips against the breast of her robe, and extended her hand to me across the table, palm upturned, inviting me to take it, which I did, marveling at the sweetness of her clasp.

"I'm glad we can bring our foolishness to each other," she said. "It's so much better than putting it in a book."

"I suppose. Of course, I never had a book."

"You can thank God for that." She disengaged her hand and stood up, tugging thoughtfully at the lapels of her robe. "Why don't I get dressed and we go for a walk? We've never been for a walk together. There's a place I want to show you."

"I can't think of a better idea. Suppose I take my things up to the house while you get dressed and you can stop by for me."

"Good. I'll only be ten minutes."

I rinsed out the dishes we had used, set them in the drainer by the sink, and carried the bag of groceries I had bought for myself up the lane to my cottage. When I had deposited them on shelves and in the refrigerator I went back out into the lane and met Sylvie coming up between the honeysuckle hedges, dressed in a pair of boots and blue jeans, her navy pea jacket, and with her watch cap pulled down over her ears.

She smiled at me and slid her arm into mine, linking our elbows.

"It's a gorgeous day."

"Yes," I said. "I think we've made it through the winter." We struck up the lane in the spring sunlight between the backs of the abandoned houses. The soil was soft with the spring thaw and the crushed oyster shell of the path gave under our feet with a pleasant spongy resilience. The dark red buds of the maples and persimmons had burst into tender, tiny, rose-colored leaves and sprinkled the path with a feathery debris that blew in the mild breeze like dust. The sky was blue and clear and smelled of earth and wet wood. In the tall, still-naked sycamore at the end of the lane a raven clung to the bare branches like a black rag, shrieking a single hoarse syllable endlessly. Sylvie stopped and listened, looking up. In a moment she stooped and picked up a stone from the path; I thought she would hurl it at the bird, but she did not; she closed her fingers tightly around the stone and plunged her hand into her pocket, moving on. Beyond the last of the unkempt backyards the lane sloped down to a strip of yellow sand that bordered the shore of the Point. We stood in the sand looking out across the estuary to the bay, very blue in the sun, between the portals of the low hills on either shore of the Patuxent. Sylvie took the stone out of her pocket and tossed it across the narrow beach into the gently lapping shallow water.

"One never gets over that impulse," she said. "To stone the soothsayers." She looked at me and smiled.

"Let's walk along the beach."

We followed the shore around the Point, sinking in the cool damp sand to our ankles. When we had rounded the Point and turned west, up the river shore, we were faced suddenly with a strong chill breeze that was blowing down the Patuxent to the bay. We buttoned the collars of our jackets and lowered our heads into the wind, striding side by side to the whisper of our boot soles and the rustle of the dune grass on the low sand hills to our right. Sometimes a shorebird, a piper or a turnstone, would run scurrying ahead of us until we overtook him, then take flight and circle landward, to alight behind us on the beach. A single gull stood on the crest of the grassy bluff above the beach, watching us haughtily, his feathers ruffling in the wind. Sylvie stopped to stare back at him, breaking into a smile.

"They're such funny things. They eat carrion, too, of course, but they still manage to be funny. A raven is a very different creature."

We stood and stared at the gull, who returned our gaze with undiminished hauteur.

"What did you mean, the other day," I said, "after they'd brought the boy in? There was a bird up in the sky. You said, 'It's one of his doves.' Do you remember?"

"One of Poppa's," Sylvie said. "He used to keep a flock of them, in a pigeon loft in the backyard. After he died, Aaron let them go. But they're still here. I see them all the time."

"The whole flock?"

"Sometimes. Sometimes just one or two. They haunt this bay." She said this in a clear, factual way, almost as if by rote, as if she had been preparing for the question for some time. "My father was a boatwright. He built the finest boats on the bay. I'll show you one someday. There are plenty of them about. They'll outlast me by a long way, or anything else he ever made." She turned her head and looked back toward the estuary and the open bay, from which direction we had walked. "He disappeared out there one day, in a summer squall. They never found his body." Then she added, as if in reply to a further question she had heard spoken inside her head, "Seven years ago, in June." I felt constrained to make a remark of some kind, but the only thing that occurred to me to say sounded very foolish the moment it escaped my lips:

"What was he like?"

"I couldn't possibly tell you. The only one who could is Jamed. And of course he doesn't explain things very well anymore." Her watch cap had slid back from her forehead; she tugged it down firmly to her eyebrows and turned her shoulders back into the wind, raising her arm to point up the beach. "There's an old boathouse up there. You see it? Let's get some driftwood and build a fire in the lee of it."

"Good. It's chilly, in this wind."

The old shed straddled the narrow beach and projected out twenty feet into the river, which tugged gently and relentlessly at the skewed pilings of its tottering walls. The roof had partially collapsed, and in the ragged cavities between the loose disheveled shingles you could see the rotting beams, like the ribs of a carcass. We walked toward it, stooping to pick up stranded twigs and branches and chunks of bleached timber from the sand. There was much debris along the beach, and by the time we had reached the boathouse our arms were nearly full. We dumped the dry wood in the sand in the shelter of the sagging gray planks of the lee wall, and Sylvie crouched to build a nest of kindling, snapping twigs from the branches and crumpling handfuls of dry dune grass. She worked quickly and expertly, adding wood of increasing heaviness until there was a pyre that reached up to our knees. She took off her gloves and struck a match from the box she fished out of her jacket pocket, dropping it into the bottom of the cross-stacked pile. It burst instantly into flame, which licked up almost vertically with a soft, snarling crackle in the shelter of the wall. We sat in the sand, facing each other through the capering sheet of flame, feeling it braze our throats and faces comfortingly. The sky had become overcast with high thin drifts of cirrus film and beyond Sylvie's back I could see the surface of the river breaking into a choppy turmoil in the freshening wind.

"There's still some winter left," I said. She nodded, drowsing her eyes in the heat. Her face was flushed from the fire and her eyes somnolent, as if the ceremony of the driftwood fire had stirred memories in her of her childhood with her brothers along the bay shore. She blinked like a cat into the fire and reached out occasionally to stir it with a branch which she then withdrew and laid across her thighs, sitting cross-legged, raptly studious. After a time she held her branch in the flames until it had ignited; then turned it at a downward angle, studying the little dancing flame that sprouted from its tip.

"Aaron went to Europe when he was twenty-one," she said. "He went to a drama school over there, in London, for three years. In all that time he sent me two postcards. And one of them had coffee or something spilled all over it, so you couldn't read the thing, and now all of a sudden he sends me this damned novel." She scowled, turning her branch carefully to keep its flame alive. "What do you think of a man who hasn't married by the time he's thirty-six? And who isn't gay? At least if he is, I'll let you chop my right arm off."

I shook my head. "I couldn't begin to say. I've never met him."

"Would you say that he liked too many women? Every damned one he ever met, maybe? Or possibly just one, that he couldn't get?"

"I think you have to know people to make any kind of intelligent guesses about them. And then you're wrong, usually."

"It bothers Momma. She wants a grandchild before she dies. And I guess she's convinced by now that *I'm* not going to give her one. And Jamed can't. Of course, if she wanted to claim some of Poppa's, she could take in half the kids running around this bay. Every time I look at anyone in this county who's within twenty years of my own age, I get the uncomfortable feeling that I'm looking at my own brother or sister. It's a damned strange feeling."

"Your father was—promiscuous?"

"He was a raving satyr," Sylvie said. "He was also a liar, and an arsonist, and a drunk." She rubbed her forehead restlessly with a knuckle. "Of course, Keats was a drunk, too."

"Keats?"

"Well, the 'Ode to a Nightingale' is in praise of drunkenness, isn't it? I think Nils was right: a man would have to be drunk to write a poem like that. Not on liquor, necessarily, but all this—" She tossed her head to indicate the surrounding universe of water and sunlight and blue air. "Maybe they saw the same things, Keats and Poppa; I never knew."

"Aaron is not like him at all?" I asked.

"Well, he drinks too much, they're alike in that. But he doesn't drink the way Poppa did. Aaron drinks like a man who's getting his leg sawed off: to stop the pain. Poppa drank like a damned Viking." She shoved her branch into the fire and watched it break into a spackling of flame all along its length, like a stalk of blossoming forsythia. "Do you know how Aaron described himself to me once? As a first-aid man on the battlefield of life. Running around through the smoke with his little box of Band-Aids, patching up the wounded. I know perfectly well what he meant, but I don't know why, exactly."

"Where is he now?" I asked.

"He's in New York, making commercials for radio and TV. I'm sure you've heard him. You know those awful Parliament Cologne things? That's Aaron. He's got a glorious voice. All that talent, and all that training, and he uses it for hawking toilet pills. God."

"Maybe it was the only thing he could get," I said.

"No, it wasn't the only thing. It was just the first thing, the easiest. I think he was afraid. Just talent alone doesn't make an artist, you know. It takes something else." She dropped her head and said bitterly, "It takes what Poppa had, I suppose."

"Would you like him to have had that?" I asked. She dug at the sand between her crossed ankles and let it sift between her fingers, her head hanging.

"I don't know. I don't know what I'd like him to be. I'd like him to be somebody else's brother, I suppose. It's a funny thing, but almost everybody I've ever loved I've wished I'd never known. That doesn't sound generous at all, does it? Or even sane. Do you know what I mean, though?"

"I'm not sure."

"It's that you want to protect those people so much. From yourself, especially. You hate the things you've done to them, and might do yet. I don't suppose happy people ever feel like that."

"I believe not," I said, and shifted my body uneasily on the sand. "I'm afraid I'm not much use to you. I know far too little about life."

"At least you know it's precious."

"I'm a bit late learning it."

She raised her eyes to mine for a moment through the gelatinous pane of heat that shimmered above the fire; then turned them aside delicately, as if not wishing to embarrass me by the length of her gaze. She dug her hand into the pocket of her pea jacket and tugged out a manila envelope bulging with what was evidently a book-length manuscript, which she tossed onto the sand in reach of me.

"That's Aaron's letter," she said. "Why don't you read it? I'd like to know what you think."

"You don't think he'd mind?"

"No."

The letter was written in elite type on what must have been an ancient and badly battered machine. Many of the letters were out of line, or clogged, or x'd out, and the sentences staggered from margin to margin in a disheveled but dauntless way that seemed very much in keeping with the tone of the letter itself.

Dear Syl:

I'm sorry I'm not going to be able to get down for Easter. I guess Jamed will be pretty upset, but I sent him a toy a couple of days ago that Momma ought to have by now, so you can give it to him on Easter morning, O.K.? It's this big pink duck that lays Easter eggs and sings. It's really great.

I hope you don't get too pissed off about me not coming home, but I'm really busy as hell right now. Anyway, I think it's about time I wrote you a letter. You gave me so much grief when I was home last time about never writing to you that I decided maybe I'd better sit down and do it, and get you off my back. I've been meaning to do it for about the last twenty years, anyway. Honest. There's a lot of stuff I want to say to you, Syl, but the trouble is, I never know how to say it when I'm there. I'm not sure I know how to say it in a letter, either, but I'll try. Not a whole hell of a lot happens to me that's worth writing home about. One day is pretty much like another in my life, and I can't make much sense out of any of them. So I decided I'd tell you about what happened one day just after I got back from London. This happened about twelve years ago, so it's not exactly news, of course, but not much has happened since that's any more newsworthy. I picked this one out because as days go in my life, it's a pretty good one. I mean I didn't fall down a manhole or find a roach in my spaghetti or lose my wallet or discover I had pellagra or anything like that, which is the kind of stuff that happens to me most days. It was a pretty cheerful day on the whole, and you looked like you could use a

little cheering up the last time I saw you, Syl. I don't know what's
going on with you down there at Solomons, but it's got me kind of
worried, and the funny thing is, I feel like I might be to blame for it
somehow, which is not a good feeling to have. So I thought I'd tell
you about this day back in '62, I think it was a Tuesday.

I don't know whether you remember or not, but right there around
that fountain at the corner of Fifth and Fifty-ninth there's a
wide-open, windy, clean space where the scalloped edges of the canopy
of Rumpelmayer's sidewalk café flap over the tables on a fall day and
there are raspy copper leaves skittering on the stone and blowing in the
blue air and salvos of pigeons going off from the sidewalk as if in salute
to someone, God knows who, some departed sovereign whose domain
perhaps you have a glimpse of there beyond the brownstone
escarpment that walls off Central Park, some lord of green places, of
granite shapes. It's the only place in New York I ever got to like, I
don't know why, what with the hansom cabs and Rumpelmayer's and
the water splashing in the sun it reminded me in some shamelessly
corny way of Old Europe, it was like a chocolate-box cover or a stage
set out of Victor Herbert, all the people were extras in costume, the air
was perfumed, just around the corner on the side streets leading down
to Madison Avenue there were guys in shirt sleeves leaning against the
walls smoking cigars and manipulating the Fresnel lights, I had a
feeling that any minute some guy was going to walk out into the
middle of the square and fling out his arms and start singing "Only a
Rose" or "Stout-Hearted Men," with Notting Hill Gate and Portobello
Road long gone I guess you settle for that stuff.

I had moved into a place not far from there between Fifth and
Madison on the east side of the park, one of those huge old
brownstones with marble stairs and velvet-covered handrails that had
been converted into single-room occupancy for ambitious young pizazz
merchants with a flair for fashion layout or advertising copy or a way of
delivering a zingy first reading, it was also just about as far as you can
get from Greenwich Village and not get your throat cut in the
elevator. It's astonishing how successful I was, inside of six months I
had it made, stereo set, a couple of prints of Picasso's erotica, black
wallpaper in the john, handsome twelve-pound edition of the *Kama
Sutra*, the works, boy, and chiefly by virtue of the fact that the English
Accent, of which I could now do about ten accredited versions ranging
all the way from Liverpool Dockside to Wimbledon Parvenu had
become in my absence practically de rigueur for commercial TV spiels,
just chic-er than hell, whether you were selling garbage bags or vaginal

spray you had to do it for some reason in a British accent, which was
O.K. with me, boy, it was a windfall, I was going to cash in before
they switched to Lithuanian. There wasn't a night went by that I
didn't get down on my knees on my zebra-striped carpet and ask God
to bless Mr. Pentingsmyth for the sacred secrets of art he had poured
into my ears in his Dialect and Phonetics class, that delicate, portly,
salmon-colored man with his fine shy eyes who was supposed to have
been the world's greatest Macheath in *The Beggar's Opera* somewhere
back around 1890 would no doubt be delighted to learn that I was
keeping the flame alive in an age that threatened everything he had
ever done.

I got out of the cab which was going east and paid off the hacker
who with a magnificent show of indifference made a lightning
calculation of the amount of the tip and then turned his head to take
in the sound truck parked in front of the esplanade across the street
which had disgorged onto the sidewalk a forest of paraphernalia, boom
mikes, camera dollies, instrument panels, light screens, about a
thousand miles of tangled black rubber cables, a little mushroom colony
of canvas-backed folding chairs, and an army of technicians,
cameramen, sound men, agency men, and startlingly beautiful girls with
snatch pads under their arms named Toni, Micki, Jodi, Bobbi, Billi, or
maybe even Leonardi or Michelangeli, there was a trend toward the
baroque setting in.

"Something's going on," the cabbie said. "Some of that TV crap.
You know what them people pull down for that crap? A couple of
thousand an hour. This guy told me."

"Well, it's a pretty highly specialized business," I said.

"It's all crap," the cabbie said. He pulled out into Fifty-ninth and
went cruising along the edges of the crowd stealthily, like a shark
looking over a shoal of minnows. I crossed the street and stepped up
onto the stone pavement where the field crew was bivouacked, this girl
Tommi or maybe Toni spotted me and started flapping her snatch pad
and yelling, "Hi, sweetie, come and get made up. Abby wants to do
something special with your nose."

I gave her a hug and dropped my script book into an empty chair
and started producing nods and becks and wreathéd smiles to
acknowledge the salutations that went up from all the folks, especially
Gerhard, the director, a very tall guy with a Prince Valiant hairdo, a
safari jacket and a lavender scarf knotted around his throat who came
toward me with outstretched arms saying, "Kid, you're gorgeous. You're
a great big sackful of semen," and then kissed me on both cheeks and

held me at arm's length to marvel. He took rapturous note of everything from my wine-colored Wellington boots to the sort of neo-Tyrolean concoction I had on my head and said, "Jesus, it's perfect. It'll sell a million bottles. That Stacey is a genius. Where did she get the hat?"

"She designed it," I said. "It's wallaby or something."

"I've got to have it. Listen, when we get through, I've got to have that *hat*. Tell her I'll give her a million dollars."

"I'll tell her," I said. "What's this about my nose?"

"I'll tell you, kid, it's not quite Anglo-Saxon enough. I talked to Abby about it and she agrees with me. We're going to build up the bridge a little. Just a pinch of putty. What we want is that hawk look, you know what I mean? Nelson, Kitchener, Disraeli."

"Disraeli?"

"That's right. This dude is all balls, see. He's come right in off the moors, all heather and fog. I want to try and capture something in this. I mean really *capture* it. England, the English character, in a brushstroke. I think we can do it."

"Listen, Gerri," I said. "I don't want to shoot down your conception or anything, but the fact is, about six Englishmen in ten have got noses like tulip bulbs."

"Maybe, baby," Gerhard said, spreading his hands like fans, "but that's the *fact*, not the *truth.*" He closed his eyes and smiled. "I don't have to tell *you* the difference between fact and truth. You're an artist." He took me by the arm and hauled me over to the location van where inside, Abby, the makeup girl, was finishing up Betsy Davenport who was the leading lady in the opus. Betsy had a blue smock on over her costume and was lying back on a sort of Récamier lounge making wide-eyed moues at the ceiling while Abby buttered her lips with a brush dipped in scarlet paste. She batted her eyes and mumbled a greeting to me.

"I've come for my nose," I said.

"I'll be with you in a minute," Abby said. "Have a cigarette. Are they set up out there yet?"

"I don't think so," I said. "They're still chalking off areas. Was that Greenspan I saw out there?"

"Yes, he's doing the camera himself. God, that man's a genius. The compositions he makes. They're like Giottos. I mean, there's something absolutely *cruel* about that man's work. He is all balls."

"He does some pretty nice stuff," I admitted. I lit a cigarette and watched her work over Betsy's face, it was a very swift and skillful job,

too damned skillful, in about five minutes she had discovered and
dramatized every element that was needed for the sixty-second role,
ambition, energy, frivolity, a kind of patented mischievous grace that
was the stock in trade of those little heroines of the marketplace, and
around the eyes just that tantalizing suggestion of sensibility that could
make the world's most cynical man sneak into the corner drugstore to
buy a bottle of whatever it was she was pushing, just *once,* for Christ's
sake, after all if there's a one-thousand-to-one chance that a girl like
that is going to be turned on by the stuff and as long as you're going
to put out five hundred dollars anyway for a Brooks Brothers suit, why
not spend another dollar and fifty-nine cents and do the thing right? It
made me feel shivery, watching that girl work.

"Talk about Giotto," I said. "You're not too bad yourself, Abby."

"Wait'll you see your nose," she said. "You'll never take it off."

She was right. After she'd shooed Betsy out and got to work on me
it took her no more than another five minutes to manufacture what
looked like an absolutely genuine Anglo-Saxon gentleman, you couldn't
tell it from the real thing, boy, there he was, hawk-nosed and
cool-eyed, whimsical, laconic, daring, with arms of solid oak underneath
the Shetland tweed and probably, just like Gerri said, testicles of solid
gold. I was mad about myself.

"Jesus," I said. "How about doing me a whole new head?"

"Anything but the brains," Abby said. "I don't do brains."

I stepped out of the van and went sauntering onto the set like a
musical comedy queen in a gold lamé squaw costume, bringing love
into the tired world.

"It's perfect," Gerhard said. "It's genius. Nose, hat, accent,
everything. It's England."

"How about a shooting stick instead of the umbrella?" I said, I was
getting the hang of the thing.

"I thought about that," Gerhard said. "But I don't know if we can
bring it in. I think we'll stick with the umbrella. It gives greater
congruity." He raised one finger, smiling like a fox. "Congruity,
darling, is the mortar between the bricks. Think about it."

I sat down to think about it, watching them chalk out Betsy's
positions on the pavement. They had finished setting up the reflectors
and positioning the cameras and a prop girl was dressing the set. There
wasn't a whole lot to dress, it consisted of a stretchered canvas and an
easel, set up in front of the fountain so that a low-angle shot would
take in the back of the canvas, Betsy painting, the fountain splashing
in the background, and far beyond and above, in soft focus, the tops of

the Essex House and the Barbizon-Plaza. The scenario went like this:
Betsy, this gorgeous but basically ascetic, basically inaccessible woman
whose attentions have turned to art because men, in their frivolity, in
the essential triviality of their passions and because none of them ever
smells quite right, have created in her a profound disenchantment with
romance. So here she is, painting away, caught in the spell of
creativity, while all these nerds who happen to be passing by stop and
wiggle their ears at her and clear their throats and jiggle their
eyebrows, trying to pick her up, but of course she is oblivious of the
clods, they're all alike, she's known them all, callow, undiscriminating,
malodorous, from now on it's just her and art. Then out of the herd,
on his Adler Elevator Wellingtons, six inches taller than anybody else
in Manhattan, comes Lord Albert Cranleigh-Passingham, *me*,
cool-eyed, laconic, whimsical, discriminating, dangerous, and reeking of
Parliament Cologne. He pauses, looks over her shoulder, and in the
steel eyes tempered in the dust of Khartoum, the galleries of Mayfair,
and the blue reaches of the Highland moors, a look of intrigue gathers,
grows into candid admiration, modestly qualified of course by the
flawless taste of the unerring connoisseur. He watches for a moment,
and Betsy, it appears, has become aware of him through some
mysterious sense which is a combination of the spiritual and the
olfactory. She pauses in her work, her hand falters, her head lifts
slightly, her eyes begin to drowse, she takes a tremendous sniff of the
suddenly enchanted air.

Then, in the golden tones of Oxford—"filtered," the script
suggested, "through a haze of peat smoke, cannon smoke, and
trichinopoly smoke"—he speaks: "It's rather lovely. But I think if you'd
add a touch of umber, just there [he points with the tip of his furled
umbrella], you'd have the power you want. The power you seem to be
searching for."

Her eyes close fully, her nostrils flare, she inhales rapturously.

"Now, *you*," she murmurs, "just *might* know what it's all about."
She turns her head to confirm with her eyes what her soul and nostrils
have just conveyed to her, finding full confirmation apparently, because
there is a close-up of her widening, beatific smile, and then as we fade
out, another, of his, *my*, cool triumphant acknowledgment of tribute,
another Bengal insurrection put down, another Everest scaled, another
Waterloo. It was a pretty slick script, it did what it wanted to do
which after all, as Gerhard was always reminding me, was the only way
that you could define successful craft. I felt pretty sure I could bring it
off now that I had the nose, the hat, and the umbrella to add to my

accent and my imperial smile, to Gerhard's satisfaction anyway, maybe not to Mr. Pentingsmyth's, but after all, Gerhard's theories were the ones you went by here, I was on the stage of the world now, you worked a little differently.

They'd finished with Betsy so she came over and sat down beside me in one of the canvas chairs and poured out a cup of coffee from the thermos jug that the commissary girl brought over with a little tray of sandwiches.

"I think it's going to be good," she said. "Gerri really knows what he's doing. I love to work with him, I feel like wax in his hands. He's a real professional."

"He sure is," I said.

We had a cup of coffee and a cigarette and then Gerhard flapped his hands for silence and said, "O.K., now we're going to have a couple of dry runs and then shoot. I think we can wrap this thing up before noon."

So we did it, a couple of dry runs first, to the impassive eyes of the technicians, the feverish, clenched-fist attention of the agency people and the smirks and gurgles of the passersby who had gathered in scores around our little wonderland to watch magic being made in the spring sunlight. I went out and sauntered, paused, smiled, pronounced, poured out my perfume and received the tribute of beauty surrendered, a thousand dollars, with residuals coming up, and a couple of hugs from Gerhard, all in sixty seconds, it was too good to be true.

"You were superb, sweetheart," he said. "I've just been in England, I've just walked over Westminster Bridge, I'm not kidding you."

"You think it was all right?" I said. "I felt it was kind of superficial."

"Oh, Jesus. When will you learn, baby? When are you going to stop knocking perfect craft just because it's commercial? Do you realize that Rembrandt painted calendars? That Wallace Stevens sold insurance? That Bill Dickey was in advertising?"

"I thought Bill Dickey was in baseball," I said.

"*Baseball?* Are you kidding?"

"You mean Jim Dickey."

"I mean Jim Dickey. Eliot was a banker. Shakespeare—"

I felt terribly sorry for him all of a sudden, and pretty goddamned ashamed of myself for shooting him down like that, who the hell did I think I was, Lord Cranleigh-Passingham or somebody? We were blood brothers, Gerhard and I, we drank from the same cup, we scavenged the crumbs of humility from the same soiled plate, he stood there with those feverish eyes, in that goddamned safari jacket he put on to hunt for beauty in the burning bush, I felt a warm liquid pity start swelling up inside me like milk into a mother's breasts, I recognized it and welcomed it, oh Jesus, boy, I welcomed it, it was aqua vitae, Jack Daniel's, pneuma, logos, it was my brand of poison whatever the hell it was, I lived on the stuff, it was what made me work. These breasts are not yet dry, I thought, which is about the best that you can hope for, after all. I reached out and clasped him on the shoulder, not patronizingly but in a sudden spasm of woebegone fraternity with the man, and said, "O.K., Gerri, I think I know what you mean. And thanks. I'm learning a lot from you." He grinned at me and winked. "Listen, I've got to run," I said. "I've got a luncheon appointment. I'll give you a ring in the morning."

"Right. It was a great show, sweetheart. Don't forget about the hat."

"It's yours," I said. I took it off and plopped it on his head and he stood there grinning like a fool in his brand-new clown outfit, vesti la giubba, I thought, we wear the same clothes, too.

I shoved through the gang of technicians and the surrounding audience of passersby who were still standing there lapping it up with various emotions ranging from highly disrespectful irony to Jell-O-eyed infatuation, I didn't have any luncheon appointment but I sure as hell had had enough of art for one day, what I had mostly was a burning impulse to work my way down toward one of the Irish bars on Third Avenue and put in an afternoon of uncompromising elbow bending. I had just stepped off the curb and pointed myself roughly in that direction when I got my feet tangled up with the feet of a long-legged girl in red satin pumps who was also departing the festivities and the first thing I knew we were both down on our hands and knees in the gutter exchanging looks of pained apology.

"Oh, gosh," I said. "I'm sorry. Are you O.K.?"

"Oh, sure, I'm O.K.," she said, which was a pretty generous remark considering that the contents of her purse were scattered all over the gutter, her teeth were clenched in agony and she had very obviously knocked the knees out of her magenta-colored panty hose, but in spite of all that she didn't seem too upset or at least not too surprised by the turn of events, you somehow got the idea that this girl spent a lot of time on her hands and knees in gutters, she had that look of patient despair of the born gutter dweller. I started scraping together the junk that had fallen out of her purse, it looked like somebody had dumped out a jackdaw's nest, I never saw such a wild batch of miscellany, there was a gum rubber eraser that had been bitten in half like a nougat, a Scorpio pocket horoscope for June, a rubber stamp whose message, BULLSHIT, was printed all over a couple of envelopes, a pencil that had been chewed to pulp, a set of poker dice, half of a sugar doughnut wrapped up in a paper napkin, and a cheap plastic lipstick cylinder that had splintered when it hit the pavement. I was kind of embarrassed by some of the items and tried to keep my eyes decently averted while I shoveled them together, I didn't know what the hell to do about the doughnut for example, I finally decided to wrap it back up and return it without comment, but I felt a kind of beatific glow, handling the junk. I love this stuff, I thought. I put the pieces of the shattered lipstick cylinder into her hand and clicked my tongue remorsefully.

"Gee, I'm sorry about that," I said.

"Oh, that's all right. It's just Woolworth's."

We were still down there on our knees, so I got to my feet and gave her a hand getting up, even through her purple cotton gloves you could feel that her hands had about the substance and temperature of a pair of wire egg whips.

"Boy, that was pretty clumsy of me," I said.

"Oh, that's all right. It was my fault. I'm almost certain."

"Golly, you've ripped your stockings. That's a shame. And look at your knees. That must have hurt like the devil."

"No, that's all right." She reached down and brushed at her scraped kneecaps and her glove came away with bloodstained fingertips.

"Look at your gloves now," I said. "Gee, that's a pity."

"Don't worry about it," she said. "It'll wash out." She gave me a sort of sidewise, stage-door look like a high school girl standing there with an autograph book and said, "I just wanted to tell you, I thought you were great in that scene. I thought you were really English."

"Oh, thanks," I said. "It wasn't so hot, though. The same old baloney."

"No, you really did it with finish," she said. "That's something I envy. I wish I could get that into my work."

"Are you an actress, too?"

"Well, I'm trying to be. I'm more of a model, really. But I'm studying at the Silvestra studio."

"Oh, yeah." I'd never heard of the place but it suddenly occurred to me that she might have been one of the extras in the scene, one of the couple of dozen passersby who kept shuffling past the fountain while I was making my pitch to Betsy. "Were you in the scene?" I asked.

"No. I wanted to be, the agency sent me down, but Mr. Wolfheim didn't think he could use me. A lot of people don't. I have this problem with my eyes."

She sure did. One of them pointed due east and the other one forgivably enough seemed to be looking somewhere in the direction of Mount Moriah, it was pretty unnerving.

"Listen," I said, I didn't especially want to pursue the subject, "don't you want a cup of coffee or a drink or something? You got pretty shook up there."

"Oh, that's all right," she said, and then after a second or two of consideration, "But, well, O.K., if you want to."

I took her by the elbow and ushered her out across Fifty-ninth Street and then up past the fronts of hotels and boutiques and French restaurants toward Seventh Avenue. There were doormen tooting their whistles in the spring sunlight and guys wheeling aluminum kegs of beer on iron-wheeled dollies and traffic palomping by and up above everything, pigeons circling in the blue sky, seeming to keep an eye on us.

"There's a little place up here where they serve real great martinis," I said. "How does that sound?" I hadn't been too sure about suggesting martinis at that time of day, but then I decided that to a girl who wore red satin pumps at ten o'clock in the morning it might sound like a first-class idea.

"Wonderful," she said. "But could I have a stinger instead?"

"Sure," I said, nonchalant as hell, I had the feeling that any relationship with this girl would call for plenty of nonchalance so I might as well get in some practice. "Listen, don't you think we ought to stop in a drugstore and get some Band-Aids or something for those knees?"

"Oh, that's all right," she said. "But, well, O.K., if you really wouldn't mind, because actually they're sort of oozing a good bit."

We went into a drugstore on the corner of Seventh Avenue and I wound up buying a complete first-aid kit because it turned out that if you bought a bottle of hydrogen peroxide and a box of swabs and a can of Band-Aids separately, it came to three dollars and twenty-nine cents and you had the problem of what to do with the stuff after you'd used it, whereas if you bought the complete kit it only cost nine cents more and you got a little pocket-sized canister that she could slip into her purse afterwards and carry around with her, which seemed like a pretty good idea because I had the feeling it was something she should never be without.

A little way up the street past the drugstore we found this place, Ciro's, that I was looking for, it was a place where I put in a good bit of time when I was uptown, one of those six-steps-down basement bars where you descend suddenly out of noisy twentieth-century sunlight into a sort of medieval murk, there's never a sound in those places except maybe some Happy Mac chortling away on the TV above the bar while he hands out shiny new Camaros to pop-eyed housewives and usually about four or five people sitting around in the gloom waiting for the game to be called on account of darkness, it wasn't the sort of place you find listed in "The Talk of the Town." We shuffled back through the fog to one of the rear booths and wriggled into it and gave our order to a waiter who came shuffling after us, he looked like he hadn't won a bet since back around 1906.

"By the way, I'm Aaron Linthicum," I said after the guy had left.

"Hi. I'm India Jones. Well, I mean it's not my real name, but it's my sort of stage name."

"It's pretty," I said. "It sounds very exotic."

"Do you think so? Thanks. I thought of making it Calcutta Jones, but then somebody told me that Calcutta is one of the most horrible places in the world, I mean people are always dying in the streets and everything, so I didn't think that sounded so good. So then I made it Bombay Jones, but everybody thought I was saying 'bomb bay,' and they'd start snickering and all. So then I decided on India. This teacher I used to have, Miss Grayson, she said it was marvelous. She said it sounded like the wind in temple bells."

"It does, sort of," I said. "Were you born in India or something?"

"No, I was born in Nebraska, but I saw this movie, *Calcutta Express*, when I was a kid and I still think it's the most beautiful movie I ever saw. It affected me tremendously. There were all these beautiful women in saris. You know, with dots on their forehead? God, it was marvelous."

"It's a pretty romantic place, I guess," I said.

"It really is. Listen, do you think I could fix my knees now? Because they're sort of starting to drip."

"Oh, sure," I said. "Why don't you let me do it? I'm pretty good at first aid."

"Oh, that's all right. But, well, O.K., if you really don't mind, because actually I can't see too well. I mean it's pretty dark in here."

I pulled a chair over and she rested the heel of her foot on it while I started swabbing the grit out of the scrape, I tried to be businesslike as hell about it because it was a pretty intimate operation and she

seemed a little apprehensive at first, as if I might be some sort of a
fetishist or something, which wasn't too far from the truth, only of
course it was the wounds that turned me on, not the kneecaps. I got
them cleaned up and then plastered squares of gauze bandage over
them with adhesive tape, which together with the fact that she was
about six feet tall made her look a good bit like a basketball player, she
didn't seem to mind though, she was too full of gratitude.

"I hate to have anything happen to my knees," she said, "because I
do mostly leg modeling, stockings and all. I've got sort of nice legs, I
guess. At least it's the only part of me they seem to want to
photograph."

"I guess it's a pretty competitive business."

"It really is. A person could get discouraged very fast. But of course
I'm not going to do it forever. Just until I get my break on the stage."

The old boy had come tottering back with our drinks by this time
so I raised my glass and said, "Well, here's to your break."

"Thanks." She took a healthy sip of her stinger and closed her eyes
and shivered. "Gosh, that's good. You know, I never heard of a stinger
until I came to New York, but I think they're marvelous. They make
your teeth tingle."

"How long have you been here?" I said.

"About six months. I still can't believe I'm here, I never dreamed
I'd get to New York. But I had this drama teacher in high school in
North Platte who really inspired me. Miss Grayson. She told me that if
I really wanted to be an actress, then I shouldn't let anything in the
world stand in my way. I mean, no kind of a physical handicap or
anything. I used to worry a good bit about my eyes, but you know
what she told me? She said that Sarah Bernhardt actually played
Hamlet with a wooden leg. Imagine that. And that if I really dedicated
myself to the theater, then nothing in the world could stop me."

"She sounds like a wonderful person," I said.

"She really is. So then I worked in a drive-in for about nine months
and saved up every penny I earned so I could come out here. Of
course it's starting to run out now, but I get a little modeling, so I'm
getting by. What I'm really happy about is that my acting is improving
tremendously. I figure that in about six months I'll be good enough at
auditions to get something. At least that's what Ben Silvestra says. He's
done absolute wonders with me."

"He's the man you're studying with?"

"Yes. Gosh, it was the luckiest thing, the way I happened to meet
him. I stayed at the Y for a while, right after I got here, and I met

this really nice girl, Alice, that I used to do all sorts of things with. So one night we decided to go to this poetry reading in the Village, and Ben Silvestra was there. I didn't know him, of course, but when we were coming out I happened to step on his feet, and he was really nice about it. I mean it must have hurt quite a lot, because of course he doesn't wear shoes, but he was just wonderful. So then we got to talking and he told me about the studio he was opening up and said that I could come and audition for him. Which was really pretty wonderful, because he only takes about five students, and of course he's very selective about them. So I've been working with him for about four months now, and I'm really making tremendous progress."

"What sort of work do you do?" I said.

"Well, right now we're working on the Ethers of Joy, which he says is the area where I need the most help. We worked on the Ethers of Agony for a few weeks, and I got that down pretty good. Do you know about the Ethers Theory?"

"Well, not very much," I said.

"It's really wonderful. It's going to replace Motivation completely. What you do is try to maintain the balance of ethers inside you, and that way you can control every vibration you give off on the stage. We do these exercises for generating the different ethers and then balancing them."

"What sort of exercises?"

"Well, like if you're doing an Ethers of Agony thing, then you have to place yourself in a situation where those ethers are going to predominate. Like if you're being raped or something, he does that one quite a lot. If you're not getting it right, then he'll actually tie you down to the sofa and go through the whole situation with you, I mean just in charade of course, until you get the balance right and start vibrating genuine agony. It's very strenuous."

"It sounds like it," I said. "What do you do for the Ethers of Joy?"

"Well, actually the situation is pretty much the same, only this time instead of being the Violator he's the Beloved, so you have to get the ethers rebalanced and start vibrating joy. You have to learn to give a completely different response to an almost identical situation. It's fascinating." She drank the last of her stinger and then ran the tip of her finger around the rim of her glass and sucked it dry with a mournful little snap of her lips. "I'm better at agony, somehow. I got that right away, almost."

"How about another stinger?" I said.

"Oh, that's all right. But, well, O.K., if you want to. I'm really enjoying talking to you, you know that? One thing I've found out about New York is that a lot of people don't really listen to you when you're talking. I mean, they're just sort of waiting for you to stop, so they can start. It's kind of depressing."

"I've noticed that, too," I said.

"I mean, I love to talk, but I hate to feel as if I'm boring people all the time."

"Well, you're not boring me a bit."

"I'll bet I am," she said. "Gosh, I haven't talked so much for months."

We had another drink and she told me about her Oedipus complex which until Ben Silvestra revealed it to her had been operating unknown, and almost unchecked, in her life. It was what was chiefly responsible, apparently, for her failure to get her Ethers of Joy properly balanced, because she had this Guilt Transference problem that automatically took over whenever she felt incipient sexual delight, so old Ben was attacking it by playing a father role in all her Joy Situations until she learned to conquer it and pour out her hitherto foolishly trammeled joy over the entire world, like Sherwin-Williams paint. I had a vision of Ben mired in the stuff like a fly in flypaper, slogging around glue-footed and giving out hoarse cries of Genuine Agony, generating ethers like a crazy man. You want to watch that stuff, you barefooted rascal you, I thought, you don't awaken a lady's joy that lightly in this world.

We had a couple more drinks and then she started telling me about the most traumatic experience of her life, which turned out to be her departure from North Platte. Her boyfriend had come down to the station to see her off, he lived on a farm somewhere outside of North Platte and he showed up at the station in this pair of faded blue overalls that really racked her up. He was too shy to kiss her or say anything personal to her because all her schoolmates and her mother and father and of course Miss Grayson were there, flapping their handkerchiefs and yelling for her to go out and conquer the world, so he just stood there at the back of the crowd smiling and nodding in his sort of humble farm boy way, and she had had a sudden terrible impulse to jump off the train and throw herself at his feet, it was one with which I was familiar.

"I think it was mostly the overalls," she said. "He just stood there in those awful blue overalls, with a bib, you know, and this sort of farmer haircut, combed back with water so he'd look nice and neat, and I just felt like dying. Honestly, I just felt all of a sudden like my heart would explode. I cried all the way to New York. I still think about that every night. I don't know why it is, but I wake up every night, about two o'clock in the morning, ever since I've been here. I think that's the most terrible thing anybody ever has to do, do you know what I mean?"

I knew only too damn well what she meant because for about the last twenty minutes I had been having a very similar vision of my own, this one was set on a station platform, too, only at Paddington, and I was standing behind the black iron gates that shut off the friends and relatives from the departing travelers, putting my hands through the bars to touch Cindy's face for the last time although she didn't realize that of course, although maybe she did, because that little crick had come back into the corner of her mouth, that little touch of irony, the salt on the melon. She was going back home to her parents to wait until I sent for her, she had decided to leave a day before I did because she couldn't stand the thought of being there alone in our room in Stanley Crescent after I had gone, and anyway who knew what the hell would happen to her if I left her alone there in the middle of London? I wanted to get her back home to Stratford before I left, get out with a clear conscience, boy, all accounts settled. She had her cardboard suitcase at her feet and her stack of movie magazines tied up with a piece of twine and a shopping bag full of odd junk, playbills of shows we had seen together and the philodendron from the windowsill which had developed leaves the color of saffron, and a music box I had given her at Christmas, with a china ballerina on top of it who pirouetted slowly to the tune of one of those corny Noel Coward numbers, "I'll See You Again," which was what the carousel used to play on Hampstead Heath. As a matter of fact the damn thing started tinkling at that very moment, it had tipped over in the bag or something, so we stood there holding hands through the bars grinning at each other and listening to those tinny little notes sprinkling out into the hollow booming roar of the station, it was not very damned auspicious. I had a bar of Droste Dutch chocolate in my pocket that I'd bought for her, it was something she was nutty about, so I took it out and gave it to her and said, "That's for you to eat on the train. Not all at once, though, or you'll get sick."

"Oh, golly," she said. "Thanks, Aaron. You're too good to me."

"Listen, nobody could be too good to you," I said. "You remember that."

"You'll write every week, won't you, love?"

"More than that," I said. "Twice a week, anyway."

"Well, just once a week will do, you're going to be busy, I know, finding a job and a place to stay and all. But once a week at least, please."

"O.K."

"I'm going to work, too. There's lots of jobs I can get in Stratford. I mean, it's not like London, where you don't know anybody. I know almost everybody there. And living at home, I can save almost everything I make. I'll bet I can save twenty pounds a month."

"That'll be great. We'll live in a penthouse."

She reached through the bars and held me tight, pressing herself as close to me as she could, with the bars between us I could just feel the curve of her forehead against my breast like the nuzzle of the new moon, I laid my cheek down on the top of her head, her hair was cool as nighttime grass, and cupped my hand around the back of her skull, knowing I had the jewel of the world there in my grasp, in my feeble fingers that could not contain it.

The guy at the turnstile yanked his whistle out of his vest pocket and started tooting on it, everybody broke away from the iron gate, there was a sudden outcry of goodbyes and a flutter of hands and handkerchiefs and blown kisses and then they were all galloping away through the clouds of dream-white steam that came billowing out from under the locomotive wheels, running away to the most distant land there is, where they could never die and from which they could never be retrieved. Cindy lifted her head off my breast and raised her face to be kissed and I could see the marks of two bars branded vertically on her forehead like the shadows of the masts of Poppa's ships. After we kissed she whispered something that I couldn't hear, so I said, "What?" but she shook her head and bent down and gathered up her junk and started plunging off along the platform through the steam. She hadn't got very far, of course, before the handle of her suitcase broke and the goddamned thing went tumbling down on the concrete with the bottom corners crumpling in a couple more inches like a collapsing accordion, fortunately I had strapped it up with an old belt so it didn't split apart completely although the next time she unbuckled it would probably be the last. She stood there with her hands full of movie magazines and shopping bag handles not knowing what the hell to do and of course everybody was in such a goddamned hurry to get a seat on the train that they just went galloping on past her, bumping into her elbows and adding to her confusion, she'll never make it, I thought, never in this world, that girl was born to miss trains. I felt furious, I felt like I was in shackles, I never felt such a fury in my life, I hated everything, the train, the bars, the heartless people, myself, the shabby suitcase she was condemned to carry her miserable patrimony in, the whole goddamned show. I started yelling, "Listen, you sons of bitches, that's a lady out there, why don't you help her? That's a lady in distress out there in front of you, why don't some of you for God's sake lend her a hand? Can't you see I can't help her anymore?"

Nobody seemed to pay any particular attention, they were all hurrying home to find out why the plumbing broke or the wife ran away with the milkman, they had problems enough of their own I guess, you couldn't blame them, who the hell can you blame, ever? I thought of crawling under the turnstile and forcing my way past the guard and going to her rescue one more time, but then I lost sight of her in a great cloud of steam as pure as mountain mist that came flooding over the platform tenderly, mercifully, as if to cloak her ignominy or to shelter her or maybe to snatch her away to a better world or at least one where the handles don't break and where there aren't any timetables, because, anyway, I never saw her again. When the cloud dissolved she was gone as if by magic, either back to glory or back to Stratford, whichever one it was they had me to thank, so I had one mark on the right side of the ledger anyway, even if it was written in left-handed.

"The funny thing is," India said, "I mean it's not really funny, it's sort of terrible, that even though I think about him all the time, like I said, I don't write to him so much anymore. Hardly at all, really, maybe once a month, or every two months. I don't know why. I just never seem to have the time, or maybe I don't want to take the time because I know it's no use, really. I just hate myself for that. I don't understand it. Is there any way to explain a thing like that?"

"I don't know," I said. "But it happens."

"He didn't even answer my last letter. I guess maybe he was trying to make it easier for me. I guess he knew what was happening."

"I guess so. People seem to understand those things. Good people do, anyway."

"I know," she said. "They do, don't they? And you know, sometimes it seems to me that you can explain yourself best just by being absent. Not to everybody, of course, but certain people. The people who care about you most, maybe. You feel almost closer to them than if you were really there."

"You're a pretty beautiful girl," I said. "Why don't we go take a walk in the sunshine?"

"O.K.," she said. "I think that would be nice, if you really want to."

It was a great idea but I could see it wasn't going to work the minute she got herself extricated from the booth and unfolded to her full elevation and we struck out through the murk toward the street door, because the fact was, she was stoned. I was pretty sure by this time that she hadn't had any breakfast so those five stingers must have dissolved a good part of her digestive system, which together with the fact that her knees had probably started stiffening up by this time and that she was wearing those 1937-style spike heels made it pretty rough going. We kept bumping into the edges of tables and knocking over chairs and by the time we got through the door and up those six steps to the street level we had had some pretty exciting moments.

"Listen," I said. "Maybe it would be better if we just got you home right now, and you had a cup of coffee and a nap. I mean, your knees must be bothering you quite a bit. It's probably a good idea to stay off them for a while."

"Well, actually, I'm sort of glad you suggested that," she said. "Because they are a little bit sore. And also I've never worn these shoes before and I'm having a little trouble with them. I just got them yesterday."

"O.K., let's do that, then. We can always take the walk another day."

"Oh, yes, I'd really love to, I mean it."

"Which way do you live?"

"Down at West Eleventh. I have to take the Sixth Avenue subway." She looked around vaguely in about six directions at once and I knew she had as much chance of making it to the subway as I did of making it into paradise.

"Why don't we take a taxi?" I said. "Wouldn't that be simpler?"

"Well, it would, yes. But actually I don't take too many taxis, because I'm sort of on a budget."

"Well, look, it's on me. After all, I'm the one that talked you into this scene. I'll go along, if you don't mind, just to make sure you get in all right."

"Oh, would you? I'd really appreciate that, because you see I live in this third-floor walk-up, and I'm not sure I could manage all those stairs. There are about ten billion of them."

I thought it might be a good idea if we walked down to Seventh Avenue where there would be a better chance of catching a cab, and she said, "Well, O.K., I'll try. Do you think I'll be all right?"

"Just lean on me," I said. "You'll be O.K. For right now, anyway. I can't guarantee forever."

So I started waltzing down Fifty-ninth Street in the midday sunshine with my stoned, six-foot-two, cross-eyed basketball player, happy as a clam. The whistles were tootling away, the jackhammers were buzzing like big contented bees, the entrance canopies were tossing their scalloped fringes in celebration, the windows were blazing like diamonds, and up there in the baby-blue air the pigeons were soaring, circling over us. All of a sudden I had the feeling that all my life, anywhere I had ever been, there were those calm-eyed doves, watching over me. It swept over me for a minute with a ghostly comfort, like the sea.

"Golly, I'm sorry we couldn't take the walk," she said. "It's a beautiful day."

"It really is," I said. "You get a day like this maybe once or twice a lifetime. But thank the Lord for that little bit. Many a man would make a meal off that."

So that's what happened, Syl, that day. I'm sorry I took so long to tell about it, but I thought you ought to know. After all, you don't get a letter from me every day. I'll see you in a few weeks, for your birthday, so take it easy, and eat something once in a while for God's sake. Give Momma and Jamed a hug for me.

Love, Aaron

The sky was overcast and there was sand blowing down the beach in the strengthening wind, making a thin haze just above the ground. The dune grass was bending eastward. I heard the bell buoy tolling above the sandbar in the river channel to the west of us. I handed the letter back to Sylvie, aware that I was smiling.

"You're amused," she said.

"Beguiled, I think. He sounds like a charming person."

"He's a very unhappy one. My God, can't you see that?"

"It seems to me," I said after a moment of reflection, "that he's trying to explain to you that we all are, to one degree or another. But that he's as happy as he can expect to be, considering his nature and the circumstances of his life. Or as content as he can be, if not as happy. He seems almost to be asking you to forgive him for his contentment."

"Contentment?" she said. "I call it resignation." She folded the sheaf of papers and replaced them in the envelope broodingly. "To forgive him? That's an odd thing to say."

"Well, perhaps that's not the right word. To understand, at least."

"You think I'm demanding an apology from him for his existence?"

"I hope not. But it obviously matters to him that you disapprove of it."
When she did not reply, I added as gently as I could, "I think he's also trying
to explain to you why he's never married, or is likely to."

Clutching the envelope, she thrust her fists into the pockets of her pea
jacket and sat with huddled shoulders, staring into the embers. The fire had
sunken to a mound of pulsing scarlet coals over which black shadows licked
and coiled like flowing oil.

"Shall we go back?" she said.

"Yes. I think we may get some rain soon."

She stood up, bending to shove the longest, unburned, ends of branches
into the heap of coals. "It'll burn out soon. You should always leave before the
fire's dead. That's a country saying down here. I don't know how good a one."

We trudged up through the sand beyond the boathouse, bending into
the wind. Gradually the narrow strip of beach widened to a broad stony
strand that sloped down from the westward bluffs of the river shore. High up
on the strand ahead of us stood a stone cairn that she had heaped together,
waist-high and solemn in the gray light. We passed it without speaking. A
hundred feet beyond, we turned up from the beach and climbed the sandy
bluffs that leveled out into the church-field meadow. It was tangled with
withered milkweed whose brown pods rattled against our trouser legs as we
broke through them. A flock of brown finches scattered before us, sailing
down the wind with a sweet thrum of wings like the raked strings of a lute.
Sylvie walked with an unrelenting lissome strength that tested all my stam-
ina. She stopped once to turn and look at me, her face almost hidden by the
blown tangle of her teak-colored hair.

"Are you all right?"

I nodded, moved to a giddy pleasure by her beauty. I would have liked to
walk beside her forever through the cool, gray, windy world. When we reached
the street and stamped the sand from our boots the flag above the post office
was raving on its shuddering staff and the balls of the weathercock above the
chandlery were spinning wildly in the wind.

"There's a northeaster blowing up," Sylvie said.

"It feels like it."

The sand hissed along the pavement and sprinkled the backs of our legs
as we tramped up the street. The lane, when we turned into it, was coated with
a lime-green film of dust from the leaf buds, and the branches swung above
us with a soft soughing sound, clean and restlessly pacific as the sound of surf.
When we reached her gate Sylvie said, "Would you like some tea? I got chilled
out there, didn't you?"

"A bit. But I'm using up your whole day."

I think you salvaged it," she said. "I'd be asleep still if you hadn't come by. Come in, Carl."

"All right." I followed her up the path and into the kitchen. We shucked off our jackets and gloves, and when she had put a kettle of water on the stove, Sylvie came and sat across from me at the table, her head turned to one side, listening.

"Do you hear that?" she said. "How this house moans?"

There was indeed a faint cry keening through the old house, under its windowsills and doorsills, through the cracks of its cupboards and swollen floorboards, rising and fading like something imprisoned there, fleeing futilely along its halls and through its rooms. "God," she said. "Houses." She stared vacantly at the wall for a moment, her eyes drifting, as if habitually, to a newspaper clipping that hung impaled on a nail. After a moment she plucked it off and stared at it briefly before she laid it on the table in front of me. "Do you know who that is?"

Above a column of print there was a photograph of a plump, mild-looking man in a beret and a bulky sweater holding a pipe between his square hands and looking out gently and judiciously, like a farmer who has been asked to comment on the harvest.

"No. Who is he?"

"Pablo Neruda. He died last fall."

"I don't know who he was."

"A South American poet who won the Nobel Prize a few years ago. He died last fall, less than two weeks after the Chilean government fell. I think they killed him."

"Do you like his work?" I asked.

"Yes. It's very beautiful. I'd like you to read that."

Beneath the photograph there was an obituary which included a brief bibliography of his work and a summary of his very active and diverse existence, his diplomatic assignments as ambassador or consul to Ceylon, Spain, and France, his involvement in the Spanish Civil War, his brief political career as a senator in the Chilean national congress, and his candidacy for the presidency of his country, in which he had deferred to Salvador Allende. Included was a portion of an interview with a journalist named Rita Guibert, which Sylvie had underlined with red ink:

My book *Residence on Earth* represents an obscure and dangerous moment of my life. It's poetry with no way out. I almost had to be reborn to find the way out of it. In that way the Spanish war saved me from a fit of despair whose depths I cannot judge today . . . I said once that if I ever possessed the necessary authority I should ban my own book and make sure that it was never reprinted. Of course I realize that's a rather shocking statement, a rather harsh thing to hear . . . But when one is writing—I don't know if this happens to other writers—one has to think where one's verses will end up. Robert Frost says in one of his prose essays that poetry should be oriented toward pain: "Leave sorrow alone with poetry." But I don't know what Robert Frost would have thought if some young man committed suicide and left one of his books, covered in blood from a bullet hole, beside his head. That has happened to me here in this country. A boy who was full of life killed himself beside my book . . . that page of my poetry stained with a young man's blood ought to give not only one but all poets something to think about.

"What a strange thing," I said. "It must be a terrible reality to have to live with. Do you know the poem?"

"Yes," Sylvie said. I laid the clipping on the table and she stared at it for a moment, her lips pressed together so that they whitened. "Does he look like an evil man to you?"

"No, not at all. A very mild, pleasant-looking man."

"Do you think it's possible to write an evil poem? Do you think it's possible for beauty to be evil?"

"I never thought of it."

"Maybe it is. Maybe what he says is true. Maybe art is a terrible, transforming thing. Maybe no one has the right to make it. You may have been right to dislike it so intensely."

"I don't think so. I think I just didn't understand it at all."

"You don't know. You have very sound instincts, it seems to me."

She put her elbows on the table, gripping her hands together and laying her face against them. "Which do you think is worse? To have had a role in someone's life and to have made a ghastly mess of it; to have, ever afterwards, to contemplate a life disordered by your presence in it—ruined, perhaps—or to have been left out of a life, entirely, that you know has been impoverished by your absence? To contemplate a vast and dreary hiatus in someone's existence that you feel you could have filled and satisfied—ennobled, maybe. Which is worse? To sin by omission or commission?"

"I'd rather not have to choose," I said.

"But one must, always. Almost every minute of one's life. I can remember sitting, countless times, in a restaurant, or a bar, or at a party, when someone has approached and spoken to me; or simply in the midst of a conversation with someone, when their tone has changed, their eyes have taken on that luminous, steadfast look of attention, of appeal, or of demand; and I've realized: at this moment I can change this person's life. At this moment I can enter it, change it utterly, bring desire into it, or friendship, or love, or dereliction, or joy. By the next few words I say. By my consent, disinterest, approval, by the lowering of my eyes or the alteration of my voice, I can change this person's destiny. In a week we can be lovers, or warm and steadfast friends, or enemies in just as dedicated a way—or I can have forgotten him, and gone my way, and let him live another kind of life. That terrible opportunity is there, almost every moment, to invade and alter another person's life; or to let that opportunity go unclaimed forever, for better or for worse. Haven't you felt that? The constant fear of it?"

"I don't think my advent into anyone else's existence would be quite as spectacular as yours," I said. "Although I can understand your concern about it, very easily."

"You're mocking me."

"No."

"Not even in your wife's case?"

"It didn't occur to me, no. There was hardly time."

"What do you mean?"

"I married in considerable haste. There wasn't much opportunity to consider the consequences."

"That doesn't sound at all like you," Sylvie said.

"It's true, however. I'd known her for less than a month."

"My God," Sylvie said. "That sounds like a very impulsive act, for a man as methodical as you've made yourself out to be. I can't believe it."

"I can hardly believe it myself, even yet," I said. "I've never understood it properly—the recklessness with which I behaved. Nothing else in my life had approached it for—picturesqueness, I suppose it could be called. It was grotesque. Terrible." I clasped the belly of the teapot with my palm and found that it was cold.

"Shall I reheat it?" Sylvie asked.

"If you don't mind. I'd like another cup."

She rose and went to the stove to relight the burner under the kettle. I became aware that there had been for some time a drumming sound of rain against the windows and a windy splash of lilacs beyond the pane. "The storm has broken," I said.

"Yes. It'll rain all afternoon. Spring is hard-won, on this bay." She dropped a couple of tea bags in the teapot and stirred them, waiting for the water to boil. "What was she like, Carl? Not like Karen, you said."

"No. Nothing in the world."

"When did you meet her?"

"About five months after Karen left the hospital. She was a patient. She was brought into the emergency room one night—like Miss Pitting. Unlike

Miss Pitting, however, she wasn't dying of love. On the contrary, she'd been raped."

Sylvie paused for a moment, holding the kettle aloft. Then she continued filling the pot with boiling water, brought it back to the table, and sat down.

"Let me have your cup." I held it while she poured it full. "You said she was raped?"

"Yes. I was on night duty one evening, in September. I had nearly finished my internship and was in charge. There were two younger interns and a couple of students under me. Unlike many young doctors, I didn't mind night duty; in fact, I found it fascinating. In spite of the lack of sleep and the overwork and constant fatigue, I actually enjoyed the atmosphere of a large city hospital at night. It was a self-contained world of suffering. There was something mysterious, even mystic, about the experience of keeping vigil in those quiet, harshly lit corridors, waiting to take in from the city streets all their nightly harvest of casualties—the maimed, the assaulted, the depraved, the desperate, the catastrophically unwary: the unblest of the world. One of whom, as it turned out, was my wife, Molly. She was admitted to the emergency room at about one o'clock in the morning, having walked something like ten blocks from the scene of the rape without assistance, bleeding, beaten, her clothes badly torn. But not hysterical. I thought that odd. Nor desperate. I don't know how to describe her state, quite. A kind of awful isolation."

In those days George Washington University Hospital was located in the most disreputable section of Washington, a district of all-night bars and run-down cheap hotels, which also housed, in very odd proximity, the old Gayety burlesque theater and the Little, the only art-film cinema the city boasted at the time. Molly had been attending a performance of a French film there with her escort. On leaving the theater, they had quarreled; she had insisted on going home alone, and he had driven away in anger. It was nearly midnight. She had walked for several blocks in search of a taxi along the deserted streets. A man had emerged from the mouth of an alley which she passed, had seized and dragged her into the shadows of its walls, raped her, snatched her purse, and fled into the darkness. She had stumbled, dazed, along the streets to the hospital and presented herself at the emergency room, which was where I first saw her.

She was lying on the examination table with her eyes closed, her face mercilessly bleached by the overhead lights, wearing that look I have tried to describe, a kind of limpid solitude. A blanket had been thrown over her, and her hands clutched the coarse material rigidly. She was shivering slightly and constantly. Her long dark hair, which was always her most beautiful feature, was streaked with its varied hues of oiled walnut and lay about her shoulders and the padded mat of the examination table in a strangely rampant, festive way, like that of a child tousled at play, only partially concealing the ripped lapel of her blue woolen suit and the wrenched and crumpled collar of her blouse. I don't know how to describe my feeling at the sight of her. It may sound like a very odd thing to say, but I think she was more—alluring—in that moment than ever again in the thirty-five years I was to know her; beautiful with a strange combination of innocence and affliction, a look of ruinous, untimely wisdom, which is somehow suggestive of abandon. She lay there in a dark beatitude that made her seem almost beyond the reach or need of any paltry arts of healing we could offer her. I stood looking down at the delicately veined lids of her closed eyes and the pallor of her still face in the wild walnut hair, and felt a bitter glamour that made my hand tremble when I touched her shoulder. Her eyes opened instantly and stared with harrowed intentness into mine. Her eyes, as I remember them now, were not remarkable at all, a meager gray, shallow and pale, but at that moment they seemed as mysterious to me as the old well of our summer house in Maine, depthless in its slime-sweet vault, full of drowned stars.

"Miss Gannon?" I said.

"Yes."

"I'm Dr. Ransome. How are you feeling?"

"I'm afraid I may be sick. I can't stop shivering."

"I'll give you something to calm you in a moment. Were you beaten?"

"I think so. Yes. My wrist hurts."

I lifted and examined it, palping the bones gently.

"Flex your finger." She did so, wincing slightly. "I don't think there's anything broken. It's probably badly bruised. Do you have any other pain?" She closed her eyes without replying. "I'm going to give you a sedative to make you more relaxed. Then we'll have a closer look at you. Try not to be alarmed."

"I don't want a sedative," she said.

"I think you'll feel much better."

"No. I'll be all right. What time is it?"

"It's five minutes till one."

"I don't want the police involved," she said. "Are you going to notify them?"

"This is a criminal case, Miss Gannon. There will have to be a report made."

"If you notify the police, I'll get up and go home." She was evidently very sincere.

"Very well," I said. "But you'll have to be examined and treated. You may have internal injuries."

"Will there be a nurse here?"

"Yes, of course."

"You can examine me," she said. "But I won't speak to the police."

She closed her eyes again and fell back into her trancelike solitude. The nurse who was in attendance looked at me doubtfully, but I raised my eyebrows and shook my head, as if to acknowledge responsibility for failure to make the report. It was injudicious, but it was done. While the admission of rape victims in large city hospitals is an all too common occurrence, it was much less so in those days than today, and I had never before been on duty when such a case was admitted. I have to confess that I was anxious to add to my experience by making the examination and providing treatment, and unless I agreed to her request it seemed pretty certain that I would lose the opportunity. And quite beyond this, there was the startling feeling that the woman had aroused in me. There was that disturbing combination of the hectic and the languid in her face, the scattered, shining hair, disordered almost as if by revelry, the groping, constant flexion of her hands that suggested both pathos and avidity.

"Help her into a gown, Miss Cauldwell," I said. "I'll take care of the records."

The procedure in rape cases is simple and routine: initial treatment for shock, an examination for physical damage and confirmation of coitus. Surgical treatment is rarely indicated. A slide of vaginal fluid is prepared and microscopically examined to confirm ejaculation, and a spermicidal douche administered. Little more can be done; the victim must then begin her long and agonizing vigil to learn whether she has been impregnated or infected by disease, or both. In most cases, where any considerable amount of time had elapsed since the assault, little or nothing could be done, in those days, to prevent either. Today, a massive prophylactic injection of penicillin is given as a matter of course, but at that time—it was the fall of 1937—no such measure was available; nor was abortion, even to terminate a pregnancy incurred by rape or incest, legally permissible.

My awareness of those facts must have added to my agitation as I dealt with the first such case in my experience. A most unusual agitation, for me. I think I've told you that I was remarkably—even legendarily—self-composed in clinical situations of any kind. Not on that occasion, however. As I performed the procedure I've described to you, I felt a delicate, vertiginous flame of sentiment for the young woman flare throughout my body, racing along my nerves as if they were ignited fuses. I had consciously to steady my hands and quiet my mind to make and record my observations: She appeared to be in good physical health, although frail and slightly underweight. She had been a virgin, but aside from the rupture of the hymen, there was no evidence of tissue damage or other internal physical abnormality. The slide confirmed that there had been intravaginal emission by her attacker. Her temperature, pulse, and respiration rate gradually returned to normal as I attended her; they had never been irregular enough to suggest a clinical description of shock. She was passive and compliant, and having been assured that the police were not to be notified, seemed generally less distressed, replying to my questions in a bleak obedient monotone, sometimes raising her hand to clasp her temples loosely and despondently with her fingertips.

"You don't seem to have any serious bodily injury," I said. "Was there a struggle?"

"Yes."

"A violent struggle? I mean, would you be likely to have sustained any internal or skeletal injuries that wouldn't show up immediately?"

"I don't think so. He had a knife. He said if I screamed or called for help, he would kill me. So I was frightened. I stopped struggling."

"Was he a powerful man?"

"Yes."

"Young?"

"Well, I should think so, yes. His voice was a young man's." She dropped her face into her palm, holding her temples between her fingertips. "I can't tell you any more," she said. "Absolutely nothing more." She seemed to gather her remaining strength together, and after a moment lifted her head. "What I'm mostly concerned about," she said, speaking with deliberate clarity and composure, "is the possibility of pregnancy."

"Of course. The odds against it are very great. Can you tell me the date of your last period?"

"A little over a week ago. Eight days, to be exact."

"That was the date of its termination, or its beginning?"

"Its termination."

"And your cycle is ordinarily how long?"

"Twenty-eight days, exactly."

"I would say the chances are very small indeed. Almost infinitesimal. I don't think you have anything to worry about."

Her lips blanched as she stretched them across her teeth.

"And of disease?"

"We've given you an antiseptic douche which will destroy any residual bacteria. Ordinarily, this should make it very difficult to contract an infection of any kind. Of course, we can't be entirely sure. It will be best if you keep in fairly constant contact with us for a month or two; or with your regular physician. You should report any irregularity at all you may experience, however minor it may seem to you. Any skin rash or eruption, for example. But you mustn't be too concerned about it. You can do yourself far more harm by worrying too much. The chances of that sort of thing developing are really quite remote."

"You're saying that to reassure me."

"I'm quite sincere."

"But it does happen?"

"Well, very rarely, yes. But there are always methods of treatment, even if it should. The important thing is to be aware of what might occur." She lapsed again into her trancelike state of solitude, her eyes wandering idly about the ceiling as if following the course of vultures in a summer sky. "I don't know whether you want to go home tonight," I said. "It's quite late. Perhaps, if you live alone—"

"I'll be all right, thank you."

"If you'd prefer to stay here, I could have you admitted for observation and released in the morning. It's only a formality."

"I don't think so. Thank you. I wonder if someone could call me a taxi."

"Of course. I'll see to it myself. The nurse will help you to dress." I went to the door of the emergency room, then turned back to face her. "If you'd like to have a cup of coffee and rest for a little while, I'd be glad to accompany you home. I'm off duty in about half an hour."

"No, thank you. If you could just call a taxi."

"Yes."

I went down the hall to the admitting office and after looking up the number of an all-night cab company in the phone book I asked to have her picked up as soon as possible, revealing my own discomposure in the process by twice, before dialing it correctly, inverting digits of the number, and twice, at three o'clock in the morning, awakening indignant subscribers. I stood outside the emergency room door and waited for Molly to appear, then accompanied her silently down the hall to the outpatient entrance, where, after fishing in her purse for a cigarette and matches, she stood at the revolving door and smoked nervously and rapidly, occasionally biting her lip and sighing deeply through her nostrils. When the taxi appeared in the gloom of the circular driveway, I ushered her out under the portico, opened the door for her, and after she had seated herself, said with a counterfeit cheerfulness that must have disheartened her even more than it did me, "Now, don't fail to call, if you have any question at all. Will you remember my name? Dr. Ransome. I'll be very happy to advise you."

"Thank you," she said, in the oddly formal tone of a little girl who has been coached to thank her hostess after a birthday party, "I appreciate your sympathy." She took the handle of the door and closed it firmly from within, and as I watched her taxi disappear into the autumn night I had the dismaying conviction that I should never see her again.

"Dismay" is just the word to use in describing the effect of Molly's appearance in my life; the kind of feverish dismay that one feels on discovering that one has, at a particularly busy and all-engrossing period of one's life, contracted a severe infection of some kind. A disabling infection, such as I had never known before, and which gravely threatened my capacity for work, for concentration, for tranquillity. The memory of that night, of the few moments I had spent with the victim of its maleficence, held me in this dismay for weeks. I could not forget the strangely festive look of her scattered hair and disordered clothing as she lay on the examining table, the hectic almost exhilarated flush of the crests of her pale cheeks, her weird, shallow, vulture-following eyes. These visions perniciously invaded my attempts to study. I would find myself staring at an opposite wall across a page of text unread for a quarter of an hour, to see her slender fingers plucking with a kind of delicate exalted haste at the edge of the blanket that covered her, like those of a little girl plucking violets or wild strawberries on a summer hillside, or clutching in agony at grass blades, her eyes staring up bewildered at the encircling dark birds, her bloody skirt wrenched up to her throat. What is it in a woman that gives her that power to fascinate—to infect—a man? I could not have listed a single truly distinguished feature about Molly to explain the spell she cast on me. Nothing, that is, except the circumstances of my meeting her; circumstances, I decided finally, which must be responsible for my obsession with the woman. It occurred to me that very often it is not people themselves that we are vulnerable to, but the conditions under which they appear, as we are made vulnerable to a viral infection by a state of physical exhaustion, by having eaten poorly for some time, by having stood for an hour in the rain on a winter day or having swum for too long in cold water and dangerously lowered our body temperature. Human beings were, after all, like viruses or bacteria, predatory organisms. The distemper she had produced in me was not a matter of choice or predilection on my part, but of debility. A bit of exercise, a bit more iron in the diet, an occasional calcium tablet, I concluded, would have made all the difference. The point of view could have been called, I suppose, the Clinical, or Pathological, Theory of Passion. I found strange comfort in it, since it accorded with my view of natural dysfunction, generally, as simple mechanical failure in the universe. It did nothing, however, to relieve my condition. I was, for the next many days, notoriously inattentive at conferences, I badly botched a laboratory experiment I had had underway for weeks, dropping and smashing two irreplaceable bottles of serum on the floor, I ate virtually nothing—thereby even further reducing my resistance to the malady that had seized me—and for the first time in my medical career I made a grossly inaccurate diagnosis of a very simply identified disease, rubella, in a child. This child, a little girl of five or six, looked up at me with eyes as pale as sapphires when I had removed my hands from her hot belly, and asked in a terrified hushed voice, "What did you do to me, mister?" I remember very clearly thinking these startled, somehow ghastly words: Nothing. I did nothing to you. Hush, or the birds will come for you. Pull down your skirt, child.

This curious condition I called love, later, when asked by Molly to define my feelings toward her; and again when I married her and promised, with insane rashness, to preserve the sentiment forever, until death should us part; in both cases, however, with a sense of fraudulence, an agonized embarrassment, in which I now take comfort. And yet perhaps it was love, or as nearly that emotion as most men are apt to experience in this world; but I hope not, and I think not. I certainly had none of the more congenial symptoms of love that are celebrated by popular convention; I did not sing, or smile unaccountably, or trip down the stairs two at a time, or behave in the unduly arch or antic manner of any of the inhabitants of Shangri-La. I lapsed, for the most part, into sullen, aching, abstracted silences, surrendered to my misery and humiliation. Romantic agony is of course a part of the traditional experience of love, but what I felt was unillumined by any sense whatever of inspiration, levity, or joy. I felt an actual, physical, arthritic pain, as if hot oil had been poured into the cavities of my bones. My teeth hurt, the roots of my hair throbbed as if I had been suspended by it for hours. Somewhere in my lower back, at the juncture of my hips and spine, there was a constant, exquisite, stringent palpitation, as if my very kidneys were infected. And worst of all was a kind of grisly tenderness, an eerie, unremitting, toxic excitement, like fumes of cyanide permeating my blood and lungs and tissue, or as if the entire network of my nerves were being caressed constantly, mercilessly, by a delicate warm rasp, like the tongue of a cat.

I wish I could report that I felt spiritual sublimity of some kind, a greatening of perception and appreciation; that sense of increased wonder in the world and of communion with it that poets have so much to say about; or of the admission into its mysteries and harmonies that music intimates; or of that growing dissolution of the estranging walls of selfhood, of the prison of individuality, that saints describe—any part of that apotheosis we are taught to expect of love; but I did not. What I felt, on the contrary, was an intensified definition of myself, of my even more conscribing individuality, a kind of gathering and greatening of energy, noxious, darkly burning energy, for which I could find no release, like that of a captured animal. There was a monstrous concentration and inversion of myself; I felt as if I were a pool of fierce vitality, too intense to shine, but rather a negation of shining and of being, like those black holes we read of in the universe, those Stygian pits of energy that devour light and matter. And with this sense of utter incarceration within myself, I felt for the first time in my life the solitude of abject sexuality, a truly abysmal loneliness that I began to realize I had to alleviate in some way, or go insane.

More than once, in the ensuing two weeks of this infernal state of mind, I came very close to taking steps toward that end. I don't know how many times I stood with the receiver in my hand and my finger poised to dial the number I had copied from her admission form, ready to confess my interest in the lady —if not to describe it in its appalling urgency—and to ask for some such modest gratification of it as dinner or a concert in her company; but invariably my sense of the ethics of the situation, or simple propriety, or my invincible prudence, would intervene and compel me to replace the receiver, standing empty-handed, empty of prospect, with clenched jaws, full of that feeling of terrible, frustrated potency. I remember in one such moment raising my eyes to the glass doors of a cabinet across the room and seeing my face reflected in the dark panes, glaring back with slunk head, like a caged wolf.

I hesitate to use the word "rescue" to express my release from this wretched condition, because the form it took lends an irony to the word which is unpleasant, if not indecent. To summarize as briefly—and decently—as possible: the form it took was Molly's fear, her impulse to confer with me in order to alleviate it, and our subsequent courtship and marriage. (God forgive my indiscriminate use of these terms.) I learned that she had been undergoing a spasm of apprehension at the same time and almost of the same degree as that she had caused to rage in me; and one evening, two weeks to the day after she had stumbled into my care and destiny, she yielded to the impulse to call me, as I had wantonly proposed, in order to relieve herself of it. I was doing a tracheotomy at the time, and the measure of her anxiety was that she held the line a full five minutes, until I had finished the operation. Fortunately I was not advised of it at the moment, or I would without a doubt have severed the patient's head. When I had closed the wound and was removing my gloves at the lavatory sink, a tap at the open door made me turn my head to see Miss Johnson, the admissions clerk, scowling at me with evident disapproval.

"Dr. Ransome, you have a private call," she said. "A Miss Gannon. She's been holding the line for five minutes. Shall I put it on Post-Op?"

"Please," I said, gasping the word as if I had been stung by a bee. I strode into the office and plucked the phone up, waiting until I heard the receiver replaced in the admissions office before I spoke, and swallowing to suppress the turmoil that swam into my throat like bile.

"Dr. Ransome?" Molly said in the strange, flat, almost arrogantly matter-of-fact voice that I suddenly remembered, a voice such as very shy or sheltered people often use to disguise their discomfort at having to make conversation.

"Yes. Miss Gannon?"

"Yes. I hope I'm not disturbing you."

"No, not at all."

"I'll call back, if I am. Or I'd appreciate it if you'd call me, when you're free."

"No, I'm not busy at the moment. I'm pleased to hear from you. How have you been?"

"I don't know. That's why I'm calling. I believe you said that if I had any questions, I could feel free to call you."

"Yes, of course. I'm glad you have. Have you been having any—problems?"

"Yes. I have a rash." There was a pause, in which I felt a slow arctic chill envelop me, as if I had opened the door of a refrigerator on a summer day. "It worries me. I think you said I should report a rash of any kind."

"Yes. What sort of a rash? Where is it located?"

"Around my—my breasts. A lot of tiny blisters, like poison ivy. It's made me very—nervous."

"How long have you had it?"

"For about a week."

"Have you been to see your doctor?"

"No, I don't have a doctor—I mean one that I see regularly." She paused again, apparently to compose herself; her voice had a constricted quality, as if on the point of breaking. "And I don't think I could tell that terrible story to anyone again; anyone who hadn't heard it, I mean. But since you know about it already, I wondered if I could ask you to—examine me."

"Well, I'm on night duty now, you see; not in the clinic. That would make it difficult. But if you came down to the clinic in the morning, someone would be glad to have a look at it."

"I don't want to see anyone else. And I'd rather not come down to the hospital. I don't suppose you could make a house call? I'd be happy to pay you —anything at all."

"But you see, I'm not in private practice yet. I'm finishing my residency. I don't take private patients." There was another pause, fragile and exhausting, in which I heard her sigh deeply through her nostrils, as she had done while waiting for the taxi. "Perhaps I could arrange—"

"No, that's all right," she said quickly. "I'm sorry to have troubled you. I won't keep you any longer."

"But, listen," I said hastily, "I could come to your home on an informal basis, perhaps. Just as a friend, you see, on a social call. And then, of course, if you mentioned that you had a slight indisposition of some kind, I could have a look at it. Just casually, you know; and give you my opinion."

She seemed to be assimilating this information, considering the extent of the imposition she was making on me; a consideration that evaporated in a little breathless gasp of uncontainable relief: "Oh, would you? I'd be so grateful. I just don't know where to turn."

"Yes. I'll be happy to. Now don't distress yourself. It's probably nothing at all. Very often anxiety itself can produce these things. I'll come around tomorrow, if that's convenient. Will you give me the address?"

I wrote it down on a slip of notepaper on the desk at which I was standing, and by dawn had memorized it; because I went to bed with the piece of paper on my nightstand and rose at two- or three-hour intervals to study it mindlessly while I brewed a cup of tea with a little immersion heater I kept in my room.

It was an address in Georgetown, one of those cavernous old-fashioned apartment houses off Wisconsin Avenue whose echoing corridors were paved with tiny black-and-white octagonal tiles and whose lobby had a cold stony pallor, like a mausoleum. I think Molly must have been standing, waiting for me, just inside the door of her apartment, because she opened it instantly when I rang and said hurriedly, as if we had arranged a clandestine negotiation of some kind, "Come in, please." Then she turned and walked rapidly away from me across the length of her living room to a pair of tall, many-paned windows that looked out onto the street, where she stood staring into the branches of a yellowing sycamore. As she had not relieved me of my overcoat, I set down my bag and began uncertainly to pare it off, looking about uncomfortably for a place to deposit it, until at last she turned and said, "Oh, I'm sorry. Let me take those."

"That's all right, I'll just put them here," I said, and set them on a heavy Victorian armchair that stood against the wall. I smiled at her and she advanced a few steps toward me across the dark oriental rug, stopping to stand with her feet set far apart on the blood-colored pile with a touching look of valor, as if she were preparing to withstand a gust of cold wind or an onslaught of some sort. She was wearing one of those colorless, shapeless woolen suits that it seems to me women of my generation wore almost ubiquitously, an equally indistinct dove-colored blouse, and a pair of very businesslike low-heeled black shoes. With the light behind her, I did not see her face clearly, but I had an impression of weakness or infirmity about her mouth and jaw, as if she might have a chronic dental problem of some kind, a severe malocclusion perhaps, which made it difficult and embarrassing for her to speak or smile. She gave the impression, when she did either, of someone who has just returned from having a tooth pulled at the dentist's, and whose lips are still somewhat numb and unmaneuverable from the effects of novocaine. This can, oddly enough, be captivating.

"I'm sorry to inconvenience you like this," she said. "But, you see, I've been very—upset."

"Yes, of course. I understand."

"I've gotten this—rash."

"Yes." I stood staring at her in a kind of craven idolatry, yearning for some scrap of small talk with which to acclimatize myself, some genial preliminary comment on any subject whatever—the weather, the condition of her abominable rug, the morguelike quality of the vestibule. None of them seemed promising as topics. It appeared there were to be no amenities of any kind, not even the invitation to be seated. I could think of nothing to do but forge ahead, into the statistics of her case. "Now, have you had any other unusual—condition—of any kind?" I asked, my voice falling into a discouragingly grave, professional tone.

"No. I don't think so."

"Good. It's probably nothing at all. I wonder—" I broke off, seeing that this bewildering woman had begun to unbutton and remove her jacket. I was stricken with mortification at the thought of suggesting that the bedroom might be a more practical place to conduct the examination.

"Yes? What?"

"I wonder—if we could have a bit more light?"

"Yes." She leaned over to switch on a lamp that stood on a small end table beside the sofa. I retreated into the entrance foyer to retrieve my bag from the chair where I had placed it, fumbling in it for a packet of tongue depressors, aware that she was proceeding with a kind of furtive, anguished diligence to disrobe herself. All this seems cruelly comic to me now, almost as dementedly grotesque as a scene from a Marx Brothers movie. Certainly it was relieved by no such recognition at the time; there was nothing at all funny about my palsied scrabbling through my kit, about the parched and strangulated feeling in my throat or the coldness and pallor of the hand in which I clenched the tongue depressor that I feverishly excavated and unwrapped. It was macabre to me, like a farce played in an empty theater, without an audience, with no witnesses to guide the actors, by their laughter, away from the abyss on which they caper. I turned back toward her and saw that she now stood naked to the waist, her bare breasts, bathed in the light of the lampshade, upswept as firmly as young pears to their delicate scarlet cusps that I could almost feel rankle the flesh of my own breast.

"Perhaps you'd better lie down on the sofa," I said harshly, "I want, first of all, to examine your throat, and the light will be better."

"Yes."

She moved to the sofa and lay down on her back in a stiff, complaisant way, still clutching in her clenched hand the crumpled brassiere which she had last removed. The lamplight fell over her naked upper body from beneath the shade in a candid wash, revealing between her breasts a rash of tiny dark red vesicles; no more malignant-looking, however, than a mild allergenic reaction of some kind, or what used to be called prickly heat.

"Open your mouth," I said. She did so, spasmodically, with a dry, desolate gasp. I knelt beside the sofa on one knee and put the depressor into her mouth, pressing my free hand, as if to steady her head, into the warm luxuriance of her hair. I held down her tongue and studied her throat and gums and palate. They were a healthy color, uninflamed, and clear of the mucus patches I had dreaded to see. Holding the depressor between my fingers like a cigarette, I palped the glands of her throat and neck; they were not swollen or, evidently, sensitive.

"Have you had a sore throat?" I asked. "Or a headache, or a feverish feeling?"

"No." She swallowed to relieve the dryness of her throat and coughed briefly.

"Well, you don't look very sick to me. Now, let me take your pulse." I took her wrist in my hand and, baring my watch, counted the soft pulsations that broke against my fingertips like the lapping of a gentle, dark lagoon. They were only very slightly accelerated, no more than might have been produced by agitation. "Yes," I said, "that's quite normal. Let's have a look at this rash." I bent over her more closely, observing, far more intently than the dermatitis, the trembling undulation of her breasts, set with their twin jewels, as hard and bright as garnets. "I don't think that's anything serious at all," I said, withdrawing my hands and rising abruptly to look down at her with a very shallow pretense of equanimity. "I think you've worried yourself into that rash. Worry can do it, you know; as well as a hundred other things: something you've eaten, chafing from your clothes, irritation from a cleaning fluid or detergent. A hundred things. If you'd like to dress now, I'll take your temperature."

"Are you sure?" she whispered huskily. She made no move to rise, but lay still clutching her brassiere, staring up at me with a steady, cheerless fortitude.

"As sure as anyone can be, from what I've seen of you. I'd like to take your temperature, though, and a little blood, just to be on the safe side. I'll take it back to the laboratory and have a Wassermann done. That way, you can be absolutely at rest about it. I wonder if there's somewhere I could drop this depressor?"

"There's a wastebasket over there."

I turned in the direction her eyes indicated, then went across the room and dropped the depressor into a raffia basket that stood beside a mahogany secretary. As I did so, I noticed that on the writing desk, which lay open, suspended by brass chains, there stood a metal-framed photograph of an extremely handsome young man, beneath whose flawless, if somewhat self-congratulatory features was the enigmatic inscription: *With my love, always, Robert T. Aldington.*

"Who is this handsome young man?" I asked as casually as I could.

"A friend of mine," she said quickly. She had risen to a sitting position on the sofa and was leaning forward, her arms bent awkwardly behind her to fasten the clasp of her brassiere. I picked up the photograph and pretended an absorption in it that was not entirely fraudulent, in order to allow her a certain amount of privacy in which to complete the process. My interest increased considerably when I discovered that the young man's name, almost unmistakably, had originally been printed on the portrait by the same photographic process that had reproduced there his winning Saxon features, and had been carefully, if unsteadily, traced over with a fountain pen to give the impression of a genuine signature; above it, the words *With my love, always,* considerably lighter in tone, had been added in a woefully imperfect forgery of his hand. I did not know who Robert T. Aldington was, but from the glossy commercial quality of the paper, I suspected that he was a minor motion-picture actor, singer, or entertainer of some kind, and that the portrait was one of those mass-reproduced publicity photos that are mailed out routinely to admirers. I set it back on the secretary, murmuring appreciatively, feeling oppressed and yet faintly, malignantly elated by the discovery. Miss Gannon, I saw, was now buttoning her dove-colored blouse.

"Will you roll your left sleeve up?" I said. "I'm going to take that blood, remember."

"Yes."

I took my bag from the hall chair, carried it to the sofa, and sitting beside her, removed my syringe, rubber tubing, a bottle of alcohol, and a packet of sterile compresses. She sat obediently while I took the specimen, shrinking with a little shiver when I inserted the needle, then watching with an awed intentness, equal to my own, as her scarlet blood welled up into the cylinder. I removed and capped the vial, set it in my bag, then withdrew the thermometer from its case and asked her to open her mouth. She did so, turning her eyes upward when she had clasped the instrument between her lips, and until I had removed it, remained like that, rigidly motionless except for her eyes, which roamed about the yellow, cloudlike stains of the ceiling and the discolored plaster garlands that bordered it like the decaying foliage of a ruined arbor. I half expected to see the great gross shadow of a vulture glide over her strained face. After a moment I murmured, "All right," withdrew the thermometer from her lips, and read it. It was normal. I put it back into its case, replaced it in the bag, and stood up.

"You seem to be in very good health," I said, speaking with unnatural rapidity, "at least as far as any serious infection goes. I think a little calamine lotion will clear up that rash quite promptly. You can get it at any drugstore; the directions will be on the label."

"Oh, thank you so much." She stood up for the first time and clasped her hands firmly in front of her in a quaint, professorial way, as if standing before a class. It occurred to me suddenly that she might be a schoolteacher, or perhaps conduct Sunday-school classes; although neither possibility seemed to accord with the business about the photograph, nor did any other profession I could think of. "I can't tell you how relieved I am. I wish I could repay you in some way. Are you sure you wouldn't be able to accept a fee?"

"Really, don't consider it. I'm glad to be able—" I could not think of any very sensible conclusion for the sentence; I smiled and nodded heavily. "I'll let you know the results of the laboratory test. It should only be a day or two."

"You're very kind."

"Not at all." I stood for a moment looking into her poignant, pale, artlessly shifting eyes, then smiled and nodded again in my lugubrious way and retreated to the foyer to retrieve my coat. As I struggled unaided and somewhat hysterically into it I found myself repeating mindlessly, "Well, then, I'll let you know the results of the laboratory test. It shouldn't be more than a day or two. Now, you'll remember to pick up the calamine lotion?"

"Yes. Thank you so much."

"Not at all. Good morning."

I opened the door and plunged out into the cold vastness of the corridor, aware that she was still standing there, following me with those harrowed, gentle eyes.

The two days that followed were fraught with a delirium exceeding even that of the two weeks that had preceded them. There were not only my previous fantasies to contend with, but the all too material memory of those naked, small, jeweled breasts rising and falling tremulously in their timid sufferance of my gaze, those sweetly abject eyes, flickering over mine like the dark sparkle from the surface of a moonlit lake. And her blood, thicker and redder, it seemed to me, than any I had ever seen, with its strange velvet viscosity, like silt-laden water gushing up from a sullied spring.

After thirty-six hours of this miasmal frenzy, I rang her, on the evening of the second day, from the telephone booth of a drugstore opposite the hospital.

"I have the results of your blood test," I said. "It's negative. You have nothing to worry about."

"Oh, thank God," she whispered. She began another sentence, but her voice caught uncontrollably.

"I did the lab work myself," I said. "Just to be perfectly satisfied about it.

Sometimes it's possible for the identity of specimens to be confused, and so on. But when you do it yourself, there can't be any question."

"Thank you," she murmured. "I'm very, very grateful."

"Well," I said, after a moment of vehement gathering together of my resolution, "I wondered if we could have dinner together, or something, to celebrate."

"Oh, that would be nice." She spoke without hesitation. "Why don't you let me fix dinner for you here? I'd really like to. That's the least I could do."

"Oh, well, that's kind of you." What a sudden miraculous placation I felt of all my agonies and execrations! What a warm, assuaging certitude! What a sense of justice and proportion in the universe! And, at the same time, what an ignominious sense of triumph, of opportunity cunningly pursued and knavishly achieved. I was too exhausted by the conflict of these unreconcilable sensations for a moment to do anything more than repeat stupidly, "Well, that's kind of you."

"Would you like to come tomorrow night?"

"Tomorrow night. Yes; as a matter of fact, that's my night off. Yes, that would be very nice. About what time?"

"Well, around six, I guess. What would you like, especially?"

"Oh, I don't know. Anything at all; I'm not much of a gourmet."

"Well, I'll try to think of something. I'll expect you around six, then."

"Yes. Fine. Thank you. I'll look forward to it."

"And I want to thank you again," she said, and hung up.

During the next twenty-four hours my understanding of my own emotions and impulses did not improve; it did not improve greatly during the next thirty-five years, as a matter of fact; it is far from perfect now. This did not deter me from presenting myself, however, at the appointed time, dressed with a fastidiousness which I'm sure would have delighted Karen: cuff links, newly purchased and very fashionable (so the haberdashery clerk assured me), a button-down collar, and in my "good suit," a shaggy, superannuated mustard-colored tweed, purchased with far more academic eventualities in mind.

It was dark when I arrived, and for some reason the streetlights were not working. It was an unusually cold September night, without moon or stars, and I had to fumble my way along the narrow sidewalk by holding out my hand to touch the branches of a hedge that bordered the meager front yards of the old town houses. Their brick porches were wrapped in blackness, bare of their summer furniture except for the wooden swings that on one or two of them blew gently back and forth in the night wind, their chains creaking. I had the disquieting illusion that they were occupied by ghosts who sat swinging slowly in the autumn night, as they would eternally. Pale children with dangling bruised legs and somber eyes who waited for the footsteps in that street of the strange companion of their wanton afternoons.

The mortuarial gloom of the lobby of Molly's building seemed almost a haven after this excursion; as did her apartment when she opened the door to me—or that small area in the heart of its Victorian vastness that was enclosed by lamplight, its forbidding rug and monstrous furniture bathed in a dusky, unexpected glamour. She herself was no better acquainted with couture than I, apparently. She was wearing a dress that I think I can be forgiven for remembering in detail: a furry-looking, navy blue garment with a drawstring waist, a file of lyre-shaped white buttons descending from throat to abdomen, and, embroidered on its left breast, a gigantic purple butterfly, an embellishment transparently her own, which inspired in me the same secret, sly rejoicing as had my discovery of the forged inscription on her photograph.

I think I've forgotten to tell you that I was bearing a bottle of murky-looking liebfraumilch wine, very perfunctorily supplied by the manager of my neighborhood delicatessen. She accepted it gravely, murmuring, "That's very nice. Thank you," and stood cradling it impassively while I struggled out of my overcoat and laid it on the hall chair.

"Is it raining?" she asked.

"No. No, there's a bit of fog, but it's not raining."

I thought it an odd question, since I was evidently perfectly dry, but nothing in me demurred at its inanity, any more than at her strange dress, or the equally beguiling malformation of her slack, tenuous jaw. I think that at that moment no conceivable banality, vulgarity, or deformity could have diminished my hopeless infatuation with the woman, but on the contrary, would have compounded and enhanced it in some inexplicable way. This may seem strange or sinister to you; I think I have suggested that it did to me—as it no doubt would to anyone with equal reason to regret my folly of that night. And yet, it is not an unheard-of phenomenon. Men have written songs to it. Which I did not realize until thirty-five years later, a few days after Molly's death, when I was packing her books to deliver to the Purple Heart and was leafing through a copy of Shakespeare that her grandmother had given her long ago, which fell open to the pages enclosing a tiny, red, faded blossom. On the verso was printed the sonnet numbered c x x x:

> *My mistress' eyes are nothing like the sun;*
> *Coral is far more red than her lips' red:*
> *If snow be white, why then her breasts are dun;*
> *If hairs be wires, black wires grow on her head.*
> *I have seen roses damask'd, red and white,*
> *But no such roses see I in her cheeks;*

And in some perfume is there more delight
Than in the breath that from my mistress reeks.
I love to hear her speak, yet well I know
That music hath a far more pleasing sound:
I grant I never saw a goddess go;
My mistress, when she walks, treads on the ground:
And yet, by heaven, I think my love as rare
As any she belied with false compare.

It is the only poem I ever learned by heart. Perhaps I was inspired to that feat by my astonished appreciation of the fact that great men—one great man, at least—had shared something of my own apparent aberration, and had chosen to make it the subject of an equally grotesque and passionate poem. But what I felt most, sitting on a packing crate in that silent, empty house, surrounded by those forlorn relics of our lost and perjured lives, was a throe of inconsolable pity for us both, for the misbegotten love that had flowed through our blood with its bitter, plaintive strain of grief and supplication, binding us together as the Miserere binds communicants.

Wisdom, in its meager portions, comes late, and always in the form of elegy. If I had had any intimation of that sad conclusion of my ardor as I stood there confounded by it in my mustard-colored suit, I would have broken out of its bonds, and out of that apartment, as if through chains of steel, leaving the tiled corridors shattered in my flight. But I didn't. I stood there with my eyes clinging incorrigibly to the soft blue mound of her one breast unobstructed by butterfly or bottle—or, unless I was mistaken, by brassiere; because in the center of the sweetly swollen bombazine, cut like a cameo and flagrant as a thimble, was the outline of the dazzling garnet gem that it concealed. When the silence had begun to grow conspicuous, I smiled in a painful imitation of cordiality and began to rub my hands together from the cold; until I realized that the gesture unpleasantly resembled one of voracious anticipation, at which I quickly and noisily began to blow on them to better illustrate the nature of my plight. The impression it gave was even more egregious. I folded them under my armpits at last, shivered, and said, "It's very cold out there," raising my eyes to hers. She seemed much taller.

"Yes. You must be very conscious of your hands. I guess all surgeons are." I nodded, cheered by the unexpected perspicacity, or generosity, of the remark. "Would you like me to heat some of this wine and put a stick of cinnamon in it? Maybe that would warm you up."

"Actually, I don't drink wine at all," I said. "It doesn't seem to agree with me. But I thought you might enjoy it." I paused uncomfortably, recognizing the insidious quality of the suggestion. "But of course we don't have to have it at all, if you'd rather not."

She looked down at the cradled bottle as if into an infant's eyes and said with what seemed like tranquil indifference to my imprudence, "I think I'll have some. I like mulled wine. My grandmother gave it to me once."

"Really? I didn't realize that you could mull white wine."

"Oh. I didn't know that. Maybe it was red. I think I'll try it anyway. Are you sure you wouldn't like a glass?"

"No, thank you. It gives me a headache, for some reason."

"Would you like a cup of coffee?"

"If you're going to have the wine, yes. That'll be fine."

"Why don't you sit down? There are cigarettes there."

"Thank you." She went into the kitchen and I sat down and began to cast my eyes about the apartment in the hope that it might yield some further clue as to her life and nature more reassuring than the last. It was old, as I've said, and had the high, ornate ceilings of buildings of its period, clouded, as the whole place was, with a residual Victorian atmosphere, torpid and vaguely insalubrious-looking, suggestive of obesity, secret odious indulgences, laudanum, florid verse, soiled underclothes. I marveled at it; only art or utter ingenuousness could have so perfectly preserved that ambiance, or felt at home in it. A conclusion I have had the never-ending desire to correct.

For several minutes the pungent scent of steaming liebfraumilch had been blending, not at all incongruously, into the atmosphere. In a moment Molly appeared, carrying a red lacquer tray on which was a glassful of the hot wine and a cup of coffee.

"Do you take cream and sugar?" she asked.

"No, thank you. I'll have it black."

She set the tray on the end table at my elbow, wrapped a paper napkin around her glass of wine, and bore it to the overstuffed chair opposite me, where she sat down and began to stir it with a cinnamon stick. I picked up my coffee and sipped at it, peering at her over the rim of the cup with diminishing discretion as I began to realize that there was something quite different about her face from the last time I had seen it. It was either flushed or rouged, inordinately; there was an almost garish glow to her cheeks that neither the fumes of hot wine nor any emotion that I dared to credit could account for. Her eyelids were shadowed with a soft purple sheen, her brows distinctly thinner and more deeply arched, as if they had been plucked, and her lips glittered with a bright scarlet paint. With a prickle of uncanny excitement, I perceived, unquestionably, that all this was so; her face had the shameless, whorish, innocent extravagance of a little girl's, dressed in her mother's clothes and high-heeled shoes and made up to "play grown-ups." I lowered my eyes to her feet and saw that she was indeed wearing high-heeled shoes, very high, spike-heeled shoes of a peculiar purple luster, evidently brand-new and giving the impression of having been confiscated not half an hour ago from her mother's closet. She raised her glass—a large, ten-ounce water tumbler—and holding the cinnamon stick aside with a crooked forefinger, drank half of its murky contents in one uninterrupted, audible swallow that rippled her white throat with a spasm of startling rapacity.

"That's very good," she said. "Are you sure you won't have some?"

"No, thank you." I glanced appreciatively about the room. "You have a nice apartment."

"It's old, but I like it." Her eyes wandered to a dark papier-mâché occasional table against the wall, on which stood a luxuriant plant in an oriental china bowl. "My grandmother left me the furniture. There was a lot more of it, a whole warehouseful, because she lived all her life in a big old house in Takoma Park. I had to sell most of it. You get almost nothing for secondhand furniture. Do you know what I got for it?"

"No."

"Less than five hundred dollars."

"Oh, that's terrible. It's a pity you had to sell it, because Victorian things are getting hard to find."

"Are they?"

"Yes." There was a considerable pause. "I think so."

"I like it," she said ruminatively. "It means a lot to me. I can still see my grandmother sitting on that sofa." It was an unsettling thought; I glanced hastily down its length, as if the lady's wraith might indeed be seated at my side, a ghostly chaperone. Molly began to speak more rapidly, with mounting energy and fluency, produced, I suspected, by that prodigious gulp of wine. "My grandmother was a wonderful person. She told me all the things I value most about life. All the things I've learned are truest. People of that generation knew a lot more about life than people do today."

"Yes," I said, and then asked gently, moved by the commanding solemnity of her tone, "What did she tell you?"

"She said it was 'a precious hard business.' That's the phrase she used. She didn't mean precious *hard;* she meant precious *and* hard, both. With a comma between them. I realized that one day. Do you see that table?" Her eyes moved back to the piece of furniture which apparently had generated her discourse.

"Yes. It's very nice."

"She used to keep a plant on it, just like the one I have there now. It's a Christmas cactus. She really loved that plant. She used to pick it up once a week and carry it in the kitchen and put it in a bowl of water, to soak the roots.

She was an old lady, and it was very heavy, so she had to hold it very carefully, from the bottom, with her hands wide open. I said to her one day, 'Can I carry it, Gramma? That must be hard for you.' She said, 'Oh, it's hard, but I can manage. I've learned how to carry it. That's the only way you can hold precious things safely, with open hands.' That's when I realized what she meant."

I felt curiously unwilling to comment on her ancestor's insight. After a moment I said, "It's a beautiful plant."

"Yes, it is. It gets beautiful little red blossoms at Christmastime." She lifted her glass, and in a swallow as phenomenal as the first, drained it to the bottom, then closed her eyes and pressed her lips together, as if the effect had been unexpectedly pronounced. After a moment she raised her purple lids and looked back toward the table. "She dropped it one day. It broke all to pieces. There was dirt all over the rug, and little pieces of china. And little red flowers. All the blossoms fell off. She gave me one of them. I remember how she sighed when she picked it up and put it in my hand." She sighed deeply, as if in illustration of her grandmother's woe, her breasts rising and falling distractingly.

"I suppose she was heartbroken," I said.

"Do you know what she said?"

"No."

"She said, 'Well, we'll put it in some fresh dirt, child, and maybe it'll come back. Sometimes they do. Sometimes they bloom even better after they're broken. Some people actually snap them off, to make them.' Then she made me a glass of hot wine." She frowned, searching her memory, and murmured in a moment, as if in answer to the question it now seemed wildly inopportune to ask, "I don't remember whether it did or not. She died a little while later. I still have the blossom somewhere. In my Shakespeare book, I think."

I had listened to this recitation with uncertain but absolute absorption. Like her apartment, it made a very ambiguous impression, of either artifice or almost divine inadvertence; and my reaction to it was very much the same as to the milieu, composed of regret for what might be considered its lamentably cunning air of pathos, its skilled but vulgar virtuosity—like that of the Victorian novels almost certainly somewhere at hand—and of delight at my equally strong persuasion of its spontaneity, of its having been excavated out of her soul and memory by simple grace, by that magical felicity that brings forth images in poems, like flowers, like Christmas cactus blossoms. I decided, for my own greater comfort—and prosperity—to give credit to the latter. Or perhaps I didn't deliberately decide it; perhaps Molly's very genuine and irresistible air of destitution was completing my already far-advanced subversion.

I set my coffee cup down and laced my fingers together in my lap, staring down at them in silent deference to the departed lady's wisdom—and to her granddaughter's surprising sensibility.

"I never knew my grandparents," I said. "I've always regretted that. I think you can learn a lot from older people. As you say."

"Yes." She raised her empty glass, glanced into it, then rose suddenly and said, "I'm going to get some more wine." I realized for the first time that she was very deliberately intoxicating herself. "Did your coffee get cold? You haven't drunk much of it."

"No, no, it's fine."

"I'll just be a minute."

She was gone for eight, in fact. Impatiently, and darkly thrilled by my knowledge of her mission, I sat awaiting her, staring sightlessly into the gloom beyond the windowpanes, feeling gather again in me, after its brief and only very partial remission, that cold, convulsive knot of energy, that ganglion of atrocious, throbbing sensitivity and power, like a black vertiginous well that sucked into its depthless, noisome vortex stars, and blossoms, and drifting voices of the dead, and its own light, unslakably.

Molly came back into the room carrying her replenished glass, from which, standing beside her chair, she took a sip considerably more moderate than the last. After a moment of what looked like restless indecision, she set the glass down on the end table and raised her hands, spreading their fingertips lightly against her breast, as if breathlessly musing.

"I'd better draw the curtains," she said. She went across the room to the window and stood looking out briefly at the natural world with a grave valedictory gaze; then tugged the cord that hung beside the sill and drew together the heavy purple drapes with a rustling, shimmering, velvet sweep, like the swift consummate closure of a theater curtain.

"It's dark out there," she said.

"Yes."

"I don't know why they don't put the lights on earlier. Maybe they're not working." She came back across the room and stood beside her chair. "I have a roast in the oven, but I've put it on warm, so it won't burn." I nodded. She raised her hand, inserted her fingertips between the two upper buttons of her dress, and brushed them gently across the cleft between her breasts.

"Is the rash still troubling you?" I asked, reciting the words like an inexperienced actor.

"It itches just a little."

"You've been applying the calamine?"

"Yes. It's much better, I think. Would you like to look at it?"

"Yes."

She began to undo the white lyre-shaped buttons slowly from the top, ritualistically, as if we were performing a ceremony, known to both of us, in which our roles were practiced, unabashed, and, if still imperfect, gathering in assurance. When she had undone the last button, she raised her arms and tugged the upper portion of her dress from her bare shoulders, wriggling them free until they shone like pearl in the lamplight. She drew her arms out of the sleeves with a hypnotic gravity and let the dress fall, hanging from its draw-string belt around her waist. As I had foretold, she wore nothing under it; her naked breasts rose and fell with her deep, rapid breathing like floating melons surging on moonlit water. It seemed as if I had never left the room, as if only a long disordered moment had interrupted my last vision of them. I had preserved them with my longing as a desert traveler preserves the memory of the jade-cool rind of globed, ambrosial, quenching melons.

"Shall I lie down?" she asked, with a nunlike, almost liturgical solemnity.

"Yes."

I rose from the sofa as she came toward me, to allow her to do so. She sat down, then raised her feet and lay back on the cushions, adjusting her body inward to give me room to sit beside her, as I did. Her eyes, from between their blue lids and bright-rouged cheeks, stared up with the fixed brilliance of alabaster into the shadowy firmament above us. I leaned forward and moved my hand to touch lightly the shallow cleft between her breasts where a pale efflorescence still barely tinged her skin. All of these gestures we performed with a disciplined, aesthetic complicity, like that of ballet dancers, like the nymph and satyr I had seen with Karen perform a scene of ravishment on the stage, abandoned but exact, every wanton motion and attitude ordained, re-hearsed, reproduced with a kind of frozen, soulless skill. There was nothing ambiguous now about her actions, or about the hushed balletic pantomime we were enacting; it was almost decorously, almost placidly precise. And yet because of that earnestness and complicity and formality, thrilling in a way that nothing extemporary could ever be, almost sickening in its excitement, almost unspeakable. I think truly that for a moment we understood. That we had the companionship of outcasts, which is like no other. For a moment we were united in the mute, outrageous candor and consanguinity of felons, lepers, renegades. And I think we may have sacrificed the rest of our lives to that moment. We may have paid for it with lifelong penance, lifelong silent, mortified, unconversable chagrin.

But when I touched her breasts, that spellbound, choreographic quality was dispelled in an instant. There was a monstrous concussion in me like the distant thunderous uproar of a collapsing dam, and then an overwhelming, nauseating, purulent, hot flux, like the discharge from a burst abscess. My mind darkened as if engulfed with a wall of cataracting fetid water. The pent-up passion of all those years of insane abstinence burst over me in a glittering black wave;

I was deluged, drenched, vitiated. It poured through every artery and nerve as if through the viaducts and channels of a ruined city; they swelled and split like crumbling masonry with torrents of uncontainable desire. Whatever might still have stood of the ordered city of my self fell in tottering heaps of smashed and smoking stone. And out of this rubble I heard my own voice crying, like the crushed, trapped victim of a flood, "Please, please, please, please, please." I could not stop saying the word. I must have repeated it a hundred times, crouching over her while my utterly ungovernable hands reached out to take her breasts, cupping and crushing them until their flint-hard nipples pressed into my palms like poignards. "Please, please, please, please, please," I muttered, while she whispered, "Oh my God, oh my God, oh my God," in a kind of crazed antiphonal. She lunged suddenly upward and thrust her thumbs into the top of her skirt, tugging it down over her hips and thighs, tossing and lurching with uplifted knees to free herself of the entangling folds of cloth. She kicked it aside at last with a desperate thrust of one white foot and then subsided, lying bewilderingly slim and pale against the dark upholstery, her breast and belly heaving as she panted rapidly through her open glittering lips. Her hips were cool as porcelain, curved subtly as the walls of a wide bowl. I clasped them in my hands and sank my mouth into the middle of them, where she held afloat between her thighs a coarse brown matrix, like a bitter sponge. She gave a lonely cry, like a bird in a dark wood, and raised her hips, shuddering, offering up to me in a consuming kiss the bruised-lipped mouth of her defiled spirit.

Of course, I knew it was inevitable that I should meet Nils again, and I think you can understand that I dreaded it. But do you know how much? I actually prepared things to say to him: bits of dialogue, courteous but firm demurrals, graceful protestations of indifference, complete with cunningly contrived transitional devices to make them all the easier to weave into a conversation, or to change the course of one. Considering my abhorrence of the prepared, the rehearsed, the political, that is pretty shocking evidence of my state of mind. He frightened me, truly, in a way that no one ever had, because he threatened me. He gave me a feeling of rather weird indignation, as if his appearance in my life, his nature, his very existence, were a presumption, an insupportable intrusion, an imposture, almost. When I thought back, as I did all too often, about our conversation under the viaduct on that rainy afternoon, a phrase he had spoken recurred continually and hauntingly to me: "Do you think he mistook his beautiful companion for someone else? Someone more beautiful? For his true love?" I heard the exact tone of his voice, echoing as if out of a dream, and could see the shifting spray of pale freckles around his peculiarly livid mouth. I resented the indelibility of the sentences, ringing away in my mind like a telephone number you've sworn not to forget, or a line from a play you've performed years before, worn into banality by their insistence, and yet becoming more oracular with every repetition.

I expected him to appear at my office door almost any afternoon, with the book he had offered to let me read, or to find him waiting for me again under the viaduct as I went home in the evening, or to see him seated somewhere at the back of the lecture hall listening very gravely to my opinions about *Adonais*. I didn't feel safe, anywhere, for weeks. And I kept on making up these ridiculous, valedictory conversations, many of which involved theatrical effects that I rehearsed shamelessly; a little trill of amused, indifferent laughter, or a sudden stern, peremptory lowering of the voice. Thank God, I never tried to practice any of them; I'm so damned transparent.

When I did see him again, it was under the most embarrassing circumstances imaginable. It was at an E.U.A. party—English Undergraduate Association—in the last week of May. They give those things every year to celebrate the end of the spring semester. It was held in one of the big projection halls that open out onto the mall and it was very well attended; people are naturally festive with exams over and the summer holidays coming up; and because it was such a warm spring afternoon, all the doors were left open and the party spilled out onto the mall. There were people sitting everywhere on the grass with paper cups full of wine or beer or strolling around among the quince bushes or leaning against the trunks of the oak trees nibbling at pretzels and laughing and chattering away in that overanimated way they have at those things—the professors cutting a figure among the students, and the students eating it up. Some of them were graduating, of course, and would never see each other or their professors again, and that gave it all a kind of magical, bittersweet quality: the soft spring air and the girls in their fresh summer dresses and the men in shirt sleeves, everyone looking surprisingly slender and cool and handsome, as they do when you see them out of doors for the first time in the spring without being bundled up in coats or sweaters. There are times when a university is really a very romantic place; when you realize that in spite of all the rubbish and politics and pedantry that goes on there, you really love it, that there is nowhere else in the world where so many attractive, intelligent, earnest, still uncorrupted people are all together in the same place for a moment, interested in the same things (and knowing quite a bit about them, really), making a kind of enchanted tableau of innocence and eloquence before they're dispersed forever into labor and meanness of spirit and connivery and compromise. You feel a kind of love for them all, for a minute, that some people never feel again, I think. It's a kind of love that Roethke expresses beautifully in a poem called "To Jane," which he wrote to a student of his who was killed in a riding accident (so she never changed, you see). It really *is* a party, you know—the kind that all of life ought to be; and maybe the last one a lot of people ever go to. And maybe the reason some of us stay is that we can't bear for it to end.

Well, I suppose I was feeling something like that, that afternoon. I had on a cotton skirt for the first time that year, and I could feel the breeze under it, and in my hair, and on my arms, and the quince was all in blossom along the paths, and every quarter of an hour the bells would toll on Chapel Hill with a molten sound. I was waiting for Ron, who was going to stop by after his class let out at four. He had become very fond of parties; he liked showing me off and he liked performing for me among the students, which he did very well, without ostentation or hysteria, but with a sense of enjoyment and genuine social virtuosity that was surprising and admirable. There was usually a circle around us, animated and attentive, in testimony to his wit and energy, and often he invited some of them home with us to share a pot of chili and a jug of wine, if it was a weekend or we had late classes in the morning. I liked all that. I was proud of him and grateful for his affection and indulgence and respect, and for the fact that I had got a great deal of work done since I had moved in with him. I had written twelve chapters of my novel, and I was very pleased with them. (I called them cantos instead of chapters because it wasn't really a novel; it was a phantasmagorical journal that wandered off into fictive or fantastic alternatives to what really happened in my life. A passage of very literally transcribed events might be followed, for example, by an imaginative one describing what might have happened if I had behaved differently at a certain point in those events, followed a different impulse, one which was just as truly and perhaps even more characteristically a part of my nature—something I might actually have considered doing, as a matter of fact, and regretted not having done. Or perhaps a kind of magical improvisation on that reality —events and personalities deformed as if by a fun-house mirror or an imperfect pane of glass into those convulsive possibilities that experience conjures in us and that memory and dreams are woven of. I tried to compose a kind of polyphony of all the roads not taken but invoked by and implicit in a person's existence, and to make a fuguelike whole of them. I called it *An Entire Life.*) All this combined to produce a feeling in me as close to peace as anything I had ever experienced. I had become almost totally absorbed in it and fascinated by it, and I didn't want any of its delicate and enchanting processes disrupted. It seemed to me to assign some purpose to my life that gave it dignity and meaning, that redeemed what had been headlong and hysterical and desperately improvised about it for so long.

So I sat there on the grass in my cotton skirt under one of the willow oaks that had broken into feathery blossom that was falling into my hair like dust, feeling a sense of felicity and fortune that was as rare in my life as a vision of paradise. And then Beth Palmer came along. That's what always happens, of course: you manage to make a composition of some kind out of your life and imagination that is tranquilly strange, full of deep, romantic chasms and cedar-covered hillsides, and then the Man from Porlock comes along, nattering about grocery bills or career opportunities or sexual politics. Beth had shared an apartment with me briefly, between boyfriends, a year before, and she knew as much about me as anyone—a fact in which I didn't rejoice at all as she came and sat down on the grass in front of me under the willow oak at the edge of the mall where I was waiting for Ronnie. I didn't really dislike her, but she disturbed me very much, because once our lives and fortunes had coincided so closely that there had been, if not really affection, at least a strong and somehow reassuring intimacy between us that she presumed on, insidiously. It was my own fault; once we had done some pretty scandalous things together, and defended each other in our commission of them; I think we drew comfort of a kind from our mutual profligacy. There was nothing comforting about it any longer, however, because I had learned, even before she moved out with her boyfriend, that although we were very alike in our behavior, it was for very different reasons, and that they made a very poor basis for a relationship. She had an impudent and agile wit which could be entertaining for an hour, or the time span of a party, but whose only real end, it seemed to me after long exposure to it, was defamation: of other people, of their relationships, of institutions, works of art—of the world in general. There are a lot of people like that—sometimes very gifted people—and they are among the saddest in the world. There is always a reason for it, of course, and I suppose Beth would have made a fascinating subject for a novel, if I had had the time or inclination to get to the bottom of her. But I didn't have the inclination, and therefore not the time or patience. You must be *very* interested in such people, I think, or else avoid them whenever possible, because they can be genuinely outrageous and disruptive. We hadn't kept up our acquaintance since she had moved out of the apartment, although we chatted occasionally over a cup of coffee in the cafeteria, exchanging the latest biographical data on our lives. She found it fascinating that I had moved in with Ron—the least predictable event of the century, she called it—and could be very gauche and garrulous about it. "I don't see why," I told her. "You did the same thing: you moved in with Eddie." "Yes, but for the very opposite reason," she said. "That's what's fascinating. I wonder which of us is kidding whom?" (She was very bright, you understand, which added to the menace I felt in her—particularly at that moment.)

She was graduating at the end of the semester, and going into the University College program in Europe. She was going to teach at Ruislip, just outside of London, where she had never been, and was anxious to talk to Ron about it, because he had spent a year there. So we were keeping an eye out for him, scanning the stretch of walk from Tydings Hall while we talked, when Beth's voice changed suddenly, dropping to a confidential hush, and she said, "Oh, Lord, do you see that boy coming toward us, across the Mall? I was mad about him last year."

I turned my head and saw Nils coming toward us across the grass, bare-waisted, holding a Frisbee between his teeth while he struggled into his shirt. He had very pale skin, literally as white as milk, and already, after an hour in the spring sun, there was a blush of sunburn across his breast and shoulders that gave him a fevered look, as if he were artificially illuminated, like an actor striding into a limelight. "What do you think of *that,* for a man?"

"I don't know," I said, almost stammering. My mind was suddenly a total shambles. "He looks—well—sunburned."

"I went to bed with him once, after a *Calvert Review* party. And never heard from him again." Then, as if somewhat tardily aware of my confusion, she gave me a gaze of mischievous gravity and said, "Yes. It's becoming, isn't it?"

I saw Nils stop at the hedge that bordered the mall and break off a spray of quince blossom, and I knew he would bring it to me. With that knowledge a kind of hushed stasis fell over the afternoon that held it for a moment in absolute suspension; the stirring of my hair against my neck in the breeze froze in an everlasting caress, the note of the quarter hour caught in the throat of the chapel steeple like a great golden ingot; and I saw with fearful, inexpurgeable clarity a shrike, perched in the foam of the quince hedge, poised to disembowel a tiny, almost hairless, pink creature—a baby mole, I think—that twitched in an endless spasm on the thorn on which it was impaled. When the moment was resumed into time, the bird was startled by the snapping of the branch that Nils broke off, and swept up from the hedge in a swift dipping flight that carried it to the top of a willow oak a hundred feet away, where it sat with a sinister elegance, like a finial ornament on a Christmas tree. Then Nils was standing above me, holding down the spray of blossom with an earnest smile.

"I thought this would look nice in your hair," he said. I took it from him, but only lowered it into my skirt, smiling up at him as composedly as I could.

"That's a fine romantic gesture for a spring day," I said. "But I don't think the grounds crew would appreciate it."

"It comes out of our tuition. I think we have a right to at least one bouquet a year."

"Thank you. Do you know Beth Palmer?"

"Yes," he said. "Hello, Beth." He shifted his glance to her in a very perfunctory way, which added to the sense of panic that had begun to bubble up in me, like an Alka-Seltzer tablet dropped into a glass of water.

"Beth is going to England this summer. She's going to teach at Ruislip, in England, in the fall."

"Hey, that's great." He turned to her with sudden genuine enthusiasm. "I envy you. I'd rather go to London than anywhere in the world. You ought to live in Hampstead, if you can."

"Why?"

"Because Keats's cottage is there. I had a friend who lived in Hampstead, and he could walk down and visit it in about ten minutes, from his house. It's right on the edge of the Heath, I think. Imagine being able to walk down and visit Keats's cottage every day."

"You like Keats?"

"Yes. More than anybody."

"Sylvie does, too."

"I know. We had quite a talk about him one day. In fact, she knows as much about him as anybody I ever met."

"Well, that's something else about her I didn't know," Beth said. "In fact, I didn't even know you two had met. You're full of surprises, Sylvie." She leaned forward and picked the spray of blossom from my lap, sniffed it briefly, then dropped it deliberately, from a considerable height, into my skirt, so that the tips of the thorns pricked my thigh through the thin cotton like a shower of delicate sparks. "They don't have any odor, do they? I thought they did." She smiled at me serenely. "I'll tell you where *I* want to go, when I get there. Newgate Prison, where Moll Flanders got her start. I think a girl could learn even more about life in Newgate Prison."

"You ought to spend a few months there," I said. "Get to really know the place."

"I suppose I could, until I find somewhere to stay," Beth said. She made a point of being unperturbed. "They say housing's a terrible problem in London. That might be the perfect solution. What would I have to do, do you suppose, to get in?"

"Assault somebody, or rob them," Nils said. "Could you manage that?"

"Oh, I don't know," Beth said. "I was hoping it would be something simple, like fornication. I don't suppose I'd be the first woman who did that, for accommodation." She raised her eyes above my head and widened them suddenly with a look of huge concern. "Here comes Ronnie. And my God, he's wounded! Now what would account for *that?*"

I turned and saw Ronnie hobbling toward us down the path from Tydings Hall, stopping to raise his cane and wave it to us above the hedge. He had sprained his ankle a couple of days before in a tennis match and had taken the opportunity to dramatize his disability by digging up a gnarled-looking briar staff somewhere in an antique shop and carrying it about with him everywhere, like Stephen Dedalus with his ashplant.

Nils, whose eyes had rested gravely on mine since my last remark, turned his head with an abrupt suavity of motion, like the bending of a branch in a sudden gust of wind, and even through my vexation, I found I was delighted with the movement. He stood rolling the edge of the Frisbee against his thigh as he watched Ronnie approach, a gesture that seemed gently judicial, as his eyes did. Coming out of the cover of the hedge, Ronnie advanced on us, stumbling picturesquely.

"What's happened to you?" Beth cried.

"Not much. It's mostly affectation. Although I turned my ankle, playing tennis." He grinned and held out his cane to tousle my hair with the tip of it. "You look gorgeous. You look like a naiad. Where did you get that skirt?"

"It's been in the drawer," I said. "Waiting."

"For this very day."

"Yes."

"Women are surprising."

"Aren't they?" Beth said. "I just said the same thing. They have so much hidden in their drawers."

Ronnie turned to her, raising his eyebrows genially in a look of mock reproof; then stuck the cane under his arm like a swagger stick and held out his hand to Nils. "Patterson," he said. "Grenadier Guards."

Nils shook his hand, smiling. "I'm glad to know you. I'm Nils Larsen. You're doing a book on Emily Dickinson, aren't you?"

"I was," Ronnie said. "But I think I'm going to have to abandon it, or rewrite the whole thing, in the light of the last hour and a half. I have just had the most astounding theory proposed to me about Emily Dickinson by a feverish young lady in the second row. It's changed my entire conception of the woman. Do you know what the mystery of the Divine Spinster is? Of that passionate solitude in which she heard the voice of the 'King who does not speak'? In which she fed on 'that white Sustenance—Despair'? Do you know what produced phrases of that kind? Psoriasis. Absolutely, I mean it. That was the young lady's thesis, at any rate. That's what accounts for her seclusion, you see, the white dresses she always wore, the long sleeves and high collars. All those harrowed, unconsummated 'Calvaries of Love.' The heartbreak of psoriasis. Or impetigo, possibly. Some noxious skin disease, at any rate."

"She doesn't actually believe that?" I said.

"Absolutely. And she's worked out a system of clinical allusions from the texts. Dickinson was always calling herself 'spotted,' 'freckled,' 'flawed,' you know—things like that. All allusions to this awful skin condition of hers, apparently. I tell you, it was a revelatory hour and a half. Of course, the relationship between poetry and disease has been pointed out more than once, but psoriasis! Psoriasis as the source of 'those boundaries of pain, capacious as the sea.'"

"I don't think you're in any position to mock the idea," Beth said. "Standing right there in front of us with your limp and your cane—all those afflictions, to give you a dashing, poetic air."

"You're right, of course," Ron said. "I'll tell you what we ought to do: get out a whole new edition of standard authors. The Dermatological Series. *Petrarch and Pimples, The Eczema Theme in 'Vile Bodies,' Shingles in Shelley.* It's a gold mine."

"Nils has a passion for Keats," Beth went on smilingly. "I suppose it's the charm of tuberculosis, in that case. Of course, it doesn't take more than a mild case of sunburn to turn some people on."

"How would you like an affliction of your own, to make you a little more fetching?" I said. "A swollen lip, maybe?"

"No, thank you," Beth said. "I already have a badly bruised ego, and it doesn't seem to be doing a thing for me."

"Suffering doesn't suit some people," Nils said. "Emily Dickinson wore her rue with a difference. Like Sylvie."

Ronnie looked at him with real interest for the first time, and when Nils could no longer pretend indifference to the length of his gaze, he asked abruptly, "Are you interested in Dickinson, Nils?"

"Yes. There's a poem of hers I like especially. 'I Died for Beauty.' I wonder if you'd say it for us?"

"Very happy to oblige," Ronnie said. He stared off into the middle distance and began to recite in the strange braying elocutionary voice he always used when he was quoting:

> "*I died for beauty, but was scarce*
> *Adjusted in the tomb,*
> *When one who died for truth was lain*
> *In an adjoining room.*
>
> *He questioned softly why I failed?*
> *'For beauty,' I replied.*

'And I for truth—the two are one;
We brethren are,' he said."

He paused and closed his eyes, as if searching his memory. "There's another verse. I don't know if I remember it."

Nils waited a respectful moment, and when Ronnie either could not or would not—I had the feeling that he would not—complete the poem, he did so, speaking the last verse in a rich vibrant monotone, like the G string of a cello being bowed insistently:

> *"And so, as kinsmen met a-night,*
> *We talked between the rooms,*
> *Until the moss had reached our lips,*
> *And covered up our names."*

He smiled at me and said, "You see? The same music that Keats heard, blowing in the wind through Amherst. In spite of their afflictions. Isn't that amazing?"

"Yes," I said. "I suppose there were shrikes in Amherst."

"Just as many as on Hampstead Heath, I'm sure," Nils said. He tugged with a kind of impatient delight at the grass, ripping up a handful of blades with a tearing sound.

"What is this about shrikes?" Beth said.

"They're savage little things with bloody beaks and beady eyes," Nils said, looking up at her with remorseless casualness. He blew the grass blades out of his opened hand and watched them fall. I could hear Beth's anger come trilling out in her voice, almost thrillingly, like birdsong:

"Well, of course, Ronnie knows more about her than any of us, but it seems to me she had a *typically* Romantic temperament, if you'll forgive the term. Didn't she regard God as 'the Blond Assassin'? That should be a caution to you, Nils; as vulnerable as you are to sunburn."

"To all of us," Ronnie said. "There's very little cut-rate comfort to be found in Emily Dickinson." He frowned, giving a distressingly effortless impersonation of the Ponderous Exegete. "Now, let me see. She was laid to rest something like sixty-five years after Keats. I wonder if they *are* talking together down there, between their rooms, this very minute?"

"If they are," Beth said, "you can bet your boots it's not about Truth and Beauty. He's far more likely to be demanding what she was doing all that time. Just what was going on between her and the Vicar."

Ronnie laughed, an unpleasant, chortling laugh of collusion with this vulgarity that made me feel ashamed of him.

"And she is no doubt protesting that it was all perfectly platonic," he murmured, turning to me. "What do you think, Sylvie?" He would never have made that remark a year ago, I thought. Such is the power of love. Such is love's transformation.

"I don't think so," I said. "I'd like to think that love was conducted a little more gracefully; in the grave, at least."

"Well, we'll never know," he said. "We can only judge by how people behave when they've spent a few *years* side by side, let alone a few centuries." He laughed again and rapped briskly with his cane at the bottle I held between my feet on the grass. "What's that you're drinking? Your private stock of ginger ale?"

"Yes. But they've got wine inside. Shall I get you a glass? You'd better rest that ankle."

"You're a very good angel." He leaned toward me and clasped my wrist. I shook my hand free with sudden fury, because the gesture, which was supposed to convey comfort and concern and intimacy, seemed like an affront to me, as offensive as the fastening of a manacle around my wrist.

I got up and plunged across the yard to the open door of the classroom, picking my way hurriedly and with a sense both of flight and of disgust among the bright, animated figures on the sunny grass. I felt I never wanted to return. I don't enjoy that kind of flagrant, public competition for my affection or attention; I don't like the entirely accidental, biological eminence it gives women or the fatuous stirrings of vanity it provokes in them generally—and is designed to subjugate them to—and all that awful, arch gallantry that operates just below the surface of so much social intercourse and reduces it to not much more than intrigue. It seems to me sometimes that much of what most people think of as civilization is nothing but a kind of wily overture to sex, and perhaps the most insidious form of vanity there is. I've felt, all my life, a terrible indignation at the thought that anyone should assume he was entitled to contend for my favor just by virtue of existing, as it were, with no invitation to do so whatever; and that anything I might have given him, out of genuine affection, or gratitude, or largesse, or caprice, was his, eternally and exclusively and beyond redemption. Anyone who entertained that idea was a pretender —as all the men I'd known were, really—all of them equally absurd and ineligible, to something that was neither theirs to hold nor mine to give them truly; that I was really only the minister of. The vulgarity and presumption of their rivalry, whether it was as artful and inspired as Nils's or cast in the ironic or abject importunities of Ron, filled me suddenly with ire and contempt. I wanted to be rid of them all, of that circle of self-appointed martyrs to my independence and intelligence and aspiration—Beth, with her nasty, bitchy jealousy, included—each of them wearing his ambition and his vulnerability like badges of sensibility, of wounded, sanctimonious idolatry! I simply can't stand having people fall indiscriminately in love with me, or indiscriminately appointing themselves my victims—which is very much the same thing. I will not be responsible for the suffering of fools, of the recklessly ambitious or audacious, and I will not accommodate the suicidal impulses of the pathologically romantic. I'm leaving, I thought, as I pushed my way through the close-packed bodies around the entrance to the classroom; maybe forever. I'm not going back there and contribute to that awful, messy, maudlin scene. I'll go back to the apartment and pack my bags and get out. I'm not going to be pecked and haggled over by these jackdaws like a crust of bread that's been tossed in their midst by the gods or something.

You can judge my exasperation—or my desperation—by the fact that it included Nils as well, in spite of what he had made me feel when I first met him, and again on that afternoon. Or perhaps—and much more likely—*because* of what he made me feel. Because I think I believed that in his case it might not end as my affairs with boys always seemed to end: in disgust and indignant reassertion of my independence, and bitter regret for the shambles that I always seemed to find myself up to the knees in afterwards, all those shards of illusion like the million broken splinters of a mirror, the whole world gone shabby and desolate, strewn with litter like a dance hall in the morning, with crumpled paper hats and confetti all over the place and wizened balloons drifting like ghosts along the floor. I remember once, in the course of an M.L.A. convention, when I was in bed with a boy whose name I've forgotten in a hotel room in a city I think was Chicago, the thought occurred to me: It's like biting the lips of a ghost. Just as insubstantial as that, if you please; not even genuine blood involved; not even mine. (You know what is really weird? I didn't bleed even when I lost my virginity. I think it must have happened during one of my menstrual periods somehow, because it certainly didn't happen the first time I ever went to bed with a boy.) And yet I would feel these—pangs—I don't know what else to call them—when I met someone who was gentle and poetic and who had that luminous quality of mind that Nils had; or someone, on the contrary, who was huge and coarse, and possibly brutal and selfish as well. I don't know what it was. Maybe it was a kind of spasmodic clutching at the memory of my mother's passion for my father; of something dumb, invariable, and eternal that made her shriek night after night in his bed when he clasped her hips with his ragged hands, and stand watch for him night after night on a wild porch with a wet shawl around her head and her eyes blown apart like begonia blossoms in the wind. Or at the memory of my little brother, his face struck white by those same hands, standing with the absolutely dauntless resolution of his worship for that man while he was scourged for being gentle, for hating pain and violence. Or of Aaron, hobbling through life on his knees from bedside to bedside of the maimed, trying to cradle the whole world in his arms, crooning to it like the demented witness of a holocaust. Perhaps I've wanted to love like that all my life, as my mother and my brothers loved, and had never found anyone or anything that was worthy of it, never experienced anything that didn't resolve itself, in the end, to vanity.

Perhaps that's why I got along so well with Ronnie, and for such a long time: because there was none of that involved; no pangs; it was simply an arrangement that was benign and useful and that I had thought, in my innocence, would survive because there was nothing very complex or passionate to decay. Evidently, however, that was not going to survive either, because he was out there on the lawn being pained and ironic and importunate; and of course, the worst thing about it was that he had a right to be, in a way, because I had done that awful thing in the Italian Gardens: I had been frightened enough for a moment to let him believe that he had that right, that he had a claim on me that he deserved, that he had earned by his kindliness and patience and generosity, and by the very modesty of his passions. Well, when you've painted yourself into a corner like that, there's no way out of it. The only thing to do is to clench your jaws and stride out of the room, resigned to the fact that you're going to leave great gloppy footprints behind you wherever you go, for the rest of your life, a blazing, great, painted trail of a fugitive, leading right up to whatever door you hide yourself behind. It seemed to me at the moment that it was the only thing to do, however; that the urge to fly from a painful, undignified, insoluble situation was just about the soundest impulse that animals possess, and without a doubt responsible for the present existence of most species of that kingdom. I wish to God I'd had the resolution to do it. I wish to God I could reduce this whole story to some such statement as "I lived with this very nice guy for a while, but we broke up because he began to get jealous and to demand commitments of me that I couldn't make." Of course, I didn't; and I couldn't.

What I did was to work my way up to the serving table, snarling silently at everybody I bumped into, feeling suffocated in that hot overcrowded room by the smell of bodies, of sweat, of damp cotton clinging to bellies and breasts and buttocks, of moist hair and breath; sunken and drowning in it, as in the fetor that comes up from a swamp, a smell that it seemed to me must pervade the farthest corner of the universe, drifting among the stars like some awful carnal rumor out of space.

When I got to the table I looked down and saw this little round wedge of Gouda cheese covered with bright red wax, with a knife plunged into the center of it as if into a heart, and beside it a jug of red wine with a splinter of sunlight twinkling bitterly inside it, and I felt sick. I picked up the jug and tried to pour a paper cup full of the wine and my hands were shaking so that I splashed it all over the table top and the front of my dress. I barely made it to the door, where I had to stand and gulp the fresh air for a minute to keep myself from vomiting, before I started back across the lawn to where they were all sitting, now, in the lacy shadow of the oak. Ronnie looked up and said, "Oh, here she is," and held up his hand to take the cup from me; but I drew it away from him and dipped my fingertips into the wine and flicked them at him, sprinkling his hair and face with red beads. Then, with a snap of my wrist, I did the same to Beth and Nils, Beth ducking her head and yelping indignantly.

"What's this?" Ronnie cried. "A libation? Are we being sacrificed?"

"It's the sacre du printemps," I said. "You know how you love ceremony." He laughed and wiped his face with his shirt sleeve, but one red drop oozed down from the center of his forehead and sank into his left eyebrow as if into a sponge. His smile faded to a frown and he pointed at my breast. "My God, what have you done to your dress? You look as if you'd been gored." I handed him the cup, plucking with my fingertips at my blouse, which clung to my breasts stickily, making them tingle. "Are you all right? You look pale."

"Yes. It's just wine."

Beth dabbled at her hair with her fingertips, hissing bitterly. "Honestly, you're a *clod*, Sylvie," she muttered. "I just bought this blouse last week."

I sat down and looked up at the tree, where the shrike sat still, awaiting his victim with brutal, bleak-eyed patience.

"You sure you're all right?" Ron said again.

"Yes. I just felt faint for a minute, it was so stuffy in there."

He took a sip of wine and said uncertainly, "We were talking about the Romantic temperament. Nils feels the word is derogatory."

"It's come to be, in the popular sense," Nils said. "And anyway, it's inaccurate. Shelley's essays on prostitution, or child labor, for example, are models of logical, moral, formal, almost scientifically rigorous thought. They're supreme examples of the exercise of intelligence towards social problems which were typically treated, in his time, with prejudice, bigotry, selfish expeditiousness, hypocrisy of every kind, in the name of correct thinking, tradition, and Christian morality. How can such essays be called 'romantic,' either with a small or capital 'r,' by men who are meretricious, equivocal, or frivolous in their treatment of the same subjects? How can a man who disbelieves in God be condemned as fanciful or illogical by one who maintains that not only is there a God, but also a Son and a Holy Ghost, as well as a hierarchy of Archangels, Angels, Seraphim, Cherubim, and Saints, all residing in a Paradise composed of seven concentric circles of varying degrees of bliss, surrounded by an indeterminate area called Purgatory, where imperfect souls are allotted a certain specific amount of time in which to make themselves eligible for entry into the above; as well as a graduated conical funnel beneath them, composed of seven concentric circles of graduated horror where sinners are confined for eternity according to the degree of their transgression. Those who believed in all that were good, hardheaded realists, Tory constituents to a man; whereas Shelley, as I say, was willfully illogical, or, if you like, romantic." There was something odd about his voice. It was full of grief and nameless indignation that had nothing to do with what he was talking about. He seemed to be crying out for mercy more than justice. I closed my eyes as I listened to him and his voice seemed to grow fainter and fainter, as if he were receding—or I were—toward the back of some vast cavernous hall; as if I were walking away from the podium on which he stood lecturing, striding up an aisle that stretched off infinitely to the blazing, sunlit rear of the auditorium, between rows of seats crowded with the motionless skeletons of students who had sat listening for centuries, until the flesh has slid from their bodies, still raptly clenching dusty pencils in finger bones that were jarred by my footsteps and fell apart on the yellow pages of their notebooks. Outside the auditorium, melding into the drone of his voice as I flew faster and faster up the aisle, there was a rising sound of wind in the persimmon leaves and of footsteps running down a grassy hill, and Aaron calling from the beach, "Sylvie! Come on, hurry! The tide is coming in!" That was my vision, the only one I've ever had. I heard my own voice crying, "Oh, I want to go back where I belong! No one knows me here. This is a place of fools, impostors, living dead men!" I think I probably fainted for a minute, because there was a kind of spinning brilliance and everything converged to a point of impossible radiance that was the almost consummate agony of my desire to be a child again, and then I found that I was sitting with my eyes wide open, seeing nothing, blinded for a moment to everything but a limitless expanse of beach that opened out inside my mind, where I saw my footsteps preserved forever in the sand, moist and fresh and tiny-toed, wandering along the shore of an old brown gentle bay. Ronnie began shaking me idiotically by the knee as if trying to wake me up, saying, "Sylvia? Hey, you're in a trance! Why don't you join us?"

"Oh, leave me alone," I said. "I'm all right. Did you talk to Beth about London?"

"A bit."

"Well, don't you think we ought to go, Ron? I think it's going to rain."

All my fine romantic conceptions about the university had evaporated in the last half hour with Beth's innuendos, the general unpleasantness of the situation, that hideous bird up there in the tree, and the other assorted omens that had appeared as suddenly and perversely as the single, swollen, livid-looking cloud whose edge crept over us now, casting shadow on the lawn, and a quick chilly breeze that stirred the fronds of the willow oaks nervously.

"God, I think you're right," Beth said. She stood up, brushing her skirt, drained her paper cup of wine and crumpled it in her hand. "Ed and I are going to see that Russian film at the Biograph. Is anyone interested?" We murmured that we were not. "Well, thanks for the advice, Ron. Sylvie, I'll call you before I leave."

"Yes. So long, Beth." We stood up as she departed across the lawn between the buildings because already there were huge drops of rain striking us on our heads and shoulders and splattering on the walk like spent bullets.

"Hey, we're going to get wet," Ronnie said. He took me by the arm and led me at a swift walk past the quince hedge and along the path beside the mall, breaking into a run as the rain began to pelt down in a dense bright shower. We galloped up the steps of Tydings Hall and stood under the portico looking out between the columns at the steam rising from the hot stone of the steps and, out beyond the hedge, Nils, who had turned into the mall, running across the grass in the rain, peeling off his wet shirt as he ran and stopping to wave it to us joyfully, like a flag.

"He seems like a nice chap," Ronnie said. "Is he one of your students?"

"No. But he dropped in to one of my lectures one day with a friend, and we talked afterwards. He's interested in the Romantics."

"Evidently." He watched Nils vaulting across the mall like a brightly polished centaur, his sunburned shoulders glittering with rain. "He's quite a handsome guy."

"Are you jealous?" I said.

"Jealous? Oh, I don't think so." He stuck his hands into his pockets, thrusting his chest out and taking a deep breath of the damp air as if to fortify himself. "I think there's a difference between jealousy and the feeling that you've been treated with a certain—lack of candor—by someone you've never given reason to be dishonest with you. I mean, one is unfounded, isn't it? Just an excess of vanity. But the other is a quite palpable insult, it seems to me." I didn't answer him. "I think I deserve a little of that truth you recommend so highly. Don't you?"

"How much of it are you prepared to accept?" I said.

He took one of his hands out of his pocket and stood looking at the back of it, flexing the fingers twice before he replied. "Well, let's start with just a little of it. Have you been to bed with him?"

"My God, Ron, I've only spoken to him once before."

"Would you like to?"

"What a ridiculous thing to ask. Honestly."

"Still, I'm asking it."

"I don't know. Well, I suppose—in a fantasy way. What woman doesn't have fantasies about going to bed with handsome, intelligent, sensitive young men? But that doesn't mean I would."

"Oh? I thought perhaps it did. Why not?"

"Because I wouldn't want to be involved with him. I'm too busy, I have too much work to do. And I wouldn't want to offend you."

"What do you mean by 'offend me'?" he said. "Do you mean it would offend me to know the truth of your nature?"

"It might," I said. "I'm not sure; because I'm not sure what it is myself. It might offend me, even more." He stared at me silently. "I remember when I first discovered that I liked raw oysters. I was horrified."

"You're being flippant."

"No, I'm not. I mean it. Do you know anyone who wants to know the truth of his own nature, no matter how much he advertises his passion to 'discover his identity,' or any of the rest of that claptrap? Most people would be terrified if they had the vaguest intimation of it."

"You're different from most people."

"Not in that."

"Yes, in that," he said. "Especially in that. And it's my misfortune to love that in you, because I never knew anyone else who had that passion, ever. I agree with you: I didn't know it was even possible."

"You're wrong," I said. "I'd be as terrified as anyone."

"No, you're obsessed," he said, and looked at me wonderingly. "You really are, Sylvia." After a minute, without having lowered his gaze, he asked, "Do you love me at all?"

"As much as I can. As much as I've ever loved anyone, except my family."

"Do you want me to love you?"

"Not if it hurts you."

"Do you want anyone to love you?"

"I don't know, Ron. I really don't. I can't tell you."

"But not me, at any rate." He sighed profoundly through his nostrils, a noise like a weary horse, and put the hand which had hung clenched against his hip back into his pocket, like a weapon he had decided against the use of. "Well, of course, there isn't really anything I can do about it, anyway," he said. "Not anymore."

I looked away toward the hedge where the shrike sat now—I was sure, although I couldn't see him—hunched and dripping, over the tiny twitching body of the baby mole, disemboweling it with murderous, innocent zeal.

"Ronnie," I said, "do you remember that conversation we had just before I moved in with you? The day we went on the canal?"

"I'm not sure," he said after a moment. "After all, it was quite a long time ago, wasn't it? Quite a lot has happened since then. Or so I thought."

I looked at him, a bit surreptitiously; measuring him, I suppose: his fortitude, his basic capacity for survival. Taking his true height, to put it cruelly
—as you do at such moments with people whose behavior in a crisis, you realize
suddenly, is quite unknown to you. And the evidence of that furtive moment
appeared to outweigh that of the previous two years, because whatever I saw
made me conclude, with very unreasonable surprise: I'm married to this man
already, whether I call it that or not. We're probably more married than a lot
of conventionally wedded couples are; and the fact that I don't call it that is
not so much evidence of my honesty as of my naïveté.

"I wonder, sometimes, if you want to go," he said.

"Sometimes, for a minute or two. Or an hour. But I won't."

"Why not?"

"I don't think I can."

"What do you mean by that?"

"I need you. You keep me sane. You've given me more than anyone else
ever did, and I don't think I could get along without it. I'm sorry if I haven't
given you as much."

"I don't deserve you," he said suddenly and harshly, as if the words had
been tearing at his throat for months, for years. "People shouldn't—" He
dropped his head and stared down at the smoking steps simmering like brim-
stone. "What's that thing of Yeats's?" He quoted the verse with such simple
and moving eloquence—without a trace of the usual magnificence, for once
—that I wanted to lay my hand on his arm, but I was afraid to multiply his
pain.

> *"The folly that man does*
> *Or must suffer if he woos*
> *A proud woman not kindred of his soul."*

The words seemed to echo between us, ringing off the columns of the rainy
portico. We stood in a kind of despair.

"Do you *want* me to go?" I asked.

He shook his head. "I couldn't bear it."

"Because if you want me to, I will."

"And what would happen to both of us then?"

"I don't know."

Far across the campus, Nils was almost indistinguishable now, running
toward the McKeldin Library at the west end of the mall. He stopped just in
front of the great bronze terrapin that sat with its bleak reptilian head raised
in a kind of emblematic aboriginal majesty on the granite pedestal in front of

the portico; there he turned and looked back at us for a moment, before disappearing up the steps between the columns.

"You're sure about this boy?" Ronnie said. "That you wouldn't like to have an affair with him?"

"I told you, Ron," I murmured.

"Because, if you would, I almost think I could get used to the idea, you know; if I had to." He chuckled, a little wildly, and then added with the solemnity, almost, of a pledge, "I think I could even dig someone up from the grave for you if you wanted him badly enough, like your John Keats."

"Don't say things like that," I said a little breathlessly.

"Oh, it might even become a passion, I suppose—procuring for a woman. From the ranks of the dead, even. That's the nature of perversion, isn't it? Developing a passion for something that's basically incongruous and repellent. I mean, when there's nothing you can do about it, anyway, you might as well learn to like it."

"I don't want to humiliate you, ever," I said.

"I know you don't." He drew another deep breath of the rainy air. "Well, maybe we can think of something else." He looked out across the mall. "Who was Yeats talking about in that poem, anyway? Maude Gonne?"

"I think so. At least you can be thankful you don't have her to contend with."

"I don't know. Do you think he would have been? I have an idea that he might have regretted it, whatever it cost him to know her. Still, he was a very dignified man, wasn't he? Only poet I know of who wore a pince-nez."

The shower had subsided to a soft incessant sprinkle and the sky had darkened to a pale disordered pewter that hung over the row of colonnades along the mall like a ragged canopy.

"It looks as if it's going to keep up all afternoon," Ron said. "Shall we strike out?"

"I think we'd better."

We went down the steps and along the walk under the dripping willow oaks. Where there was a wide puddle on the walk, he took my hand and helped me to leap across. When I had done so, he kept my hand in his, held as lightly as one would hold a flower to keep from crushing it.

"There's not much in the house for dinner," he said. "Shall we eat out?"

"Oh, I don't think so. I'd like to eat at home tonight."

"O.K. What would you like?"

"Let's just have a fruit salad. The Granny Smith apples are in now."

"Great. Listen, there's a thing on Channel 26 tonight about Malcolm Lowry. Why don't we take the night off and watch it?"

"I've got to read *Perkin Warbeck.* That awful play."

"I can tell you everything you need to know about it in fifteen minutes. Then we'll watch the Lowry thing."

"All right. And drink mocha."

"That's the idea," he said. "Mocha and cinnamon toast at midnight. A bacchanal."

That was what we did, and I took a great sheltered sense of comfort in it, like someone coming in from a storm to hot chocolate and an open fire. After the Lowry film we sat on the rug in front of the coffee table and dunked our cinnamon toast, talking about the magnificent scenes of Mexico, where he had written *Under the Volcano.*

"Listen, how much money do you have?" I said.

"Money? More than I can count. Why, what do you want?"

"No, really. How much?"

"I don't know. Three thousand dollars, I suppose. Something close to that."

"And I've got almost two thousand that I've saved since I moved in with you. What are we saving it for, anyway?"

"Well, there's a piece of metal sculpture in a gallery downtown that I'd love to have; but I suppose it'll really go into a secondhand car, or a down payment on this apartment when the place goes condominium. What about you?"

"Oh, I don't know. Something for Momma, or Jamed, I guess. I've been trying to talk her into an air conditioner for years, but I know she'd never use it."

"Well, my God, Sylvie, you send her half your salary already. And you're always buying things for Jamed. You deserve something for yourself once in a while."

I munched my toast for a moment. "All right, then; why don't we take part of it and go to Mexico this summer?"

"Mexico?" He stared at me and frowned, then raised his eyebrows very high and tilted his head thoughtfully.

"Yes. It's much simpler than Europe. We could drive down. And in the summer it's cheap. We could spend a couple of months down there. God, I need to get away from this place. I've been on this campus for years now, without a break. And so have you. I think it would be marvelous."

"By God, you may be right," he said. "Puerto Vallarta. Guanajuato. Tacos." He frowned and shook his head.

"No, really, I mean it. We'd have a marvelous time. We could drive from Yucatán to the Pacific. Just get away from everything: U.S. 1, the Italian Gardens, Howard Johnsons, Dr. Middlemeyer. Everything."

"And everybody. You may be right, you know. I've always wanted to take a picture of you sitting right on top of the Pyramid of the Sun. That would be worth the trip alone."

"Well, why don't we do it?" I reached out to take his hand and tugged at it with a sudden feverish urgency that stilled his features. "It would be something we had together, Ron. That we could keep."

"Do you think so? I'd like that. I think you're right, Sylvia. It's really a great idea." He set his cup on the table and leaned forward to take my head in his hands and kiss me on the forehead.

I'm not a man who has had very many emotional crises in my life—although perhaps my life itself could be called one long, languid crisis. There have been one or two, however, of such terrible extravagance that they make up in drama what they lack in numbers—if such a happy rarity can be called a lack. One of these was my frenzied suit of Molly, that unaccountable passion I felt for her on the disastrous September evening I've described to you. It lasted, I suppose, a month or so; and then it waned and disappeared, forever. When, six weeks after that evening, she announced that she was pregnant, I received the news, and offered her my hand in marriage, with an impassivity that would have astonished anyone who had witnessed the two events. It may have been testimony to my rectitude, but absolutely none to my credentials as a spouse. I was surprised myself that a woman could accept such a spiritless proposal. I do remember that she asked if I loved her, and that I said I did, with misgivings that were overcome by my desire to dignify the madness of my behavior on that night, and to preserve my conception of myself as not only honorable but sane. That unbridled passion had been, no doubt, an excess of love—a possibility to which the whole history of romance, from *Aucassin and Nicolette* to *Lost Horizon*, testified—about which I knew far too little to dispute the hypothesis. That it never reappeared, or was resumed only sporadically or perfunctorily enough to satisfy the meanest definition of connubiality, I didn't consider a contradiction, or a crisis. I don't suppose I dared. I suppose I chose to consider it another of nature's numberless phenomena, no more aberrant than my profligate seduction of her had been. When circumstances —her brooding silences, her baffled, questioning, often piteously, distastefully importunate eyes—obliged me to examine the situation, I did so with the objectivity and logic I applied to all the natural phenomena I investigated in my laboratory. I think my conclusions went something like this:

The male of the human species is by nature unpredictable, fickle, not to say promiscuous in his sexual behavior. His attention to any one woman is necessarily and by design short-lived, and succeeded almost immediately, and profitably, by his interest in another, in order to promote production of the maximum amount of progeny of which he is capable, in accordance with nature's firm intentions. In her anxiety to ensure the survival of the species—and thus provide a constant supply of food for some other species—she has ordained that he shall fertilize as many females of his kind as possible, that his interest in any one of them shall be neither exclusive nor interminable. All this is just and good; and if marriage, which lies entirely outside the interests or requirements of nature, suffers in consequence, it is a matter of absolute indifference to the grave and orderly processes of the universe—processes which, if they had not prevailed from the beginning, would have evolved no such creature as man to challenge them with his capricious, oddly perverse institutions.

All of which might have done much to reassure a libertine, but seemed to offer very little in the way of comfort to me, whose libido, apparently, was exhausted not only by a single woman but by a single such event—or by so few more, and of such rapidly diminishing enthusiasm, that they were hardly worth the counting. The fact was that in spite of nature's machinations to the contrary, there were a great many long and happy marriages—which were also disconcertingly prolific; it was difficult to regard them all as anomalous. Exceptional, perhaps; and progressively so as mankind became increasingly aware of the economic and ecological consequences of overpopulation. After all, the mean birthrate among educated, middle-class people was something like 2.2 children per couple. A very modest rate of propagation, which was not yet entirely beyond my reach. That its modesty might be due to contraception rather than to apathy I hardly paused to consider, since reliable data were not yet available. Considering such evidence as was available, my experience was probably very close to universal. That any very much more impassioned marital state existed, or was common, was merely the hyperbole of romantic legend, smilingly—and perhaps a tiny bit cynically—propagated by state and church alike in the interests of order. Which was perhaps not quite so cynical a deception as it might seem: order was after all the first concern of the responsible citizen. Marriage must and should settle into the measured, sober serenity that made all things possible, that was the very bedrock of society. (There was something about the look in Molly's eyes that made me a bit uneasy about my use of such terms as "order," "serenity," "sobriety," etc.; but I hurried on, in the best forensic fashion.) This estimable serenity was not only the natural, inevitable, indispensable, but the supremely productive, condition of matrimony. That its onset was a bit premature in my case was no doubt due to the circumspection of the disciplined and inherently discerning mind. A lifetime of undiluted ecstasy? Not if you pleased. Judging by the three weeks' worth of it I had enjoyed after meeting Molly, I would sooner have spent the rest of my days in the throes of a grand mal epileptic seizure. Life was largely interlude, as it should be; the insistence upon epiphany was a disorder of youth and of the poetically deranged mind. An allotment of one epiphany per lifetime was all the reasonable and prudent man should expect or demand. Indeed, it was munificent: anything like a nightly recurrence of the events of that autumn evening off Wisconsin Avenue would have rendered me hors de combat in very short order, driveling among splintered racks of test tubes and madly bubbling retorts, as the original instance of them very nearly had. If I had failed in anything, it was in being perhaps a bit overscrupulous in my regard for the demands of civilization.

I was pleased with this analysis. It was exhaustive, succinct, and salutary. If I still had a few niggling reservations (those words "serenity," "order"), the demands of my dignity and my respect for the powers of deductive thought were great enough to dispel them. With much less at stake than faith in my virility, I was a gifted enough polemicist; in the present case, I swept myself away. I managed to absolve myself almost entirely of whatever guilt or consternation I felt at the fact that three weeks after our marriage I was able to watch my wife peel off a pair of silk stockings or musingly apply cologne to her bare breasts—those same enchanting, ruby-nippled breasts!—with an indifference bordering on disapproval, on reproach for her immodesty.

I remember thinking it possible, as well, that I had somehow transmuted a portion—a very considerable portion, evidently—of my tardily awakened carnal energy into a heightened, sublimated passion for my work. Considering the nature of that carnal energy, as I've described it to you, the idea may seem just as specious as any other part of my apology, but it was an appealing one to a man in my position, and certainly supported by the facts. Because I began, with startling immediacy, to plunge myself into my studies, my experiments, my duties at the hospital, all my professional interests and obligations, with a fervor that, even for me, was phenomenal. It began, grotesquely, almost uncivilly, on the very day of our wedding; after which ceremony, performed with icy bureaucratic brevity in a registry office in downtown Washington, I escorted Molly home in a streetcar in pensive, inauspicious silence, took off the mustard-colored suit of my infamy, and within thirty minutes had boarded a second streetcar, bound for my laboratory, through an autumn morning of limpid beauty that stirred me not at all. I was evidently a man far more moved by the mysteries of nature than by her largesse.

I remember Molly saying as I came out of the bedroom in my working clothes, "You're not going back to the hospital this afternoon?"

"Oh, I've got to, I'm on duty until eight. I took the morning off, as it is."

"Can't somebody substitute for you?"

"There isn't anybody. Residents are scarce. And there's a very interesting case I've been involved in from the start. Lupus. You don't get the opportunity to see much of it." Her eyebrows writhed with disappointment. I took her by the shoulders and kissed her on the cheek. "But I'll tell you what we'll do: we'll rent a car and drive down to Williamsburg this weekend, if the weather holds. That's just about all we can afford, right now, in terms of time or money. We'll have the rest of our honeymoon when I graduate. Isn't that what I promised?"

"All right. But don't be late, Carl. I'm going to have roast veal for dinner, just like we did when—well, you know—when we met."

"Oh, yes. Yes. Fine."

On that same morning, I had moved into her apartment, bringing with me in a footlocker strapped onto the roof of a taxicab all my worldly goods; we had decided that the most prudent, economical—indeed, the only possible— thing to do, considering my present circumstances, was to consolidate our lives and fortunes under that grim Victorian ceiling, among the potted flora and mahogany monoliths of Grandma Gannon's legacy. Every morning I departed it at dawn, arriving at the hospital at eight o'clock, where for the next twelve hours I was gratefully, obliviously immersed in the enchantments of mephitic kidneys, ruptured spleens, encysted ovaries, contaminated blood and urine, morbid tissue, fever, disrupted metabolisms. When I came back at dusk or after, Molly, who would have arrived considerably before me, would serve me up, with growing solemnity and reticence as the days went by, her veal cro-quettes or chicken fricassees or stuffed peppers or, on particularly poignant occasions, her roasted veal, and I would appreciatively, murmurously devour it while I entertained her with accounts of the progress of an especially stub-born case of encephalitis or the latest statistics on the incidence of gout. Or while she described to me with hopeful, humble uncertainty as to their charm the details of her day's adventures at the Department of Commerce, where she worked as a stenographer, or her noontime excursion to the library, or the condition of the philodendron on the windowsill or the *Monstera deliciosa* on the radiator. Already, within a month of our marriage, there had developed between us and all around us in that vast cavernous arboretum we inhabited a miasmal, vapid, verdurous gloom, like that of a tropical rain forest, and almost as enervating in its effects. It was heavy and humid and fitfully illuminated by little lightning flashes of attempted gaiety, of the desperate pretense of enthusi-asm or contentment, or a desperate, strangled effort at communication or of longing, like the cry of a bird in the depths of jungle mist; and, occasionally, the startling hiss of a poisoned blow dart whistling through the foliage. Even in those first months there were such sounds; infrequent and usually, by mutual consent and mercy, unremarked; but unmistakable. Sudden, involuntary, expletive expressions of impatience, unwitting ironies, spontaneous, sharp insinuations of inadequacy, cruelty, deception; all followed, in those days, by instant agonized contrition, regretful, supplicating looks, quick little effusive demonstrations of affection, respect, the promise of patient understanding. The atmosphere was charged with a sense of bewilderment which no one was able to define or willing to acknowledge, a sometimes almost sordid embarrassment.

I don't mean that this situation was without respite, thank God. There were diversions and excursions, such as our trip to Williamsburg, a notable and providential success, since the weather was fine, the city, with its charm and historical significance, of equal interest to us both, the hotel accommodations inexpensive and surprisingly agreeable, and especially because Molly, who was the only one of us who could drive, did so, and assumed in the exercise of that faculty a faint but positive distinction, the possession of a skill I did not have, which put me at her disposal in however subtle a degree, and which seemed modestly miraculous to me, like her ability to perform somewhat stiff-fingered, oppressively cadenced but competent renditions of Bach on her grandmother's monstrous old upright piano. I admire skill of any kind, especially one I do not have. However mechanical, however merely kinetic it may be, it is the product of training, diligence, hours of patient, arduous application, the imposition of form on fearfully vacuous time and matter. I liked to sit beside her while she drove, watching her minute, mindlessly reflexive but critically delicate adjustments of the wheel, any one of them the difference between life and death for us; and on the piano bench beside her, watching her hands while she played in her ponderous, percussive, movingly resolute way. At those moments I felt a strange, almost grief-stricken admiration for her, for her humble virtuosity and the aspiration in her, glorious beyond the reach of her facility; and if I murmured, "You drive very well," or "You played that part very nicely," I would sense something in her gather and well up as I used to sense the upwelling of water when I was priming the pump at the summer house in Maine, and then would feel an almost palpable outpouring of emotion from her, of felicity and grace, cool and plentiful and clement as well water. And knowing that this was beautiful, that I might have drunk and bathed in and been refreshed by it, I felt only an ignoble resentment and regret that I could not do so; I could not accept it; something in me disparaged it remorselessly. She did not appear to understand that this was not what I desired of her, this sweet, sane plenitude; nor was it that I desired her to be more physically beautiful; because, in Karen's case, for example, it had been her physical beauty that I could not accept, that I could be moved by only in the callow, clandestine way of the voyeur, the connoisseur, who cannot consecrate himself to what he finds beautiful by service and sacrifice and long devotion and by the submission of his vanity to it, but which he can only surreptitiously, inconsolably admire. Perhaps the state I longed to spy her in was some stark nudity of spirit, some immodesty more genuine and startling than the simple womanly baring of her breasts—which was grace, was magnanimity itself.

On Sunday afternoons we would often walk along Wisconsin Avenue to the Cathedral (I admire Gothic architecture; all other seems frivolous, insubstantial, and impermanent to me) and we would wander about the grounds among the huge cut blocks of stone, freshly delivered from the masons and runically inscribed with small red-painted numbers, that lay in ordered rows, with dandelions sprouting between them, waiting to be fitted into the unfinished walls. It was the only remotely ceremonious thing we did together, and perhaps in the augury of that fact and of those mellow afternoons, she could be almost winsome, leaping from one great polished slab of granite to another, or spreading a tablecloth on one of them and opening a paper bag to set out in the sunlight sandwiches and plastic coffee cups. A Renoir would have immortalized her, very likely. I had no such impulse; not even in those momentary glimpses that I had of her beauty, or in the momentary efflorescence of it. What I might once have hungered to depict in her was evidently veiled forever in that shroud of embarrassment and grief by which we were appalled; or perhaps had been extinguished or uncannily transformed by some strangely sacramental act in which I had participated almost without my knowing it. I think I understood in some dim way that while I had bewildered her by my desire, I had, as well, delivered her from it, had put her beyond the reach of it forever; and this was part of my resentment, my disparagement, my renunciation of her.

An equally curious paradox—so curious that it discouraged exploration—was that the imperfections I had originally found so enchanting—her weird laxity of jaw and afflicted diction, her tastelessness in dress, her aridity of conversation, her almost hilariously extravagant manner of applying makeup —now produced in me a distaste that was equally intense. Although the photograph of Robert T. Aldington had disappeared even before my absorption into the household, it was survived, or possibly succeeded, by other oddities, banalities, vulgarities which I could not have guessed at. She used cologne in quantities and of an odor that were bizarre; she bought magazines called *True Romance* and read tediously lurid Gothic novels by the bushel, most of them in paperback editions whose covers were illustrated with moonlit Cornish mansions from which a girl with flying hip-length hair, generally barefoot and clad only in a nightgown, fled down a manorial lawn toward a grove of willows where a figure in a black cape, mounted on a white horse, waited statuesquely in the shadows. (That she felt some compunctions about her taste in literature was attested by the fact that she would bring these books home tucked stealthily into the recesses of her grocery bags, and that if I entered the room unexpectedly she would often slide one of them hastily behind the sofa cushions.) She bought cheap, sad costume jewelry, little garish earrings, bracelets set with glued-in, partially missing brilliants, brooches of a despondent yellow luster, which she kept in an overflowing treasure chest of soiled quilted satin over which she pored by the hour, stirring the livid, artificial stones and tangled, tarnished chains with her fingertips in a kind of hopeless rapture.

There was a numberless assortment of objects around the apartment commemorating places and occasions better left forgotten; a plaster fish of vile proportions set rampant on a pedestal inscribed TARPON SPRINGS, a gilded bust of Franklin Roosevelt, his cigarette holder snapped off, cast for his inauguration, souvenirs of Ocean City, Scranton, Hackensack. Gradually these things disappeared, one by one, as my disapproval of them became evident. I thought for years—until her death, in fact—that they had been obediently consigned to the garbage bin or the incinerator, but after her funeral I found them all, augmented by relics of our years together, in trunk trays, cardboard cartons, shoe boxes, become almost intolerable in their wracking, gimcrack eloquence. This passion of hers for souvenirs was almost a madness, a tragic, desperate obsession beyond her control or understanding. She could not walk with me to the drugstore without pausing to snatch up a dandelion to take home and press; her purse bulged with match covers, cubes of sugar, wrinkled red balloons, and candy-apple sticks from Glen Echo, theater tickets—even (as truly as I speak to you!) the shoelaces from a pair of sneakers I wore on a trip we took once to the Skyline Drive. It was as if she felt life slipping away from her with its ruthless, terrible volatility and swiftness, its moments flying past as the twinkling, pied, rhapsodic world flies past the rider of a spinning carousel, its lights and sounds and the laughing faces of friends and lovers only half perceived before they have sped by forever; and she wished to snatch something out of it as the rider of a whirling, painted pony snatches at a brass ring in its flight, trying desperately to seize and hold a bright fragment of that fleeing world forever. But in spite of what I took to be the pathos of this instinct, I felt an aversion for it even greater than I did for her cologne and costume jewelry and romantic novels. It was not only morbid but exasperating—and sometimes dangerous—to be confronted in the course of a stroll through Rock Creek Park with her request to climb that tree and fetch down that abandoned bird's nest; or, of a picnic, to take off my shoes and socks and wade out through the slippery rocks to retrieve the cork, bobbling in the foam, that I had witlessly tossed away a moment earlier. Or to see her secretively fold up and store away my paper napkin, or expired library card, my letters, grocery lists, hotel receipts —my shoelaces, for God's sake (and perhaps, who knew, my bath water and toenail clippings as well)—all seized and stored away to salve her desperate nostalgia, bottled and beribboned and bound in twine like totems, ugly little mummified mementos of our mortality. They reminded me of bits of excised kidneys or lung tissue in formaldehyde.

When I expressed this exasperation, she would fall silent for a moment and stare at the backs of her hands or furtively pleat the front of her blouse with her fingertips, and then perhaps look up with a quick supplicating glance, like a scolded dog, and say something so humble or bemusingly ambiguous— "Maybe if I varnished it, you'd see," or "It would only be this one; I wouldn't want any more"—that I would have, scowlingly, mumblingly, to concede to her. (Later, my concessions became fewer, more graceless and impatient; and her suppliant glances, level stolid looks of resignation.)

The most egregious manifestation of this mania of hers for souvenirs was an absolutely ungovernable passion for photography—or snapshottery, I should call it; there was certainly nothing like aesthetics involved. She carried an old-fashioned box camera, everywhere and always. When I see Molly now, in my mind, that camera is a part of the image, swinging from her wrist by a black leather thong, like an iron weight manacled to a prisoner. It seemed terrible to me, a symbol of the penal solitude of her existence, of her bondage to those phantasmal moments of imagined joy or illusory, or barely glimpsed, or cruelly promised happiness to which the hundreds of thousands of snapshots that she took bore such desperate, spurious, artless testimony: scenes slightly out of focus, murkily underexposed, or washed by too much light almost into extinction, as if bleached by the glare of her yearning beyond recognition; nothing clearly beheld or cannily composed; nothing salient or surpassing captured in attitude or event; faces blurred as if seen spinning by from a carousel, grinning agonizedly, or agape with dismay or cretinous delight, or bearing imposed upon them pale, ghostly succubi; many were invaded by great cancerous blobs of brown, like a lichenous mold, creeping over housefronts, descending upon unwary picnickers, dripping from the ceiling like some awful emanation, threatening or defiling almost every occasion of her life, every place she inhabited, everyone she knew. And there were blood-curdling cutenesses: dogs engaged in various indecencies, or sitting abjectly with Christmas bows tied around their necks or pirate patches over one eye; or Elizabeth, our baby daughter, ecstatically gnawing a very phallic-looking cucumber, or sitting on a potty with her face seductively concealed behind a fan, or of myself, stitching up her disemboweled teddy bear with a gigantic knitting needle and a length of yarn, or emerging from the bathroom with a towel clutched to my loins in startled, furious embarrassment, or standing on a ladder beside a Christmas tree, impatiently attempting to repair a tattered fairy with badly damaged wings and a tinsel halo that had slipped down like a blindfold across her eyes;

all travesties of joy, of a legendary peace and love and plenty of which they were such painfully invalid evidence. But there was truth in them, if not the beauty she longed to perpetuate; which may be why, after her death, I saved them; why I flung them into the footlocker I had bought for the purpose in shabby armfuls, in scores of dusty albums, or curled up in wan decrepitude in shoe boxes, or bursting free of their bonds of rotted rubber bands to spill out in a shower of irrepressible ironies and mockeries and parodies across the floor.

I thank God she was not religious, at least not in any rigorous, ceremonial way. She was nominally Lutheran, I think, but we went to church very rarely, and for theatrical rather than spiritual purposes, and she did not seem to regret at all the fact that in our haste to marry we had forgone a church wedding. But she had a solemn, pietistic strain in her nature that I suppose was the result of her midwestern heritage (she had spent her youth in Grand Island, Nebraska) and of her grandmother's influence. It expressed itself in comfortable, often memorably acrid, folkloric adages and platitudes and grave endorsements of loyalty, honesty, trustworthiness, and all the other verities and virtues of which the Boy Scout Creed is such a convenient compendium. When we listened to news broadcasts on the old Atwater-Kent radio that was a part of her inheritance—as we did with growing frequency, at mealtimes and on those evenings that we spent together—she would issue occasional solemn interpolations to the day's events in a tone of voice that seemed not so much to express the fervor of any very principled or animated moral attitude as a dour disappointment with human nature and the world's behavior in general, mordant reminders that hard work never hurt anybody, that dancing in the kitchen meant fallen dough, that honesty was the best policy, that you could get used to hanging if you hung long enough. But I don't think any of their lugubrious sentiments really mattered to her; they were a lore, a tribal literature, like fairy tales or country proverbs, that she recited as tonelessly, predictably, and often as confusedly and irrelevantly as a child recites the catechism or the few remembered verses of "Hiawatha," or "Red Rover," or the Pledge of Allegiance to the flag. Often I had the uncomfortable impression that they were directed obliquely at myself, either as prescriptions or reproach or perhaps as examples of the consolations of philosophy to which I had somehow driven her for refuge. I had the feeling that she would have forsworn them all instantly and on the spot if I had proposed our abdication to Tahiti, or a bottle of wine by firelight. But occasionally she could make use of them with a startling, scriptural incisiveness that was chastening in its aptitude, its revelation of the vision and rough art of some beleaguered ancestor, whose travail she seemed to appreciate, in those moments, with equally unsettling insight. Once, when Elizabeth cried out in petulant frustration that she could *not* solve a problem in arithmetic, I heard Molly offer the soft, stoic counsel: "Well, try again, honey. You'll get it before you get married; if you're smart at all." It took me years to unriddle the implications of that laconic phrase. When I read to her one morning from the newspaper President Truman's injunction to get out of the kitchen if you couldn't stand the heat, she murmured, with a vernacular eloquence equal to his own, "Well, there's more truth than poetry in *that.*"

Our lives were as simple and frugal as our conversations. Molly went on working for a time as a government stenographer, and I was ever more immersed in my duties at the hospital. If I were on a day shift, and our working hours coincided, we would share one of the enormous breakfasts that were as firm a fixture of her moral universe as punctuality or industry, exchanging bits of information from our respective sections of the newspaper—selected with growing discretion on my part—discussing my preferences for dinner, or the possibility—increasingly eminent—of my being late for it, expressing our concern or confidence about the weather; and, having cleared away the dishes, would walk down to Wisconsin Avenue together and board a streetcar for a thirty-minute ride of stuporous constraint whose most adventurous remark might be the observation that the traffic was very heavy that morning. She debarked a few blocks before I did, murmuring goodbye in a hasty, curiously apprehensive way, as if she anticipated her almost invariable buffeting by the accordion-action door and her flustered, red-throated descent to the pavement. More often, I would have night duty, and leave the apartment at five or six in the evening, not long before her re-arrival at it. I would make myself a cup of tea and a piece of buttered toast, feeling a strange sense of prosperity, of mute, buoyant elation at the silence of the place, the freedom from accountability with which I boiled my egg, and from the obligation of making cautious, dutiful conversation, rejoicing in the blissful resumption of the solitude to which I was incorrigibly accustomed. On those days I would eat dinner at the hospital cafeteria after I had finished my night duty, in the early hours of the morning, and arrive back at the apartment just after her departure from it, sinking with a vast sense of thanksgiving into the blessed privacy of a fresh-made, vacant bed.

On Sundays we would stroll to the Cathedral or to Rock Creek Park, or on the rare occasions when our budget permitted it, we might go to a concert at Constitution Hall, to which she would sit and listen with the same evident enchantment as that with which she stirred her artificial gems or read her Gothic novels. I could forgive her furtive slipping of the program into her pocketbook for the look of genuine serenity, of grateful transport that possessed her for an hour, stilling her features with an ardent, shy receptivity as she listened to Rubinstein or Rachmaninoff, almost as if she were being courted by the man—perhaps because I considered it respectably induced and could allow myself respectably to approve of it. It was the quality about Molly that so plaguingly and reprovingly redeemed her most unprepossessing traits—and was probably responsible for some of them—that immediate, innocent response to whatever was gallant, generous, spirited, or picturesque—whether or not it was commensurately skillful. And along with my covert admiration for her, born of such an evening, that would last an hour or a day, I would feel something inexplicably like resentment, or indignation, or even envy, at that capacity in her. It invaded, and diluted, and perhaps contaminated whatever physical passion I might momentarily feel for her when we returned to the apartment—it certainly abbreviated it—so that we would turn aside and lie in a kind of haunted epilogue to our luckless grasp at glory, staring up into the murky depths above the bed while I heard the magical opening bars of Grieg's Piano Concerto in A Minor sprinkling out into the darkness with a ceaseless, harrowing insistence—DUM dee dee DUM DUM / DUM dee dee DUM—the phrases, one of five, and then one of four, clear notes, separated by a rest as poignant as a sigh, spilling through the silence like jewels from a shattered coronet; or great crystal raindrops after a summer shower, dripping from wet leaves; or the separate, ecstatic stages—at each one the petals extended another quivering fraction of an inch—of the opening of a rose; or footsteps stumbling in awe and exhaustion up the last nine steps of a flight of silver stairs; or a volley of arrows embedded, one by one, into the shuddering breast of a deer at bay; or the final nine convulsions of a dying heart. Or like the fingertips of a lover tapping at a windowpane some coded, urgent invitation to fulfillment, to amnesty.

In spite of everything that happened there, what I remember immediately and always about Mexico is its landscape: the aching, ecstatic emptiness of those deserts and sierras, those awful silent expanses over which the clouds stand motionless, pitilessly pure in the vacant, blue, phantasmal sky. The broken cairns and sheer, uplifted stelae that stand lividly acute, arrant, totally explicit against the depthless indigo of space. The mounds of stony rubble where a column of rock has fallen and lies shattered, the measurelessly stretching, jagged ranges that ravage the horizon, that wander across leagues of barren plain ravined with dusty, leached arroyos, spread out at the feet of ruinous, ashen hills. A loneliness as utter as this is consecrated. The heart quails before it, not as before an icon, in the reverence of communion, but in the spell of some enthralling disenchantment. These are not icons, these tumbled cromlechs and brutal buttes and starkly towering megaliths; they invoke nothing, sacred or profane. There is nothing beyond them, no truth concealed or symbolized; nothing pervades them or is occulted in their burning stones and shadows. This desolate, fervid place is the symbol only of itself; of nothing else, neither heaven nor hell; nor is it the abode of any supernatural being—god or demon. There is nothing called good or evil being perpetrated here, there is only the bitterly earnest exercise of faculty. Nothing is supernal to this burning, vivid, base, but somehow hallowed reality. And life here, of whatever kind—the scurrying armadillos or bleakly gazing lizards or silent, spiring cactuses—is as phenomenal and as inane as the unmoving clouds, each form of it exquisitely articulate, uttering all of itself and no more, conveying only to this great silent gallery of forms its own inimitable shape. Mexicans have chosen two of these shapes, the eagle and the serpent, as their emblems—ironically, I think, because they know as no one else can know that these are emblems of nothing so little as of nationhood: of communal pride or power or progress, or any human, lyrical delusion. One is a traveler in dust and one in air, but neither is either a pilgrim or a vandal. They might, with no more irony, have chosen the stone-eyed iguanas or the great, slow-moving tortoises to ornament their flag and their aspirations; and perhaps the Mexicans know this, too. Because it is only the madly poetic, madly polemic heart of man that would try to confiscate the beauty of these things, to demand eloquence of them, or testimony. They have none to give; they are only messengers of silence, and it would degrade them to be impounded in a poem or a metaphor—like lions in a cage—if they could be degraded; but they cannot. They survive all pathos; they burn through its syntax like hot stones through gauze and will stand blinking in the desert dust, unscathed, august, mute, servants of no beauty or passion but their own. Their lives are an endless fugue of languor and desire, of satiate torpor and the lust for food or sex. If a living thing approaches another in that wasteland, it is either to kill or to copulate; no other relationship exists or is conceived of, no other state aspired to. Life augurs or reveals nothing but its own momentary ecstasy or indolence; neither fraternity, nor charity, nor play, nor art, nor any creed but stealth.

Once, when we were driving from Mexico City to Guanajuato, I got out of the car and crouched down beside the road to urinate. There was a huge hard-shelled land tortoise there, stretching his leathery neck to gnaw a spiny, dark green leaf of a plant. I watched his indomitable, bitter-mouthed, quartz-eyed, reptilian head munching the succulent plump leaf, and thought of the great bronze statue of the terrapin on the granite pedestal in front of the McKeldin Library that is the emblem of our university; and I thought: This creature beside me is the reality that that, and all, emblems represent. This desert is its ark and sanctum. Nothing can be more true, because all else is its fragile simile; there is nothing else, but dreams.

And then I stood and tugged up my pants and saw a little dusty pueblo in the distance, scattered along the barranca of a torpid yellow stream, the walls of its houses showing pink and white and pale blue in the sun, the spire of its church rising against the merciless azure crusted with ornament like icing on a cake in that desperate Mexican baroque that seems to shriek or sob against the sky, and I thought: but how valiant, how exquisite those dreams are. Because in spite of the terrible still air in which they bleach and crumble, there is lofty artifice in those towns, and revelry, and a yearning, unutterably mournful music, and a kind of gallant, nefarious ambition. There are many such villages on those blasted plains; they lie like coral reefs, pale, pitted, pastel-colored shoals rising out of the desert which has cast them up and which laps at them ceaselessly, gently, pitilessly, slowly eroding and consuming them, calling back the aberrantly poetic, insanely ingenious life that has crawled out of it and been sheltered there for a moment and transformed, that has learned to chip arrowheads out of the mother rock, to pound corn seed into flour in stone bowls, to mold and bake clay pottery, to cut combs out of tortoiseshell to smooth out its shining, night-black hair, to operate a treadle sewing machine and make white communion dresses and fiesta frocks.

When we drove into those villages and I would get out of the car and stand listening to the gusts of guitar music from the stinking, foul cantinas, and the wheezing of concertinas or the brass bands playing in the shabby, faded, blue-and-coral plazas in the evening, and watch the boys and girls parading counter to each other around the bandstand and the petunia beds, I would think: Nothing out there beyond the barranca feels sorrow. And I would remember a line from a story of Balzac's called "A Passion in the Desert": "In the desert there is everything and nothing; there is God without humanity." But it is a humanity different from that we know in College Park or Washington, because it is a kind of tidal life, still lapped by that oceanic solitude from which it has emerged, still washed over by the silence in which it seethes and bubbles and glitters like cockles streaming in the sand. It tastes of the white brine of those leagues of crystal distance in which it is enisled, the brazen stillness that falls out of the sky on the pink cathedral spires and the broken bougainvillea loggias, and that leavens their festivity with a commemorative, tortoiselike solemnity, a flashing, snake-bright brilliance, and an unholy candor. The eyes that watch you crossing the plaza in the sunlight are scarifying in their shameless, scalding candor; contempt and desire burning in them like the twin concentric arcs of a flame tip, one white, one blue. They sear your bare legs, your arms, the pale, vulnerable nape of your neck, as mercilessly as the light of that blue sky; they leave a kind of sunburn on your body—an eyeburn—that darkens your flesh forever with its blazing recognition of the ecstatic blue void of your heart.

I felt that even in Mexico City when we first arrived, even in the glitter of the Reforma and of the fashionable, tree-shaded streets behind it, where you would see camped on the sidewalks outside the boutiques and hotel fronts and the canopied, tinkling street cafés of the Zona Rosa, a family of Indians, lean and dark and stunted as sierra pines, and with that impassive, firmamental brilliance in their eyes, holding out their delicate brown hands, demanding restitution from those whose chivalry had dispossessed them. And at that distance, a peso's toss away from the table at which we sat drinking margaritas in the shade of a pink-striped canopy—and already—I did not think of them as picturesque: I feared and was thrilled by them, and shuddered to acknowledge that these people lived more honestly, with less pretense or guile than any I had ever known. These are the children of truth, I thought. The innocent of the earth. I have sought them everywhere. I longed to touch them, to stroke their glistening, clay-colored skin, to fit the arcs of my curled fingers into the hollows of their throats and temples, to drink their dark breath, to taste their blood; but I did not want to love them, to acquit myself of the claims of their poverty by a charity more imposing than the few centavos' change that lay on the tablecloth; I wanted to be of them. I wanted to feel the sparkle of their bitter patience in my heart, their stealthy vitality running in my veins like lye, but I was afraid. And doubly afraid, because I felt that they recognized me, and that what they despised in me was not myself, but only the appearance of disparity between us, my clothes and circumstances and my language—and my fear of renouncing that disguise, of ever transcending it; my knowledge of the impossibility of descending or ascending, without shame or disaster, to the miasmal, radiant anonymity in which they squatted like vultures or coyotes around our café tables, in which I could be naked and nameless as a lizard, and slay and steal and fornicate impenitently, with the savage innocence in which they slew and stole and fornicated in order to survive in the forsaken pueblos that they came from. I think they saw my awe of that capacity and that necessity in them, which no circumstance could ever permit me, or admit me to; and my regret, at least, they respected. I felt that terrifying kinship confirmed in the café waiters who although they spoke good Spanish and wore white bolero jackets and bow ties and were nimble and courteous, were Mexican, too; but mestizo, not full-blooded Aztecs. In them was blended the blood of the two peoples they maneuvered so dexterously between with their expertly balanced trays—the Europeans at the tables and the Indians at their feet. But it was not the ragged aborigines on the pavement who had committed the acts of savagery, the rape and pillage, out of which they were born, but we, the Europeans. It was we who had ravished and plundered those silent desert children; and the slender, imperturbably respectful, nimble young men who bore us our iced drinks were the offspring of that rapacity, and living proof that our seed mixed readily enough with theirs, that our blood flowed in easy consanguinity. I remember Ronnie saying to me as we sat there on our first evening, "Not a lot of Americans realize that we took almost exactly half of this country—Texas, and New Mexico, and Colorado and Arizona and the whole state of California—by force of arms, by the Mexican-American War and the Treaty of Guadalupe Hidalgo that followed it. But General Lee knew it, and even old Ulysses Grant. Abraham Lincoln knew it, and lost his seat in Congress for saying so. Thoreau knew it, and went to jail because he refused to contribute to the villainy." But it began long before then, I thought; with Cortez, who betrayed the king of this old barbaric culture, looted his gold and silver and emeralds, desecrated his gods and burned his codices, tore down his temples, enslaved and debased his people, and slaughtered him. But not in innocence. These were the deeds, not of a desert wolf or mountain lion, but of a cavalier of Spain, a gentleman educated at the University of Salamanca and baptized into the Faith, a product of the glory of Western civilization; and they were done, not out of hunger, not out of the heart's and body's honorable need, but in the name of Jesus Christ and of Their Imperial Majesties Ferdinand and Isabella. I looked furtively at the victims of those deeds on the sunny sidewalk at my feet, at the bleak and feral fortitude of their onyx eyes, and thought: Their only creed is stealth, and they are right; it will serve them just as well here in the Zona Rosa as in the desert. It is no wonder they recognize me; like their despoiler, I am baptized, well clothed, and university-bred; and, like themselves, I am a sun worshipper, stained with wilderness, born on the shores of an ancient blue bay, out of whose vastnesses of sky and water the same ethereal silence by which they are enchanted has seeped into my heart.

In Mexico City we rented a car and drove north through the deserts to the old hill towns of San Miguel de Allende and Guanajuato. It was a journey of two days, but before we had been on the road an hour my possession by that country was complete. We drove out through the Valley of Mexico in the fresh morning light that bathed the stones like water and flooded the ravines with cool shadow and set aglow like quicksilver the clouds of mist out of which the snowcapped peak of Popocatepetl rises above the valley and the city with an eerie majesty that is almost fantasy, that disorders, that sets one almost imbecilically abroad into the heart of that spectrally elemental region over which it reigns. I sat and watched the land sweep toward us in its unvarying austerity, its limitless lavender reaches cloaked with sage and swollen with barren tumuli and stricken with gaunt pedestals that uphold nothing; brutal, ancient, rapt; and I thought: It is wrong to call this land mysterious. There is no mystery here. This is absolute exposition, absolute definition. This is as near to revelation as we come on this planet. Those monstrous dolmens entomb nothing, not even bones; those great stone monuments commemorate nothing but themselves; those obelisks that seem to point to heaven or the stars, to personify enigma, signify nothing but their own shapeliness, their beautiful idiosyncratic concord with that numb, livid vault against which they stand. This place is beyond redemption, because already totally redeemed from nothingness, all of its being manifest, consummately itself. And beyond execration, because it contradicts or affirms nothing; nothing is inherent in it any longer; all that was intrinsic has been translated into sublimely finite rock and blazing sand and radiant, radical, serpentine vitality. It exists; absolute, imponderable. There is nothing here but an awesome, incomprehensible simplicity that confounds all complexity, all art, all personality.

I had never felt so excruciatingly aware of the fragility and uniqueness of myself, and yet that feeling was born out of the passion that the place created in me, the terrible enchantment that I felt in that speechlessly, soullessly voluptuous wilderness that lay everywhere around me, that called to me as no man ever had with its grave, inexorable demand for intercourse with it, its mute, appalling offer of union, of unutterable consummation.

When we stopped the car and stepped out to take a photograph, I saw a snake slither swiftly away in a glittering, furtive flash into a clump of mescal. I stood watching dumbly, and thought: I will follow him. I will ask to share his stony sanctuary. My brother infidel, admit me. Oh, let me come in. I am a fugitive from love and mystery, as you are.

A little later we passed an old man in a ragged straw rebozo with a face as vacant as the desert sand who raised and swung a heavy gnarled staff; patiently, mercilessly flogging a gray burro, its back piled high with faggots of firewood, that stood in patient immobility with downcast, drowsily indifferent eyes. Nothing matters to them, I thought. They are bound in a passionate apathy that has consumed their hearts away; it is like the sadness after love.

It swept toward us as unchanging as the sea, billow after dusty billow, mile after mile, as we moved into it, hypnotizing in its monotony, and I thought: Soon we will reach the very heart of it; the epiphany. But as we went further into it, and into the waxing noon, as if being swept over by a tide of land and light and time, I thought: No, there is no heart to it, as there is no heart to the sea or sky or time; it is infinite, and no acre of infinity is more beautiful or true than any other. Truth is not concentrated or confined in any one inch or instant of eternity; it is homogeneous, totally solute; and it is everywhere; and that thought is as true as any human thought can be, and I must be content with it (and then, for some reason, I turned and looked at Ron, beside me in the car, and, in panic, and with a desperate resistance to the thought, completed it) and with this man.

Lord, what shame I felt, what ignominy! For a long time I was scarcely aware any longer of the desert that surrounded us; I sat burning with remorse, with the piercing awareness of my pride and contumely in an incandescent self-consciousness. It was as if I bore through that dumb, sublime indifference that lay everywhere about us a kind of blasphemous, bright immanence, a chalice, brimming with my shame.

And then, a little later, the really frightful thing happened, the thing that was after all, perhaps, the apotheosis I had yearned for, or had dreaded. As we followed the curve of the road around the point of a great crumbling headland that sloped down from the mountain whose base we had been circling, there appeared with horrifying suddenness and clarity in the thin bright air, not thirty feet in front of us and hurtling swiftly, inevitably into us, a mound of hideous shattered flesh, the carcass of a burro, its legs dangling brokenly, its swollen putrid abdomen burst open in a reeking, cavernous wound; and all around, and huddled ravenously on top of it, tugging with their beaks at its mangled flesh and coils of ruptured, spilt-out, glittering entrails and at scraps of offal they held clenched in their talons, a flock of filthy, avid, red-necked vultures. The ghastly sight grew almost instantaneously huger and closer as we bore down upon it, the brakes shriekingly, shudderingly echoing our horror, until it filled the windshield like a scene flashed on a motion-picture screen by a demented projectionist. I held out my hands to shield myself from that mass of corruption, of obscene squalor that hurtled into us, and as we struck it, the glass was splattered with pink and gray and scarlet gore in a strangely abstract, strangely exquisite composition, almost like a Pollock painting, whose beauty, in that dreadful instant, I agonizedly perceived.

There was a sickeningly soft, yet violent impact, a liquid, loud, lubricious thud that wracked the silence like the sound of moist, huge bodies frenziedly colliding, a ragged, witchlike clatter of wings from the startled, fleeing vultures; and as I was flung forward into the dashboard and crushed there in paralyzed, instantaneous suspension of all motion, a pain ran into me like the blade of a gigantic poignard, from my loins to my heart.

I was in darkness for a moment, and then I heard Ron's voice coming to me from infinitely far away, as if blown by ocean winds across empty leagues of water: "Are you all right? Sylvia? Sylvia? Are you all right?" I felt as if I were awakening from a dream: what had happened drifted only in phantasmal rags of vapor in my memory, like the torn mists of an imperfectly remembered nightmare. But my breast hurt still, and I pressed my hand to it, thinking that I would find it soaked in my own blood; it astonished me that it was not, that it seemed only to be bruised from the dashboard's blunt impact. I unbuttoned the top two buttons of my blouse, idly, unremonstratively, in a kind of trance, feeling with my fingertips the blade of my sternum and the ribs above my heart.

They were apparently intact. Even the skin, mysteriously, was unbroken.

"Are you all right?" Ron said, his fingers wandering gently over my face.

"Yes. I think so."

"Thank God. You're sure?"

"Yes. Only bruised. Are you?"

"Yes. Banged my knee a bit, that's all." He rubbed it absently, turning to stare at the soiled windshield. "Oh, my God. Oh, my God, what a mess." We sat without moving or speaking for several moments. "Oh, my God," he said again. "I suppose I'd better get out and see what's happened." He opened the door and stepped out onto the asphalt of the road, then hobbled to the front of the car and stood staring for a moment. "It seems to be O.K. The fender's just dented in a little." He made a low, choked sound of revulsion in his throat. "My God, I never saw anything so—foul—in my life." He limped back to the open door, got into the car, put the gearshift into neutral, and reached down to turn the ignition key. "Let's see if this thing will start." It did, miraculously. I watched everything with bleak indifference, idly, in my trance. He put the gear into reverse and, looking up into the rearview mirror, backed cautiously away, fifteen or twenty feet along the road. Then he opened the door and got out of the car again and stood looking back. On either side of the narrow strip of asphalt there were deep, rain-washed gullies that would capture a car wheel to its axle, and beyond them the boulder-strewn floor of the canyon was, in any case, impassable.

"There's no way we can drive around it," he said. "I don't know what the hell to do." He closed his eyes and shook his head in frustration. "Well, I suppose I'd better clean this mess off the windshield first, before it dries." He took a handkerchief out of his pocket and, leaning across the bonnet of the car, swept it, crumpled into a pad, across the glass. It was obviously not going to suffice; after a single stroke it was soaked and clotted with gore. He tossed it into the gully with a croak of disgust. "I'll have to get a towel out of the suitcase." He opened the bonnet and then the suitcase that he found inside, and after fumbling about for a moment, hobbled back to the windshield with a bath towel wadded in his hand. Squinting with revulsion, he scrubbed the glass clear. I watched, something stricken in me to see the unimaginably beautiful composition erased before my eyes. He threw the towel into the gully and then bent down to scrub his hands with the sand of the roadside. I watched, unmoved, while he rose and, clutching his thigh, hobbled up the pavement to where the carcass of the burro, even more gruesomely mutilated, and shifted slightly by our collision with it, lay now almost in the center of the road. He studied it disconsolately for a moment, then leaned forward and seized one weirdly uplifted hind leg just above the hoof and tugged at it fiercely for several minutes, his body arched and lurching backwards, grunting and panting with the effort. The huge limp carcass shifted only an inch or two across the pavement. He paused and stood upright with a great gasp of exhaustion, raising the back of his arm to his dripping eyebrows. "I can't move the goddamned thing," he said. "It must weigh five hundred pounds."

"I'll have to help you." I opened the door and stood up on the road, feeling nakedly encompassed by the hot bright silence of the desert air. I stumbled as I walked toward him, swearing at my own frailty and the furor in me, like nausea.

"You'd better go back and sit down," Ron said. "You're pretty shaken up."

"No. I've got to help you. We've got to get out of here."

Near to it, I saw that the burro was freshly slain but already putrefying in the ruthless light. There was a swarm of glittering green flies buzzing about it and into the red maw of its ruptured belly with a shrill, insensate fervor. It stank of the fecal smell of bowels and blood. I took hold of the leg above the hoof.

"You sure?" Ron said. "My God, it's an awful thing to have to do."

"Listen, I'm strong," I said. "Don't you know that yet? I hauled jib sheets for years. Can you sing?"

"Sing?"

"Yes. We've got to sing a chantey, and haul like hell on the beat."

"Couldn't we just count?"

"No. Chanteys do something for you. We've got to sing. Get hold of it." He placed his hands above mine on the leg. "O.K., let's start with 'Shenandoah.' You ready?"

"All right."

So we sang "Shenandoah," which is probably the most beautiful song ever written, and by its melody we were able to unite our strength to do the loathsome job. There was a terrible, Brueghel-like comedy about it: the two of us heaving at the leg of that noisome, stinking corpse, on that empty, desolate highway, in that sea of silent imperturbability while we chanted out the lovely, sorrowful words: "Oh, SHEN-andoah, I love your DAUGH-ter. ROLL away, you ROLL-ing river." And after maybe half an hour of our grotesque labor, we had done it; we had managed to drag the dead beast inch by inch, grating on the sandy asphalt, far enough from the center of the road so that there was room to drive around it. We staggered back to the car and I leaned against it for a moment, panting, my heart bursting in my breast.

"Jesus," Ron said. "You're some girl, Sylvie. You may have saved our lives, you know that? There might not be a car along this godforsaken road for the next month."

When we came to San Miguel de Allende we stopped at a posada at the side of the mountain road that wound down into the town, and before we got out of the car Ron took out of his pocket and handed me a little cake of soap in a paper wrapper that he had taken from the bathroom of the hotel in Mexico City.

"You'd better take this," he said. "There probably won't be any soap in there."

I took it wordlessly and went into the dingy, yellow-painted lavatory and washed my hands for fifteen minutes at a tiny, chipped, antique basin stained with a rusty rivulet from the single shattered porcelain faucet, inscribed CA-LIENTE, which gaspingly produced a frigid murky trickle, the color of tea. Outside the barred window a bird was singing in a jacaranda tree with ceaseless undulating rapture. I went out through the cool whitewashed dark of the posada to the terrace, where Ron was sitting at a table in the shade of a bougainvillea arbor with a pair of margaritas in front of him on the red checkered tablecloth.

"I thought you'd want something," he said. "So I went ahead and ordered these. And a little lunch."

I nodded gratefully. There was a pale stone floor and huge Cinzano ashtrays and sprigs of vivid, papery bougainvillea blossom stuck in mineral water bottles. Below us we could see the bullring, its arches hot and white in the sun, and the spires of cathedrals shrilly vertical against the sky, and the tiled roofs of the houses with pots of geraniums blazing on the grilled balconies that hung over the silent midday streets, and off beyond the village, the shimmering desert we had driven through, and the distant purple mountains. We drank and sat fingering our icy glasses silently.

"I'm sorry about what happened," he said. "My God, what an ordeal."

"It doesn't matter. It certainly wasn't your fault."

"No, but it's one hell of an introduction to this country. Are you sure you're all right?"

"Yes. I've just got a sore wishbone, that's all."

"You don't think you ought to see a doctor?"

"No, for God's sake, don't fuss about it."

"I wish it hadn't happened," he said. "I'd give a million dollars if it hadn't happened."

"It doesn't matter. It had to, I guess."

"No, it didn't," he said. "There's something perverse about it. It didn't have to happen at all." He sat for a moment looking down at the wavering transparent pall that billowed up from the stony distant sand. "Well, we escaped, anyhow. Thanks to you."

"This time," I said.

"Christ, don't say that. If anything like that happens again, I'll go out of my mind."

I looked at him across the table in the brazen, shadowless midday light, trying to see him truly, with total clarity, in that most absolute illumination I would ever see him in, wanting to confirm or refute the furtive vicious candor of the thought that had sprung like a serpent out of my mind in the desert. He wore a full beard now that was a pale ginger color, lighter than his russet hair, and his eyes seemed paler than I had ever seen them, as if vitiated by those hours in the desert. I'm writing a book, I thought, in which this man is a character—one of the two most important characters—and I can't afford to make mistakes about him. I have to see and understand him, and how I feel about him, truly. I must. If he can make me ashamed of not loving him, then perhaps he is the only true measure of my conscience, and of my consciousness. There is some terrible paradox here that I must unravel. If I misrepresent anything at all, it is a disservice to our lives, a subversion of them, and better left unwritten. But after the first moment of my scrutiny, I gave it up as being useless and unfair and delusive, realizing that in people light reveals almost nothing but deformity—the depth of the lines of their faces, the coarseness of their flesh and pores, the hitherto unsuspected hairs sprouting out of ears and nostrils, the sag of cheeks and jawlines. It tells nothing about gentleness, or charity, or abnegation, I thought. Maybe it isn't strong enough, even yet. Or maybe moonlight reveals us better. And then, ludicrously, I thought of an idiotic song that I used to be crazy about when I was a kid, that would make Aaron grunt with disgust when I bellowed it from the bowsprit while we were sailing: "Moonlight Becomes You." I turned my eyes from his face and looked out at the desert. After a while, I felt his hand laid on my wrist and heard him say, "Are you sure you want to go on, Sylvia? You look—well, exhausted—already."

"What do you mean, 'go on'?"

"I mean with the trip."

"My God, don't be ridiculous," I said. "We have to, of course."

"No. We can turn back if you want to."

"My God, that's an absolutely craven idea. I wouldn't turn back for anything on earth. Would you?"

"Well, I suppose not, but I think we've had enough for today, anyway. Thank God we didn't make reservations in Guanajuato." He turned and nodded toward the door of the posada. "The patrón in there told me just now when I went in to wash up that there's a fiesta of some kind here tonight. It's a saint's day. I thought we might take that in, if you feel like it."

"Will there be a moon?"

"I don't know if I can promise you a moon, but there'll be mariachi music, and fireworks, and dancing in the street, most likely."

"Oh, Lord, I'd like that," I said. "After a bath, and a long nap. That sounds heavenly."

"Good. I think so, too." He raised his drink and sipped at it judicially. "No, it's the only way to do things, really: with no itinerary, no time schedule. Just spontaneously, on impulse. Just take things as they come. We were wise, to decide on that."

"I hope so," I said. I took a sip of my margarita, holding it in my mouth for a minute to let the harsh, bright, stony taste of the tequila sink into my tongue and cheeks and palate like a stealthy toxic attar, lurking under the bouquet of lemon and vermouth. It was made, I had been told, from the juice of the maguey, a desert cactus that the Aztecs used for everything: to shingle their houses with, for needles, for thread and rope, for alcohol. It was the distillation of the desert, its essence, bleak and omnipotent; but not really intoxicating, I thought; it doesn't so much inebriate as put one in a state of exalted, wanton sobriety. I closed my eyes in the trance it produced in me almost immediately, remembering that heap of stinking carrion laid like an offering before us in the road.

"How is it," Ron said, "that you've begun to drink?"

"This is a vacation, isn't it? I'm entitled to a little depravity."

"Oh, absolutely. I'm not objecting, I'm just a bit surprised. I'm delighted, actually. It's good to see you let your hair down, leave it all behind."

"Oh, it is?"

"Yes. I've been wondering what it took."

"By the time we get to Guadalajara, I'm going to be drinking straight tequila," I said. "This stuff does strange things to me."

"It seems to."

I closed my eyes again, and again I saw that reeking altar in the sun.

"What are you thinking?"

I shook my head. "Nothing. Just about this place. About today."

"I hope it's not going to throw a pall over the whole damned trip. That would be awful."

"No. It can't. I learned too much."

"What did you learn?"

I shook my head again. "I don't like talking about it, and I'm not sure you'd like to hear about it. That's part of what I learned: that I can't tell anyone what I learned."

"But you just have," he said, and smiled at me.

"I know. And how paltry it sounds. You see, I'd have been wiser to say nothing. Talk seems to cheapen things, out here. I'm learning the majesty of silence. Silence preserves things better than words."

"It's golden," Ron said. "But not the best policy for an artist."

"Oh, I don't know. I wonder if the very best thing a writer could do wouldn't be to write nothing at all. To present his publisher with five hundred blank sheets of paper under a title page called *Silence,* and ask him to publish it. It might be his masterpiece."

"And don't think he wouldn't do it, today. Everyone would be enchanted. It would sell a million copies. Just don't let Andy Warhol get ahold of the idea."

"I know. I guess the best thing to do is not even to report in. Not even to answer the census, like Salinger. You know, his silence speaks more to me —I think it's far more eloquent—than all the effusions, all the noisy, clamorous, ephemeral opinions that get printed these days. All that awful vanity. 'Me, *me!* Look at *me,* listen to *me!*' It's appalling."

"I don't think you really mean that," Ron said. He had begun to turn a fork on the tablecloth with distressed quick movements of his fingers.

"I do. My God, didn't you feel that today? It seemed to me that almost the greatest horror, the greatest profanity out there in that desert was my vanity. That place is so—clean. I don't know how else to say it."

"Clean?" he cried in an astonished, grating whisper. "*Clean?* My God, I never saw anything so filthy in my life!"

"But not like human vanity. It's clean of that, and the products of that vanity. It isn't filthy like Buchenwald, or Harlem, or Chapultepec, where we were yesterday—that palace that Maximilian built on the bodies of these people. It doesn't desecrate, it isn't wanton. It doesn't kill to feed its vanity, but only its body. And it doesn't invent all kinds of fraudulent, grandiose pretenses—political or theological or ideological—to excuse its crimes. It doesn't want to rule, or be celebrated, or worshipped, or to persuade. It doesn't demand luxury or tribute. It simply says, 'I'm hungry.' It's chaste, utterly. My God, you only have to look at a picture of Richard Nixon, or of his White House guards in their Graustarkian uniforms, or of Hitler or Mussolini shrieking away on a balcony, or of Napoleon or Caesar, or Cornelius Vanderbilt, to know that ninety percent of human misery is the direct result of men's personal vanity."

"Still," Ron said, his face humbly declined, "they manage to love each other, now and then."

"And much of what they call love is vanity, too. 'Look at *me!* Love *me!* Kiss *me!* If you feel any affection or tenderness or desire for anyone else in the world, I'll kick you; or kill you.' It's the most terrible form of vanity of all. The desire to possess or dominate another human being. Nothing out there demands the tribute of love."

"Well," Ron said. "You're getting quite a lot out of your system, aren't you?" He set the fork carefully parallel to the knife in front of him and looked up into the bougainvillea leaves that had begun to stir in a warm breeze, then out at the desert. "There's a story I think you'd like," he said, "by an Argentine author named Eduardo Mallea. A novella, called *Chávez*. Do you know it?"

"No."

"It's about a man who never speaks. His child is desperately ill one night, and he goes out into the street to get the medicine she needs to recover. But it's a Sunday night, and all the pharmacies are closed. He runs from shop to shop in gathering desperation, pounding at storefronts, at the doors of doctors' offices, but they're all shut and silent. He can't find the medicine anywhere, and so the child dies. After that, Chávez leaves his wife and their apartment in Buenos Aires and wanders about the country in lifelong silence. He never speaks again, to anyone. He manages to find work on a lonely ranch, but his silence begins to infuriate his foreman and his fellow workers. He doesn't respond to their jokes, their friendly overtures, their questions about his life, his pleasures, his opinions. They grow to despise him, they consider him antisocial, stupid, malicious, maybe even diabolical. One day he approaches a woman, the foreman's wife, to whom he is drawn by her loneliness, as she is drawn by his. She is pleased, she believes he will console her, perhaps make love to her. But he says nothing, he's dumb, he can't speak to her; and she is disappointed, and then puzzled and angered by his silence. 'You never speak!' she says. 'Have you nothing to say? Are you inhuman? Speak! Will you never speak?' And then Chávez speaks, at last. 'No,' he says."

I sat enchanted by his story, staring out at the desert with tears welling in my eyes.

"Why didn't you ever tell it to me before?" I asked at last.

"Oh, I don't tell you everything I know," that man said.

"No, you don't. Thank God." He smiled at me shyly, and I lowered my head in humility. "Did you say he was an Argentine?"

"Yes."

"They have those pampas there, don't they? Those great empty plains?"

"Yes, I believe that's what the country mostly is."

"It's a beautiful story."

"Yes, it is." He raised his hand and stared into its palm. "And suppose he'd never written it?"

After a moment, I asked, as nearly lovingly as I had ever spoken to him, "Shall I tell you what I really learned today?"

"Yes, I'd like to know."

"That I have two loves," I said. "As all women do, I suppose."

"Oh?" He looked startled and grave.

"Yes. That the two things I love most in the world are savagery and gentleness. And that I love them equally. That's my dilemma."

Instantly I felt bereft, because what I had owned and cherished as a small, hard, simple truth, something won by a combination of perseverance and luck, like a shark's tooth or a small blue pebble that is the treasure of a whole day's vigilant wandering along a beach, was lost; had become merely a sententious nugget, delivered up at a café table for general admiration and then cleared away with the other debris of our sophistication, the lipstick-stained cigarette butts and the strips of orange rind in the ashtrays.

I saw the waiter, a solid leathery old man like a tightly filled wineskin, approaching us between the tables with a huge wooden tray which he held pressed against his hip while he removed from it and set down in front of us a platter of sliced avocado and tomato and bowls of mole poblano, and then a bottle of mineral water, which he uncapped and poured sizzling into our glasses.

"Gracias," Ron said, when he had finished.

"Que tengan buen apetito," the old man murmured, and shuffled back into the door of the posada.

I watched Ron lift slices of avocado and tomato onto my plate with a wooden fork and spoon, very soberly and winningly absorbed in serving me.

"What did *you* learn today?" I asked him.

"Oh, I don't know if it was anything really new. It was more like having something confirmed that I've always believed, ever since I began to love literature."

"What is that, Ron?"

"That men must speak." He waved the fork at a fly that had settled on the tablecloth. "That's where we differ, I suppose."

"Yes." I lifted a slice of tomato in my fingers and munched on it for a moment. "You know what I've almost decided? To give up that stupid book I'm writing." He paused, holding the fork aloft, and looked at me in shocked immobility.

"I don't believe you're serious. My God, it's your life."

"No, it isn't. My *life* is my life. It's much more important."

He continued staring at me for a moment, then resumed briskly serving out the salad to our plates. "Well, I'm not going to talk about it now," he said, "but you'd better do a lot of thinking about it. I want to read that book someday."

"I don't think so."

"Hey, this doesn't look too bad," he said. "Come on, now. You'll feel a lot better after you have something to eat."

I thought: Oh, God, why do they always say that? In all crises, after all disasters, at every funeral, after every hurricane, earthquake, train wreck, desertion, death, or infidelity: Have a cup of coffee and a sandwich; you'll feel better. And of course he was indecently, insanely right. I did.

We decided not to go down to the village and try to find the pension we had located in *Mexico on $5.00 a Day*—we were too tired—but to stay there at the posada, which was much less than modest, and oh, God, how elemental in its amenities! And after I had had a shower in a moldy cubicle infested with little gray chameleons that lay flat against the splintered blue and yellow tile and made impudent kissing sounds while I soaped my breasts, and had slept for hours in a small white room of penitential bleakness, under a wooden-bladed ceiling fan that stirred the dull air with a groan, and had awakened and gone out again onto the terrace, I saw that the world had been tenderly, nocturnally transformed. Night had descended over San Miguel de Allende, and in the sable blackness there were stars above the mountains, and a scent of jacaranda in the dark, and from the town below a thin, twinkling tintinnabu-lation of distant laughter and cornets and burro bells and rockets splashing heartbrokenly against the night. I put on perfume, and little winking garnet earrings and a dress of diaphanous green chiffon, and we drove down to the town in the cool dark with the windows open and the night air whispering into my hair like a lover.

I think the early months of our marriage were the most painful of all. There had not yet been time for that sordid sense of embarrassment at finding ourselves married to each other to transpose into resignation, or almost indiffer-ent equanimity, or the candid habitual rancor that came later. There were still those dismaying cycles, on Molly's part, of anxious solicitude, tortured, inar-ticulate appeals for faith and patience, and the growingly weary forbearance that began to express itself in ironies and adages. All this was inevitable, I suppose, considering the events of that unfortunate night she invited me to dinner—and to so much more, which, like the withered, desiccated roast of veal we finally sat down to consume between my mumbled, transparently insincere congratulations, was already blighted by the calamitous hour of pas-sion that preceded it. I don't suppose any woman relishes the thought that the man who marries her is driven to that extremity by the rashness of his own behavior; especially when nothing afterwards confirms that rashness as the magnificent eruption of an ungovernable, eternal love, but only as the aberra-tion of a grotesque and infamous hour. In the weeks and months that follow, she has time to meditate on the fact that rectitude in a man may enable her to conscript him as a husband but is a very poor credential as a lifelong lover; on the fragility of remorse as the foundation of a human relationship, and the

215

power of resentment to undo it; on the folly and impermanence of lust; and the greater folly of that form of penance for it which is so often expressed in matrimony. "Lust" was not a word that would have embarrassed Molly, ever; and in the wake of our brief, strange moment as servants of its madness, she might even have taken a kind of tortured pride in dramatizing our unhappy example of its consequences. There was much in her nature and background that suggested it.

On the other hand, pregnancy is a period in which a woman's emotions are notoriously unstable; there are dramatic shifts of mood ranging from euphoria to despair, and this may have accounted for many of Molly's darkest, most lugubrious moments. I heartily hoped so. From what I remembered from my residency in obstetrics and gynecology, after the first trimester a woman's outlook improved greatly. Her body adjusted gradually to the hormonal disruption produced by pregnancy, and the mental turmoil that accompanied it began to dissipate. The reality of the child she was about to bear became constantly more substantial, more imminent, more all-absorbing. Her doubts and fears were growingly supplanted by her delight in the most profound of womanly functions; all apprehensions were eventually extinguished by her joyful anticipation of bringing new life into the world. This prospect was my chief consolation. I daily snatched at the slightest evidence of it, hungry for the relief it promised from the sense of indecent bewilderment that besieged us: a gentle word, a moment of musing serenity, a momentary failure to detect, or invent, or exaggerate, my indifference or absence of affection. In Molly's case, however, any such demonstrations were delayed by the lack of dignity in which they struggled to be born, and meanwhile the dense, miasmal gloom that clung to the Victorian furniture like the mist of a rain forest was only deepened by my daily fugitive flight from it into the haven of my work, my constant, obsessional immersion in my duties at the hospital, and, most of all, the impending completion of my residency and the prospect of my commission, in the coming fall, as a Passed Assistant Surgeon in the U.S. Public Health Service. It was far more important to me than the birth of our child.

I'll tell you something that may seem as incongruous—and as quaint—to you as it does now to me: when I was a young man, I had heroes. I had forgotten that until I drove up to Prince Frederick a couple of months after I arrived here to renew my automobile license. Halfway there, I passed through a village on Route 2 and saw the sign above the post office door that reads ST. LEONARD, MD. Suddenly the realization came flooding over me that this was the childhood home of the man who had been the model and idol of my apprentice years in medicine, Dr. Thomas Parran. I'm not sure at all that I had forgotten that fact; it may have been part of some subconscious complex of motives that drew me to the place originally, and that worked in a profound, subliminal way in my orientation to it. I certainly remembered it *then;* there was an aura about that name on that weather-beaten sign that was as magically and powerfully stirring as the smell of the sea, and the realization that I had found my way at the end of my days to the obscure birthplace of a man who was one of the gods of my youth left me mysteriously moved.

I don't know if you are aware that Thomas Parran was born and grew up not thirty miles from here—or if you ever heard of the man. There's not much reason to know his name unless you're involved in his profession; but he was one of the greatest men of medicine of the twentieth century. Parran was Surgeon General of the Public Health Service from 1936 until 1948. It was under his direction that the National Institutes of Health were organized, and took the course they did as one of the great research centers of the world. The Center for Disease Control in Atlanta was his conception and creation, and under his guidance the vast, pioneer programs for research in venereal disease, tuberculosis, cancer, malaria, sylvatic plague, mental illness, and a host of other historical afflictions of mankind were instituted and developed. After the war, he organized the World Health Organization, which bears the stamp of his vision as surely as the public health system of this country. He was born on a tobacco farm here in Calvert County, about thirty-five miles from St. Leonard, but in spite of the seeming obscurity of his birth, he came from a long line of distinguished physicians, one of whom was a medical officer on Washington's staff during the Revolution. Parran went to St. John's of Annapolis for his undergraduate work, and then to Georgetown, in Washington, for his medical training, helping to pay his way by working in the summer in the laboratories of the District of Columbia Health Service.

He entered the U.S. Public Health Service in 1917, and spent the early years of his career in rural sanitation in the southern states. In 1926 he was appointed head of the Venereal Disease Division of the P.H.S., and for the next several years put into effect an intensive and unique program of research and control in the network of clinics across the country that had originally been financed by the Red Cross. In 1930, Franklin Roosevelt, who was then governor of New York, appointed him Commissioner of Health of that state, and after Roosevelt became President, he made Parran head of his advisory subcommittee to study the research possibilities of the Public Health Service. It was Parran who hand-tailored Title VI of the Social Security Law of 1935, which authorized the expenditure of two million dollars annually for the investigation of disease and the problems of sanitation—a sum that up to that time was unheard of. In 1936, Roosevelt brought him to Washington as Surgeon General of the Public Health Service, and in that position he was able to proclaim the new era in public health made possible by the legislation he had fathered. It was the beginning of the modern national health program in this country. He reshaped the Public Health Service to fit in not only with the Social Security Act but with all other New Deal projects relating to public health. He created a strong enough public opinion for venereal disease control to secure the passage of the National Venereal Disease Control Act by Congress in 1938, which greatly increased the appropriations for federal assistance to state health systems and the number of new local health units and consulting services. Grants-in-aid made possible by the Social Security Act went into venereal disease control in every state of the union. In fact, all modern research in venereal disease, and especially in syphilis, is the direct result of Parran's leadership.

In December 1936, at the end of his first year as Surgeon General, the Public Health Service held a national conference on venereal disease in Washington, attended by almost a thousand health officers, clinicians, and nurses. It was a landmark in public health and medical history. I was an intern at George Washington University Hospital that year, and I went to that conference. Listening to Parran speak, I was thrilled by the power of his imagination and his absolute, undeterrable dedication. I think it's the first time I was ever in the presence of a great man, and I never forgot the experience. It made me burn to work under his leadership and to take part in the campaign he had inaugurated. I remember the quiet fervor with which he set forth the principle of government responsibility for the health of its citizens—a concept I had never heard publicly expressed before—and while the proposition itself seemed curiously radical, the sober passion of his advocacy sent a chill of excitement through me that the antics of no ballet dancer could ever have awakened. In that speech he named syphilis and tuberculosis as the two major preventable causes of sickness and death in the world at that time, and made clear his absolute commitment to eradicate them. You can have some idea of the forces of hypocrisy, prudery, and fear he fought against in that commitment by the fact that he was interrupted in his speech by a reporter from the Associated Press who rose with the objection: "But, Dr. Parran, the AP never uses the word 'syphilis.' "

"It will use it from now on," Parran said, "or it will have to omit all the pronouncements of the Surgeon General of the Public Health Service." Here is a man of truth, I thought. Here is a man who will speak it in the face of all dread and all shame.

He had demonstrated that fact before in his career. As early as 1934, when he was New York State Health Commissioner, he had been invited by the Health Education Committee of the Columbia Broadcasting System—of which Parran was a member—to give a lecture over that radio network. From his office in Albany, he sent an advance copy of his speech to CBS in New York. When he arrived at the studios, he was greeted by a very agitated young man who protested that he could not possibly use the word "syphilis" on the air. "I didn't ask to appear," Parran said. "I was *asked* to appear by CBS." "We've just got to cut it off," the young man replied. He went out of the studio and brought back a girl to play the piano, and while she was tinkling out popular melodies, he announced over the air, "Due to circumstances which we cannot control, the speaker scheduled for this program cannot appear."

In his indignation, Dr. Parran sent a telegram to CBS, resigning from its Health Education Committee. The telegram found its way to the national press associations, the New York newspapers, and the radio networks; and the incident became a cause célèbre. For the first time in the history of America, the word "syphilis" was spoken over the air on a public radio broadcast, and Dr. Parran's name entered into legend and into my consciousness.

I was aware of it, and of his career in public health, because the period of his most dramatic achievements corresponded with the years of my internship and residency at George Washington, and because of my consuming interest in syphilis. Being situated in Washington, I was close to the seat of his operations and to the site of the new campus of the National Institute of Health in Bethesda, only a fifteen-minute bus ride from our apartment off Wisconsin Avenue. By 1938, the first three buildings of this vast complex had been completed on a tract of land in the Maryland suburbs of Washington contributed to the P.H.S. by Mr. Luke I. Wilson and his widow. By the time I had begun my internship in 1936, and after hearing Dr. Parran speak at the venereal disease conference in Washington at the end of that year, I was already interested in trying to make my future with the Public Health Service. Nowhere would I find such extensive facilities for research, an organization so entirely philosophically committed to the type of work I wanted to do, or a leadership and animating spirit so powerful and inspiring as that of Thomas Parran's. When I finished my internship I was invited to stay on at G.W. for my residency, and decided to do so because of its proximity to N.I.H. and also because of the presence on its staff, as professor of pathology, of Dr. R. M. Chrisser, who was one of the world's outstanding figures in research in treponemal diseases at the time, especially in yaws and bejel, exotic forms of syphilis which have become endemic in many tropical countries. I learned a great deal from this wise and eminent physician, and my zeal did not escape him. He gave me a letter of introduction to Dr. Lewis Thompson, who was head of the Division of Scientific Research at the institute in Bethesda, and Thompson invited me up one day to meet him and see their new laboratories, of which he was greatly and justly proud. He was a marvelous man, Parran's right-hand man, and his peer in energy and vision; it was very largely through his determination and administrative genius that the land for the institutes had been acquired from the Wilson family, and that the N.I.H. and the old Division of

Scientific Research had been merged into a single powerful and prestigious unit. I liked him immediately, and was gratified that he would give such a considerable amount of time to acquainting an obscure young physician with the institution he was erecting. It was obvious that he had a great respect for Dr. Chrisser and that my professor's endorsement of my abilities carried weight with him. He invited me to lunch, and very much encouraged my interest in a Public Health Service career.

"Dr. Chrisser tells me you've done some fine work in dermatology and syphilis," he said. "You know, that's Dr. Parran's big field. There are research programs going on in the Service right now in venereal disease that I think will revolutionize our approach to syphilis. Mahoney's work with this new drug, penicillin, and the sulfa drugs, up in New York, and some fascinating studies in epidemiology in the South. I think you'd be very much at home with us, and very valuable to the Service. Why don't you sit for the exam for the Commissioned Corps?"

I told him that that was becoming increasingly my chief ambition.

"Good. We need men like you. It'll be given in Washington in August. I think I can promise you a very interesting post, if you make out all right. There'll be positions open in research right here in Bethesda, and there's a special training program in syphilis that we give, over at Johns Hopkins, with J. E. Moore. Of course, working with a man like that would be a marvelous opportunity for anyone who qualified."

"It would indeed. I'd give my right arm for the chance. How long is the program?"

"It runs for an academic year, from September to May. It's not an easy exam, you know, but from what Dr. Chrisser says, I shouldn't think you'd have any trouble."

They were the most portentous words I'd ever heard spoken. They seemed to bring my whole life into focus. I felt that my destiny was determined. When I made this known to Molly, she had no difficulty controlling her enthusiasm.

"That's very nice," she said. "Does that mean you'd be working for the government?"

"Yes. The Public Health Service. And we wouldn't have to move for a while, at least, because Dr. Thompson says I might qualify for a special training program at Johns Hopkins. It just runs from September to the middle of May, and I could commute, to Baltimore, for that time. Of course it wouldn't be until next year, when I finish my residency."

"I'm glad of that. I wouldn't want to move, with the baby coming."

"No. Of course, I wouldn't make anything like the money that I would in private practice."

"Well, that doesn't really matter, does it? As long as you're happy."

"No. As long as we're *both* happy. Of course, it would be much more than I make now, as a resident. We'd be able to take trips and things. Buy a car. We might even be able to start saving for a down payment on a house."

This moved her to a dim, ironic smile which would have been equally consistent with the offer to make her Princess of Cathay. None of our prospects had for Molly the power to absolve the present of its pain, as they had for me. Her confidence in the future was as vague and inconstant as a child's summertime belief in Christmas: it would come, if one was good, and kept one's room in order, and ate one's vegetables; and there would be lights and bells and pretty packages, but on some morning so inconceivably remote, so veiled in myth and distance that it would not serve to lessen the sting of the present splinter in one's toe or viper in one's bosom. Only when it had come close enough to be called the passing present or had fled irrecoverably by could Molly take the future to her heart. For her, Christmas was never so true or beautiful as when she swept into a dustpan the last brown needles of the vanished tree or plucked from the carpet with welling eyes the bright splinters of a broken ornament. We lived in a present whose possibility of joy was mortgaged, by me, to the consolations of the future and, by Molly, to the solace of the past. The only present that she could have cherished would have been some suspended moment somehow eternally imbued with the glamour of its past, that served as its own imperishable souvenir and was, like Christmas, the commemoration of its own legendary joy. I suppose the single human state approaching that condition is pregnancy, and it was Molly's great good fortune to be in it and for a little while to rejoice in it. The joy did not last; but for those final six months of her pregnancy and the first few months of Elizabeth's infancy there was a brief and wonderful remission in her disenchantment with the present, her inconstancy toward the future, and her pathetic infatuation with the past. For a little while, she had all she asked of life: a present, continuous —and unmistakably palpable—blessing, which would resolve itself into its own enduring souvenir.

If I have put this at all sardonically, Molly would forgive me that much. However inadvertent, her pregnancy was my chief contribution to her tenuous prosperity. And to my own, since it relieved me greatly of further responsibility for hers. As it advanced, she withdrew more and more deeply into a state of private, mystical contentment and repose. It was now her belly she would fondle hour on hour, rather than the contents of her jewel casket, but with the same look of stuporous placidity. She became something close to dulcet of eye and voice; the tone of irony began to dissipate, as did the proverbs. Sometimes, from a long glowing silence, she would seem to waken smilingly and turn to gaze at me, reaching out to lay her fingers on my arm, as if gratefully to acknowledge my complicity in her condition. The embarrassment this made me feel was more than compensated by my relief from even the pretense of sexual interest in her, and from feeling myself the author of so many of her disappointments. As far as her pregnancy was concerned, I was, like Molly, more indifferent to its consequences than to its present blessings. I would have been delighted if she could have remained pregnant forever, not only because of the relative peace it brought into our home, but because I had some reservations about her capacity for motherhood—and about my own, for fatherhood, a vast and utter skepticism. The traditional happy fantasies that other prospective fathers were evidently prone to—of Fourth of July picnics and fishing trips and Saturday-morning games of catch with sturdy, freckled scions—were simply inconceivable to me. I had been frightened of fireworks from the day I was born, had seldom held a baseball in my hand, and detested fish in any condition, especially death—which glazed their eyes with that terrifying, pale, translucent film. Whatever appeal bicycles or electric trains or roller skates may once have held for me, it was long spent; and I could not imagine the nature of a relationship between myself and anyone for whom it still burned bright. I suppose if I had been capable of any conception whatever of an heir, it would have been of a small, owlish laboratory assistant in sneakers who would enthusiastically and devotedly help me to prepare specimen slides and perform flocculation tests. But not even this genial travesty presented itself to me. I was unable to consider my son's inevitable advent at all, except in fiscal terms: there would be certain expenses for his delivery, crib, food, wardrobe, medical attention, a fund set aside for an insurance policy and his education and, later, for his amusement, toys, summer camps, Boy Scout uniforms, and the like; all blessedly calculable—as the nature of our relationship was not— and urgent and complex enough to absorb all of my attention as far as his eventual existence was concerned. The possibility that he might be a girl I did not even consider. If Molly suggested it, as she sometimes did, I would indulge her with a grandly amused amenability to whatever she proposed in the way of preparation.

"My grandmother's name was Elizabeth," she said once. "Do you think that's a nice name for a girl?"

"Very. A good, straightforward, old-fashioned name."

"Everyone called her Libby. I liked that."

"Yes."

"Of course, there are so many nicknames for Elizabeth that a girl can almost take her pick. That's nice, I think."

"Yes."

"There's Libby, and Liz, and Liza, and Betty, and Betsy, and Bess; and of course Lillibet, like the Queen."

"Oh, she should have a queen's name, I think."

"I do, too. Lillibet." She pronounced it musingly. "It's cute, don't you think?"

"Yes, it's very cute."

"You really wouldn't mind? If she were a girl, I mean?"

"Not if it makes you happy."

"But does it make you happy? Really?"

"Very happy. But I won't be happy long, if I don't get this letter off to Edmundson."

"All right. I won't bother you anymore. I'm glad you like Elizabeth, though."

Two weeks before her expected delivery date, she took leave of absence from her job, and twelve days later, on a bright June morning that cast a shower of shifting, striated sunlight through the kitchen curtains across the breakfast table, she thumped down the syrup pitcher suddenly with a look of combined anguish and delight and said, "Oh, my goodness, I think I'm having pains." We went together in a taxi to the hospital, where I registered her and installed her in the delivery ward, and then went about my rounds on the lower floors. Between visits to my patients, I would go up again and check on her condition. She was damp and pale and pathetically delighted with the attention she was receiving. I stood at her bedside, holding her hand and smiling down at her, suddenly grotesquely moved by the fact that until that moment I had been unmoved by the entire event, that my only satisfaction in our impending parenthood had been in its convenience. This knowledge made my lips tremble astonishingly; I don't know why, exactly. Perhaps for Molly, in the sad but stately eminence of her motherhood, which could not be denied. Perhaps for myself, for my barren forfeiture of what I might have claimed from life for months. Perhaps for our child, innocently clamoring for admission into the strange world and strange household our benighted natures had designed for him. At any rate, I didn't trust myself to speak. Whatever I might have said, I could hear myself pronouncing it with a fatal and transparent lack of joy. I nodded, endlessly, feeling a distinct physical contraction in my breast, as if my heart were closing like a fist.

At lunchtime I bought a sandwich and a pint of milk in the cafeteria and sat in a little waiting room next to the delivery room, where she had now been taken. I read a tattered copy of *Time* magazine from cover to cover, concentrating with a curious passionate absorption on accounts of forgotten football games, the ceremonious signing of treaties by now thrice violated, long-dissolved marriages of movie stars, hurricanes whose fury was only a memory any longer in the still, purple silence of Louisiana dawns. I studied countless photographs of important-looking men in pin-striped suits carrying briefcases, getting on and off of airplanes, all wearing a look of outrageously self-conscious

Destiny, on missions long ago discredited. I took my fountain pen out of my breast pocket and, turning the pages slowly, crossed out with a large bold X the face of every fifth such man. I had eliminated eight of them before Dr. Pasmore, Molly's physician, came into the waiting room with a firm smile, shook my hand, and announced that I was the father of a fine baby daughter. "A fine baby daughter," he repeated, nodding vigorously, as if to forestall the protest he saw gathering in my eyes.

None of the nicknames Molly had proposed was ever used for her. From the moment of her birth, she was called Elizabeth by both of us, by unspoken, unexamined, mutual consent, with a punctilious intonation of the name unabridged by any hint of gaiety, of impetuous, delighted dotage. Even if she had more conspicuously inspired it, I think I would have been unable to pronounce any such set of syllables as "Lillibet"; or to toss her merrily into the air and babble to her fondly by a pet name. But the fact was, she was a very solemn, silent child from the beginning. She seldom cried or laughed, at least not in my presence, and not in the robust, wholehearted way one expects of healthy children. Her only—and almost constant—expression of discontent was a dispirited whimper, like that of an ailing puppy, and the most nearly joyful demonstration I remember her ever making in her infancy was a kind of cautious, gargling chuckle. Perhaps in some extraordinary way my own lack of enthusiasm for the relationship communicated itself to her and subdued her natural exuberance. Or perhaps I don't remember very well; perhaps I prefer these impressions of her for some convenience of my own, or imagine them. Judging by Molly's attitude, this is possible, because in spite of the fact that she was never moved to adopt any of the affectionate soubriquets we had discussed for Elizabeth, she was evidently more than satisfied with her baby daughter. She was, to my gratification, as absorbed in her as I had anticipated. More so; I no longer had to fear, on my daily journey home, a greeting that would be either fulsomely effusive or dolefully aloof, or to deliver over a plateful of stuffed cabbage a vainly spirited account of the fascinations of a case of mononucleosis, or to feign indifference to her solemn-eyed obliviousness to them, or to pretend appreciation of her lugubrious annotations of the evening news. As often as not, she would fail to answer the door to my knocking— something that had never happened before—and I would have to let myself in and call out my arrival, to hear her answer briskly from the nursery, "I'm in here with Elizabeth, honey. Make yourself a glass of ginger ale. I'll be in in a minute." Our mealtimes now were dominated by Molly's animated, if not actually gay, accounts of the child's daily progress, of her ability to digest solid food, of her artful dismantling of a celluloid toy, of her unquestionable ability to distinguish tunes. Most of these achievements seemed less than phenomenal to me, but I nodded or smiled or exclaimed in what seemed suitable appreciation of them, very pleased indeed to have relinquished my role as the chief source and object of my wife's concern, and more than willing to admire my daughter's ingenuity in providing me with that relief. Molly seemed forever to be dressing or undressing her, like a doll, applying talcum powder to her, administering ointments or formula, brushing her sparse damp hair, dangling before her vapidly beholding eyes a little ivory bell that tinkled in the apartment with the perpetual sound of a lost, bewildered sheep.

Soon there was the even more tangible diversion of her actual presence at the dining table when we ate, in an old-fashioned ladder-back high chair that had been Molly's own, lovingly preserved by her grandmother. Elizabeth was installed in it with great ceremony one morning at breakfast, her great, baffled, querulous blue eyes gazing at us with a look of unassuageable dismay over a horrid plastic bib. From that day on, the atmosphere of our mealtimes was permanently altered. For the better, I suppose I would have said; since I continued to enjoy immunity from the corrosive evidence of Molly's disillusion; but it was a very mixed blessing: there were spoonfuls of unpleasantly colored mush to be stuffed into her mouth to spuriously enthusiastic recommendations of its deliciousness, and to be wiped from her chin and bib when she stolidly resisted this deception; there were spoons to be excavated from beneath the table or across the room where she had flung them; there were constant improvisations of strategy, anxious hurried consultations in which I was addressed embarrassingly as "Daddy," and in the third person; and there were Molly's constant cries of approval or reproach or her invocations to me to bear witness to my daughter's virtue or iniquity ringing through the room like the clamor from a rookery. Still, I found it preferable to sitting across the table from each other, as we had done for months, in our nightly auto-da-fé, insidiously giving vent to our disaffection or making cumbrous efforts to disguise or repair it.

All through this period—the final months of my residency—I worked and studied like a man possessed, preparing for the Public Health Service examination I was to take in August. My domestic obligations and vicissitudes became bearable, even trivial, bleached into insignificance in the light of my ambition to distinguish myself in that test of my eligibility to enter Parran's legions. I became even more perfunctory, or indifferent, or briefly and unpersuasively apologetic in my disposal of them. I had sufficient reason. I often did a thirty-six- or forty-eight-hour shift of duty at the hospital, during which I snatched no more than three or four hours of sleep, in twenty- or thirty-minute intervals, on a cot in the residents' quarters; and when I got back to the apartment would sit up for the remainder of the night with a pile of textbooks at the dining-room table until I fell asleep and woke to the cooing of pigeons outside the window in the gray of dawn or the clatter of teacups and cutlery as Molly prepared breakfast in the kitchen.

In August, I sat for my exam in a conference room of the old P.H.S. headquarters in downtown Washington. It was an arduous four-day affair, with one day devoted to each of the four main branches of the science: medicine, surgery, obstetrics, and pediatrics. At the end of the fourth day, I laid down my pen and looked out at the strangely insubstantial world shimmering in the summer heat outside the window. I had a solemn sense of accomplishment; I knew I had done well, and I had. Out of a group of twenty-five applicants, as it turned out, I had come in second. When I received the notice of this result and reported it to Molly, there was a curious diffidence in her congratulations.

"Well, that's very nice," she said. "But I'm not surprised at all." And then, after looking out the window for some time, she added, "Whatever you may think, I'm proud of you. I wish I had had a little more to do with it."

"You had a great deal to do with it," I said. "I couldn't possibly have got through it without you."

"Well, it's nice of you to say that. I'd like it if you told Elizabeth that someday."

On the third of September, I completed my residency at George Washington and was congratulated by Dr. Chrisser and unoccupied members of the staff, at a modest ceremony in the consulting room, attended by three of my fellow residents and a sprinkling of nurses and aides who stepped in for a moment in the course of their rounds to wish me well and to share a bowl of champagne punch, at which I sipped with growing recklessness in my discomfort at finding myself the center of much inescapable badinage. Dr. Chrisser presented me with the print of Blake's "Isaac Newton," which he had had handsomely mounted in an oak frame. He set it on the consulting table and turned it to catch the fall sunlight that filtered through the grimy city windows.

"To me it represents the spirit of science, in a way that no other painting does," he said. "I thought you'd appreciate that, Carl."

"It's very fine," I said, although I remember my chief reaction to the picture at the time being a sense of dismay at its anatomical inaccuracy. The ribs and deltoid structure seemed to me to be grossly misrepresented. The painting was unwrapped, so that, embarrassed at the prospect of having to carry home on a public streetcar a large, imposingly framed portrait of a naked man, I stopped in the gift shop in the lobby and bought a copy of the Washington *Post,* in which I bandaged it awkwardly. Sitting in the streetcar with the front page of the newspaper spread out flat across the pane of the portrait in my lap, I experienced an elation such as I had never felt before. My life was at last assuming the form and significance that was the reward of years of patient labor and commitment. My gratification, I ventured to believe, was more than merely vanity: it was the just appreciation of those benign, imponderable processes of equity in which the universe revolved. It was as nearly luminous an emotion as I had yet experienced: a sense of purpose, of fruition, of progress towards fulfillment, as exact and irrepressible as the clarity of the early-autumn light in which the streets were bathed, through which I swayed and jolted, undisturbed, in my piety. Overcome almost to the point of tears by my felicity, I lowered my eyes; they fell on the headlines of the newspaper spread out across the picture in my lap:

ENGLAND AND FRANCE
DECLARE WAR ON GERMANY
Von Rundstedt Drives into Poland
Lodz, Cracow Threatened

The news seemed so remote to me—in place, in time, in spiritual or moral relevance—that the nearest thing I felt to alarm or indignation or dismay was perhaps a faintly chastened acknowledgment of my geographical ignorance. It occurred to me that I had only the very faintest idea of the locations of those cities, of their histories, chief industries, populations, political importance, physical appearance, or language. This fact produced a second, and my only measurable, discomfort at the news of their imminent disasters. A great many totally anonymous people were about to suffer and die in places about which I knew next to nothing, and I resented the importunity of the fact. As if in testimony to the verity of their existence, they demanded recognition of their death and suffering—as they had not succeeded in doing of their lives and pleasures—a recognition that intruded upon unpleasantly and diminished gravely the sense of pious eminence in which I had only just rejoiced. If they had had the tact—or wit—to suffer and die in the same obscurity in which they had lived, I could more readily have appreciated the pathos of the experience. I sat uneasily examining this paradox for the next eight blocks; for greater than which distance, evidently, the misfortunes of imaginary Poles and the metaphysical problems they arouse cannot compete, for gratification, with the study of one's own good fortune. By the time I disembarked on upper Wisconsin Avenue, I was again immersed in my faintly delirious absorption with my own far fairer prospects. Perhaps not so faintly. Burdened as I was by Sir Isaac Newton, who was ominously lunging to escape my embrace in the chill wind that had sprung up, I made my way to a neighborhood delicatessen and bought a bottle of wine with which to celebrate the commencement of our new life. I had no sooner left the shop than I regretted the impulse, because the familiarity of the proprietor's features and the assurance with which he had recommended the bottle of Lacrima Christi suddenly clarified into the realization that it was he who had proposed and sold to me with equally forbidding insistence a bottle of liebfraumilch on a winter evening almost two years ago. To add to the cheerlessness of this discovery, the wind began to blow even more cuttingly; I clutched my oddly assorted burdens to my breast and lowered my head into it, reflecting that I would be a very strange subject of speculation by a casual visitor from space: there goes a typical denizen of this planet, plunging into the night wind with a bottle of Lacrima Christi and a portrait of Sir Isaac Newton. A raggedly dressed man approaching me on the sidewalk evidently shared that startled view; his eyes widened as if in unexpected fascination, or possibly admiration, or hope, or delighted recognition of my poetic soul, my capacity to redeem that dreary, stony sphere across which we wandered. He removed a hand from the pocket of his baggy, soiled trousers and thrust it out toward me as if in congratulation or blessing; but then, as we approached more closely and our eyes met, he withdrew it hastily and stuck it back into his pocket, his face falling, his shoulders resuming their hunched and weary opposition to the wind.

I hoped that, as so frequently of late, Molly would fail to answer my tinkling of the doorbell, that I could let myself into the apartment and dispose prudently of my two unprepossessing bundles in the hall closet before she appeared. It was not the case. She opened the door to my initial signal, dressed in a fresh, flowered apron and smelling inauspiciously of Polynesian Night.

"What have you got?" she asked, relentlessly surveying in turn the brown paper bag and the arrantly enigmatic square of swaddled picture frame that I had set on the sofa to remove my overcoat.

"This is a painting that Dr. Chrisser gave me," I said, whisking away and crumpling under my arm the sheets of newsprint to unveil Sir Isaac Newton, whose nudity, it seemed to me, was startlingly magnified by the surroundings. Molly gazed at it with a look of shocked distaste. "It's the Spirit of Science," I explained. "By William Blake. It's Isaac Newton, actually."

"Do you mean he posed for it? Like that?"

"No. It's an—imaginative conception of him. I don't think they ever met."

"Well, we can't have it in here," she said. "It's not—suitable."

"No, I suppose not. I don't care for it too much myself. He's done the torso all wrong. Maybe I'll take it down to my new office."

"And what's this?"

"Ah! This—" I picked up the paper bag and plucked out the bottle of wine with an uncertain flourish. "This is a bottle of Lacrima Christi. To celebrate."

" 'The tears of Christ,' " she said, the words echoing hollowly, as if from the bottom of a well. She raised her eyes to mine. "Do you mean to say you're going to drink some wine?"

"Well, I thought we'd have just a glass together. To celebrate. After all, it's an occasion."

Her eyes clung to mine for a moment like those of an animal seeking shelter in a cave, equally beset and wary, poised for instant flight from what it might discover there.

"It should be chilled," I said with unnatural emphasis. "The man told me that, specifically." I moved my eyes abruptly to the kitchen door and sniffed, raising my head appreciatively. "Something smells very good in there."

"It's a ham. I got it especially. It won't be long. Let me have that. I'll put it in the refrigerator." She took the bottle from me and stood studying the label for a moment, lifting her hand to brush from her forehead a fallen wisp of damp, oak-colored hair. The gesture was suspended, her hand held stilly, the palm turned inward as if to shield herself from a blow as she raised her head to listen with sudden absolute attention to a peal of restless whimpering from the open bedroom door. "Elizabeth is awfully fussy," she said. "I wish you'd have a look at her."

"Oh? Does she have a fever?"

"No. But she's hardly eaten anything. Her stomach seems to be upset." She followed me into the bedroom and handed me the thermometer which she had carried in the pocket of her apron, apparently only recently employed. I felt the baby's neck and belly and pried open her mouth to peer into her throat, then turned her over to insert the thermometer into her rectum. Molly stood holding the bottle of wine to her breast while I completed the examination. The child's abdomen was a trifle taut, but she had no fever or other signs of infection; and yet, as she lay plucking restlessly at the bedclothes, she looked unaccountably unhealthy to me: alien, bathed in a curiously unpleasant aura, like the morbid luster that envelops a decaying fruit, unrelated to me by anything but disaster. I had the sudden appalling conviction that the child was not mine. My hand recoiled from her forehead, where it had lain, and she broke into a howl.

"What's the matter with her?" Molly said, her voice thinned by a harsh, unnatural tension.

"Nothing very serious. Why don't we leave her in here tonight instead of bringing her to the table?" I raised my eyes to hers and saw that she was watching me fixedly, her face gaunt-looking and very pale.

"It must be something serious, the way you look."

"No. Her stomach's a little upset, that's all. I'd feed her lightly. Just a little thin formula."

"I don't believe you. You're keeping something from me."

"Why would I do that, for God's sake?" I saw that I was holding the thermometer away from me with a delicate aversion, as if it were contaminated. "I'll go and wash up. If you put that wine in the freezer it will chill quicker."

I went into the bathroom, washed off the thermometer, restored it to its case, then washed my face and hands carefully, dried them on a towel, and stood combing my hair before the mirror, studying my face with more than casual interest for the first time in many years. I was very nearly thirty years old. I was about to embark on a career that would be fascinating, fruitful, and perhaps distinguished. The face appeared to be adequate to the destiny. The mouth was firm and circumspect, the eyes clear and determined, and although I would have preferred that they be not quite so deeply set (to ameliorate somewhat the look of lanterns in a cave), the vault above them was honestly vertical, not swept romantically upward to the brows with that look of tender, frail convexity, peculiar—I remembered with sudden curious exactitude—to those of Robert T. Aldington. And yet it was not a face to which I would have gravitated in adversity. If I had been a derelict on a winter street, the owner of this face, I realized, was the last person to whom I would have appealed for charity. I would very likely have voted for him in a political election, and would no doubt have been reassured to read beneath his photograph in a newspaper that he had been newly appointed Admiral of the Pacific Fleet; but I would not have clipped those features from the paper to set on my dressing table for heartsease. And just as well, I decided brusquely; a very promiscuous appeal to justify.

I went out and across the living room to the door of the kitchen, where Molly was heating a bottle of formula in a pan of boiling water.

"I'm just getting this ready for her," she said. "Why don't you go and read the paper while I feed her?"

"I don't feel much like reading it tonight. The news is very bad."

She raised her head to look at me with an expression of steadfast inquiry. "You mean the war," she said after a moment, and then added tonelessly, "I suppose we'll get into *that* next."

"I suppose we will, eventually. I don't see how we can avoid it."

"Will you have to go?"

"Oh, no. Not with you and Elizabeth."

"Oh. Well, at least—" She dropped her eyes and moved her hand suddenly to switch off the burner; then, with a dish towel, plucked the bottle from the boiling water. Her face was flushed slightly, evidently from the steam.

"I think I'll put on some Bach," I said. "I'd like to hear some Bach tonight."

"All right. I won't be very long."

I went into the living room and put a record of the Toccata and Fugue in D Minor on the phonograph. While Molly fed our daughter I sat on the sofa and listened to the icy notes crystallize and then thaw instantly in the darkening room, leaving behind the faint, pure echo of the perfect, lucent pattern they had woven across the silence. It was first conceived of, I reflected, in 1707; and when Napoleon stormed Ratisbon, a century later, he might have listened to that imperishable clarity ring out into the salon of his headquarters at night, above the thunder of the guns. Through the ghostly precipitate of the dead German's mind I heard the cries of my daughter trickle like the wail of Polish children through a winter mist. Outside the window the slow September dusk was possessing the tops of the sycamore trees. It enveloped them as stealthily as the sorrow that enveloped me like a vague nausea. As the crystal thread ran out and the piece wove into the silence, I became aware that Elizabeth's whimpering had been extinguished with it. There was a moment when the room rang thinly with only the two frail echoes, tossed between the walls like a cloud of blown rime; then an agonized infantile shriek rose from the bedroom, throbbing in the air like a nerve pierced by a dentist's drill. I leapt up from the sofa and plunged in through the open door to where Molly stood above the crib, her hands clutched to her throat, staring down at Elizabeth, who lay convulsed, her face purple with an indrawn, long-held scream of pain, her forehead just above the left eye disfigured by a pale blue, already swelling contusion, like a plum.

"God in heaven, what happened?" I whispered. Molly turned her head to stare at me, her eyes glittering.

"I dropped the bottle," she said. "It hit her on the head." As I moved toward her, she snatched the child up and held her clutched against her breast, swinging her back and forth in desperate, quick half circles, showering her face and throat with kisses, mumbling to her in passionate contrition. I reached out to touch the baby's head, to reassure, and if possible, examine her.

"Leave her *alone,*" Molly shrieked. "If you don't love the child, leave her *alone!*" She turned her back to me, hugging and caressing her daughter with a hysterical tenderness, shielding her from me.

"You'd better let me look at her," I said in bitter astonishment. "That looks like a nasty bump."

"I couldn't *help* it!" Molly cried. "The bottle was full, and it was slippery! She didn't drink a bit of it! It was heavy! What do you *care,* anyway?" I stared at her in desolation, feeling the entire length of my intestines writhe like a great constricting serpent waking inside of me.

"Well, you'd better put some peroxide on it," I said voicelessly in a kind of serpentine, sustained hiss. "And give her one of the children's aspirins. And it may need bandaging." I went out of the room and stood in front of the living-room window, looking out at the black branches swinging restlessly in the wind across the streetlights and the housefronts. Somewhere in Poland tanks were rumbling across the wheat fields toward the streets of Lodz and Cracow, where people peered through their darkened windows toward the west, the curtains clenched in their clammy, rigid hands.

From San Miguel de Allende we drove west through the deserts and mountains to Guanajuato and Guadalajara, old gray cities of blunt, rain-pitted stone, thick-walled buildings brutal with their weight, and colonnaded squares where we sat in the cool stone-smelling shadow and looked out through the arches at the blazing zócalos, their hedges and canna beds and wrought-iron rococo bandstands quavering under a sky that was one vast violet flame. All around those cities I could feel the silence and lonely immensity of the deserts and crumbling barren sierras we had driven through to reach them. It washed against the great stone buildings like a wave and seeped between their blocks like water through the masonry of an ancient dam, sliding in shimmering sheets over the polished cobbles of the narrow streets, seeming at noontime to gather in pools in the hushed plazas or in the patio of a hotel, where I would look down through the iron bars of the slotted window and see the stone figure of a Virgin standing sunken in white silence, her drowned eyes gazing through the haze like those of a sunken figurehead.

Then it was an almost agonizing delight to see a group of little girls in pretty pink and blue and yellow Sunday dresses, as sweet and bright and ephemeral as spoonfuls of sherbet in the sun, being herded across the plaza by a nun, their voices and laughter tinkling like a flurry of wind chimes in a breeze. In the brutal stony silence their delicate evanescent fragility made my heart ache as icy sherbet makes the palate ache on a hot day, or when, as when the noontime tide of silence receded up the streets and between the huge, stained blocks of stone, there would be a burst of birdsong in the tamarind trees or a sudden peal of angelus bells, as wracking as a birth cry in the air. I wandered for hours over the cobbles of the serpentine walled streets, stained and sour with the smell of basin water and dung and rotting rinds of fruit, and across the foot-worn paving stones of secret inner plazas, held in the congealed gray convoluted entrails of those ancient cities like petrified, barely beating ganglia, throbbing with old, slow lusts and impulses. I preferred to go alone, and once or twice I managed to—although he fumed about it mightily—when Ron would leave me in the hotel room and go out to change traveler's checks or buy theater tickets or a bottle of aspirin. Then I would slip out for an hour or two and roam through the endless mazes of the barrios, wandering deeper and deeper into the labyrinthine tangle of streets toward the heart I knew not to exist but whose soundless throbbing drew me toward it like a silent drumbeat, like the pounding of pure, invisibly pale blood. I was followed once for blocks by a speechless, unmotioning, impavidly persistent figure with a face as gaunt and sorrowfully possessed as those of the plaster saints who stared out of the chapels of the musty, gilded churches; and once by a cringing yellow dog with the look of craven cunning of a jackal which, when I stopped to dip my hands into the stone basin of a stagnant fountain, crept up and licked the calves of my legs with an avid, feverish ardor that scalded and sickened me.

And always there was the sudden, magically tender descent of dusk with an uncanny faint perfume of sage and night-blooming cereus blowing from the desert in the cool dark air, and the calandria carriages clopping along the Calzada Independencia under a sky shivering with starlight like altar candles and the girls with gardenias in their hair and their teeth glowing like alabaster in their shy dark faces as they smiled and murmured, "Noches," drifting by like blossoms on a stream; and the couples strolling with the fingers of their brown hands twined together with an almost cruel intensity, as if stricken by the glamorous soft wind that blew against the heart like a bewildering gust out of ancestral fields.

When we left Morelia and drove south into the Sierra Madre del Sur toward the coast, I would look down from the bend of a mountain road and see those towns and villages lying in the floor of a valley like stone blossoms in a dry lake bed, motionless petrified flowers, their spires rising slender and startling as pistils from the cup of lapping, slate-blue petals, roses of frozen silence. And then when I thought my heart would be parched and calcified forever like those terrible burnt stones and those spellbound flint cities, we drove up through a zone of transfiguration as sudden and gentle as the desert night, plunging into rustling, green, jungled heights, cool gulfs of shadowy foliage with mountain streams and waterfalls gushing down through moist, ferny, fragrant glens and pouring into moss-bound tranquil pools that overflowed their slippery velvet boulders in a sweet, ceaseless ebullition, murmuring swollenly. I felt a great pure diastolic rush of life into me with the surge of air into my desperately distended lungs and of warm, resuscitating blood into my desiccate, dilated heart. I laid my head on my forearm on the sill of the open window and let the cool air lave my face, lapping my throat and temples and my parched lips and eyelids with an avid, almost bestial tenderness, like the tongue of an animal, of that yellow dog in the barrio. My head lolled in a kind of shivering stupor, watching the tangled mountain forests grow more dense as we crossed the crest of the sierra and went down the coastal slopes into the green depths of the Pacific jungles. There were banana trees with huge, primordial leaves, and banyans, dripping with hairy, savagely contorted vines, and mahogany trees with their burnished bronze trunks glowing like gold pillars in the gloom, and sometimes a dazzling rumor of violence: a hectic, frenzied flurry of foliage, ripped open with a splashing sound of torn silk, and then a flash of blue and scarlet plumage like a wound, like a ruthlessly bared vulva, and the shriek of a macaw ringing through the radiant green vaults, and afterwards a palpitant silence that beat against the ears like blood.

We came into Zihuatanejo in the middle of a still white afternoon, into a light that hung like a blazing platinum mist over the hot mud in the street and the tattered banana trees and beyond the ragged huts of the sleeping village the incandescent, indigo expanse of the endless, silent, burning sea. We parked in front of a *taller*, a little general store with mud-splashed adobe walls and a Coca-Cola sign nailed to a post. I couldn't move for a while; exhausted by the brilliance, I sat staring through the windshield at the few soft clouds standing in the sky like mountains above the violet sea.

"How about a Coke?" Ron said.

"Is this the place?"

"This is Zihuatanejo." He pronounced it with malicious elegance. "But I think the hotels are up the mountain. I hope to hell they are. I'll ask inside."

"Yes, I'd like a Coke."

"You want to come?"

"All right."

I got out of the car and stood on my shivering, very naked legs until they had stilled themselves, and then followed him up the wooden steps into the little dingy shop and stood drinking a Coca-Cola while he asked directions to the Catalina from a stout brown lady in an undershirt with a gentle gold-toothed smile. There was a very strange assortment of merchandise: plastic fans and tee shirts stamped ACAPULCO in silver-glitter letters and magnificently hand-embroidered linen rebozos and dusty bottles of tequila and savage-looking wooden-handled machetes.

"Yes, it's up the mountain," he said. "But probably full, the lady says, and pretty expensive. She recommends a quinta called the Zapata, in the middle of the bay."

"What is it? Cottages?"

"Yes. Casitas, she calls them. With kitchenettes. There's a hotel, too, I guess."

"Then we'd better buy some food. And a bottle of tequila."

"That's a good idea. Basics, anyhow."

I went out and sat in the car while he made the purchases. A child driving a snorting, plodding pig before him with a stick paused to stare at me.

"Buenos días," I said.

"Buenos días." Standing on one leg, he scratched the calf of it with the toes of his other foot. Beyond him, a battered trawler with the name ROSAURA written on its bow in pink letters nodded gently at the end of a dilapidated pier. The heat lay like hot wet towels draped all over me. Ron came out of the *taller* carrying a string bag that bulged with boxes and bottles.

"What did you get?" I asked when he got into the car.

"Elementals. Sun lotion; Metazín, for the trots; bug spray, tequila, and a bottle of margarita mix, lemon and all. Saves a lot of work."

He turned the car around, thumping in the muddy potholes, and drove back up the length of the street to a dirt road that forked off through the village. It led between a huddle of huts of mud-splashed concrete blocks with tin roofs over which drooped great ragged blades of banana leaves and coco palms whose pale trunks bowed stilly toward the sea. There were pigs and chickens wandering among the flat-roofed houses and children in torn undershirts with brown elfin faces standing in the doorways. The village reeked of the sour, ubiquitous stench of tropical poverty.

"It's called the Last Resort," Ron said, turning to grin at me.

"I've heard of it."

"According to Terry, it's very beautiful; in the suburbs, I guess."

The road began to rise steeply between walls of steaming vegetation, the ravaged muddy corduroy giving way to a patched and crumbling asphalt, and then halfway up the mountain, broke clear of the strip of jungle to our right, and we could look down onto a little half-moon bay of emerald purity, its pellucid calm green water rimmed with a strip of salt-white sand, like melon rind, and then a narrow canopy of coco palms that merged into the vine-tangled silent jungles that rose up the mountain slopes to where we sat in the parked car, staring down in humbled jubilation.

"My God, it *is* beautiful," Ron said. "Don't you think?"

"It's unbelievable."

Far out at the open end of the bay the crystal green of the water blended into the depthless lucent indigo of the Pacific, stretching out forever, everywhere, in a numbing totality of blessing that made me for a moment utterly unafraid, utterly faithful to its blue, immeasurable beatitude. I felt as if a part of me would stay there forever, rescued from everything.

"Oh, I love this place," I said. "I love it here." I laughed and caught Ron's hand and kissed it all over his wrist and fingers with quick crazy kisses of delight. "Oh, thank you for bringing me here! Now I owe you everything."

"Oh, I don't know," he said with a solemn shyness. "Maybe we'd better have a look at the Quinta Zapata before you say that."

He put the car in gear and we drove further up the open crest of the mountain above the bay shore. Here and there the jungled slopes had been cleared to enfold small private villas, and, in two places, the grounds of luxury hotels, their many-layered tiers of sun decks bright with striped umbrellas, and the vine-clad loggias of dining terraces and iron-balconied cabanas, their red tile roofs sprinkled between the foliage along the track of a funicular railway that plunged almost vertically to the beach below. We passed the stuccoed Moorish gates of their entrance driveways that led off from the road, and drove beyond them, descending again into enclosing walls of vegetation until we came to a huge, faded, barely legible sign that bridged what was apparently the last length of the dwindling, once again decrepit pavement. It said: QUINTA ZAPATA—*Posada*—*Casitas*.

"More our style," Ron said.

"I think so, too. I'm going to love it here, I know." I felt an almost hilarious excitement at everything.

The road wound in between beds of ornamental cactus and poinciana trees splashed with scarlet blossom to an old two-story hotel that enclosed a blue-and-yellow-tiled patio, open to the roadway, with a dripping fountain and a gigantic royal palm whose fronds rustled above the red tile roof and the flaking stucco of the scabrous, white-plastered walls. There was no one anywhere in sight, and the sound of the dripping water and the rustle of the palms was as clear in the dense, white, saturated silence as if cut into crystal. We got out of the car and walked into the patio. There was an ancient, darkly shining mahogany bar, and behind it, pasted on the chipped blue and yellow tiles, a pair of photographs, one of a priest, in a black cassock and biretta, squinting in the sunlight, and the other of a torero, in a bicorne hat and gold-embroidered fighting suit, both young and slender and with the same look of proud, shy ambition. Against one wall there was a serape-covered cot, and underneath it a coatimundi crouched, staring at us with bright, bitter eyes. The rim of the fountain basin dripped into a slime-green tiled pool in which four pale, blotched goldfish hung dreamily. Ron tapped the button of a call bell on the bar and called out, "Frente," but the only thing to appear for some time was a shabby red rooster, who walked into the patio and paused with one foot uplifted, muttering and shaking his comb at us. We sat down on a pair of barstools and giggled at each other.

"There's a bar, after all," Ron said.

"Yes. It's marvelous. One of those quiet little places where you can sneak off and really talk."

"I know," he said. "Why don't you tell me about yourself?"

"Oh, there's nothing much to tell. Of course, I have my dreams, like everyone."

"Yes. Do you come here a lot?"

"No, not very often. Only on special times, when I want to really think."

"I know what you mean. It's a place where you can really have long thoughts."

"Yes, it is. I'm glad you feel that way about it, too. Somehow I've always known I would meet someone like you here."

"I've always felt that, too." He reached out and laid his hand on mine on the bar top. I drew my hand away and lowered my eyes.

"Please, not yet. It's too soon. Let's talk a little first."

"All right. What shall we talk about?"

We broke into peals of laughter that rang around the little patio, both full of our sudden dizzy gaiety that was like a shower of rain sprinkling onto hot desert sand.

"Oh, God!" I howled. "How did we *find* it? There's not another place like it in the Western Hemisphere."

"Oh, everyone who knows where it's at comes here." He tossed his hand grandly. "Jackie, Ari, Johnny Carson."

"Schopenhauer."

"Schopenhauer. Rasputin. Spengler—this is where he wrote *The Decline of the West,* you know. Oh, everybody."

An old man in a sagging undershirt and a pair of stained white trousers, and wearing a pair of mirror-lensed sunglasses, limped painfully through an arched doorway that led out of the dim, tile-floored recesses beyond the patio.

"Buenos días, señores," he murmured.

"Buenos días," Ron said. "Estamos buscando habitaciones."

"Sí, claro." He nodded and wandered back of the bar, where he bent down and disappeared from sight for several minutes, apparently arranging bottles and glasses with a clinking sound. "Hay habitaciones," he murmured, still out of sight. "Cinquenta pesos la noche. Y con comida, ciento."

"Fifty pesos," Ron said. "That's about four-fifty. Nine dollars with dinner."

"My God," I said. "Let's stay here forever."

"I think you're right."

The old man reappeared, leaning with his palms against the bar and panting for a moment. "Están de acuerdo? Is that agreeable?"

"Sí," Ron said. "Muy de acuerdo. Very agreeable." He nodded vigorously and swept his open hand around the patio. "Muy lindo, el hotel. Nos gusta mucho. It's beautiful here. We like it very much."

"Sí." The old man nodded and turned to point to the photographs pasted on the wall behind him. "Mis hijos. My sons."

"Muy guapos," I said. "They're very handsome."

"Sí, guapos. Y sabios. And wise." He pointed, first to the priest, then to the bullfighter. "Éste es Raúl. This is Raúl. Y éste, Porfirio. Se lo llaman El Tigre. And this, Porfirio. They call him the Tiger."

"Ah, sí." I nodded admiringly.

"Fué el año en que fueron ordenados ambos. It was taken the year they were both ordained." Ron and I murmured appreciatively. "Tener hijos es buena suerte. To have sons is good fortune. ¿Los tienen ustedes? Do you have any?"

"No," I murmured: "Ningunos. None."

"Se equivocan. Sin los hijos, la vida no vale la pena. You're making a mistake. Without children, life isn't worth the trouble."

The coatimundi began to make vicious chirruping noises underneath the cot. "Cállate, hombre," the old man muttered tranquilly. "Shut up, boy." He opened his mouth and tapped his brown, broken teeth warningly. "Le fastidia la gente. He doesn't like people."

"Ah," Ron murmured. "Nos puede hacer una margarita, señor? Tenemos mucha sed. Could you make us a margarita? We're very thirsty."

"Sí, cómo no." He began to do so, digging about in the zinc bowels of the bar and fussing abstractedly with bottles and glasses, pausing to hold aloft a plastic bag of ice cubes and announce proudly, "Purificado," which meant that it was made from distilled water.

"Ah, bueno." Ron nodded gratefully.

It took the old man at least ten minutes to make the drinks. When he had finished, he set them on the bar and held out his open hand, saying, "Diez pesos." Ron dug into his pocket and put a ten-peso piece in the old man's hand.

"Gracias. Y entonces hay las casitas, con cocinas. And we also have cottages, with kitchenettes. Pero están todas ocupadas al momento. But they are all occupied at the moment. Mañana habrá una. Pero son mas costosas. Mil pesos la semana. There will be one available tomorrow, but they're more expensive; eighty dollars a week."

"La tomamos," Ron said. "We'll take it."

"Bueno. Pero esta noche se tienen que quedar en el hotel. Good. But tonight you'll have to stay in the hotel."

"De acuerdo," Ron said. He nodded and saluted with his drink.

"Bueno. Ahora les voy a preparar la habitación. Fine. Now I'm going to go and get your room ready. Would you like to stay upstairs? Hay vista del mar. There's a view of the sea."

"Ah, sí, ¡arriba! Oh, yes, upstairs!" I cried.

He nodded and shuffled out from behind the bar and back into the arched doorway, calling out, "Socorro. Socorro."

When he came back, half an hour later, we were even giddier, having finished the margaritas, which were about ninety percent tequila, sipping them slowly from the salty glass rims while we sucked lime slices and listened to the dripping of water in the sunny silence, and the soft clatter of the palms, and sometimes, when the breeze blew up the mountain from the bay, the gentle hollow clap of the rollers breaking on the white sand far below. He led us in through the arched doorway and up a flight of bare, worn stairs and around the wooden-railed inside gallery of the hotel that looked down onto the patio and the bar where we had sat. There were geraniums with white-and-scarlet blossoms hanging in tin cans, and from under the red tiles of the roof a muttering of doves. He opened a door that bore an enameled metal plaque with the number 9 printed on it and waved us into the room. It was bare and white, with cheap pine furniture and on the wall a small wooden crucifix with a frond of dry palm stuck behind it. There were narrow double doors that opened onto a tiny iron-railed balcony that looked out across the tops of palms and banyan trees to the vast violet sea, stretching from horizon to horizon. I went out and stood with my hands on the hot iron of the railing, and looking down, I could see, far to the left, the rocky gnarled cape of the southern horn of the bay tumbling down into the green water and the gentle translucent combers rolling in in a tranquil endless procession, and on the distant beach a few palm-roofed huts among the coco palms and a canoe pulled up on the sand. There was a path winding down through the jungle to the beach, a hundred yards below, lined with pink-and-white oleander bushes and blood-bright poinsettia blossom.

"Está perfecto," I said. The old man came to the door of the balcony and stood at my shoulder. "Sí. Muy bella, la vista. The view is very beautiful." He pointed to the point of rocks at the far end of the bay. "Over there it is called Los Gatos—the Cats. When I was a boy one could stand here and see the big cats—the jaguars—come down to the beach in the morning and run on the sand. Such beautiful animals. Now they are gone."

"You've been here since you were a boy?"

"Yes. I was born in this house. My father was patrón before me." He handed me the key to the room, a huge old skeleton key, attached by a piece of wire to a square of smooth dark wood. "You will be happy here." He nodded and went back into the room and stood at the door, pointing out into the hallway. "Down there is the bath. There is a shower. Will you want to eat?"

"Yes," Ron said.

"It is served at nine o'clock. I'll have your bags brought up."

"The car is unlocked," Ron said. "Thank you."

"It is nothing." He opened his hands and bowed above them slightly, then thumped down the gallery toward the stairs. Ron came out onto the balcony and laid his hand on my shoulder.

"I hope it isn't a mistake to eat here, but I don't know where else to go, for the moment."

"It will probably be very good home cooking."

We stood looking down at the bay in the sun and the green roof of leaves of the jungle that surrounded the hotel. In the hot silence I could hear a woman singing softly and the clatter of a bucket on tiles and the occasional splash of water and the grinding of a scrub brush on stone.

"I feel as though I've been here forever," I said. "Or as if I'd just come back from a long trip to somewhere else. Oh, God, I'm tired." I went back into the room and lay down on the bed, staring up at the ceiling fan that turned slowly, shifting my hair about my temples gently and ceaselessly. I closed my eyes, and after a moment I felt Ron take off my shoes, and then a moment later heard someone enter the room and a girl's voice asking if we would like ice and flowers.

When I woke up it was dark in the room and the curtains were blowing inward from the balcony doors in a breeze from the sea. I could smell jacaranda, and charcoal smoke, and roasting corn, and the faint, distant scent of the ocean, like the veil of brine that lay over everything when I was a child. I have never slept so profoundly in my life; I had a sense of refreshment and restoration that was like metamorphosis; my body and mind were brand-new, limp and moist and pink; I was like a soft-shelled crab or a snake in his new, shining skin, or a locust spreading its fresh wet wings in the summer dark. Ron was sitting beside me on the bed. He put his hand on my hair and said, "You're very damp. Are you too hot?"

"No. I feel very cool and fresh. And terribly hungry. Have we missed the comida?"

"No, but they're eating. Do you want to go down now?"

"Yes. I'll just comb my hair." I reached up and took his hand and smiled at him like a child recovering from a fever. "What have you been doing?"

"Well, I unpacked the clothes and put them in the wardrobe, and read a couple of chapters of Terry's guide."

"You were good to let me sleep. Can I have my green dress?"

"All right."

I brushed my hair and put on the fresh dress that he brought me from the wardrobe, feeling a quiet virginal splendor in these acts, and we went down to the patio, where they had covered the tables with cloths and other guests were eating in the light of candle lanterns in the warm darkness. They all seemed to be acquainted; there was conversation between tables and an atmosphere of friendliness and intimacy; one could sense that they were drawn together by the distinction of having discovered the hotel for themselves, as we had—it was not advertised in any of the guidebooks—and rejoicing in its seclusion and economy, and the excellence of the food, and the hospitality and charm of the proprietor, whose name was Esparolini and who had had his kneecap blown off by a grenade, fighting with Zapata as a boy of fourteen. We were seated with a German family, a middle-aged engineer from Berlin and his wife and son. The wife was the single exception to the general air of congeniality—a plump silent woman with dusty white hair, a tragic-looking face, and slowly moving, downcast eyes, who seemed to regret her presence there and took consolation only in the food, to which no one could have objected. We ate huachinango—red snapper—caught that morning and grilled over charcoal, with baked bananas and roasted corn and chiles rellenos, chili peppers stuffed with meat and cheese and fried in batter as delicate as frost. We were served by two of the patrón's sons, dark, slender youths who moved like panthers, and a pair of sweet, merry girls named Socorro and Miquelina, who giggled with delight every time they were spoken to, and brought us bottle after bottle of ice-cold Carta Blanca beer.

We must have eaten for two hours, and then we drank beer until midnight, sitting at the littered tables under the stars. The German boy went upstairs and brought down a mandolin and played "Muss Ich Denn?" and "Du, Du, Liegst Mir im Hertzen," singing the folk tunes in a trembling tenor voice that he seemed to project out into the darkness beyond the patio with a sentimental passion that grew more and more candid as he drank. An exquisite blond-haired girl with a Swedish accent, seated alone against the wall, listened raptly, her head bowed in the candlelight like a Caravaggio madonna. His mother sat with downcast, slowly roving eyes, tapping tragically with her fingertips on the tabletop. After a while the boy leaned his mandolin against the table and wandered out across the patio to the road, where he stood with his hands wedged into his hip pockets, staring up at the sky. I could hear the tide change suddenly in the bay below us; there was a gathering intensity in the sound of the incoming surf after the long idle lapse of slack water. I said to Ronnie, "Shall we go for a walk on the beach before we go to bed?"

"That's a great idea," he said. "I'll just go up and get the flashlight. It'll be dark on that path."

We sat in silence for several minutes after he had gone. The engineer's wife watched bitterly as her son paced back and forth on the worn grass beyond the patio and then turned suddenly and disappeared up the crumbled pavement of the road into the shadows of the forest.

"You should be careful," she said, turning to look at me directly for the first time in the evening.

"Why? Do you mean it isn't safe?"

"Oh, yes, yes, it is perfectly safe," her husband said. "My wife does not like the tropics. It is perfectly safe. A lovely spot." He raised his eyebrows with a hint of irony, as if somewhat amused by his own confidence, and laid his hand on his wife's arm.

"I won't come again," she said. "Last year it was Guatemala, and there were the earthquakes. All night the ground trembled. Do you know what it is to wake up at night with the earth shaking beneath you?"

"No," I said.

"Is terrible. And there is that stink, always. Like dead bodies. And the snakes. The creatures. Here, of course, the insects are not bad; but there is that filthy animal."

"A coatimundi," the engineer explained, smiling. "He is very peaceful, unless approached."

"A filthy, savage thing. And that depraved girl."

The engineer sighed humorously. "Uta does not understand that depravity is not confined to the tropics. I prefer the tropical version because it is undisguised. One is safer."

"There are so many decent places to go," the wife said. "There is Athens, the Aegean."

The engineer's eyebrows shot up wildly. "Ah—Athens!" He broke into a long guttural chuckle, patting his wife's wrist and nodding enthusiastically. "Yes, Athens. And Rome. And Alexandria! Have you been to Alexandria, Miss Lindekomm?"

"No."

"Or this famous Aegean of Uta's?"

"No, I haven't been to Europe at all."

"Ah. Or Berlin itself. You should have visited Berlin in the thirties. I can describe it to you, if you like; I was there." There was a considerable pause, during which his wife removed her arm from beneath his hand. "And where are you from, Miss Lindekomm?"

"I come from College Park, Maryland," I said. "It's a suburb of Washington, D.C."

His eyebrows shot up again, with even greater enthusiasm. "Ah! Washington, D.C.! This, too, is a remarkable city. All those imitation Greek temples everywhere. A kind of Athens on the Potomac, it seemed to me. Do you find that the spirit of Aristotle resides there, too?"

"It isn't conspicuous," I said.

"No, that was my impression. Still, we were not there long enough to have discovered it, perhaps."

"The cherry trees were very beautiful," the wife said. "And there was much lilac. It reminded me of Berlin in the spring. Such beautiful cities, they are. Such a good hotel, we were. The Carleton. Do you know the Carleton?"

"I know where it is," I said. "But I've never been in it."

"Such a fine hotel. So good the service."

Ron came back into the patio with the flashlight, and I stood up and excused myself.

"Yes, yes, you go. Enjoy yourself," the engineer said effusively. "We see you in the morning."

We went across the patio to where the path opened out of the hillside forest and down the trail to the beach. In the dark masses of foliage around us we could see orchids glowing in the starlight with a haunted pallor, like faces suspended in the night. At the bottom of the path we came out into the grove of coco palms that bordered the beach and heard the soft soaring of the branches, and then the sea breeze swept over us, cool and steady and salt, and we saw the long luminous rollers curling in from the Pacific, breaking into radiant white foam on the flat hard sand. We took off our shoes and socks and walked through the edge of the foam along the shore, feeling it lave our ankles and swell up to the calves of our legs, almost as warm as milk. Far up on the mountain were the lights of the grand hotels, looking as fragile as Christmas-tree balls in the fumes of jungle vegetation that swarmed around them, and below them, rippling in the water, the harbor lights of Zihuatanejo. At the end of the bay there were a few grass huts among the palms of the coconut grove, with kerosene lanterns shining yellow through their windows and the sound of guitar music pulsing out, beating into the sea breeze.

When we came back up the path from the beach the patio was dark and the hotel stood square and silent against the starlight. Ronnie switched on the flashlight and we made our way cautiously across the patio, touching the edges of the tables, around the fountain and toward the arched portal that led in to the stairs. He stumbled against the cot that stood against the wall, and there was a sudden hissing intake of breath, as shrill as a cat spitting, and then a wail like the cry of a cougar. He swung the beam of the flashlight onto the cot and we saw the girl who had been sleeping there, crouched now like a cornered animal against the wall, her hair set into incandescence like a great snarled spiderweb, her eyes bright with terror, pawing at us with her fingers curled like talons.

"You son of a bitch," she whispered hoarsely. "You think you can just tramp on my life like a roach? You think you can do anything you want to me, don't you? I'll kill you, you horrible person." She was wearing a halter top and denim shorts, and in the instant that the beam of the flashlight fell on her I could see a deep scarlet scratch across her bare left shoulder, raked by a thorn or talon, running down across her throat and disappearing into the cleft of her breasts. "Where is my passport?" she said in a strangled, desperate whisper. "You sold my passport, didn't you? You think I'm just going to die for you like an insect?" She struck out at him with her clawed hand, knocking the flashlight to the floor. The lens and bulb tinkled apart on the tile. Ron backed away from her and she leapt up from the couch, slashing wildly at his face with her hands before she fled sobbing across the patio, past the fountain, and out into the forest beyond.

"God in heaven," he muttered. "What was that?"

My heart and my breathing had stopped entirely for an instant and my breast was a still void, empty of anything but a wreath of cold mist that drifted through my throat like the mist that curls lingeringly through the throat of a cold, freshly emptied bottle.

"I don't know," I whispered. "Did she hurt you?"

"No. Just a scratch on my wrist. Who the hell was she? She wasn't at dinner."

"No."

"She's out of her mind."

"Yes. It sounded like it."

We stood for a moment, staring into the darkness beyond the patio.

"Jesus," Ron said. "Scared me to death. Did it scare you?"

"Yes."

"I guess we'd better go on up."

I followed him through the arch and up the stairs in the dark, holding tight to the railing to support myself on my trembling legs. We had left the balcony doors open and the curtains were flapping softly in the breeze from the bay. Ron went out and stood looking down at the tops of the dark trees. I sat on the bed, feeling emptily contained by a hard cold carapace, like the glass shell of a turtle.

"I guess she's in there somewhere," he said. "Do you think we ought to tell somebody?"

"They're all asleep. It wouldn't do any good."

"I suppose not. She must be a vagrant or something. It's weird." He came back into the room and went to the bureau, where the bottle of tequila stood beside the water pitcher and the pair of plastic glasses. "Shall we have a nightcap? I think I could use one."

"I guess so." I had been trying to remember a phrase that the girl's hair, lit into savage, snarled brilliance by the flashlight, had reminded me of. I sipped at the tequila and suddenly thought of it; a phrase from a poem by Dylan Thomas: "This spun slime."

I fell asleep a little drunk and had a terrifying dream of being that girl—of being stranded in an exotic, savage country whose language and laws were unknown to me, without a passport, penniless and friendless and deranged and in desperation to escape, to recover my passport somehow or secure an exit visa. But I could not find the embassy of my own country. I sought for it for hours, for weeks, for months, running, at last, in panic through the mazes of silent, stone-bound streets. And when at last I found it, it was locked and barred, the iron gates chained, weeds growing through the cobbles of the drive, and a sign, bleached and illegible, dangling from the rusted bars. I turned and stumbled through the streets to a police station and wandered through its marble-floored corridors to an office whose door was labeled MINISTRY OF ALIENS and asked for aid, for information; but they could tell me nothing. I went from office to office in growing terror and confusion. I was told to fill out endless forms, subjected to endless, arcane, bewildering interviews with ministers and police officials and bureaucrats who gazed at me with astonishingly beautiful, black-eyed, inscrutable faces, but whose hands, when they lit cigarettes and offered them to me or pushed papers across their desks for me to sign, were leathery, wrinkled, taloned, like the claws of crocodiles or iguanas. Sometimes they were impassive, unmovable; sometimes voluble, effusive, insidiously sympathetic. Sometimes they blew smoke into my face and smiled; sometimes they leaned forward across their desks to stroke my arms or shoulders, insinuating that for a certain fee, a certain consideration, arrangements could be made, the web of regulations sidestepped, my freedom expedited. Sometimes they became stern, abusive, threatening; there were intimations that I had violated sacred statutes, that I was an intruder, an illegal, seditious alien, a spy; that my crimes were punishable by lifelong imprisonment, vile servitude, the amputation of my hands and breasts, by decapitation. Confessions were demanded, torture hinted at; my photograph and fingerprints were taken, my hair cut off. I was made to stand naked in the center of a room and to bend over, to spread my legs, to open my mouth wide while every crevice and orifice of my body was searched and probed with cruelly rigid, taloned fingers. My clothes were flung back at me contemptuously, stained with the dung and urine of my inquisitors. I put them on, shuddering, and when they motioned for me to leave the room, I leapt through the window onto the cobbles of the street below and ran for hours, pursued by dogs and shrieking urchins, through muddy, labyrinthine passageways, my feet bruised and bleeding, my clothes wearing into rags, while people mocked and spit at me, tossing basins of foul liquid onto me from windows, reaching out to snatch at my tattered clothing, hurling stones that thudded against my skull and spine with agonizing impact. At the end of a walled alley I saw a man emerge from a flight of cellar steps and beckon to me with a gentle, magisterial gesture. I ran to him, sobbing with exhaustion and relief, and he motioned me to follow him down the flight of steps. They seemed endless; I held his hand while we descended for miles into the damp, dripping entrails of the earth until we came to a great oak door, which he opened with an iron skeleton key fastened by a length of wire to a slab of smooth wood. I followed him into the darkness of the cellar and when he turned to snap the switch beside the door the room was flooded with a glorious empyrean light. I saw that it was a vast, crystal-vaulted ceremonial chamber, prepared for a rite. There was an altar of glowing alabaster and silver sconces filled with great white magnolia blossoms whose perfume filled the chamber. Across the back of a tall, thronelike chair there were vestments laid ready for me. Stately smiling girls in white robes advanced toward me and removed my foul, ragged clothing and bathed me in liniments from crystal basins and anointed my bruised skin with sweet-scented oil out of shining vials. I was dressed in a diaphanous robe of palest amethyst and my hair was combed and bound into great soft sheaves with gold twine. I was led to the altar by the man who had brought me to the place, and he lifted from a scarlet pillow a wreath of woven marigolds and nodded to me in command. I began to sing, miraculously, magnificently, in a voice of searing, silver timbre the most beautiful and sorrowful of Mexican songs, "La Golondrina":

> *¿A donde irá, veloz y fatigada,*
> *La Golondrina que de aquí se va?*

> *Where will you go, swift and weary,*
> *Swallow who flies from this place?*

He smiled and set on my head the wreath of marigolds. It numbed me instantly, extinguishing my mind in a blaze of white oblivion. All that endured of the dream was the sound of my own voice singing in mysterious, angelic purity, surviving the last frail webs of the vision, sewing it into reality; because when I found myself awake, staring into the dim, dawn-lit air of the hotel bedroom, it continued, undiminished, weirdly disembodied from me now, but floating still into the room through the door that led out to the gallery.

I got out of bed and went barefoot to the door and opened it and went out onto the gallery, looking down into the patio. The wild girl sat on the edge of the fountain basin in the soft light of dawn, bending to wash her hair in the silver water. She gathered it into thick wet strands and wrung them in her hands over the stone bowl, singing in the pure soprano voice that in the dream had welled out of my own throat:

> *También yo estoy en la región perdida*
> *—¡Ay, cielo santo!—y sin poder volar.*

> *I, too, am in the lost regions*
> *—Oh, sacred heaven!—but unlike you, I cannot fly.*

I stood watching with the ghostly sense of seeing my own apparition. She finished the song and raised her head suddenly. When she saw me she smiled with the sweetness of a child, and I felt an eerie tingling pall sweep over me. I turned quickly and went back into the room, standing with my hand on the old porcelain knob of the door until my heart had quieted. I crept back into the bed carefully, so as not to waken Ron, and lay looking up at the crazed, flaking plaster of the ceiling and the fan blade turning slowly, creaking like a mill wheel as it ground reality to dust, to a luminous golden pollen that glowed like a nimbus in the light that welled through the drawn blinds of the balcony doors. When Ron awoke he mumbled dazedly and groped with his hand to find my hair and grasp a handful of it gently.

"Are you awake?" he murmured.

"I believe so."

"Did you hear singing?"

"Yes. It was that girl. She was downstairs in the patio."

"My God. She must live there."

"I think she haunts the place."

In the mornings we sat on the veranda of the little villa we had moved into, drinking café con leche with hot bread and guava jelly, looking down at the blue water of the bay and the mist rising from the jungles on the hillside and laborers from the grass huts in the coconut grove driving their burros along the beach to the forests and cane fields beyond the village, the pale-faced dainty animals plodding briskly and haughtily through the white sand while the men followed at a stolid, rapid walk, rapping their haunches occasionally with the flat of a machete blade. In the bright hot stillness of the morning the clap of the long green translucent rollers on the sand was like a constant scattered volley of rifle shots, sometimes distinct and startling, and yet, in their ceaseless indolent monotony, as hugely comforting as heartbeats, as were all the morning sounds of that place: the bleat of a burro when it was tapped too sharply, the clatter of palm fronds when a breeze sprang up from the sea, even the creak of the rattan chairs we sat in, when we leaned forward to butter a roll or lift a coffee cup. At the corner of the veranda there was a gigantic cactus that stood with its upturned branches spread against the blue of the water like the arms of a giant menorah; sometimes butterflies alighted on it and clung there with their wings opening and closing rapturously to some ecstatic rhythm of the place. In the center of the bay a rocky headland ran out from the shore; the incoming rollers broke against it in a ceaseless girdle of white foam, and when the breeze blew strongly from the sea there would be rainbows hanging in midair in the mist above the rocks, dissolving as swiftly as the memory of dreams. Sometimes a pair of boys would row out to the rocks in a log canoe and drop the large stone that they used for an anchor with a cool splash through the clear water, and then dive and wade for hours among the rocks, hunting for langosta, the giant crayfish that they would lift, wriggling and glittering in the morning light, to drop into a bucket in the bottom of the boat. In the late morning smoke would rise, fragrant and pale blue, from the palms at the bottom of the path where their mother, a stout, sweating, happy-faced, infinitely industrious woman, had lit her charcoal braziers to bake the langosta and the red snapper and banana fritters that we would eat for lunch, seated at picnic tables under the grass roof of her tiny open cantina, with the sea breeze blowing cleanly and the palm fronds flapping and the sand cool under the tables on our bare feet.

There was a huge family from Mexico City occupying two of the villas on the hillside, a pair of brothers, both doctors, and their wives and eight or ten children, who were annual visitors to the place and who kept a sailboat berthed in Zihuatanejo. Often in the mornings we would see the little white sloop ghosting in the light air across the tranquil water to the cluster of huts of the village of Los Gatos, held in the curve of the left arm of the bay shore, the men standing and waving in the cockpit across the water to their wives and children, who watched and waved back from the verandas of their villas. The Swedish girl who was staying alone at the hotel went down to the beach very early every morning to bathe and body-surf, coasting swiftly and expertly shoreward in the curl of the gentle green rollers to sprawl deliciously on the smooth, salt-white sand, and then rise and race back splashing through the sunny, jade-green water to her waist, tirelessly, for half an hour or more. Then she would spread her towel and sit waiting for her friends, a boy and girl who wandered along the beach from the cantina in the late morning, selling iced beer from a bucket they carried between them, lurching and stumbling with its weight through the deep hot sand. She would buy a bottle of beer, which they would open for her, and she would drink it while the three of them sat cross-legged, conversing gravely, until she finished the beer and gave the empty bottle back to them. Then they would get up and totter on along the beach with their bucket and she would lie out on her back, slender and brown-skinned and very beautiful, her wet hair shining like silver in the sun.

When we had finished breakfast we would put on our swimsuits and fill a thermos jug with margaritas and pack a plastic bag with beach towels and suntan oil and diving masks and the copy of Emily Dickinson that Ron was annotating, and would go down the path between the rustling oleanders whose pink blossoms trembled at our passage to the beach, plodding across the white sand that was still cool beneath the dewy crust of morning to our querencia, as we called it (a lovely word that means a homing place, a place to which animals return by instinct, the spot in the bullring in which the bull takes his stand and to which he will return, invariably, when he is wounded). We would drop our things there and race down to the crystalline, warm water to be delectably rebaptized, as we were every morning, splashing and shrieking with a wild hilarity. Then we would stagger back across the sand to our belongings, waving to Annaliese, the Scandinavian girl, who sat with clasped knees watching smilingly, and collapse with glorious exhaustion, wet and cool and panting, to stretch out on our backs in the sunlight, feeling our skin warm and tighten sweetly in its rime of brine while we stared up through a depthless, dark red, throbbing sea that laved our closed eyelids. We would bathe in sun and water alternately, sitting up sometimes to munch apples and sip icy margaritas out of paper cups, feeling the merry, juvenile morning grow into the grave, full luxury of noon, ourselves growing more solemn with it, our pulses slowing, a kind of conformation taking place in us, a shapely stillness stirred only by a subtly growing, zephyrous hunger that at last was strong enough to recognize. Then we would trudge across the sand to the little cantina in the coconut grove, toward the smell of red snapper broiling over brazier coals, where we would embrace the stout, damp, gleefully smiling señora who had become our great friend, and sit at the trestle table under the roof of palm leaves and eat dizzyingly savory broiled fish and vinegary ceviche and ripe yellow chunks of avocado, listening to the hollow clap of the long rollers on the shore and the creak of the hammock where a beautiful, narrow-faced dark girl lay smiling while an ecstatically snarling puppy tugged at the tips of her dangling black pigtails. Sometimes a young, newly married couple from the hotel would be there, a pair of schoolteachers who had driven down from Texas in a van, lingering for hours over the scarlet shards of their langosta shells while they drank cold bottles of Carta Blanca beer. They had the delightful shy formality in their manner to each other that people who are newly in love and on their first holiday together often have in public, as if afraid that the wealth of their feelings might be discovered and somehow stolen from them. But they were very attentive to others and extravagantly appreciative of everything anyone said, as if their happiness were welling out of them unstemmably. Annaliese was also there sometimes, and although she smiled and murmured to us pleasantly, she sat shyly apart and conversed only with the patrona's children, who would clamber up on the bench beside her while she ate, chattering to her, snatching morsels from her plate with a giggle, stroking her long blond hair, which fascinated them, tickling or kissing her with impulsive impudence. She spoke to them in a fluent, vernacular Spanish to which they listened with a kind of careless, intimate inattention, as if she were an older sister or a pretty aunt whose opinions and reprovals they were used to, and tolerated, but whose simplicity and grace it was that really ruled them. I loved to watch them.

We would finish our beer and then drift back, hand in hand, to our querencia, where we would lie drowsing for an hour, and then the afternoon would have taken hold of the beach, a full-blown, ripe, hot consonance that rang off the waves like bugles and jellied the air above the sea and sent people cringing across the sand to shelter. We would swim again for an hour or so with our masks on, floating face-down in the lymph-clear water among the rocks that ran out into the center of the bay, through showers of little blue and scarlet fish that swept away as if blown by a wind before our bodies, over pulsing, gently tossing clouds of velvet seaweed where the tips of tiny periwinkles twinkled in the moss and sometimes a giant dusky grouper drifted like a phantom over his shadow on the sand. Then we would dry out again in the sun and sip the last of our margaritas and sit staring out at the sea that stretched in its violet infinitude beyond the bay, feeling a glorious languor flooding slowly through us, hushed and humbled by the royal afternoon. Later, we might wander for a while along the moist sand at the water's edge searching idly for pretty shells or pebbles, or if Ron went up to the veranda to read his Dickinson for an hour or two, I would put on my beach robe and drift along the shore toward Los Gatos, past a mile or more of jungle that sloped down from the enclosing hills and which I would sometimes venture into for a hundred feet or so and stand listening, looking up into the tangle of liana and giant acacia leaves, feeling a gentle tumult toss my heart lightly, like a floating coconut. Often I wandered as far as the village itself, drawn by the allure of the life that swarmed among the tin-roofed houses. I would sit on the gunwale of one of the outrigger canoes pulled up on the sand and look up through the trunks of the coconut trees into the teem and swelter of the village, of women crouching with their skirts between their knees to pound cornmeal in stone mortars with a sound like heartbeats all through the sultry afternoon, the neighing of heavy-uddered goats that tugged nervously at their tethers while they were milked implacably, and the ring and splash of milk into the metal pails, the chiming cries of children kicking a football or playing rayuela in the sand, the barking of dogs and the shriek of macaws swinging in the wind in bamboo cages, the steady brutal thump of machete blades chopping firewood, and the crackle of flames under great black iron kettles where women stood and stirred their boiling laundry with long, bleached wooden paddles.

One day I saw a pair of children crouching in the sand under the coconut trees at the edge of the beach, digging furiously, tossing the sand desperately while they raked it with their fingers. Behind them a very old woman with a wrinkled brown face squatted patiently in the sand, staring at the sea with milky blind eyes. The smaller of the two boys was wailing, trembling, his teeth bared in a grimace of despair. I walked to where they were and bent to lay my hand on his head.

"¿Que te pasó, niño? What's the matter, child?" I said.

"Perdimos un diez-pesos," the older boy said. "Y se va a poner rabiosa mi mamá. We lost a ten-peso piece, and my mother will be very angry."

"¿Esta señora es tu mamá?" I asked. "Is that lady your mother?"

"No. Mi abuela. No, my grandmother."

"Pues, cálmate. Les voy ayudar. Well, take it easy. I'll help you find it."
I knelt down and began to sift the sand with my fingers. "Fué por aquí? Was
it here?"

"Aquí mismo. Right here."

After a few moments of searching I felt the weight of the coin in a handful
of dry sand I had plucked up.

"Tén, chinito," I said. I took him by the wrist and held his hand out,
pouring the sand into it until the coin fell into his palm.

"¡Ay, que suerte!" he cried, his face breaking into a jubilant smile. "Ay,
gracias, señorita." He leapt up and ran to where the old woman sat, seizing
her by the hand and putting the coin into it. "Mire, Nana. Se nos lo halló la
señorita!" The old woman clutched the coin, raising her fist to her face and
kissing it, murmuring delightedly, "¡Hola, hola, hola!" She reached out toward
me gropingly in abject gratitude. "Mil gracias, señorita. Usted es muy
benigna."

I took her hand and felt a dark thrill run through me at the clutch of her
impassioned, dry, reptilian fingers. "Mi hija se hubiera puesto rabiosa. My
daughter would have been furious. Hubiera matado a los niños. She would have
killed the children."

"No es nada," I said. "¿Se quiere levantar, señora? Do you want to get up?"

"Sí, gracias." I drew her to her feet almost effortlessly; her frail body felt
weightless as a phantom. She held me close to her, clutching my arm with her
hard clawlike hands. "¿Le conviene ayudarme a la casa? Mis piernas son muy
flojas. Do you think you could help me to the house? My legs are very weak."

"Sí, claro," I said. "Yes, certainly."

She clung to my arm, her own withered, fragile ones wound around it like
vines as we trudged slowly through the deep sand. An odor floated from her
clothing, sweet, fermented, of an old brown shrunken apple, clenching in its
wrinkled rind the last drop of its brandied succulence. The two boys ran ahead
of us, shouting and chattering, their despair forgotten. I followed them, leading
the old woman to the house, where they stood beside a round-faced, smiling
woman in a bleached pink cotton dress who stood holding the elbows of her
crossed arms, awaiting us.

"¿Qué tal, Mamá?" she said when we had paused in front of her.

"Bien, m'ija. Figúrese, la chinita ésta se les halló la moneda para el arroz
que perdieron los muñecos. What do you think? This young lady found the
money for the rice that the kids lost."

"Ya me dijeron. They told me," the woman said. She held out her hand
to me and, when I clasped it, squeezed it in both of her own. "Usted es muy
amable. You are very kind."

"De nada," I said. She took out of the pocket of her dress and held out to me a pair of plump yellow guavas.

"Tómaselos. Es muy poco, pero lo agradecemos mucho. Take them. It's very little, but we are very grateful."

"Gracias," I said. "Usted es generosa. You are generous."

I carried the guavas back to the quinta in my hands, raising them occasionally to my nose to smell their fragrance, as delicate as a perfume. We ate them the next morning at breakfast, warm from sitting on the veranda railing in the sun.

"They're delicious," Ron said. "But I think you're foolish to go up there alone."

"No. I'm neither foolish nor brave," I said. "I love it there."

After that I went up into the village every day, feeling, every time I went, less intrusive, or shy, or patronizing. Sometimes Carlos and Benito, the boys, would run to meet me and tug at my hands as I walked up between the trees, taking me to see their goat, to watch them climb palm trunks, offering me the stick of sugarcane they were gnawing to bite into, leading me to the little plot of ground outside their house where their grandmother sat sometimes on a log mixing tortilla dough in a wooden bowl or plucking a chicken, her face blindly averted, a little flurry of white feathers clinging to her dress and hair. She would set aside whatever it was she was occupied with and take my hand in both of her own, patting it affectionately and crying merrily, with a toothless, leathery-lipped smile, "Buenos días, china!" The first time she called me by the word, which was so familiar and endearing that she would never have used it with a foreigner, I felt a sudden bating of my blood to realize that because she could not see the color of my skin or eyes or hair, she thought I was an Indian like herself.

Then I could walk freely through the sharp and dizzying incense of the village that I breathed drunkenly: the reek of earth packed hard with pot water and urine and soapsuds, eddied through with sweet astonishing wisps of scent from giant, voluptuous, scarlet cannas that blossomed beside the splattered plaster of the doorways and the savory, coarse, maizey smell of pulverized dry corn, and the bewildering bittersweet medley of animal smells, of swine and chickens and rankling, dank burro sweat and a dusty, darkling stench of captured iguanas, staring bleakly through their wire cages, and the soapy, humid cleanliness of boiling cotton in the wash kettles, and an innocent, enchanting scald of allamanda and faded, fragrant linen from a passing girl. There was a constant faint perfume of wood smoke drifting through the village, and the rich, spicy pungence of bubbling chili sauce and saffron-tinted rice and steaming onions from the ollas, and the herbal, oily tang of citronella candles smoking under the corrugated-iron roofs in the dim interiors of the houses, swarmed under with a damp, raw musk of mold and rotten wood and sour mud.

The smell of the village was no longer repellent to me, nor debased, as it had seemed when we first drove into Zihuatanejo, but a profound, primordial fetor, of life rendered down to its seething, redolent essences in the crucible of poverty and pain, past the reach or recognition of the callow sensibility I had come there with and which seemed to me more and more contemptibly fastidious, more a disability than a faculty. I shed it, day by day, like a lizard skin, and was able at last to visit the village unselfconsciously, with none of the sense of privilege or immunity or inquisitiveness of an itinerant artist or an academic or a tourist, and without being treated with resentment or suspicion or the licensed rapacity that the wretched practice on the rich. People looked at me and spoke to me casually, with the intimate, almost inattentive equality that the patrona's children showed toward the Scandinavian girl. Sometimes other Americans or Europeans would come up among the huts to buy coral trinkets or necklaces of seashells or to inquire about the rental of the pirogues that were drawn up on the sand beyond the trees, and I saw that they were dealt with by the villagers with an excessive, fraudulent courtesy and deference that was not shown to me; perhaps only because they'd learned that I didn't come to purchase souvenirs or services—but perhaps because I walked there in an ignominy and poverty of spirit that they recognized as genuine.

In the center of the village they had built a shrine or chapel that was no more than a low wall of cinder block painted a pastel blue and rising in the center in a narrow shaft, two cinder blocks in width and six feet high, against which was fixed a cheap plaster crucifix of the kind that are mass-produced in commercial bisque-ware molds and painted in crudely vivid colors; it had salmon-colored flesh and scarlet lips, and wounds that dripped with garish blood, like fingernail enamel. But what appalled me most about it was its eyes, which were horrifyingly open, black and glittering with rage and pain. And then I realized that on every crucifix or in every painting of Calvary that I could remember, the Christ was dead, the eyes closed, the head downcast, the body pitifully slumped and limp, the spirit extinguished or fled. But this awful thing was alive, livid and writhing in its agony, the gouts of hot blood still pulsing out of it; not merely pathetic, but terrible and tragic, the head raised in its dauntless wrath, the black excruciated eyes staring in a steadfast glare of outrage and defiance at its torturers. Those lips could never have uttered, "Father, forgive them, for they know not what they do"; they seemed to hiss, "Damn them, they know too well what they do." This was not Christ; this was some scurrilous son of sorrow whose ecstasy was indignation. It was almost profane, and their worship of its shocking vulgarity made me feel an awe, an infatuation for them as ineffable as their own for the crucifix. In front of it there was a low cinder-block altar on which stood tin cans of potted geraniums and votive candles that had been reduced to lumps of melted wax in the sea wind; and in front of that, six rows of palm logs laid in the sand. I would sit there sometimes, listening to the creak of palm branches in the wind above me, and the distant tumbling rumor of the sea, and the incessant throb of a guitar, like an arthritic aching of the air. Old women would come and kneel in the sand among the coral pebbles, whispering through their wrinkled gray lips while they fumbled at their rosaries, the black beads slipping through their gnarled fingers like nuggets of a precious dark ore whose worth they counted endlessly.

One afternoon I cut my foot on a piece of coral rock and hopped to the doorstep of a house, sitting down to twist my foot sole-upward to examine it. A man came to the door and stood silently for a moment, and then went back into the house and reappeared with a damp rag and a strip of cotton cloth; a plump-faced, somber man of forty, perhaps, with lustrous eyes and tallowy, pitted skin. He squatted in front of me in the sand and bathed my foot and wrapped it carefully, and then brought me from the house a mug of pulque, a sour, milky broth that made my throat contract. When I had drunk he took the mug from me and sat beside me on the step, sipping from it and passing it back to me, pointing to a pair of ragged children who clambered on the trunk of an almost horizontally bowed palm in front of us.

"Mis nietos," he said. "My grandchildren."

"Son guapos," I said. "They are good-looking."

"Sí." He nodded and wiped his lips. "Y fuertes. And strong. El mayor mató un perro con sus manos. The older killed a dog with his hands." He rose and took the empty cup from me, then nodded at my wound and laid his hand on my head and went back into the house.

Another day I stopped to watch a young man crouching with a machete to split the shell of a coconut. He pried out a chunk of the moist white meat and tossed it to me, saying, "Tén, china"; and when I caught it and murmured, "Gracias," and bit into it, he broke into a glittering smile whose arrogance I could not resent because it was so different from that ominous, ironic deference I had come to fear—and that the wealthy and powerful of the earth would do well to fear also, I thought, because it would demand requital. I loved the audacity of his smile and his stance as he stood and watched me eat, as I had come to love the irrepressible and fervent life of the village that had begotten it, compared to which my own was an obscene frivolity. I felt ashamed of the bright, peach-colored beach robe that I wore; it seemed to me an emblem of my obliviousness of that life that lay wrapped in its flamelike obscurity. It had come to seem to me almost the only human reality I had known since my childhood, and I felt a sickening repentance for my lazy, willful complicity in

its destruction; because it was people like these whose slaughter and subjugation the government of my country had methodically subsidized for decades,
in Chile, Guatemala, Nicaragua, Haiti, El Salvador—all over Latin America
—by sending arms and money—*my* money, arms bought with *my* wages—to
men like Cabrera and Somoza and Duvalier and Carías and Batista, by engi-
neering the crushing of their protests and the assassination of their leaders,
beginning as long ago as with Madero and including God knew how many
others. I felt abject with the guilt of my indifference and complaisance, and
I thought: If I have been wanton in anything, it is in my ignorance of life, of
this uncouth, sovereign thing that cannot be denied or subjugated or taken in
vain, and that will not forgive my ignorance of it.

I would walk back to the villa in the cool of the late afternoon with the
sun low across the water and pools of shadow deepening on the sand. A
clemency had come over the world, a surcease; the mild waves plashed on the
shore and there were soft, stray zephyrs that stirred my hair and frilled the bay
like breath. The laborers would be coming back along the beach, their burros
plodding before them briskly with the zeal of homecoming, the canteens and
pruning hooks and tins of kerosene lashed to the faggots of firewood on their
backs lurching and clanking in the quiet air. There were pelicans settling to
roost on the rocks out in the bay, sitting hunched and still, their great grotesque
beaks drooping. A lavender haze was gathering in the palm grove and voices
came tinkling out from the huts among the trees, and ripples of easy evening
laughter. I would walk up the path to the casita in the cool dry sand, bowed
and limp with a luxurious fatigue, my muscles and bones gone soft as if
marinated in their daylong bath of brine and sun. I would stand in the shower
with my eyes closed, holding my breasts in my hands like little tart green
apples, letting the cool water spray over me as sweetly as spring rain; and then
would dress idly, vacant-mindedly, in a fresh cotton frock, and brush my hair
and put my pink beads around my neck; and then go out onto the veranda and
sit with Ron to drink my evening margarita, feeling purged and fragile and
surfeited, gazing out at the endless calm that lay across the water. There was
a perfume of bougainvillea in the air and a tissue-paper rustle of the little
plum-colored lanterns of its blossoms. A soft flashing roamed across the water
in the low light, waning to a purple gloom as the sky darkened and the stars
came out above the sea. Then we would walk up the path to the hotel and dine
in the patio with shadows roving over the stuccoed walls in the candlelight and
the vast black velvet dome of tropic sky above us and the steadfast glittering
stars.

When I fell asleep at night with the jalousies open and the cool air fondling
my nakedness, yielding to the last dark throe of the day's long rhythmic thrall,
I lay enfolded in a speechless faith in the morrow's revelation of its abiding,

plenary images: the naked children galloping in the surf, the burros jangling their way to work, the sweet wet morning leaves, the misted, glinting sea, the fresh, blithe, matinal clarity that lay burgeoning in the heart of every night like a silver seed.

The life of the beach and village made me ache with its sacramental, idly transpiring ritual; it was almost like reliving my childhood on the bay, its sunny indolence almost beyond time, an endless reenactment of something imperishably remote and innocent, preserved forever by the green, guardian mountains from the vanity and hypocrisy and counterfeit dignity and vile, venal ambition that strutted and screamed for tribute beyond their silent crests. When I thought of the mad girl who slept sometimes in the hotel patio at night, it seemed to me there must be some inviolable sanity in her that had led her there, that her torment must be dissolving into the place, its cruel brilliance extinguished slowly like a knife blade rusting into nothingness in the fathoms of solvent, saline air and water and light that laved me to the bone. I had never felt so nakedly, royally tranquil, as if some clamorous skeleton in me were being unclothed gently, irresistibly, delightedly, of the stale, bitter, smog-stained flesh it wore in College Park to keep it warm; as if the ruthlessly transitive, ravishing light were seeking to leach clean and illuminate at last the long white letters of my secret name. I longed for them to be spelled out, to be laid bare and blazing on the sand to dazzle passersby: the burros, who would neigh and nose at me in wonder; the dark, wild children who would run with my teeth rattling in their pockets to play jacks or hopscotch with; the paisanos who would hang my ankle bones above their beds for amulets and string my knuckles on agave thread to decorate the brown throats of their sweethearts; my skull would be a lair for scorpions and my long thighs pestles to pound yellow grain in stone bowls. I wanted to be scattered in a thousand anagrams of joy through the barrios and fiestas and hovels of that white land. I was enamored of and in a trembling conjugal harmony with everyone and everything I saw; I was dangerously, shamelessly amorous, like a bride. I felt betrothed to everything, and possessed by a cool, convalescent gaiety, like that one feels after a long, feverish, delirious struggle with disease. I think my blood changed; it felt colder in me, brighter, slower-moving, and there began to gather in me like the growing viscosity of my blood the saturnine serenity of the great land tortoises we had seen in the deserts in Jalisco. And I could feel, also, the whimsical perversity and pride of a burro; I was obdurate and dainty and indomitable; and enchanted by these new dimensions and configurations of myself, as a young girl is enchanted by her own nubility. There was a serpentine brilliance in my eyes and a glitter on my skin that startled me sometimes when I looked into the mirror. I let my hair hang loose around my shoulders for the first time in my life and one day in Zihuatanejo I bought a necklace of cheap pink beads that delighted me, whose dental coolness soothed my throat, that I fondled endlessly and wore to bed at night. I was very conscious of my teeth. I bit things—bread and meat and apples—with a piercing awareness of the act, the dire sound of it, the strength of my jaws. The Mexican men began to seem beautiful to me; I loved their swarthiness, their silence, the hard, short-legged compactness of their bodies, their somber faces that in an instant could be transfigured by a look of outrageous childish cunning or hilarity or of a bold and sorrowful cupidity that stunned me like a blow. Sometimes we were served at dinner by the grandsons of the patrón, supple, smooth-skinned boys in their twenties who laid our silverware and filled our wineglasses with an insensate grace that changed the rhythm of my breath, and it took an act of conscious will for me not to bend and kiss their splendidly naïve, bewildering, chocolate-colored hands. I longed to run and play with the naked children who splashed and galloped in the surf in the morning, to clutch their glittering bodies to my own and roll and wrestle gloriously with them in the limpid, warm, green water. Even Annaliese, who had become somehow a native of the place through the passion that she shared with me for it, struck the same coolly promiscuous sparks of desire in me with her humbly royal beauty that clashed against my bones like flint.

One evening she dined with Ron and me in the patio of the hotel, dressed in a sheath of pale blue silk, with her hair, still moist from her afternoon swim and shower, swept back in a silver swath across her ears and pinned with a tortoiseshell clasp at the nape of her brown neck. With her tanned face, the shape of a philodendron leaf, and her clear, ocean-colored eyes untainted by a trace of makeup, she looked so innocently exquisite that I felt a calm, utterly guiltless, imperious desire to hold her in my arms, to stroke her warm brown skin. And when we left the patio and walked down the path from the hotel to our villas together, I yielded to it, reaching out to take her hand in the darkness; and I felt something like the sudden chill of starlight sweep my heart when her fingers closed quickly and delicately over mine. Then, when we had reached our cottage and Ron had stooped to unlock the door, I turned to her and laid my hand against her cheek and pressed our mouths together for a moment. She gasped and murmured, reaching out to clasp my waist gently with her fingertips in startled, shy acceptance of my homage; and I felt again an icy ague shake my skeleton, like a cold fluttering pallor at the heart of flame.

In spite of my apprehension, I think Ron understood that moment, and granted it to me, without jealousy or rancor, because the next morning when we watched her surfing on the beach from our veranda, he turned to me to speak; but seeing my face, he paused and raised his cup to finish drinking his coffee; and then set it down again, and after several minutes, said in a gently constrained way, "She's very lovely."

"Yes. Everything is equally lovely here," I said. Feeling his eyes cling to me, I turned to him. "You aren't sorry that we decided not to turn back, are you?"

"No. Not if you're not. I want to see you happy."

"I'd hate you to regret it."

"I couldn't regret your happiness," he said. "Only your concealing it from me." He made a gesture like a withered shrug, and turned away to look out at the sea. "That's the only real treachery there is, I think."

After a moment I said as lightly as I could, "That's a very brave thing to say—before your first margarita of the day."

"I wouldn't trust it, afterwards."

We sat watching Annaliese glide like a burnished bronze spear toward the shore on the slope of a smooth green wave, plunging headlong aground in a happy sudden scattering of her slender arms and legs and a burst of jeweled spray. She stood up and swept her drenched hair backwards across her head in her spread hands, staggering joyfully; and then raised her arm and waved to us. We waved back, lifting our coffee cups in tribute.

"Well, you'd better not leave me alone with her," I said, "or I may do something very foolish."

"I can't tend you like a sheep dog all my life," Ron said. "And I certainly wouldn't want to."

I leaned forward to lay my arms along the rail of the veranda and rest my chin on top of them. I felt somehow haunted by myself, consumed by myself, by some unspoken thought or creed that had been gathering in me lifelong, feeding on my life and deeds, accreting words and images to itself to be spoken in, as an inseminated egg devours its mother in order to grow and manifest itself, to transform its ethereal energy into flesh.

"I wish I could be someone else—" I began; and when Ron said quickly, "Well, I don't," I saw that he had either fearfully anticipated or generously misunderstood me; so I closed my mouth and bit my lips.

"*I* certainly don't want to change you. I don't want you to be one of those people with—'dimity convictions,' as Emily Dickinson called them. I wouldn't love *her,* if she'd been."

"No, I suppose not," I said; and thought with grief: But that's where I'm so terribly unfair, because I *do* want to change *you.* But not only selfishly, I hope; not only because I want you to be conveniently invulnerable to me, so that I needn't feel any guilt about humiliating or abusing you, but because I would like you to be someone whom I could love, and whom I could deserve. Which is to say, I suppose (I added sadly to myself, looking at him sidelong), that I would like us to be equal in passion and intelligence and energy and resolution. God, is there any such pair of people in the world? Is it possible to love at all without compromising something dear to one? I hated being human at that moment. I hated having a mind, and personality, and something —whatever it is—that could be called a spirit, and instincts so intractable and ill-fitting with dignity, or prudence, or comfort. He laid his hand on my bowed head and smiled at me wincingly.

"And I love you most," he said, not cynically or speciously, but in a touchingly confounded way, "when you most nearly escape me. When you're most nearly treacherous. Now, why do you suppose that is?"

"God knows. The creator of this world was a very, very tricky customer."

"Yes. I hope to God"—he paused to chuckle wearily—"I hope to God he didn't make many others like it. Perhaps he was just experimenting wildly. I suppose we can be forgiven for doing the same."

"That's not fair!" I cried, jerking my head free of his benedictory, oppressive hand. "I don't believe in 'wild experiments,' and you know it. 'Experiment!' That's the damnedest, most theatrical, most ignoble, most craven, most —political—of all the bloody buzzwords they use back there. That's an awful thing to say!"

"I know," he said in a very chastened voice. He withdrew his hand and laced its fingers into those of the other, staring at them for a moment solemnly. "That's not what I meant. I know you're not frivolous, or vandalistic. Or that you hold life cheap, God knows—your own or anyone's. In fact, what I love about you most is your seriousness, and complexity, and absolute integrity. I think you're more—conscious—than anyone I ever knew. I really do, Sylvie. And, you see, I can't stop watching you—exercise those things." He frowned at his laced hands and turned them over, making them into a kind of empty basket. Then he made me feel a fresh remorse for my misconception of a few minutes earlier—that he had misunderstood me—by saying, "Maybe I'm only a sort of midwife, really. Maybe all I really want to do is to preside at your birth. Fetch the basin, boil the water, count the throes—"

I plunged up out of the chair and fled into the villa, throwing myself face-down onto our wickedly uproarious bed, whose mockeries—strangely intestinal, and skeletal, and vocal, as if its whole being were convulsed with sardonic mirth—made me, in a moment, feel like giggling. I heard Ron come in and open the refrigerator and move about the room for a time, fiddling with ice trays and cans and drawers and bottles. Then he came and sat down beside me on the bed and laid his hand on the small of my back.

"We have the nastiest, evilest bed in Mexico," I said.

"I know. It's seen too much, I suppose. Listen, I've got the jug filled with margaritas, and the bag packed. Are you ready to go down?"

"Apples?"

"Yep."

"And the snorkel? I want to go out by the rocks."

"Yes." We didn't move or speak for a moment or two, and I heard one of the little lizards that clung to the wall make ironic kissing noises in the silence. "There really isn't any end to it, you know," Ron said. "Not unless one of us *decides* to end it. So we might as well just accept things as they are."

The longer that blunt platitude rang in my ears, the more it sounded to me like revelation, like the only totally irrefutable thing that could be said about life, and the only possible kind of contract that two people could make with each other. "We have to remember that vision and virtuosity are very different things," I heard myself saying at a lecture long ago, and I remembered a pretty dark-haired girl in the third row nodding enthusiastically.

"I hope you made the margaritas good and strong," I said.

"I think you'll find them adequate." He dabbled at my back with a piece of cloth. "Here's your suit. You want to put it on?"

"Yes." I rolled over and stood up and took off my dressing gown and dropped it on the bed. He sat watching me, his face gone pale and stricken. When I picked up the bathing suit to step into it, he leaned forward to seize my hips in his hands and press his face against my belly.

"Oh, Jesus Christ, you're a beautiful woman," he whispered hoarsely. "Oh, Christ, I'm mad about you, Sylvie." He kissed my belly wildly, locking his arms around my waist and hugging me against him. I took his head in my arms and held him to me while he murmured agonizedly, rolling his face against the line of tan below my navel where the white outline of my bikini pants began.

"Let's go out on the veranda," I whispered, bending down to him. "I want to make love in a hammock."

"But there are people—"

"I don't care if they see." I clutched his hair and dragged him to his feet and began to undress him quickly and skillfully, my fingers marvelously nimble and zealous. When he was naked I led him out through the door and across the veranda to the hammock that was flooded now with morning sunlight and we lay and made love in sight of the Scandinavian girl and the two ragged children who sat cross-legged and solemn on the sand below. I cried out soundlessly as he brought me to an excruciating orgasm: Look! Look at me! Look at this dazzling indecency that you have conjured! Do not turn away. Look till you are safely blind.

When we had finished we lay exhausted, running with sweat in the hot sun, drifting off to sleep with the hammock swinging idly, its hemp cables creaking like the rigging of a ship in passage.

One morning when we drove back from Zihuatanejo with a fresh supply of margarita mix and guava jelly and a felt sombrero that Ron had promised to take back to a friend, the Volkswagen behaved oddly. Ron had to turn the wheel a full revolution to bring the car around a very gentle curve in the road.

"What's the matter?" I asked.

"I don't know. The steering seems to be shot."

"God, where will we find a mechanic?"

"I don't know. I'll ask the patrón."

We learned that the nearest competent mechanic was in Playa Azul, about sixty miles beyond Zihuatanejo. He had no telephone, but Señor Esparolini called a hotel in the town whose proprietor he knew, and who consented to hunt down the mechanic and ask him to call back. He did so, two days later, and agreed to drive up to the quinta the following day with a tow truck. There would be a charge of two hundred pesos for the trip. He arrived a day later, very cheerful and agreeable, and towed the car away, assuring us it would be ready the following afternoon. Two days after that he called again and said that the car could be picked up on Friday, the day after tomorrow—not tomorrow, unfortunately, that being the feast of the Assumption, a celebration he never failed to observe. Also, there had been unexpected difficulties: the repairs had been far more extensive than he had believed, parts had had to be brought from Acapulco. The cost would be considerable: fifteen hundred pesos, which should be brought in cash.

"Jesus Christ," Ron said. "These people are bandits. That's a hundred and twenty dollars."

"It's quite a lot. But there really isn't anything we can do, is there?"

"That's the trouble. They've got you at their mercy."

The young couple with the van, who had learned of our plight at the dinner table, offered to drive Ron in to Playa Azul when the car was ready, and as a week had now elapsed since it had broken down, they also offered to take him to Zihuatanejo in the morning to replenish our supplies. I didn't go with him because, for the first time since our arrival, we woke to the sound of rain drumming on the leaves outside the open windows and cool, earthen-scented drafts of moist air sighing through the villa in the gusts of sea wind and a booming thunder of surf from the beach below. We rolled down the split-bamboo weather screen on the veranda and had breakfast in slacks and sweaters, feeling oddly metamorphosed, deformed by the bulky clothing. Through the blind we could see the bay below us, gray-skinned and dimpled with rain, heaving hugely under the low, fast-moving cloud that swept in from the sea. The surf was mountainous; great smooth combers of foam-laced water rolling swiftly landward, uprearing into glossy opaque alps as they reached the shore and thundered down upon the sand in a wild uproar of boiling foam and shattered form.

"At least you won't miss a morning on the beach," I said.

"No. You sure you don't want to come?"

"I don't think so. Do you mind? I'd like to read, and write a couple of postcards."

"O.K. There'll be mud up to the hubcaps, anyway. You'll be better off."

"I've just started *The Heights of Machu Picchu*. It's incredible, even though I only understand about half of it."

"It's a good way to learn Spanish," Ron said. "And a good place."

"It's the only place to read Neruda. I never knew what he was talking about before."

"I'll be back by noon, I guess. If we don't get washed away."

When he had gone, I lay in the hammock with a pocket dictionary and the paperback edition of Neruda I had bought in a bookshop in Mexico City. The epic poem was like the ocean and the jungle that surrounded us; swollen and savage and heaving with huge elemental rhythms; it seemed to have come fuming up out of tossing palms and rain-swept forests and blue Andean vastnesses that stretched out over misty chasms smoking with the spoor of jaguars. I shivered as I read it, recognizing in the wild tumultuous imagery a vision of the same eternity that rang like crystal in the cold New England speech of Emily Dickinson; as if from their antipodean lives their sight converged on the same high star, the same chaste shard of timelessness, whose light they had metabolized, one into poems of alabaster and one, of anthracite. The dark poet's voice called to me from the pages:

> *Come up with me, American love,*
> *Among flint roses stained with the sperm of condors.*

I dropped the book on the floor and stared out through the blind at the oceanic surging of the jungle foliage in the rainy wind. The blind flapped restlessly against the railing. The clouds were thinning and there were long pale rifts among them, and far out on the ocean, shoals of gleaming light like pools of mercury. The pound of the rain had softened to a tinsel whisper on the vines and now I could hear a steady dripping from the tiled eaves. I went inside and heated myself another cup of coffee and brought it out to the veranda and stood sipping it at the railing, looking down at the beach, where a gray cat tripped daintily across the stuccoed sand. Out in the bay there was an empty canoe drifting that had been washed out from the beach by the surf. A boy swam toward it from the shore, lazily, his brown arms splashing flat on the lead-surfaced water. He reached the canoe and climbed up into it, his naked haunches gleaming like wet copper. I watched him paddle back toward Los Gatos, bowing forward and then lunging back with each paddle stroke, trailing a wake of addled silver through the dark lead of the unillumined water. A dog began to bark somewhere. I felt an exhilarated, solitary freedom. I went back into the villa and sat down at the desk and took out of the drawer a sheaf of postcards we had bought at the hotel. They were photographs of the bay and the mountains and the harbor at Zihuatanejo, formal, flagrantly vivid, conventionally picturesque scenes of crimson sunsets and flaming bougainvillea and strangely catatonic, almost inanimate peasants and stuffed, stiff-legged burros that had evidently been carried out and placed on the sand for the occasion. They looked like time exposures of anthropological exhibits in a museum case. My God, I thought, they'll think we never left town; they'll think we just sneaked down to the Smithsonian. I picked out one for Beth that was a view of the villas and the hotel taken from the beach, in which our casita could be seen, nestled among its cactus and oleanders. I drew an X above its tile roof, and turned it over and wrote: *This is where we are, and I hope will remain until the Apocalypse. Let me know when it's over, and I may come back, but you won't know me. The smear is not a tear—it's a drop of tequila: the true and blushful Hippocrene. Tell everyone to go to hell for me. Sylvie.* Then I picked out another, the only genuinely recognizable one, that showed a sweep of jungled hillside falling down to the bay with a plume of smoke rising through the palms clustered on the sand. I turned it over and wrote: *Site of a recent immolation;* and then scratched out the words in furious embarrassment. I tore up both of the postcards and dropped the little shiny scraps into the wastebasket. The sound of the light rain on the foliage had faded almost entirely, so I opened all the jalousies and rolled up the bamboo blind on the veranda. Now there were long rifts in the clouds, through which the bright azure of the sky could be seen like a blue cyclorama behind a window in a stage setting. Rays of light slanted down from the torn cloud like great plated chutes, spilling pools of silver into the sea. Down on the beach the German engineer and his wife stood in flapping yellow raincoats, staring at the surf. The gentle dripping around the villa had slowed to intermittency, and there was a fresh-minted merry peeping sound of tree frogs everywhere. There was steam rising through the vegetation and already a gathering sense of calm and the suffocating humid heat that would come with the sunlight on the warm, drenched earth. I picked up the books from the floor where I had dropped them and took them into the villa and put them in the beach bag with an apple from the refrigerator, and a towel, and my bathing suit, which I plucked, still moist, from the railing of the shower stall. I sat down at the desk and took out of the drawer the key to the casita and a sheet of notepaper. I wrote on the paper: *Ron: It's cleared up, so I've gone walking. Go on down to the beach, I'll meet you there for lunch. S.* I laid it on the desk and then picked up the key and the beach bag and went to the door, where I paused and turned my head to read, in its entirety and as if for the first time, the placard tacked against the wall. On it there was a message printed in Spanish and in its tortured English equivalent:

THE GUEST IS PLEADED TO TAKE
WITH HIM HIS PASSPORT, MONY
AND JEWELS. THE MANAGEMENT
IS UNRESPONSIBLE FOR THE LOSS
OF THINGS OF VALUE.

I went back to the dresser and took out of my purse my passport folder and wallet and the velvet drawstring bag in which I carried my costume jewelry. I put them in the beach bag and then went out of the casita and locked the door, stretching up on my toes to lay the key on the strip of molding along the top of the doorframe where we had agreed to leave it in such a situation.

There were already ragged patches of sunlight on the bay as I went down between the glittering wet leaves that hung bowed above the gray sand of the path. The German couple were coming up from the beach, and they stood aside to let me pass, the man smiling effusively, his wife nodding perfunctorily to me.

"Good morning," he said. "A real storm we had last night. You heard it?"

"No. I slept like a log."

"Ah. To be young." He turned and pointed out across the beach. "There was a boy there swimming chust now. You saw him?"

"Yes. He was pretty brave."

"They are abominable," the wife murmured. "Filthy, naked savages." Her face was flushed. I smiled at her and went on down the path to the beach, the soles of my feet grinding suavely in the wet cool sand. I walked down to where the sand was smoothed and washed flat by the backsliding ebb of the smashed waves, and bent down to roll up the legs of my slacks; then I walked toward Los Gatos through the shallow bright glissade that raced up the shore in lace-edged tongues and then paused and slid back swiftly in glassy, marbled panes that rippled over my feet deliciously and dizzied me to watch. There was a cool mineral freshness in the air from the salty mist that blew in off the pounding surf, and far out over the ocean a straight sharp line where the silver canopy of overcast was scissored off and the faultless azure infinity of blue sky stretched beyond. I felt a childlike, ancient happiness effervescing in my blood like mineral water and realized that I was smiling ceaselessly, my face raised to the magnificent fresh tumult of the morning, like a child entering a fairground. I loved myself, and wanted to walk hand in hand with my reincarnated self, whom I suddenly discovered pattering beside me with fluttering yellow hair and nimble spindly legs, like an immortal and unaging friend. I hoped I would be able to find her always, in whatever dark hour, and hear her say to me—as my best friend, Paisley Offut, used to say to me, on the bay, when I was miserable—"But I *love* you, Sylvie!"

When I had walked halfway to Los Gatos, the clouds had blown in across the mountains and the blue canopy of clear sky broke suddenly above the bay in a scalding bath of light that flashed on the water and brazed my hair and sent steam curling up from the jungle in pale, disintegrating wisps in the bright air. I came to a little rill of clear water that was flowing down out of the jungle and across the beach into the bay, cutting a winding hard-packed bed across the sand. I stopped beside it and crouched down to dip my cupped hands in the cold water and splash my face with it. Then I sat down in the sand and unbuttoned my sweater and twisted out of it, feeling the blow of sunlight on my skin through my light blouse like a hot wind. The beach was empty for a mile in either direction, and I felt in splendid, private possession of it. I took the towel out of my bag and rolled it up with my sweater for a pillow and lay out on my back in the warm embrace of the sun, and in a little while fell asleep to the boom of the surf and the creak and clatter of the palms behind me in the wind. When I woke up the sun was almost overhead in the mercilessly brilliant sky and I was soaked with sweat, my slacks clinging to me like steamed towels. I sat up and saw, far down the beach, a scattering of people on the sand in front of the quinta, but no one walking. I dug my swimsuit out of the bag and went up into the edge of the jungle above the beach and, standing in its shadow, took off my slacks and blouse and dropped them on the ground with my bikini and then crouched down naked to urinate, on all fours, like a dog, feeling the scalding flow of urine run down the insides of my thighs with a stinging astringency. Then I rose and, leaving my clothes in a heap on the sand, I walked naked along the bed of the stream into the green, shadowed forest. The sound of the surf faded into the green silence as I padded through the icy water, pushing my way through fronds of huge lacy ferns and smooth broad leaves that slid along my thighs with cool, lingering caresses. Fifty yards into the forest a great bleached log, naked of bark, pale gold and subtly curved like a giant torso, lay across the stream. I climbed up onto it and lay stretched out face-down with my body pressed to the warm, soft, rotten wood, watching little ragged spangles of sunlight that filtered through the foliage dance and flicker on the ferns and sparkle in the running water of the stream. There was a labial murmur of water from beneath me and high up in the treetops a soft seething of leaves in the sea breeze. Far off through the forest I heard the laughter of a woman peal out like a bird cry from one of the grass huts in the palm grove, and then a man's voice calling in a searing, velvet obbligato, "Vén, linda, vén." I was sweltering and faint from the humid earthen weight of the jungle air. I slid down from the log and as if performing an ancient, dimly remembered rite of purification or of consecration, I knelt down in the stream and splashed my breasts and thighs and belly with the cold water, gasping and cringing, until my flesh burned with an icy flush. There was a sudden turmoil in the leaves beside the stream, the crash of foliage and thudding footfalls of a body plunging through the brush toward me. I rose and stood watching in a kind of awe, my hands pressed flat against my breast, my breath held frozen in my lungs, staring at the wall of foliage through which the thing must burst in a moment. Then the leaves shuddered wildly and swept apart to reveal the black, sleek-snouted, majestic head of a huge wild hog. It halted and stared at me, blinking hotly, its cloven feet sunken in the soft, mossy soil, its leathern ears toppling forward, its glistening, flat, black nostrils twitching fiercely. A series of brutal, menacing grunts rumbled in its throat, almost like a command. I stood and stared into the creature's pink, tiny, implacable eyes until it snorted again and, as if satisfied that it had subdued me, turned and went lumbering off into the jungle. When it had gone I swayed and caught the log to keep from falling; but I was not afraid, and I had felt no fear or disgust; only a kind of ceremonial secession from myself that left me empty and vertiginous.

I leaned against the log breathing heavily until I felt my personality gather again in me like the coalescing of a vapor, and then turned and wandered back weakly through the jungle to the beach, stumbling and splashing in the black mud of the stream bed, the snarled fronds of foliage lashing at my thighs like whips, branding them with flushed, stinging stripes. The blood was still pounding so loudly in my ears that I was hardly conscious of the growing thunder of the surf as I came nearer to the palm grove on the shore, but I felt the coolness of the sea breeze rinse my body as the foliage grew less dense, as cool as liniment. I found my clothes and bent down to pick up my bikini bra, my arms and fingers working feebly as I tied its string into a bow between my shoulder blades. As I stepped into my pants I raised my head and looked down through the palms to where I had left the beach bag on the sand. A man stood over it, eating something, a red, plump fruit, a mango, looking down. As I watched, he bent down to pick up the bag, holding it against his chest with one hand and searching through it with the other. He was twenty-five or -six, and wore a straw sombrero with a leather chin thong dangling loosely and the loose white camisa and baggy cotton trousers of a paisano. For a moment I was paralyzed with a bleak panic that raced along my nerves like acid, a bitter, mournful sense of destitution darkening my mind as swiftly as the shadow of a vulture. I saw him take out my passport case and flip it open, studying it for a moment before he closed it and slid it into the hip pocket of his trousers. He looked about briefly and then with the bag held under his arm he began to walk along the beach toward the quinta, raising the fruit to his mouth to bite at it. I tugged up my bikini pants and snatched up my clothes from the ground and went running down through the coconut trees across the sand toward him, shouting, "¡Hola, hombre, hola! ¡Basta! ¡Alto!" He stopped and turned instantly, standing motionless as I raced toward him, unfrightened, making no attempt to flee. I came to a gasping stop five feet in front of him, the dry sand sprinkling his trouser legs, and for a moment could not think of a word of Spanish. He said in a resonant dark voice like the humming of a wire in the wind, "Is you bag?" He had a wide, brown, fine-cut face that glistened like a chestnut shell and very sharp black eyebrows set high on his broad forehead above his somber, quartz-black eyes, and a glistening thick mustache through which the tips of his upper teeth showed when he spoke, square and blunt, like kernels of white corn.

"Yes, it is," I said. "And you've got my passport. I saw you take it." My voice had a harsh, breathless fearfulness that I could hardly recognize.

"Sí." He nodded gravely. "I think somebody forget this bag. I want to know who he is, so I can tell the hotels. So he get it back. O.K.?"

"I see," I said pantingly. "Well, thank you. Can I have it back?"

"You stay the Villa Zapata, no?"

"Yes." When he did not speak or move for a moment, I added, "Why, do you work there?"

"No. But I know señorita there. I come there sometime." His eyes roved over me expressionlessly, from my face to my feet, lingering on my bare belly for only a fraction of a moment, then drifting languidly aside to rest on the bundle of clothing clenched in my hand. He set the bag on the sand and took the passport out of his pocket and opened it, studying it for a moment with an ominous, almost official self-assurance, raising the soft, red, heartlike fruit to his mouth to gnaw at it while he did so, holding the passport aside to avoid the dripping red juice. "No so good picture," he said, raising his eyes to mine. "You more pretty than you picture." He bit into the fruit again and then raised his arm suddenly and flung it out into the surf with a gesture so violent and unexpected that I stumbled back a step in fright. He raised his hand to his mouth and sucked the red juice from between his fingers with his dark, cordovan-colored lips, his onyx-black eyes gazing steadily into mine.

"Here you passport—señora." He held it out to me, pausing in the gesture to emphasize the last word, but with a carefully toneless absence of irony, his eyes falling to my naked ring finger as I reached out to take it from him.

"Thank you."

"You stay with you hosban, sí?"

"Yes," I said, my eyes faltering. He wiped the palm of his hand along his trouser leg and knelt down beside the bag, holding up his hand to take the crumpled clothing from me. "You like I put you clothes in the bag, señora?"

I handed them to him silently, watching him fold them with an ostentatious care and lay them ceremoniously in the bag. "You passport, too?" I nodded and handed it to him, feeling numbly idiotic, vanquished by his gallantry, which was grave enough to seem genuine and yet discolored by a tint of parody, barely presumptuous enough to be provocative.

"What is your name?" I said. He looked up at me with a steady, inquisitive dismissal of the question. "I wanted to leave you a little reward," I mumbled. "Un premio—at the quinta. For finding my bag. I'll leave it with Señor Esparolini, so you can pick it up."

He stood up, holding the bag by its handles, letting it hang against his thigh, his dark eyes gazing indolently into mine.

"I don't find you bag," he said. "You don't lose you bag. What you think my name is?"

"I don't know. How would I know your name?"

"Maybe you guess." I stared at him blankly, feeling my blood begin to burn. "Abél," he said, and smiled with an invincible formality, as if he had just been introduced to me at a diplomatic reception.

"How do you do? My name is Sylvia," I murmured.

He nodded and said, "Encantado," smiling gently. "Maybe I come for my premio tomorrow. I like you give to me youself. Maybe I don't get it if you don't. You be there?"

"Yes, I think so."

He nodded again and handed the bag to me, his fingers holding on to the handle for a moment with a taunting persistence, tugging it gently when I took it from him.

"Hasta mañana, señora," he murmured, and then turned and walked away from me in the direction of the quinta, turning, when he had gone twenty feet, to raise his hand to me. I stood looking after him, feeling a kind of flagrant ease come over me, a white composure, as orderly and lambent as the sea and sky and clean, washed, ardent sand.

When I came back to the strip of beach in front of the quinta, Ron was sitting up on his towel watching my approach. He waved as I came closer, slogging to my ankles through the hot sand, and held up the thermos jug encouragingly. Further down the beach, Annaliese was lying face-down, her head turned to the side to listen to the German boy, who sat beside her with crossed legs, making earnest, animated gestures with his hands. The wives of the doctors from Mexico City had set up a red-and-white striped parasol at the bottom of the cliff and sat with fluttering skirts in beach chairs in its shadow. In front of them a band of sunburned, narrow-bodied children were digging an enormous pit with red tin shovels. Two of them were down inside the pit, and only their heads and frail brown shoulders could be seen, bobbing busily as they tossed up spadefuls of damp sand that were pounded into a parapet by their companions. I trudged up to where Ron sat and collapsed beside him, dropping the beach bag in the sand. He handed me the paper cup of margarita that he had poured out for me, and when I had taken it, reached out to clasp the back of my neck gently with his cool hand.

"You have a good walk?"

"Yes. It was too beautiful to stay up in the casita. I had to get out."

"I know. It's cleared up beautifully. I didn't think it would."

"Did you get the stuff?"

"Everything but the peanuts. They didn't have any."

"What time is it, anyway?"

He turned his wrist to see. "Just after noon. Are you hungry?"

"I'm starved. But I'll have this first. I'm thirsty, too." I sipped the margarita, blinking at its wryness. We drank them almost straight now. "Was it muddy?"

"Not too bad. There's one bad spot, just outside town. We had to get out and push a little, but we made it. Did you do the postcards?"

"No. I was reading, and then it cleared up, so I left. The surf's fantastic."

"Yes. It runs high for a day or so after a storm, the patrón says. Annaliese tried it, but she got wiped out. Where did you go?"

"I found a little stream and followed it up into the jungle for a way. It's beautiful in there."

"That's pretty risky," Ron said. "There are skin parasites in there, snakes, poison plants, God knows what-all."

"I suppose so. I suppose I'm verminous, and poisoned, and maybe snake-bit. But it feels marvelous."

"So they say." He grinned and tossed a handful of hot sand onto my thighs. "My God, you're getting brown." He wiped the sand from my thighs, his hand lingering tenderly. "Your skin's like satin. God, you're getting more beautiful every day, you know that?" He raised his eyes to my face, a sudden gravity welling in them. "You know, we ought to come here every year, Sylvie."

"Do you think so?"

"I think I do."

When we had finished our drinks we went up to the cantina in the palm grove and ate an enormous lunch of broiled snapper and guacamole, staring out at the brazen silver-plated sea. The doctors' white sloop was idling across the bay from Zihuatanejo to Los Gatos under motor power, its sail furled and bunched along the boom. It left a mild bubbling wake in the glazed green water. When the high, sleek rollers swept under it beam-on from the sea, it wallowed deeply, dropping almost out of sight, the tall aluminum mast sweeping across the sky as it rolled broadside into the steep troughs, then straightening swiftly as the sloop rose to the next incoming crest. Four men and two of the older children from the quinta clung to the lifelines in the cockpit, waving exuberantly shoreward as they rose and fell rhythmically in the heavy sea. On the beach the señoras had risen from their chairs and were waving to them; the children stood flapping towels and waving their tin shovels seaward.

"They should have on life vests," I said. "That's idiotic, in a sea like that." A cold gust blew over me out of my childhood.

In the center of the bay the boat slowed, its bubbly wake dissolving in the plated water to its stern. One of the men leaned over the outboard motor on the transom, lurching with the roll as he fiddled with the throttle.

"What have they done, cut the motor?" Ron said.

"They haven't cut it. It died."

The boat drifted gently, coming almost to a halt in its eerily slow course. It was now almost directly opposite the point of rocks in the center of the bay where the swells smashed up in a wild, exploded spray. I stood up at the table, raising my hand and clutching my hair gently. The man bent above the transom was working frantically now, pulling the starter cord in a series of desperate, violent lashes of his arm, lunging backward with each frenzied tug. The others crouched, clinging to the lifelines, reeling and staggering helplessly in the heaving cockpit.

"Jesus Christ," Ron said. "They're going to go aground. On those rocks." He stood up beside me, staring. The patrona wandered down weakly to the end of the table, murmuring, "Ay, no! Se van a matar." On the beach, the two wives swayed, withered, blown by the wind of their horror like dry leaves clinging to a stem. A screaming child tugged at the skirt of one of them; another was running hysterically down toward the surf with an older sister racing after him; the other children tottered in strengthless terror, their fists pressed to their bellies, shrieking, with contorted faces.

"Madre de dios," the patrona whispered. She put her hand out, touching my shoulder. The sloop had come to a complete stop now in its forward course and paused for a moment, breaching slowly, its bow turning idly seaward, washing with an awful languid inevitability toward the roaring turmoil of the surf on the gray rocks that streamed with foaming torrents of back-running water, not ten yards to leeward. Annaliese and the German boy had risen and stared out at the scene, motionless. No one moved again at all until the sloop, rising on the crest of a huge shining billow, smashed down onto the rocks in a spasmodic, suddenly arrested lurch that snapped the mainmast and sent a wild sheet of spray and white spume cataracting up into the blue sky. We heard the hollow crunching boom of the splintered hull and the clatter of the broken mast catapulting onto the rocks, and then the anguished chorus of screams rising from the beach like the wailing of a pack of harpies. Three of the men aboard were hurtled like sacks of grain out of the cockpit and disappeared into a glazed uprearing wall of green almost without a splash. Two others were flung spinningly askew, clinging to the wire lines like trousers flapping from a clothesline, and then, with their hold broken, splattered down upon the rocks with a shocking rubbery resilience of their bodies, among jets of shallow froth. Suddenly the beach was streaming with people I had not seen, or who had mysteriously multiplied or been evoked out of the air; the patrón's two slender sons came hurtling down the path from the quinta and across the sand toward the surf, carrying between them a gigantic black rubber inner tube, their arms hooked through its center; the German was plunging out through the surf in a boiling confusion of flashing arms and legs; the boy from Texas ran, hobbling, kicking off his shoes, toward the water, the sand spraying from his feet; a man on a red rubber raft, already out beyond the line of breakers, paddled frantically toward the foundered sloop; and I saw Ron, galloping through the boiling white foam to his waist, raise his clasped hands above his head and dive down through the marbled swell that rose before him. I kept my eyes on the long, flat, foam-streaked trough that hollowed out behind the breaker he had plunged into, and saw him reappear, shaking his head to snap the drenched hair from his face, and strike out strongly, swimming without haste or confusion, toward the wrecked sloop that skewed and tottered, helplessly uplifted, its hull grinding on the rocks. The heads of the castaways could be seen now, drifting swiftly in the current that ran shoreward along the line of rocks. Two of them had evidently managed to snatch life vests from a locker before they were thrown overboard, because I could see the bright, orange-colored fabric clutched to their chests. The third man was foundering, his arms slashing at the water senselessly as he struggled frenziedly to keep his head above the rise and fall of the huge, polished, weirdly magnificent swells that lifted and swiftly lowered him like a floating bottle or a patch of seaweed. Ron swam toward him steadily, with an unhurried stoic ease, rising with a look of exaltation on the shining, sunlit crests and then vanishing for a moment when they swept under him. The drowning man's head disappeared just before he reached it; I saw him dive, and then in a moment reappear, clutching the man's hair, heaving upward with both his hands to raise the man's head above the sea, and then turn, and in a strong, slow sidestroke begin towing him toward the shore. I looked back to the rocks and saw three of the castaways sprawled clinging to the streaming boulders, edging their way down with terrified caution to the two Mexican boys who had maneuvered the huge black inner tube to the rocks below them and held it there, rising and falling in the ebb and wash on the lee side of the boulders. In a moment two of the stranded men had tumbled down onto it, clutching the wet black rubber frantically, twisting and writhing until their bodies were securely athwart the ring. The third, an older man with white hair and a frail, shrunken body, plunged into the sea toward the man on the red raft, who paddled swiftly toward him and in a moment had seized him by the wrist and tugged his hand to the yellow line that ran in loops along the edges of the raft.

This bright, terrible flow of images seemed timeless in its passage, like those dreams teeming with innumerable events that transpire in an instant's drowsing; and hardly had another instant passed before the shipwrecked men were being dragged up through the gently bubbling backwash to the sand, staggering and drooping, collapsing in the rippled slide of water with heaving ribs, their fingers dug into the streaming beach like claws. They lay outstretched and panting while their women and children ran down to crouch and clutch at them, weirdly like a flock of vultures descending on carrion. The two wives fell full-length across the bodies of their husbands, sobbing with demented joy, their skirts and hair flowing landward in the shallow wash of the shingle. I saw Ron reel and collapse with exhaustion into a sitting position on the sand, his head bowed between his knees. The man whom he had dragged ashore crawled on his hands and knees up the slope of the beach, where he fell flat and lay gasping.

Then the spell that had bound me like a delicate taut net fell apart in a shower of shattered filaments, and I found that I could move again. I started to run down across the sand to where Ron sat panting with his forearms dangling from his knees, and I saw that the beach was now teeming with more mysteriously evoked people: a dozen boys and men and brown-legged girls in flapping skirts from the huts in the palm grove, and guests from the hotel in slacks and sports shirts and cabana clothes, were running with me or had already gathered about the shipwrecked men. One of the survivors was now struggling to his feet with the aid of their outstretched hands. Another sat hugging to his breast and stroking with tender vehemence the black heads of his wife and a pair of sobbing children. The woman clung to him, her hands wandering over his head and shoulders in gentle, bewildered gratitude. The man whom Ron had brought ashore had risen and was loping off down the beach, his arms dangling loosely. I dropped beside Ron and slid my arm around his knee and hugged his leg.

"Are you all right?" I said. He nodded, reaching out to take my hand. "My God, you were marvelous. I didn't know you could swim like that."

"I didn't either. God. Did they all get in?" He raised his head to glance up at the crowd that had gathered around the survivors. Between their legs we could see that the old, white-haired man lay groaning, reaching down to clutch his bleeding, twisted knee. One of the doctors knelt over him, examining the joint. The backs of his own hands were scraped raw.

"He seems to be the worst off," I said. "They've got some scrapes and bruises, but I think they're all right."

"What happened to the guy I brought in?"

"I don't know. He's gone off down the beach." I pointed to where the man loped away in a feeble trot toward Zihuatanejo. A girl in a red dress ran beside him, reaching out to hold his arm.

"Well, I guess he's all right, if he can run," Ron said. "I'll be damned if I could right now." He looked at me and grinned. "My God, I'm glad to see you again. There was a minute there when I wondered if I would."

"It was strange."

"It really was. I thought he was going to drown me, a couple of times. He was so damned crazy to stay alive, he didn't seem to realize I was trying to help him." He shook his head as if trying to clear it and stared out at the foundered sloop, skewed and heaving ponderously on the rocks. "Those things happen so fast. It's like getting put in the batting order all of a sudden, when you didn't expect it."

"You better come and have a hot shower," I said. "You got your man home safe."

That night at dinner in the hotel patio we and the other men who had aided in the rescue were feted by the physicians and their families. They brought bottles of champagne to all our tables, accompanied by their wives and children. The youngest daughter, a beautiful little creature of nine or ten in a white dress and with tiny gold earrings in her earlobes, put the bottle in Ron's hand and said in a merry tumble of words: "For you heroísmo, señor. For you save my papá's life. Lo agradecemos very much. You very good man." She stood on her toes and kissed him on both cheeks. Then everyone clapped, and the ten children lined up and sang to us, to the tune of "Cielito Lindo":

> ¡Ay, ay, ay, ay!
> ¡Gracias, señores!
> Que sean benditos por haber salvado
> Las vidas de nuestros padres!

Everyone, the physicians told us, was in miraculously good condition with the exception of their father, who had broken his leg and had been sent back to Mexico City in the airplane from Acapulco. His younger son had set the bone and stitched the gash in his knee—not very well, he said, smiling broadly, because he was a gynecologist; but the old man was very strong and would perhaps survive. The man whom Ron had brought ashore and who had disappeared afterwards was a paid boat hand, an employee of the marina in Zihuatanejo, where they kept their boat, who often crewed for them. He had been confused and embarrassed, they explained, but they had learned that he was well, and they knew he would wish them to add his blessing to their own.

They were full of the gracious gaiety of people who have experienced the greatest of all good fortune—salvation—and whose gratitude is too profound for any question. They were convinced that their rescue was a miracle and that everyone who had aided them was an instrument of God. Well, of course, whatever you believe, you have to be moved to solemnity by the events of such a day, and when we went back to the casita after dinner we sat on the veranda for a while, looking out at the black sea that was growing calmer now under the vast, jeweled sky.

"They're so certain God smiled on them today," Ron said. "I suppose they'll believe that for the rest of their lives."

"Yes."

"I suppose you could find vanity even in that."

"I don't want to argue."

"No, but there is. You've taught me that. How could one help feeling gratified by the belief that God had paid such very special attention to his welfare—interceded in destiny on his behalf? You couldn't help feeling distinguished." I didn't answer him. "It must be wonderful to have faith," he said after a moment. "It must be absolutely the most wonderful thing in the world. Real faith, I mean; not the kind you gain from miracles. I mean the kind that Kierkegaard was talking about in *Fear and Trembling*. That exists beyond reprieve, or even the hope of it. Beyond even the vanity of gratitude. I wonder if anyone does anymore."

"Jamed does," I said.

"Yes, I guess so. I was just going to say that, as soon as I asked." He sat for a moment and then asked suddenly, "How is he, Sylvie?"

"He doesn't change."

"No, I don't suppose he ever will." He reached out to take my hand. "I don't know which of you I envy most." Then after a long silence, he said, "I'm glad that man didn't come to thank me. I hope he never does."

I remembered the night after Poppa had been lost at sea and Ron had come home with me for his memorial service and we had sat on the front porch with Aaron, staring at the black sea, as we were now. That man would be out there now, like Poppa, I thought, if you hadn't brought him ashore; tumbling on the hard white corrugated sand of the ocean bottom, being scrubbed clean of all his lust and pride and agony. Would that have been a greater grace to conjure by?

In the morning when Ron went to Playa Azul to pick up the Volkswagen, I got up to make toast and coffee, and after he had gone, got back in bed and read Neruda until the the light coming through the window made the printed poem dissolve in a diaphanous blur that blinded me. I closed the jalousie and

lay in the dark room dreaming of Inca history, of the high walled eyries of
Macchu Picchu and Cuzco, and of Atahuallpa, the golden son of princes, and
Pizarro, the swineherd from Estremadura who had betrayed and slain him. The
thunder of the surf had softened to a heavy, restless wash through which I
could hear sometimes, when people passed on the path outside the casita, the
murmur of voices and sudden low laughter that startled me. I must be mad,
I thought. I'm a mad, unworthy woman. Ron should sell my passport and leave
me here to rot. I got up and put on my robe and tried again to write postcards,
but I found myself staring at them with the pen in my hand for half an hour
or more, distracted by the thin bright turmoil that trickled through me like
the aching of a tooth. He had not said what time he would come. I might sit
there all day; and it would please his pride to think that I would wait, in
growing impatience and anxiety, but abjectly. To add to my irritation, my
watch had stopped because I had forgotten to wind it when I went to bed, and
I could not tell the time exactly. I went out onto the veranda to look at the
shadows; they lay half the length of the villa and the trees that cast them; so
it was an hour or more yet until noon. On the bay, I thought, I would know
what time it was without a moment's calculation, without a single clue but the
shadows in my blood.

On the beach below, a crowd had gathered to watch the salvage of the
foundered sloop, which was being hauled from the rocks by a stubby-looking
battered little workboat. Six oil drums had been lashed to the bared keel to keep
her from righting, and she lay on her side, washing heavily, to windward of the
rocks, her gored port beam upraised, showing a ragged hole the size of a bass
drum. A cable had been connected to her bow from a derrick on the stern of
the workboat and was being reeled in slowly onto a drum amidships to the
steady purring of an electric winch. There was much flapping of hands and
shouting from the crew of three aboard the workboat, and on the shore the
physicians and their teen-aged sons stood gesticulating briskly, calling out
instructions and encouragement. A pair of Mexican boys were kicking a soccer
ball on the sand. I reached out to pluck a spray of bougainvillea from the vine
that grew along the eaves of the veranda, and stuck it in my hair. Above me
on the hillside, I saw Annaliese coming down the path toward the beach with
her towel draped across her arm. She waved to me, and when she had come
opposite the veranda she stopped and said, "Good morning," tossing her hair
back in a restless, self-conscious way and smiling shyly.

"Good morning. It's a lovely one."

"Yes. You are coming down?"

"After a while. Ron's gone into town."

"You are alone?" I nodded. "You have had breakfast?"

"Yes."

She waited for a moment and said, "You have flowers in your hair. They are pretty."

"Thank you."

She turned to look down at the salvage operation on the beach. "They are getting the boat off."

"Yes."

"It was a terrible day, yesterday. But it came out well. Your husband was very brave."

"Yes, he was."

She raised her eyes to mine and after a moment said gently, "You would like to have a cup of coffee with me?"

"I can't," I said. "But thank you very much, Annaliese." She lowered her eyes and stood in a kind of humble uncertainty. "I'm waiting for someone," I said deliberately.

"Oh. Good morning, then."

"Good morning."

She turned and went quickly down the path. I watched her walk across the beach at the bottom, away from the crowd gathered by the rocks. She tossed out her towel on the sand and raised her head to look up at me quickly before she stretched out in the sun. I went back into the villa and dug out of my suitcase the notebook in which I was writing my novel. I sat down at the desk and slipped through the pages I had written in Mexico; there were only fifteen of them. I read the last few pages twice, biting my lips:

because there was something about Neil that suggested madness and poetry: the lividness of his lips and the strange albino blondness of his eyelashes, which gave his eyes a look of pale, repressed ferocity. I didn't feel either guilt or self-contempt at inventing such a fantasy, because I had virtually been invited to indulge in it by Gowan's strange, convulsive declaration to me that day on the steps of Tydings Hall. He had in fact invoked it (and probably much more than merely fantasy) by that agonized, unconscious confession of his desire for complicity in it, which I accepted as a definition of his status. In fact, it didn't take very much inventing, because the basic incident had actually happened to me once, when I was going to high school on the Western Shore. A boy had taken me to the old stone quarry on the Shady Grove Road on an early summer day, the last week before graduation. It was one of the few real dates I ever had in high school, and I went with him because he had that same quality about him of something suppressed and ecstatic that was beyond his ability to express except in some scandalous way, through some form of outrage. And so I had only to substitute Neil in his role, and change the circumstances a little—the occasion, the nature of our acquaintance, our ages and appearances—and I found myself there at the quarry again, with the summer heat crimping the leaves, and the May apples ripening, and the stone cliffs over the deep still water, and the voices of picnickers from the oak grove on the opposite bank.

When Neil went back to the car to get the beer, I sat there throwing pebbles down into the water twenty feet below—such a nice sound they made; a kind of revelatory liquid sundering of an element—trying to remember exactly what it was that Gowan had said to me that day in the rain. But I could only remember his last words, which were not his at all, but the speech he had quoted to me from Joyce's play *Exiles;* a line that Richard speaks to Bertha in the last scene: "It is not in the darkness of faith that I desire you, but in restless, living, wounding doubt." Those words scarified me, like a canker on the tongue. They seemed almost heraldic, like the motto on an escutcheon. I even tried to translate them into Latin, and had had to grimace with frustration because they sounded so absurd in my barbaric syntax.

Then Neil came back with a six-pack of beer, and the rifle in his hand. He sat down beside me with the rifle across his knees and ripped the cap off a can of beer. It was warm, and came frothing out of the open hole with a bitter hiss.

"Why did you bring the rifle?" I asked.

"I want to show you something in a minute." He handed me a beer and I held it without drinking. "I come up here a lot. People leave sandwiches, eggshells, all kinds of garbage. It makes for interesting sport." He sipped at his beer and stared down at the can. "You told me once that the very basest act conceivable could be redeemed by the beauty that is in it, if we know how to seek it out. Do you remember that?"

"Yes."

"Do you really believe it?"

"Yes. That's the only thing I know. If I don't know that, I don't know anything."

He sipped again, blinking for a moment. (And I saw him, so clearly, in this fantasy, that I think sometimes it may have actually happened: The words slipping out between his bright, barely moving lips as if he were afraid they might lacerate them if spoken too loudly or quickly; his white eyelashes fluttering with an odd, fragile artificiality when he blinked.) He set down the can and picked up a rock from the bank. "O.K., watch now," he said. "I want you to see this. Watch when it hits."

He threw the rock across the water onto the opposite bank where there was a sodden heap of brown paper bags among the boulders. A huge gray rat came plummeting down the bank and plunged into the water with a plunk like a falling apple. It swam swiftly toward us, its head leaving a rippled V across the surface. Neil raised the rifle and fired quickly three times, the head disappearing in a murky spurt with the impact of the last bullet. A red stain spread out in the water like an unfurling silken ribbon. Neil stared at it, his white eyelashes fluttering.

"I wonder if we could make a poem out of that," he said. "I made some out of Vietnam."

"Somebody could," I murmured. I dropped my head and closed my eyes.

"Well, let's just see. You know what I'd like you to do? I'd like you to take off all your clothes and swim across that quarry, and then back. Right through that blood. But you better hurry, because it'll be gone in a minute."

"I can't do it," I said. "I'll be sick."

"I don't think so. The water's cold. It'll clear your head."

"Neil, there are rats in there."

"Well, I've got the gun, if they bother you."

The bushes on the far side of the quarry shook and parted, and then a man—one of the picnickers, I suppose—pushed his head between them and stood looking out, startled by the shots. Neil waved to him.

"Go ahead," he said to me. "I'm waiting."

"There's a man watching over there."

"He won't bother you. Remember, I've got the rifle."

I stood up and began to unbutton my blouse, my hands trembling terribly. When I tell Gowan about this, I thought, I'll put his hands on my breasts while I describe it to him, and make him hold them there, so he can feel the nipples getting hard, as if it were happening to me then, for the first time. I want him to understand what I feel for a crazy poet who has been driven mad by life and whose innocence I cherish enough to swim through rat blood, naked, to provide him with a poem.

I sat for a long time with the pen in my hand, staring at the page, and finally added these sentences:

If he doesn't love that in me, then he doesn't love me, and can't claim to. And I won't permit him to.

Then I closed the notebook and took it back to the suitcase and shoved it down inside under a pile of dirty underclothes. I went to the door of the veranda and stood for a time, looking down at the beach. The sloop was gone

from the rocks and the crowd had dispersed. The physicians' wives had set up
their umbrella at the bottom of the cliff; I could see the top of it, and the
children splashing in the surf, and Annaliese wading out to where the breakers
began, her brown shoulders glittering in the sun. It was bright and still, and
the shadow of the villa had withdrawn from the oleander bushes in front of
the veranda. I went into the kitchenette and took the bottle of margarita mix
out of the refrigerator and poured a glass half full and then filled it with tequila.
I'll drink this, I thought; and then, if he hasn't come, I'll go. I've waited long
enough so that I can't accuse myself of pride or coquetry; and so that he can't.
I carried the margarita to the bed table and set it down; then I went into the
bathroom and took my razor out of the cabinet and came back and sat down
on the bed and began to shave my legs, pausing occasionally to lift the glass
and sip the cold sour liquid. I had finished one leg and had taken a few strokes
at the other when there was a knock at the door.

"Come in," I said. "Entre."

The door opened hesitantly, halfway, and I looked up and saw Abél standing outside in the sunlight with his hand on the knob. He was smiling at me
through the open door, the straw sombrero worn very low on his forehead, so
that it almost touched his eyebrows. He had a paper bag in his hand.

"Well, come in," I said. I lowered my eyes from his and went on shaving
my leg. I saw the widening lane of sunlight on the floor when he opened the
door, his shadow falling almost to my feet, and then it narrowed and vanished
and I heard the click of the latch when he closed the door behind him. I lifted
the razor and blew the hairs out of it and looked up at him without smiling.
He was smaller than I remembered—not very much taller than I was—and
more delicate of feature, and his skin had a faint purple tint to it, like cordovan
leather.

"I didn't know whether you'd come or not," I said. "I was just going to
leave."

"I have to work this morning. Then I come." He took off his hat and held
it by the brim, looking around the room, his gaze pausing on one of the little
brown lizards clinging to the wall above the desk. He pointed to it with his
hat brim, breaking into a broad smile.

"Besaderos. Pweef, pweef." He made a kissing noise, puckering his lips. I
nodded. "You like him?"

"I don't mind them." I picked up my glass and sipped from it. "What do
you have in the bag?"

"Limas." He opened the bag and held it toward me so that I could see the
green limes inside.

"Are they for me?"

"Sí."

"Thank you." He shrugged and twisted his mouth wryly, turning to set the bag on the table.

"Would you like a tequila?" I said. "¿Quiere tequila?"

"Sí, gracias."

I took the bag of limes into the kitchenette, sliced one of them, and poured tequila into a glass for him. He turned to watch me, setting his hat on the table. I slipped the split lime slice onto the rim of the glass and picked up the salt cellar and carried them out to him. He took the glass very carefully in both his hands, and I saw that there was grease on his fingers and his knuckles were scraped raw.

"¿Sal?"

"Sí." He held out his hand and I sprinkled a little mound of salt into his broad, soiled palm. He raised it to his mouth and, craning his neck slightly, licked it with the tip of his flickering, glittering scarlet tongue, smiling at me over his cupped hand. Then he raised the glass to me, nodding slightly, and said, "Salud, pesetas, y amor. You know what it mean?"

"Health, money, and love."

He nodded, smiling broadly, and drank the tequila in a single swallow, his brown, upraised throat rippling smoothly. He plucked the lime slice from the glass and chewed it for a moment, swallowing it rind and all. "¡Qué bueno! La tequila vence todo." He set the glass on the table and sucked air shrilly and appreciatively between his teeth, wiping his lips with the back of his hand. The air smelled of the sweet, acid perfume of the fresh-sliced lime. I moved to him and stood with my hips touching his. I felt very self-possessed and certain but I was trembling furiously. He reached out to take the sprig of bougainvillea out of my hair and kiss it and drop it into the pocket of his shirt. Then he took the lapels of my dressing gown in his thumbs and fingers and parted them, gazing sorrowfully at my bared breasts.

"Qué linda," he said, "how beautiful," almost without expression, as if in simple confirmation of some verity. I stepped away from him to let the dressing gown fall open, and looked down at my bare belly and hips and thighs, enthralled by my own nakedness, so that I gasped.

"Qué tu eres linda," he said. "Caraje." He lifted the gown by the lapels and let it drop down over my drifting arms and then seized me against him, my face crushed painfully against the blunt knobs of his collarbones, pressing his lips against my hair in a savage slow welter of kisses that stunned and hurt me. I could feel his teeth against my skull as if he were gnawing at the stone of a peach.

"My God," I said. "Wait just a minute." I went reeling across to the bed and sat gasping, my hands laid flat on the mattress, my head sunken between my shoulders, staring up at him in a harrowed way, like a hound waiting to be beaten, while he took his clothes off, folding them carefully as if to demonstrate his good breeding, and laid them, piece by piece, across the back of a chair. I watched while he sat down and took off his blue canvas sandals, his penis hugely erect, trembling rigidly while he removed his shoes. When he stood up and came toward me I saw that there was a patch of gauze bandage strapped to his left side with adhesive tape. He stood in front of me, clasping my ears lightly with his fingertips, and drew my head against him. I raised my hands to hold the weight of his testicles like warm dark plums and kissed his genitals lightly and delicately, brushing them with my lips like blossoms, holding them like heavy, succulent, warm fruit.

"Tu eres lindo," I murmured.

"Y tu."

"Vén conmigo." I took his hand and lay back on the bed, drawing him down beside me, raising my free hand to shift the jalousie and let the sunlight spill over us. I loved the glistening, oxblood planish of his skin and the flowing current of muscle under it, like the scurrying of velvet moles. He bit me gently everywhere, my ears and lips and eyelids and fingertips and nipples, saying in a persistent, augustly quaking voice, "Mi china, mi guapa, mi estrella."

"Ay, sí. Sí, sí, sí, amor, hermano," I murmured in answer to him, pressing him down to me with my hands against the suave nape of his neck and the great undulating tendril of his spine. The rhythm of his love was grave and oceanic, like the endless surge of Pacific swells, pounding over me until I was limp and bleached and shriven; and when at last his passion ebbed majestically like a great withdrawing sea, calm in its vast, shining surfeit, I drifted in its tidal pools with floating hair and billowing broken limbs and vacant, skyward eyes, like a clump of pliant wrack, in utter noble destitution. I lay for a long time stroking the sleek brawn of his back, clutching the moist black curls that clustered on the nape of his neck, trailing my fingertips over the hard swell of his buttocks and through the graven furrows of his ribs. I felt the strip of bandage dangling from his side, ripped loose by our writhing, and he winced when I touched the deep moist gash that lay exposed below his ribs. I drew my hand up and saw that my fingers were glistening with fresh blood.

"Estás herido," I said. "You're wounded."

"Un poco. No es nada. A little. It's nothing."

"¿Que te pasó, amor?" I said. "What happened to you, love?"

"De las rocas. From the rocks. Trabajo por la marina a Zihuatanejo. Estuve al bordo del barque del doctor Zuleta cuando fracasó ayer. I was in Dr. Zuleta's boat when it capsized yesterday. I work for the marina." He rolled onto his back and lifted his hands into the sunlight from the window. "Las manos son los peores, porque es difícil trabajar. The hands are the worst, because it is difficult to work."

I took them and drew them quickly to my mouth, kissing their raw, lacerated backs lightly, over and over.

"¿Huyiste, después? Did you run away, afterwards?"

"Sí."

"¿Porque?"

"Me dió mucha vergüenza," he said with a shy, childish candor. "I was ashamed. Nos apagó la gasolina. We ran out of gasoline. Fué mi culpa. No averigüé el tanque antes de salir. It was my fault. I didn't check the tank before we left. Fué bruto. It was stupid." He turned towards me and laid his hand against my cheek, gazing at me with a sorrowful intensity. "No, la culpa es tuya. No pude pensar. No, it was your fault, I think. I couldn't think clearly. Fuí pensando en esta cara, estos senitos. I was thinking about this face, these little breasts." He lowered his hand and cupped my breast, bending to crush it gently to his cheek. "Ay, caraje, qué lindeza. Oh, Christ, how beautiful." He lay quietly for a time while my hands strayed over him, stroking his sunlit skin, as silken as river silt, gathering in my hand the flower of his reawakening desire, the great swelling purple amaryllis bud that sprang like a scepter from his loins, until he sighed vastly with a sound of incoming tide and took me in his arms, and the sea of his passion swept over me again and I lay ravaged, huddled in his arms.

We fell into a numinous white sleep, from which I arose in nameless exultation. I led him across the cool tile floor to the white cubicle of the shower stall; and with the water turned on full to a cataracting coldness that drummed against our skulls and pummeled our tense skin, we stood shuddering, clasped in each other's arms, pale blue and slick and icy, pressing our cold lips to one another's throats and ears and eyes, murmuring frenziedly. He sank to his knees, his hands slipping down the wet length of my body, and clutched me to him, pressing his face into the cleft of my thighs. I closed my eyes and stood plucking idly at his hair, my head dangling with its inexplicable weight, as if it were a great ripe melon drooping from the white vine of my neck, a golden cassava splashed with summer rain. Inside the rind of its skull my mind seemed to have come to an ambrosial, glistening fruition, a moist, delectable firmament sprinkled with glittering onyx-bright seeds, like constellations of black stars.

Ron did not get back from Playa Azul until almost five o'clock. I was sitting in a rattan chair on the veranda, my arms akimbo, my face raised to the afternoon light in a slumbrous, trancelike peace. He closed the door of the casita loudly and came out onto the veranda in weary silence, standing at the railing for a moment before he greeted me with a sullen "Hi."

"What happened?" I said. "Why are you so late?"

"The goddamned thing still wasn't ready, of course. And then he wanted two hundred pesos more. Honest to God, there's a limit to the patience you can have with these people."

"Oh, Lord. I suppose you had to wait around that town all day."

He nodded bitterly. "Counting the pigs. There are three thousand two hundred and twelve of them. Eighteen three-legged ones. And a cantina with a rest room in it that I think Dante must have visited."

"You better have a drink. We're out of mix, but there are some fresh limes there. They're marvelous when you take it straight."

He went into the kitchenette and I heard the rattle of an ice tray and the clink of cubes in a glass. When he came back out with the glass, he carried a quartered slice of lime in his fingers and its fragrance permeated the air of the veranda.

"Where did you get them? They're delicious."

"From Los Gatos."

He sipped the tequila and then sucked the pale wedge of fruit, shuddering, looking down at the bay. I felt an almost desolate affection, watching him.

"I'm sorry you had such an awful day."

"Well, this'll put it right. I suppose it was bound to happen, sooner or later. What have you been up to?"

"Just loafing. Drenching myself in this place. Dreaming."

He turned to look at me, swirling the ice in his glass. "You look a little drunk. You been drinking straight tequila all afternoon?"

"Not all afternoon. I managed to do a little writing."

"Well, I'm glad to hear that. I won't forgive you if you give it up, you know." He sat down and looked sidelong at me for a moment, then reached out to grasp a handful of my hair. "After all, that's what you took up with me for, wasn't it? So you could write?" I murmured vaguely, blinking in the sun. "Your hair's wet," he said after a moment.

"I didn't dry it. I took a shower earlier."

"It looks marvelous. It's gotten three shades lighter since you've been here."

"I'm sorry you had such a rotten day."

"You just said that." He grinned at me. "It's practically over. Just a fit of pique. Anglo-Saxon indignation, I suppose. After all, we have to keep reminding ourselves who we are. How things ought to be done."

"Who are we?" I said. "How ought things to be done?"

"Damned if I know. But I have the very strong illusion that I do whenever I'm abroad and things go wrong." He swirled the ice in his glass, staring down at it. "Actually, I got quite a bit done. I took my books along, and found a spot under a palm tree and finished annotating a couple of the poems. It's just that

I felt—restless—suddenly. As if I'd finished with this place or something. I don't know."

"Why don't we go, then."

"Why do you say that? I thought you loved it here."

"I do. But after all, we've been here almost a month. And if we want to see a bit of Oaxaca and Taxco, we've got another ten days' driving ahead of us."

"Do you mean it? You really wouldn't mind?"

"No. We can always come back, if you want to. I mean, another year."

"Yes. Good, let's do that, then. I'll settle with the patrón tonight, and we'll get away early in the morning. We can spend tomorrow night in Acapulco. You sure you don't mind?"

"No. I'm ready to go when you are."

So that was what we did. And it was not until we had stopped for lunch the next day at a grass-roofed restaurant on the end of a pier that went out into a lagoon at a place called Puesta del Sol, a few miles north of Acapulco, and we were finishing a bottle of wine, looking out from the cool shelter of the roof at the sparkle of sunlight on the water, that I said to him, "I lied to you about the limes, Ron. I didn't get them at Los Gatos. A man gave them to me."

"A man? What do you mean? What man?"

"A man I met the day before yesterday. On the beach. When I went up into the jungle, I left my bag on the sand, and when I came back he was looking through it. He was looking at my passport, as a matter of fact, so he knew my name. He gave it back to me, though. I suppose he would have kept it if I hadn't surprised him, I don't know. I wouldn't have blamed him. It was a stupid thing to do. But he was very pleasant, and said he'd meant to ask at the hotels if I was staying there, and return it to me. So then, yesterday, when you were at Playa Azul, he came up to the casita, with a bag of limes for me. Of course, it was presumptuous, but I felt I owed him courtesy, at least."

"Yes, I suppose you did," Ron said. "Just how courteous were you?" His voice was thin and unsteady.

"I went to bed with him." I turned my eyes from the water, which I had been watching steadily while I spoke, and looked at him. His face was pale under his tan, so that it looked made-up. His lips were closed and he was breathing with a steady soft shrillness through his nostrils.

"So that's why you wanted to leave," he said. "I see."

"Yes. I didn't want it to go any further. Really."

"I don't know how much further it could go," he said. "I mean, you were pretty thorough already, weren't you?"

"I mean I didn't want to see him again. I didn't want there to be any unpleasantness about it."

"Oh, unpleasantness." He stared at his silverware, reaching out to straighten the pieces carefully, laying them side by side.

"I don't want it to hurt you," I said. "Really, Ron."

"No, I understand."

I raised my glass and drank the bit of wine that was left in it. "Could I have a little more wine?" He reached for the bottle and poured my glass carefully half full, steadying the bottle with his left hand. When he had set it down he stared at the label studiously for a minute.

"I don't know exactly how much I'm allowed to ask," he said. "I don't know what the protocol is, exactly."

"You can ask anything you like. You know that."

"Well—" He sighed and squared his shoulders, straightening his back in the chair. "I assume it was—satisfactory."

"Yes. I suppose whatever was supposed to happen did. If that's what you mean."

He raised his head and looked out at the water. The waiter, a boy of twelve or thirteen who had been leaning against a post at the end of the pier watching us, approached alertly, evidently believing that Ron had summoned him with his glance.

"¿Señor?" he said.

"No. No queremos nada," Ron said. "Gracias."

"A sus órdenes, señor." He returned to the post and took up his position with folded arms.

"They're wonderfully accommodating," Ron said. He turned to look at me directly. "Do you feel any different about me?"

"I like you better. I appreciate you more. I mean that." I laid my fingertips on the table and stared at them. "I wish it could be the other way around. I mean, I wish you'd done something I could be as nice about."

"I wish I wanted to." He turned his face away and stared out at the water. "Well, I don't think we'd better say any more about it, just now. Or ever, maybe."

"I haven't lied to you," I said. "I promised you I wouldn't, and I haven't."

"No. I can't accuse you of that. I can't accuse you of anything, really. And you wouldn't like to see him again?"

"No."

"You're sure?"

"There's nothing to see him about. It was meaningless. Perfectly meaningless."

In 1940, Tallacoochee, Alabama, was a shadowy, sun-stilled town of fifteen hundred people in the south-central region of the state, twenty miles above the Florida line. It had a wide main street lined with live oaks from which Spanish moss hung like rags of rotted bunting over the blunt, rouge-red bricks of the swollen sidewalks and the ruptured, sandy street. No building on the street was over two stories high, so that the tops of the live oaks stood level with the line of the dentiled red brick and white wooden cornices of the old Georgian façades of the offices and stores, and the dusky, grape-blue shadow of the foliage lay always against the front walls of the buildings and in a wash of blue-and-silver chiaroscuro on the glass panes of the store windows. The names of the proprietors and the identity of their businesses were printed in bold, black-edged gold-leaf letters on the windowpanes: BLOOD'S DRY GOODS, J. R. WINSTON DRUGS AND NOTIONS, MURCHISON & SON HARDWARE. The pitted and flaking gold leaf glowed with a tarnished luster in the shadow, like sunken coins. The second floors of the buildings were offices, with sash windows set in deep sills and lettered with the names and professions of the town's lawyers, dentists, real estate agents, and the Hackett County *Sentinel*, "The Voice of Freedom in the Bayou Country." At every corner there was a streetlamp upheld by a pillar of fluted cast iron crusted with a hundred coats of dark green enamel and decorated with garlands of scabrous acanthus leaves. There were slatted green wooden benches under the live oaks in whose shadow dogs lay sleeping in the summer afternoons and where old men in battered, sweat-stained felt hats sat in eternal witness and coarse, saturnine colloquy, like the chorus of a Greek tragedy.

The first thing I noticed about the town and the last thing I will remember was its silence, a strange, spellbound stillness through which the click of an acorn dropping on the pavement, the whine of a dentist's drill from an upstairs office window, the tinkle of a bell from an opening shop door, or the sudden distant shriek of a circular saw from the lumber mill outside the town penetrated in the startling, ghostly way of a sound that awakens one from sleep. Sometimes on a still, hot day, I have stood at the window of our laboratory in the Hackett County Health Clinic over Winston's pharmacy and listened to the tapping of a woman's heels approach and then recede along the pavement underneath with a weird, cryptic sound, waxing out of, and waning into, the silence like a coded message from some veiled, unattainable universe that had brushed for a moment against our own. I can still hear in my head, if I shut my eyes and lean my head back against a chair, the ceaseless, canny muttering of the old men on the benches underneath the open window, a bleak, admonitory strophe that floated in the air like a lament while I drew from the distended vein of a quietly horrified black man a slowly welling cylinder of bright, polluted blood.

Tallacoochee was the county seat of Hackett County. The courthouse stood at the center of Main Street, set far back behind a pair of ancient, huge-boled white oaks on a wide, shadow-clad lawn through which a walk of red octagonal tiles coated with slime-green moss flowed like a stagnant stream toward the street. It was an old crumbling red brick building of stately Palladian architecture with a great, gloomy two-story portico that smelled of damp stone, its entablature supported by four white wooden columns streaked with pigeon lime and scarred with initials whittled into the soft, dry-rotted wood. In front of it a limp, faded flag clung to the top of the white staff above the lawn like the trophy of a hunt lifted lifelessly on a lance point. The building faced west, so that in the late afternoon, when the sun had sunk below the foliage of the oaks, its windows blazed with a hellish red glare, as if it were on fire inside. I passed it every evening on my way home, and sometimes at night I would dream of it: the walls of its chambers bathed in sheets of silent flame, tapestries fringed with flickering yellow fire sliding down to fall across blazing oak tables and elegant Adams cabinets where the yellowed chronicles of the Confederacy burst into scarlet blossom.

Beyond the courthouse I would turn left and walk for three blocks between the old white clapboard houses that lay north of Main Street and through a small melancholy park with an iron drinking fountain whose rusty basin was damp with a constant trickle of warm, sulfurous water. There were gigantic magnolia trees in the park, the odor of whose still, ivory-petaled blossoms floated through the town in tendrils of sweet, narcotic scent. Under the trees the bare, moist clay showed through the thin grass, and the pale boles of the trees were coated with a film of lime-green lichen, like the slime of rush stems. The park was enclosed by black cast-iron palings, chipped and rusted, and in the center there was a statue of Andrew Jackson, commemorating his victory over the Creeks at the Battle of Horseshoe Bend. He was mounted on a rampant bronze horse that stood almost upright on its hind legs, pawing frenziedly at the sky. The general had a look of startled preoccupation—as he might well have had, in his situation—and seemed to be waving his sword desperately for balance. The statue's travesty of gallantry made me very uneasy for some reason; I didn't like to look at it, and yet I never failed to raise my head to do so as I walked along the cracked concrete of the path beneath it. The faint, tingling discomposure it made me feel was somehow morbidly titillating, like touching the edge of a ragged tooth with the tongue, or pressing a sore gum with a thumbtip.

The quarters the Service provided me with were no worse and no better than any I could have found in the town: a Victorian white frame house with a half second story centered above the sloping red tin roof of the wide veranda underneath, its windows shadowed by the live oaks of the street, so that the rooms were always dark and smelled of damp carpeting and moist, ancient plaster. There was a huge, enameled metal oil heater in the center of the parlor, and directly above it, in the floor of the bedroom that Molly and I used, a steel register through which the heat came shimmering up on winter mornings, acrid and gaseous, like the miasma from a swamp or the fumes of some smoldering region into which the house was sinking slowly, its walls collapsing inward, the plaster buckling, the ceiling splitting imperceptibly, the beams issuing sudden hoarse cries of despair at night in the hot, damp, jasmine-scented silence. The veranda underneath was surrounded with a wooden rail swaying in the toils of a ravenous, pullulating Virginia creeper vine whose savage, shining tendrils had begun to coil up the columns at the corners of the porch like a horde of newborn vipers from a pit. Molly ripped them loose and clipped them periodically with grass shears, her lips pressed together with a look of harassment that deepened at every such operation to an eventual one of bitter apathy. There were a pair of rocking chairs on the veranda with deep-sunken cane seats and ruptured backs whose raveled fibers I used to sit and finger while we stared out at the dusk gathering in the tattered shrouds of Spanish moss that hung from the live oaks, and the pale, eerily floating magnolia blossoms glowing in the dusk among the houses, and the slowly rising spectral glimmer of lightning bugs among the branches. Every evening an old Negro ragman pushed his barrow up the street beneath the trees, and I came to listen for the creaking of the axle and the clatter of the ironbound wheels on the pavement bricks, an ancient, mournful, and somehow reverend sound that became a kind of coarse angelus of my days.

The street ran out past the line of shambling, veranda-clad wooden houses to the edge of town, and then, beyond the shadow of the oaks, into a bath of sudden, dazzling sunlight, to Tuskegee and Bibb, past shabby, peeling billboards and straggling roadside pines with rusty 666 signs nailed to their bleeding trunks. At the city limits, in a flurry of Kiwanis, Civitan, and American Legion signs pocked with stones and rifle bullets, the brick pavement gave way to the crumbling gray asphalt of State Route 25, which was joined at intervals of a mile or two by a pair of sandy tire tracks winding back into the silent pine barrens that surrounded it in depthless, paralyzed monotony. One of the sand roads led a mile back through the pines to a teeming, smoky hamlet of bleached, spindle-legged shanties huddled in a black willow grove beside a slow, sad, yellow river. I have spent hours of many days in that place, and of more than one night, watching a man die slowly, by the light of a kerosene lamp, amid the endless, throbbing shrill of hot-bugs in the willows. Sometimes the smell of the place reaches me even yet: pork grease and soapsuds and wood smoke and sour earth, the stink of privies and the warm, fecund reek of river mud, a musky, fetid vapor that still drifts and rankles in my breast. If I awaken to the memory of that smell it sends, even yet, a faintly nauseated thrill of fear running over my flesh like a caress.

The still, silent pines with their slowly running amber blood were the chief sustenance of Tallacoochee; it drew from them its own rapt, nearly static life and the rhythms of its own slowly pulsing veins. The thick-crusted brown bark of almost every pine of the county forests was slashed with a downward-pointing, chevron-shaped scar from which a stream of shining yellow sap oozed into a clay pot wired at shoulder height to the trunk. The pots of resin were collected periodically by crews of the Kindred Lumber Company and shipped to distilleries in Montgomery to be made into turpentine, and the forests were systematically harvested by gangs of lumberjacks whose flatbed trucks hauled the chained cargoes of great brown logs into the mill at the north edge of the town, where they were sawed into planks and stacked in tall, clean, fragrant piles inside the chain link fence of the company compound. All day there was a faint, distant shriek of the circular saws from that end of the town, and the golden mountains of sawdust grew higher beside the tracks of the spur line of the Southern Railway that ran into the lumberyard. Periodically the towering piles of sawdust were bitten into by steam shovels and dumped in streams of yellow meal into empty cars shunted into the spur line, that carried it to factories in Birmingham and Montgomery to be made into sheets of pellet-board and cellulose and paper pulp.

South of Tallacoochee was bayou country: the Coosalatchee River flowed into it and disappeared, merging into a wilderness of cypress swamps and miles of desolate mangrove hammocks and acres of saw grass threaded by the channels of sluggish tea-colored creeks and broken by scattered hummocks of high ground on which a few gaunt, tattered pines stood bitterly against the hard blue sky. If you climbed the fire tower at Broadwater you saw it stretching out in purple, endless, unutterable solitude beyond the reach of your eyes and almost of your sanity, past the southern border of the state and through the Florida panhandle to the Gulf. It was inhabited by shanty-dwelling, bearded wild men, trappers and moonshiners and alligator poachers, who came into town on Saturday nights and roamed the streets with eyes jellied by a lonely, crazed ferocity that burned in them like fever.

To the north of the town were scattered, small, poor truck farms that sucked their meager crops out of the sandy loam below the cotton belt and the rich blackland farms of the central midlands. They were worked by tenant farmers or black sharecroppers whose bare, weather-silvered cabins stood tottering like headstones in the sun-scorched sweet potato and peanut fields.

Only on Saturdays did Tallacoochee break out of its eerie trancelike somnolence. In the early afternoon the street began to fill with broken, dusty automobiles, angle-parked along the brick sidewalks in the shade of the live oaks. Men in straw hats and faded, pale blue overalls climbed out of them and filed through the streets in a solemn, ceremonial way, like pilgrims, carrying back from the shop doors sacks of fertilizer and chicken feed and lime, which they slung across the fenders, or spades or axes with fresh, clean wooden handles, which they stacked inside the cars or lashed to their bumpers. When they had finished their business they sat with dangling legs on the fenders of their cars, drinking liquor out of bottles wrapped in wrinkled, damp brown paper bags and talking quietly, with soft, occasional laughter, while their women shopped for groceries and brooms and cheap bright cotton dresses, and their children ran among the parked cars playing tag or hide-and-go-seek, chattering like chipmunks in the failing light. The murmur of talk and the soft laughter grew in volume and raucousness as the warm, black, jasmine-scented night enfolded the town, and then the streetlamps and the shop lights went on, casting great soft globes of shadow from the live oaks and lacing the darkness under the trees with a filigree of shifting radiance, like the sand of a shallow, moonlit lake. Then the boys and girls would appear, as mysteriously as acolytes at their appointed advent in a rite, clean, fine-boned, tight-skinned, and delicate, full of harsh, innocent enchantment, dressed in soft summer frocks and faultlessly ironed fresh white shirts, casting into the warm air an incense of gardenias and peppermint and drugstore cologne. They would disappear up the side streets into the shadows of the magnolia trees in Jackson Park, or down the length of Main Street in stuttering, spoke-wheeled roadsters, their laughter ringing from the rumble seats, toward the picnic tables and barbecue pits of the eucalyptus grove at Broadwater.

The black people were almost invisible, and yet everywhere, a host of silent-footed, gentle-handed incubi who flowed like dark wraiths through the shadows from shattered automobiles parked at the far ends of the street, or in silent, spectral files out of the pine woods and along the edges of the highway in the darkness to the lighted town, noiselessly entering the shop doors and whispering with soft, occultly tender voices while they stood waiting humbly to be served. They gathered in murmuring covens at the entrances of alleys and around the drinking fountain labeled COLORED at the far end of the street, chuckling with a sound of bubbling oil in the darkness and withdrawing like schools of languid minnows if they were approached by a group of white men or an unsteady, adventurous youth, or replying with patient, wary obsequiousness if they were spoken to; or they sat silently in the depths of their parked cars and watched the flow and commerce of the street with great, sadly glowing, opaline eyes. They did not linger in the town; they did their drinking and their reveling in the Negro tavern on the Tuskegee road or in the pine grove of the Church of the Divine Redemption, a mile outside of town. If you drove by there on a Saturday night, you would see the strings of colored lights above the picnic tables and hear the dark, wild laughter and the sound of fiddles and harmonicas.

There were never altercations between the Negroes and the whites, only a pulsing play of energy, like the shift and writhe of iron filings in a magnet's spell; but sometimes a thing that had been welling up slowly all through the long hot afternoon and the growing hubbub of the dusk would erupt in the velvet darkness with sudden livid vehemence, like the bursting open of a scarlet moonflower blossom in the night: there would be a snarled burst of oaths, the blundering thud of bodies against the metal doors of automobiles, the brutal smack of fists on flesh, the splintering glassy smash of a bottle against a brick storefront; and then subdued, grave murmurs and somber, quick advice: "Git him up on the car seat," "Git that coat under his head," "Goddamn, that eye looks bad," "We better git Doc Proctor, have a look at this." In the morning someone would sweep the splinters of glass from the gutter and hose the bloodstains from the bricks, and the silence of the town would close over its bright wound of violence as the sunlight clenched shut the moonflower blossoms on the backyard fences. Then there would be only the cheerless peeping of sparrows in the live oaks and the far-off wail of disk saws from the mill and the muttering of the old men on the benches, ceaseless and dire as the drone of wasps.

How could I have come to feel at home in such a place? Although I had spent my youth in a small Maryland town, it was north of the Potomac and not far from Washington, which made its atmosphere as different from that of Tallacoochee as from that of rural Maine. And yet, the town, with its dust and its silence and its air of destitution, came to seem my home more truly than anyplace I had ever lived. It was, of course, the only place where I could have carried out the research to which I dedicated the next ten years of my life; but even if that had not been so, I think I would have become a part of the town, of its rapt, slumbrous life. I liked to walk under the cool umbrellas of the live oaks in the blaze of noon; I came to relish the slightly sulfurous taste of the water that trickled out of its old porcelain faucets, the damp, ancient odor of its buildings; the endless lull of its heavy, flower-scented air. The town lay like a pool of shadow in the midst of the blazing savanna that surrounded it, and I felt myself transformed slowly into a creature of its warm, forgotten waters, swayed by the slow, clandestine currents that stirred the Spanish moss like gently flowing seaweed and lapped with soft, lubricious sounds at the shores of light that enclosed it like a flame.

Those things I felt later, after I had come to recognize the place and something in me had yielded to it. At first, I loathed the town. I arrived on a late May afternoon in a wave of heat in which the buildings at the end of Main Street quavered like a mirage and the gingerbread gables of the old Gothic railway station shuddered as if sunken in fathoms of translucent water. No one else got off the train and there was no one waiting on the deserted platform. I had sat for four hours, from Montgomery, in an ancient day coach with gritty windowsills and musty crimson-velvet upholstery that emitted clouds of coal dust into the stagnant air if you struck it with an elbow; and the town seemed to offer, or promise, no relief. I stood beside my bags for ten minutes, staring off beyond the station at the chimneys and gables floating on the mass of blue-gray foliage like the flotsam of a jellied sea. Heat billowed up from the red bricks of the platform in a merciless, infernal flow that raised wisps of pale steam from my sweat-damp clothes. There was a waiting room on either side of the central bay of the building; the door of one was labeled COLORED, and the other, WHITE. I went in through the WHITE door to the musty, silent room. Behind the grilled window of the office a man wearing a green celluloid eyeshade that cast a gangrenous shadow over his pink, congested face sat eating a ham sandwich, watching me silently. The room was so still that the crackle of the waxed paper on which he rested his wrists was startling and ominous, like flame in an attic.

"Someone was supposed to pick me up," I said. "Dr. Proctor, from the County Health Department. I wonder if you've seen him, or if he left a message?"

"No, I ain't," he said. "There's a phone yonder. You can ring him." He nodded to the phone, mounted on a wooden plaque against the wall. It was an old-fashioned phone with the receiver hanging in a metal fork, its soft cord dangling.

"There isn't any dial," I said.

"No, they ain't. You just ask the operator for your number."

A lady with a voice as sweet and slow-flowing as sorghum connected me with the number I had been given for the clinic, and I listened to the phone ring endlessly. After several minutes, she said, "I reckon Dr. Proctor's done left to pick you up. He been having car trouble all week, I reckon that's it. Miss Thurmond be having lunch about now, and I reckon Mrs. Farris be out on a case, they won't be nobody there. Why don't you git a Coke? He be along."

I carried my bags out through the waiting room to the lumpy red-clay compound in front of the station and stood under a lone eucalyptus tree whose dusty leaves hung motionless in the heat. Beyond it there was a stretch of gray asphalt road, its crumbled edges overgrown with sandspur, and above it a burning blue sky in which three clouds of unbelievable whiteness and definition floated with ghostly immobility. After another fifteen minutes I saw a car approaching, an old square-bodied sedan, growing larger at the tip of the funnel of red dust that billowed up behind it on the road. It pulled up into the red clay of the station yard and a slender, gray-templed man in shirt sleeves and a pair of baggy white-twill trousers got out of it and came briskly toward me, smoothing back his fine, blown hair.

"Dr. Ransome?" he said, and held out his hand to me. "I'm Liam Proctor."

"I'm glad to know you. It was kind of you to come down and meet me."

"I'm sorry to be so late. Damnedest thing happened. I hit a dog, and I had to stop and take care of it. Broke both its back legs. The vet was off on a case."

"You do the vet work, too?"

"We do damn near everything. They didn't tell you that in Washington, did they?"

"No, they didn't."

He seemed about to laugh, but the expression failed, apparently for lack of practice, or out of preoccupation, or from some acquired, habitual constraint, perhaps the sense of seeming inauspiciously jovial in a less than merry world—something that invariably reduced his impulse toward laughter to a flickering, half-lipped, strangulated smile. I can't talk about Liam without seeing that smile of his, like that of a child in a thunderstorm, whose anxious valor is a curious, indelible reproof to one's own callow confidence. It is difficult for me to speak of Liam at all, not for the least reason because I helped to kill him—a consideration that blights my memory of more than one of the people I have known. To say that I miss him is a strange confession, because when I think about the time we spent together I don't remember ever feeling conscious comfort or pleasure in his company. He wasn't a man with whom it was easy to feel comfort, because he himself appeared to have lost the capacity for it. All he seemed able to accept of it were wistful moments of truancy from the afflictions and confusions of a world whose real essence—or whose most illustrious possibility—I think he believed, were those wistful—or faithful—moments themselves, extended to infinity: a time when one might laugh without shame or apology, when his own strangulated smile would expand into the gentle, universal mirth out of which it had apparently been born, whose lost, phosphorescent gaiety glimmered sometimes in his dark gray eyes like fox fire in a mist. And yet he seemed to be mortified by the intimation of any such millennium, or by the untimely aspiration to it, in his own nature. He had very fine and restless hands, which he sought constantly to conceal, as if their delicacy were an embarrassment to him, and with which he was constantly touching and adjusting things: stroking back his soft, loose hair, plucking his damp shirt away from his chest, fingering the rough cuticle of a thumbnail, snapping his fingers silently for a moment and then plunging them hastily into his pockets to rattle the smooth, lavender-colored chips of seashell that he always carried there. He was forty-six when I met him, and four years later, when I followed his coffin to the clay chasm that awaited it under the cedar trees of the Baptist cemetery, I had the impression that he was being awarded, for the first time in half a century, the opportunity to smile without remorse, and was more than ever embarrassed at his impulse to do so.

"Let me take some of those bags," he said. "This all you've got?"

"Yes. I only brought enough for a month or so. My wife will be following shortly."

"Good. You'll be well set up by that time."

Before I could object, he had bent to take up two of my three suitcases and, limping slightly with their weight, led me to the car. I followed him with my portfolio, bulging with documents and correspondence, and when he had opened the back door and tossed the bags onto the seat, I got into the front seat beside him in the huge old Studebaker touring car. It had wooden-spoked wheels, a wooden steering wheel, and a panel full of dials whose needles spun wildly while the motor coughed and gargled into tremulous animation. When we had pulled out of the yard and got underway down the straight narrow strip of asphalt toward the town, I said, "Why do you suppose they built the station so far out of town?"

"I don't know. I guess they thought the town would expand. Victorian optimism. Did you have a good trip?"

"It wasn't bad to Birmingham. From there on, it was pretty hellish."

"I know. I think those coaches were built around 1850." He reached down to rub his knee, cringing slightly. "Banged my knee, with that damned dog. Have you had lunch?"

"No."

"Good. We'll stop and get a bite at the Bayou. You'll be more comfortable if you take that jacket off, I think."

"I'm all right, now we're moving."

"Janet's got you a place to live. I believe you asked about that in your letter. Janet Thurmond. She's our lab technician, secretary, caseworker, everything you can think of."

"Oh, good. I hope it wasn't a lot of trouble for her."

"Not for Janet. It's out on Choctaw Street, east end of town. Walking distance of the clinic. I hope you'll find it convenient. I don't know about luxury. It's not too bad, though. Not after you've been here a while." He turned again, and the left half of his upper lip fluttered in its ambitious smile. "How long do you intend to stay?"

"I'm not sure. I think we should be able to get things wound up in about six months, if all goes well."

"I hope no one's given you any illusions about the place."

"I think I know what to expect, generally."

"Ah. They told you about the Bayou Restaurant?"

"No, I didn't hear about that."

"Crafty devils." He smiled again, and nodded in grave, mock homage to their cunning.

"Are we going to pass the hospital?" I asked.

"No. It's on the other side of town. I'll take you around tomorrow and introduce you to Dr. Kidd. I believe he's expecting you."

"He knows I'm coming down, but I don't have an appointment. I'll call him this afternoon and make one. What sort of a man is he?"

"Very pleasant, very efficient. And very young to be a hospital administrator. Thirty-eight, or something like that, I suppose. He went to Howard, in Washington."

"Yes, I know. Would you call him cooperative?"

"Well, he's always been very cooperative with me." His eyebrows constricted slightly as he appeared to consider the question. "Of course, Negro professionals have a rather odd position in the South. They develop a sort of protective—I don't know what you'd call it—equanimity, I suppose. Among whites, anyway. The university faculty is a world of its own. There's virtually no social fraternizing with white intellectuals. Not that we have all that many intellectuals to fraternize with."

"Some of them, I suppose, are very ambitious?"

"The Negroes, you mean? Oh, yes. Isn't everybody?"

We entered the end of Main Street, jolting onto the bricks out of the sunlight into the tunnel of shadow and silence under the still gray drapery of the hanging moss, and for the first time I saw the shadow-bathed storefronts and the cast-iron drinking fountains and the old men scattered on the benches, watching us with bleak, sapient, slowly following eyes. I read the burnished, sunken signs on the plate-glass windows and the lettering of street names on the iron plaques below the lamp globes: Tuscaloosa, De Soto, Rive Verte, Coosahatchee. On a deep lawn, in front of an old white two-story mansion, an elaborate, glass-paned sign equipped with a pair of flood lamps facing it from brackets in the lawn read: LE FEBRE FUNERAL HOME.

"Is that the only funeral home in town?" I asked.

"No, there's another, over on Creek Street. Caldwell's. You're not feeling that bad already, I hope." He turned to smile at me again.

"Oh, no. No, I was just digging into the demographic facts a little, but I don't think they were very up-to-date."

"I've put a few of them into that summary Dr. Turner asked me to write up, about our public health situation. I don't know if it'll be of any use to you. Things never look the same on paper." He pulled the car in to the curb and switched off the engine; then extended his hands, palm up, in a wry, proffertory way and said, "Tallacoochee." The glass pane in front of the car was labeled BAYOU RESTAURANT—STEAKS—CHOPS—CREOLE DELICACIES. We got out and went in through the curtained door to a dim, high-ceilinged cavern with pale blue checkered tablecloths and malacca-backed chairs and a wooden-bladed fan turning slowly high up under the pressed-tin ceiling. Liam pulled out a chair at a table by the window and turned to nod toward the rear of the room.

"You want to wash? It's back there."

I hung my jacket on the back of a chair and went across the room between the dozen or so seated customers, bulky businessmen in shirt sleeves and suspenders whose eyes followed me with nonchalant interest, to a washroom in an alcove beside the kitchen door. Standing at a foul-smelling urinal clogged with cigarette butts, I unbuttoned my trousers and relieved myself lengthily, staring out the open window into a backyard shaded by a huge catalpa tree under which a shabby white rooster scratched listlessly at the potato peelings fallen from a stuffed and battered zinc garbage pail. There was a stirring in the branches of the tree and I raised my eyes to see a little girl of nine or ten in a bright pink dress, clinging to a high branch and holding aside the leaves that half concealed her face to stare down at me through the window with arrantly unblinking eyes. I turned away from her with startled haste, splashing my shoes and the front of my trousers with urine, and reached out to snatch away the stick that held the unweighted window open. It dropped with a sharp clatter onto the sill. I plucked a brown paper towel from a stack of them set on the windowsill and, shaken by a dismal agitation, I wiped the front of my trousers and my shoes and washed my hands in tepid water with a palmful of gritty borax from a wobbly dispenser.

When I went back into the dining room Liam was carrying on a quietly genial conversation with a vivid-eyed, black-haired girl in a waitress's uniform who sat perched on the edge of the chair beside him, nodding and chuckling languidly, with one arm resting on the table. She stood up when I approached and flipped the cloth clean of crumbs with a tea towel.

"Mildred, this is Dr. Ransome," Liam said. "You'll be seeing a lot of him, so you'd better treat him right."

"Hi!" She gave me a swift, easy smile. "Welcome to Tallacoochee, Doctor. I sure hope you like it here."

I nodded and sat down, murmuring, "Thank you. It seems like a very nice town."

"You'll get to like it," she said. "Everybody does."

"Have you got something good for us?" Liam said. "How about some chili?"

"We sure do. Jimmy fixed it before he went to softball practice. You know how he fixes chili."

"Yes, I do. How does that sound, Carl?"

"Fine," I said. "Anything."

"It's real good," Mildred said. "Everybody says so."

"O.K., we'll have chili and a pitcher of iced tea," Liam said. "As fast as you can make it. This man is starving."

"Well, you know we not going to let him starve. You just keep him going for about five minutes, I'll be back."

Liam smiled at me silently for a moment when she had left.

"That's a very nice uniform you people wear," he said. "Do you have to buy them yourself?"

"Yes."

"Costs a penny, I'll bet."

"About twenty-five dollars."

"My God. That would buy me three suits. Still, I suppose they wear very well."

"I don't know. This is the first one I've ever had."

"Oh? You haven't been in the Service long?"

"Just a year. I finished my residency last fall, and I've been training for this assignment at the syphilis clinic at Johns Hopkins, with J. E. Moore."

"Oh, yes. A very fine clinic, I understand. Where did you go to school?"

"At George Washington."

"Oh, in Washington. That's a beautiful city. I went there in '36, to that V.D. conference that Parran held. I had a great time. A wonderful gallery, the Mellon. Do you know the Post-Impressionist collection there?"

"No. I'm not a great art enthusiast."

"Oh, that's a pity. I'd never be out of the place, I don't think, if I lived there. It must be terrible to have to get through medical school in a city like that. God, there's so many things to see. You could spend a week in the Smithsonian."

"I was pretty busy, as you say. I didn't spend much time in the museums."

"No, there isn't time to do anything, if you're a doctor. It's the curse of the vocation." He brushed salt from the tablecloth with the edge of his hand, then dusted his palms together. "Well, we're very glad to have you with us. I'm not sure I'm quite clear, yet, about the nature of your project, but of course we'll be glad to help in any way we can. I hope you understand we have very limited personnel."

"Yes. We realize you're working under difficulties, and we certainly don't want to put any added strain on your facilities. I don't think we will. We do need your cooperation, of course; but if there's any significant added work or expense, the P.H.S. is prepared to assume it."

"I see," Liam said. "I'm very glad to hear that. Are you all right?"

"All right?"

"Yes, you look a bit pale."

"No, it's just the heat, I guess. I'm not used to it. You made me out a summary of your department organization and history, I think you said."

"Yes. I have it here." He rolled forward in his chair and dug out of his hip pocket a damp, folded sheaf of typewritten pages which he unfolded and spread on the table in front of him. "Gotten a bit damp, but I think you can make it out. Outline of our department structure, personnel, activities. Bit of county history, one thing and another. I'm not much of a writer, but I think you'll find the facts pretty accurate." He peered at the sheets, squinting. "Well, you can read it for yourself, I won't bother to go over the whole thing. Briefly, we have a staff of twenty-three people, and an appropriation, this year, of about thirty-seven thousand dollars. Of that, state and federal money comes to over nineteen thousand. The Rosenwald Fund came in with eleven thousand. The rest of it is local. We have a per capita expenditure for health services that's above the national average, which is pretty impressive when you consider the economic condition of this county." He pushed the typescript toward me across the table. "Hope this'll be of some use. I wasn't just sure what you needed."

"I'm sure it will. We just wanted to know what your present clinic facilities were, the extent of your V.D. program, the number of personnel, and so on. That's why I asked about Kidd. We're counting on a good deal of help from the hospital. You say he's cooperative?"

"Very. They have a very good hospital there. One hundred beds. Their school of nursing is as good as any in the country. And they've just built a fifty-bed Crippled Children's Hospital with money they got from the National Infantile Paralysis Foundation. Kidd's worked with us on all sorts of county projects. I suppose the biggest thing we've done together is the Maternity Health Clinic. We put that together back in '34. It's been a great success. Last year we had a hundred and fifty in-hospital deliveries. Back in '36 we had three, I think. It's pretty miraculous, when you think that these people have used midwives since the year one."

"I'm glad to hear that," I said. "That's a pretty generous attitude for a private hospital."

"Well, of course, it's in their interests as much as ours. More. When you talk about public health in this county, you're talking about Negro health. The population of Hackett County is eighty-five percent Negro, as I suppose you know."

"Yes."

"It's hard to realize what things have been like in this part of the world up until about four years ago. I helped organize the Hackett County Health Department back in '28. We had a staff of four people: one Health Officer, one Sanitation Officer, one nurse, and a clerk. In '29, we got a part-time Meat and Milk Inspector, financed by the city of Tallacoochee. But when the economy collapsed, he went. It was hell raising a dime in those days to buy a bandage with." He smiled at me crookedly. "It's not what you'd call a glamorous profession."

"No."

"It wasn't until '36, after Parran became Surgeon General, that things began to improve. I don't think anyone really knew what was going on in this country until he woke them up to it. This year we have a federal appropriation of ten thousand dollars, which is over a quarter of our total budget. Do you know what I've been able to do?"

"No."

"I was even able to buy a sixteen-millimeter sound projector this year and eight films on health education, that we take around and show at the public schools—those that have electricity. My God, what a luxury." He lifted and twisted a fork between his long fingers, looking into my eyes with the sudden youthful enthusiasm of a schoolboy talking about baseball scores. "You should see how those kids respond to it. My God, all they need is education. It's worth all the medicine in the world. All anyone needs. We have their parents come, too. It's gotten to be a real social function. Janet has gotten together a crew of women who make cookies and lemonade. People walk in for miles out of the pine woods. We're getting to them, slowly."

"I understand you won an Award of Merit from the U.S. Public Health Association last year," I said.

"We did, by God. I was tickled to death. I think we deserved it, you know. Do you realize that twenty years ago this corner of Alabama was the unhealthiest place to live in the United States? That's true. Birmingham had the highest death rate from typhoid of any city in America. And infant mortality rates, from diarrhea and enteritis, were almost as bad. And that's in Jefferson County, which is well off compared to ours. When our department was organized, the typhoid death rate was something like a hundred twenty-five per thousand. Last year there was only one known case reported in the county. There hasn't been a case of smallpox here for over ten years."

"I suppose syphilis is your big problem."

"Oh, yes. It's a damned scourge. The number of new cases goes up steadily every year. Last year we had five hundred and fifty, against only a hundred in 1928, and the death rate has gone up from around ten per thousand to over twenty per thousand. We've got to lick it, somehow." He plucked at his sideburns for a moment, frowning at the tabletop. "Not that we're not trying. In the last three years, the number of patients we've treated for the damned thing has risen from around three hundred to over a thousand. We've given seven times as many treatments as we did then—over thirteen thousand, compared to about twenty-five hundred three years ago. And something like seven thousand serologic tests, compared to about three thousand in '37. And keep in mind that we only have about seven hundred live births a year in this county. Can you imagine what that's doing to the prevalence figures?"

"I think the Rosenwald Study, back in '32, discovered something like thirty-eight percent," I said.

"That's right. Thirty-eight percent of the population syphilitic. That's a pretty tragic statistic, for the richest country on earth. I don't know what it is now. I hope it's not as bad."

"That's one of the things we want to find out," I said.

"That's what I gathered from Dr. Turner's letter. I'm glad to hear it. I'd welcome a new survey, to learn just what the situation is now, compared to then." He raised his eyebrows delicately. "Of course, what we'd really like is not just to find them, but to treat them. That's one of the things I've tried to do, as Health Officer: keep our V.D. budget pretty well balanced between the two, case-finding and treatment. But it's hard. Case-finding really gobbles up man-hours and money. You find one early acute case, and you know damn well it's just the tip of the iceberg. Just one in a whole chain of contacts and possible infections. Ten or a dozen, very often. And then you've got to persuade them all to come in and get examined, and treated, if they need it. That's where you need good personnel. Real people, not just timeservers. There isn't anybody in this department who doesn't earn three times his salary."

Mildred had arrived with our chili and a bowl of crackers and a pitcher of iced tea. The chili lay seething in the bowl like lava and when I took a mouthful of it, the fumes soared through my nostrils as if through a chimney draft. I blinked and brushed the tears from my eyes with my knuckles.

"We use this stuff instead of bismuth on very far-gone cases," Liam said. "It works wonders."

"I can believe that." I rapidly drank a glass of iced tea. "You have a new clinic here in Tallacoochee, I understand."

"Right. Just opened last year. This is the county seat, so I make it my headquarters. Our offices are just down the street. Up until last year, the bulk of our syphilis control work was conducted through clinics. We had a full-time clinician who held weekly diagnostic and treatment clinics over at Cardozo and at seven points in the county. It was rough. You know there are only sixty-seven miles of paved road in this county? Just getting people to the clinics often took a whole working day for each patient. They had to come by foot as often as not, because the clay and gravel roads are nothing but bogs in the winter. Then, last November, when you gave us that mobile lab, the whole picture changed. My God, what a blessing. Now we can reach almost anyone in the county— anyone who hears about us and can be persuaded to come in. The truck crosses the whole county on a regular schedule, and stops at thirty-three different places—stores, schools, crossroads, churches, post offices. This year we were able to assign a clerk to the truck, for better record-keeping, and also a full-time student nurse, from Cardozo. They not only operate the clinic but they drive the damn thing. Great people." He smiled a long, fluttering, lopsided smile, and spooned up chili for a few moments in enthusiastic silence. "They know damn near everybody in the county. Sometimes when they pass a pregnant woman's house, they'll stop and give her a lift to the clinic point, and bring her home again afterwards. We're able to make a real attack on congenital cases that way. Oh, it's going to work out well, I think. But last year, when we began to get federal money, the Board of Censors talked it over and decided that although the rural areas were getting very good service that way, the town of Tallacoochee was getting pretty short shrift. After all, something like one-sixth of the total population lives here, and the single clinic we had going in town, over at Cardozo Hospital, just wasn't adequate. So we decided to put in a new one for the city. We run it on a per-clinic-session basis, with a public health nurse. They're held every Saturday morning and Thursday night, and lately I've been holding a Tuesday-morning session as well. We need it; and I like to keep my hand in, you know."

"This is a Negro clinic?"

"It's open to anybody, as the ones on the mobile lab circuit are. But the whites just weren't coming in to the mobile lab. This clinic in Tallacoochee is the only one they really use. Cardozo is the only hospital in the county, and because it's Negro, there weren't any facilities for whites here. They still don't have a hospital. Any white person who needs hospitalization has to go over to Birmingham, in Jefferson County; or down to Mobile." He lifted his iced-tea glass and raised his eyebrows at me above its rim. "Yes, we have forced integration in our clinics," he said merrily, setting it down. "You know, it's amazing how they get used to the idea. There's nothing like misfortune to make brothers of people. Maybe by the time this war is over, we'll be a little bit closer to the New Jerusalem."

"You think we'll get in it?" I said.

"How can we stay out of it? We should be in it already. Not that I'm any great enthusiast about war, but Christ, in one like this, there's no standing above the fray. You've got to get counted." He lifted his spoon and tapped for a moment at his iced-tea glass, staring at the dusty curtains of the window.

"It's going to be a different world afterwards. I really believe that, you know. It had better be." A yellow cat with a stiffly erect tail stalked across the floor of the restaurant to the front door, where it sat and began to wash its face languidly with a curled paw. Liam watched it abstractedly, then turned his face back to the table and studied a bouquet of faded paper flowers in a waterless vase. "Look at these damned things," he murmured. "Awful." He fingered the dusty petals, his eyebrows constricting in a painful, melancholy way. "Do you sail?" he asked in a moment.

"Sail? No."

"Ah, that's too bad. It's a wonderful sport, especially for a doctor. It's so clean, sailing."

"I used to spend summers in Maine," I said. "But we didn't have a boat."

"Did you really? I spent a summer there once, first year of medical school, with a friend who had a place up there. Little town called Sedgwick, near Bar Harbor. I've never forgotten it. Most beautiful place I ever saw. I can still smell it sometimes, the cold mornings and the sea." He narrowed his eyes, as if into the memory of a sea mist. "I have a little day sailer I keep down on the Gulf at a cottage where we go. My wife's down there now. I'd like to take you down sometime, if we get a weekend off. I could teach you to sail in an afternoon. It won't be very often, I'm afraid."

"Thanks," I said. "I'm not much for the beach, though. I'm not the best of company on a vacation. I don't like being idle."

"Oh, really? Well, you've come to the right place."

"I never learned the art of relaxation, my wife says."

"Well, maybe you'll learn something about it in Alabama. Although we'll keep you busy enough to stay happy, you needn't worry about that." He crumbled a cracker into his bowl and then brushed his palms together nervously. "How are you on orthopedics?"

"Not very good. I only spent about three months on the orthopedic service during my whole residency."

"Same with me. And that was twenty-odd years ago. I was going to ask if you'd have a look at that dog. You can imagine what kind of a job I did on her. Probably be walking around backwards for the rest of her life."

"Where is she?" I asked.

"Up in the office, in a box. I'll have to take her home this evening, I suppose. It's a good thing my wife's away; she'd raise holy hell. I'll take her over to the vet tomorrow, let him have a look at the casts."

The front door swung open with a tinkle and a young woman in a pale blue blouse and a wrinkled white linen skirt came into the restaurant and looked about until she saw Liam. "Ah, here's Janet," Liam said. She came quickly across the floor toward our table. She had large sober dark eyes in a pale and delicate face, and a body that seemed not to match it at all, a wide-hipped, short-boned body that would be plump in five years, and soft brown hair cut very short around her ears that bounced briskly as she walked. Liam rose and drew back a chair for her. She sat down quickly and smiled at me across the table, saying, "Hello, you're Dr. Ransome."

"Yes."

"I'm Janet Thurmond. It's nice to have you with us." She plucked a cracker out of the bowl and turned to Liam. "Can I have this?"

"Looks like you've got it," Liam said.

"Listen, I hate to interrupt you, but Dr. Kavanaugh's got a patient in the office that he wants very much for you to see. I thought if I took Dr. Ransome home, you could run up and have a look at him. I think you'll be interested."

"Maybe I should. How's the dog?"

"She's still groggy, but she's come out of it now. I got her to drink some water, and she wagged her tail, so I guess there's hope." She raised her eyebrows and cocked her head at him dubiously.

"It's a miracle. You sure you don't mind taking Carl home?"

"No. I'll be happy to. Things are pretty well under control right now." She turned to me, nibbling at her cracker. "I hope the house is all right. There isn't a lot of choice, really."

"I'm sure it's fine," I said. "Houses are much alike to me. I appreciate it very much."

"You'd better have a look at it before you say that. Did your wife come with you?"

"No, she's coming down in a month or so. We had to sublet our place in Washington and put some things in storage, so she's taking care of that."

"Well, we just took it on a monthly basis until you had a chance to see it. If she doesn't like it, I'll help her look around later."

"Thanks very much. Molly isn't hard to please."

"I'd better have a look at this patient," Liam said. "Hate to run out on you, but I'll come around this evening after you've unpacked, and fetch you back to dinner. We'll have a decent talk then." He rose and fished in his pocket for a moment, dragging out his car keys and a crumpled five-dollar bill, which he set on the table in front of Janet. "There's the car key. And for the chili. Don't let him have more than three bowls of it, or you'll have trouble with him. I'll see you this evening, Carl."

"I'll look forward to it," I said. "Thanks. And thanks for picking me up."

"Not at all. Pleasure." He strode across the floor to the front door, where he stooped to stroke the cat for a moment before he went out into the street.

"A very nice man," I said.

"Yes."

"Have you worked with him a long time?"

"I've been here for three years, and in the County Health Department for eight. I guess Liam told you what I do."

"Almost everything, he said."

"You learn to improvise. We're a very ragged bunch."

"You've done a very good job, from everything I understand."

"It's Liam's doing. He makes people proud of what they do. He's turned the department into one of the best in the country in the last ten years." She plucked up the car keys, regarding me steadily with her intelligent green eyes. "I won't even ask you about your trip. You had to change to that awful day coach in Birmingham, I guess."

"Yes. I'm glad I don't have to do it every day." I found myself considering her face almost judicially; measuring its intelligence and equanimity; the evident incongruity of a blue celluloid barrette clasping back a lock of her hair from her right temple. Her very dark, almost plum-colored lips were unusually contrasted with the pallor of her face. In those days almost no woman went without lipstick in public; I think she was the first woman I ever saw who did so, and there was a curious look of nudity about her naked mouth. I lowered my eyes and poured myself a glass of iced tea. "Would you like a glass of this?" I asked.

"Yes. Thanks."

"I'll ask the waitress for another glass."

"That's all right. I'll use Liam's." She held it out to me while I poured it full, and then drank briefly, licked her lips, and resumed her candid and disturbing level gaze, fingering the car keys gently.

"Liam doesn't strike me as a typical Southerner," I said. "And yet I understand he was born right here in the county."

"In Mimosa Springs, fifteen miles up the road. What is a typical Southerner?"

"I'm not sure I know. I come from Maryland myself. But it's different." She smiled at me. "Are you a Southerner?" I asked.

"No. I come from Michigan."

"How did you happen to wind up in the Hackett County Health Department?"

"I went to Vanderbilt. Liam lectured there one semester, and I found him very impressive. Do you have any children?"

"Yes. A little girl, just over two years old."

"She won't have much trouble adjusting, then. I mean, no friendships to break off or anything. I believe they're very adjustable at that age."

"Yes, I believe so."

"I hope your wife isn't disappointed. She's apt to find it very dull, after Washington."

"She's never been terribly social," I said. "And she has the baby to take care of. That seems to occupy her pretty thoroughly."

"Of course, you can get in to Birmingham occasionally, if she wants to see some bright lights. There's a paved road all the way."

"Well, that's good to know. Do you get in often?"

"No, almost never."

I finished my iced tea and set down the glass. "Listen, I don't want to hold you up. I know you have to get back to the office."

"All right." She looked across the room and waved the bill at the waitress, who was delivering a sandwich and a glass of beer to a distant table. "Millie, I'm leaving this for Dr. Proctor," she called.

"O.K., honey," Mildred called back. "Goodbye, Doctor. Mighty nice to meet you. I'll see y'all later."

We got up and went out of the restaurant into the dense, still heat of the street. Standing beside the automobile, I put one arm into the sleeve of my jacket.

"Why don't you leave it off?" Janet said. "You'll get that beautiful new uniform all wrinkled."

"All right. Thank you." I took it off and got into the car beside her, sitting with self-conscious stiffness while she turned the key and stamped the accelerator impatiently. When the motor had sputtered into life, she backed the car out and drove through the mottled shadow of the street which flowed across the windshield like the ripple of wheat in wind.

"Those are our offices," she said, and pointed across my body upward through the open window of the car. I looked up and saw the lettering HACKETT COUNTY HEALTH DEPARTMENT across the shadow-cloaked pane of the second-story windows. On the windowsill there was a white china bowl, on the rim of which a sparrow sat drinking. Above the building, the same three clouds that I had seen from the railway station hung motionless in the scalding blue of the sky. A feeling of sadness came over me.

We passed the courthouse, and between the pillars of the portico I saw on the wall of the façade beside the fanlighted Georgian entrance a flaking horizontal stripe painted on the crumbling brick, and the words: HIGH-WATER MARK, SEPT. 1921.

"Was there a flood?" I asked.

"There have been several, but that was the worst. In 1921 a hurricane came out of the Gulf, and the bayou flooded. There were snakes swimming all through the streets of this town, and muskrats, and other things. In Stansell's dry-goods store there's a stuffed alligator hanging on the wall that was trapped in the basement. I think some of them are still breeding here."

We passed the gigantic dark green magnolias of Jackson Park, standing eighty feet against the sky. The scent of them drifted through the car in clinging dizzying strands of sweetness, like the sachet from Molly's open lingerie drawer. The odor made me narrow my eyes slightly, as if in defense against it. Janet drove silently. Once a hanging streamer of Spanish moss swept across the roof of the car with a swift, caressing whisper.

"Well, here we are," Janet said. She slowed the car and pulled in to the curb in front of the house. The Virginia creeper was full of scarlet blossom that cloaked the veranda, and a pair of Cape jasmine bushes in the front yard were splashed with still, cream-colored flowers. When I had set my bags on the sidewalk Janet took one of them and went ahead of me up the concrete walk to the front porch. I did not protest. As we approached the house a squirrel leapt from the back of one of the rocking chairs to the porch rail, leaving the chair nodding emptily, back and forth, with a gentle, fading sound, like the grinding of departing footfalls.

"I have the key," Janet said. She set down the bag and took the key out of the pocket of her skirt and unlocked the front door. The hot gloom of the parlor smelled of damp and must. A pair of overstuffed chairs and a sofa were draped in white sheets, like crouching specters. "I was going to come in this morning and take those sheets off and open the windows, but I got so tied up with that dog and everything that I didn't have time." She set down the bag and pulled the sheet from an easy chair, revealing the worn brown cut pile of the upholstery.

"Don't bother. It'll give me something to do for the rest of the afternoon. You've been very kind." I looked around the room and nodded. "It looks very nice. I think we'll be very comfortable."

"I hope so. There's an extra bedroom upstairs that I thought you could make into a sort of study, so I had an extension phone put in up there. There's another in the kitchen."

"Thank you."

"The landlady's name is written on a pad on the kitchen table, with her phone number, in case you have any questions. I did start the refrigerator on Saturday morning, and put water in the ice trays. And there's butter and a dozen eggs and some bread and strawberry jam, for your breakfast. And the beds are made. You'll be having dinner with us tonight, so you won't have that to worry about. Liam invited me over."

"Well, you've certainly taken care of everything. I don't know how to thank you."

"There isn't any need to." She set the key on a table that stood against the wall. "Well, I'll leave you the key. You have our office number."

"Yes."

"I'll see you this evening, then. Goodbye, Dr. Ransome."

"Goodbye."

When she had gone I sat down on the sheet-covered sofa and stared out of the parlor window between the posts of the veranda to the shadowed street. The squirrel had returned and crept in a flowing walk along the porch rail, stepping daintily among the leaves. I stamped my foot on the floor and he leapt into the air and vanished. The dust that I had raised rose swirling through the two thin rays of sunlight that fell through the parlor window, forming slender, incandescent shafts whose tips set a pair of trembling golden disks on the front of my shirt. I raised my hand and held them in my palm like pale, warm coins. The sense of sadness rose in me like ruin. I had the feeling that I had made a disastrous decision, that I had come to the wrong place, that I was among alien gods and foreign faces, that nothing was understood.

I sat on the sofa in the silent house holding in my palm the pair of shimmering, weightless coins that cooled and melted gradually away, until my impatience with my own idleness and melancholy made me get up suddenly and pluck the dusty sheets from the overstuffed furniture. I tumbled them into loose bundles and carried them out onto a small screened back porch that adjoined the kitchen, where I dropped them onto a shabby glider that looked out through the rusty, billowing metal screen to a wooden shed beside which the upturned flat-bottomed hull of a wooden scow sat on a cradle of bricks and two-by-fours. Across the yard, in a huge, tattered mulberry tree, a flock of birds foraged noisily. I went back into the parlor and carried my bags upstairs to the largest of the three bedrooms. A pair of floor-length windows looked down over the top of the mulberry tree in the backyard and, beyond it, a vacant lot, in which the red clay paths of a baseball diamond showed through the knee-high weeds. There was a smaller, central bedroom, with a window facing south to the clapboard second story of the adjoining house; and a bathroom with an enameled cast-iron tub whose ball-and-claw feet had sunken deeply into the linoleum carpeting. Two porcelain-spoked faucets dripped rusty rivulets into the crazed, chipped basin of the sink. A third room at the front of the house looked out over the red tin roof of the veranda into the leathery foliage of the live oaks. A wooden swivel chair and a rolltop desk had been set adjacent to the window, and a bookcase with sliding glass panes, along the abutting wall. On top of it stood a telephone and a local and state directory. Above the desk a calendar for 1939 illustrated with a painting of an Indian maiden rowing across a moonlit lake was fastened to the wall with thumbtacks.

I rolled back the slatted cover of the desk and spread on top of it a sheaf of correspondence, reports, and documents from my portfolio. The window frame was swollen tight in the sill; I had to tug at it for several minutes before I managed to raise it a foot above the sill to let a faint, sweet-scented breath of air into the musty room. I set the telephone on the desk and leafed through the local directory to the listing for the Banneker Institute, from which I copied into my notebook the numbers for Willoughby F. Horgan, Ph.D., Principal; and Benjamin D. Kidd, M.D., Medical Director, Francis Cardozo Memorial Hospital. I called Dr. Horgan first, and was connected with him immediately by his secretary.

"Dr. Horgan, this is Carl Ransome, of the U.S. Public Health Service," I said. "I hope you remember our correspondence."

"Of course I do. Are you in town?"

"Yes, I just got in this afternoon."

"Well. Welcome to Tallacoochee. Did you have a good trip?"

"I wouldn't want to make it again very soon," I said. "But I've arrived intact."

He laughed easily. I was disconcerted by his accent, which sounded vaguely Princetonian. "The Gulf and Mobile Railway is a very conservative organization," he said. "It's rooted deeply in the past."

"Evidently. I don't think the windows had been opened for twenty years."

"Oh, at least. Like many in these parts. Did you try the ham sandwiches?"

"No, I wasn't quite that hungry. Dr. Horgan, I wonder if you've heard from Dr. Kidd yet, about our project?"

"Yes, I have. He was away at a conference when your letter came—or was it Dr. Turner who wrote to him?"

"Dr. Turner, originally. I wrote him also, to let him know I was coming down."

"Oh, yes. He just got back on Tuesday. I suppose you haven't had his reply yet?"

"No, I haven't."

"No. Well, I talked to him on Tuesday afternoon, and he seems, generally, to be favorably disposed toward your project."

"Oh, good. I'm glad to hear that."

"Of course, we're neither of us quite sure yet what the exact nature of it is. But that's what you've come down here to tell us, isn't it?"

"Yes. And to get it started, of course. If we can be assured of your cooperation."

"Yes, so I understand."

"What we want to do, basically, is to make a follow-up study of the syphilis cases that were revealed by the Rosenwald Study a few years ago."

"I see."

"We want to determine the present condition of those patients, the ones we treated at the time and the ones we didn't—"

"There were some who weren't treated?"

"Yes. Unfortunately our resources ran out before we had an opportunity to treat many of them fully, or at all. We want also to do an additional study, of people who've never yet been examined at all. To compare the incidence of the disease today and seven years ago. We especially want to make a study of untreated cases, which, as I believe Dr. Turner pointed out, there's a unique opportunity to do in this county." I waited for his reply, which, after a moment, came as a gently murmured "Umm." "It will add tremendously to our knowledge of the pathogenesis of the disease," I said.

"Yes. Well, of course, it's something that we ought to sit down and discuss at length. I'm afraid I'm going to have to rely pretty much on Kidd's advice. I'm not a medical man, you know."

"No."

"We talked only very briefly about it. He'd been away, and barely had time to unpack his bags when I saw him."

"I see. But he seemed favorably disposed, you said."

"On the whole. Why don't you come around and talk to me tomorrow? Are you free?"

"Yes."

"Good. Why don't you meet me in my office around noon, then? Have you got a way to get over?"

"Yes. Dr. Proctor offered to drive me over. I wonder if I could bring him along? He's going to work very closely with us, so I think it would be useful to include him in our conference."

"By all means. I was going to suggest it myself. He's agreed to help you, has he?"

"Well, of course, we haven't yet discussed it fully, but I'm sure—"

"You'll have talked it over with him by tomorrow?"

"Yes, we're having dinner together tonight."

"Ah, good. I'll look forward to seeing you tomorrow, then."

"Thank you. So will I."

"Goodbye, Dr. Ransome."

"Goodbye."

I hung up the phone and sat frowning for a moment before I called Dr. Kidd, feeling somewhat discomfited by Horgan's air of gracious reserve. Kidd, I sensed immediately, was a different order of man, one with whom a certain amount of flattery might be profitable.

"Oh, I'm glad to hear from you," he said. "I've just been up to Washington, you know. To a conference. I wrote to Dr. Turner a few days ago. Did he receive my letter yet?"

"I don't know. It may have arrived after I left, so he wasn't able to relay your feelings to me before I left. I understand from Dr. Horgan that you think well of the study we propose."

"Yes, I do. It's very interesting. Very worthwhile, from what I understand of Dr. Turner's letter. Naturally, there are some points that I'd like to talk over with you, to get a clearer picture of the whole thing. I'm not quite sure of the extent of participation he expects from us. We have a very long list of priorities, you know."

"I know you do. And I'd like to say that we think you're doing a splendid job. Your work with the County Health Department has been exemplary. Dr. Proctor's been extolling you to me this afternoon."

"Well, it's gratifying to hear that. I think we've helped to make life a little better for these people in the last few years. I hope we can continue to."

"I'm sure of it. And this is a real opportunity. Dr. Kidd, I'm coming over to the Institute tomorrow at noon to talk to Dr. Horgan. He suggests that you join us for our discussion. Would that be convenient?"

"Yes, I think so." He paused, apparently to consult his calendar. "At twelve?"

"Yes. Dr. Proctor will be with us, too. He'll be working with us very closely, of course, and I think it'll be useful to hear his observations."

"Yes, Liam's a good man. He'll be working with us, too?"

"Oh, yes. I think it would be impossible to get along without his coopera-tion. Without all of your cooperation, of course." ·

"Yes. Well, good. Fine. I'll see you tomorrow, then."

"Yes. Goodbye."

When he had hung up I opened my notebook on the desk and wrote a summary of my conversations with the two men:

Spoke to Horgan and Kidd by phone, Monday, May 20. My impression is that Kidd's advocacy will be easier to secure than Horgan's consent. Kidd can be managed, Horgan needs very prudent persuasion. Odd accent. Would call it phony Princeton, but there's nothing phony about that man. Look up biography, education, interests. Has great respect for Proctor. So does Kidd, but may be touch of envy in his case.

I turned the page and wrote at the top of the next:

Proctor is another matter. Great intelligence and sensitivity. Curious com-bination of idealism, practicality, anxiety, and whimsy. Fits of daydreaming. Tremendous energy, but appears overworked. Likes animals. Racial feelings untypical for Southerner, be very careful on this point. Is much admired by everyone, especially Janet Thurmond. Never speak unguardedly with this man. Nor, on the other hand, express false sentiments. Basically, I think will yield, but not at all predictable.

After a moment of reflection, I added this postscript:

Dinner party this evening will be interesting, and critical.

I closed the notebook and took out of a labeled folder in the file of documents I had assembled in preparation for my assignment several pages of historical abstracts and textual summaries and a brief curriculum vitae of Liam's career. I tilted back the swivel chair, backed it to the window, and with the light of the late afternoon falling on the pages, began to read:

Liam Proctor: B. Hackett Co., Ala., Jul. 19, 1894. Father schoolteacher. Elementary education public schools, Hackett Co. 1908–12, attended Dufresne Private Academy, Mobile, Ala. 1912, matric. U. of Ala., full academic scholarship. 1916, B.S., U. of Ala., summa cum laude, entered Med. Sch., Vanderbilt Univ. 1920, grad. Med. Sch., Vanderbilt Univ. 1921–24, residency, Vanderbilt Univ., syphilis clinic (Dr. Rudolph Kampmeier). 1924–28, private prac., Hackett Co. (Tallacoochee, Mimosa Springs). 1928–29, lecturer in dermatology and syphilology, Vanderbilt Univ. 1928–30, priv. prac., part-time clinician, Hackett Co. Health Dept. 1930, elected Health Officer, Hackett Co. Has contributed widely to medical journals: *Journal of Chronic Diseases; Archives of Internal Medicine; Archives of Dermatology* (see especially "Syphilis in Southern Rural Areas," *Jour. of Chr. Dis.*, 17, 210–21). Mentioned with much respect by Parran in *Shadow on the Land*, Reynal & Hitchcock, 1937. Amateur painter and bibliophile. Badly wounded by shotgun blast from hunter in Dec. 1932 in unusual circumstances. In June 1918 married Paula Le Febre (old Hackett Co. family), one child, daughter, b. Jul. 1920.

I set the sheet aside and opened a folder of typescripts stapled together under the title sheet "Historical Background":

In 1767 a Scottish surgeon named John Hunter, in order to study firsthand the effects of gonorrhea, obtained pus from a patient suffering from that disease and inoculated himself. The patient from whom he secured the gonococcus bacillus was also suffering from syphilis; Hunter consequently infected himself with that disease as well. When the chancre appeared on his body, he observed and described it so meticulously that the primary lesion of syphilis is today called the Hunterian sore. As he had inoculated himself concurrently, however, Hunter mistook the symptoms of syphilis and gonorrhea as being those of a single disease, and attempted to demonstrate his belief by inoculating volunteers with the serum of his own lesions. That he failed in his attempts to reproduce the Hunterian sore in these subjects was probably due to the fact that they had been previously infected and were immune. In 1787, Hunter published the results of his experiments in a book entitled *Treatise on the Venereal Diseases*. He developed classical syphilitic heart disease, from which he died in 1793.

In that year, a book entitled *Treatise on Gonorrhea Virulenta and Lues Venerea*, which clearly differentiated the two diseases, was published by another Scottish surgeon named Benjamin Bell. Bell succeeded in demonstrating the distinctness of the two conditions by inoculating not only himself but several of his medical students. His book was little noted, however, and it was left to an American-French investigator named Philippe Ricord to demonstrate conclusively, in a report published in 1838, that the two conditions were separate clinical entities. His report was based on experiments in which he inoculated more than 2,500 human beings with either gonoccocal pus or the serum of syphilitic chancres.

A further contribution to the knowledge of the etiology of syphilis was made early in the nineteenth century by an Irish physician named William Wallace, who succeeded in transmitting the disease to a group of subjects by inoculating them with the serum of secondary lesions, which had formerly been regarded as non-infectious. Our present knowledge of the etiology of syphilis is founded largely on the work of these three men.

THE BOECK-BRUUSGAARD STUDY

Between 1891 and 1910, Dr. C. Boeck, professor of dermatology and venereology in the Oslo, Norway, Hospital, kept medical records on the course of untreated syphilis in 1,978 persons admitted to his hospital with primary or secondary stages of the disease. He withheld treatment from them because of the inadequacy of available therapy. Instead of being treated, they were hospitalized until their symptoms disappeared. The study group was composed largely of persons living in the eastern section of the city, a section of laborers and underprivileged. Females outnumbered males by approximately 2 to 1. In 1929, Edvin Bruusgaard, his successor, compiled an analysis of the subsequent medical histories of 473 of these

patients. This study is the major source of information we have today on
the course of untreated syphilis.

When I had read twice through these and several other pages of abstracts,
I put them back into the folder and spread out flat on the desk the folded sheets
of typescript that Liam had prepared for me. Most of the material was a digest
of what he had already told me in the restaurant, some of it crossed out and
scraggled over with handwritten addenda in a lurid violet ink. In its tone of
combined exactitude and whimsy, and in its sometimes startling non sequiturs,
I could hear the sound of Liam's voice:

Hackett County is mostly hilly, with sandy or clay soil. It was settled in
1832. Population in 1940: 27,654, of which approximately 85% are Negro.
Tallacoochee is the only town with more than 1,000 inhabitants. Next is
Mimosa Springs, with 987.

11,496 (40%) of the inhabitants of the county are gainfully employed,
one half in agriculture. Lumber is the primary industry. There are 20
lumber mills in the county, the largest in Tallacoochee.

Remuneration for day labor is 50¢ a day.

In 1940 the number of relief recipients was 367. The no. of workers
on W.P.A. projects was 469. God bless Franklin D. Roosevelt.

You may be surprised to notice a lot of wagons, mules, and horses
hitched up to posts on side streets in Tallacoochee. It is a sight not seen
in many parts of this country today. It is because our roads are so bad. There
are 67 miles of paved roads in the county.

No. of children in public school:
  White—1–12 grades: 1,098
  Colored—1–12 grades: 5,910
There are 70 schools in the county.
Private medical facilities:
  M.D.s—10 (1 colored)
  Dentists—5
  R.N.s—2
  Pharmacists—5
  Midwives—50
There are 23 eating establishments in the county. Permits are granted
by the State Health Dept.

There are 20 meat markets, 1 candy factory, 1 Coca-Cola plant & one
slaughterhouse.

6 dairies produce milk. 3 supply raw milk and 3 pasteurized. The
percentage of urban milk properly pasteurized is 75%. One pasteurization

plant is located at Banneker Institute, and assures faculty and student body of a safe supply. I wish I could say the same for the entire population. The County Inspector in our dept. examines cows for both Bang's disease and T.B.

Hackett Co. is 1 of 8 counties comprising East Alabama Health District, established early in 1938 by State Health Dept. with assistance from Rockefeller Foundation and Commonwealth Fund.

An Alabama state law, passed in 1928, requires the reporting of all discovered cases of venereal disease to State Health Dept. authorities, and the assignment of such cases for treatment either to a private physician or to a state or local clinic. Drugs for such treatment will be supplied free to private physicians by the State Dept. of Health.

In the summer of 1939, federal funds were made available for all V.D. clinics operated by the County Health Department and staffed by local physicians. Clinician fees for treatment of V.D. are:

1–50 patients treated = 1 clinic session. Fee—$5.00
51–100 pat. treated = 2 clin. sessions. Fee—$10.00
101–150 pat. treated = 3 clin. sessions. Fee—$15.00
151–200 pat. treated = 4 clin. sessions. Fee—$20.00

In addition to treatment sessions, separate examinations are paid on a fee basis of $5.00 for 3–6 patients. Examinations must be complete enough to evaluate the patient's physical status and serve as a guide for the type of treatment needed.

This year we began the treatment of gonorrhea in our clinics, and next year we hope to begin the treatment of chancroid. Last year we treated 952 patients for syphilis, giving 13,332 treatments. In cooperation with the P.H.S., we are experimenting with the Eagle-Hogan 8–12-week schedule of arsenotherapy. Best results were with bismuth and oxophenarsine together. Patients receiving 21 or more milligrams of mapharsen per kilogram of body weight responded better than those receiving less.

At some time late in the afternoon, I fell asleep and was awakened, still sitting in the swivel chair with a sheaf of papers fallen in my lap, by the ringing of the telephone. The shrill peal of the bell in the silent, empty house startled me, so that for a moment I was totally disoriented. I didn't recognize the sound as a telephone bell; it seemed to be an alarm of some kind, a protest, a pealing disruption in nature; or as if the house had screamed suddenly in warning, or in indignation at my intrusion into it. I dropped my pen and sat trembling in the silence that followed, until the phone rang again. When I snatched it from the cradle and spoke, my voice was strained.

"Hello?"

"Hello, Carl? How's it going? You got squared away there?"

"Oh, Liam. Yes. There wasn't a lot to do. I've been writing letters."

"Good. It's not too bad, I hope."

"No, it's fine. Very comfortable. Janet took care of everything. She even put some food in the icebox for my breakfast."

"She's a great girl. Well, look, I thought I'd come pick you up and bring you over to the house for dinner. We have a marvelous cook; I think I can promise you something better than the Bayou."

"That sounds fine."

"Good. I'll be around in fifteen minutes."

"I'll meet you out front," I said.

"Right. See you then."

I went down to the front porch and sat in a rocking chair until I heard the hoarse grinding of his motor and saw the square old sedan limping up the street. Liam leaned across the seat to unlatch the door for me, and when I got in, said, "Well, have you had a good day?"

"Yes. I got in touch with Horgan and Kidd, did some reading, got unpacked. I was going to come down to the office after I ran out of things to do."

"Wish you had," Liam said. "Very interesting case in there." From the back seat I heard a dog whine, and turned to see it lying in a cardboard box, a small, brown, smooth-furred mongrel bitch, her hind legs encased to the hips in plaster casts. Liam reached across the back of the seat and stroked her head. She licked his hand passionately.

"How's she doing?"

"Not bad, considering she's had a taste of my orthopedics. Sweet little creature. You going to have room in the house there?"

"Oh, plenty. More than we need. We only have one child, and she's just two years old."

"I see. Well, if there's anything else you need, just let us know. Janet will handle it."

He swung the car in a full turn and headed back toward the main street, the late afternoon sunlight falling warm through the windshield on our breasts and thighs. "I'm over west of Main a few blocks, on Water Street. We've got a real Charles Addams place, with about ten gables on it. Don't need half the room, now our daughter's gone, but most of them are like that, these old town houses. Made for Victorian family life, when everybody had ten kids and they all stayed home till they got married."

He drove for a while in silence, turning occasionally to reach across the seat and stroke the dog's head, murmuring, "Hang on, lady. Almost there." When he had pulled up in front of the towering old Gothic frame house in which he lived, he opened the back door of the car and lifted the dog out carefully, holding the box by the hand holes he had cut in its sides and carrying it like a basket up the walk between the azalea hedges. We went up the front steps and I held open the screen door for him while he went into the hall. Inside, the house was not very different from the one I had moved into: the parlor was high-ceilinged and dark, with painted floors and waist-high wainscoting, but, very unlike my own, it was a handsome, graceful, beautifully appointed room, a fact that was borne slowly to one, like the contours of an ancient temple buried under leaves and fallen vines, from beneath the layer of litter and debris that covered it. The furniture, I realized gradually, was not the malassortment of Victorian relicts with which my own was filled, but carefully selected pieces of early-nineteenth-century antiques in pale golden woods and the modest, elegantly simple style that I believe is called Biedermeier. The old gas lamps projecting from the walls were not encrusted, as those in my house were, with yellowing layers of cheap enamel, but restored and polished to their original gleaming brass chastity and furbished with fine cut-glass shades. The rugs had the lustrous depth of pile and slightly irregular authenticity of design of genuine, handwoven Persian carpetry, and the books that lined the solid wall of shelves at the rear end of the parlor were bound in Morocco leather and stamped with gold-leaf lettering. All this, I came to assume, was Paula's doing, and in her absence was almost obliterated by the litter of journals, textbooks, empty bottles, overturned ashtrays, sweaters, neckties, and other abandoned bits of clothing that were the detritus of Liam's unsystematic passage through the world. His contribution to the decor, I deduced in the course of the evening, was a bust of William Blake with a coonskin cap fitted tightly over his marble curls that gazed down dauntlessly upon the room. That and the original oil painting of the sea seen from above the rooftops of a Mediterranean village that decorated the wall above the sofa, a bright, reckless, and exuberant tribute to a world of sun and water and provincial peace which, when I went and examined it closely while he carried the dog out to the kitchen, I saw was signed with the letter L entwined by a pair of serpents and fashioned of what looked like a badly bent caduceus. While I was looking at it I heard his voice from the kitchen issuing greetings and then instructions about the care of the animal to a black woman with a soft, merry, solicitous voice. When he came back into the parlor he shut the kitchen door carefully and carried a silver ice bucket to a liquor cabinet against the wall.

"Is this yours?" I asked.

"Oh. Yes, I used to do a bit of dabbling."

"It's very good."

"Oh, I don't know. It's—earnest—I suppose you could say. And free of gloom, at least. Which is about all you can ask of a young man."

"Do you still paint?"

"No, no. I haven't the steadiness of hand required anymore." He held up his hand and wobbled it exaggeratedly in the air. "Or vision. What will you have?"

"I don't drink. I'll have a Coke or something, if you've got one."

"Oh, you must need something stronger than that, after that train ride. You sure?"

"Yes, a Coke would be fine. How's the dog?"

"Seems to be settling down, poor little creature. I'm going to have a julep. We keep a bed of mint out back. I make up a batch of syrup and let it brew for a whole day. Never without a pitcherful in the icebox. You sure you won't have one, as an introduction to the South?"

"No, thanks."

He made the drinks with lingering absorption, as if deliberately and somewhat wistfully protracting the process, speaking abstractedly above the tinkle of ice cubes and the splash and sizzle of liquid. "Hope that house of yours is not too hot. May's bad enough, but I'm afraid it'll get worse yet. Right up through October. We'll have to find you some fans." He brought me the Coke and sat down across from me in a straight chair, lifting the glass. "Well, here's to your arrival. Welcome to Tallacoochee." I nodded and sipped at my Coke. Outside the window of the parlor there was a constant massed droning sound, like the turmoil of a distant army. Liam turned his head to the window and listened, his face still.

"Carpenter bees," he said. "They're all up under the eaves, eating the place to bits. I'll have to get after them, but it's a nasty job. Is that all right?"

"Yes, fine."

"We'll have some roast lamb, not too long. I think you'll find it an improvement over the chili." He took a very long drink of his julep and closed his eyes for a moment, his face gone entirely expressionless, as if he had fallen into a profound and instant sleep. When he opened them, he smiled and nodded, his eyes touching mine in a quick, disconcerted way, like those of a man exchanging a sudden glance with someone in a waiting room. From the open window came clinging, delicate threads of intoxicating scent of magnolias. I breathed out heavily through my nostrils.

"Everything all right?" Liam said.

"I just find that smell a little overpowering."

"The smell?"

"Yes. The flowers everywhere. It's rather like a funeral home, or a brothel."

"I suppose it is, yes; if you're not used to it." He turned his head to the window. "Could close the window, but it's so damned hot I think you'd suffer more."

"No, no. I don't mind it, really."

He listened for a moment to the droning from the eaves, then jiggled the ice in his glass and lowered it into his lap. "If you have a minute on Friday morning, you might like to have a look at this man who was in this afternoon. I've asked him to come back then. Trophic joint changes in the left knee and elbow. Could be diabetes, could be syringomyelia. Might even be arthritis. But more than likely syphilis."

"Charcot joints?"

"Yes. It isn't something you see every day."

"It would be interesting to see," I said. "Do you get much of it?"

"A certain amount. Although late syphilis is generally cardiovascular in these Negroes. See plenty of that. Although not until autopsy, all too often."

"Because they don't get treatment?"

"Yes. Very often don't realize what they've got. We don't see them sometimes until it's too late."

"Do they know the term 'syphilis' at all? Or its implications?"

"Not generally. That's the trouble. So many of them are impoverished, ignorant—often illiterate—worn out by overwork, or wasted by indigence and cheap liquor; generally suffering badly from malnutrition, run-down from a host of endemic diseases like hookworm, malaria, tuberculosis, dengue fever, every damned thing you can think of; and inveterately promiscuous, as anyone would be under those conditions. And of course, the first two stages of the damned affliction—the only time when you have a hope of absolutely curing it—are short-lived, and disappear spontaneously without treatment, and are often so mild or inconspicuous that they're hardly noticed by people who live all their lives with things like pellagra and ringworm and impetigo and scabies. They get a blister on the genitals or lips, and then perhaps a mild skin rash or a sore throat, both of which clear up in a few weeks, and they think it's all over, think they're fine. 'Bad blood,' they call it; or 'haircut.' They don't realize that in anywhere from three to forty years they're apt to go blind, or mad, or that their arteries will explode, or their faces and toes rot away, or their lungs turn into concrete. So they go on infecting each other, bearing congenitally syphilitic children, blind and half rotten with the stuff. It's a goddamned nightmare." He set down his glass and leaned forward to pluck from the shelf of the end table beside his chair a newspaper, folded open to the editorial page. He handed it to me across the coffee table. "Look at this. This is the Birmingham *News-Age-Herald* for last week. That's their lead editorial." I took the paper from him and began to read the section that Liam had encircled with red ink:

The presence within our nation of more than 5,000,000 men and women suffering from syphilis in an infectious form constitutes a danger of far greater significance than any possible "fifth column" or unsound political philosophy with which we are likely to have to deal. The concentration of men in the huge and expanding military establishments, apart from the normal modes of life, will inevitably intensify this problem. . . .

For example, as the result of blood tests recently made of registrants for the local draft boards, more than five times as many active cases of syphilis are now known as can possibly be treated by all the clinics now provided by Birmingham and Jefferson County. Let us assume for the moment that it would be possible to convince all these known cases of infectious syphilis that as a patriotic duty they should submit to treatment, to render their disease non-infectious, and to conserve their physical strength for the national defense. Surely this ought to be possible; the advantages and even the necessity of this action are obvious. But most of these people are from low-income groups totally or partially unable to pay for the rather expensive course of treatment involved. And our public clinics have facilities for less than one-fifth of the number of known cases —not to mention those not at present on record!

"Yes," I said. "It's a very grave problem. That's why I'm here, of course." I handed the paper back to him and took up the folder that I had set beside me on the sofa. "When you identify a case, and begin treatment, do you tell the patient what it is he actually has? Are you able to make them understand?"

"Oh, yes," Liam said. "These people are not morons, you know; they're just uneducated. They're only too anxious to get treatment, when they know the possible consequences. And if you're starting a course of treatment that will require an individual to report once a week to a clinic, for the next eighteen months, maybe ten miles, by foot, through bogs and mire and palmetto scrub, you've got to be damned well able to make him understand the importance of it. They do, for the most part. But of course, the conditions of their lives make it impossible for some of them to continue treatment to the end. Still, we're able to stay with most of them long enough to render them non-infectious, and to greatly reduce the severity of later complications, if there should be any."

I opened the folder and took out a sheaf of typewritten papers. "You mentioned the Rosenwald Study this afternoon. I'd like to review that for a minute, if you don't mind. It has a lot to do with my project."

"All right. It was a very good study. I helped work on it, with our local clinics, when they were getting the statistics together."

"I realize that. It couldn't have been done at all without your assistance. Let's just go over the figures again." I plucked a page of notes from my folder. "That study was concluded in 1933. At the time, you had a Negro population of 22,320. Of these, 3,684 received serologic tests for syphilis; and of this number, 1,466 had a positive reaction, roughly thirty-eight percent of those tested. That's an astonishing figure."

"It is," Liam said. "Astounding and horrifying."

"Of those with positive reactions, 1,400 were treated through facilities your department and ours made jointly available. Only thirty-three of those people gave a history of any previous treatment, and those had had an average of only 4.3 doses of arsphenamine. Far from adequate."

"Yes," Liam said. "That was pretty much the state of things seven years ago."

"Treatment for all positive reactors who would accept it was carried on for a period of twelve months, which represented forty percent of the amount of total treatment planned. The total planned was twenty arsphenamine injections and one hundred ninety-two mercury rubs, over thirty-four weeks, at a cost of $8.60 per case. Well, as you know all too well, the economy fell apart at that point, and our resources went with it, so the project had to be abandoned."

Liam nodded. "Still, a great many of them were treated sufficiently to arrest the course of the disease, or reduce its later complications greatly. That's not a small achievement."

"No, it isn't." I laid the sheet aside. "But what we're contemplating now is a new study, an independent one. We want to examine another four or five thousand individuals and compare the incidence of the disease at present with what it was in '33. Naturally, some of the people who turn up will be individuals who were included in the Rosenwald Study. But we'll have records, and a reliable history of them. We'll be able to identify them and compare their present health status with what it was seven years ago. That will give us a lot of very valuable information about the efficacy of the amount of treatment they received. Some of those people in the Rosenwald group, of course, received no treatment at all, and probably haven't since, which will give us equally valuable information about the course of the disease when it remains untreated. Of course, there's only one really reliable piece of literature on that subject available today."

"The Boeck-Bruusgaard Study," Liam said.

"Yes. I don't need to tell you what a mine of information it is on the pathogenesis of the disease. Morbidity and mortality rates, secondary relapse, types of tertiary involvement, socioeconomic influence, male-female ratios of morbidity, virtually everything we know today about its untreated course."

Liam nodded; not overenthusiastically, I thought. "Yes," he said. "It was a very useful study."

"But, of course, that information was all relevant only to the white race, and in a cold climate, and under urban circumstances. And because the sample was quite small—I believe Bruusgaard studied the subsequent histories of only 473 of the original patients—its findings are far from exhaustive. We need to know much more."

Liam nodded again; then frowned and shook the cubes in his glass.

"There's a point I'd like to emphasize," I said. "Of the 1,466 people found to be syphilitic in the Rosenwald Study, only thirty-three had had any previous treatment whatever. And so little that it was insignificant. I realize that that was a good many years ago, but do you think that's anything like the case today? How many present cases go undiscovered or, if they are discovered, inadequately treated? What would your estimate be?"

"It's very hard to say," Liam said. "That's what I've been talking about. According to that editorial, so many active cases are showing up in draft board examinations that they can't possibly be handled by all the existent clinical facilities in Jefferson County. Five times as many as they're able to take care of. I suppose we're in much the same situation. Many of those people would never have taken a physical examination at all if they hadn't been required to. And, in normal times, they never would."

"That's the impression I get from what you've been telling me. I suppose many of them consider 'bad blood,' as they call it, just a temporary inconvenience that will clear up by itself, so they never bother to get medical attention."

"That's true," Liam said. "A lot of them think it's nothing more serious than a case of boils, or poison ivy. Sometimes they use home remedies. Poultices, 'spring tonics,' drugstore lotions. Or they drink a lot of sassafras or some damn thing. After all, it's a lot of trouble to get to a county clinic on Saturday morning when there's a field to be plowed, or a day's wages are at stake. And if you try to convince a very uneducated man that his Aunt Ida died of a ruptured aneurysm last week, at the age of fifty, because she had a skin rash when she was sixteen, he's apt to think you're out of your mind. And if the skin rash *he* had three years ago has cleared up, and he's felt fine since, he's not very apt to walk five miles through the mud to get a blood test. And if he never *had* any symptoms, or has forgotten about them, he's even less likely to. I'm afraid a hell of a lot of them never get within ten miles of a clinic all their lives, in spite of everything we do to try and reach them." He leaned forward, resting his forearms on his knees and staring into his glass. "I suppose that less than ten percent of all the syphilitics in this county are ever tested or treated, even with the gains we've made. I don't know. It would have to be a guess."

"But it's possible that in as many as ninety percent of them the disease runs its course?"

"It's possible, yes. It's a damned sad thing to think about."

"How many of them have what you would call a 'spontaneous cure,' " I asked, "without any treatment at all? Never show any tertiary symptoms?"

"I don't know how you'd find out," Liam said. "Not in my circumstances. If I find someone who shows any symptoms at all, clinical or serological, I treat him. So if he becomes asymptomatic later on, you can hardly call it a spontaneous cure. And if a man of thirty, or forty, or fifty shows no symptoms, how do you know he ever did? Unless he gives you a history of it—which is bound to be very imperfect, badly remembered, conjectural at best. On the other hand, I've seen late latent cases that don't seem to have had any difficulties. I've been treating one man who's had positive Klines and Kolmers and a positive spinal reading for eight months, and he gets up every morning and plows five acres of land, or chops cotton all day. He's fifty-five years old, and has never had a clinical symptom that I could find. Call it anything you like: spontaneous cure, remission, subclinical latency. Maybe it will make him more vulnerable to something else that comes along; maybe his life span will be reduced considerably, but it's hard to prove." He drank, draining his glass, and sat back in the chair, staring out of the window. "That's something I'd like to know: why some people are more resistant to it than others, or at least suffer far fewer effects. It seems to me if we could identify something in their blood that makes them resistant, or immune, it's possible we could come up with a vaccine. That's what I'd work on if I were doing research. God, what a blessing that would be."

"Those are the questions that only long-term studies can give us clues to," I said. "Boeck was fortunate, in Norway, because he had the perfect conditions. A ready-made study in nature, right there in front of him: a population with a high percentage of infection which was also very stable, very easy to keep track of. They were located in a small geographical area, a single section of a single city, and didn't have either the money, the inclination, or the tradition to travel very much. Even if they moved out of Oslo, Norway was a very small country. All he had to do was watch, and keep careful records. He could follow most of them right through to death and autopsy. An ideal situation. He had their lifelong medical histories available for study and interpretation. It's a classical study in nature." Liam gazed out of the window without replying. "In fact," I said, "the situation was very similar to what you have here in Hackett County. That struck me immediately, when I was going over the demography. What's fortunate is that he had the intelligence to make use of it."

"That, and the fact that any treatment he could have given them, back there at the turn of the century, would probably have done them as much harm as good," Liam said.

"Yes." I considered for a moment possible extenuations of his comment. "Yes, I think as many people died of treatment in those days as died of the disease. My God, the things that used to happen with mercury. Symptoms of mercury poisoning used to be so common that they were considered part of the tertiary stage of the disease itself. At one time, I think, every professor at the University of Heidelberg had to take an oath that he'd never use any form of the stuff. Of course, we're not out of the woods yet on that score. We're still giving mercury inunctions regularly. We used them on the Rosenwald people. And arsenic and bismuth are almost as toxic. I've seen cases of arsenic and heavy-metal poisoning at Johns Hopkins that were hair-raising. I suppose you have, too."

"Yes," Liam said, "I've seen some very bad reactions." He shook his glass, sipped at it again, and stood up suddenly. "How's that Coke?"

"Fine."

"You wouldn't like another?"

"No, thanks."

"Well, I think I've got time for another before Janet shows up. She's joining us for dinner, did she tell you?"

"Yes."

He went across to the liquor cabinet and poured bourbon and then syrup from the pitcher into his glass, his movement fastidious and slow, as if he were performing a delicate operation. He sipped at the drink, staring up at the bust of Blake. "I've seen patients go into Herxheimer reactions, anemia, horrifying dermatitis. As you say, it's poison we're pouring into these people. I have a case now that I'm worried about. Pregnant girl, nineteen years old, with a bad liver." He came back to his chair and sat down, restlessly adjusting a framed photograph on the table beside him. "These three or four thousand additional people you want to examine in this new study," he said. "If you get the same percentage of positive reactors that they did in the Rosenwald Study, that would come to—what?—something like eleven to fifteen hundred people. Are you prepared to treat that many cases?"

"As many of them as possible." I replaced my notes in the folder carefully. "Of course, if we found anything like fifteen hundred cases, at a cost of approximately nine dollars a case, that would come to around thirteen thousand dollars. That's an awful lot of money. As far as I know, the P.H.S. has no fixed budget for this study, but of course there are limits to everything." I paused to observe the effect of this statement on Liam. He began to stir the cubes in his glass with a fingertip, a kind of melancholy conformation taking possession of his features. "Fortunately," I said, "a private source, the Dunedin Memorial Foundation, has agreed to assume some of the expenses connected with the project. Just how far they're willing to go, I'm not sure. We'll have to wait until we get some figures before we're able to estimate anything like exact expenditures, make a definite requisition. Certainly, all the early, acute cases will be given treatment, to reduce the spread of it any further. That much I can promise you."

"And the remainder?"

"The remainder would be put into an observation group, for careful periodic examination and study. As I say, these would all be late or late latent cases, well beyond the infectious stage." There was a considerable silence. I finished my Coke and set the glass on the coffee table in front of me. Liam put his hand into his pocket and rattled the chips of seashell for a moment.

"You have no idea of what actual percentage of the discovered cases this would be?" he asked. "This 'observation group'?"

"There's no way of telling. We don't know how many cases we're going to find, or how many we're going to be able to treat. In fact, we don't know how many it would be advisable to treat, even if we were able." I opened my folder again, and shuffled its pages to my notes of the Boeck-Bruusgaard Study. "Bruusgaard found that, by 1927, twenty-seven point nine percent of the patients included in the original study had undergone spontaneous cure; they no longer had any symptoms whatever of the disease. Moreover, he estimated that as many as seventy percent of all syphilitics went through life without any inconvenience from the disease at all. It's very possible that the morbidity and mortality rates for people treated in late stages of the disease are higher than for late-stage patients who go without any treatment whatever, because of the toxicity of the therapy. One of the very possible conclusions of this study is that it would be better to do nothing at all in latent cases." I laid the sheets aside and sat back on the sofa. "I won't disguise the fact that we find the situation here in Hackett County a very unique opportunity to study the effects of untreated syphilis in black males—"

"Males," Liam said. "You're going to restrict it to males?"

"Yes, that's our intention."

"There's no question of a woman—who may become pregnant—going untreated?"

"No. Since at present we don't have the resources to treat every case of syphilis that comes to our attention, and since most of these people would, in the natural course of things, receive no treatment anyway—I think you said as many as ninety percent of them—the Service feels, and I feel personally, that it would be a serious neglect of opportunity to ignore this ready-made situation, which nature herself has presented to us. It might almost be called delinquency. Any early infectious cases that come to our attention will of course be treated, and a certain number of late latent cases as well; as many as we have the resources to take care of. The remainder, however—a group of, say, three or four hundred—will be put into the observation group for regular examination and study."

"Three or four hundred," Liam said.

"Yes. What must be remembered is that none of these people will be any the worse off for the study having been made, and a great many will be much better off. The situation, in general, will be much improved from what it is now, and a great deal of invaluable information will have been gained. Don't you agree?"

Liam hitched himself up in his chair as if the note of challenge in my question had sent a throe of vast unease through him. "I understand you've contacted Dr. Pearson, at the State Department of Health, about your project?" he said.

"Dr. Turner has, yes. He's very much in accord with it. I believe I have a copy of his reply here." I began to shuffle through my correspondence file again.

"Did you say you got in touch with Dr. Horgan and Dr. Kidd today, at the Institute?"

"Yes, with both of them. They're very favorably disposed, I'm glad to say. Their help is indispensable. We hope to make use of their clinic and laboratories and radiology facilities, and their personnel to some extent." Liam rose, carried his glass to the window, and stared out into the hot, droning, sweet-scented somnolence of the afternoon. After a moment he set his glass on the windowsill and turned to the bookcase that abutted it. He ran his forefinger along the spines and then plucked out a volume and opened it.

"You say that the patients put into the study group for observation would be late latent cases. 'Well beyond the infectious stage,' I think you said."

"Yes."

"I believe you said you were trained for this study by a year of work with J. E. Moore at Johns Hopkins."

"That's right."

"I have a textbook of Dr. Moore's here," Liam said. *The Modern Treatment of Syphilis.* I often refer to it. I'd like to read you something." He leafed through the pages for a moment, holding them to the light. "Here it is: 'Though it imposes a slight though measurable risk of its own, treatment markedly diminishes the risk from syphilis. In latent syphilis, as I shall show, the probability of progression, relapse, or death is reduced from a probable twenty-five to thirty percent without treatment to about five percent with it; and the gravity of the relapse, if it occurs, is markedly diminished.' " He turned from the window to face me. "I'm sure Dr. Moore must have conveyed that opinion to you while you were studying with him."

"Yes. But of course there are different views."

"He goes on to say—just a minute; I'll find it." He leafed over a few more pages, then paused and held the book again to the light of the window. "Yes, here it is: 'Another compelling reason for treatment exists in the fact that every patient with latent syphilis may be, and perhaps is, infectious for others.' " He closed the book and looked up at me. "I think Stokes has a very similar point of view. And others."

"I've read his book, of course," I said. "But, as you know, there's a great deal of difference in the way syphilis manifests itself in the white and black races. No one should realize that better than you. In fact, as Moore himself has pointed out, in Negroes syphilis can almost be regarded as a different disease from syphilis in whites. It may interest you to know that Dr. Moore has been advised of our intention to make this study, and he's agreed to act as an expert consultant to us."

"Moore has? Really?"

"Yes. He believes it to be of enormous potential value. As far as infectiousness in late syphilis goes, as I understand it, there's a great diversity of opinion on that point. You went to Vanderbilt, I believe. I think Dr. Kampmeier, at the syphilis clinic there, has a very different view. As I remember, Kampmeier states unequivocally that anyone who has had syphilis for over four years is no longer infectious. He also has strong reservations about the efficacy of treatment in many late latent cases. Just as Bruusgaard has. His opinion is that in many circumstances it is unnecessary to treat such cases, and perhaps preferable not to treat them at all. I think many other authorities agree with him. And certainly no one is more circumspect—or has more experience with the disease —than Rudolph Kampmeier."

"No, that's true," Liam said. "I've heard it often enough. No one has greater respect for the man than I do. Or for Moore, as far as that goes. As you say, there's a great diversity of opinion." He turned back to the bookcase and replaced the volume on the shelf. "It just seems to me that if there's any doubt at all, about either the indication for treatment or the infectiousness of the particular case, we always ought to decide in favor of treatment. That's been my philosophy, in any case. God knows who's right." He inhaled deeply and gave a breathy snort of consternation, then looked across the room at me with his ragged smile. " 'Now we see through a glass, darkly,' " he murmured.

"A glass that only knowledge can wipe clean," I said.

"I certainly won't argue with you about that." He raised his glass and seemed discouraged to find it empty. "Just what part do you expect me to play in this experiment—this study?"

"A large and indispensable one. I hope that doesn't discourage you; I know you've got plenty to do already. But we'll need to operate through your clinics, of course; yours and the Cardozo Hospital's. In the first place, that means getting the people in for testing. You have their confidence, you know them, you understand their way of life, their psychological reactions, better than anyone else in the world. We'll need a great deal of advice on how to go about inducing them to come in for examination, about setting up clinic dates and procedures, actually taking the samples. After that's done—which we calculate will take six months or so—we'll need someone to be in continuous charge of the study. I'm not sure yet whether the Service intends to assign anyone permanently here to Tallacoochee, but I don't think it would be possible or practical. But someone will have to keep track of the patients, maintain contact with them, see that there is no interruption in the course of the study. We'd like very much for you to assume that job. If it means extra work, extra personnel to keep records and maintain contact with the subjects, we'll provide them to the greatest degree we possibly can."

"I see." He carried his glass to the liquor cabinet and began to refill it, lifting the lid from the ice bucket and dropping a couple of cubes into the glass. He added bourbon and filled the glass, rather carelessly this time, with syrup from the pitcher. It ran over the rim onto the tabletop, and he dabbled for a moment at the pool of liquid with a paper napkin. "I can see a great deal of thought and planning has gone into this thing already," he said. He leaned against the liquor cabinet and stared at his shoes.

"A great deal, yes."

"I wish I were ten years younger. I wish I were your age. You'll live to see the great breakthrough in this disease, I feel sure of it. Perhaps even an effective vaccine. I won't."

"Why do you say that?"

"I don't know. You get feelings about things. The feeling that you're coming in on the crest of something, or that you've just missed it. There are rhythms to life, I think. Don't you feel that?"

"I don't know whether I've thought about it in just those terms, but I suppose you're right."

"This war, for example. You've been able to feel it coming on ever since the Spanish business, in '36. We'll be in it this time next year. There's a kind of sickly excitement takes possession of the world, I don't know what it is. Military men can sense it like a hound. They have a nose for it, the way some doctors have a nose for syphilis. They can almost smell it, and you can see that they're excited by it. It's a funny damned thing."

There was a knock at the front door, and then the creak of the screen door being pushed open, and Janet called into the hall, "Hi. Can I come in?"

"Come on in," Liam said. "I'm just about to build you the biggest mint julep in the world. I guess you've been down at that office slaving away all this time."

"Well, I had to finish doing those Suggs tests, and then I had to take a shower. I'm no good without a shower in the afternoon." She sat down on the far end of the sofa, smiled at me, and said, "Hello"; then got up almost immediately and went across the room to a gigantic pothos plant suspended by a chain from the ceiling beside the parlor window. She reached up and dug with her fingertip into the soil of the hanging pot. "Did you remember to have Viola water this? Paula will kill you if it dies."

"I think so," Liam said. "Yes, I'm sure I did."

"Well, I'm not." She went to the end of the hall and opened the door that Liam had closed, calling out into the kitchen, "Viola! Hi!"

"Good evening, Miss Janet," Viola said from the kitchen. "You do look nice."

"I look like a crow," Janet said. "Listen, did Dr. Proctor ask you to water the plants?"

"Yes, ma'am, he sure did," Viola said. I saw her standing beyond Janet in the doorway, a heavy, merry-faced woman in a blue apron, with skin that shone like onyx. Janet stared at her sternly, her hands on her hips, until Viola broke into a spasm of soft, helpless laughter, bending double as if she would collapse.

"I'll bet he did," Janet said. "You two are as thick as thieves."

"No, ma'am, I swear I telling you the truth!" Viola said. She slumped against the doorframe in strengthless mirth. "He say to me, 'Viola, you water them plants now, you hear me?' And I say to him, 'Yes, sir, Dr. Proctor, I sure will.'" She retreated into the kitchen, clutching with one hand at the doorframe and flapping weakly at the air with the other. Janet came back out into the parlor and stood beside Liam, staring at him ironically while he stirred her drink. When he handed it to her, she said, "You bribe them all. That's what you do."

"I never bribed anyone in my life," Liam said. "I have far too beautiful a nature."

"Oh, yes. Very beautiful."

"I do. Just this evening a woman stopped me in the street and said, 'My goodness, what a beautiful nature you must have, young man.' Everyone realizes it but you."

She nodded and sipped at her drink, then closed her eyes gratefully. "Well, maybe you do. It takes a beautiful nature to make a julep like that. How's the dog?"

"Right as rain," Liam said. "She was purring like a kitten when we brought her in. Wasn't she, Carl?"

"She seemed pretty happy," I said.

"I'm going to call her Enitharmom. It's the only thing she responds to at all. How's that Coke, Carl?"

"Maybe I'll have another."

"Good. I'm going to have another julep. A woman shouldn't drink alone."

Janet carried her drink to the couch and sat down again on the far end of it. "Did you get straightened out?" she asked.

"Yes. It was only a matter of unpacking a couple of bags. Thanks for having the phone put upstairs. It was a godsend."

"He's spent the whole afternoon up there, administrating," Liam said. "We've got to teach this man the restorative powers of the julep, or he won't last a month down here." He turned from the table with a fresh drink, swaying very slightly, holding a sprig of mint in one hand which he waved delicately across his nostrils while he inhaled deeply. " 'Oh, the beautiful witchcrafts of Albion,' " he murmured. Janet frowned at him very slightly.

"I suppose Blake had something to say on the subject of mint juleps, too," she said gently.

"Oh, yes. As he did on all the verities. Obliquely, of course. That was his method." He held the sprig of mint aloft and addressed it lyrically:

"I am a watry weed,
And I am very small, and love to dwell in lowly vales;
So weak, the gilded butterfly scarce perches on my head;
Yet I am visited from heaven, and he that smiles on all
Walkes in the valley and each morn over me spreads his hand,
Saying: 'Rejoice, thou humble grass,
Thou gentle maid of silent valleys,
For thou shalt be clothed in light, and fed with morning manna.' "

He dropped the mint into his glass and nodded at Janet. "Of course, some people deny it was mint he was talking about, but there's no doubt about it whatever, as far as I'm concerned." He came back to his chair carrying a Coca-Cola for me, and set it on the coffee table; then sat down across from us and plucked at the knees of his trousers, his downcast eyes falling into sobriety. "You did the tests on Lucy Suggs, then?"

"Yes. I'm not sure you want to hear about it."

"Oh." He closed his eyes and raised his brows, shaking his head lightly as if to clear it of fatigue or mild pain. "I guess I'd better."

"I got a negative Kolmer reading and a reactive Kline; eight dilutions."

"What about the spinal fluid?"

"Less than four cells on the Kolmer, doubtful in 0.2 cc on the Wassermann, with a negative mastic curve." She paused for a moment, watching him. "I did them very carefully."

"When did you not?" Liam said. He turned his head to the window and stared out for a moment. "Such a nice kid." He stroked his hair and turned back to look at me across the coffee table. "This is the one I was telling you about, who's five months pregnant."

"She doesn't have any clinical symptoms at all?" I asked.

"Well, she came in to see us because she was turning yellow and felt very bad. Bile in the urine. But she doesn't remember any primary or secondary lesions; or else she's lying. I don't think she is. Now, the jaundice itself, of course, could be a secondary symptom, but I don't think it is. Not in the absence of any others, and with such an ambiguous serological report. I've seen some syphilitic hepatitis, and this doesn't look like it to me. I'd call it a very lively case of catarrhal jaundice. Also, she's very badly run-down. And pregnant. Pregnant women's organs are carrying a heavier than normal load already. I sure as hell don't want to pour arsenic and heavy metal into the girl if she's getting a false-positive reaction. Aside from the physical damage we could do her, there's the psychological damage, which can be a damn sight worse." He sipped at his drink and frowned. "I think despair and suicide claim almost as many syphilitics as the disease itself. I knew an eighteen-year-old girl who threw herself in front of a bus after she'd been given a positive laboratory report that I'm almost sure was faulty. And I've known patients who became absolutely obsessed with the idea that they still had the thing even after they were cured, as far as their physicians were concerned. They go from doctor to doctor, demanding treatment, all their lives sometimes, convinced that they're rotting away inside. If you treat them, they know they've got it, and if you refuse, they think it's because you've given up on them, that you've decided they're incurable. Syphilophobia is a terrible thing. It destroys the personality just the way syphilis destroys the body."

"Even with these people?" I said.

"Yes, even with these people," Janet murmured.

"You've got to be damned careful about telling anyone he's got syphilis," Liam said, "if there's a chance in a hundred that he doesn't. On the other hand, I wouldn't like this girl to have a stillbirth, or a macerated syphilitic baby." He set his glass down and plucked at his eyebrows.

"You say she's five months pregnant?"

"By my calculations. But we could still get very good results with treatment, even this late. Probably save the baby. There'd be less than a twenty percent chance of its being syphilitic if we began treatment immediately. But I'm not sure she has the disease at all."

"Of course, some women don't show any primary or secondary symptoms if they've gotten infected during pregnancy," I said.

"I know. That's strange, isn't it? Something about the hormonal changes, I suppose, that inhibits the early symptoms. They get them later, of course.

And the baby, too. I just don't know whether to take the chance. Or whether she should, rather. She's the one who's got to take it. We're just the ones who decide."

"How is it you didn't know about the positive reaction until she was five months pregnant?" I asked.

"We didn't know she was, so none of our prenatal nurses ever visited her, and she never reported to a clinic till she was five months gone. Every public health nurse on my staff visits prenatal cases, and every one of them is able to take blood pressure and give Wassermanns and urinalyses. We have an in-hospital maternity service that includes ten days of hospitalization, at a cost of only five dollars to the patient. We have a maternity education program that gives demonstrations all over this county on a regular monthly basis; and yet some of them escape us. If she hadn't had this jaundice problem, I don't suppose she ever would have come in."

"Is she married?"

"No. That may be part of the reason. Afraid she'd get in trouble with her parents. They're very strong church people."

"We've tried to check her sexual contacts," Janet said. "She swears there have only been two, both in the last year. We've managed to get one of them in for a blood test, and he's negative on both the Kolmer and Kline, and has no history. The other one seems to have disappeared, so we don't know anything about him, but she swears 'there wasn't anything funny about him' while they were intimate."

"I suppose she could be a congenital case herself."

"No," Liam said. "Not a sign of it. Neither parent has a history, and she has no Hutchinson's teeth, no rhagades, no Clutton's joints, no interstitial keratitis, nothing at all. Of course, you often get hepatosplenomegaly in very early congenital cases, but I never heard of it developing after the age of two. I'm sure she's not congenital. If I thought so, I wouldn't do anything right now; not until the child's born. Chances of its being infected would be so remote you could forget about them. No, if she has the disease, it's acquired. In which case, there's a better than fifty-fifty chance that she'll have a congenital infant. If it's born alive. More likely, we'll get a stillbirth or an abortion."

"She may be latent."

"She may, but considering her age, it's not very likely, is it? And I've been over the girl with a fine-tooth comb, and can't find a late symptom anywhere. She's had a few episodes of vomiting, but what with jaundice and pregnancy, it would be odd if she hadn't. Gastric syphilis is so rare, you can pretty well forget about it. I suppose I've seen ten cases of it in twenty years of practice." He came back across the room to his chair and sat down, a little unsteadily, setting his drink on the coffee table that stood between us. After a moment he raised his eyes to mine, lifting his eyebrows in a curious, harried but penetrating expression of inquiry. "Just as a matter of information," he said, "what would you do, Carl? I'd be glad to have your opinion." I returned his gaze steadily, trying with a very conscious effort to invest my own with a combination of earnestness, modesty, and candor. Under the weight of Liam's gaze, this was not easy; almost equally composed of humility and catechism, it seemed to be both an appeal to me for counsel and the demand to be assured that I was worthy of that appeal.

"Do you mean exactly?"

"Exactly, yes. Sometimes it helps to have a disinterested opinion. I'd be very glad to know."

"How many weeks does she have till term?"

"Twenty, by my calculations."

I raised my glass and stared into the pale, oxblood-tinted dregs of the Coca-Cola that curled about the cubes like diluted blood. "I think I'd start treatment. With neoarsphenamine and bismuth. A first course of eight weekly injections, bismuth with the first four. Then four weeks of bismuth alone. And a final course of eight weekly injections, right through to term. I'd start with a small introductory dose of the neoarsphenamine and watch her very carefully for a Herxheimer reaction or any toxic effects. No more than 0.10 gram per thirty-five pounds of body weight, in 20 cc of cool, distilled water, administered intravenously, using at least four minutes for the injection. If there's no adverse reaction, I'd increase that to 0.15 gram per thirty-five pounds of body weight. After delivery, I'd follow up for at least six months with a pair of regular monthly blood tests, one flocculation and one complement-fixation, and at least two spinal fluid tests, on both the mother and the child."

He raised his eyebrows and smiled at me with a long, flickering, ruminative smile that was succeeded at last by a protracted, slowly subsiding nodding of his head.

"Yes," he said at last. "You wouldn't use arsphenamine?"

"I wouldn't, no. Not with a history of jaundice."

"No. Well, that sounds like very good advice. I'm glad to have it." He drained his glass and turned to Janet in an energetic way that I didn't yet know the man well enough to interpret either as approval or as gentle irony. "I think you've got your work cut out for you in the morning, Janet."

"Getting her back, you mean?" Janet said.

"Yes. With a rope, if you have to. After that spinal tap, I don't think it's going to be easy."

"I'll get her back," Janet said. "Don't worry about it." She raised her glass and sipped at it uneasily. "Why don't we drop it for a while now? Sufficient unto the day."

"Very sufficient," Liam said. He nodded thoughtfully while we sat in silence for a moment, listening to the droning from the eaves outside the window.

"You've still got those damned bees," Janet said.

"Yes. I'll get at them on Sunday, for sure."

"No, you won't. All you need is a mess of bee stings all over you. I'll get Carter or one of the boys to do it. They'll be glad to pick up a couple of dollars."

"Maybe you're right." He smiled at us crookedly. "I'm scared to death of the damn things, to tell the truth." He plucked the mint out of his glass and nibbled at a leaf. "Blake had something to say about syphilis, too, you know. Do you know 'London'?"

"*I* don't," I said.

> *"But most thro' midnight streets I hear*
> *How the youthful Harlot's curse*
> *Blasts the new-born Infant's tear,*
> *And blights with Plagues the Marriage hearse.*

" 'The new-born Infant's tear.' That's an allusion to blind, congenital babies, of course." He sighed deeply. "Well, in the New Jerusalem—"

"In the New Jerusalem they won't have roast lamb for dinner," Janet said. "Not if Blake can help it. But *I* think it smells wonderful. I'm going to see if I can help Viola speed things up." She got up and carried her drink down the hall and out through the kitchen door. Liam smiled at me.

"She's not quite sure about Blake," he said. "Thinks he may have been an idle crackpot."

"I take it you don't," I said.

"No. He knew about life, that man. What it was, and what it could be. And should be. You like Blake?"

"I don't know anything about him. Although I have a picture that he painted of Isaac Newton. My professor gave it to me when I finished my residency."

"Really? Who was that?"

"Dr. Chrisser. He was my pathology professor."

"Isn't that remarkable," Liam said. His eyes lit up with a look of sudden, delighted animation. "He's the man who did all that work on bejel and yaws, isn't he? My God, you were lucky to have him. I'd forgotten he was at G.W. Well, you must have learned *something* about syphilis."

"As much as you can learn secondhand, I suppose."

"Yes, there's a difference. Still, we wouldn't learn anything without men like that. They're the ones who push back the boundaries. He gave you Blake's

'Newton,' did he? Isn't that remarkable." He nodded, smiling as if greatly refreshed, until almost the tips of his teeth showed between his lips. "I'd like to meet that man. Maybe he'll be at the next V.D. conference. I think there's one in Houston, in February."

"I'm sure he will," I said.

"Maybe I'll be able to make it. I doubt it, though." He swung his glass up to his lips rather loosely, spilling a few drops on his trousers. He brushed at them clumsily.

Janet came back into the parlor from the kitchen and clapped her hands briskly. "To the table, gentlemen," she said. "I think we're ready."

"Ah, good," Liam said. "Now, I've got something here to add a glow to this occasion." He rose and went to the liquor cabinet, where he knelt and took out a bottle of dark red wine, rising with it held triumphantly aloft on his fingertips. "Bodegas Bilbainas, Spanish claret, 1930. I brought it back from San Sebastián in my luggage, five years ago, almost to the day." He picked up a corkscrew from the cabinet and waved us ahead of him through the arched portal that divided the parlor from the dining room. "Carl, why don't you sit here? And, Janet, I think we'll have you over here." We sat, I to his right and Janet to his left, at a fine, honey-colored Biedermeier table under a small brass-and-crystal chandelier. Liam stood at the head of the table in the sprinkle of soft evening light that fell through the leaves of the mimosa trees outside the long western windows of the room, uncorking the wine in a solemn, ceremonial way. We watched him silently, spreading our napkins in our laps. The cork made a muted popping sound, like a gunshot in a distant wood. Janet's face was still and sad. He poured full two of the wineglasses that stood in front of him and measured carefully an inch of wine into the third, setting it before me with a flourish.

"Only a taste, if you insist. But you can't go to your grave without having known the flavor of the Spanish earth." He set a glass in front of Janet and then raised his own, saying gently, "To the very good health of everyone in the world." I sipped at the rim of my glass, feeling my throat constrict slightly against its musty, earthen acerbity. Liam, when he had drunk, nodded and held his glass up to the light of the chandelier, gazing appreciatively into its sparkling scarlet depths. It cast a feverish blush across his face.

"I bought that in a bodega in the Old Town, in the summer of '35, at the foot of a mountain with a castle at the top that looked out over the Cantábrico. I used to climb up a great cliff, three hundred feet high, to the castle wall, and sit there, every morning, and look out at the sea. There were anise bushes growing among the rocks, and when you came down, your hands and clothes had the faint smell of anise on them, all day long, like perfume. Do you know what Paula said?"

"Shall I guess?" Janet said.

"Oh, you couldn't guess. She said it made her sick. When she was a kid she used to buy those black licorice candy ropes at a store on the corner, and she ate so much one day that she got sick and threw up. I suppose it does smell like that." He sat down and drank again. "We used to go to Spain every summer. That was the last summer we were there."

Viola came into the room with a serving tray on which there was a leg of lamb surrounded by baked potatoes and slices of syrup-coated carrots. The smell of it came with her in a savory cloud. She held it proudly aloft for a moment, saying, "How do that look, Dr. Proctor?"

"Absolutely heavenly, Viola. You have a magic hand with lamb." She chuckled softly. "This is Dr. Ransome, Viola. He's going to be working with us at the clinic."

"How you do, Doctor?" Viola said. "I hope you going to be happy with us."

"Thank you," I said.

"I wonder if you'd carve it for us? I'd hate to mangle anything as beautiful as that."

" 'Deed I will." She set the tray on the side table along the wall and began to do so, deftly and rapidly, a soft congenial murmur welling from her continually, like the cooing of pigeons in a loft. Liam watched her in a beguiled, musing way.

"We went to France the next year," he said. "Little place on the border called Pau. It was weird. You could hear the shelling in the mountains, just across the border, where they were blowing up all the places where we used to drink wine and lie in the sun. Guetaria, Santander. They used to bring in truckloads of Basque children. Refugees. Scared to death. Didn't know if they'd ever see their parents again."

"They be blowing up everybody 'fore they get through," Viola said. She grunted in soft indignation, setting plates before us. "What they do best. Blow up people. Don't know how they find so many reasons to blow up folks."

"Nor do I," Liam said. "I never understood politics. You don't have the time for it in this job." He cut and chewed a slice of lamb meditatively, raising his eyes in awe, when he had swallowed it, to Viola. "Oh, that's the best ever," he said. "The very best. You've outdone yourself, Viola. That would bring a man back from the grave. That would restore a creature to health."

"Just like you get every Wednesday night," Viola said. She was busily spooning out vegetables onto our plates. "It ain't no different. You ain't getting around me. I know what you up to."

"What am I up to?" Liam said.

"That dog ain't getting none of this lamb, now I tell you that for sure. That dog is getting cold scrapple."

"It's marvelous," Janet said. "You know where to come if this man ever gives you any trouble."

"He ain't about to give me no trouble," Viola said. "Don't you eat them potatoes till you put some gravy on 'em. I'm going to get you-all some hot bread." She went out through the arch and down the hall. Liam raised his eyes to me and asked, "Have you ever been to Spain?"

"No, I've never been out of the States at all. I haven't had the time for it."

"No, that's what I say. There isn't time to do anything, really. Like politics. You just don't have the time to learn what's happening in the world. Then one day you find that they're blowing it up all around you, and you don't have any idea why. Even what side you ought to be on, really. You're too damn busy patching up all the casualties. We're so damned naïve, we doctors. We can only do one thing well. And not even that well enough, too damned often. Don't you find that?"

"I'm afraid I haven't worried about it a great deal," I said. "I've always had the idea that if everyone in the world did his job well, there'd be a lot less trouble generally."

"Well, that's it," Liam said. "We're all Aristotelians, I guess. Aristotle never worried too much about why; only how. How things are done, how things work. Leave it to the Platonists to wonder why. He may have been right, of course; but I'm not as sure of it as I used to be."

"You worried about 'why' enough to want to run off and join the Abraham Lincoln Brigade," Janet said.

"Oh, well, not really. It was just a little burst of—" He waved his hand vaguely. "Just a last flare of adolescence." He looked very embarrassed. "Plenty to do right here."

"Don't make fun of yourself," Janet said with startling severity. "Don't patronize yourself. It's awful."

"Not patronizing myself. Just accepting my limitations. Isn't that how they define maturity?"

"Some people do," Janet said. "Usually people without any imagination, and with more money, and leisure, and good health, and good looks, than they ever earned. Or deserved."

"Oh, well, you can't blame people for that," Liam said. "Having more than they deserve. We all do, if it comes to that."

She lowered her eyes to her plate and stared at it stilly while her indignation subsided. It subsided very slowly. Meanwhile, I ate studiously. The lamb was really excellent. After a moment I said, "I wonder if I could have a glass of water?"

"Good Lord, yes," Liam said. "I forget about it, because we never drink it here. It tastes of sulfur, you know. Maybe you'd like a glass of iced tea; you don't notice it so much in tea."

"Water will be fine."

He turned his head and called out through the hall, "Viola, will you bring a glass of water for Dr. Ransome?"

"Yes, sir, 'deed I will," Viola called back from the kitchen.

"There are very large sulfur deposits in the soil," Liam said. "They say it's good for you, I don't know. They may be right: after all, people still take sulfur tonics every spring. And all these new drugs, the sulfonamides. There may be something in it."

"Yes."

We ate in silence for several minutes, until Liam said suddenly, "Been trying to think of that woman's name."

"What woman?" Janet said. A look of attentive concern came over her face.

"Used to be the sweetest little woman in the pension where we stayed. Every morning she made us a gigantic omelette, full of onions, potatoes, tomatoes, cheese—everything you can think of. She'd wrap it up in waxed paper for us, with a bottle of wine, so we could take it along for lunch. Merced! That was it. I wonder what's become of her. You see those awful pictures of Spanish towns after the fighting. All the bodies in the street."

Viola came into the room with a glass of ice water, which she set in front of me. "There you are, Doctor," she said.

"Thank you."

"That dog is very indisposed," she said to Liam. "That dog is puling some."

"I'll have a look at her," Liam said. He stood up quickly and went out through the arch and down the hall to the kitchen. Viola followed him. Janet and I sat across the table from each other, eating wordlessly. The click of our silverware on our dinner plates was startlingly clear in the silence. I could hear the grinding of my jaws, an unpleasantly ominous sound, like rats in an attic. When Liam returned he sat down and resumed eating without speaking.

"She all right?" Janet said in a moment.

"Yes. I gave her some aspirin in a piece of meat." He refilled his wineglass, drank, and said in a moment, "Do you know that syphilis was practically epidemic in both armies during the Civil War? Everybody had it. Abraham Lincoln had it. Herndon believed he gave it to his wife and his children. And that that's what accounts for his terrible sadness."

Janet exhaled heavily through her nostrils and set down her silverware. She reached into the pocket of her skirt and took out a small package wrapped in tissue paper and tied with string. "Here's something for you," she said. She laid the package on the table in front of him.

"What's this?"

"It's a present for you. From Harold Perkins."

"Really?" He set down his fork and picked up the tightly bound square packet, weighing it in his palm. "He brought me this? Really? Isn't that nice." He plucked vainly at the knotted string for a moment with his fingernails. Janet took the packet from him, untied the string quickly, and set it back in front of him. Liam unfolded the paper and lifted carefully out of it a small hand-carved model of a square-rigged sailing ship, whittled out of hard white wood. He held it in front of him, studying it with a look of boyish delight. "Isn't that lovely," he said. "Isn't that a lovely thing." He looked up at us in a quick, radiant way. "These people are so damned nice. Just look at that." He handed the model to me carefully, holding it in both his hands, touching the tips of the tiny masts with his fingertips when I had taken it. "Look at that work. Must have taken him weeks."

"He came in last month and said he wanted to whittle something for you, and asked me what I thought you'd like; so of course I said a boat. He brought it in this evening, just before I locked up."

"What a nice thing to do," Liam said. "The man's a real artist, don't you think so?"

"It's very well done," I said. "Who is he?"

"Patient. Very bad iritis, which we got straightened out. Never saw anyone so grateful. The man's famous around here for his wood carving."

"It's very skillful." I handed the carving back to him.

"I'll put that on the mantel," Liam said. "Look very nice there. You've seen it, Janet?"

"Yes. He showed it to me in the office."

"What a nice thing to do." He set the model on the table in front of him and smiled at it as he went on eating. "It seems to me the less people have, the nicer they are. It isn't as if we didn't get paid very well as it is."

The vaporous melancholy and abstraction that drifted across his thoughts increasingly as he drank seemed to have been swept away, and the phosphorescent gaiety that flickered through it from time to time, like flashes of distant summer lightning through a mist, prevailed more and more. He seemed sometimes on the point of laughing aloud. We finished the meal talking about folk music, about the charm of New Orleans, about the pleasures of bass fishing from a skiff in the bayou. Liam did, rather. I said very little, put increasingly and—for that evening, at least—irredeemably ill at ease by his confounding volatility and by the conspicuousness of his relationship with Janet. I didn't quite understand the nature of it but whatever it was, it depressed me, and I felt very much an intruder. I remember that when we had finished dinner and sat drinking coffee in the parlor, he told with great enthusiasm the story of

Blake's altercation with an English private named Schofield who had invaded his garden at Felpham, and whom he had ordered out. When the man replied with threats and curses, Blake shoved the soldier fifty yards to the inn where he was quartered.

"I like the picture that conjures up," Liam said merrily. "This 'fuzzy-minded visionary' driving a hulking bully of a Royal Dragoon down the lane to the public house. He wasn't all milk and water, that man. I'll bet you anything that if he was alive today, he'd have fought in Spain, along with Hemingway and Orwell and the rest of them."

"I don't think it would be hard to find men ready to go to war anytime, about anything," Janet said. "But it's no reason to rejoice."

"Oh, I think it is, in this case," Liam said. "I find it very encouraging."

I found myself resenting the woman, almost irrationally. I was justified, to some extent, by the fact that she had interrupted my discussion of the study with Liam, and had apparently postponed, for that evening at least, his definite commitment to it. But apart from that, I felt the weight of her somehow forbidding intelligence and forthrightness of manner, her oppressive and judicial silences, the air of prerogative with which she criticized and counseled him, and that suggested either impertinence or a licensed and disconcerting intimacy.

"If you're going to treat this girl in the morning," I said, "perhaps it would be better for me to take a cab over to the hospital. Is there a cab service in the town?"

"Oh, I'll be free by lunchtime," Liam said. "You'll have her in by then, won't you, Janet?"

"I hope so," Janet said. "I'll go over first thing in the morning."

"Yes, I'll have seen her by that time. I'll go along and introduce you to Horgan."

"All right, if it's no inconvenience. I think it's important for you to join in our discussion."

"Yes, there'll be no problem at all. Maybe you'd like to come up to the office in the morning and have a look around. Like you to have a look at Lucy, too, if you've got the time. Shall I come over and pick you up?"

"That would be fine," I said. "I'd like to see your setup here."

"Good. Then we'll go over to the Institute together."

"Well, you'd better get to bed now," Janet said. "You were up till two o'clock this morning."

She insisted on driving me home, over all of his protests. He walked with us down the front path to her car. It was a soft, still summer night with patches of black and silver cloud curdling in the moonlight above the trees. He stood looking up at it while we climbed into Janet's ramshackle roadster, his face plated with a mercurial glow.

"It was a very pleasant evening," I said. "Thanks, Liam."

"Yes, it was. It's good to have you here. I'll see you in the morning."

When we drove away he was still standing there, his hands in his hip pockets, his elbows jutting out, looking raggedly incandescent, like a floodlit Pierrot on an empty stage.

Janet drove without speaking, in what seemed to be a determined and melancholy silence. After several minutes she said, "I have the impression that he has confidence in you. I hope you can make him take it a little easier. He's killing himself, that man."

"I thought he seemed quite well."

"You haven't known him very long. He never stops. He hasn't had a vacation in three years. Ever since the war in Spain, he won't go anywhere, except down to the coast once in a while for a weekend." She turned her head to look at me. "You didn't think he seemed ill at all?"

"No. Do you think he is?"

"I suppose he'll be up to his ears in this study you're going to do."

"Well, we've counted on his cooperation. But I don't think it will add too much to his usual duties."

She did not speak again until she had pulled the car in to the curb in front of my house.

"Thanks for the lift," I said. "I suppose I'll see you in the morning."

"Yes. Good night, Dr. Ransome."

"Good night."

The house was full of the damp heat of a shower room. I went upstairs to the study, switched on the light, sat down at the desk, and opened my notebook to the paragraph of analysis I had written about Liam earlier in the afternoon. After several minutes of thought, I added these lines:

His opposition to the study is now quite clear, although we seem to get along well personally. On what I think was sound judgment, I virtually promised him to treat a certain number of cases. I think the best plan is to offer to treat all positive reactors not actually included in the study group, and to limit the untreated patients to a reasonable proportion of these, so there will be some demonstrable immediate benefit to the community. I don't think we will have his cooperation otherwise. The man can be persuaded, however; there is a softness about him that will yield to determined argument. He is harried, works too hard, drinks too much, and appears to have demoralizing personal problems. He seems only to be demanding reassurance as to the reason, necessity, and value of the project. Which I have no doubt I can supply him with; after all, he is a scientist.

Janet Thurmond may be a very real problem. She has great influence with him, and seems to share his doubts about the study, without his pliability. Seems also to have an inordinate sense of her own virtue. Women of this kind I find abhorrent. There are more and more of them in our profession.

After seeing Horgan and Kidd tomorrow, I will write to Dr. Turner with definite proposals along these lines, and ask for authority to proceed.

I closed the notebook and went into the bedroom and undressed. There was no closet in the room, but an ancient Victorian wardrobe, whose creaky, swollen doors would not close tightly. I hung my clothes in it and went into the bathroom to brush my teeth. While I did so, I watched a horde of small black ants dissecting the body of a cricket that lay belly-up on the linoleum behind the toilet stool. I replaced my toothbrush in the water glass, plucked up the cricket and its scavengers in a wad of toilet paper, and flushed them down the toilet. I washed my hands, went back into the bedroom, switched off the light, and lay for half an hour on the damp and lumpy mattress without being able to sleep. I switched on the bedside lamp, went down the hall to my improvised office, and brought back a textbook from the shelf beside my desk. I lay down again on the bed and, opening the book at random, began to read:

gummatous inflammation in bones may cause necrosis and liquefaction, thereby forming irregular necrotic cysts, filled with a grayish gelatinous fluid or a caseous material. The bony tissue about the necrotic foci in many cases becomes very dense, due to proliferation of osteoblasts and gradual deposition of calcium. This dense periphery may be considered as corresponding to the connective tissue capsule of a gumma of the skin. On relatively flat surfaces the eroded areas appear in outline not unlike those of serpiginous lesions of the skin.

Something disturbed me. I lowered the book to my chest and stared at the ceiling. After several moments I set the book on the table, got out of bed, and went back down the hall to the office. I switched on the light and leafed through the telephone directory until I had found Janet's name and telephone number. I dialed the number and stood on the damp, worn carpet in my bare feet, listening to the repeated hoarse purr at her end of the line. When it had rung five times, I replaced the receiver, switched off the light, and went back to the bedroom. I sat on the edge of the bed to brush off the soles of my feet with my palm, then took up the book, lay down again, and resumed reading:

Commonly the affected bone shows a combination of sclerosing and gummatous lesions and of periosteal, endosteal, and medullary injury. The skull, if attacked in this way, characteristically presents one or more irregular tumors depressed in the center with a hard, roughened, bony periphery. If superficial, an osseous gumma may break through the skin, forming an ugly sore with a discharging sinus. Besides the tibia, clavicle, and skull, other bones may be affected by gummatous changes: the hard palate may become perforated, most of the bony septum of the nose may be destroyed and cause a "saddle-nose," or one or more of the phalanges of the fingers may have spindle-shaped enlargement. Syphilitic spondylitis, although rare, undoubtedly . . .

I was awake at dawn, staring at the swollen plaster of the ceiling, the gaunt, arthritic tallboy, the armoire with its cracked and mottled mirror, all doubly decrepit in the sallow light that slunk into the room and enfolded them like an incubus. I arose from the damp, hot bed whose gray sheets carried the curious coarse granulations of the mattress embossed upon them like the surface of the moon, then went into the bathroom and shaved myself, peering into my own eyes from the depths of the scrofulous mirror like a man peering at his warden through the cobwebbed transom of a dungeon door. I showered, standing on the scarred, tea-colored porcelain of the iron tub and noticing with distaste how the dough-white roll of flesh about my hips jiggled while I soaped my body. I went back into the bedroom, put on a fresh shirt from the drawer of the tallboy, and then my dress uniform. Looking into the wardrobe mirror, I saw that it was badly wrinkled from my train ride in the heat. I went down to the kitchen, and after much searching through closets and cabinets, discovered an old flatiron on a shelf underneath the sink. I lit the oven, set the iron on the metal rack inside, took off the uniform, and, dressed only in my underwear, boiled a pair of eggs and toasted a slice of bread. I found that Janet had provided me also with a pound of coffee and a jar of excellent Scottish marmalade. Accustomed to Molly's extravagant breakfasts, I was gratified by this bounty. The woman is intelligent, I thought, munching my second slice of toast while I watched a mockingbird breakfasting in the mulberry tree outside the window. She thinks of things, she does everything well, with great attention to detail. She is probably an excellent lab technician. A woman like that would be a great aid and comfort to a man in almost any circumstances, any relationship. She is just plain enough, and just indifferent enough to her own physical appearance, to be unquestionably reliable. Women without vanity are intractable; they make undeviating disciples and dangerous adversaries.

I felt a flush of consternation sweep over me at having permitted my thoughts to be diverted so strenuously and unproductively by Janet Thurmond; I had far better be thinking of Drs. Horgan and Kidd. I cleared the kitchen table, switched off the oven, removed the flatiron with a pot holder, and, laying my uniform on the oilcloth cover, sprinkled it with my fingertips from a pan of water and pressed it, inexpertly and apprehensively, but to some effect; when I put it back on and regarded myself again in the mirror, it seemed measurably improved. The cap did not fit well, however; it never had. In my haste to behold myself in the regalia of the Corps, I had been virtually cozened into the purchase of it by a cunning outfitter in Baltimore who enjoyed the city's only franchise for furnishing our uniforms. I detested the insidious insight of the man. Standing at the bathroom mirror, I lined the sweatband with successive strips of toilet paper until the shiny, patent-leather visor sat with a respectable degree of stability above my eyebrows. I was reassured to reflect that people generally were not familiar enough with the uniform of the Public Health Service to recognize the insigne of a Passed Assistant Surgeon, the lowest grade of commissioned officer in the Corps.

It was still very early. I went into the study, added several candidates to my list of correspondents, and drafted letters to two of them, the president of the Hackett County Medical Association and the District Director of Selective Service—both still unknown to me by name—and composed a brief, modestly rhetorical peroration suitable for concluding my conference with Drs. Horgan and Kidd. I reviewed my notes for the discussion, slipped them back into my briefcase, and at nine o'clock left the house. The day was clear, relentlessly blue above the umbrageous silence of the street and already suffocatingly warm. I walked under the live oaks to the clinic, the handle of my briefcase clamped damply in my fingers, my forehead constricted by the effort of memorizing my epilogue, as well as by what soon proved to be an excess of toilet paper in my cap. Beside the pharmacy which occupied the ground floor of the building there was a door with a sign above it that read: HACKETT COUNTY HEALTH DEPARTMENT. Inside, a flight of steep, worn wooden steps led up to a narrow, railed landing onto which a door with a frosted-glass pane labeled CLINIC stood open to a high-ceilinged waiting room with a row of wooden benches around its walls. Above the benches there were hung several of Liam's paintings, mounted in cheap drugstore frames and fitted with mattes cut somewhat unsteadily out of children's construction paper. On a low central table there was a stack of tattered *National Geographic* magazines. A huge floor fan droned in one corner, its wire cage oscillating shudderingly. At one end of the room there was a door with a glass-paned transom above it that was tilted open, its hanging latch cord swinging idly in the breeze from the fan. Through the open transom I could hear the distant murmur of Liam's voice.

"Anyone in?" I called.

"Oh, Carl. Be right with you."

I picked up a magazine and leafed through it until the door opened and Liam appeared in a white lab coat with a sheaf of papers in one hand and a cup of coffee in the other. "You got here early. Come on in; I'll show you around."

I followed beside him down a narrow hallway that connected, on the right, to his office, and on the left, to a door with a frosted-glass pane labeled LABORATORY. At the end of the hall a third door stood open to an examination room, in which I could see a floor scale and an examining table. He opened the laboratory door and ushered me inside. It was a huge old sunlit room that looked as if it had had a wall knocked out and been converted from a pair of upstairs bedrooms and that still smelled faintly of its fresh white paint. There were a pair of long, old-fashioned sash-weighted windows that reached almost from floor to ceiling, and because they stood above the tops of the live oaks in the street the sunlight slanted through them in lustrous parallelograms that lay across the floor and glowed on the zinc top of the lab table and glinted on the steel surfaces of trays and instruments. There were a pair of very good Bausch microscopes, one furnished with a dark-field stage; a high-speed centrifuge; a Wassermann bath; a bacteriologic incubator; cabinets of flasks, pipettes, chemicals, tubes, Bunsen burners, and what seemed to be every necessary for performing blood, globulin, and colloidal tests.

"You seem to be very well equipped," I said.

"We're not in bad shape at all, thanks to Mr. Rosenwald, the F.H.A., and you people. Of course, I'd like to have an EKG machine and an X-ray; we have to use Banneker's right now. We have the room for them, though, when things get better. Maybe someday. Come across the hall, I'll give you a cup of coffee."

He led me out of the lab and across the hall into his office, which was as bright and pleasant and almost as large as the lab. At one of its windows a middle-aged Negress stood looking down into the branches of the catalpa tree in the alley behind the pharmacy. On the wall beside her, facing Liam's desk, were hung a pair of parchment scrolls inscribed with epigraphs in hand-done calligraphy. One of them read:

> While there is a lower class, I am of it, While there is a criminal class, I am of it, While there is a soul in prison, I am not free.
>
> —Eugene Debs

The other, much more recently executed, by the freshness of its ink, read:

> We have reached a stage in our civilization when we must accept as a major premise that citizens should have an equal opportunity for health as an inherent right with the right of liberty and the pursuit of happiness.
>
> —Thomas Parran, Surgeon General, U.S.P.H.S.

The Negress turned from the window and smiled at me. "The ice truck is down there," she said. "John William is back at work."

"He's hard to keep in bed," Liam said.

"Indeed he is."

"Esther, this is Dr. Ransome, from the P.H.S. He's going to be in charge of the study I told you about. Carl, this is Esther Farris, our statistician, caseworker, and house mother. She's practically a one-woman maternity clinic." She chuckled, smiling broadly.

"How do you do," I said.

"I'm glad to know you, Dr. Ransome."

"You have a very nice place to work," I said to Liam.

"I do. I'm very fortunate." He raised the sheaf of papers in his hand and scanned the top one quickly. "Esther is running down some delinquent patients for us this morning. Let's see; you have Julia Berry, Nancy Partridge, and Leola Hooks on here. You say Leola has gone off to Tuscaloosa?"

"That's what I hear. I'm going to talk to her mother this morning. If she's gone up there, I'll try and get her address. Get her to go to the Creary Street Clinic. Dr. Elbert up there gives us good cooperation."

"How much treatment has she had?" Liam said. He shuffled the sheets, frowning at them.

"She's had mapharsen, .06 $\times$ 2; and bismuth $\times$ 2."

"When is she due?"

"December 28. She needs a lot more."

"She sure does. I hope you find her, Esther."

"I think I can. She's a good girl. I think that man just talked her into going up there. I think her mother has a right good idea where she is."

"What about Julia and Nancy?"

"Julia just loses track of time. She has trouble that way. I don't know about Nancy. I think their wagon might have broke down."

"Well, good luck. If you have time this evening, I'd appreciate it if you could stop off and have a look at Georgia Mae Burrocks. She had a nasty-looking throat."

"I'll do that for sure, Dr. Proctor. You want me to set up for Lucy now?"

"Yes, please, Esther. That girl is going to need you. I think she's going to be pretty nervous."

"Yes, sir, I know that."

"I hope I'm not making you late."

"No, sir, I've got time." She crossed to the door, turning to smile at me. "I'm glad to meet you, Dr. Ransome. If there's any way I can help, you just let me know."

"Thank you," I said.

Liam turned his head to follow the sound of her footsteps down the hall. "That's the best nurse I ever had," he said. He waved at a heavy old platform rocker that sat facing his desk. "Sit down. Janet ought to be here any minute. I hope she isn't having trouble, after that spinal puncture."

"They're painful," I said.

"They're awful. I hate to give them." I sat down in the platform rocker, taking off my cap and laying it on the arm of the chair. "You want a cup of coffee?" Liam asked.

"I don't think so, thanks. I've had two already. Janet left me a pound in the cupboard."

"She doesn't overlook much," Liam said. The phone rang. He picked it up, murmuring "Sorry" to me, and then said into the receiver, "This is Dr. Proctor. Oh, hello, Walt." He sat down on the edge of the desk, his eyes roving to the window while he listened. After a moment he said, "Listen, Walt, Jerry Daniels promised me that hall six weeks ago. No, we can't do it at Sandy Landing, because they don't have any electricity there. I gave him the whole damned schedule. Well, call Billy Tennery at the Moose Lodge in Notasulga. Yes, he's been very cooperative, helped a lot. O.K., and call me back around two this afternoon, will you? I've got to go over to Banneker now. I think Jerry'll come around. It just sounds to me like he's having trouble with Billy Jean again." He laughed softly. "So long, Walt. Good luck." He hung up the phone, closed his eyes, and massaged the lids for a moment with the balls of his thumb and forefinger, then picked up his coffee cup, drained it, and set it down on the desk. There was a brief light clatter when it touched the desk top, and I saw that his hand trembled. His face was sallow. "Trouble about getting a place to show the film," he said. "It takes a hell of a lot of manipulating sometimes." He carried his coffee cup across to the filing cabinet and poured it full from a percolator that stood steaming there. "Did you sleep all right?"

"Yes."

"Good. You got a good bed there?"

"Oh, yes."

He sipped at the coffee, leaning on the file cabinet with one elbow and staring beyond me through the open window. "Odd, sleeping in a strange bed. Something terribly romantic about it. Do you know what I think is absolutely the most wonderful sensation in the world? To wake up in a strange bed, in a hotel room, in a foreign city, and look out the window at a place you've never seen before in your life. All those mysterious streets and rooftops, full of people you've never met. Adventures, possibilities. So damn glamorous. It's like being born again. I'd like to do that every morning of my life."

"Yes," I murmured, very perfunctorily.

He turned his head to me and twisted down the corners of his mouth in his wracked smile. "Of course, it's not a feeling that waking up in Tallacoochee is very apt to produce in one. I realize that."

"Oh, I look forward to being here," I said. "It's a great opportunity."

"Yes, I suppose it is. It's your first real assignment, isn't it?"

"Yes."

There was the sound of the waiting-room door closing at the end of the hall and then the multiple light tread of footsteps along the corridor toward his office.

"It sounds like we have success," Liam said. He turned to the door and stood listening until Janet appeared, peering around the frame at him and rapping on it with her knuckles. Behind her, a slender young Negress in a faded blue cotton dress stood humbly with dangling hands. In one of them she clutched a worn white beaded evening bag.

"Come in," Liam said. "Hello, Janet. Hello, Lucy. Come on in. I was hoping you'd get here."

"Lucy was busy putting up beans," Janet said. "But she agreed to come when I told her how important it was. For her baby especially." She laid her arm lightly on the small of the Negress's back and ushered her gently into the room. The girl stepped forward hesitantly, her great lustrous eyes furtively exploring the room. Her skin was black as sable and with the same silvery glimmer playing over the crests of her bare arms and her high, taut cheeks and brow. Her hair was cut short as a boy's, fitted like a tight mossy cap over her magnificent skull. The swell of her belly was barely visible: a delicate distension of the pale blue fabric of her dress, like the soft globe of a lupine. Esther Farris came into the room behind her and stood with her hand resting lightly on the girl's back.

"Lucy, this is Dr. Ransome," Liam said. "He's going to be working with us for some time." She raised her eyes to mine with the brief liquid glitter of moonlit oil.

"How do you do, Lucy," I said.

"How you do," she murmured.

"Would you like a cup of coffee?" Liam said. "We've got a potful of it here."

"No, thank you kindly," the girl said. "Miss Janet said I might have that disease. Is that right, Dr. Proctor?"

"We don't know for sure," Liam said. "But the blood tests we did indicate that it's possible. It's a very serious disease, and if you do have it, and you're not treated for it, your baby will be very sick. It might even be born dead. And that's something we don't want to happen."

She raised the purse and clutched it to her waist, lowering her head.

Her eyes drifted sorrowfully along the floor, following a seam of the painted planks.

"I don't want no more of them spine shots," she said. "My head like to bust. I don't want no more of that."

"No, we're not going to do that again," Liam said. "That was part of the test." She raised her eyes to his and stood without speaking in a kind of stately humility.

"What would happen to my baby?" she said in a moment.

"Well, all kinds of bad things. It could have bad sores everywhere. Its bones and blood vessels and heart could be damaged. And its lungs. It might even go blind. I don't say this to frighten you, but because it's true. It's a bad disease. But it can be cured, Lucy. If you're treated for it, there won't be any danger to you or your baby."

"What kind of treatment I got to have?"

"Well, quite a lot of it, and I'm not going to pretend that it's pleasant. But it's not nearly as bad as the spinal puncture, I can promise you that. We have to give you a series of shots, at least two a week, for the next six months. Maybe more, but I don't think so. We'll see, at the end of that time."

"And you don't have to worry about how you'll get here every week," Janet said. "I'll come and get you, or Mrs. Farris will, and take you home again."

"Indeed I will, honey," Esther said. "I'll be glad to. Why don't you come on back now and I'll get you ready for Dr. Proctor?"

The girl stood, plucking at the white beads of her purse. Liam put out his hand and touched her on the shoulder.

"We want to make sure you don't get sick, Lucy," he said. "We want you to have a fine, healthy baby." She looked at him for a moment and then turned and went toward the door. Esther put her arm around her shoulders and led her out into the hall. When she had gone, Liam raised his eyebrows at us and nodded happily.

"You two have a cup of coffee," he said. "I won't be long. You're a good girl, Janet." As he went through the door he reached out to touch her hand quickly. Janet went to the file cabinet, opened the top drawer, and took out a white china mug.

"Will you have a cup?" she asked.

"No, thank you. I've had my quota this morning. I want to thank you for leaving it."

"You're welcome."

"I hope you kept a list of all those things. I want to repay you."

"I'd appreciate it. I hate to say that, but you know we're always strapped for money here." She poured out the coffee, sipped at it, then set the cup on top of the cabinet, opened the second drawer, and riffled through the index

tabs, plucking out forms until she had three of them clenched against her ribs
with her elbow.

"How is the dog this morning?" I asked.

"Much better. Liam said she had a good night. He took her over to Mimosa
Springs, at dawn practically, to have the vet look at her." She closed the drawer
and turned to look at me. "I have to do some cell counts in the lab. Would
you like to come in?"

"All right. If I won't be in the way."

"No."

We went out of the office and across the hall into the laboratory, Janet
carrying her coffee cup and lab reports, I my cap and briefcase. She set her
cup and papers on the lab bench and slipped on a white work frock from a coat
hanger that stood beside the door. On the bench beside the microscope there
was a rack that held three test tubes of spinal fluid, each labeled with the name
of its donor, and a steel tray holding pipettes, tongs, and bottles. Janet washed
her hands at the sink, nodding at the rack.

"Those are pregnant women. Liam did them this morning." She dried her
hands with a towel from a linen cabinet and sat down on a lab stool, drawing
it in to the bench. "Sit down and be comfortable. How did you make out last
night?"

"I slept quite well."

"You didn't hear any strange noises?"

"No. What sort of noises?"

"Lots of people get squirrels in their attics this time of year. Especially in
old houses. I hope you don't."

"So do I. I don't think Molly would like that at all."

"If you do, there's a man over at Broadwater who's a genius at getting rid
of them. It's quite a job." She looked up at me seriously. "We get raccoons,
too, sometimes. They're even worse, because they're so intelligent." The remark sounded vaguely ominous. She turned back to the bench and worked for
a moment in silence. I watched her rinse a white, blood-counting pipette with
glacial acetic acid, leaving .05 cc in the bulb, then take a tube of spinal fluid
from the rack and shake it vigorously. She filled the pipette with spinal fluid
and shook it also for a moment, discarding the first three drops into the sink.
Beside the microscope there was a Levy-Hausser counting chamber; she placed
a drop from the pipette on the chamber and slid it onto the stage of the
microscope, switching the objective to low power. She studied the slide for a
moment, then switched to the high-power objective to verify her count. She
took a pen from the pocket of her lab coat and entered the cell count on the
topmost sheet of her file of lab reports.

"Three," she said. "That's all right."

It delighted me to watch her work. There was such skill, assurance, and precision in everything she did that I felt a faint prickle of admiration rippling along the backs of my hands and neck. It was a response I often had to a demonstration of great skill. When she had drawn fluid from the third tube and examined it in the counting chamber, she sat back stilly on her stool and stared at the microscope for a moment.

"Would you look at this?" she asked.

She leaned aside to make room for me above the microscope. I bent above the instrument, resting my palms on the zinc top of the table while I peered through the lens. I added carefully the visible cells in the nine large squares of the chamber. There were twenty-four of them.

"I count twenty-four," I said.

"That's what I make it." She sat motionless.

"Some of those nuclei look a little odd. I'd do a differential if I were you."

"I will."

She drew fluid from the labeled tube, dripped it into a glass-stoppered flask, and carried it to the centrifuge at the far end of the lab bench. She set the machine at high speed and when it had begun to spin softly she came back to the table and took a bottle labeled *Ammonium Sulfate, Sat. Sol.* from the tray.

"This is Corabelle Crockett we're doing," she said. "She's fourteen years old."

"And pregnant?"

"Yes."

I watched her place half a cc of the ammonium sulfate solution in a serum tube with a pipette. She laid the pipette aside and with another drew half a cc of spinal fluid from the Crockett tube. Holding the tube of ammonium sulfate inclined in one hand, she overlaid it carefully, letting the spinal fluid run very slowly down the side of the slanted glass. It was a delicate and critical operation. She watched with a look of moving intentness. A whitish ring of moderate thickness developed slowly at the zone of contact of the two fluids in the slanted vial. She set the tube at the far end of the rack and sat down, staring at it gravely, her cheeks supported by her fists, her elbows resting on the table.

"That's a marked increase in globulin," I said.

"Yes."

"Of course, it could be almost anything. A virus, tuberculosis. Tertian malaria will give you those kinds of readings very often. I understand there's a lot of it down here."

"Yes." She stood up, took a pack of cigarettes out of the pocket of her lab coat, and went across to the window. She lit the cigarette and stood looking down through the branches of the live oaks at the main street of the town. The centrifuge hummed softly, a sound like the wind in telephone wires. I had a peculiar sense of oppugnancy in the room, a bodiless animus, like foul air.

"When I told Liam I wanted to work for him," Janet said, "he tore up my application form and said, 'I don't need to read all this; I just want to ask you one question: Why is gold so valuable?' I said, 'Because it's so rare.' 'That's right,' he said. 'Don't forget it. It applies to everything.'" She drew strongly on the cigarette and let the smoke drift from between her lips out through the window.

"I suppose that's a good text for a physician," I said.

"Or an exterminator. There's something that abhors life. I'm certain of it. Liam says that's nonsense. He says disease is simply a process of transformation: life changing itself from one form to another: devouring itself, the way we devoured that lamb last night for dinner. But I think there's something that abhors life. All forms of it." She inhaled deeply on the cigarette and again the cloud of pale blue smoke was swept gently away into the morning air. "It seems to me there are only two forgivable reasons for killing anything," she said. "Hunger and passion. Do you think that's irreligious?"

I took up my cap and turned it in my hands. After a moment, I said, "The only piece of religious dogma—or dicta, or whatever it is—that ever made any sense to me at all is 'Laborare est orare.' That seems to be all the metaphysics I require."

She turned her head and smiled at me faintly. "The last thing in the world I expected to hear from you was Benedictine theology."

"Oh, is that Benedictine? I didn't realize that." She leaned her head against the window frame and looked up at a cloud in the blue of the sky. "I take it this girl means something to you?" I said.

"Yes. She's Viola's daughter."

"Oh. Where is she?"

"She lives in a shack with a man of forty, out there in the pine woods somewhere. She ran away."

"Can't she be made to come home—legally?"

"There's very little recourse to law in these parts," Janet said. "Other than natural law, of course." She crushed out her cigarette in an ashtray that had been set on the windowsill, apparently out of her practice of standing there to smoke, and came back to the lab bench, switching off the centrifuge. With the sudden silence, time seemed to be suspended in the room; the gentle pulsing whir of the machine had been the only process dividing it into units; unmeasured, it seemed not to exist. A small, seamless infinity possessed the room, and we stood in a kind of basal disposition of ourselves, Janet and I— and Liam, who in the course of that measureless moment had appeared in the door of the laboratory and now stood smiling across the room at her. They held their eyes united, timelessly, it seemed to me, with a look of gravity that I found offensive in its total disregard of privacy. It seemed to imply, in its very innocence of any such intent, an opprobrium of me that was almost humiliating. When Liam turned his eyes to me and spoke, the impression was dispelled and seemed only an embarrassing illusion.

"Carl, would you come in here a moment, please?" he said. "I'd like you to have a look at this girl."

"Yes." I stood up, setting my cap down on the stool.

"Is everything all right?" Janet said.

"Oh, yes. I just want Carl to take a look at her eyes."

I went out of the laboratory and followed him down the hall. Halfway to the examining room he paused and turned to me. "There's a very slight inflammation of the conjunctiva that I didn't see at all the last time she was here," he said. He frowned, his eyes dropping to the buttons of my tunic. "I think it's a very slight nitritoid reaction, because she has a mild dyspnea as well. But I haven't seen a syphilitic conjunctivitis for quite a while. You've been at Johns Hopkins all year; I thought you might be more familiar with it."

"Have you given her epinephrine?" I said.

"Yes. And it seems to be subsiding, but there's still some redness." He raised his hand and started to brush back his hair, then suspended the gesture and lowered his hand to midair, staring for a moment at his fingers, which trembled very slightly. "I want to give her bismuth, too; but I was wondering—"

"I shouldn't think there'd be any problem," I said. "Not if it's subsiding." He closed his eyes and raised his brows as if dispelling a tinge of nausea. I saw that his face was quite pale. "Are you all right, Liam?"

"I'm feeling a little woozy, as a matter of fact. Don't know what it is." He raised his eyes to mine and smiled shyly. "Maybe a drop too much of the julep last night."

"Would you like me to give her the bismuth?"

"Oh. Would you mind? I'd hate to get into a vein or something."

"Not at all. Maybe you'd better sit down for a minute."

"No, no. Let's see what she looks like." He took my arm and led me into the examining room. The black girl was lying on the table in a hospital gown, staring at the ceiling with her great liquid eyes. Esther Farris stood beside her, holding the girl's right wrist and studying the watch on her own raised arm.

"Well, how are you feeling now?" Liam said.

"I'm fine, Doctor," the girl said in her dusky voice.

"Why, sure she is. She's just as right as rain," Esther said. She laid the girl's arm on the table and patted it.

"Dr. Ransome is going to have a look at your eyes," Liam said. "It's just possible you have a slight infection there, and I'd like him to check it." She said nothing, watching expressionlessly as I took the flashlight that Liam handed me and moved to stand above her at the table.

"Have you had any trouble with your vision?" I said. "Has your sight been cloudy, or have you had spots in front of your eyes?"

She shook her head silently. I bent over her, depressing the right lower lid with my fingertip, and examined the conjunctiva. It was very slightly flushed and the lid seemed a little swollen. The iris was clear and there was normal light-near accommodation of the pupil. The other eye presented virtually the same appearance.

"I'd like to have a look at your throat, Lucy. Will you open your mouth?" She stared up at me somberly. The swell of her breasts was steady and slightly accelerated under the white cotton of the gown. The sleek black column of her throat rippled as she swallowed. I tapped her jaw gently with my fingertips. When she parted her lips the bright red lining of her mouth and throat was startlingly vivid against the glistening blackness of her face, like the secret scarlet heart of a melon. Her tongue lay like a huge pistil in its center, convulsing in a gentle, throbbing spasm as I clasped her throat between my fingers and compressed it softly.

"Is that tender at all?" I asked. She shook her head, murmuring negatively. "Does your throat feel swollen, or your tongue?" She shook her head again. I released her throat and straightened up above her. "Is it difficult at all for you to breathe?"

"I was panting there a little bit, but I ain't now."

"Well, I think you're all right. Those eyes should last you another hundred years." She blinked slightly without smiling. I handed the flashlight to Liam and nodded to him. "I think you're right; just a little nitritoid reaction, but I think it's all over."

"Yes, that's what I thought; but since you were in the office, I just thought I'd have you check." He raised his arm and with the cuff of his sleeve blotted the faint dew of sweat on his forehead. He did not look well at all. He smiled at the black girl and reached out to lay his hand on her arm. "Dr. Ransome's going to give you another shot now, Lucy. Then it'll be all over for another week. Miss Thurmond will take you home."

The girl's eyes gazed at him with a steadfast, solemn recalcitrance. "I ruther you was to do it," she said.

"Well, you see, I've—I've hurt my hand," Liam murmured. He held it up, wiggling his fingers as if they ached. "And we want to be sure it's done right. Dr. Ransome's had a lot of experience at this. He's very good at it."

She stared at him silently. I waited for a moment for her to express some further objection, or approval, but she said nothing, her eyes moving to mine with a kind of sorrowful hauteur. It was a look that fell so little short of scorn that I found myself addressing Mrs. Farris rather than the girl herself.

"I think she'd better turn over on her side," I said. "Will you help her, Mrs. Farris?"

"Yes, I will. Come on, honey, you going to have to turn over, so Dr. Ransome can give you your shot. He's going to have to inject it in your buttock. That means your sitting-down place, you know?" She took the girl's shoulders gently to assist her, but the girl turned swiftly, with a single, lithe contortion of her body, lying with her back to me, the backs of her black thighs and legs hard-muscled with a defiant tension. She glittered as if carved out of anthracite. I turned to the instrument table and took up a bottle of alcohol, unscrewed the cap, and soaked a cotton swab.

"Will you raise her gown, Mrs. Farris?"

"Yes, sir." She took the hem of the gown and raised it to the girl's waist to bare her buttocks. They were hard, globed, swelling with a smooth black luster from the backs of her thighs. I reached out with my hand and clasped her naked flank. It was warm, resilient, and yet firm with a marvelous mineral suavity. With the wet swab I gently scrubbed the flesh of the upper outer quadrant. She drew a deep breath, a faint tremor running down the length of her body, her buttock quivering slightly in my palm. Mrs. Farris patted her shoulder, murmuring reassuringly, "Now you just relax, baby. It ain't going to take a minute."

I turned from the table, dropped the swab into a wastebasket, and took from the instrument tray the 2-cc syringe that lay beside a bottle of bismuth salicylate. It was a savage-looking thing, fitted with a 2½-inch, 20-gauge needle. I took up the bottle of bismuth and shook it vigorously, conscious that the girl had twisted her head to watch me with her great olive-black eyes.

"I think we'll need .13 gram," Liam said. His voice startled me.

"All right."

I aspirated the dosage into the syringe and, holding it outwards and upwards in my fingertips like a dart about to be thrown, I turned back to the table. The girl turned her face to the wall. I clasped the buttock I had cleansed and, drawing it down firmly with my hand, I plunged the needle deep into the muscle. She gasped; a soft, stricken sigh, and a shudder ran down her spine and through her hips. For several seconds I made traction on the plunger to be certain that a blood vessel had not been entered. She lay trembling while I slowly depressed the plunger with my forefinger; I could feel the faint, fibrillating current of the fluid entering her body. When the syringe was empty I withdrew the needle rapidly and stood above her for a moment. She lay shivering, her face turned to the wall. I set the syringe on the instrument tray.

"Now, if you'll rub that for a few minutes with an alcohol swab, Mrs. Farris," I said.

"Yes, sir."

Liam moved to the girl and laid his hand on her head. "There now, it's all over," he said. "This time tomorrow, you'll be dancing. And you won't have to worry about being sick. Mrs. Farris will help you to get dressed. Will you stop by the office and see Miss Thurmond before you go home?" The girl nodded, murmuring her assent. I went out into the hall and stood waiting for him. When he came out he nodded to a door in the hall adjacent to the examining room.

"There's a lavatory in there," he said. "I'll be in the office. Thanks, Carl."

"Not at all. I think she'll be fine." I went into the lavatory and washed my hands carefully and dried them on a paper towel, staring at my face in the mirror above the sink. There was a brilliance about my eyes that I thought remarkable, considering the night I had spent. I combed my hair and adjusted my tie.

When I entered Liam's office Janet was standing at his desk looking over his shoulder at a lab report she had evidently just set before him. He picked it up, then becoming aware that it trembled slightly in his hand, set it down again.

"Well, we'll have to get her back," he said. "Maybe I'd better go over there with Viola. It's just possible that man could get ugly."

"That's a very good reason why you shouldn't," Janet said. "I'll go over, and take Buddy with me. We'll get along just fine. Now, for God's sake, Liam, why don't you go home and lie down for an hour? You don't have to go over to Banneker today."

"Yes, I do. Horgan's expecting us," he said. He looked up to see me standing at the door. "Oh, you're here. Are you ready, Carl?"

"Yes, when you are." I raised my arm and glanced at my watch. "I told Horgan we'd be there by twelve."

"Good. We'll just make it." He stood up and came around his desk, rolling down his sleeves, to join me at the door. "We'll be back early this afternoon," he said, turning back to Janet. "I'll be with Horgan, if there's anything I need to know."

She nodded soberly.

"Thank you for letting me observe," I said to her.

"Thanks for the advice. Is that your hat?" She pointed to my cap, which hung suspended from a wooden scroll of the hatstand at the door.

"Oh. Yes. I thought I left it in your lab."

"I brought it out," she said.

I plucked it from the hatstand and set it on my head. "Thank you."

"You're welcome. Don't forget your briefcase."

"No." I bent to pick it up from where she had set it beneath the hatstand.

"Please take it easy, Liam."

He nodded and went a step ahead of me along the hall, through the waiting room, and down the stairs to the street. Outside the pharmacy, the druggist, a stern-looking little man in a white apron, was scrubbing his windows with a pail of water and a long-handled squeegee. He said to Liam, "I got that sulfanilamide."

"Good. Good," Liam said.

"What the hell does that stuff do, anyway? That Marjie Dodds won't set still till she gets some."

"It cures bad breath," Liam said.

We crossed the street and got into his car. He backed out, murmuring reassuringly to the shuddering vehicle, and we drove eastward along the main street of the town.

The commercial buildings gave way to comfortable homes that stood back from the street in wide, landscaped grounds planted with ornamental stands of eucalyptus, magnolia, and scarlet oak, their soft green lawns graced occasionally by a sundial or a stone bench. At the far limits of the street a black cast-iron paling enclosed the grounds of Banneker Institute. We drove in through an open portal between a pair of red brick pillars and then between the black locust trees that lined the drive. There were six buildings, clustered loosely around Washington Hall, which housed the administration offices and was the only building of the original Institute, a three-story Victorian red brick mansion built in 1875, its four octagonal chimneys rising above the gray slate mansard roof among the crowns of the locusts and scarlet oaks that east their shadow on the soft rust-colored walls. Adjoining it was the Cardozo Memorial Hospital, which was built in 1910 in the same morose design of turn-of-the-century institutional propriety. The other buildings were very similar; they might have been post offices, foundries, or textile mills; all but the latest of them—the Crippled Children's Hospital—which had only just been completed and was constructed in a kind of standard Academic Doric. In spite of the banality of the architecture, the place had an atmosphere that was distinct and dignified; I don't know what accounted for it; perhaps the soft, antique patterns of sunlight and shadow that mottled everything, like the stains and crazings of old chinaware, or a startling and charming anomaly, like the addition of a wide screen porch, furnished with white-painted wicker rocking chairs, to a Victorian Gothic structure; or an ivy-covered gazebo settled among beds of azalea and rose of Sharon with empty music racks twinkling through its railings and a weathercock turning idly above its shingled roof. A more startling and less beguiling anomaly was that the students wandering about the campus were black, exclusively so, and possessed of a formidable equanimity and ease in the face of that fact. The varsity style of their clothing, their banter and laughter, their youthful vigor and enthusiasm all were disconcertingly ordinary. They seemed almost perversely unaware of the privilege they enjoyed, of the miraculous convolutions of destiny and fortune that had made it possible for them to stroll among those trees and academic halls with copies of Tacitus and treatises on calculus, that had set them so fortuitously inside the iron palings that separated them from the ignorant, ragged, syphilis-ridden ninety percent of their race who were to be the subjects of our study. The poise with which they assumed that distinction had a disturbing nonchalance about it—not indifference; something more luminous and sure—that made the distinction itself appear illusory, or so ephemeral that it did not deserve their recognition. It was as if they had transcended the disorder that surrounded them, out of which they had arisen, and in their magnanimity were able to dispute its reality, to disavow the difference between them and its victims, out there in the savanna, and to refute the rubric of the iron paling that divided them. In the presence of their strange tranquillity I felt bereft of something: a form, a premise, a conviction by which I verified my role as a witness of the world's phenomena. Where there is no diversity there can be no definitions, nor aberrations, nor anomalies; as where there is no substance there can be no configuration.

Liam had said to Janet that disease did not exist: it was only change, life transforming itself, as these students were being transformed in the still, strange light of this place. Did he mean by that that nothing could be described by so callow a conception as disease? That was either a vagary or casuistry of his romantic nature, or evidence that he could regard such realities as ulcers, rotten bones, and ruined organs with a serenity that was almost divine. Disease was disorder; the man knew that as well as I. He had spent his life contending with it, as these students would spend theirs. Out of what conviction? That it did not exist? It was preposterous.

I looked at his face beside me in the car, moved by my agitation to the chimerical belief that I might find it black. It was not black, however; but plated with a strange metallic pallor that in spite of its abnormality was striking, perhaps beautiful; and I saw it was the look of something that has been purified by fire: the delicate, chaste, tempered look of surgical steel or of brass annealed in flame, across whose surface a volatile, iridescent burnish plays like light on silk, like the luminous patina of a scar. He is healed, I thought. They are all healed. And I felt myself threatened or diminished, the warrant for my practice confiscated.

I had what I suppose could be called an experience of unreality. A kind of bleak hysteria swept over me like nausea, and I took hold of the handle of the door and clenched it to assure myself of my own sensibility. This discomposure accompanied me into Dr. Horgan's office, where the calm and benignity of his manner and the unsettling elegance of his accent did nothing to dispel it.

From the moment his secretary opened his office door to us and I saw him rise and come across the carpet from his desk to greet us, I felt an intense discomfort and artificiality of manner take possession of me that I had to make an embarrassingly strenuous effort to suppress.

I had given little thought to what manner it would be most productive to assume with the man; I had no faith in manner; my belief was that a scrupulously prepared brief was its own best advocate, and that administrators, almost by definition, shared the conviction. Everything I had learned about Horgan assured me that he was a man of perspicacity and a very effective administrator. No amount of animation, ingratiation, or social or forensic virtuosity could persuade such a man of the truth of a frail or faulty premise, or substitute, with him, for facts, solemnity of purpose, and, of course, institutional endorsement. With all these at my disposal, I was dismayed by the unnaturally spastic vigor of my handshake and the low, inauspicious rumble of my voice—like the sound of distant thunder—that his calm, penetrating, oddly whimsical gaze produced in me when Liam introduced us. It occurred to me that the problem with my hat might be conspicuous. I removed it quickly, and in spite of my resolutions about virtuosity, clamped it underneath my arm with an artful air of modesty, letting the gesture serve to inflect my ominously orotund profession of pleasure at meeting him and my admiration of the grounds.

"Thank you," he said with chastening amiability. "It still looks a little raw around the new building because the plantings aren't in yet. But give it another six months, and it'll be in better shape." He turned and pointed out of the window behind his desk to the new hospital that faced the administration hall across thirty yards of campus. The bare clay at the base of the building was fine-haired with a soft green haze of seedling grass. In front of the Doric porch a naked marble pedestal, five feet high, stood on a square foundation slab. "There will be a statue of Dunbar on the pedestal," he said. "It's the Dunbar Memorial Hospital. There will be, if we can find one that isn't too embarrassing. We've been holding a competition for its design, and there have been over fifty drawings submitted by black sculptors. I've been going over them all week. My God. I never before appreciated Joyce's epigram about statues. Do you remember it? He had categories for statues. One of them is this kind—" He assumed a mock-heroic attitude, holding one arm vaingloriously outstretched as if to measure the altitude of something in which he took inordinate pride. "The kind that says, 'In my time, the dung pile was this high.' "

Liam laughed for the first time I could remember: a merry ripple running through his throat like the plashing of a stream.

"It's a problem you don't have with soldiers," Horgan said. He turned from the window with a burdened air. "A man in a cocked hat with a saber seems perfectly comfortable with such sentiments. But you've no idea how forsaken a poet can look standing on a chunk of marble in a winter rain with his arm stuck out as if he were trying to hail a cab."

"It makes trustees uneasy," Liam said.

"It does. One definition of 'a pile,' of course, is a venerable and stately building, an institution. I'm finding that the chief job of an administrator is to keep it from becoming the other kind. You gentlemen may have discovered that."

"I work for the government," Liam said, raising his eyebrows innocently.

"And so does Dr. Ransome, I believe." I smiled painfully. He seemed to have a heretical disregard for the tenets of his profession. He was also very large and very black, I had had time to discover, and the quaintness of his nature further expressed itself in a Phi Beta Kappa key worn rakishly askew on what looked like a length of soiled cotton cord across the center of his vest. The only thing at all reassuring that I could find in his appearance was the fine, hairline mustache that ran along his upper lip and that was vaguely associated in my mind with venery: it reminded me of photographs of gamblers, pimps, and bogus ministers, and this thought, with its implications of delinquency, comforted me.

"Why don't you gentlemen sit down?" he said, to my great relief; it seemed to me that I had been shifting my feet and smiling for centuries. "Dr. Kidd should be here shortly. I don't think we'll get into this thing until he arrives, because I don't understand medical matters; I have to rely on his advice about them." I accepted his invitation, settling into one of the three chairs of reassuring severity that he had had drawn up in front of his desk. Liam went to the window and stood looking out.

"The hawthorns are dying," he said.

"They're very old. I think we disturbed their roots with the excavating." I saw that Horgan studied Liam's face for a moment in the subdued light that fell through the panes before he asked, lifting his intonation of the question in a curiously gentle way, "How is the health education program going?"

Liam raised his hand and wobbled it noncommittally in midair. "We could reach so many more of them if there were proper facilities." He turned briefly to the principal. "Do you know how much a generator costs?"

"About the price of an Enfield automatic rifle, I would think."

"Yes, just about."

I sensed a laconic intimacy between them, like that of the fellow veterans of a long, obscure, and arduous campaign in some unpleasant, unpronounceable colonial outpost: they had scars, and recurrent fever, and perhaps bad dreams that united them beyond the need of any dissembling, or the power of any convention to diminish. It seemed to me that there was something subtly invidious in the satisfaction they took in the relationship at the moment.

There was a tap at the door and it opened hesitantly to disclose the face of Dr. Kidd, who stood peering in as if making reconnaissance, a look that transposed swiftly, when my eyes fell on him, to an extravagant, convoluted smile. This was a very different order of man, I saw. He was tall, undernourished-looking, with something about his body and face and abnormally attenuated hands that suggested both ardor and affliction, like a pious tubercular. His responses to everything, I learned shortly, were immediate, and canny, and often categorical, as if his mind were already made up and he wanted only formal assurance on certain vital points to corroborate his judgment.

"Come in, Ben," Dr. Horgan said.

"I hope I haven't kept you waiting. I had an admissions problem. Hello, Liam." Liam nodded, turning from the window.

"Ben, this is Dr. Ransome," Horgan said. "Carl: Ben Kidd."

"How do you do." I stood up and held out my hand, which he took eagerly, peering with unnerving intentness into my eyes.

"You made it all right, then. I just got back from Washington myself. I had a conference at Howard. If I'd realized, I could have offered you a ride."

"Oh. That would have been—pleasant."

"Well, what do you think of Alabama? I hope it's not too cold for you."

"No, I can't complain about that."

His complicated smile materialized swiftly. "I hope we won't give you anything to complain about. Have you—gotten into things yet?"

"We thought we'd wait till you got here," Horgan said. "I didn't see any point in making Dr. Ransome go over things twice. Why don't you gentlemen sit down, and I'll read you the letter I got from Dr. Turner." He stretched out his hand to the desk top, where a folder of correspondence lay open.

"Yes. Good," Dr. Kidd said. He and I sat down in two of the armchairs that faced the desk. Liam remained at the window, sitting on the sill. He plucked at the knees of his trousers, his face declined. Dr. Horgan took up a letter from the folder and adjusted his glasses.

"Now, this is dated May 10," he said. "Dr. Kidd received a similar letter from Dr. Turner at about the same time."

"Yes," Kidd said. He turned to me. "Dr. Horgan and I discussed the matter by telephone. Only briefly, I'm afraid. I was on my way off to Washington." I nodded.

Horgan lifted the letter and read to us, mumbling over passages which he evidently considered irrelevant: " 'The recent syphilis control demonstration carried out in Hackett County with the financial assistance of the Julius

Rosenwald Fund revealed the presence of an unusually high rate in this county and, what is more remarkable, the fact that ninety-eight percent of this group was entirely without previous treatment. This combination, together with the expected cooperation of your hospital, offers an unparalleled opportunity for carrying on this piece of scientific research which probably cannot be duplicated anywhere else in the world. . . . The results of these studies of case records suggest the desirability of making a further study of the effect of untreated syphilis on the human economy among people now living and engaged in their daily pursuits. . . . It is expected the results of this study may have a marked bearing on the treatment, or conversely the non-necessity of treatment, of cases of latent syphilis. . . . You can readily see, therefore, that the success of this important study really hinges on your cooperation." He laid the letter on the desk, took off his glasses, and held them by the stems, looking across the desk at us with an air of mild confusion.

"Now, I'm not a medical man, as I say," he said. "So there are a few rather simpleminded questions I'd like to ask you gentlemen. Dr. Turner speaks of 'latent syphilis.' What does that mean?"

"It's a period following the secondary stage of the disease," I said. "It can extend from a few weeks to as much as thirty years or more. In this stage the disease is—'underground'—in a manner of speaking. There are no clinical symptoms, but an attack may be generating on any of the vital organs of the body, the skin, the bones, the central nervous and cardiovascular systems, including the brain and eyes; every part of the body, in fact. If these possible invasions and complications occur, the disease is said to be in its late, or tertiary, stage."

"Is it contagious in this stage?"

"No."

"But in the primary and secondary stages, I believe, it is."

"Yes. Extremely."

"Is the study to be confined to these late, or latent, stages?"

"Yes."

"Women, I believe, in whatever stage of the disease, are apt to bear congenitally infected children."

"That's true," I said.

"Will the study include women?"

"No. We want to identify and select a group of approximately four hundred males, ranging in age from twenty-five to sixty years, who have had no previous treatment whatever and who have passed well beyond any infectious stage. If it were possible to treat every identified case of syphilis, we would be delighted to do so. Unfortunately, this is economically impossible; at least at present. This being so, we can nevertheless make use of the circumstances by studying the later consequence of infection, the frequency with which it attacks specific systems, the morbidity and mortality rates, and the gravity of tertiary lesions. We know that in many cases, after the secondary stage, the disease never reappears. There is what appears to be 'spontaneous cure,' or at any rate a remission of such duration that the patient has no further inconvenience. We want to know what percentage of cases this is, and what the factors are that predispose to the development of late complications in some patients, and why others simply outlive the disease. There is another factor of great importance: present methods of treatment are very toxic; they often involve an element of risk to the patient that may be greater than that of simply allowing the infection to run its course. We want to know the morbidity and mortality rates that can be expected if it does, and balance them against those resulting from arsenic and heavy-metal therapy. There is a vast amount of knowledge to be gleaned from the study of untreated cases."

He listened, nodding occasionally with a mild frown of intelligent absorption.

"How many people do you intend to examine in all?" he asked after a moment.

"As many as is necessary to isolate a group of perhaps four hundred untreated, latent cases. And also to find a group of uninfected people who will serve as a control population: perhaps two hundred. It is important to compare the subsequent histories of these people with those of the infected ones. If we have available the health records of an equivalent group—people who lead the same kinds of lives, eat much the same food, do the same kind of work, are subjected to the same environmental influences as those suffering from syphilis —we can make an intelligent study of their relative morbidity and mortality. We can compare, for example, the incidence of such things as aortal aneurysm, arteriosclerosis, hepatitis, in the two groups."

"How many examinations would this require, approximately?"

"It's very difficult to say. Perhaps as many as three thousand. Perhaps as few as one thousand."

"And if you discover, in the course of these examinations, other cases of syphilis, cases in primary and secondary stages that don't qualify for your study group, what do you intend to do about them?"

"We'll treat as many of them as we can. As many as we have the means to treat, and for as long as we have. A full, anti-recrudescing treatment for syphilis can require as long as ninety-six weeks and cost as much as several hundred dollars. Now, obviously, we don't have the resources to treat three or four thousand people to that extent. The disease, however, can be rendered non-infectious, and often put into remission by as few as eight or ten inoculations, over as many weeks, at, of course, a far lesser cost. This isn't what anyone would consider ideal, but it comes much closer to a practical possibility. I can assure you that we'll give them the absolute maximum amount of treatment that we have the money, personnel, and facilities for." I paused and took up my briefcase from the floor. "I think you'll be glad to know that Dr. Pearson, of the State Health Department, has offered to put a very considerable amount of arsphenomine and bismuth at our disposal for this purpose. And of course the P.H.S. itself will contribute everything it possibly can."

Dr. Kidd stirred and leaned forward in his chair. "I think it would be well to point out," he said, in a modest and punctilious tone, "that without the study, most of these cases would never be located or treated at all."

"Exactly." I nodded enthusiastically, opened my briefcase, and began to pluck out sheets of data.

"How long do you intend to study these people?" Dr. Horgan asked.

"Again, that depends on economics. It would be profitable to study them right up until their deaths. That, of course, is the only way we can determine their relative mortality rates, as compared with the life span of the non-syphilitics. As a matter of fact, the most valuable information the study could possibly yield would be what was learned after their deaths. At autopsy."

"At autopsy," Dr. Horgan said. He unbuttoned his jacket and sat back in his chair, lowering his gaze to examine his shirtfront, on which he discovered, evidently with little surprise, a large violet inkblot. He leaned forward and drew toward him a metal carafe that stood on the desk, unstoppered it, laboriously excavated a crumpled handkerchief from his hip pocket, and pressed it, firmly wadded, to the mouth of the carafe. He inverted the flask, dampening the handkerchief, and then sat back in his chair and began to dabble, with a meditative look, at the inkblot. "You intend to perform autopsies on these—what is it?—six hundred people?"

"Well, we'd like to. Of course, that's looking a long way into the future. Many of these people will survive another forty or fifty years, and what the situation will be at that time, no one can predict. But much tertiary syphilis, perhaps the bulk of it, is subclinical, or at least can't be detected by physical examination of a living subject. A great deal of damage to internal organs and bones and tissue doesn't reveal itself even to X-ray. Autopsy would be the ideal resolution of the study. It's something to consider as a long-term goal. Although there are many problems connected with it."

"There's expense, for one thing," Dr. Kidd said, twisting in his chair to face me.

"Yes, it's expensive. And of course it requires a careful and constant monitoring of the subjects. One must be sure of where they are at virtually every moment, and just how—moribund—their condition is." I stirred and shifted the sheaf of papers I had taken from my briefcase. "What I mean to say is that the body must be immediately available for postmortem examination. And in a good condition. The climate here is very warm a good part of the year, and there is rapid deterioration."

Dr. Kidd nodded, murmuring his concurrence, a faraway look mildly dilating his eyes, which drifted to the open window. "Of course, some of these people won't survive anything like forty or fifty years," he said. "If you're going to include men of sixty, I suppose some of them will be passing on within a matter of months."

"That's possible," I said.

"Which means that provision for their autopsy will have to be made imminently."

"Yes, that would be desirable." I separated a sheet of data from my folder. "Now, with respect to that, I'm happy to say that we've received a commitment from the Dunedin Memorial Foundation to provide a sum of fifty dollars per postmortem procedure for every patient who dies in the course of the study. This is renewable, yearly, as a matter of course; it requires only annual approval by their board of directors. And, as far as we can anticipate, it will extend indefinitely."

"Ah, that's splendid," Dr. Kidd said, his eyes returning, reanimated, from the window. He nodded vigorously, turning to face Dr. Horgan, who seemed more deeply preoccupied than ever with his shirtfront. "Don't you agree, Dr. Horgan?"

"Yes. Yes. You've evidently impressed a great many people with the importance of this study." He leaned forward, squeezing a trickle of pale violet fluid from the handkerchief into an ashtray. "Are these people going to be told that you intend to perform autopsies on them?"

I cleared my throat, referring again to my data sheet. "The Dunedin Foundation has also agreed to provide a fund of fifty dollars for burial expenses for every person participating in the study. Now, you must remember that participation is entirely voluntary. No one will be forced, or in any way intimidated, to take part in it. And I gather, from the demographic data, that a great many of these people don't have the money to provide for their own burial expenses. In many cases they must rely on charity. And they're going to die, sometime, in any case. This fund that the foundation has put at our disposal is a kind of burial insurance for them. One that they couldn't possibly afford, privately, and that I think most of them would welcome. I'd also like to point out that we will offer them, within our means, free medical attention for the balance of their lives for any condition not relating directly to syphilis. That is to say, if they should develop some unrelated ailment—hookworm, psoriasis, some minor physical injury—they will be given treatment, medication, as much attention as we can possibly fit within our means. This is something they wouldn't otherwise enjoy, something that will remove a great many of the ordinary physical discomforts of their lives. You might say, in a sense, that they will be privileged members of their community. They'll receive many benefits unavailable to most of those people out there." I turned to nod toward the nameless, miserable blacks who teemed beyond the open window, my glance—perhaps because it traversed Liam, in his perverse isolation there —assuming a tincture of asperity that also seemed to leak into my voice. No one said anything for several moments. Then Dr. Horgan began to straighten out his handkerchief, stretching it taut between his clenched fingers, and observed gently, "Dr. Turner says that this study depends for its success on our cooperation. I wonder if you could tell us just what he expects in the way of cooperation?"

"We intend to initiate the study by assembling as many adult males as possible at one place in clinics, schools, plantations, and other selected sites, and do a preliminary Wassermann. The blood samples will then be sent for evaluation to the state laboratory in Montgomery. Dr. Pearson has agreed to this procedure. The positive cases we would then like to bring to the Cardozo Hospital here for thorough examinations consisting of a complete history, a Wassermann recheck, X-ray of the chest and of the bones when indicated, and a routine spinal puncture on as many cases as will consent to the operation. For this we will need the services of your interns and nurses; the loan of an office and examination room; and the use of your X-ray facilities and technicians. We will provide the necessary plates. In those few immediately occurring cases where an autopsy is required, we would appreciate the facilities for performing it, and if possible, the services of your pathologist. Dr. Blakemore, I believe his name is." I turned to Dr. Kidd for confirmation.

"Yes," he said. "He's an excellent man. I'm sure he'd be happy to cooperate." He turned to Dr. Horgan. "I feel it would give our interns and nurses extremely valuable experience," he said. "I spoke about it to Miss Waters only the other day, and she was anxious to include it in the training program."

"You don't feel it would add unduly to their present duties?"

"I think it could become an integral part of them. A very useful part. And it will cost us nothing. You say you'll supply the plates, Dr. Ransome?"

"Yes. As we will all drugs and incidental materials. We don't want to impose any unnecessary burden on you at all. Certainly no outright expense. For example, it may be necessary for you to engage in a certain amount of official correspondence in connection with the project. Rather than have you bear the cost of postage, we'll furnish you with a supply of official stationery, with a government letterhead and franked envelopes. In fact, it's occurred to me that some aspects of the situation could be expedited by having you made a temporary government official, Dr. Kidd, so that you would have federal authority behind your decisions and in support of any action you might take in connection with the study. I spoke to Dr. Turner about this, and he agrees with me. He thinks it would be to our advantage if you were given a nominal commission in the Public Health Service in the grade of Passed Assistant Surgeon. I'm afraid it would have to be only nominal. You'd have all of the prerogatives and authority, but unfortunately, a salary of only a dollar a year." I smiled at him ruefully.

"Will he be entitled to wear one of those handsome uniforms?" Dr. Horgan asked.

"Oh, yes, if he chooses," I said promptly, failing for the moment to appreciate the dryness of his tone.

"Oh, well, I couldn't miss out on an opportunity like that," Kidd said. He hoisted himself up in his chair with a satirical parody of pride that I thought unnecessarily extravagant; then glanced at me quickly, as if concerned that I might take offense at his jocularity. "Still, it might be advantageous, as you say." A profound gravity descended on him suddenly. "It's never a *dis*advantage to have a government imprimatur."

"We don't consider it one."

"I take it, Ben, that generally speaking you're in favor of our participation," Dr. Horgan said.

"I think so," Dr. Kidd said. His gravity deepened. "It would cost us nothing. It would be a valuable extension of our training program, for both nurses and interns. It would give us the opportunity to contribute to what I think is an undertaking of worldwide significance. One that I believe may well become a part of the literature and history of medicine. Our hospital, and the Banneker Institute, will receive a large part of the credit for this research. And most important of all, the community in general will benefit from it."

Dr. Horgan nodded, folding his handkerchief into four successive squares and pressing it down heavily with his palm on the blotter pad that lay before him. He set the ashtray on top of it and sat back in his chair, lacing his fingers together dreamily. "I suppose what one has finally to consider, as a pragmatic man, is that more people will benefit, if this study is done, than if it is not. And, presumably, no more will suffer. That seems to be a persuasive basis for a decision." He tapped his thumbtips together and fell into a moment of reverie. "We have an institution here that I believe in, that I know is a force for good, and that I've served for a good part of my life. My duty, as I see it, is to preserve its effectiveness, its dignity, and its purpose, which is to advance knowledge. From what you gentlemen say, I believe the study you contemplate will advance knowledge, in conformity with that purpose. I suppose I am obliged to offer our resources to it." He raised his eyes to Liam, who sat with folded arms on the windowsill, his face declined. "I believe you're going to help with this work, Liam?"

"Yes," Liam said. He raised his eyes briefly to meet Horgan's.

"Well, I think we can consider that we've reached an agreement," Dr. Horgan said. "I think I can promise you the cooperation that you've asked for, Dr. Ransome."

"I'm very glad to hear that," I said. "I'm very pleased indeed. And I think I can speak for the Public Health Service, and the government—which is, after all, the people—in expressing my appreciation." I cleared my throat to deliver the peroration I had prepared, to garnish the occasion. "After all, as Dr. Kidd says, history is nothing but the recitation of memorable names and events—" Dr. Kidd gave a puzzled frown at this point as if surprised to hear himself credited with the sentiment. "The history of our nation is a recitation of names like Plymouth, Concord, Valley Forge, Jefferson, and Washington. The history of medicine, one of names like Pasteur, Koch, Panama, Walter Reed, and Hunter. I have a strong belief that in the future it will include those of Kidd and Horgan and Tallacoochee. And Proctor," I added hastily, casting a wry smile in Liam's direction, intended to imply that the omission was a drolly conscious one. He smiled genially.

"That's a pretty long list," he said. "If you're pressed for space, I'll be happy to be left off it."

Dr. Horgan rose and buttoned his jacket. "Well, I've enjoyed this conference. I've learned a good deal from it. I hope we'll work together very fruitfully." He came around the desk and held out his hand to me. "I'm pleased to have met you, Dr. Ransome. I hope this community, and the world, will profit from our partnership."

"I'm sure it will." I stood up and took his hand, transferring hurriedly to my free one the sheaf of papers I had held and spilling several of them onto the floor in the process. Before I could intervene, he had stooped to pluck them up for me, pausing to let his eyes roam along the lines of the topmost and murmuring them aloud: " 'In Cooperative Clinical Group, thirty-five percent maintained serologic fastness in spite of treatment. Drop in titer of reagin in blood under treatment not so precipitous in latent as in acute phases.' Fascinating. Pity we didn't have time to hear more of this. Perhaps another day. I'd invite you gentlemen to lunch, but I know Liam has his heart set on the Bayou."

"Nothing could dissuade me," Liam said.

"Fortunately, it's a temptation that does not present itself to me. One of the very few advantages of the present social arrangements."

"You can consider yourself privileged," Liam said. They exchanged a benevolently ironic glance. Dr. Kidd offered me his eager, bony hand.

"This has been a pleasure," he said. "I look forward to working with you."

"Yes, so do I."

"I wonder if we could arrange an appointment, one day soon, and go over particulars?"

"Yes, I think we should. I'll call you on Monday."

"Good, good. Liam." He held out his hand to Liam, who shook it quickly. "Have a very pleasant afternoon, gentlemen."

"Thank you," I said, and turned back when we had reached the door to add, "And thank you once again for your cooperation."

Outside, the noonday light cast blue labyrinths of shadow on the campus grass. We strode through them to the car and I watched their arches collapse and flow over Liam's shoulders like the shambles of a vast obscurity he toiled through in a kind of long-legged, artless errantry that left his hair in perpetual disarray and his gray eyes moiled with misgivings. He paused beneath one of the shabby hawthorns whose leaves shivered like flakes of scurf in the blue air. He bent to pick up a dead thorny twig and pressed the tip of one of its black spines against his wrist.

"I didn't expect to outlive these trees," he said. He laid his hand against the trunk and turned to look eastward through the buildings of the campus. "That was woods when I was a boy. I used to hunt squirrels out there, with a slingshot. There was a stand of sassafras by a stream. I used to sit with my feet in the water and chew sassafras twigs and watch the trees for squirrels. Did you ever kill a squirrel with a slingshot?"

"No."

"I used mockernuts. It's amazing how much damage you can do with a green mockernut." He broke one of the thorns from the twig and threaded it through his shirtfront like a brooch. "Well, are you hungry?"

"I could use a bite."

We got into the car and drove in silence back toward the town for five minutes or more. He said at last, "Well, it looks as though things are working out for you. Were you satisfied with Horgan's reaction?"

"Yes, I was very pleased. He seems fully committed."

"I don't see what more you could have asked of him. Or of Kidd, either. I think you sold them both."

"I don't know that I 'sold them.' I think they saw the value of the project."

"Well, you heightened their appreciation of it, let's say. You did a good job of it. Horgan's not a man who can be proselytized against his will."

"He seems to be very sound. I think the Institute's in good hands."

"Yes, and Kidd's a damned good doctor, don't be deceived. A bit nuts-and-bolts, but it takes that to keep a hospital going. God, look at that crepe myrtle."

"Yes. It seems to me the next step is to arrange a conference with all the practicing county physicians. I think you said there were nine of them."

"The county physicians?"

"It's very important that the subjects—the patients—not receive any inadvertent treatment from anyone who doesn't know the study is in progress. It's possible that some of them could. Not very likely, perhaps, but possible. I think the local medical society should be informed fully about the nature of the study and given a list of everyone participating in it. That will assure that there isn't contamination by treatment. It might be a good thing to notify those in neighboring counties as well." When he did not reply immediately, I turned toward him. "Could you manage that?"

"Yes. Will Monday do?"

"Yes, whenever you get around to it. I'd appreciate it. Another thing: some of these men may be called up for draft physicals. That's something we need to be particularly careful about. If they're found to be positive on their draft exams, they'll be required to take treatment before induction. And we don't want any of them being inducted. Or treated. Do you know the local Selective Service officer?"

"Ted McDermott's in charge of this county. I know him pretty well."

"I'll have to get in touch with him, too." I took my notebook out of my breast pocket and wrote down his name. "Who's the president of the Hackett County Medical Association?"

"Ousby. Willard Ousby."

"Is he here in Tallacoochee?"

"Yes." I wrote down the man's name. "You know, I think I'll just have a cup of coffee and a sandwich in the office," Liam said. "I'm anxious to hear the results of those tests Janet's doing. Do you mind if I run out on you?"

"No, not at all."

"Can I drop you off at your house?"

"No, I don't really have anything there for lunch." I drew back my sleeve and looked at my watch. "What time is it? One o'clock. Maybe I'll stop off at the Bayou."

"You're kidding." He turned to grin at me. "Jimmy's chili two days running will give you the trots."

"Oh, it wasn't that bad. I'll have ham and eggs or something. I'd just as soon get it out of the way, and then I can have an unbroken afternoon; I've got a lot of letters to write."

"Whatever you say. I really should get back to the office. Suppose I give you a ring in the morning."

"Fine."

"You don't mind walking home?"

"No, I enjoy it. I make a point of walking at least a couple of miles a day."

We rattled over the bricks to the corner of Main Street under the clinic windows, and Liam nosed the car in to the curb. When we got out he spoke to me across the roof.

"Well, I'll talk to you in the morning, then. I'm going to run up and see what Janet's found out with those tests. Have a good lunch."

"Thanks."

I walked across the street to the Bayou and went in through the curtained door to the dim, high-ceilinged room with the blue checkered tablecloths. It smelled of spice and steamed shrimp. I took my jacket off and hung it on the back of a chair at the table where we had sat the day before. Millie came in through the swinging door from the kitchen with a tray, headed for a tableful of businessmen. She gave me her bright, lacquered smile.

"Hi, Doctah," she said. "Good to see you. I'll be with you in a minute."

"Fine. I'm just going to wash up."

I went across the restaurant to the washroom at the back. Inside, there was the same rank stench of urine and sodden cigarette butts. Water still hung in rust-red beads from the bloated dark paint of the overhead pipes. The window stood open and the stack of brown paper towels on the sill rustled in the breeze. I went to the urinal and stood in front of it, unbuttoning my trousers and taking my swollen penis out with a bleak, methodical flagrancy. From the tree outside the window there came a lewd, elfin giggle that blew a chilly ripple across the surface of the dark pool in my breast. The giggle dropped to a guttural, gleeful croak and then rose in a chime of scalding brilliance that rang against my nerves like witch hazel spilling on a wound. I closed my eyes and stood trembling in the fumes of the ordure in the bowl below. I felt precipitated by the eerie childish laugh into a region of spume and shuddering horses and women with smoking loins and eyes of obsidian, scavenging through starlight.

A few days after we got back from Mexico, which was just before the fall semester began, we went into the Italian Gardens one afternoon for a drink after our four o'clock classes and discovered Nils sitting there with a look of patient expectation, as if he had been awaiting us for the past six weeks. He stood up immediately and beckoned us to join him, and as there was no very good reason not to, we did. I was agonizingly uncomfortable and didn't want to stay any longer than civility demanded; but Ron, out of some perverse impulse, ordered a liter of wine—although he had a seminar that night—and settled down to delivering the little formal travelogue we had collaborated, very delicately and judiciously, in composing for that kind of situation. Nils was a political science major—I don't know if I told you that—and he'd taken a couple of courses in Latin American history, so he was interested in our impressions of the political climate of the country. Of course we didn't know anything about the political climate of the country, and I've always thought political science was something of a joke, anyway (I'm not even sure there *is* such a thing; the phrase seems to me to be a flagrant oxymoron), so I didn't have much to add to the conversation, and what with my raging impatience to be gone, I wasn't following the course of it too closely. But then Nils said something that seemed to ring out like a gunshot, and that I never forgot: that the stability of every government in history has depended on the resignation of the poor. It was one of those few statements about human affairs you hear in the course of a lifetime that have about them the ring of absolute irrefutability and that seem to reveal something sovereign about the workings of human nature that demands attention. A verity of that sort reduces me to a humbly astonished and usually oddly feverish contemplation of it; the way I used to feel when I discovered a shark's tooth in the sand at Port Federation when I was a child. I didn't know enough about history to challenge the proposition, although I found myself making an urgent, agitated review of the few facts in my possession to see if I could discover any examples to the contrary. *I* couldn't think of any, and the kind of darkling confirmation that I felt at that fact was increased when Nils went on to expound the idea that, every now and then, this abjection of a great part of the populace which is necessary to the functioning of government spills over, erupts, breaks out in a paroxysm of revolt and indignation, and then you have revolution or reform, a violent change of some sort in the political system. This was the course of things, he went on to explain, that Spengler had elucidated in *The Decline of the West,* the almost metabolical process by which society revolves through endless cycles of monarchy, autocracy, democracy, and anarchy. Somebody usually got deposed or killed in the process, he added.

He went on to remind us of the fact that this was the basic structural system that Joyce used in *Finnegans Wake* (that vast, cyclical book which begins in the middle of a sentence and ends with the beginning of that same sentence), that Goethe had used as a pattern for his work, and Giambattista Vico, before him; and that corresponded, radically and essentially, to the seasons of the earth—spring, summer, autumn, winter—in their eternal alternations. I think I've told you that he was a very good speaker, full of information and enthusiasm, and with that magical ability to make connections between apparently disparate facts or bodies of fact that integrates them, that lets us see suddenly their continuity and wholeness, the majestic configurations of things that is revealed by the power of imagination and memory. This, of course, is what art does; which is why I loved it, and do; but sometimes it can be done, in a lesser way, by logic—if logic has imagination for its handmaiden. (I don't *mind* dialectics, you know; I just suspect it as the supreme human faculty. G. K. Chesterton said once that the last thing the insane lose is their capacity to reason.) Nils's thought had both of those qualities: passion and intelligence, in very large and almost equal measures, and I suppose that's why it had the ability to provoke me to fits of seething cogitation. That or the way the freckles danced around his lips when he spoke, or the way his lips themselves seemed to brighten and glow with vitality, and his eyes almost to incandesce with the intensity of his beliefs, the kind of wounded outrage that spoke through them.

As I say, I didn't have much to add to the conversation, and I'd pretty well lost track of it by the time he got into Spengler and Giambattista Vico, because I'd fallen into a brooding fascination with the idea he had used to preface his discussion: that there has never been a period in history whose peace or apparent prosperity was based on justice or genuine equity or general content, but only on the resigned submission of the poor. It was a powerful idea, and I think the truth of it would have compelled almost the same spellbound respect in me even if it hadn't been expressed by someone as personally fascinating as Nils was. Ron didn't seem to share my fascination with it, however; in fact, he seemed offended by the idea—or perhaps by Nils's impassioned expounding of it—because he went into one of those scowling, silent spells of dudgeon that extravagant, categorical remarks usually threw him into, especially any that had a vaguely nihilistic odor about them. He started tearing his paper napkin into strips and rolling the strips up into little pellets that he piled up on the table as if he were stockpiling ammunition for a ridiculous little onslaught of some kind, God knows on what, or whom. Maybe his reaction helped to form my own—very likely, I'd say, now that I've had two years to think about it—although the idea didn't occur to me then; because right away I stopped thinking in terms of seething proletariats and wicked monarchs (or hapless plutocrats and avenging mobs) and started thinking about him and me. If it was true of nations, it was probably true of people, and of every relationship between them, beginning with the primary, connubial one: that there was no such thing as genuine equity between them; that even the semblance of tranquillity or equilibrium was based on the subjection of one and the domination of the other, whether there was consent to that condition or not. It was undignified, and dastardly. Perhaps even more dastardly if there was consent, because in that case the subjugated party was deprived even of the dignity of protest; he was demoralized into a state of soulless servitude, whether by bread or circuses or the promise of eternal life. We are bribed into conformity and slavery, I thought, even by love. Especially by love, or by the fear of losing it.

There is no such thing as peace, for living people; and there shouldn't be. One should refuse to suffer or inflict degradation in the name of peace.

Nils went on talking in that hectic, softly buffeting way of his and I listened to him the way I used to listen to a northeaster blowing outside the house on a rainy night, shifting the fences, thumping the cliffs with surf, tugging at the shingles. I could almost see Momma outside on that windy porch with a wet shawl wrapped around her head, staring out across the bay for Poppa's running lights in the dark. The whole of humanity, he said, was paired up into those wretched, bitterly conjugal groups—some of them composed of a single couple, some of them multitudinous, all of them founded on inequality: on oppression, prosecution, or overt tyranny: the governed and the governing, the criminal and the policeman, the child and the parent, the sinner and the priest, the laborer and the employer, the heretic and the saint, the beloved and the lover. They were all species of the same dilemma, and what was even more appalling than its universality was the peculiarly voluptuous relationship that existed between its antagonists. There was a dark vitality that flowed between them, bred out of their conflict, that joined them in a strange, passionate bond, almost a complicity. An agon worked through their fatal unions that bewitched them, and the fact that it would almost always be shockingly or bloodily resolved was probably a part of its allure. He provided us with some very dramatic examples of *that,* from the French Revolution to the slaughter of Agamemnon. History and literature, he said, teemed with the names of its doomed couples, yoked together in the spell of their tragic affinities: David and Absalom, Hester Prynne and Arthur Dimmesdale, Lönnrot and Red Scharlach, Jason and Medea, Caesar and Brutus, Elizabeth and Essex. Even Sadie Thompson and the Reverend Davidson.

Even Ron and me, I thought; and the idea would have been hilarious if it weren't so sad. I looked at him, converting his paper napkin into ammunition, and thought how surprised everyone would be if I ripped open my blouse and bared my breast to that ridiculous little fusillade. As if he were as conscious as I of the travesty of it, he swept the pile of paper pellets off the table with his hand and said suddenly to Nils, "You don't see anything but strife, do you, anywhere?"

Nils looked at his hands for a long time, moving his fingers slowly as if they had been bruised and hurt him; then he said, "That's what I've mostly seen. That and a rotten, nefarious peace, which is even worse, I think." It was almost like a blow, and I blinked at it.

"Even in love," Ron said. There was a kind of poisonous insistence in his voice, like a police inspector's questioning someone he suspected strongly of a felony.

Nils went on looking at his hands, moving the fingers painfully and slowly, as if he were suffering from arthritis. "I think there may be peace in the heart of love," he said. "Or an illusion of it. There's a stillness in poetry that makes me think so. It's the only place time stops." Then he managed to look up, rather furtively, above our heads, as if he wished to avoid our gaze, and his eyes fell on that vapidly preserved vista of Pompeii that decorated the wall behind us—that dowdy illustration of eternity that seemed to be all that the time and place were able to provide him with. He looked at it for a moment, his white eyelashes fluttering like faded butterflies, and said, "Do you know what the last words Victor Hugo said were? 'Je vois de la lumière noire.' 'I see the black light.' Then he died. That was his last poem."

After a little silence I said, "I've left a leg of lamb in the oven." Nils lowered his eyes to me and very gravely considered that for a moment before he nodded and said, "I understand. I'm very glad to have seen you. You look better, both of you. The trip has agreed with you."

We went home from the restaurant cold with these thoughts through a September evening magnificently impervious to them, and to a dinner very much shaped by them: the spinach was sandy, the biscuits were badly burnt, the lamb dripped ghoulishly and had a charnel smell.

"I wish we were in Zihuatanejo eating huachinango at Vermela's," Ron said.

"Maybe we'll go again, next year."

"I wonder if we will."

"We can if you want to. We did very well. We have sixty-three dollars left. We didn't overspend our resources at all."

"You don't think so?" He sawed at a charred biscuit for a moment, then put it down and looked out the apartment window at the distant, simmering broth of Washington. "Maybe we should go somewhere else next summer, like Singapore or Bora Bora. People should go to a different place every summer, so they would never find their own footprints. That boy is very fond of you."

"Oh, well; so is Dr. Beddow."

"I don't worry too much about Dr. Beddow. I know for a fact he wears a corset."

I cleared the table silently and began to wash the dishes. He took an envelope out of his pocket and began to scribble on the back of it, humming a song I had come to love in Mexico, "Jalisco."

"Aren't you going to help with these?" I said.

"I can't. I'm in the throes of creativity. What rhymes with 'gay'?"

"Flay. Slay. Dismay."

"You're a dark-minded woman."

I scrubbed the oven rack and dried it with paper towels while he wrote silently. When he had finished he came to the sink, set the envelope on the Formica shelf, and standing back with one hand on his hip, like Dr. Beddow at his lectern, he read it off grandiloquently:

> *"Dr. Beddow went out to the meadow to pray,*
> *To seek divine guidance as to where his course lay.*
> *(He suffered from irresolution, a gray,*
> *Sad inertia, like Hamlet's; a torpor—which may*
> *Have been due to constriction; I've heard people say*
> *That the foundation garments he wore in that day*
> *Were tighter than blazes, and* very outré.)
> *He vaulted the stile, and in vast disarray*
> *Spied four rustic maids, pink and plump, pitching hay.*
> *They, all in their artless and bucolic way,*
> *Had flung off their frocks, and with cries blithe and gay*
> *Were wielding their pitchforks like naiads at play.*
> *Such a wanton, provocative déshabillé!*
> *He was swept with a fervor that naught could allay*
> *Short of deeds. Brave, bright deeds! Pausing only to say,*
> *'Lord, I thank thee, devoutly, for this clear display*
> *Of thy Infinite Will. Who am I to say nay?'*
> *He ripped off his corset and cried, 'It's time to make hay!'* "*

He tapped the envelope majestically. "Well?"

"There's something the matter with the last line," I said. "It doesn't scan properly."

"Rubbish. The poem is sublime. It speaks of the relationship between God and man. It also contains a great deal of useful information about rustic customs, agricultural methods, climatic conditions, and couture. It's a mine of spiritual, meteorological, horticultural, and ethnic truths. There's been nothing like it since 'Paradise Lost.' I'm going to call it 'Paradise Briefly Reglimpsed.' Between the two works there lies only a wasteland."

"It's also profane," I said. "It reduces God to a sort of procurer."

"You know what's the matter with you? You're passé. You're a slave to convention, to outworn creeds."

"That's the first time I've heard *that* complaint," I said. "I thought my creeds were all too novel for your taste."

"Don't pride yourself. There is no new thing under heaven. And nothing older than the pride of heresy." He picked up the envelope, folded it, and tucked it into the pocket of his shirt. "I'm going to take this to my seminar. It will be more properly appreciated there."

"Well, you'd better hurry. It's a quarter of eight already. You can't keep them waiting for revelation much longer."

"My God, is it really? Where are my books?"

"On the hall table."

When he had kissed me on the forehead and gone, I went into the bedroom and dug out from under my underwear in the dresser drawer the notebook of my manuscript. I carried it back out to the kitchen and sat down at the table, and after rereading the last passage I had written in Mexico, I added this one:

That was one of the ways we preserved the fragile equilibrium between us: with whimsy, facetiousness, oblique, urbane references to our plight, merrily allusive and composed. I suppose it was preferable to floods of tears and rhetoric, but it was also more ignoble in a way, because more devious, and sadder, really. Sometimes I would stand and listen to us as if I were a third person in the room, and be aghast at the sound of our cunning, tinny badinage. It was like that chic, shiny advertisement of their misery that you hear from married couples at a suburban cocktail party, tinkling all around you in the room like the bells of a hundred happy, pie-eyed lepers.

After Gavin went out I made a pot of coffee and sat down at the kitchen table and drank the whole thing. It held four cups, and I told myself that after either that much caffeine or the amount of time required to consume it, I would have made a reliable decision of some kind; but of course what I was really doing was outwaiting Neil: making *him* decide just how much longer he would sit there drinking wine in that restaurant, waiting for me to come back. (Because I knew he would be; his eyes had told me so when we said goodbye to him.) After the fourth cup, I washed out the pot, scrubbing it very painstakingly with Brillo, and then I went and put on a cardigan and my Mexican jeans, and transferred to the pocket of them from my skirt the stone I had found in the desert in Jalisco. Then I went out of the apartment and walked along University Boulevard to the restaurant. It was windy and warm and felt as if there might be rain coming, that soft, restless rain that blows out of low, running cloud on autumn nights and brings the last smell of summer with it, of wet brown gardens and fields gone to seed and goldenrod and a kind of aching, valedictory sweetness. University Boulevard is a pretty grimy street, but it looked beautiful that night: the soft, rosy lights from the bar signs rouging the sidewalks and the people standing bent over books inside the bookstores and even the plastic pennants flapping in the wind outside the shopping plaza. I felt so free and blithe and tranquil that I could have sung, and probably would have if I hadn't thought it would be hard to account for *that,* if I ever told Gavin about this. I think I knew, already, that I never would. I don't know just when I had decided that—maybe somewhere in the course of those four cups of coffee; although I think it was long before that, really—but I was pretty firmly determined by that time that it would have to be a genuine betrayal of him. I owed him that much, at least. I could not do him the indignity of demanding his complaisance—his collusion, in fact—whether he offered it or not, in his craven anxiety to hang on to me. That might be the more peaceful arrangement, and maybe even the more civilized (and there was plenty of room for argument on that score), but it certainly didn't coincide very well with the visions of splendid manhood I had been cherishing about him. It would do him a lot more good to be in love with an old-fashioned whore than with a newfangled swinger of some kind, and he would just have to learn to take the consequences. Maybe not everybody would benefit from it, and it might not be exactly a heroic role, but anybody with Gavin's love of tradition, it seemed to me, would be a lot happier in the fellowship of Agamemnon and King Arthur than of some torturous Lawrencian explorer of the labyrinths of love. Gavin was no prophet; he was a good, kind, rather simpleminded man who had made the mistake of taking a bitch unto his bosom, and the sooner that was understood all around, and he had decided whether or not it was worth the risk, the better off everyone would be. As far as I was concerned, honest harlotry seemed far more in keeping with my nature than the role I was being forced to play in the paltry, demoralizing, makeshift peace we were becoming addicted to, like pot or Perrier water or Humphrey Bogart movies. It was becoming evident to me—a little tardily, you might well say—that the situation I was tangled up in was considerably more grotesque than those from which I had fled to it for refuge, and that maybe any I would ever flee to I would manage to gum up somehow, with that same awful, turgid ichor that seemed to start oozing out of people, like molasses, whenever I came near them. Maybe my great mistake was in believing relationships with people would ever be a refuge or a resolution of any kind for me. Maybe I was a landscape artist, and should spend the rest of my life in the middle of oceans or deserts or in abandoned houses. It seemed to me a perfectly reasonable thought: lots of people had far more passionate relationships with places than they did with people. There were great landscape painters, and they were not regarded with scorn. Nobody in his right mind thought of Turner as merely a picturesque renegade of some sort with a romantic distaste for reality or a puerile misconception of where it lay. But if you were a landscape *writer* you were considered vaguely reprehensible, or infantile, or old-fashioned— "regional" was the current term of derogation. You were not supposed to devote a lifetime to literary descriptions or studies of sky, or sand, or stone, or waterfalls, or primroses, or the quality of light across the sea at evening.

But maybe there was more reality, and more divinity, in those things than in a month of Sundays in the Italian Gardens and all the beery self-preoccupation and self-deception that passed as reality or honest colloquy, or even love.

You should remember that all the time I was thinking these thoughts I was headed for those very Italian Gardens, where I knew that gray-eyed Viking would be sitting with his bandaged heart and his hands that would ache forever from wielding the rifle butt forced into them by those purveyors of reality whose marble chambers, a couple of miles away on Capitol Hill, would stink forever with the deed. Well, this night belongs to me, I thought; and a plague on all your houses. I never liked your game, but I've done the best I could at it.

I wrote the passage very fast, in perhaps fifteen minutes, and without pausing to make a single alteration or strike out a single word. Just like Shakespeare, I thought; and even while I thought it I could hear Ben Jonson's rejoinder to that fulsome praise start ringing somewhere in my mind like a cricket in a silent house. Maybe I will live to wish I had struck out a hundred, I thought. I closed the notebook and took it back into the bedroom and salted it away underneath my panties in the drawer, and then put on a cardigan and my Mexican jeans, and transferred to the pocket of them the stone I had found in the desert in Jalisco. I wrote a note for Ron saying I had gone to Susie Temple's to review the English Honors candidates, and left it on the kitchen table, clipped in the clothespin holder where we left our notes. Then I went out of the apartment and walked along the avenue to the Italian Gardens in the windy dark.

Nils was sitting there watching the door, and when he saw me come in he didn't smile. He watched me walk across the restaurant to his table with a look that was almost sorrowful in its joy. I sat down across from him and said, "Hi."

"Hi," he said. "I hoped you'd come back." Then he smiled rather shyly and picked up his glass. "I'm finishing up Ron's wine. It's not a good thing to waste wine."

"Can I have a glass of it?"

"You don't drink wine."

"I'm going to drink some tonight."

"I thought you just finished your holiday," he said. He poured some wine into an empty glass and set it in front of me.

"I've decided to go on celebrating." I raised the glass and sipped it. "This isn't very good. You make better wine than this."

"I think so, too. My grandfather would be pleased to hear you say that." He watched me drink, smiling. "What did *you* like best in Mexico?"

"The desert," I said. "And making love with a Mexican man."

"Did you do that?"

"Yes."

"Does Ron know?"

"Yes."

"Did you tell him?"

"Yes."

"Do you tell him everything you do?"

"I won't tell him about this," I said.

"Why not?"

"Because I think it would be undignified to make him submit to it. I'd rather he felt genuinely betrayed, if he found out."

"What would he do?"

"I don't know. Something—worthy—I hope. And earnest."

"I think he loves you very much."

"I think so, too."

"Do you love him?"

"I don't love anyone," I said. "No one I can name."

"Why haven't you left him?"

"Because I needed him too much. Now he needs me. It wouldn't be fair. Maybe I still need him, too; I don't know. Maybe I'm still afraid."

"Of what?" Nils said.

" 'The undiscovered country from whose bourn no traveler returns.' It 'puzzles the will, and makes us rather bear those ills we have than fly to others that we know not of.' " I sipped some more wine and set the glass down. " 'Thus conscience does make cowards of us all.' "

"But you came back," he said.

"I wasn't there very long." I put my hand in my pocket and took out the stone. "I brought you something."

"What is it?"

"A stone." I put it in his hand. He held it curiously, studying it, then pressed it against his cheek.

"It's warm," he said.

"I had it in my pocket."

He smiled at that and sat looking at me for a moment, holding the stone clutched in his hand. "I don't know anything about you at all. I don't know how old you are, or where you were born, or whether you have any brothers or sisters, or what your parents did. I don't know anything about you at all."

"Yes, you do. You know more than almost anybody. I'm not going to tell you any more." I watched him sip the wine, and when he had set down his glass I put my hand out and laid it on his wrist. He bent his head down and kissed the back of it.

"I love you," he said, his lips moving lightly and warmly on the skin of my hand. I put out my other hand and laid it on his hair and pressed his head down, crushing his lips lightly against the backs of my fingers.

"Do you have some place where we can go?" I said.

"I live with a roommate, and he's in right now, studying."

"Then we'll go up on the campus, by the culvert. There's a quince thicket there."

"That's a pretty thorny place," he said; and then raised his head and smiled at me.

We went out of the restaurant and walked up the avenue to the campus entrance, holding hands and glancing quickly at each other sometimes in the delicate, deeply pacific way of people whose delight is very new and yet as old and assured and certain as the sunrise. Oh, you can put old wine in new bottles! It is never sweeter. We went through the old brick gateway and up the paved path for a little way, before we left it and went out across the grass under the great dark oaks and sycamores and across wide, milky swaths of open lawn. Down near the avenue wall a boy was playing a guitar with a circle of listeners sitting around him on the grass, singing softly the words of "Blowin' in the Wind." You could smell pot smoke in the air and hear the wilting, tenderly intricate chords of the twelve-string guitar. We came to the arched passageway where we had met, and went through it, musty and cool and silent, and forged our way into the quince thicket that lay between it and the chapel on the hilltop. The thorns caught at our clothing and we had to stop and disengage them sometimes, murmuring while we helped each other in gentle, patient complicity. There was a place in the center of the thicket that was clear enough to lie, under a gigantic sycamore whose heights almost disappeared into the warm, cloudy sky above us. We stopped there and embraced, and with our arms about each other I felt so nearly utterly restored to the true peace and rhythm of the great, dark, slowly turning world that I cried for a little, tasting my own tears, like sea foam, on his cool, fair throat.

Within a week of my arrival in Tallacoochee I had mapped out a network of examination centers in the county, arranged a schedule for performing the blood tests, and composed a circular advertising their free availability that was posted in schools, clinics, churches, the meeting halls of a black religious group called the Brotherhood of Christ, on fence posts, and in country stores. It took me the better part of an afternoon to compose, and its effectiveness, I thought, was testimony to the amount of consideration I gave to it:

Several years ago the United States Public Health Service carried out medical examinations to find out how many people who live in Hackett County were suffering from the disease called Bad Blood. It was found that a good many people had this disease, and they were given free treatment to cure them of it. The Government Doctors believe that since that time a good many more people have caught this disease, and they want to give a new set of blood tests to locate these people and give them treatment for it. The blood test will be given free, and it is important that everybody should take it, because it is very possible to have Bad Blood and not to know it. Examinations will be given at the times and places that are listed below. If you have trouble getting to one of these places, let Mrs. Farris, the County Visiting Nurse, know about it, or get in touch with the Hackett County Health Department or the Cardozo Hospital in Tallacoochee, and arrangements will be made for your transportation. Free hot lunches will be served to everyone reporting for examination.

REMEMBER, THIS OFFER IS ONLY GOOD FOR A FEW WEEKS. IF YOU FAIL TO TAKE ADVANTAGE OF IT, YOU WILL MISS YOUR CHANCE TO BE EXAMINED AND TREATED FOR BAD BLOOD.

When I showed it to Liam, he expressed his reservations by an uneasy, meditative rattle of the chips of seashell in his pocket and a long gaze out of his office window.

"I thought the study wasn't to include women or children," he said.

"It won't. But the thought occurred to me that if we limited the examinations to adult males they might think they were being lured in to take draft exams. A good many of them have been delinquent in reporting to their draft boards, McDermott tells me, and they might think this was a piece of subterfuge to get them listed for induction."

"Subterfuge."

"Yes. The last thing we want to do is create a lack of confidence in us. So I think it's better to include women, and all males over eighteen."

"You say in the circular that people found to be positive will be given treatment."

"Some of them will. All of the women, and a great many of the men. More than not, in fact. But as I've pointed out, it's impossible to treat everyone. And there's no point in discouraging anyone who is eligible for treatment from receiving it. We'd be defeating our own ends."

He laid the circular on his desk and stared at it for a moment. "You want my people to distribute this around the county?" he said.

"Yes. We need an official notice of some kind. Do you think it's worded effectively? So that they can understand it?"

"Oh, it's worded very skillfully," he said. "But I don't know about them understanding it."

"You have reservations about it?"

"I don't know, Carl. I suppose medicine is the art of the possible, as much as politics, but it doesn't add much to either of them's charm."

"Fortunately, we're not required to be charming," I said. "Charm is for courtesans. Or movie actors." I added the last category with unexpected acerbity, born of the sudden, inexplicably vivid image that floated into my mind of the photograph of Robert T. Aldington that had once decorated Molly's writing desk. "What we're interested in is knowledge," I said, more gently. "Truth."

The word seemed to startle him. He murmured it to himself, twice, like a student attempting to decline a Latin noun. Then he turned to the window and said, "Well, have them printed up and I'll give them to Mrs. Farris. Galbreath's the only printer in town, but you might get them done cheaper in Montgomery."

"He's already given me a price. It seems quite reasonable."

"All right. She'll get them posted around the county when they're ready."

"Good. Monday night, Ousby's arranged this meeting of the County Medical Association. We're meeting in one of the lecture rooms in Banneker, and Kidd's agreed to speak to them. I'd appreciate it very much if you could be there to introduce me and say a few words about your part in the study."

"What time?"

"At eight-thirty. I think it's important that they're assured of your participation."

"Yes, all right. Do you want me to drive you over?"

"It would be a help."

"I'll pick you up at eight."

I picked up the circular from his desk and slipped it into my briefcase. "Would you like a copy of this for your files?"

"No, I don't think so."

"I appreciate your help very much," I said.

"That's all right. It's my job."

He was not niggardly with it. With his assistance and advice, I organized a team of clinicians to which he contributed Mrs. Farris; Dr. Raymond, the young Negro physician who operated the county mobile unit; Janet; and a pair of nurses from his Venereal Disease Control Division. Dr. Kidd put the Cardozo clinic at our disposal and assigned to the project two of his interns, a Dr. Phillips and a young man named Geoffrey Jakes, whom I appropriated as my team assistant. He was zealous, meticulous, and with a quick intelligence and enormous self-possession of a kind that I could see immediately would be very useful and tractable. We selected sites at strategically located county schools, those with electricity and running water, at Cardiff, Appalachicoosa, Sandy Landing, and the permanent county clinic in Mimosa Springs. Examination sessions were scheduled at one or more of these sites on every weekday morning and all day on Saturday.

All these developments I reported by letter to Dr. Turner, who wrote back promptly, expressing his pleasure at the dispatch and skill with which they had been carried out. His single reservation was about expense. "It never occurred to me," he wrote, "that we would be called upon to treat a large part of the county as return for the privilege of making this study. I am anxious to keep the expenditures for treatment down to the lowest possible point, because it is the one item of expenditure in connection with the study most difficult to defend, despite our knowledge of the need therefor."

I replied:

I understand your reluctance to invest large sums of money in treatment for these people, since it is really quite beside the main purpose of the study. However, I hope you understand my conviction that it would be impossible to secure the cooperation of the Banneker Institute without making them a guarantee of at least a minimum amount of treatment for cases not included in the actual study group. As I have pointed out, this is also the position of Dr. Pearson of the State Health Department. As for Proctor, he has perhaps the strongest feelings of any of them on this point, and he has contributed so greatly by assigning personnel to us, putting his clinics and laboratories at our disposal, and by the investment of an enormous amount of his own personal time, activity, advice, and interest, that I would be very loath indeed to disappoint him in this respect. I think it would be impossible to proceed without a firm commitment to these people to give at least a minimum amount of treatment to the discovered positive patients not included in the demonstration group. I have managed to leave unspecified the exact amount of it, or the form it is to take, and I think it may be possible to satisfy their requirements by administration of a few mercury inunctions or pills and perhaps five or six injections of arsphenamine as a gesture of good faith. Dr. Pearson himself is making available a certain amount of it, as I told you, and we cannot very well let it go unused. In fact, we may find these supplies sufficient for the number of active cases we identify. It is my hope—and expectation— that we will be able to isolate our demonstration group with relatively few examinations. Everything Proctor tells me about the prevalence of the disease at the moment leads to this conclusion. Next week we begin our Wassermann campaign, and I will be able to confirm or deny the accuracy of that prediction. I think we must proceed with a cautious sense of the realities of the situation, and with a keen awareness of the attitudes of these men, however provincial or limited they seem to us.

I enjoyed my correspondence with Dr. Turner. It gave me not only the opportunity to assess the progress of the experiment, and to codify and evaluate my own feelings and methods of procedure, but it was in a real sense the only genuine conversation I was able to engage in about our work with someone who was identically oriented and disposed toward it, to express my enthusiasms and misgivings without a constantly inhibiting—sometimes strangulating—exercise of prudence or the need for tedious propitiations. I was even able to express occasionally the elation I felt about the progress of the study to someone whom I knew to share my sentiments. When I sent a copy of my circular to Dr. Turner, he wrote back to congratulate me on the text: "You evidently have a great understanding of the mental processes of these darkies, and a talent for communicating with them in the vernacular." I was moved to acknowledge his approval in his own lighthearted tone of exhilaration: "As you suggest, I find it relatively easy, already, to adopt their syntax. Let's hope I don't adopt some of their more visible characteristics as well."

Liam suggested to me that it would be profitable to augment the circular campaign with a series of public addresses to black audiences to inform them about the proposed examinations and urge them to attend. With the help of Mrs. Farris and other members of his staff, he arranged for these, and at my request, agreed to appear himself. We drove together to these meetings—five of them—in the clear, cool, often magically luminous nights of the late spring. The moon was full, and the bare, ramshackle shanties in the cotton and peanut fields were silvered by its light, silent and fragile, sometimes with a torn, diaphanous pennant of smoke clinging to a chimney, a delicate, mysterious decrepitude about them, like the glimmering flotsam of some ill-omened passage. The Negroes walked or came by horse and wagon to the meeting places along pale roads through clouds of mist that hung above the fields, singing sometimes, with rich, sable-soft voices that beat like an angelus against the dark. They came in scores and sat in ceremonial rectitude, clasping their ragged straw hats to their breasts, their faces upturned with a look of almost reverent solemnity, as if they were attending a sermon. If a child stirred or whined, it was quieted with a whisper, a light slap, or rocked in an embrace. Sometimes there was a swelling antiphonal murmur of appreciation or assent, and a nodding of dark heads, and a gentle, jubilant chorus of amens, as if they were reciting a liturgy, as if they were indeed being promised salvation.

They asked occasional, soft-spoken questions to which we replied in simple, practical, colloquial terms, designed to convey our purpose without creating confusion, anxiety, or suspicion. The disease we were combating was "bad blood"; its signs were sores on private parts, sore throat, fever, skin eruptions, falling hair, complaints general and common enough for all to have suffered from them at one time or another, whose universality I felt would guarantee large turnouts at our blood-testing sessions. Liam disapproved of this, as I had foreseen he would, from observing his manner with Lucy Suggs. He thought we should be more candid about the nature of the disease, its scientific name, its complications, and the length and complexity of treatment. I persuaded him that our basic purpose was to get these people in for blood tests, not to provide them with a medical education or a set of criteria with which to judge our methods. He submitted to my point of view, as he did eventually to most of my convictions; not bitterly or resentfully, but with a kind of troubled forbearance, as if he recognized both the subordinacy of his position and the intelligence and practicality of my methods and opinions; perhaps even, occasionally, their fervor—or something he was generously prepared to construe as fervor —because he listened to them at times with an air almost of uneasy conversion, or at least of disturbed deference, like a Christian stirred by the recital of a Moslem creed. That his judgment did not always prevail with me did not diminish the energy, industry, or loyalty that he gave to the study; he was a man who, having made a commitment, lived up to it. Whatever perished along the way in the form of protocol or nicety of scruple he seemed to accept as the inevitable loss of another shred of grace in the endless struggle to bring grace into a fallen world.

There was a week of these meetings. On Saturday morning Liam called me to say he could not attend the seminar with the medical association on Monday night.

"Something's gone wrong down at the beach," he said. "Paula called to ask me to come down for the weekend and get it straightened out. Septic tank's boiled over, or some damned thing. I'm sorry, Carl. Do you want me to ask Janet to drive you over?"

"No, that's all right. Kidd offered to do it, when we talked about the meeting. He'll be glad to."

"Oh. Well, good luck with it. I'm sorry to beg off on you."

"That's all right."

Dr. Kidd picked me up at eight o'clock on Monday night, and seemed to share my sense of anticipation about the conference. He was a man, I felt, who had only one genuine preoccupation in his existence, and that was the welfare of his hospital. He thrived on any form of activity, planning, procedure that involved and would advance it. It was a fine clear night and there were bonfires burning in the back lots behind the houses, casting the sweet, dry scent of wood smoke into the warm air.

"I'd like you to open the meeting," I said. "I think it's appropriate, since you're the local institution most involved. I think you should describe the nature and purpose of the experiment in general terms, and the role you're to play in it. Since Liam won't be there, you can speak for him, too. Give them some idea of the extent of his department's participation. Give yourself half an hour or so; and make it clear we need their help."

"Yes. Good. I'll be prepared to do that."

"Then you can introduce me, and I'll try to outline the ways we think they can contribute to the study. There's one thing I'd like to mention, in that respect, that we haven't really got straightened out yet. That's autopsy procedures."

"Autopsy procedures."

"Yes. We touched on it when I met with you and Dr. Horgan, but I don't feel it was satisfactorily resolved. You remember I mentioned that the patients would have to be very closely monitored, in case any of them became terminally ill and there was a question about securing the bodies for a post."

"Yes."

"I've been thinking about it since, and it seems to me the most satisfactory arrangement would be to have them transferred to your hospital as soon as we learned they were in critical condition, so that when they died the bodies would be immediately available. That's where the private physicians could be of great help to us: contacting us immediately when they become aware of such a case. I realize there would be some additional expense involved."

"Yes, there would. The problem is, there's no way of knowing how long these people are going to survive after they've been brought in for terminal observation. It might involve a week or more of hospitalization. That could be very costly."

"It could, of course. But the point is, yours is the only facility in the county we could use for that purpose. I suppose we could make arrangements with the local funeral homes to do our postmortems there, but the patients would have to have expired first. There'd be a great delay there. And there'd be a lot of time wasted getting consent of their families for the posts; even being advised about their deaths. It would be far from satisfactory."

"Yes. You realize it's not a decision I have the authority to make myself. I'd have to speak to Dr. Horgan about it. It's the expense that will concern him most, I'm sure. We have to depend very greatly on endowments, and that means keeping our trustees appeased about the nature of expenditures."

"I understand the problem. And it's possible that in those few cases—I don't think there'd be many of them—we could help to meet the costs. Maybe part of the funds the Dunedin people are allocating for autopsy procedures could be consigned to terminal hospitalization—I don't know. It'll have to be worked out some way. That's why I'm so glad to have your help, Ben. You see these problems and know how to address them practically and firmly. It's not a common gift."

"Well, I want to contribute any way I can. I think it's a vitally important piece of research. I'll speak to Horgan about it tomorrow. I'm sure he'll realize the significance of it."

"Good. I'll follow up with him next week. We just can't afford to lose so much valuable autopsial evidence."

"Well, let me have a word with him first. Give him time to digest the idea."

"It's a blessing to have a man like you aboard," I said. "Vision is something you can't buy."

He justified the confidence I expressed to him. The Hackett County Medical Association was made up of the county's entire body of ten privately practicing physicians, and Kidd evidently enjoyed their respect. They were dignified, informal, easygoing country gentlemen, very proud of the fact that their association was one of the oldest in the nation, with a charter dated 1879, and Kidd was intelligently aware of that fact. He was an effective speaker: brisk, brief, and articulate, with a fine sense of what was salient and what was better left unsaid. He clearly understood the diplomatic necessity of securing their cooperation and blessing, and he appealed for it with nothing of either condescension or servility in his manner, but with a sound regard for their opinion and for the conventions of their mutual profession. He stressed the fact that the State Health Department and the Hackett County Health Department were participants in the experiment, and that it thus enjoyed the sanction of health officials at the federal, state, and local levels, as well as the leadership of the Banneker Institute. It lacked only the support of their association to gain full community endorsement. They manifestly appreciated our solicitation of their help and approval, with its tacit recognition of their eminence. Kidd spoke for half an hour and then introduced me, with the promise that I would detail the specific ways in which their cooperation was needed to assure the study's success.

There were several points on which I wanted their firm understanding and consent: that any black male patient whom they discovered in the course of their practice to be suffering from syphilis was to be reported to us; that no such patient was to be given anti-syphilitic treatment by them; that they would receive from us complete lists of all subjects of the study, in both the demonstration and control groups, and that these names would be checked against those of all black male patients who came to them for care; that any included on the lists would be routinely referred to myself, Dr. Kidd, or Liam; that any found to be critically or terminally ill would be reported with especial diligence and speed, so that they could be transferred without delay to the Cardozo Hospital, where, when they expired, their bodies would be immediately available for autopsy. I explained that the details of this last provision were still being ironed out, but that they could be accepted as a modus operandi for the present. All of this, I explained, made up the protocol of a continuous study-in-nature of international significance, in which we were all partners and which would redound to the credit of all of us.

They listened with much interest and sympathy, moved by the appeal to their authority, their scientific vision, and their good will. There was nodding of heads and murmurings of approval. Following my proposal there was an open general discussion, to which they contributed lively and generous questions and suggestions. No one inquired about referral fees or compensation for the clerical and clinical services involved. I had the feeling that there was a very genuine concern among them for the welfare of their community that we had judiciously invoked. Dr. Ousby, the president, a pleasantly rumpled, white-haired man in a broad and shaggy cardigan, rose to congratulate me on the conception and design of the experiment, and on behalf of the association, pledged his support to it. Far beyond the simple accord I had hoped to promote, there was an atmosphere of fraternity and expedition in the room that was unmistakable; we were partners in high enterprise.

Dr. Kidd drove me home, and considering the success he had helped to achieve, I thought he was subdued in manner. He drove for a while in silence, watching the distant glare of bonfires behind the black trees and houses of the street.

"You made a fine address," I said to him. "The members were very much impressed. I think you made them see the significance of the study, and the importance of their cooperation."

"Well, I hope so. Of course, I don't know what major objection they could have had. The possibility of them being called on to treat any of our subjects is pretty remote." He breathed deeply the fragrant smell of wood smoke in the streaming air.

"What are the fires?" I asked.

"It's graduation. It's a custom with the young people around here. When they get out of school all hell breaks loose." A group of distant, white-robed figures fled across our headlights into the shadows of the trees. "You've been working with J. E. Moore at Johns Hopkins?"

"Yes."

"I suppose a great many of the clinic patients there were Negro people?"

"Oh, yes. The majority, by far."

"Was it your experience that syphilis manifests itself very differently in the black race than in the white?"

"I don't think there's any doubt about it," I said. "Of course, Dr. Moore has very firm convictions on that point, and out of vast experience. He's found that neurosyphilis, for example, is far more prevalent in white people than in black. And that bone and cardiovascular complications are far more prevalent in black people. We don't know why, exactly. It's one of the things this study can help to elucidate."

"It's difficult to quarrel with the theories of a man like Moore," Dr. Kidd said. "But I find that very strange."

"It is. But we've discovered stranger things than that in this profession. It's probably more difficult to accept some of them as truth than it is to discover them; and just as much our duty." His sobriety had communicated itself to me; I felt the need to make propitiation of some sort, a solemn utterance, an adjuration. "Some of our discoveries are very delicate points for people who aren't trained scientifically to accept them. I'm glad that's not the case with us. If we're not prepared to deal with the truth of our discoveries, there's no grounds for our profession. The ability to do that is what makes us a community, separate from all other communities, no matter what superficial or social distinctions we may have. I felt that very much tonight, when you were speaking to the association: that we were members of the same fraternity; one dedicated to the good of mankind as a whole. We've taken the same vows, we have the same faith. I don't know how you feel about it, but it makes me feel that our work is—blessed—in some way. That if anyone on this sorry planet has divine sanction for anything, we do. I think a lot of doctors are embarrassed by that notion, but I never have been. Maybe that's why I went into public health work in the first place."

"I understand that," he murmured, as if he himself were somewhat embarrassed.

A white-robed figure leaped suddenly into the rays of our headlights and stood prancing mockingly, the crooked fingers of one outstretched hand waggling balefully at us. It wore a death's-head mask and dragged a limp, shaggy object at the end of a rope. Dr. Kidd gave a startled snort and swung the car away into the center of the street. The figure leapt nimbly aside and swung the rope toward us, hurtling its burden into the windshield. It smashed against the glass with a sodden thump, leaving a florid blotch of flesh and fur.

"My God. What was it?" he muttered.

"A cat, I think. If you stop a minute, I'll wipe it off."

He pulled the car up to the curb and I got out and walked to the front, assuming an air of composed impatience. I plucked a handkerchief from the pocket of my trousers and leaned across the hood to scrub the windshield clean, clenching my nostrils closed against the stench; the cat had been long dead. A howl of mockery rose from the shadows of the trees beside the road, and a shower of chicken bones with shreds of glutinous flesh still clinging to them rattled on the car roof and rained against my shoulders. One of them lodged against the back of my collar; I snatched it off and flung it to the street.

"You'd better get in," Dr. Kidd said. "No telling what they'll do."

I dropped the handkerchief to the ground and got back into the car. We drove the few blocks to my house in silence. When he stopped I got out and spoke to him through the open window: "Thanks very much. I'll call Dr. Horgan tomorrow and see if I can arrange an appointment with him about the hospitalization."

"Yes. I'll have a word with him in the morning. You're starting the tests tomorrow?"

"Yes. Your people are meeting us at the county clinic at nine o'clock."

"Good luck with them."

"Thank you. Good night, Ben." I extended my hand to him through the open window. He seemed surprised by the gesture, fumbling for my hand in the darkness and taking it with perceptible diffidence.

The house was oddly cool, luminous and full of swart shadows from the moonlight that fell through the tall windows. In the lot beyond my backyard fence there was a wallowing carmine glare against the sky from a bonfire in the abandoned baseball field. It threw long shuddering shadows on the grass from the broken pickets and the tool shed and cast a tremulous, hectic glow on the bedroom walls. I stood at the window and saw black figures cavorting against the firelight, tossing what looked like sticks and boxes and shapeless, ragged chunks of offal into the capering glossy flames. Someone ran from the shadow of the tool shed and leaped the backyard fence, crashing into the top of it and falling in a clutter of splintered pickets, then rising and running on into the darkness. I went downstairs and switched on the porch light to flood the yard. There were hoots and yells of defiance from the darkness beyond its wide, wan bath of light. The porch screen was splotched with dripping scarlet gouts of paint or tomato juice or blood. I went back upstairs and pulled down the ragged blind, switched on the lamp, and lay down on the bed in my clothes. It was an hour or more before the revelry outside had subsided sufficiently for me to pick up my copy of Hinton from the bedside table and attempt to quiet my mind with its stately prose:

In its fully developed condition, a Charcot's joint is greatly disorganized: the ligaments are lengthened; the capsule is thickened in some parts and thinned out in others; and the articular surface of the cartilages is partially worn away. The onset, which may be coincident with or may begin after the ataxia, is rapid in most cases and starts with a sudden effusion in the joint that may swell within even a day. Though this swelling may disappear and then recur, in most cases the disorganization of the joint is rapid and may complete itself in three or four weeks. In a typical case the joint is greatly swollen, sometimes to more than twice its normal size, is painless, creaks and grates, and shows marked hypermobility, so that an affected knee, for example, may be superextended, superflexed, and may be moved laterally in either direction like a flail. The overlying skin is stretched, pale, and shiny; the muscles above and below the joint are usually not atrophied, though they may appear to be because of the marked enlargement of the joint itself. X-ray films show a characteristic, but not pathognomonic, disorganization of the joint caused by the pathologic changes described. Tabetic arthropathy often requires orthopedic appliances, and, in the opinion of some surgeons, occasionally amputation of the limb.

When I look at you sitting there in the light against the window, stirring so uneasily as I tell you these things—as you have every right to do!—I wonder if I would have them to relate, if they would ever have been done at all, or done, at least, in the form and spirit they were, if you had been there to share the knowledge of them with me. Sometimes I have the feeling that I committed these things almost in the search for a confidante to reveal them to—or to reveal the possibility of my committing them—as if I wished to create, with the complicity of someone willing to live in utter, ardent candor with me, a world of our own: secret, fervid, strange, in which we could exist as a consecrated cult of two, breathing its fiery, clandestine air, bound together by our occult, private faith, dwelling in a sanctuary of prodigal intimacy and consanguinity.

I say this because I was often aware of loneliness. I don't mean solitude, which I think can be an exultant state, and which I often, consciously and ecstatically, enjoyed. (That kind of solitude is very close to obscurity, an obscurity in which the self blazes like a flame with a brilliance and absolute configuration it can never achieve in the sunlight of society.) I mean loneliness;

the need to share my exultation with someone, and to increase and propagate it by the sharing; almost, indeed, to foster and nourish it in anticipation of the sharing of it, as a bird builds a nest in the dream of dwelling in it in exalted seclusion with a mate. It may be that I designed and carried out the study in that way: out of so great a longing for a fellow communicant of my faith and fervor that her existence was almost ordained by it, so passionately evoked that she seemed to have inspired the deeds and rituals that gave birth to her; as if, by creating either paradise or hell, we could conjure up a necessary Eve or Lilith to dwell in it with us, to confirm and vindicate and rejoice in it, almost to share in its invention. If we could, if such a being appeared, called forth by our desire, would then the heaven or hell we created to evoke her disappear? Do we build worlds in order to inhabit them with lovers, and then find them absurd, or obsolete, or ugly; and ourselves in exile from them, or in bewildered love with ghosts among their ruins?

That may be what happened to Molly and me and to our momentary world of rapture; I suspected it, as I think I told you once. Perhaps if a man found such an ideal companion, and could recognize her, he would be content, forever, with her perfect reality, the warmth of a hand, a caress, the faultless finitude of eyes and hair that requires no affirmation. There would be no need for desperate deeds or vows or volumes of inane creeds or incantations to summon and sustain her, or for the doomed, precarious worlds he invents for her to walk in. That's why I say that if I'd known you then, Sylvie, I might not have this tale to tell you now. Or if I'd had a sign from someone as beautiful. That's theory, of course; and perhaps a plaintive or meretricious one. But I know that there were moments of loneliness great enough to move me to uncharacteristic overtures for affection, understanding, or approval, such as my curiously humble, almost courtly appeal to Dr. Kidd on the evening he drove me home from our conference with the medical association, or to inspire the inordinate, almost voluptuous pleasure I took in my correspondence with Dr. Turner, written as if I were conversing with a kindred soul. I don't mean that it was a constant, conscious, or agonizing affliction—I don't know that loneliness of that chronic kind is ever any more than the ceaseless, stealthy gnawing of a maggot in the heart—but there were moments, in the flood of high affairs, or on the occasional peaks of triumph, in the middle of a speech to colleagues or to civic dignitaries, or pausing to record the data of a significant and gratifying clinical procedure, when I would feel for an instant the sudden minuscule prick of tiny jaws, a fleeting, mordant stab that terrified me far out of proportion to its pain, like the ominous, almost imperceptible symptom of an insidious disease. It came like a stitch between the ribs, that grim, elfin memento that makes one pause for an instant with held breath in the middle of a jest or gesture.

For the most part, I was happier, I suppose, than I had ever been before. I was engaged in the medical research that I had yearned to practice all my life, that was the culmination of all my years of study and apprenticeship. I had at my disposal the power, prestige, and facilities of a branch of the most powerful government on earth. I was exercising all of my intelligence and imagination in the investigation of the single most fascinating subject in the world; there was an opportunity to plumb a mystery—perhaps the greatest, darkest mystery—that had confounded my race from its beginning. I had been born at a moment in the history of our planet and of the universe in which some vast, inscrutable, and perhaps divine concatenation of events had made it possible for me, among the millions of men who had ever lived or would ever live, to set my mind against one of the densest shadows in the boundless fields of space, with a hope and prospect never known before of unraveling it, of separating the dark warp threads of that black fabric that had bound our eyes and hearts for centuries. I often had to repeat those facts to myself with awe —an awe that no maggot prick of desolation in the heart could diminish.

I found that I had an unexpected talent for organization, and a psychological acumen that would have been hard to predict in a man capable of being disquieted by a graduation prank. I was able to influence and guide the behavior of people—not all people, certainly, but many—who were older, more experienced, and far more sagacious than I, to a degree that I found as exhilarating as it was profitable. These were simple pleasures, and I thought myself intelligent enough to judge them for what they were: expressions of a common, healthily robust vanity, no different from that displayed in any Fourth of July oration or the satisfaction of the village butcher in disposing of a pound of stringy veal. Also, as I think I told you, I was becoming fond of my environment, of the town itself, the physical look of it, its atmosphere, and, as the study progressed, of the gravely satisfying ritual of our work, of rising at seven o'clock of a pearl-dim morning and driving out along clay roads to a school or wooden church or country store in the western reaches of the county through pine and palmetto barrens smoking with mist in the morning light.

The summer was dry and the dust of the roads enfolded our passage in boiling yellow clouds whose soft, saffron-colored powder coated the metal surfaces of the automobiles and lined our features and laid a delicate roseate rime, like an aura, on our clothes and hair. There was a Brueghel-like festivity, an air of pilgrimage about the throngs of black people making their way along the country roads to the meeting places, in twos and threes, or single, steadfastly trudging figures, or quietly jocular groups in rattling wagons whose iron tires rumbled and gritted in the clay, or astride lank mules that plodded with nodding heads between the beggarweeds and gopher holes. Our information campaigns were a great success; they came in scores and milled about the old bleached wooden buildings that we used for clinics in groups of two or three hundred, from nine o'clock in the morning until two or three in the hot, still afternoons, the dust rising, the bleak, dry scent of sun-baked foliage, like smoldering paper, drifting from the cotton fields, the pools of shadow shifting under the stands of black locust trees where they squatted whittling, or nursing babies, or crouched in stately impassivity for hours, raising a hand to brush away a gnat or wipe a rivulet of sweat from the corner of an eye, or mouthing harmonicas in their cupped and fluttering hands, the dry leaves tingling with the tinny, sobbing wail of "Steal Away" or "One More River to Cross." They stood in patient lines at our canteens, beside the coffee urns and gasoline stoves set up in the shade of the trees, waiting to be handed a paper plate of grits and fried Spam and a cup of hot yellow coffee. I was glad we fed them; the act of eating intensified the carnivallike profundity of the testing days. They addressed their food with a solemnity I had never seen before, spooning the salted grits into their mouths with a measured, ceremonial hunger, holding the smoking paper cups of coffee clasped between their palms like chalices, bending to them with the reverence of communion. I don't know where, outside of a medieval fair or feast day to glorify the memory of a patron saint, one could have seen such a congregation of wretched, ragged, devoutly animated people, gathered in humble, hopeful celebration of their salvation. When they had finished eating they shuffled forward in the lines that led to the tables where Dr. Jakes and I and Mrs. Farris stood with our syringes and swabs and numbered vials, rolling up their sleeves and baring their black arms as they approached us with the gravity of communicants offering an oblation of their blood. Whatever I might have been accused of, it could never have been of indifference to those people. I could pick out their individual faces, today, from an album; I could almost draw them: the leathery black lips compressed, pouted forward in a tense, stern grimace; the sad, brimming black eyes clenched in reptilian folds of wrinkles, focused blindly upwards in a kind of decorous fortitude as the needle was plunged into their veins. I can see them bending over the open register at the table, murmuring their names to Mrs. Farris or Janet, watching with an eager awe as the mysterious flow of written symbols recorded their names on the pages, as if they were witnessing their enrollment among the blest. I participated with them in this rite; no one could do so and not be moved by it; no one could take part in that immolation ceremony of blood and salted meal and not know its solemnity. When I saw their eyes move up to mine from that portentous inscription of their names in the register of our subjects, or close in a spasm of dulcet pain when I pierced their flesh with the glittering syringe, I understood with an absolute and numinous understanding the mortal thrall in which I held them. They worshipped my omnipotence, my wisdom; they offered their lives to me in witness

of their faith. And I accepted their lives. They believed in my goodness and
mercy; they offered their wounds to me in witness of their trust. And I accepted
their wounds. Sylvie, you should have seen the wounds they heaped like floral
offerings on the sad shrines of our clinics! Great, dripping, scarlet flowers of
corruption! Ulcers blossoming in luxurious rosettes of glistening, putrid flesh.
Sores like huge purulent chrysanthemums. Eyes swimming in the milky scum
of blasted irises. Limbs crusted with a scabrous slough of filth like gangrenous
lichen. Palates coated with gummy mucus and punctured with ragged holes
through which a stinking sinal discharge oozed. These were the bouquets they
brought, their votary offerings, the chaplets of their ruined bodies. And I
accepted them; I cherished and preserved them, like flowers pressed between
the pages of a book. I described them in my letters to Dr. Turner like a delirious
belle describing to her confidante the tribute of a swain.

> I had not dreamed there was so much untouched, virgin syphilis to be
> found in this country! It is a truly heady experience. Much of it, as we
> expected, is evidently cardiovascular—although, of course, there will
> need to be a great deal of roentgenogram and diagnostic work to
> confirm this. But there is also an astonishing amount of osseous and
> cutaneous involvement, with some manifestations unknown to me
> before. I am speaking now about late symptoms, not primary or
> secondary ones, which we are obliged to treat to some degree; these are
> cases that we can preserve in their pristine splendor and study without
> interference. Yesterday I uncovered a case of saccular aneurysm of the
> thoracic aorta which is the most dramatic in my experience. It has
> eroded up through the ribs and clavicle and erupted at the right base
> of the neck, where it is mounted on the patient's shoulder like a gourd!
> Thank God we've reached an agreement with Horgan about
> hospitalization of these terminal cases. I'm having this one transferred
> immediately to Cardozo, as I am sure the aneurysm will burst within a
> very few days. I look forward to the autopsy, and will forward the
> results to you without delay.

The work was prodigious. We sometimes examined six hundred patients
a day, moving our makeshift clinics to as many as three or four different
localities, working from dawn until four or five o'clock in the afternoon. Their
blood was taken, they were given superficial clinical examinations, and their
histories were recorded according to a brief but thorough and effective interview procedure I had designed with the help of Liam and Janet. Because the
blood samples were shipped to Montgomery for analysis, we had no way of
knowing in the field which or how many of the people examined were infected,

but there was often visible clinical evidence of syphilis that required only academic serological confirmation. When the results of the specimens began to come in from the capital, we found that perhaps a hundred and twenty out of a day's batch of six hundred were positive; this was disappointing; we had expected something much closer to thirty-five percent. All positive male cases under the age of twenty-five, and all positive female cases, were assigned for subsequent treatment. All positive males between the ages of twenty-five and sixty were placed in a special file to be recalled for a second Wassermann and an exhaustive physical examination at Cardozo, including X-ray and spinal tap. Those found to be in primary and secondary stages would be treated and excluded from the study; those in late and latent stages would be placed in our final demonstration group, which I came to refer to in my thoughts and in my correspondence with Dr. Turner as the Select. I did not use the term with Liam or the other fieldworkers, who would not have appreciated its austerity. All males between the ages of twenty-five and sixty whose tests were negative and who had no clinical evidence or history of the disease were placed in a separate file for possible inclusion in the control group. An exact statistical procedure was adopted for keeping scrupulous account of all of these categories. In this, Janet and Mrs. Farris were invaluable; they interviewed the subjects according to our pattern, making skillful and effective improvisations where they were necessary, and kept the completed questionnaires in loose-leaf notebooks which we reviewed daily. This meant that we often worked long after we had returned to Tallacoochee from the clinics, sometimes for fifteen hours a day continuously. The perseverance of the workers was formidable; they did not complain, although I often saw that at the end of such a day they were exhausted. I never was. An indefatigable energy pulsed through me constantly, like streams of lightning in my blood. My mind was so afire that I found it difficult to sleep at all. I would lie awake for hours, caught in an obsessive recitation of the day's events, reviewing in my mind the implications of cases of exceptional interest, drafting letters, framing analytical procedures, getting out of bed at last and going into the study in my bathrobe to pore for hours over our casebooks, compiling statistics, roughing out charts of data to be sent to Washington. I felt a constant fever of excitement, an insatiable desire to pursue the work. I had no thought of leisure; I had almost forgotten that I was married, or that I had a child. I was startled one morning to find a letter from Molly in the battered black metal mailbox that dangled from one of the porch posts. I opened it and read it as I walked to the clinic to arrange the working schedules for the day.

Dear Carl:
I'm writing to tell you that I have managed to sublet the

apartment. I'm lucky to have rented it so soon since things are so bad everywhere. I ran the ad in the Washington *Post* for six days and there were only five answers to it. Most of them I wouldn't have wanted to live here. They were either single men or young couples who would be liable to have parties, but this is a widow lady of about 60 yrs. of age who is very quiet and refined and I think lives on a pension. She even says she would like to keep the plants! Isn't that wonderful? I would hate to think of them all dying in some rubbish heap! She wants to move in on the 15th of July and so I agreed to date her lease from the first of August and let her have two weeks' rent free. A lot of places are giving a month's rent free now, with things so bad. So Elizabeth and I will be coming down to Tallacoochee at that time. We leave Washington on the 14th of July and will arrive in Tallacoochee on the 15th at 4:27 P.M. That is a Wednesday, is that all right? I'm sorry to be coming in on a weekday because I hate to interrupt your work, but otherwise I would have to come down the weekend before and there is so much to be done that I don't know if I could get ready in time.

Elizabeth is fine. She is sitting right here and wants me to say hello to her Daddy. She has eight teeth now and they are all nice and straight.

When I told Mrs. Rambaugh, the lady on the third floor, that I was leaving, do you know what she did? She had a little party for me and Elizabeth, and made some brownies and fruit punch. She's the lady that has the trouble with her leg, remember? The one that used to take care of Elizabeth when we went to the concerts. She has always been so considerate and is such a good, kind, Christian person that I will be very sorry to say goodbye to her. In fact I hate to leave Washington at all, it is going to be a terrible ordeal for me. I know I will feel lost down there in that strange part of the world with all those strange people, but I suppose it is a woman's duty to follow her husband and try to make a home for him, and I have never shirked my duty, I can say that much.

I hope your work is progressing favorably. It sounds as if you are kept very busy indeed. I know that what you are doing will contribute to the good of mankind and that gives me comfort. I constantly remind myself of what you have accomplished in the past two years!

If you think about it, the next time you go to the grocery store I'd appreciate it if you bought a can of a product called Grime-Go, so it ˉ will be in the house when I get there. This is a cleansing product that I use on sinks, drains, tiles, toilet bowls, etc. etc. It comes in two sizes, one a 67¢ size and one a $1.19 size. I think you better get the $1.19

size, because we can use it in an old house and it is more economical.

I will have to close now because your daughter Elizabeth seems to want her supper. She says to tell you she is very anxious to see her Daddy! I have missed you very much, although we struggle along. It is good to know that we will see you again in 13 days.

Love, from Molly

Such a sense of sadness and oppression came over me when I read this letter that I closed my eyes in a momentary surge of desolation. I did not want them to come. Their presence in that house and in that town would be an intrusion; more than an intrusion: a trespass, on ground that had become my domain, whose rhythms, ritual, codes, and shibboleths I had decreed, even in the short time I had been there, and which I felt indignant at having to defend from Molly's inevitable disapproval and very probable dismay. The letter itself was an invasion and impugnment of my world. The suggestion about the "cleansing product," it seemed to me, was an entirely gratuitous aspersion, not only on the state of my living quarters, but extending somehow, by virtue of its weary, habitual, and transparent umbrage, to my eating habits, activities, aspirations, and general spiritual condition as well. It was astonishing how she managed to express antipathy in every sentence—every phrase, word, syllable —she wrote. Even her congratulations were tainted with it; even her brief, banal reference to Elizabeth managed, in spite of its perfunctory exclamation point, to convey a further, cheerless implication of my delinquency, in this case as a father. In fact, the writing of the letter seemed to have served her primarily as an occasion for expressing a wholesale disparagement of my life and nature that assumed, in its universality, a strangely missionary quality, as if she spoke as a delegate of mankind in general, assigned to censure me for my offenses, and perhaps inspire me to penitence. It was framed, of course, in that gray tone of longanimity, as if she murmured these indictments reluctantly and from the heights of Christian charity. (Mrs. Rambaugh was such a "good, kind, Christian person"—not like *others* I could mention!) I crumpled the letter in my fist and shoved it into the pocket of my jacket with a shudder of indignation so close to fury that it startled me even while I made the gesture—perhaps because I sensed, however remotely, piously, or captiously misrepresented, some justice in her insinuations. The possibility moved me to take out the letter, smooth the crumpled sheet as best I could, fold and replace it in its envelope, and return it with a semblance of decorum to my pocket. It lay there all day, generating a vague sense of discomfort, like a mass of unpleasant, undigestible food in the duodenum.

We worked for eight hours in a tiny church in the southwest corner of the county. The paint was peeling from its clapboard walls and it had a square, truncated wooden steeple that listed dangerously, like a battered tea crate toppling from its roof. There was a small, ancient cemetery at one side of the church, its blunt, gray, tottering headstones shadowed by a grove of dusty cedars that straggled to the wall of the church itself, their roots uplifting gently askew the concrete-block pilasters on which it stood. In front of the church a metal gate sagged between a pair of crumbling brick columns, and from it a sandy path, sprinkled with acorns, led to the three worn wooden steps of the church door through the shade of a magnificent white oak whose branches flared upwards eighty feet into the sky in a vast, voluminous fountain of foliage. There was no fence surrounding the churchyard; only the lonesome gate in front of it. The building and cemetery and the grove of trees were clustered together in the center of a barren flatland pimpled with the yellow mounds of gopher holes and snarled with thistles and ragged strands of joe-pye weed, brown and bedraggled in the summer light. Far away a pine forest stood, sad and silent. Across the center of this mournful plain a clay road ran straight to the church like a plank fallen among the waist-high weeds that were limp and powdered with a brick-dust red along its edges. The road was corrugated like the surface of a washboard, and the two cars of our caravan jolted over it with a furious joggling clatter that bounced us in our seats and rattled our teeth together and buried us in turbulent hellish clouds of carmine dust. There were Negroes tramping across the open fields toward the church with cautious, dogged steps, clutching their skirts away from the thistle stems, stepping over gopher holes; others trudged in broken files along the edges of the road, standing back when we passed to shield their eyes with upraised arms. We stopped sometimes to let some of the younger and nimbler of them step up onto our running boards, where they stood swaying precariously, clutching the gutters of the roof and waving with grinning jubilation to their comrades as we drove on.

In front of the church there were already twenty or more people gathered in the great deckled globe of shadow that lay beneath the oak: children flinging acorns against the wooden walls, women patiently jouncing babies on their hips, old men sitting with canes between their legs, fanning their faces slowly with their ragged hat brims. Someone was playing a harmonica and a man was dancing to the music, a slow, stately soft-shoe, hanging stationary, his limbs joggling as if he were suspended from a set of twitching marionette strings. A circle of watchers stood clapping with a measured smacking of their palms.

We stopped in front of the church and got out, Dr. Jakes and I and Mrs. Farris and Calvin Hooks, one of Liam's black caseworkers, from the first car; Liam and Janet and a young black nurse named Gwyn Thomas from the second. Liam opened the back door and reached in to lift down the dog, Enitharmom, who now had recovered to a grotesquely ambulatory stage and followed him everywhere, one hind leg still encased in a plaster cast, hobbling behind him like a battered dinghy towed through a high sea. When he lifted her from the seat she stretched out her head to lick his face with cravenly passionate caresses of her tongue as he set her on the ground. We began to take our equipment from the automobiles, smiling and nodding to the assembled Negroes. The music stopped, they stood watching us with a shy, reverent air, some of them moving forward to offer their assistance. Two of the children came and crouched grinning in front of the dog, reaching out to stroke her sleek, toffee-colored head. There were coffee urns and kettles of soup and baskets of doughnuts to be placed on folding tables under the tree, and cartons of medical supplies to be carried into the church. The clinic was set up quickly and expertly; we had developed an effective system in our two weeks of experience. Inside, two tables were organized as lab benches, with portable sterile cabinets and a camp stove and racks of tubes and vials, each attended by a pair of clinicians and a registrar. Twin files of Negroes shuffled up to them through the open doorway of the church from the dusty heat of the morning outside where Calvin doled out cups of soup and hot coffee and doughnuts. It was hot and muggy and the dust swirled idly through the shafts of sunlight like silt in roiled water. Outside, there was a constant tidal murmur of voices, and the distant tinny sob of the harmonica. We worked in short-sleeved shirts and sleeveless dresses that grew damper every moment, clinging to our backs and breaking out in tea-colored stains of moistened dust. At my table, Mrs. Farris took down the names of subjects and made careful, involved mementos of their dwelling places, and filled out their questionnaires. I examined them briefly for skin eruptions, sore throats, heart and respiratory abnormalities, checking off the columns of symptoms on their case sheets; Dr. Jakes swabbed their arms, took the blood samples, numbered the labeled tubes to correspond with their registration, and kept the samples and equipment table in order. We worked at the steady, leisurely pace of assembly workers, almost without conversation, adjusted to the rhythms of our roles with the skill of practice. The Negroes filed into and out of our hands at a constant, orderly pace, their bared arms outheld, their great soft eyes wandering to follow the movements of our hands with a docile awe. Most of them spoke only when questioned, in gentle, taciturn murmurs; but some of the older men and women were garrulous and more bold; they chattered lengthily about their ailments: twinges that "took them bad," shingles, "summer complaints," colic, back miseries. We spoke patiently to them, nodding gravely, murmuring consolation. I had discovered that nothing reassured them so much as being dispensed an innocuous placebo of some kind, a vial of sugar pills or a bottle of aspirin. I kept a large supply of aspirin in half-grain tablets, colored a bright blue and packed in quantities of a dozen in small envelopes labeled *Salicylic Acid.* They were a great success.

Most of the Negroes had never taken aspirin before, and the almost immediate relief it gave them for a huge range of complaints, from headache to malaria chills, had made the miraculous "blue pills" famous already throughout the county. People asked for them eagerly, smiling and muttering with delight as they shuffled happily away, clutching the envelopes between their fingers. It was a good policy: effective, inexpensive, and it produced a vast, general good will for our work. The problem was that everyone wanted them; it was difficult to convince some of the applicants that the pills would do no good at all in their cases.

By noon, my back was stiff from having stood for so long. I left the table in charge of Dr. Jakes and went outside to drink a cup of coffee and lean for a few minutes against the wall of the church in the shadow of the oak. The crowd still milled around the canteen tables or had wandered out to sit among the headstones in the shade of the cedar grove. Far down the clay road I saw a mule pulling a wagon toward the church, its head nodding between the shafts, its pale gigantic ears flopping rigidly. The wheels rumbled distantly with a sound of barrels tumbling in a hold. Two men sat on the wagon seat, one with the drooping reins held loosely in his hand. On the wagon bed a man with close-cropped white hair sat in a cane-backed rocking chair holding a ragged umbrella over his head and fanning his face slowly with a palm-leaf fan. A woman in a red skirt stood behind him, holding the chair steady on the lurching wagon bed. A funnel of red dust raced ahead of them, spinning in a small whirlwind across the road and out into the meadow. High above the field a buzzard coasted in lazy circles in the Wedgwood blue of the sky.

Beside the church wall to my left four boys and a little girl sat squatting around a captured gopher, a huge, hard-shelled tortoise, turned onto its back, its leathery neck and beaked, reptilian head and black-nailed, stubby feet scrabbling at the earth, spinning in a slow circle as it tried to right itself. One boy reached out to poke at it with a stick, rapping it across the head. It disappeared instantly and entirely—head, feet, and tail—into its helmetlike carapace. The boy leaned forward to spit into the dark orifice where the head had been withdrawn; the white froth of his spittle seethed like spilled beer. The children giggled and whooped. Liam's dog lay in the yellow sand under the floor joists of the church, watching with a bemused and genial gaze, her ears limply erect, her head cocked quizzically. I reached down and gathered up a handful of brown acorns and tossed them gently, one at a time, at a headstone whose eroded inscription I could barely make out on the chipped gray stone: OUR LAMB IS GONE. I saw that an old man was watching me expressionlessly from under the brim of his sweat-stained felt hat. I dropped the acorns and dusted my hand against my trousers.

In the road, the wagon had rumbled abreast of the iron gate of the churchyard. The driver tugged lightly at the reins and the mule came to an instant halt, blowing a shuddering sigh and stamping in the road. The two men on the wagon seat stepped back over it onto the bed of the wagon and bent down to slide a pair of two-by-four poles under the seat of the chair on which the white-haired man sat stilly. With one of them at each end of the paired pole handles, they carried the chair like a litter to the back end of the wagon bed, then jumped down to the ground and reached up to lower it with rigid forearms to the clay of the road. The young woman crouched at the rear end of the wagon and held the spindles of the back to steady it as it descended. The white-haired man sat imperturbably upright, holding his umbrella, fanning himself gently. The left leg of his trousers was cut off at the thigh, and I saw that his knee was grossly swollen. When he had reached the ground the young woman jumped down from the wagon and the four of them moved in a small, stately procession through the gate and into the churchyard, the two men staggering slightly with the weight of the litter poles, the old man seated in the chair, the young woman in her red skirt and white blouse following gravely. The crowd parted to let them through. They set him down in the shade beside the bole of the oak and the young woman took his umbrella, folded it, and laid it in his lap. Then she and the litter bearers picked their way down through the crowd to the canteen tables and stood with paper cups and plates, waiting to be served.

I crumpled my cup and tossed it into a garbage pail and went across the yard to where the man sat fanning himself with the calm, judicial air of a visiting magistrate. He was fifty-five, perhaps, or sixty. Below the sheared gray poll of his hair, his forehead and face were webbed with a mesh of lines as intricate as the patterns of crazed porcelain. A pair of deep smooth furrows ran from his nostrils to the corners of his mouth, and his skin shone with the smooth hard luster of carved and polished ebony. His lips were very finely cut, with sharply crested ridges, and his eyes had the composed calm brilliance of a hawk's under the exact gray arcs of his brows. They followed my approach with a steady, disconcerting gravity. I stopped beside him, nodded, and murmured, "Good afternoon."

"Aftahnoon," he said. "You d' doctah?"

"Yes, I am. Dr. Ransome."

"I come to see could you do somethin' fo' mah laig. I got a right bad laig."

"I can see you do," I said. I moved my eyes down to his swollen knee. It was huge, the size of a Persian melon, the skin stretched tight and shining with an unnatural, almost iridescent luster, the weight of the enclosed fluid making the knee sag heavily, like a filled wineskin. "How long have you had that?"

"I reckon it fo', five weeks now. It come on right quick. I done tried the black poultice, the hog grease, ev'thin' I know. I can't do no good with it."

"Does it hurt?"

"No, it don't hurt so bad. But it sho' messed up. I cain't walk no ways. Cain't git to d' privy, cain't git out of bed."

"Do you have pain other places?"

" 'Deed I do. I got the rheumatism bad. Shoot all down mah laigs an' arms like lightnin'. But the knee don't hurt all that bad. Seem like it kindly dead."

I took the pencil flashlight out of my breast pocket. "Let me look at your eyes," I said. "Lean your head back against the chair." He did so, staring up into the sky while I illumined the pupils. They were small, unequal, and reacted sluggishly to the light. I lifted the lids with the tip of my thumb and they drooped again, with their hawklike, hooded look.

"Close your eyes," I said, "and try to touch the tip of your nose with your finger."

The movement of his hand was wavering and uncertain; he touched his right cheek, beside the nostril.

"Cain't seem to do that no ways," he said.

"Can you move back in the chair a little? Let your legs hang. That's right." I knelt in front of him and rapped his right leg, the good one, just below the patella. The reflex was very weak, repeatedly. I felt a gathering sense of excitement and confirmation, as if a rite moved through its stages toward epiphany. "I'm going to take your shoe off now," I said, "and scratch the bottom of your foot. I want you to tell me if you feel it."

"Yes, suh."

I untied the lace of his right shoe and tugged it off. As I did so, the two men and the girl moved up through the crowd and stood beside him, holding cups of soup. The man's feet were gray with calluses, thick-soled and gnarled. I ran the tip of my flashlight along the sole. "Do you feel that?" I asked.

"No, 'deed I don't," he said. I scraped his instep and then the calf of his leg. "Jest a little whispery feel," he said. "I ain't real sure."

"All right. Now I'm going to feel this knee," I said. "You let me know if I hurt you." He nodded. I pressed the great bloated sac gently with my fingertips. It gave to the pressure with a sickening liquid resilience, like a rotten cantaloupe. "Does that hurt?"

"No, it don't. Jest feel kindly soft."

I pressed more firmly, trying to locate the patella. When I touched it, it slipped away with an oily suavity, as if floating in a bag of slime.

"Can you lift your leg at all?"

" 'Deed I cain't, don't I take holt of it. Seem like it too weak to move."

"I'm going to lift it," I said, "and try to move the joint. You let me know if it hurts." I took hold of his ankle and raised it gently; it moved with an eerie, disembodied ease. His face remained impassive. "Now I'm going to move it sideways." He murmured, nodding. I swung the lower leg gently from side to side, bending down to press my ear against it as I did so. There was a distinct grating sound of the malarticulating joint, like the creaking of an oarlock. "That doesn't hurt?"

"No, suh, it don't."

I raised the shin slowly, hyperextending it far above a straight line with his thigh, lifting it until it formed a shallow V at the junction of his upper leg. "You don't feel any pain at all?"

"No, suh, I don't. Seem like I ought to, but I don't."

I felt a tiny, tapering glow of elation, like the tip of a gas flame lighted in my mind. The monstrous affliction was a classic example of the complication I had read about in Hinton only recently. It might have been used to illustrate the text, it corresponded so exactly with the distinguished doctor's description: the massive effusion, the malarticulation, the hypermobility, the cutaneous tension, the appearance of muscular atrophy. In the light of this example of the trauma, there was something oracular about the passage, a miraculous precision in the way it prefigured the condition of the bloated, ruined knee I saw before me. Or about the way this diseased knee conformed to the august universal Dr. Hinton had fashioned in his mind from his study of a thousand such particular cases. I was always moved by that phenomenon of medicine, that magnificent exactitude of faultless diagnosis and prognosis; the perfect observation of a state of imperfection. It was to me an apparent evidence of congruity in nature, a harmony between mind and matter born out of their disparity. Where, in nature, was there a perfect thing to match a conception of perfection in the mind? Nowhere at all. It was only through the study of disease, of imperfection, that man could conceive of the health, the flawless functioning, the perfection that existed nowhere under heaven. It was almost as if the natural world were confirming the physician's vision of disease by conforming to it, offering up its deformities and corruptions as tokens of the perfection they evoked and of the unanimity of God and man in recognizing them. Only through the mystery of disorder were they brought into consonance. I think there was always something almost revelatory to me about the lesions of the body, a kind of gnarled, cryptic eloquence that needed only to be read; and I never felt it more than at that moment.

"Ah, that's fine," I said. "Fine. You sit there and have some soup now. I'll be back in a minute with Dr. Proctor and ask him to have a look at you. What's your name?"

"Walter Lubby," he said. "Kin you do any good fo' me, Doctah?"

"Oh, I think we can, yes. I think we've got some medicine that'll ease your pain a lot. Do you have it right now?"

" 'Deed I do. The mostest in mah othah laig. Mah han', too."

"Well, I'll bring you some pills in a minute. I won't be long."

I strode across the yard to the church and pushed through the crowded door between the lines of waiting Negroes to the table where Liam was working in the close, dusty heat. His shirt was soaked and his forearms running with sweat. He plucked the stethoscope out of his ears and raised his eyebrows quizzically when I tapped him on the shoulder.

"Liam, come out here for a minute, will you?" I said. "I want you to look at something. Bring your mallet."

He turned to the young black nurse who was assisting him and said, "Gwyn, do a couple of Wassermanns, will you? I'll catch up when I come back."

"Yes, sir."

He picked up the rubber reflex mallet from the table and hooked the stethoscope around his neck, following me out through the crowd into the churchyard.

"There's a man over here with a knee I'd like you to look at," I said. "It's quite a sight."

"What's his name?"

"Lubby, I think he said. Walter Lubby."

We went across the yard to where the patriarch sat in his chair under the oak, sipping vegetable soup out of a paper cup. His sons and daughter stood beside him, eating silently.

"My. Lubby, this is Dr. Proctor," I said. "He's going to have a look at your knee."

The man nodded impassively, saying, "Doctah."

"Hello, Mr. Lubby," Liam said. "How's the soup?"

"Real good. I 'preciate it."

"Too hot, for a day like this."

"No, suh. It's real fine."

"Let's see what you've got here," Liam said. He knelt in front of the man and clasped the swollen knee joint gently. I watched silently while he went through much the same procedure as I had, cautiously raising and articulating the leg, examining eyes and reflexes, asking soft, casually framed questions. He stood up when he had finished and shoved his hands into his pockets, rattling the seashells faintly, looking down, unsmiling, at the knee.

"Are you a carpenter?" he asked suddenly, raising his eyes to Mr. Lubby's.

"Yes, suh, 'deed I am. Many a year."

"I think you worked on a house for Mr. Newcomb over at Bibb, back around '26."

" 'Deed I did. Put him four dormers in his attic and a new roof. Cedar shingles."

"That's right," Liam said. "That's a fine-looking house. I went by there a couple of weeks ago."

"Is that a fact? I heard he done passed on."

"He did," Liam said. "His son-in-law lives there now. Charley Connors, runs the Coca-Cola bottling plant."

"Oh, yeah. Mr. Connors, yeah."

"You used to split wood at the fair," Liam said. "I've heard my daddy talk about you. He said you could split green oak one-handed."

The old man's lips spread into a long-lipped, leathery smile. "That's a fact," he said. He nodded, chuckling softly.

"Are these your boys?"

"Yes, suh, they is. My boys Moses an' Micah. This my daughter Becky."

"How're you folks?" Liam said.

"Real fine," the older of the young men said. They nodded to him, shuffling their feet.

"You live with your father?" Liam asked.

"Yes, suh."

He turned back to the patriarch. "They take pretty good care of you?"

" 'Deed they do. They good chirren. We real close family. I thank the Lord for that."

"Well, you're lucky that way," Liam said. He lowered his eyes to the knee. "You've got a bad leg there, Mr. Lubby. I'm going to talk to you man to man. I don't know if we can make that leg better by next month—or next year. We'll do what we can for it, and I hope we can make you a good deal more comfortable, but I'm not going to promise you any miracles."

"No, suh."

"We do the best we can. Anything else is up to the Lord. I guess you know that as well as I do."

"Yes, suh," Mr. Lubby said. " 'Deed I do." He nodded simply, looking into Liam's eyes. Liam took his hand out of his pocket and held it out to the black man, who set the cup he was holding between his thighs in order to clasp it, austerely and unhurriedly, with no show of surprise or diffidence, although I felt certain it was the first time in his life he had been offered a white man's hand to shake. His face was immobile, darkly shining in the shadow.

"You finish your soup," Liam said. "Dr. Ransome will be back out in a minute, to give you a blood test. It'll be easier for you out here than coming inside." He stared at the ground for a moment, then turned quickly and strode across the yard toward the church. I followed beside him, touching his arm when he had reached the door. He turned to face me, his face expressionless.

"It's a Charcot knee," he said. "There's not much doubt about it."

"That's what I think. You don't think it could be diabetes, or syringomyelia?"

"No. With those reflexes, and those pupils, it's almost certainly tabes."

"Yes. Kidd's an orthopedist, isn't he?"

"Yes."

"I want him to see this. We'll have to get this man in to Cardozo sometime this week. Do you think Janet or Mrs. Farris could manage it?"

"Somebody will."

"Good. I'll speak to Mrs. Farris about it."

Liam nodded and turned away, making for the door. "I've got to get back in there," he said. "Gwyn's up to her neck."

I followed him into the church and went to my table, where Mrs. Farris and Dr. Jakes were processing the line of Negroes. I washed my hands in a basin of water, dried them with a paper towel, and took a syringe and a bottle of alcohol from the table.

"Mrs. Farris, will you come outside with me, and bring your book?" I said. "There's a man out here with a bad knee. It'll be easier to talk to him out there."

"Yes, sir," she said. She picked up her register and followed behind me through the crowd and across the yard to where the man sat in the shade of the oak. He had finished his soup and sat now, watching us approach with his steady, hooded gaze, fanning himself again, slowly, imperturbably, like a seated monarch. I did not feel able to interrupt that leisurely, regal motion.

"Mr. Lubby, will you hold out your arm?" I said. "I want to roll up your sleeve and take some of your blood, for a test."

He did so; and while I rolled up his sleeve, inserted the needle into his vein, and drew the blood, he watched aloofly, still waving the fan before his face.

"Now, Mrs. Farris is going to ask you some questions about your health, your age, where you were born, where you live. We want to know how to get to your place, because we'd like to bring you in to the hospital in Tallacoochee next week, to give you some treatment. Could you make it on Monday or Tuesday?"

"Yes, suh. Either one."

"Good. You give her the information, then. Now, before I go, I want to give you some medicine. I think it's going to help a lot." I took three envelopes of aspirin out of my bag and unscrewed the cap of my fountain pen. "There are twelve pills in each of these envelopes. I want you to take three of them every morning at eight o'clock, three of them at noon, three at four o'clock in the afternoon, and three at eight o'clock at night. That's one whole envelope a day. I'm going to write that down here so you won't forget it. Can you read?"

"I kin read," his daughter said. "He won't forget, nohow."

"Good." I wrote the directions on the back of one of the envelopes and handed them to him. "You'll feel much better if you take these regularly. Then on Monday morning we'll come over and bring you in to Tallacoochee. About nine o'clock; will that be all right?"

"Yes, suh. I thank you kindly."

I nodded. "I'll see you on Monday morning, then."

I smiled to his children, then turned and walked back to the church, consciously limiting the length and speed of my steps so that they should have no appearance of haste or retreat. Beside the church the circle of children surrounding the captured tortoise had grown in number and maliciousness. They crouched now around the upturned, desperately scrabbling creature in attitudes that seemed overtly savage to me, their black, baleful faces contorted with a mindless glee, their eyes glistening with a kind of miasmal delight while they watched its torment. One of them held out a lighted cigarette, manipulating it with delicate, exultant skill to touch the hotly glowing tip of it to the creature's twitching, stumpy tail. The turtle spun and rocked on the crest of its inverted shell, all its immediate instinct to defend itself by disappearing abandoned in its pain. I felt a sudden rabid indignation sweep over me at the sight. Filthy little creatures, I thought; primitive, bestial. Far more brutal than the animal they tortured. I clenched my jaws and strode up to them, feeling my face pale with anger.

"What do you think you're doing?" I said shrilly. "Do you get pleasure out of that? Torturing that turtle? You ought to be ashamed!" I kicked at the cigarette in the boy's hand. They fell away from me, tumbling backwards on the ground in fright. "Now get away from here, all of you. Find something civilized to do." I reached down to pick up the tortoise, which expressed its gratitude by expelling a lump of dripping, dark brown excrement across my wrist. The children gurgled with delight. I carried the turtle in my outstretched hands across the churchyard and out into the weedy, sun-blasted field, where I set it down among the sandy yellow mounds that marked the tunnels of its fellows. It sat for a moment, all its appendages invisibly withdrawn, before its head cautiously emerged from between the roughly plated dark halves of its carapace; then it began to lumber off among the weeds in its slow, primordial fortitude.

I can't tell you how beautiful that autumn with Nils was. Such a glorious carnage everywhere! The oak trees stood like gaunt, stricken heroes, Agamemnons clothed in bloody rags that fluttered in the wind, and shreds of tattered banners and caparisons streamed past, torn bits of cloth of gold and russet damask, skittering along the stone and smashing lightly into walls and startled faces. You could wade through knee-high piles of them along the campus walks, your legs crashing through them, dry and hoarse as parchment, raising a shower of brittle crumbs that whirled away into the blue air like battle dust, the rubble of looted palaces and towers. The ivy turned crimson and ran down the walls of the chapel like spilled wine, and that year the clematis bloomed twice, the stubborn, demented blossoms splattering the backyard fences all through October until the first frost turned them dry and pale, and they rattled in the wind like faded red and purple rosettes, wasted trophies. The world was falling into splendid ruin, and I exulted in it; I ran through it like Helen running through the streets of smoking Troy, full of wild glee, scattering the bones of princes and broken helmets and gory scraps of satin from the gowns of ravished dames.

And there were days of lucid stillness so absolute that my heart hung in it like a hanging pear, waiting to be picked and bitten, or to fall and be trodden on, crushed into succulent mire that would seep back into the damp, dark soil like a nectar, to lave the roots of glistening junipers and barbed, bright holly. The sky was so blue and still and clear that it was haunted, suffused along the horizon, just above the tops of the bare trees, with a pale silver glow, cool and luminous, that darkened, as you raised your head and eyes, into the unplumbed violet purity above you that pealed with silence, like a seashell or an empty cathedral. The black, bare elms beyond Taliaferro Hall were like charred, gigantic bones dangling in a gibbet against that ashen glow of the horizon or against the crimson wash of twilight; they made me think of that line in Yeats: "Oh, sages, standing in God's holy fire as in the gold mosaic of a wall." Everything made me think of poetry; poetry ran through me like liquor, it splashed inside my skull like wine in a tumbled cask, and raced up my thighs like lizards and sprayed my breasts like lye, like the spume of white seas that seemed to be breaking in silent tumult everywhere. I wanted to run naked, and I did; on fine, warm nights full of sharp stars we went to Greenbelt Park and I took off all my clothes and ran down a long grassy hill until I stumbled and fell and rolled over and over in the moonlight. Nils came running after me and crouched over me and kissed me everywhere, from my toes to my eyelids, while I giggled like a kid and twitched and jerked and tumbled.

"You crazy thing," he said. "You wild thing. You'll get us arrested."

"What did I do wrong?"

"You're indecently exposed."

"Oh, my God. And I thought I was decently revealed, at last."

I frightened him sometimes with my craziness, but it only added to my gaiety to see him grow grave and circumspect in the way men do when they think a woman is getting out of hand, especially one who won't talk about love. I never would, because I knew what was coming, sooner or later, and I dreaded it: the talk about my leaving Ron and moving in with him, the apartment we would share, the pictures we would put up on the walls, the number of bookcases we would need. It actually started once: we went to his room one evening when his roommate was away, and after we had made love we lay on his rickety daybed, smoking cigarettes and looking up at a poster he had made of little cut-out squares of colored photographs pasted to a piece of fiberboard. They were pieces of butterflies' wings, taken by a naturalist, that he'd found in a magazine, the *Smithsonian,* I think. In the design of each wing there was a letter of the alphabet revealed in a contrasting color, none of them quite perfectly formed but all of them distinguishable, although no one who had not been searching for them—as this photographer had—would ever have discovered them. He had cut the letters out and pieced them into words to form a phrase from one of Roethke's poems: ALL FINITE THINGS REVEAL INFINITUDE. It was dazzling.

"I love that," I said. "I wish I had it."

"You can, if you want. I mean, we could share it, couldn't we? If we had a place together."

"I have a place," I said.

"But with a man you love."

"I don't love anyone. I told you that."

He smoked and frowned, groping for the coffee can to rub out his cigarette in.

"You never talk about love," he said. "I don't see how anyone can live without love. Especially you."

"Well, you haven't thought about it very much, then. Love is a luxury, like running water. Life goes on very well without love. As you would realize if you'd pause to consider the iguana, or the black widow spider, or Mr. Adolf Hitler."

"Well, you don't resemble any of those creatures, thank God."

"Don't look too closely," I said, and turned my face away when he took my chin to do so.

We would walk in the rain, for hours sometimes, under the black, dripping trees along the shining paths, my hand clasped in his and both of them tucked into the pocket of his jacket, where they lay together like slumbering moles, and come back to his room damp and chilled, and take off our clothes and sit with blankets around our shoulders in front of an electric heater, our skin growing glazed and pink like suckling pigs while we drank hot wine and he read his poems to me: such sad, gnarled poems for such a glistening young man to write. They were full of blazing villages and screaming brown children and disemboweled oxen and banana trees stripped like asparagus, all the flowers of our youth. I loathed them and loved them for their awful beauty; but there were other poems, about me, more and more of them; gallant, rather naïve, tremblingly tender poems that made me lean to him to press his head to mine in gratitude. Why don't I remember them better—when I remember those terrible, graceless passages of my own so well? There is only one I can say now; it sticks in my mind like a little piece of stained glass from one of the broken windows of that autumn:

> It is not like a red wheelbarrow, really;
> Although there is the stillness;
> But not the desuetude. It is a new invention, always,
> Whose wheels turn on axles of ether,
> Revolving soundlessly, with the ease of planets.
> And it is not red (although that may be your favorite color)
> But the cool hue of glycerin.
> Comet-colored,
> And immobile, as they are, in their unimaginable velocities,
> Trundling through the black barrows of this barren fief
> With grapes and bolts of silk and piled attars,
> Making no shadow, anywhere.
> And still, as light is,
> In its consummate speed.

That's the only one I can remember whole, although I remember the part of one that I told you once, the fragment of my "Birthday Poem" that he wrote when I told him I was born on the summer solstice; the one in which he said I came floating in on the full tide of the world, like a frangipani blossom out of tropic seas.

"Why did you write it *now?*" I asked him. "It's only October."

"June is such a long way off. I don't think I can wait to celebrate." And he gave me a bottle of champagne and a purple orchid, which we ate, dipping it into our glasses and munching it luxuriously. "Poems and orchids and champagne," I said. "It's a wonderful regimen. We should live on it."

"You don't consider it a luxury?"

"Ah, that's mean. What do you expect from me? Logic? Very logical *you* are. You spend half of your G.I. allowance for the month on my birthday, and expect *me* to be *logical.*"

"You said I made the most logical political speeches you'd ever heard."

"Well, you *talk* logically. But that's very different from *acting* logically. For example: why are you studying political science, anyway?"

"Because I don't want there to be any more Vietnams. And I don't think I can stop them by writing poetry."

"Do you think you can stop them by practicing political science? Men have been politicking a lot longer than they've been writing poems—my God, it's almost the only thing they do!—and look at the state we're in."

"You think this would be a better world if everyone was a poet?" he said, turning his head to watch the rain against the window.

"Oh, Nils, what a stupid question."

"Plato didn't think it was stupid. He wouldn't even *allow* poets into his perfect Republic."

"Yes, there's an example of what logic can lead you to. How would you like to live in Plato's Republic? A society founded on slave labor, with a nasty, rigid class system and a vast suspicion of the arts; where literature is censored, and poets expelled, and people are punished for having anything uncomplimentary to say about God or the government; where children are taught the 'art of warfare'—actually taken out to see battles by their parents—and women are considered naturally inferior to men, and 'barbarians' to 'citizens.' My God, it sounds just like Hackensack to me. The Republic is a very nice example of what you get when you try to construct a state by logic."

"Maybe he just wasn't a very good political scientist," Nils said. "After all, he didn't go to the University of Maryland." I scowled at him; I didn't think it was funny. "What do you want me to do, then?" he said, reaching out his hand to touch my face.

"I want you to write poems. And make love to me."

"You think there's a future in it?"

He said this with a tone of rebuke that made me drop my head, but I was still indignant enough to say softly, "Do you think those people who sent you to Vietnam gave a damn about your future? Do you think the people who are turning the Great Lakes and the rivers and the oceans into stinking, stagnant pestholes, and turning the rain into poison, and cutting down the trees and ripping the earth to pieces, for profit, give a damn about the future? Only the poets live in the Eternal City, and if you don't understand that, you don't know anything. Really, you don't, Nils." I raised my head and stared at him for a minute, and then stuck out my tongue. "You political scientist."

Then we would go to bed, and after making love he was always bonelessly, supplely still with the exhausted languor of a sleeping child. He would lie with his head on my breast, his hair rustling faintly with my breath, his arm stretched across my breasts to clutch my shoulder in a strengthless, surfeited clasp, smelling of moist hair and skin and that marvelous cologne and the mossy, oaken fragrance of his breath, and I would close my eyes with an ineffable gratitude, and an unholy grief, knowing that that moment was the best life had to give, the best that I or anyone would ever receive from it, and that still—oh, insanely! shamefully!—it was not enough.

That was, of all things, the most mysterious to me, and the most unassuageable: knowing that that moment was as full as any moment of time can be, almost overfull, bursting with sweetness that spilled out beyond its mystic borders into the next, and the next, and all of them saturated with delight like drops of ocean water sweetened by a pitcherful of nectar poured into the sea; feeling it spread out through the hours of those autumn days like a glistening ambrosial pool that sparkled on the surface of the sea; and yet knowing it was not enough; it would not serve some awful ambition I had to season the whole boundless sea of time with the liquor of our days and hours. I wanted it to permeate the mercilessly vast ocean of moments that stretched beyond the stars, in which they drifted like lost, floating islands; and it couldn't, I knew. It couldn't convert those measureless leagues of brine into ambrosia. It would be diluted, at last, swallowed up like a poor, pale tincture, leaving not even the faintest taste of honey, anywhere, in the unplumbed, salt, estranging sea. Because I knew, even while I tried to stretch them into eternity, that the sweetness of those autumn afternoons lay in their impermanence, their brevity, their precious rarity. Their spell was not the long spell of the desert or the open sea that sets the soul nakedly and perpetually abroad on endless routes of brine or dust, but the charm of islands and oases, of water, wells, figs, flowers, groves of gushing trees, soft, spice-scented air, that invited me to indolence and ease. I lived in the house of flesh but I had two names: one that I was called by in that house, and another name that my kinsmen did not know, that someone was calling always in the sea wind and the desert wind, and that made me tremble when I heard it keen out like the distant splitting of a rock or the howling of a ghostly raptor who roamed the waves. I have always heard that calling of my secret name, but never more clearly than through the sunlit corridors and scarlet chambers of that radiant autumn. Once, on the clearest and loveliest and last winter of my childhood, I broke an icicle from the eaves and looked through it at the world I knew: the cottage on the cliff, and the dovecote, and the orchard, and down below, the docks of Poppa's boatyard with the masts of his vessels tilting against the blue water of the bay. It was more beautiful than I had ever seen it, and I wanted to keep it forever, like a scene inside a crystal paperweight. I put it in the freezer compartment of the refrigerator, so I could take it out in ten years, or twenty, or on the day I died, and look through it and see the world that way again, preserved forever in the crystal water of that season. But then Poppa burned the house down, and the vision was gone forever. That autumn with Nils was like that: it had that crystalline and almost motionless beauty of moments so nearly perfect that they seem to cease in time, because they are so brief their span cannot be measured. The light that plays upon them in their instant of almost absolute beauty is the sacred scintillation of desire, that cannot be divided and cannot endure.

There is no solution to that mystery but submission to it; I learned that, in sixty-seven days. God, what a desperate, paradoxical prudence I practiced —in the midst of my reckless pleasure—trying to make that gloriously brief moment longer! Even if I had succeeded, I would have destroyed it in doing so, because the longer it lasted, the more certain Ron was to find out about it; there was no way a campus romance as flagrant as ours could go undetected forever, but I wanted that patch of honey in the sea to be a little larger, to have a circumference one second greater. I didn't know how it would end, and I didn't really care, except for the fact that I knew Ron would be hurt, terribly, and perhaps irreparably. There was no other consequence I could imagine that I really feared; I would have accepted anything that happened in exchange for that bright season. I thought about it sometimes, and wondered, idly, with the kind of spellbound immunity to its events with which one reads a novel, what would happen to us. Ron would leave me, I supposed; and yet, he might not; he might cling to me in spite of anything, bowed even lower, in even greater abasement, unable to let me go. Or I might leave him; or Nils; or both of them, in grief or desperation—it wasn't inconceivable that what I was really seeking, in the strangest of all ways, was liberty from both of them. And neither was it beyond belief that the three of us would wind up welding ourselves together, even more tightly and inscrutably, into a ménage à trois, or at least experimenting with some such arrangement for a while. It wasn't an uncommon permutation, and evidently it worked very well in certain cases, if you could believe the intimations of books like *Women in Love* or *A Man and Two Women* or movies like *Jules and Jim,* or the citations I vaguely remembered hearing of modern anthropologists and psychologists who asserted that a constellation of three people was a historically conventional one and basically stabler than one of two people, or four, or any other number. If something like that evolved out of the revelation of my perfidy, I would accept it, but not as the conclusion of a bland and bloodless dialectic. The only thing I was absolutely determined about was that Ron should not find out from me, or through any action of mine designed, however subtly or overtly, to let him know. It had to happen naturally, inevitably, according to ordained circumstances and to whatever dark laws reigned over the ways of treachery. Whatever he might suffer in that way was less than he would suffer through the cunningly, brazenly selfish exploitation of his homage with which he tempted me.

Nils said to me once, "I think the reason you don't tell him, really, is because it would be a kind of obedience to him if you did. I mean, it wouldn't be an independent act, then, would it?"

"What do you mean?" I said, indignantly, although his meaning was mercilessly clear.

"I mean he'd be *allowing* you to be unfaithful, wouldn't he? He'd be giving you his permission. Which of course would destroy the very possibility of infidelity. You'd be sharing it with him. It wouldn't be private any longer. You'd almost be doing it *for* him, and you don't want to do that. You want to do it as a privilege, not a dispensation. You want to do it secretly and defiantly."

"That isn't true!" I cried. "It isn't! If I did it, and knew it hurt him, and told him about it anyway, *that* would be defiant. That would be demanding his consent, because I know he wouldn't dare refuse it. That would be dishonoring him."

"I don't think he thinks so. I think as far as he's concerned his honor depends on your telling him the truth, not on what you do; not on how much you sleep around. I think he's decided that's inevitable." He sounded angry, as if he were confronted with an arcane confederacy of some kind he didn't know how to deal with. "I think that's the only thing he asks from you. The only thing you're not willing to give him."

"If that were true, the last thing in the world you ought to want is for me to tell him. If I did, I'd be keeping faith with him, and being false to you."

"I know that," he said. "Christ, don't you think I know that? I really ought to thank God that you don't tell him; and I would, if it didn't keep me from having you."

"You have me."

"No, I don't. Nobody does. You keep telling me that."

"I mean right now. Right now, you have me. That's all I can promise."

"Why? Promises are necessary, don't you know that? Even if we know we're never going to keep them. They're what hold the world together."

"Campaign promises?" I said. "They may get politicians what they want, but they'll never hold the world together."

"You don't know. The world is held together minute by minute. Just one minute hanging to the next. If you can keep this minute glued to the next one, the whole thing hangs together somehow."

I leaned over and picked up the little yellow cat that we had found wandering in the rain and brought back to his room bundled up inside my sweater. "I know a way we can glue this minute to the next one," I said.

He ignored me. He watched me stroke the cat for a moment, wretchedly;

then he said, "All I know is that you're living with him. Not me. That's the only thing that matters."

"And suppose I did live with you, and did the same thing to you that I'm doing to him. And then to the next man, and the next. My God, it could go on forever."

"You mean there's not really all that much difference between any of us."

"No, that's not what I mean. There's nobody like you, and there never will be. Really."

"You mean we all have our special little delights, which you intend to sample one by one, evidently."

He was justified in that remark, I thought, because with the kind of nature I had, it seemed very possible that what we would have, before very long, was a ménage à quatre, or à cinq, or even à vingt, if I had a very prosperous summer. We would have to find quarters in an abandoned armory or warehouse, if I kept on the way I was going.

It seemed grimly funny like that, sometimes, and I was saved from despising myself entirely, because I think I believed, truly, that it wasn't all my fault. It was as much Ron's as mine, and as much Nils's; or it wasn't anybody's. It was some inevitable piece of irony, or comedy, or idiocy, cast up out of the imponderable workings of the world and of our immutable natures, and our only duty was to submit to it.

So I put the cat down and lured him to the daybed, where we glued that moment of time gloriously to the next, and our little pool of honey spread out an instant wider in the icy sea that splashed against the windows and rattled the panes and set the headstones on the hills adrift. Then we would lie lulled and drunken in the moment of irreproachable peace that I felt I had, somehow, in spite of everything, earned for us with my intransigence. And then, for a while, he would be gentle with bewildered gratitude, and indulgent of my fear that we would be discovered, and yield smilingly to my insistence that we avoid streets or paths or places where we might be apt to encounter Ron, for whatever unforeseeable reason—because he had canceled a class, or dismissed one early, or because he hoped, out of some well-concealed suspicion that I wasn't yet aware of, to waylay us. We stayed well away from the Italian Gardens, or the Varsity Grill, or any other of his haunts, where he might stop to have a drink with a student or a colleague; although the fact that Nils and I might meet and have a drink in one of those places occasionally could very easily have passed as innocent if we had been discovered. It wasn't really difficult to avoid being seen by him, or by anybody else we knew, because the campus is enormous; it occupies two or three square miles and is full of nooks and crannies, building complexes and fields and gymnasiums, where Arts and Humanities students almost never set foot. We would meet in the most wildly unlikely places: an abandoned greenhouse in the experimental garden back of the Agriculture School, on the roof of Taliaferro Hall, where we got by climbing up a fire ladder in the inner court; even in Byrd Stadium, vast and shadowy and silent in the moonlight, where he chased me down the middle of the football field one night, and caught me and made love to me in the shadow of the goalposts to the cheers of a thousand silent angels. When we had finished we lay with the dew misting our hair like the breath of our holy, hovering witnesses, looking up at the crossbar that divided the raving autumn stars, and he said, "You're a pretty strange lady."

"Yes. You didn't know how strange, did you?"

"No. I knew it would be deep, though. But I didn't know how deep. I've never been out this deep before." He turned his head to look at me and put out his hand to let his fingertips wander over my hair and lips and throat in a kind of timid awe. "Jesus, you're beautiful, Sylvie. You're the most beautiful thing in the world. I didn't know women could be so beautiful."

"Don't worry, baby. Really."

"All right. Whatever you say. Anyway, it's a kind of interesting life we lead, I guess." He looked around the ghostly, empty bowl. "I wonder if they give a letter for lovemaking?"

"If they do, you deserve one," I said. "You can tell your children you used to perform in Byrd Stadium."

"My children," he murmured. "God." He was silent for a while, plucking grass blades with his fingers, staring up at the sky. "I couldn't have any children that weren't yours. God, that's an awful thought."

"You'd better stop that."

"It is, though."

"Well, you'll wait a long time to have any children with me," I said. "God help any children I ever had."

"You'd make a wonderful mother," he said. "You really would. A kid would be blessed to have you for a mother."

"All right, now stop it."

He rolled over suddenly to bury his face between my thighs and clutch my hips, muttering something over and over to himself like a kind of senseless mantra. Then he took my hand and pressed it against his cheek and said, "Oh, Jesus, Sylvie, I love you so much. Listen, take it easy on me, will you?"

"Hush. Hush," I whispered, and gathered his head in my arms and kissed his hair. "I can't belong to anybody. I just can't. I don't know why. I guess I don't have any soul or something. You have to know that."

"No, that isn't so," he said, and raised his head to look at me. Then he lowered it and laid his cheek against my belly and murmured deeply, so that the words echoed in my entrails, " 'Thou still unravished bride of quietness. Thou foster child of silence and slow time.' "

Can you imagine going home to Ron after an evening like that? Going home as I did, night after night—being scrupulously careful either to arrive a few minutes before he did or to have a very good excuse for not doing so —and making a pot of mocha, and heating up some cheese Danish in the oven, and maybe setting out the chessmen? *I* couldn't have imagined it, before; but I was amazed at how easy it was once you got used to it, and I began to understand why it was such a popular process. I would sip my mocha and brood spuriously, with my hair hanging fetchingly and my eyes soft as the mist of silent stadiums, over the question of whether it would be wiser to castle at that moment or advance my queen's pawn, wondering how many million women in America were doing the same thing, with perhaps a Scrabble set or a backgammon board between them and their troubled lords. Most of them, of course, were not Guineveres or Clytemnestras or Isoldes, or even Anna Kareninas, but Emma Bovarys, or something even humbler, as I was, and that they all ended up choked on their own black vomit I very much doubted, or there would almost certainly have been some notice published by the U.S. Public Health Service about the mysterious, practically universal feminine ailment raging in the land. It's so much easier than truth, I thought; but I don't know yet if it's more beautiful.

I suppose Ron must have suspected, even then; I think there were clues and maybe even insinuations that any fully functioning woman, especially one trained in the business, would have detected and probably expertly allayed. But I was either very far from fully functioning, or functioning at such breakneck, oblivious speed, or else so little trained in deception or so naturally inept at it that I failed to observe or recognize them. I really wasn't very good at the role of suburban infidel in spite of its simplicity; I left out or botched up so many of the little tricks and travesties that generally mark its passage. I can thank God for that much, anyway. We were spared a certain amount of squalor by my ineptitude, or ingenuousness, or bad acting.

I don't know why neither Aaron nor I was any good at acting. With the kind of man we had for a father, you'd think we would have won a couple of dozen Oscars between us. I guess, basically, we both felt the way Dylan Thomas did about the business: "The strut and trade of charms on the ivory stages." We both paid for it.

In bed, especially, he must have suspected; but I had always been so nearly perfunctory in my performances in bed with him that I suppose I assumed he wouldn't be able to tell the difference. That was just plain stupid, and it was an affront to him that I regret as much as I regret anything. The difference between a companionable, habitual sexual relationship and one fraught with a kind of livid, tense submission must be transparent to a man, even to one who has never had reason to nourish any very great pretensions in the matter, and I should have realized it. That was the only thing that wasn't easy, that ugly pantomime of sexual pleasure; it was where my amateurism must have been most glaring, I suppose, and what gave me cause for a certain admiration of the skill of my sisters in perfidy. How do they manage it? I wondered. I mean, it's very different from a one-night stand with someone who has no criteria with which to judge your enthusiasm and in which case nobody has any particular concern, anyway, with the possible damage to anybody else's sensibilities or immortal soul; a certain degree of impersonality sometimes added to the success of a situation of that kind, and even a certain amount of fraudulence could be excused on everybody's part, unless it was of dimensions that involved contempt or despair, for which contingency you could always keep a pack of peanuts handy. But to put Ron in the same category with that grad student in tight jeans that I told you about would have been a calumny —one, at least, for which I'm glad I don't have to weep.

I know that doesn't make very much sense: to be concerned about wounding him with the realization that I was feigning pleasure in bed with him, when all the time I was so damned determined that it would be a genuine infidelity, which of course he would have to discover eventually, anyway, and which would wound him all the more, when he realized how successfully I had deceived him. But I couldn't let him know myself; I couldn't tell him. That would be either a concession to what it seemed to me he was abjectly proposing, or else a devious demand for his sanction for the kind of ravenous, makeshift existence I had fled to him from, and a devious, dreadful attempt to involve him in that kind of existence—to corrupt him, if the phrase doesn't embarrass anybody, I thought, and if he wasn't already corrupted by knowing me. That was such a wanton, pernicious idea that it appalled me.

None of it made any sense, and Nils's indignation and confusion at the fact that I couldn't explain it to him any better was more than justified.

"How in the hell can you keep on like this?" he said to me. "What good does it do him, being ignorant of what's going on?"

"I don't want him to be involved in it. I don't want him to be corrupted by it."

"*Involved* in it? My God, it seems to me he's almost *sponsoring* it already. He's going to be destroyed when he finds out you've been doing it without his knowledge, anyway."

"He'll have to deal with it," I said. "It's what people have to deal with in this world. It's natural. You can't interfere in nature."

"Nature is whatever *happens,*" Nils said. "Whatever happens in the natural world is *natural.* How in the hell can you get around it?"

"People try. Some people have a terrible ambition to convert the whole world to fit their nature. Or to corrupt it; whatever you want to call it."

"Is that what you want to do?"

"I don't know. Maybe. I know it's the most terrible vanity there is. And maybe the only real profanity. It's a much more terrible deed to corrupt someone than to kill him."

"What does it mean: corrupt someone?"

"It means what Delilah did to Samson. Despoiling him of his strength, and enslaving him and blinding him. Making him desert the things he loves."

"Jesus Christ, you think you'd do a thing like that to anybody?" He snorted indignantly. "Sometimes I think you do it just for kicks. You want to know what it feels like to be unfaithful. You like the thrill of it."

"Oh, God, there's no thrill to it," I said. "It tastes like vinegar; I know that already. I've never been anything else but faithless, all my life." He didn't say anything to that, but he watched me wonderingly for a moment, and I felt his question hanging in the air above me like a sword. "Except when I write," I added in a moment, softly; very, *very* humbly, as if in fear that I would be stricken with a bolt of lightning for that presumption.

"But you told him about everybody else. About the man in Mexico."

"That was different. It didn't threaten him. It couldn't possibly have gone on. And, anyway, it wasn't really a betrayal, of anybody."

After a little silence, he said, "He must have been quite a man." I didn't say anything. "You say it couldn't possibly have gone on. Well, just how long can *this* go on? I mean, if there *is* anything going on. I don't suppose there is, really, since you can't love anybody."

"Now, I can. Right now, I love you as much as I'm capable of. I just don't think I can belong to anybody, forever. How can I tell you how long it will last?"

"Well, roughly? I mean, until four-thirty this afternoon, or next March, or what? I'd sort of like to make plans."

"I don't know. You can go now if you can't stand it. There must be several thousand girls on this campus who'll promise to love you forever, right this minute, if you want someone to make plans with. And if you'll promise *them* that. I just don't want your plans to be disappointed, ever. I care too much about you."

"The funny thing is," he said, "that I believe you. I think you really do."

"I wish you knew how much," I said.

He put out his hand and laid it against my face. "I know what you mean. But don't you think it's kind of—inhuman—to expect yourself to have that kind of faith? It really is, Sylvie. People build perfectly good, respectable lives on much less faith than that. They have to, or there wouldn't be a single family to inhabit this world. That's what the world is built on."

"I know it is," I said. "But I don't much like the kind of world they've built. I lived in one of those families."

"It must have been a hell of an experience," he said.

"I don't think it was any worse than yours."

"That's different. That was a war."

"Love is war, too," I said. "That's what you were telling us that night in the Italian Gardens. Everything is war, you said."

He dropped his head sadly and said in a moment, "Well, maybe you're right. Maybe the most we can expect out of life is a few minutes of genuine passion and tenderness. And then to say goodbye, kindly and honorably. But it seems indecent to admit it, somehow. Even if it's true."

"Oh, love, I'll always feel tenderly toward you," I said. "As long as I live. If somebody told me fifty years from now that you were ill, or unhappy, or in trouble, I'd worry so much. I'd do anything in the world I could to help you. I *can* promise you that much. I know *that's* true."

"And you'd feel the same about Ron. About lots of people."

"I think so. I hope so. Don't you?"

"I guess so," he said. "I guess that's as nearly love as anything. I talk too much about love, I guess. I forget what it means after a while. If I ever knew."

"It doesn't mean possessing someone, I'm sure of that."

We sat facing one another on the hot, bright grass. He raised his head to look at me after a moment and laid his hand on mine.

"And of course that's what makes everyone want you so much, because you say that. You understand that very well, don't you?"

"Now don't go accusing me of coquetry," I said. "That's one thing I'm *not* guilty of!" I drew my hand away and slapped the one that he had laid on it. "You bastard."

"Well, do you think we could keep it together through next weekend?" he said. "The weather is supposed to stay great, and I have a very modest, short-term plan."

"What's that?"

"I've got a tent—a real nice one—that we could take over to Assateague and pitch on the sand, up there in the dunes. It may be the last good weekend of the fall."

"Oh, that sounds marvelous. Nils, what a wonderful idea!"

"We could walk along the beach, and gather shells, and build campfires in the dunes. We might even be able to swim, if it stays as warm as this."

"I'd love that. I haven't been to Assateague for years."

"Could you get away for the weekend? What would you tell him?"

"I don't know. I'll tell him something. Maybe Susie Temple will help me out. She likes me. And she does things like that: rock climbing and beachcombing. I could say I was going with her."

"You think he'd believe it?"

"Yes. He knows we're friends. She wouldn't actually have to say anything, anyway; but if we ran into her sometime, she'd back me up, I know."

"Christ, I don't know how you can say things like that, so cold-bloodedly. It sounds so absolutely unlike you."

"Don't you want me to?"

"I wouldn't ask you if I didn't."

"Then don't complain about it. You get me the way I am."

So that's what I told Ron that evening when he came back after class. I had called Susie earlier and asked her to lie for me, and the instant, cheerful equanimity with which she had agreed shocked me; I felt like scolding her. I wanted to explain that it wasn't really necessary for me to deceive Ron, but that I chose to, for his good. It sounded so idiotic that I decided it was better to let the whole thing pass as ordinary academic infamy.

"Won't you be cold?" Ron said.

"No, it's glorious weather. It's supposed to be in the middle sixties all weekend. And we'll pitch the tent among the dunes, out of the wind. Susie goes there a lot in the fall. She says it's wonderful. There's almost no one there."

"It sounds great," Ron said. "We'll have to do that sometime, Syl. Or rent a camper, even. They're not very expensive to rent in the off-season. We could spend the Thanksgiving weekend there, if the weather's good. Shall we do that?"

I was washing a cauliflower for a salad at the sink. I turned the water on full and let it splash over it through the colander, pretending not to hear.

"What did you say?" Ron said.

"I said if you'd like to."

"I think it would be great. Or maybe we could go down to Hatteras. It'd be a good bit warmer there. It might be fun to take somebody with us; another couple. Don't you think so?"

"I don't know. I haven't thought about it. It might." I set the wet cauliflower on the cutting board and began to slice it, hectically.

"Listen, why don't I ask Nils? Maybe there's a girl he'd like to bring along. He can play a guitar, can't he? That might be fun."

I sliced through the cauliflower and on into my finger, and when I jerked my hand away, the blood splashed down onto the divided white globe, whose halves rocked gently on the cutting board. I raised my finger to my mouth and sucked at it.

"What have you done?" Ron said. He came and took my hand, bending the knuckle to examine the wound. "My God, that's pretty deep."

"It isn't anything."

"You'd better have a Band-Aid. Run some water over that. I'll go get one." He went into the bathroom and came back in a minute with a can of Band-Aids and a bottle of hydrogen peroxide. "This will fix you up."

"Oh, God, stop fussing. It's just a scratch."

"You can't tell. These things get infected."

I stood impatiently while he splashed hydrogen peroxide on the cut and wrapped the Band-Aid around it.

"You're careless," he said. "It's a wonder you haven't maimed yourself before now." He picked up the snow-white lobe of cauliflower on which the scarlet blood-splash was seeping into the crannies and convolutions, like a bleeding brain. "That's kind of beautiful," he said.

"Let me have it. I'll wash it off."

"I think I'll eat it, like this." He raised it to his mouth and bit off a chunk and began to chew it, staring at me quaintly, a little spot of blood staining the corner of his lip.

"That's barbaric," I said. "That's awful." He took me by the shoulders suddenly and kissed me on the lips. "Ron, honestly. You're getting crazy. What's the matter with you?" I twisted away from him and picked the knife up from the cutting board. "I've got to cook." I shuddered suddenly.

"Are you cold?" he said.

"No."

"What is it?"

"I felt the edge of that blade hit the bone. It's an awful feeling."

"I know. Maybe you'd better sit down. I'll finish that."

"Oh, don't be silly. I'm not going to faint or anything."

"You can't tell. Come and sit down and have a glass of tequila. I'll do the salad." He took the knife out of my hand and led me by the elbows to the table and sat me down. I sat watching while he took down from the shelf a bottle of tequila that we had brought back from Mexico. He poured a couple of inches of it into each of a pair of glasses. We had not touched it since we came back to College Park. "Do we have any limes?" Ron said.

"No."

"Then we'll have it straight. With just a little salt."

He sat down across from me and picked up the salt shaker, then reached across to take my hand and spread the fingers open and sprinkle salt into my palm. "Salud, pesetas, y amor," he said, and raised his glass. We drank, and I shuddered again.

"It's bitter. I'd forgotten how bitter it was." I raised my hand and licked a dab of salt out of my palm and drank again. The two tastes, of brine and of dusty gray agave, drenched my mouth and then my mind, like the instantaneous flowering of a memory.

"I hope you haven't lost your taste for it."

I shook my head. He drank and set down his glass, and the bottom of it rattled lightly on the table, as if his hand trembled. It sounded like a faint tapping at a door. "Well, what about Thanksgiving? You want me to ask Nils about it?"

"If you want to."

"Who was that girl he was talking to one day? Beth."

"She's gone to London. He doesn't see her anymore."

"Oh, that's right. Well, maybe there's some other girl he'd like to bring."

"Maybe."

"Well, think about it. I'm going to finish the salad. You'd better keep that finger dry." He got up and went to the sink and began to chop the cauliflower into pieces, the knife blade thumping rhythmically on the cutting board.

Of the four hundred people whom I shepherded to death, Walter Lubby was by far the most interesting, in many respects; not only for the extraordinarily complex manifestations of his disease but for those of his character as well. Both were challenges to me, profound and imperative challenges; one of which, at least, persists, as far from solution as it was on the first day I met him. I came to know his body very well, having examined it repeatedly, observed meticulously the course of its decay, and, eventually, assisted at dismembering it, eviscerating it, cutting it up into pieces and studying it under a microscope. His character, undiscoverable by any such procedures, eludes me still—although I have spent many years attempting to subject it to them. Perhaps there is no one else in the world the contemplation of whose nature has occupied so many hours of my life. The man is unforgettable, and I am evidently incurable of the fascination he cast upon me.

The first time we brought him to Cardozo for a comprehensive examination, I discovered that he was suffering from a compound condition in which the two classic forms of late neurosyphilis, tabes dorsalis and paresis, exist concurrently. This is called taboparesis, and although uncommon, is far from rare. The signs and symptoms of both forms of the disease are present contemporaneously and often cause confusion among diagnosticians. There is no fixed preponderance of symptoms, or any single easily distinguishable syndrome; each case is unique, and therefore particularly interesting and rewarding to study. If, in late syphilis, the chief damage is to the parenchyma—the white or gray matter—of the brain, the result is paresis; if to that of the spinal cord, the result is tabes dorsalis. In taboparesis, both these neural areas have been invaded by treponemas (or perhaps, in the case of tabes, only by their toxin), so that there is, combined in differing and fascinating proportions, a concurrent symptomology of the two forms. In tabes dorsalis, the principal signs and symptoms are ataxia (locomotor disturbances and anomalies), areflexia (absence or irregularity of reflexes), paresthesia (anomalous pricking, tingling, or creeping sensations of the skin in the absence of appropriate stimuli), bladder and bowel disturbances, gastric crises involving acute abdominal pain and persistent vomiting, trophic joint changes (such as the Charcot knee which first brought Walter Lubby's case to our attention), ptosis (the typical drooping eyelid), strabismus (inability to coordinate the focus of both eyes), the loss of deep pain sensation, and mal deformans (perforating ulcers on the soles of the feet or toes). Those of paresis are equally numerous: headache, vertigo, tenderness of the head, epileptiform seizures, tremor of the tongue, lips, and hands, speech disorders, transient paralysis of a hand, arm, or leg, bouts of unconsciousness, and personality disorders of every conceivable kind, from mild loss of memory or general irritability to frankly psychotic and often ungovernable stages of insanity. Many symptoms are common to both forms of the disease, especially ocular ones, ranging from minor pupillary deviations and the classic Argyll-Robertson pupil, to optic atrophy and blindness. To further complicate the picture, taboparesis is almost invariably associated with yet a third form of late neurosyphilis, generally classified as meningovascular, which involves injury to the blood vessels of the brain, spinal cord, and meninges, or to the meninges and their supporting structures themselves, a condition attended by an additional spectrum of symptoms. In the whole protean range of syphilitic expression, there is perhaps nothing so complex or endlessly engrossing as the form of it which afflicted Walter Lubby. Nor, in my experience of human psychology, an example more so than that of this man. He grew in mystery to me, in strange, phantasmal fulgency of spirit, in direct proportion to the corruption of his body. It was not that he was brave, or inscrutably resigned, or piously submissive to his fate, or hopelessly indifferent; he seemed to be undergoing some strange, almost miraculous transfiguration, to be disintegrating, depurating, dissolving before me, as salt dissolves in water, or radium in time. I remember once, when I was curetting and disinfecting the enormous ulcer that had opened on the sole of his foot, scraping away the crumbling, dark purple, necrotic flesh at the rotten edges of the sore, I looked into the glittering, opalescent crater that had eroded to the bone and thought: This man is evanescing, like a phantom. He is turning into light, which is the ruins of matter. I was so startled by the thought that my scalpel sliced into his flesh, which could no longer feel any violation.

He seemed to understand that he was dying, that he must die, and that I was in some appointed way a minister, a dark angel, of his deliverance. After his first examination at the hospital, he refused to come back; not out of fear or distress, it appeared, but out of some calm, supernal understanding of its futility, perhaps even of its profanity. I was never able to persuade him to return. Even in his last few days, when he had fallen into a semicomatose condition from electrolyte imbalance and I was very anxious to get him to Cardozo so that his body would be immediately available for autopsy, he was immovable in his refusal ever to leave again the house that he had built beside the yellow river and the swamp, whose solemn currents and fabulous depths he was returning to. A flamelike serenity grew and towered in him, as if his body were being used to feed his spirit, which grew taller and brighter as his flesh was consumed, with the growing intensity of a flame whose fuel is almost exhausted, rendered almost completely into ash.

I don't know exactly when that process began; the first time I went with Mrs. Farris to bring him in to Cardozo he seemed perfectly amenable, and came with us without any hesitation or demurral, as he had promised to do, five days before, at the country church where I had seen him first. He lived in Black Willow Grove, that clutch of weather-beaten huts along the Coosa-latchee River at the end of a wagon road that wound through the pine woods, five miles out of Tallacoochee. His house was larger than most in the shanty town; it had three rooms and a screened-in front porch that looked down through the curtains of Spanish moss that hung from the black willow trees to the slippery red clay of the riverbank and the slow-moving yellow water beyond. He lived there with his two sons and his daughter and her husband and a grandchild, a fey, speechless little girl of six or seven who sang spirituals to herself, almost endlessly, in a gasping, high, harsh whisper that rustled through the house like the rasping of bracken in a wind. The two sons worked as day laborers in the cotton and peanut fields; the son-in-law fished the river and hunted the swamp for muskrats, moccasins, and foxes, and went daily in to Tallacoochee to gather and deliver the laundry that his wife washed in a pair of soot-blackened washtubs set on an iron grate supported by bricks in the sandy yard. The house stood high up on poles of cypress logs sunken into the yellow sand of the riverbank, so that you went up a flight of five wooden steps, worn smooth as velvet by bare feet, to the screen door of the front porch, where the old man sat, all day long, in the cane-backed rocking chair in which they had brought him to the church, fanning himself with his palm-leaf fan. He was sitting there the first time I came to see him, and greeted me with the same •

magisterial composure he had shown at our first meeting, as if he had been awaiting me since that day; or for even longer; for years, or decades.

"Good aftahnoon, Doctah," he said to me through the screen of the front porch, when I had parked the car and stood below him in the yard. "Come on up. The do' is latched to keep the crittahs out, but do you pull the string, she'll come loose."

I went up the steps and tugged the string that hung through a hole in the doorframe, and as he said, the door swung open. I went in onto the porch and closed the door behind me and took off my hat and smiled at him. He looked at me oddly for a moment, with a long, firm, level look of recognition, and nodded. He was wearing the same denim trousers with the cutaway leg that he had worn to the clinic, and the gross deformity of his knee, sagging like a balloon full of water, startled me as if I had not seen it before.

"You care to set down?" he said. He nodded to a chair that sat parallel to his, separated from it by an upturned orange crate on which there was a pipe, a can of tobacco, a tin can that served as an ashtray, a pair of wire-stemmed spectacles, and a frayed, much-thumbed Stanley tool catalogue.

"Oh, I won't stay," I said. "Mrs. Farris is down in the car." His silence and immobility were imperial. "Well, I'll sit for a minute, thank you." I sat down in the chair and picked up the catalogue, riffling the pages and remembering with curiosity, as the photographs of handsaws, chisels, and wrench sets fluttered past, that he could not read.

"Are you ordering some tools?" I said.

"Not no mo', no, suh. Don't have no use for no mo'. But I do like to look at 'em."

"You were a carpenter, I heard you tell Dr. Proctor."

"Yes, suh, 'deed I was. Many a year."

"You must miss that work."

"No, suh. Not no mo'. I kin rimemble it, and it's just the same like I was doing it. Doing it still." He put on his glasses and leaned toward me, taking the catalogue gently out of my hand. "Let me show you something, Doctah. Something real fine." He turned the pages with the familiarity of much usage to one on which was illustrated in a full-page photograph a spokeshave with a gleaming, beveled blade that joined the leatherbound handles. He held the catalogue open across the top of the orange crate. "Just look at that. Ain't that a beautiful thing?"

"Yes, it is. It's a fine-looking tool."

"That there is a piece of work. Yes, Lord. What do it say there, Doctah?"

I squinted at the printed item description and order form below the photograph. "It says: 'Finest forged Swedish steel, leatherbound, ash-handled,

8-inch spokeshave. Cabinet quality. Detachable handles fit blades of other dimensions. $5.75. Shipping wt. 8 oz.' "

"Five seventy-five. That's what I reckoned. That is a deal of money. Still, that is a tool a man would be proud to own. A man could leave a tool like that to his son, and his grandson. 'Deed he could."

"Yes, I suppose he could."

"Kin almost feel it in yo' hand. Almost feel her peel through the wood, come off in little white strips, smooth as willow." He nodded and took the catalogue from me, looking again at the photograph for a moment before he replaced the catalogue on the table and took off his glasses. His daughter came out of the house and stood in the doorway to the porch, eating a strip of fried grits. The little girl came with her and stood clinging to one of her mother's thighs, humming in her hoarse whisper "Jesus, Savior of My Soul."

"Good aftahnoon, Doctah," the young woman said.

"Hello, Becky. Is this your little girl?"

"Yes, suh, she is. You say hello to the gemman, Tuney."

"Graawh," the child croaked. She tugged at her mother's dress and the woman handed her a piece of the hard, batter-fried grits. She put the food into her mouth and chewed hungrily.

"My granddaughter," Walter Lubby said. "Child has got the Word."

"She has the Word?" I said.

" 'Deed she do. The Lord done talked to her. Done stirred up the child's mind." He nodded and rocked, fanning himself with the palm-leaf fan. A shiny strip of flypaper, hanging from the ceiling beam above his head, stirred gently in the breeze of the fan. He seemed in no hurry to go. Below the porch, I heard the car door close, and Mrs. Farris got out and came to the foot of the steps, where she waved up to him through the screen. "How you doing, Mr. Lubby?"

"Right good, thank you, ma'am," Mr. Lubby said. "You care to come up?"

"I thought I would. I thought I might help you in the car, if your sons not to home."

"No, ma'am, they working," he said. "You come on up."

"We won't stay," I said. "We have a pretty busy day ahead of us. How have you been feeling, Mr. Lubby?"

"Some better," he said. "Don't have the headache so bad."

"How about the shooting pains?"

"They some better."

"Good. The pills have helped, have they?"

" 'Deed they have. I been taking them regular. They do me real good. Just pull that latchstring, Miz Farris."

She came in onto the porch and stood smiling, at the rail. "Well, you're looking real good, Mr. Lubby. Real good. How you, Becky honey? That medicine the doctah gave you helped, did it?"

" 'Deed it did, ma'am. But I done run out. I was took right bad a couple of days ago, and took some extry."

"Well, I have some more for you," I said. "And we're going to take you over to the hospital now for a treatment that I think will help some, too."

"I'll be obliged for that," Mr. Lubby said. " 'Deed I will."

"He do real fine when he have the pills," Becky said. "Sleep real good, don't you, Daddy?"

"Yes, I do, thank the Lord." He nodded, fanning himself, rocking gently, looking down through the screen at the yellow water of the river between the trees. I stood up and put on my hat.

"Well, I think we'd better get going," I said. "Do you think you can manage those steps, with a little help?"

"I reckon so. I kin git outa bed, if they's somebody to he'p me." He reached to the table and took up his spectacles, tucking them into his shirt pocket. The little girl darted suddenly to his chair from her mother's side and crouched beside him, whispering in his ear. He leaned toward her, listening and nodding. " 'Deed he did, child," he said. "That's just what he done." He turned his eyes to me. "Child want to know did the Lord send you," he said. "I told her he did. I wonder would you folks like a little berry wine?"

"Oh, I don't know—" I began; but Mrs. Farris said lightly and gracefully, superimposing her words on mine with no evident intention of contradiction or rebuke, "Why, that would be fine, Mr. Lubby. I think we got time for just a glass of wine, don't you, Doctor?"

"Yes, I suppose so," I said. "A quick glass of wine."

"Have some real nice wine," Mr. Lubby said. "Blackberries was good last year." He seemed not to be uneasily postponing our departure, or to have any sense of anxiety, but only a desire to protract our visit fittingly, if briefly; to celebrate it in some formal way. "Becky, you bring that wine," he said to his daughter. "Some glasses for the lady and gemman."

"Yes, suh," she said, and went back into the house.

I took off my hat again and said to Mrs. Farris, "Well, I suppose we'll sit down for a minute."

"Yes, suh," Mr. Lubby said. "You folks set down. She be right out." There was another chair in the corner of the porch, facing inward. I sat down there, surrendering my previous place to Mrs. Farris.

"You have a nice place here," she said, having looked smilingly around the porch.

"It's tol'able. Do we git a little breeze. Used to be you would see the gators in the river. Come right up on the bank sometime. Don't see 'em no mo'. I reckon they near hunted out."

"Oh, Lord, that would've scared me!" Mrs. Farris said. "I wouldn't've stayed here long, with no gators. Not fifteen minutes, I wouldn't've stayed! Lord, no!" She chuckled hugely.

He turned to me, rocking gently with his good leg, the heel of the afflicted one resting on the floor, so that the great liquid-filled bag of the ruined joint wobbled gently with the motion. "Do you be feared of the gators, Doctah?"

"I don't believe I've ever seen one," I said. "I don't imagine it's a very pleasant experience, having one in your front yard."

"Do you be feared of the snakes?"

"The snakes? I've never liked them too much. Are there snakes in the swamp?"

" 'Deed they is. Cottonmouths. Rattlers. They is snakes, and scorpions, and red ants. They is bats hangin' in the trees. And they is a loogaroo back there in the big cypress, which you kin see his eyes in there when the moon is full."

Mrs. Farris nodded, her face falling solemnly. "Indeed they is," she said. "Indeed my daddy has told me that, many a time. They is folks that has seen the eyes."

"I has seen the eyes," Mr. Lubby said. He said it without emphasis, rocking impassively.

"Oh, my Lord, that would've scared me right outa my skin!" Mrs. Farris cried. She swung her head from side to side weakly, as if incapacitated by the thought. "My Lord, that must be a fearsome experience! I don't know how you wasn't scared right outa your skin!"

"You don't feel no fear, do you see the eyes," he said. "Eitherwise you dies, or you ain't never scared no mo'."

His daughter came back onto the porch from the house carrying four small fruit jars clutched together with a finger inserted into each, and a gallon vinegar jug filled with a dark scarlet wine. She set them on the orange crate in front of her father. He took his spectacles out of his shirt pocket, wound the springy stems around his ears, and peering through the small round lenses, unscrewed the cap of the vinegar jug and poured carefully into each of the small jars an identical level of the dark red wine, halfway to its rim. We watched this ceremony silently. His granddaughter, clinging to her mother's thigh and staring with huge pale eyes the color of sunlit milk, sang in a hoarse whisper:

> *"You got to walk that lonesome valley.*
> *You got to walk it by yo'se'f.*

Nobody else kin walk it fo' you.
You got to walk it by yo'se'f."

She had perfect pitch and an uncannily exact ear for phrasing and diction. The verse floated out of her like the harsh, inhuman emanation from an old-fashioned hand-wound phonograph. When the glasses were filled, his daughter handed one of them to each of us. We nodded and murmured our thanks. The old man raised his glass to the light that came through the screen of the porch and studied its color for a moment reminiscently; then he brought the rim of his glass to his lips and sipped delicately, closing his eyes. We followed his example, tasting the sleek, sharp wine gravely.

"Oh, that is fine," Mrs. Farris said. "That is fine wine, Mr. Lubby. Do you make it yourself?"

" 'Deed I do," Mr. Lubby said.

"That is the recipe he was give," his daughter said. "He don't tell nobody what it is."

"You got to be give it," the old man said. "You cain't be tole."

"It's very good indeed," I said. "Very unique." It was, unquestionably. It had an herbal bouquet, like crushed rosemary, and a heavy, syrupy suavity, like perfumed blood; I could not get the taste of it out of my mouth for days.

The old man held out his hand to the little girl, who moved to his side, still singing softly. He put his glass into her hand and guided it to her mouth, tipping it gently so that the viscous, scarlet fluid trickled into her lips. She did not drink, but went on chanting hoarsely, imperviously:

"With its cris-sal waters eh-vah
Flowing by the throne of God."

The wine dribbled out of the corners of her mouth and ran down the front of her faded blue cotton dress. The old man watched, nodding.

"I reckon we kin go now," he said. "Anytime you ready, Doctah."

"Fine," I said. "That was very nice. Very kind of you, Mr. Lubby." I set my glass on the porch rail and stood up, putting on my hat again. "Let's see if we can get down these steps now, without too much trouble."

"I he'p him," Becky said. "I know how to do it, don't I, Daddy?"

"Yes, indeed, sweet child," he said.

Between us, we eased and guided him down the five steps, his useless leg dragging and thumping heavily on the treads, to the yard. Mrs. Farris went ahead and opened the rear door of the car. It was a difficult job, hauling and prying him into the back seat as gently as possible, so that the knee joint should not be damaged further, as it might well have been, unknowingly, in its painless condition. His daughter stood in the yard and waved as we drove away. The little girl clung to her hip and keened harshly, the words following us faintly up the sand road between the pines:

> "Who's that yon-der dressed in blue?
> Must be the in-no-cent a-comin' through.
> Who's that yon-der dressed in black?
> Must be the hy-po-crites a-turnin' back."

When we got him in to the clinic at Cardozo, Dr. Kidd, who was an orthopedist, made a thorough examination of the knee. His diagnosis was grave.

"The joint is a total wreck," he said. "This is fulminant arthropathy in the worst stages. He's evidently been moving around on it, and the damage is tremendous. All the stress-bearing portions of the cartilage have undergone fibrillation and fragmentation. The joint capsule is full of fragments, and they've become the nidi of osseous bodies. The tendons and ligaments have lost their tone entirely, so you have an astonishing peripheral growth of cartilage, which has matured to form bone. Look at this picture. You see these long struts and bizarre craggy masses of bone in the joint spaces, the capsule, and even extending far beyond the joint along the muscle planes? These are so gross that there's liable to be perforation eventually. And look at this: there is grinding down and eburnation of the end of the femur shaft. You've got subluxation, and the beginning of dislocation. And these look like fractures to me—you see these rays?—through the joint and in the contiguous bone. It's totally useless. I think the leg should come off."

"When?"

"Whenever you can get him to agree. What sort of a man is he?"

"Rather strange," I said. "I mean, he's not the sort of man whose reactions you can predict."

"Have you finished with him?"

"Not quite. I've got the Wassermann to do, and the spinal. Are you going to be in here for a while?"

"Yes. I want to look at some more of these joints."

"I'll talk to you when I get through."

A spinal puncture is a delicate, dangerous, and often excruciating procedure. Not only is there frequently intense pain at the time it is performed, but there are resulting complications in the form of severe and persistent headache, numbness and stiffness of the neck, temporary—and sometimes permanent—paralysis; even, in some cases, death. These consequences are not uncommon, and there is very little margin for error in the performance of the operation.

A clumsy or careless practitioner may have to repeat it two or three times, and if the fluid taken is contaminated by blood, positive serologic tests or other abnormalities cannot be accepted as significant. Globulin tests may be positive, the cell count may be increased due to blood cells, and a false positive Wassermann may result, depending on the amount of blood in the fluid. The most common method of performing the procedure, and the one I used in Walter Lubby's case, is to have the patient straddle a straight chair, facing the chair back and arching his spine posteriorly. The lumbosacral area is cleansed with iodine, followed by alcohol. A sterile spinal needle is then inserted into the third, fourth, or fifth lumbar interspace and six to eight milliliters of fluid are withdrawn. I used a golden 20-gauge needle, which is very large and very painful.

When I inserted it for the first time, he shuddered and drooped forward, his head sagging and his weight falling onto his forearms, which rested along the upper rail of the chair back, as if he were about to faint. In fact, subjects often do faint during the procedure, and it was the last thing I wanted to happen. When the syringe filled with fluid, it was obviously stained with a faint tincture of blood. I saw Mrs. Farris's eyes close briefly above her surgical mask. I resented this involuntary silent censure as much as I did the trembling of my hand that had evidently accounted for my astonishing, unprecedented ineptitude.

"Are you all right, Mr. Lubby?" I said. He nodded. "Now, I'm going to have to do that just once more," I said. "I want you to be ready for it. Would you like a drink of water?"

"No, suh," he said. "I is ready, if that is how it got to be." He stiffened his back again into a convex arc and raised his head. I laid the syringe aside and took another from the sterile cabinet. I inserted the needle, lowering it to the next lumbar interspace, and as it sank into his spine he gave a long quivering sigh, his body bending slightly to the right, as if flowing with a current. The fluid appeared to be clear. He sat with his head bowed, unmoving.

"There. We've finished the treatment now," I said. "That's all we'll have to do today, Mr. Lubby. Would you like to lie down for a few minutes and rest?"

" 'Deed I would."

We helped him to the examination table, where he sat while I lifted his legs up onto it. Mrs. Farris supported his shoulders, lowering him gently onto his back. He lay looking up at the ceiling, his arms along his sides, his fingers plucking gently at the light cotton blanket we had drawn over him.

"Would you like a glass of fruit juice or a cup of coffee?" I asked him.

"No, suh. I won't take nothing."

Notes of birdsong, as clear and pure as globes of tinkling crystal, suddenly pervaded the room. The pane of the window seemed to tremble with them. He closed his eyes and lay listening. When the song had stopped, he said, "What kind of bird was that? I never heard no bird like that."

" 'Deed I didn't neither," Mrs. Farris said. "Now, wasn't that pretty."

"I wonder would you look in that tree outside the windy? See what kind of bird that was?"

"Why, yes, indeed," she said. "Indeed I will." She went to the window and looked out, peering up into the branches of the mimosa that shaded the window of the room. "Why, there he is," she said. "Ain't that a pretty bird."

"What color would he be?" Mr. Lubby said.

"He's red, Mr. Lubby. Big old red bird sitting there singing himself to death."

"He ain't black?"

"No, he ain't black. Look like a cardinal bird. Pretty thing."

"Yes, ma'am. Thank you kindly."

"Yes, indeed." She came back to the table where he lay and fussed with the blanket, drawing it up across his chest. "You feeling all right now, Mr. Lubby?"

"Yes, ma'am," he said. "I just going to lay here for a minute."

"Yes, you rest for a minute," I said. "I'm going into the radiology room and have a look at those pictures we took of you. I'll be back in a minute."

"Yes, suh."

Kidd was staring at the hanging roentgenograms in the radiology lab with Dr. Peterson, his radiologist, an unhappy-looking young black man with very fine features and straightened, shining hair. Dr. Kidd held a small notebook in his hand and was making marks on it with a fountain pen.

"Have you done the spinal?" he asked.

"Yes. What have you found here?"

"There's something up here in this right shoulder," Dr. Peterson said. He tapped one of the shiny hanging plates with his fingertip. "This bursal synovia looks a bit thickened. There seem to be some changes going on."

"The tendon sheaths seem to be enlarged," I said.

"Yes. Does he report any pain there?"

"No. What about the major organs?"

"They look all right to me. I don't see any significant changes. What have you found?"

"Areflexia: practically no knee-jerk reflex on either side. Cutaneous numbness in lower extremities. Third-nerve paralysis. Argyll-Robertson pupils. A history of severe headache and lightning pains. Sphincteric bladder disturbance. Intermittent slurred speech. Vertigo, memory lapses. And what I would call euphoria, I suppose. He has—spells."

"What sort of spells?"

"I don't know. He sees things. It's a paretic euphoria, I'm sure. What is a loogaroo?"

"Loup-garou," Dr. Kidd said. "It's the werewolf of the bayou. He's seen that, has he?"

"Evidently."

"Well, he's not the first around here. The Kline test you got back from Montgomery was positive?"

"In all dilutions. I've done another, and the spinal. I don't have any doubt that it's taboparesis. It will be a very interesting case to observe."

"Yes," Dr. Kidd said. He screwed together his fountain pen and slid it into his breast pocket. Dr. Peterson peered forward at an X-ray photograph, murmuring delicately, "Of course, syphilitic bursopathy is quite uncommon. What we might have here is early tuberculosis. Or a simple traumatic condition. It might be a good idea to take another set of plates."

"I don't really think it's necessary," I said. "We have to consider expenses. Those plates are very costly, and we have plenty here for a valid diagnosis as it is. We can take more later on, to measure the development."

"Yes, I suppose so," he murmured, his voice trailing away.

"What kind of prognosis would you make, considering his present condition?" Dr. Kidd said.

"I'd say he had eighteen months to five years. Of course, this kind of thing can fulminate very rapidly."

"Yes."

"He's a rather odd man. I mean, he can be a bit difficult to deal with. It might be a good idea if we didn't spring the amputation on him today. Maybe we should wait a few days, until we get the serology reports back. I think I'll have Janet Thurmond do the spinal tests, instead of sending them to N.I.H. She's a first-rate serologist. I'll drop around and see him afterwards, and let him know. About the leg, I mean. He might take it better. Would you mind if I did that?"

"No," Kidd said. "Not at all." He raised his arm abruptly to look at his wristwatch. "I have an appointment, anyway. It might be the best thing. Is he going to stay overnight?"

"I don't think so. He seems very anxious to get home."

"I see. Well, I'll talk to you tomorrow, then."

"Yes. Thank you very much. Dr. Peterson, we appreciate your assistance."

"Oh, not at all," Dr. Peterson said. "Not at all." He raised his hand and patted his hair vaguely, declining his head. He seemed anxious to minimize his part in the procedure.

"Well, I'll leave you, then, gentlemen," I said. "Mrs. Farris and I will take him back. Good afternoon."

"Good afternoon," Dr. Kidd said. Dr. Peterson nodded, raising his hand to examine his thumbnail and coughing gently.

The drive back to his cabin by the river was agonizing to him. I sat with him on the back seat while Mrs. Farris drove. When we left the paved highway and began to jounce and skid over the clay bumps and through the soft sand of the corduroy road between the pines, he closed his eyes and clutched at me, moaning softly. Although she drove so slowly that I could have walked beside the car, the slightest bounce of the badly sprung seat of the old sedan jarred his spine and sent him into a spasm of pain that made him clench the lapels of my jacket and writhe against my breast. I was afraid he might go into convulsions. I held him as tightly as I could and tried to ease the concussions of his body as the car thumped over the ruts. I can remember, now, telling you this, the smell of him as he clung to me: a faint, dusty, aromatic pungence like that of wintergreen and crumbled bay leaves, the smell of an old-fashioned pharmacy; as if the scent of the herbs he used to make his wine clung to his skin and hair and clothing. He opened his eyes once and stared at me like a child awakening from a dream in its father's arms.

"Did you hear the whistle?" he murmured.

"The whistle? No, I didn't hear any whistle."

"Oh, Lord, I heard the whistle. The long train is a-comin'."

"Well, try to relax," I said. "We'll be there soon. It isn't much further."

"No, Lord, it ain't," he murmured, and closed his eyes again, lying motionless for the rest of the way.

When we got him back to the cabin we put him into his bed in the rear room—a shed-roofed addition he had built onto the original one-room shanty —and advised his daughter to keep him there for two days. We had brought a bedpan, which Mrs. Farris instructed her in the use of, and I left a copious supply of aspirin for her to give him. For the sake of his comfort, and the appearance of therapy, I rubbed his arms and shoulders with alcohol. The little girl clung to the top rail of the white-painted brass foot-gate of the bed, bending her knees and swinging slowly back and forth while she croaked in her idiot-savant voice:

> "My Lord calls me.
> He calls me in the thun-dah.
> The trumpet sounds within-a my soul.
> I ain't got long to stay here."

A few days later Molly and Elizabeth arrived, on a blazing blue day in the middle of July. Their train was half an hour late. I sat on a bench on the waiting platform and with my briefcase on my lap composed the opening paragraph of an article I was writing for the *Journal of Venereal Disease Information*. It was to be the first official piece of literature relating to the experiment, and would cause, I felt sure, a considerable stir in medical circles. I wrote scrupulously, with absolute absorption, modeling my syntax on Hinton's, whose style, I felt, was an almost faultless model of scientific prose. I was hardly aware that time was passing; when I glanced up, having finished my introductory paragraph, at the huge circular clock mounted on an iron pole at the far end of the platform, I was astonished to find that I had been sitting there for thirty-seven minutes. I put my papers back into my briefcase, watching the movements of my fingers as I did so with a strangely foreign fascination, wondering if they were measurably less nimble, measurably more decrepit, than they had been when I removed the papers with them. A train whistle blew in the distance, to the north, where the rails converged infinitely to an endlessly compressed ribbon in the hazy distance of the cotton field across which they stretched. It was a heart-startlingly mournful and imperious sound, pealing over the flat field toward the shabby, gingerbread-gabled building that seemed to hang crystallized with its magically speeding clock in the veils of shimmering haze. I wondered if it was the train that Walter Lubby had heard a few days before; we had taken him home at almost that exact time.

In a moment a cloud of tumbling black smoke appeared above the tracks on the rim of the horizon, unrolling toward me as the train approached, the earth trembling perceptibly as it advanced, the face of the locomotive, with its grilled cowcatcher and single smokestack and huge glass headlight, growing from a tiny toy to a rocking, thundering monster that heaved at last, steaming and subsiding, in under the scalloped wooden canopy of the waiting platform. It seemed as if all the powers of the universe had combined to shake me into recognition of the existence of my wife and daughter. A porter leaned down from the open door of a parlor car to set a flight of metal steps in place, descended them, and held up his hand to give assistance to Molly, who appeared at the top, clutching the rail with one hand and Elizabeth to her breast with the other as she stepped down, fearfully, awkwardly, with a kind of mortified but dauntless hope, covered with the dust and lint of its scarlet plush, out of the shabby limbo from which I had summoned her.

Although she did not seem changed at all by the two months of our separation, I was startled at her appearance. I don't know why; startled, perhaps, at having my memory of it confirmed so ruthlessly. Elizabeth, however, had undergone visible and inauspicious alterations: her plump face had settled into an expression that was now not so much vapid as stoic; an almost grim acceptance of the earth and its atrocities that was alarmingly unchildlike and that made me cringe with pity for an instant when I saw her. I felt a vertigo that made me put out my hand to touch an iron pillar of the platform and steady myself. Molly set the child down on the concrete and gave her a little push to send her forward in a mechanical, much-rehearsed, tottering flight toward me. I crouched down, holding out my arms to her in a grinning travesty of welcome. She came and placed herself obediently between them, encircling my neck loosely with her damp, fat arms and laying her chin perfunctorily on my shoulder while she gazed off toward the gables of the town and muttered, "Hello, Daddy. We missed you a lot." She smelled strongly of vomit.

"Well, I missed you, too," I said. "My goodness, how you've grown!"

"We thought about you every day. We brought you a pleasant."

"A present," Molly said, standing nervously and impatiently behind her.

"A present. We brought you a present."

"Oh, that's very nice. My goodness, I don't want any present but you. That's the best present I could get." I disengaged her gently; the smell of vomit was overpowering.

"I got sick," she said. "I threw up."

"Well, that's what happens to people sometimes, on trains." I stood up, taking her hand, and smiled at Molly, who stood uncertainly apart, an anguished smile twisting askew her lips, which were painted an ungodly pinkish bronze.

"She had train sickness," she said. "It was so hot in that coach."

"I know. It's an awful ordeal." I moved to her and put my arm around her shoulders. She closed her eyes and tilted her head up, pouting her lips grotesquely. I kissed them lightly, patting her back in a vague, congratulatory gesture.

"Well, it's good to see you again," I said. "You look good, Molly. You've gotten prettier than ever. How did you do that, in just two months?"

"I don't think I'm any prettier," she said. "If you could have seen me in that toilet mirror, you wouldn't think so."

"I know. They're awful, aren't they? Those cars must be a hundred years old. Well, welcome to Tallacoochee."

"Is this it?" she said. "We seem to be way out in the middle of a field."

"No, there's a little more of it than this." I laughed a small uneasy laugh. "The station's out of town a way. I guess they expected the town to expand. Victorian optimism."

"Victorian optimism?"

"Something like that, I guess." The porter had set four suitcases on the platform at her feet and stood lingering over them. I took out my wallet and handed him a dollar bill. "Are these all the bags?"

"Yes, suh. That's all they is. Thank you very much, suh." He smiled expansively and lifted the peak of his cap.

"Most of our things are in the trunk," Molly said. "I sent that on ahead by Railway Express. They said it would be here in just a few days."

"Well, I guess it'll show up soon. You gave them the address?"

"Yes. They said they'd notify us."

"I threw up all over my dress," Elizabeth said. "My real new dress."

"Well, we'll get that washed up as soon as you get home," I said. "Just wait'll you see your new room. You'll love it here."

"I liked my old room," she said. "I didn't want to leave."

"Elizabeth," Molly said.

"Well, I did."

"I've got a car outside," I said. "I had to rent one, finally. I was borrowing Liam's all the time."

"Who is Liam?"

"He's the doctor I work with. The head of the County Health Department." I bent down to pick up two of the bags.

"I can bring those other two," Molly said. "They're not very heavy. There's mostly Elizabeth's toys in one of them."

"You sure? I can come back, in just a minute."

"No, that's all right. I've gotten used to doing things for myself." She picked up the two smaller suitcases and walked beside me to the door of the WHITE waiting room, where I set down my bags and held the door for her while she went inside.

"Why are there separate waiting rooms?" she said.

"Well, that's just the custom down here."

"It seems like a very funny custom."

She did not like the town from the minute she first saw it; it was unrelievedly "funny" to her. When we drove down the main street she said, "It certainly is a funny little place. It looks like it's falling apart. What are those funny trees?"

"Live oaks," I said. "I think they're rather pretty, really. They're evergreens, you know. They never lose their leaves."

"What's that stuff that's hanging off them?"

"Spanish moss. It's everywhere down here."

"It certainly is gloomy-looking."

"I guess it is, but you get used to it," I said. "It makes lovely shadows. That's the county clinic, up there, where we have our offices."

"Up over that drugstore?"

"Yes."

"That's a funny place to have a clinic."

I dreaded her reaction to the house, but except for the fact that it "smelled funny," she did not put it into words. She didn't need to; when we had unpacked the bags she wandered through its rooms in a growingly indurated gloom that was expressed eloquently in the tics and twitchings of her lips and nostrils. These became especially pronounced in the bathroom and kitchen, where she lingered in a kind of wan, strengthless disbelief, casting her eyes about despondently, touching with revulsion a piece of stained, cracked linoleum that hung from a shelf edge, and then a rag stuffed into a hole in the ruptured plaster of the wall. On the back porch she fell into a kind of trance, staring out through the rusty screen at the walk that ran from the back steps to the tool shed under the branches of the mulberry tree. It was spattered with the droppings of birds who had feasted on the berries, great vermilion splashes that reappeared every morning on the cracked concrete, although I hosed them off daily. The tin roof of the wooden shed and the hull of the rotting rowboat were mottled with them. It looked as if the sky had been raining blood.

"Did you get the Grime-Go?" she asked.

"Yes. I got the large size. It's under the sink." She nodded desolately. "Of course, I haven't had time to get the place in order, really. I'm sorry about that. I wanted to get a woman in this week to clean up before you came, but I just wasn't able to get to it."

"I know. You must be very busy."

"It's basically a nice old house. I think we'll be very comfortable here, once we get straightened up. I'll try to get a woman in this week."

"What is that boat thing?"

"Well, it's a *boat*. I guess the people used to fish a lot. There are beaches close by, and a picnic grove. Liam has a place down on the Gulf where he's invited us to come and stay for a few days, if you like. His wife's been there all spring. She's the lady who loaned us the crib for Elizabeth."

"Well, that's nice of them. Are the people nice here?"

"Well, of course I don't know many of them. The townspeople, I mean. Just the people I work with, mostly. But you'll have a chance to meet some of them on Saturday night. Paula—that's Liam's wife—is giving a welcome party for you."

"That's very nice. I don't know whether I'll feel like going, though."

"I hope so. She'll be disappointed if you don't."

"What would we do with Elizabeth?"

"I don't know. I hadn't thought about that." We stood together for a moment in desperate silence.

"Is it always this hot here?" she asked at last.

"I guess so, in the summer. It's been pretty hot ever since I got here. But they say the winters are very mild."

The prospect, like Christmas, seemed too distant to comfort her.

We ate dinner very early and put Elizabeth to bed immediately after. Along with the Grime-Go, I had bought steaks and baking potatoes, which Molly prepared stoically, with an air of heroic fortitude, in the gloomy, unfamiliar kitchen. Every moment or two she would ask me where something was. "Where is the grill pan?" "Where are the pot holders?" "Where is the butter dish? Is this thing what you use?" I had never before eaten in the dining room, and was as dismayed as she by its dust and dark and its ominous, anthropophagous-looking furniture with taloned feet and sinister, gleaming thews and bloated, ventricular curves. Elizabeth ate in a high chair that Liam had dug out of his attic for us, as silent and ravenous as ever in spite of her ordeal, or perhaps because of it. Molly busied herself with attending on her; without enthusiasm but dutifully, cutting up her meat and mashing her potato with a fork, closing her own eyes frequently with exasperation when the child unexpectedly spit out a piece of meat, or spilled her milk, or plunged her fork into the tabletop. I became aware, in the course of that meal, that her entire absorption in Elizabeth, her indulgent and solicitous preoccupation with her every move and gesture and expression, had declined into something very different: a weary, almost acrimonious impatience that seemed directed, with baffling obliquity, at me. I was able to deduce—it was impossible to overlook —a kind of dark, subtextual implication in her air of afflicted, undisguised intolerance that I translated something like this: You see what is happening to me? Do you see how you have incapacitated me, even for motherhood? Do you see how our child is suffering because of the way you have undermined my love for her? You are demoralizing all of us.

I was so dismayed by this implication that I began hastily to refute it in my mind, watching her surreptitiously in the mirror of the sideboard as she silently devoured a piece of beef. Of course, she may not be implying anything of the kind, I thought. She's tired. She's had a long and exhausting journey. She's very justifiably depressed by the condition of this house, by her anxiety about the future. No one could be expected to behave very cheerfully under those conditions. Not even Janet Thurmond, if Liam were sitting in my place. I wasn't at all sure of that conjecture; and both its uncertainty and the unexpectedness of its occurrence increased my discomposure. This was followed by indignation, a gust of inward fury at the silent censure I endured from her, from Liam, from Dr. Horgan, from Janet, from the world. Why doesn't somebody think about *my* problems once in a while? I thought. *My* needs, *my* comfort? Am I such a dreadful man? I work hard, I have little or no thought for my own pleasure, I'm dedicated to a project of worldwide scientific importance. Why should I be subjected to these people's self-righteous disapproval? Doesn't a man have the right to expect a little sympathy from his own family, from his colleagues? God in heaven, I get more understanding from Walter Lubby than I do from these people.

Still brooding on the strangeness of that thought, I washed up the dinner dishes in the cracked and leaking sink and scoured out the broiler pan while Molly took Elizabeth upstairs and put her to bed. Afterwards I went out and sat in a rocking chair on the front porch, my indignation transposing slowly into a weary melancholy that seemed to embrace the whole sad, damp, incontinently fragrant world. Molly came down shortly and lowered herself with an air of distaste into the shabby rocker beside mine. We sat and watched the dusk gather in the silent trees. There were pale stars in the deepening violet of the sky. Molly raised her head to stare up at them and said after a moment, "I don't know. I expected something so different."

"Well, of course, it isn't Washington. Or Palm Springs. But I have to work here. There happens to be a great deal of disease in this place." The inopportuneness of the remark struck me the moment I had uttered it; I added hastily, before she had a chance to profit by it, "And it's my duty, unfortunately, to —to study it."

"I know that," she said. "I know you have to study these things. It's your work, and I knew that when I married you, so I'm not complaining."

A pair of wrens flew, one after another, into the Virginia creeper vine that enveloped the vertical railing supporting the porch roof. We heard their peaceful rustling among the leaves as they settled for the night into the tranquil domesticity of wild things, unblighted by sensibility. Molly leaned forward quickly to peer into the foliage.

"Oh, look, Carl," she whispered. "They've got a nest in there, I think! Those sweet little birds! What are they, wrens?"

"I don't know. I think so."

"Oh, isn't that adorable! I'm going to watch them every day. I'll be able to see the little ones hatch out."

"Yes."

"How long have they been here? Did you see them build it?"

"No. I don't know. I hadn't noticed them before. Quite a while, I suppose, if they've got eggs in there already."

"I just love to see them fly back and forth all day with bugs and things for the little ones. They just seem so busy and happy. I'm so glad I'll have them to watch." She sat back in her chair and rocked it gently a few times. "You know, it *is* nice to sit in a rocking chair. I don't think I'll mind at all, when I get old."

"They're very comfortable."

"I really worry about Elizabeth, though. She just hated to leave. She cried and cried when I told her we were coming."

"Oh, children adapt very quickly. She'll forget all about it in a month or so."

"I hope so. Will you go up and say good night to her, Carl, before she goes to sleep? She wants to give you her present."

"Yes, I'll go up."

But when I went upstairs she was asleep, holding a cheap, cast-metal replica of the Washington Monument mounted on a flat, felt-covered base as a paperweight. Her plump fingers were clutched around that sad, arrant, phallic symbol of man's vanity and lust like a scepter, an odious wand held out to me in tribute, or mockery, or some innocent, vile conjuration cast at me even from her sleep.

Paula, Liam's wife, was a vivid, reverberant woman who seemed made of some resonant alloy of zinc and steel; she rang and sparkled and spoke very rapidly in rippling, dizzying arpeggios, like the sound of a mallet being run swiftly and gaily up and down the keys of a vibraphone. I always found myself frantically attempting to decode the previous phrase of her conversation while recording the present one, like an official translator keeping desperately, and barely, abreast of the remarks of a foreign dignitary. Most of her suggestions and importunities one yielded to automatically, with a helplessly congenial murmur, not only because they were delivered with such a bewilderingly euphonious speed, but also because there was something about her of the slender, willful tension of a whippet, and, as with that animal, one felt it would be safer to give her whatever amount of leash she demanded than to lay oneself open to a graceful, volatile outrage or embarrassment of some kind, impossible to predict or forestall. This was the case when I told her, over the telephone, that we wouldn't be able to attend her party because we didn't have a babysitter, and, in any case, Molly didn't want to leave Elizabeth in the care of someone she didn't know, in a strange house, so soon after her arrival.

"Well, honey, just bring her *with* you," Paula said. "We can put her to bed right upstairs, in Lucy's old bedroom. You can check on her every ten minutes if you like. That's what everybody *does*. There's even a Raggedy Ann doll up there she can cuddle up with. She'll be snug as a *bug*. Now, you let me talk to Molly; it's not going to *be* any party unless she's here."

It was curious to see Molly succumb as quickly and totally as she did to the woman's unarguable charm. She even smiled once or twice, murmuring shy and grateful expressions of assent while she twisted the phone cord helplessly around her finger.

"Well, maybe it'll work out," she said when she had hung up. "She seemed very nice, I must say. I guess Elizabeth would go to sleep all right. We could check on her every now and then."

I was pleased. I've always detested parties, as I think you know by now, but I felt that if it were possible for Molly to make the acquaintance of one or two women with whom she could shop or have luncheon occasionally, we would all be infinitely better off.

I had met Paula for the first time only a few days before, the evening after my examination of Walter Lubby. I had stopped by Liam's house, after taking Mrs. Farris home, to report the results of the examination to him, but he was not to be found. Paula had opened the door to me, her face wearing a look of merciless, glacial anticipation that had shocked me. I remember, in one of the Bibles I was awarded by a maiden aunt for my adolescent zeal, a colored illustration of Delilah inviting Samson into her chamber with just such an expression on her face. Perhaps, in Paula's case, I imagined or exaggerated it, because it transposed instantly into one of such genial and animated hospitality that I found myself deciding, later, that it could only have been the product of my own disordered state of mind, which at the moment was considerable.

"Oh, excuse me," I said, for some reason. "I was looking for Liam."

"Well, I bet I know who *you* are," she said in a tone of long-delayed delight. "I just bet you're Carl Ransome. Now i'n't that so?"

"Yes, it is. I guess you're Liam's wife."

"I *guess* I am," she said merrily. "I *hope* so, or there's going to be a certain amount of confusion around here. My goodness, you're just a *boy*. From what Liam's been saying about you, I thought you were an older *man*. Come in, Carl." She held out her hand and clasped my own meltingly in it while she led me into the room, which had undergone many small but very visible and dramatic changes. The scraps of badly chewed rawhide and the bowl surrounded by crumbs of dog food on the carpet had disappeared, and the clutter of newspapers, medical journals, and textbooks marked with ragged strips of paper or bulging with inserted matchbooks had been replaced, on the coffee table, with a copy of the latest best-seller and a gigantic edition of an art book whose glittering waxy jacket was illustrated with a magnificent full-color print of Picasso's "Les Saltimbanques"; the books had been straightened in the bookcase, and, above them, the bust of Blake shorn of its coonskin cap.

"It's nice to meet you, Mrs. Proctor," I said when I had seated myself cautiously on the sofa, whose summer slipcover had been removed to reveal its flawless golden velvet upholstery. "I hope you've had a pleasant time at the beach."

"Oh, I had a *lovely* time," she said, seating herself opposite me and leaning forward with one forearm resting on the knee of her elegantly crossed, slender legs. "But you better call me Paula, because I'm going to call you Carl whether you like it or not. Now, I don't want us to have any *trouble.*"

"No, I hope not," I said with an uneasy smile.

"Just look at my *arms!*" She thrust one of them out and ran her fingertips lingeringly up the smooth golden skin to her shoulder. "I just got *black* down there! I bet you thought I was a nigra when I opened the door. That's why you looked so funny!"

"No, I didn't. Not at all. Nobody could make a mistake like that."

"I bet you thought I was the *maid!* Now, didn't you? Oh, but that's right —you've met Viola, haven't you? Well, it would be hard to tell us apart right now, in the dark. Let me get you a little drink."

"No, thank you. I don't drink."

"You *don't!* My goodness, I never heard of such a thing. You don't drink *anything?* Well, I can see Liam hasn't been treating you right at *all.*"

"Oh, I can't complain about that. He's been more than hospitable. Is he in, by the way? I just stopped by to tell him about a patient I saw this afternoon."

"Oh, Lord, i'n't that a pity? No, he's not. He went down to the office for a while after dinner. You know how that man is. You just can't keep him away from that lab. He ought to be back real soon, though. You want me to call him?"

"No, that's all right. I'll see him in the morning. It's nothing urgent."

"All right. I'll be real happy to call him, though, if you want me to. You can call him yourself if you like. Why don't you do that? The phone's right over yonder on that table. Now I'm going to get you a cup of coffee whether you like it or not. I *know* you drink coffee; I never knew a doctor that didn't." She stood up, forestalling my protest with an outstretched hand. "Now don't you say a word. I want to *talk* to you; I don't often get a good-looking man all to myself this time of night. I'll be back here before you know I left."

"All right, thank you."

While she was out of the room I sat restlessly for a moment, my eyes drifting to the marble-topped phone table that stood beside the arch. After a few minutes, I got up and went to it, lifting the receiver to dial Liam's office number. When it had rung five times, I hung up the receiver as gently as possible and went back to the sofa.

"You know the number, Carl?" she called from the kitchen.

"Yes. That's all right. It's nothing very important." I opened the art book and began to leaf through it, pausing to stare at a startlingly voluptuous Modigliani nude sprawled across a divan in the light from an open blind. I closed the book hurriedly as I heard Paula's Cuban heels striding back up the hall from the kitchen. She carried a lacquer tray on which were a silver-plated coffee service and a pair of cups and saucers. She set it on the coffee table in front of me, and while she leaned over to pour the coffee, raised her free hand to make the perfunctory and very inadequate gesture of clasping to her bosom the low-cut neck of her blue silk blouse, below which the firm brown swell of her tanned breasts was plentifully visible. When she had finished she sat down across from me again, perched on the edge of her chair, her elbows resting on her knees, her arms extending forward, her hands drooping at the wrists, the fingers loosely laced, smiling brilliantly. She was forty, perhaps; a very striking woman with bronze-colored, glowing hair worn loose and long, almost to her shoulders, which was unusual in those days; but with a mouth whose thin bright lips, in their few and unexpected moments of repose, fell into a crumpled, garish line, like a scar made by a ragged instrument: a piece of tin or a dull can opener.

"Now, you taste that coffee and let me know what you think," she said.

I sipped it obediently, and nodded immediately and extravagantly. "Oh, that's fine. That's really good coffee. Excellent."

"Well, I'm glad to hear you say so. I wouldn't've trusted you far as that door if you hadn't. I do know how to make coffee, if I say so myself. That's one thing my mother *did* manage to teach me." She gave a little trill of amusement, as if titillated by this confession of her own legendary imperviousness to convention, her splendid intransigence. "Now, tell me: What do you think about this little old hick town of ours? I reckon you're just pining away here for some kind of civilized entertainment."

"Oh, no. Not at all. I've been much too busy to be bored." I sipped at my coffee and then gulped, adding hastily, "Although I wouldn't have been bored, by any means. Far from it. It's a charming town. I already feel very much at home here."

"You *do?* Well, my land, that *does* surprise me. A man like you, that's used to Washington, D.C. I think Washington's one of the most wonderful places on *earth*. I have a cousin that lives up there, in Georgetown, and I used to go and visit her sometimes, at Easter, when we were in school. Oh, I used to look forward to those *visits!* You know what girls are like, anyway. We just went everywhere together. Picnics in Rock Creek Park, down there by that old mill —what's the name of it?"

"Pierce Mill."

"Pierce Mill, that's right! My Lord, I haven't thought about that place in years! And down there by the Tidal Basin, where all the cherry trees are? Oh, that's just the most beautiful place in the whole *world* in the spring. And that wonderful old museum, that looks like an old red brick castle?"

"The Smithsonian."

"The Smithsonian. Where they have Lindy's plane? And all those dinosaur bones? Lord, we don't have anything like that around here. We've got plenty of *bones,* but we keep 'em in the closet; we don't put 'em on public exhibition." A stealthy, gamine smile rippled her lips while she made this confession, breaking into a brilliant, ravenous grimace, the expression of a seal which has just performed a particularly clever trick and expects to be tossed a herring in reward. "Well, now, I'm going to *try* and relieve your boredom a little bit the weekend after next," she went on rapidly. "I don't know how successful I'm going to be, but I'm going to try; because Liam tells me you're the hardest-working man he ever did see. And when *he* says that, it's something."

"I think he's exaggerating," I said. "I've worked no harder than he has."

"Uh-huh. Well, just the same, it's time you had a little fun. We do have some *fun* down here once in a while, believe it or not. Liam says your wife is coming down next week, is that right?"

"Yes, she's coming in on Wednesday."

"I'n't that wonderful? Well, what I'm goin' to do is get together a few folks I think you'd both enjoy meetin' and have a little welcome party for her on Saturday night, after she gets in. You think she'll be rested up by then?"

"Oh, yes, I'm sure she will. It's very kind of you."

"Well, it i'n't any more than I *ought* to do. I know how a woman feels when she has to move into a new community: just like a fish out of *water.* Especially if it's some little one-horse place like this. Well, we're not goin' to let that happen to her, and you can count on it."

"She'll be very pleased, I'm sure."

"It'll give you a chance to meet some of our interestin' folks, too. We *do* have a few, you know. You heard of Lacry Tulliver?"

"No, I don't think so."

"Well, he wrote a book about the role of Hackett County in the Confederacy. *The Thin Gray Line?* It's sold out two or three editions already; I thought you might have heard of it. Well, I thought you'd enjoy meetin' him. And Professor Malory? He's head of the History Department over at Birmingham."

"Oh, yes."

"And I thought you'd particularly like to meet some of the Board of Censors. That's the executive body of our medical association here in Hackett County. You'll probably be working with a lot of 'em before you get through, and it might just be worth your while to know some of 'em personally. You never can tell when you're goin' to need a friend."

"I'd like to very much. I think I did meet some of them, very briefly, over at Cardozo one evening. When Dr. Kidd and I explained the project to the medical association."

"Uh-huh, you would have. Still, it's a nice thing to be able to sit down with a drink and have a real personal talk with folks like that—that you might need to know better."

"Yes. You have a very old association here. It has a fine reputation, all over the country."

"Well, i'n't it nice of you to say that. *We* think it should. Dr. Prescott—he's the chairman—is the oldest living member. There i'n't *anything* about this county he can't tell you."

"I'll look forward to meeting him," I said.

"Well, now, don't you forget about it. I'll skin you alive if you do!"

"No, I won't."

"I'm lookin' forward to meetin' your wife. I can't tell you how much. Molly, i'n't it?"

"Yes."

"Be nice for her to meet some of the ladies in town, too. Now, you tell her I'm goin' to call her on Thursday, will you, Carl?"

"Yes, I will."

We talked for another fifteen minutes or so; or rather, she talked. Not quite so banally as any attempt to reproduce her conversation sounds, because I became aware, gradually, that it was sprinkled skillfully with invitations for correction or interpolation that one accepted at his peril. She set down her coffee cup with a sudden clatter and raised her hand to stare at the jeweled watch on her brown wrist. "I don't know *where* Liam is!" she cried in a gaily plaintive tone. "Have you figured out yet how many nights a week he goes down there to that lab and works himself to death?"

"No, I haven't," I murmured. "He works very hard, there's no doubt about that."

"He always was bad, but I think he's gettin' worse, the older he gets. Haven't you noticed that?"

"I don't suppose I've known him long enough to judge."

"It must be a *mighty* interestin' project you've got him involved in. Still, I suppose we'll all share in its glory someday. I *hope* you're going to let us share in its glory, Carl, because if there's one thing this town could use it's a little fresh glory. Most of ours is getting a little frayed around the edges by now."

"I think there'll be enough to go around," I said. "It's a remarkable piece of work; and Liam is making a great contribution to it."

"Well, I just hope he doesn't work himself to death. I don't know how you-all keep it up. And the *ladies,* especially! I swear, that poor Janet Thurmond! She must have the strength of a horse. Don't you think she's a remarkable person?"

"Yes, she is. It would be very hard to get along without her. Liam's very fortunate—to have a worker like her."

"I'n't he? I keep tellin' him that."

I set down my coffee cup and stood up. "I'm afraid I've got to get along," I murmured. "I've still got some paperwork to do tonight, and we'll be out on the circuit by eight o'clock in the morning."

"Now, you see what I'm tellin' you? Well, all right, then. I reckon I better let you get home and have a little sleep. I'm real sorry Liam wasn't here. I'll sure tell him you came by."

"Well, I'll see him tomorrow. It's not that important. Thanks very much for the coffee, Mrs. Proctor. I'll look forward to your gathering."

"Now, that's a week from Saturday night, about eight o'clock. And don't you dare eat any dinner before you get here! I'm goin' to fix a Creole jambalaya you won't forget for a long time, if I do say so."

"I'm sure we won't."

When she opened the front door for me we saw Liam's car standing by the curb halfway up the block, one headlight shining. In the wide glare of it, Liam was lurching mildly down the sidewalk toward the house, his long spindly shadow unreeling waveringly behind him like a slowly unrolling spool-length of tattered black ribbon. He paused to stand and urinate unsteadily against a tree, raising his head and calling out, while he unbuttoned his fly, *"Enith!* Enitharmom! *Enith!"* We heard the rapid uneven patter of the dog's toenails on the concrete, and in a moment saw her dashing in her wildly lopsided gallop down the sidewalk to him, whining joyfully, leaping up to plunge her forepaws against his breast. They both tottered back against the tree and were evidently liberally splashed, since Liam howled out gaily, "Goddamnit, now look at that! Got us soaking wet. You crazy little bitch." He hugged her to him, holding one of her paws out as if he were leading her in a dance, the two of them staggering back and forth across the sidewalk in a ludicrous, unsteady waltz.

"I think, as they say in the novels, we had better 'close the door mercifully on this episode,'" Paula said. She did so, and leaned against it, closing her eyes with a sardonically humorous expression of extremity.

"I guess he's had a bit too much to drink," I said, idiotically.

"You know, I think you're right. You're quite a diagnostician."

"I mean, when you're very tired, and haven't eaten properly, it goes to your head very fast. Why don't you tell him to take the day off tomorrow?"

"Why don't you tell him that?"

"Well, I'll see what I can do."

"All right. Shall we try again?" She opened the door and said very loudly, "It's just been lovely meeting you, Carl. I *wish* Liam was here."

"Well, I'll see him tomorrow," I said, with false, booming innocence. "Until next week, Mrs. Proctor." She kissed the tips of her fingers to me in weary gratitude and closed the door.

Out on the sidewalk, Liam was buttoning his fly, trying with one hand to suppress the ecstatic Enitharmom, who still vaulted wildly against him.

"Carl!" he said as I approached him. "I'll be damned. Missed you, did I?

Still, you've had the pleasure of a tête-à-tête with Paula. Now, that's something to cherish. How the hell are you?"

"Fine," I said. I took the hand which he held out to me, unpleasantly wet.

"Sorry about that," he mumbled. "Matter of natural necessity. Which after all is the great disposer of human affairs. And there is no affair like a human affair, although I think this little bitch might give a man more fun than a lot of the human ones. Get down, you hussy."

"You've left your lights on," I said. "One of them, anyway."

"You're very observant, you know that, Carl? You notice things. That's your strong suit. You're a great observer. Did you notice anything about Walter Lubby this afternoon that you found interesting?"

"Yes. We took him in to Cardozo, and Kidd and Peterson and I went over him pretty carefully. The knee's in very bad shape. Kidd wants to amputate."

"Oh. I thought he might. What's your opinion?"

"I think he's right. He seems to be a very competent orthopedist."

"Yes. He is. So you're going to chop the man's leg off. What does he say about that?"

"We haven't told him yet. I left the spinal fluid for Janet. I don't know if she told you."

"Yes. She did. It's full of cells. Thousands of them. Positive mastic curve. Buckets of globulin in every drop. The man's riddled with it."

"That's what I thought. The knee's in very bad shape. There's danger of perforation, Kidd says, from the neo-osseous formations."

"I see. And suppose it develops in the other one?"

"Well, we'll have to wait and see."

"And then the elbows? And the hips?"

"As a matter of fact, there seem to be some changes in the right shoulder," I said. "At least that's Peterson's opinion."

"Oh, yes. Listen, why don't we just cut his head off and set it on a plate? Feed him an aspirin once in a while. Save a lot of trouble." He lost his balance and lunged suddenly backwards, banging his shoulder against the tree trunk. " 'Eppur, si muove,' " he muttered. "It does, too. No good denying it. Right, Carl? Men of truth."

"Why don't you take the day off tomorrow?" I said. "You've been working too hard. Or come over at noon. Claxton's working with my team now, so we've got plenty of personnel. Get a little rest. You've got Paula pretty worried."

"Yes, I know that," he said. "Paula worries a lot. She's got what's called Southern Discomfort. Hey, how did you two get along, anyway?"

"Very well," I said. "She's charming; you're a lucky man."

"Yes, I am. A lucky man."

"Let me walk you to the house," I said.

"No. No, thanks. I've got my faithful guide dog here. She's lucky, too. All I did to *her* was *break* her goddamned leg. She got off lucky." He swung himself away from the tree trunk and plunged for a step or two along the walk, pausing to turn back unsteadily to me. "G'night, Carl. Sweet dreams," he said. I watched him lurch toward the house, the dog following in an equally incongruous stagger behind him, the two of them proceeding like a pair of maimed, inseparable derelicts under the wan midsummer moon. When he reached the front door it opened almost immediately and I saw him stumble toward Paula in the light from the living-room lamps. She withdrew from him and he followed her into the house, turning to bang the door closed behind him. I walked over to the parked car and opened the door, leaning down to switch off the headlight. I left the key in the ignition. The dog slunk past me, her tail between her legs. When I shut the door she accelerated into a terrified scurry and disappeared into the shadows of the street.

On the morning after Molly's arrival I went to see Walter Lubby again; alone this time, since I would not need Mrs. Farris's assistance. As I drove up the road between the pines, I saw an animal spoor in the yellow sand between the tire tracks: the paw prints of a large dog, or perhaps a bear or panther; I didn't know enough about animal tracks to identify them. I followed the road in through the cluster of shanties by the riverbank to his cabin. There was wood smoke in the air from the iron kettles and the smell of it blended with the musky reek of the river and the faint, distant fetor of privies in the willow grove. There were women tending the wash kettles, poking with wooden paddles at the clothing that bubbled in the soapy water. The gray moss hung very still from the willow branches and the smoke from the kettle fires drifted into it and was absorbed as if into a sponge. In the yard below the cabin Walter Lubby's daughter stood with one hand on her hip, stirring the boiling clothes in the black kettle. The little girl squatted beside her in the sand, poking the burning wood of the fire with a stick. The woman watched with a languid, expressionless air while I parked the car and got out.

"Good morning," I said to her.

"Mo'nin'. Daddy's up yonder on the porch." I looked up and saw him sitting in the rocking chair, watching me silently through the screen. I waved to him and he nodded. I took my bag from the seat and went up the steps without awaiting his invitation, tugging the latchstring to unfasten the door. When I opened it and went in onto the porch he said, "Yes, suh. Good mo'nin'."

"Good morning," I said. "You ought to be in bed."

"Cain't see the river from in there. Don't feel easy in my mind do I not see the river." He was wearing his glasses and held the tool catalogue open in his lap. I sat down across the orange crate from him in the empty cane-bottomed chair and set my bag on the floor. He took off his glasses slowly and laid them on the crate and massaged his eyelids with thumb- and fingertips.

"Are your eyes bothering you?" I asked.

"It the headache," he said. "I got the headache bad."

"Have you been taking the medicine?"

"Yes, suh. It do help, but the head is powerful bad."

"You can take two of the pills every two hours. It won't hurt you."

" 'Deed I will do that."

"You ought to be in bed."

"I got to see the river," he said.

"I wish you'd stay off that leg. You're going to do yourself a lot of damage."

He stared out through the screen for a moment and then said without emphasis, "Ain't no good talkin' about it." A moment later, when I had failed to reply, he added, " 'Deed not." We both sat silently for a few moments, watching the slow-sliding current of the yellow river through the trees.

"Did you sleep last night?"

"Some."

"You haven't been out prowling around the swamp again?" I made my voice humorously stern.

"No, suh. I sho' ain't."

"You don't want to run into that loogaroo again, with a bad leg."

"No, no. You don't see it but once."

"Only once?"

"That's all." He stared out at the river, not turning his head to me. Out in the center there was a stranded log, stripped bare of bark and smooth as driftwood. The slender end of it was raised like a crooked finger above the slowly gliding surface, trembling slightly in the current. On the tip of it a bird sat, looking down into the water. It had a bulky body and a crested, short-necked head. In the center of the river there was open sunlight, and the shadow of the log and the perching bird lay pale gray on the yellow water.

"Kingfisher," he said, as if he had heard the question in my mind.

"What is he after?"

"You cain't tell. Needlefish, brim, river cat."

"How do they see? The water is so dark."

"They see. They don't miss."

Down in the yard a pair of large white ducks waddled out from the corner of the house across the sand toward the river. They had bright orange bills and legs and they quacked gently to each other, smiling happily as they waddled through the sand.

"You've got some nice fat ducks," I said.

" 'Deed they is. I was a boy, you coulden let 'em swim loose. Gators would git 'em. Had to keep 'em penned up."

"The gators are gone now."

"Near so," he said.

"You said the other day there were panthers in the swamp still, and bears."

" 'Deed they is. But you got to git back in there a ways fo' you see 'em."

"They don't come out this far?"

"Naw. Not regular. Though they was one hit on the hard road, 'tween here and Bibb, not too long ago. Thirty-seven, thirty-eight. Now, I never did see it, but I heard that said. I woulden want to hit no bear."

"No, I wouldn't either."

He turned his head to me slowly. "Is you a huntin' man?"

"No. I've never hunted anything."

"I woulden of knowed that," he said.

"Why? Did you think I was?"

"Someways."

I leaned over my bag on the floor, opened it, and took out the stethoscope.

"I'd like to listen to your heart again," I said. "Just see how you're getting along. Will you unbutton your shirt?"

He began slowly to unbutton the front of his faded blue work shirt with his slender, big-knuckled black fingers, pausing to feel a broken button, the third one down. "Gittin' all split up," he said. "Go through the wringer too many time."

I stood up and moved to where he sat in the chair, putting the earpieces of the stethoscope into my ears and bending to set the metal disk against his thin, hairless, black chest. The ribs were deeply furrowed under the tight skin. He stared out through the screen toward the river. The beat of his heart was regular and low, a sound almost like the steady murmur of speech; serene, oracular syllables addressed to me out of a dark cavern. I listened with an intentness and for a length of time that must have seemed unusual, even to him, because he said after several minutes, "What do it tell you?" I withdrew the disk abruptly and stood up.

"It tells me that you're a very unusual man. A very strong one. And that you have a very good heart."

"It kin do all that?"

"Yes. It's a very sensitive instrument."

He began to button his shirt, watching while I took the headset from my ears. "That is a fine-looking tool," he said. "If they is one thing I do admire to see it is a fine tool. I wonder would you mind if I looked at that thing?"

"No." I handed him the stethoscope. He took it slowly and carefully, like a man entrusted with an objet d'art, and turned it in his hands to examine its details, the workmanship of its strange parts and fittings, his eyes alight with a profound interest and respect. "Now, ain't that some kind of a thing," he murmured. "Ain't that a fine-lookin' tool. What would you call a thing like that?"

"A stethoscope."

"Stethoscope. I reckon you got to know how to use a thing like that."

"It isn't difficult to use," I said. "But you have to learn to understand what you hear."

"Yeah. That is the thing." He set the black bulbs of the headset very gently into his ears and slipped his hand along the length of black tubing to take hold of the metal disk and press it against his chest. He listened for a moment, frowning with wonder, and lowered his eyes to the floor. "Listen at that," he murmured. "Lord, Lord." He turned his eyes to me. "I wonder could I listen to yo' heart, Doctah?"

"I guess so, if you like." I undid reluctantly the center button of my shirt and took the disk from him, placing it against my chest. He listened, his eyes roaming about the porch in somber fascination. After a moment he turned them to me and sat looking up into my own, listening, with an unnerving gravity.

"Lord, Lord," he said softly. "I has done heard yo' heart."

I removed the disk from my chest and reached out to take the instrument from him. He took the plugs from his ears and handed it to me, watching wonderingly as it exchanged hands. I coiled it slowly and leaned down to replace it in my bag.

"Well, what's your diagnosis?" I said. "Do you think I'm going to survive?"

" 'Deed I coulden say. It ain't my business."

"No." I coiled the stethoscope, slipped it into its case, and replaced it in the bag. Then I stood up and looked at him. "It isn't an easy trade, you can see."

" 'Deed it ain't. I kin see that. They ain't none of 'em easy. It ain't nothing so kindly mysterious, no ways, as how a man use his tools."

"No, that's true." I knelt in front of him to examine the knee. Every time I looked at it, it seemed huger and more unpleasantly soft below the cutoff leg of his dungarees. He sat back in the chair and watched while I felt with my fingertips the great slumping sack of the ruined joint. I decided in that moment to explain to him the necessity of amputating the leg; while I formulated the words in my mind, the explanation transformed itself into a question: "Do you still have your tools?"

" 'Deed I do. Would you like to look at 'em?"

"If it isn't too much trouble."

"It ain't no trouble fo' *me*, 'cause I cain't stir outa this chair. But do you not mind fetchin' 'em yo'se'f, I be proud to show 'em to you."

"Not at all," I said.

"They back there in the house, under my bed. Big tin box."

"I'll bring them out."

I stood up and went into the house and across the main room to the slant-roofed addition at the back where we had put him to bed several days before. I knelt beside the bed and pulled out the toolbox, a very old one, its baked gray enamel chipped and dented. The pin of one of the hinges had been lost, and replaced by a piece of wire. It was very heavy; my shoulder slumped with its weight as I carried it across the cabin to the porch. I set it on the orange crate beside his chair.

"You've had that for some time," I said.

" 'Deed I have. Twenty-eight years." He removed the whittled stick that was stuck through the loop of the hasp and raised the lid. There was a clean smell of oiled metal from the carefully nested, darkly gleaming tools. "I kin rimemble where I got every one of 'em," he said. "Kin rimemble the day. Whether it was rainin', or shinin', or what. Kin rimemble what they cost, mostly." He took out a small hand drill and turned it over in his hands. "This here is a Black and Decker drill. Used to be I would use it mostly for settin' screws in hard wood. Oak and chestnut. Used to be you would use a lot of chestnut inside. But they ain't no chestnut no mo'. Then they took to makin' ratchet screwdrivers, and I didn't use it a whole lot no mo'. But fo' metal drillin', stone, like that. Inside work. Make a good clean hole." He handed it to me across the crate. I examined it carefully. The beveled grooves of the drive wheel were worn by years of use and fitted loosely into the cogs of the shaft gear.

"You've done a lot of work with that," I said.

" 'Deed I have. Bought that drill up to Gregory's in Montgomery, wasn't but sixteen year old. Never did need no other one. Dropped it off a scaffold one day and chipped one a the teeth. You see where she's chipped there?"

"Yes. Here."

"That's right. You got a good eye fo' what is broke. You know how I come to drop it?"

"No."

"They was a wasp nest up there under a beam. Bugger bit me on the back of the neck. Oh, my Lord!" He chuckled gently, replacing the drill in the box and taking out a small aluminum level fitted with a hook at either end. "This here is a line level. I made this here one. You hook her on a line, see do she run straight. Brick line, chimbley line, like that." He handed it to me across the table. "I didn't use it all that much. I had a right good eye for a true line. Could jest stand back ten feet, see did she run true. Didn't need no level, most times."

We sat for twenty minutes looking at his tools, one by one. They were all fine tools and in perfect condition, very lightly oiled, those with edges honed carefully over many years until their blades were smoothly hollowed at the center, the wooden handles sandpapered and varnished, the rivets tapped flush, the screws set firmly, the shafts burnished. Each was accompanied with a brief history or anecdote or a grave reminiscent silence. When he had put them back into the box we sat and watched his daughter out in the yard wringing and hanging onto a clothesline the washing from her kettle. Beside the kettle there was a wooden stand that held two large zinc washtubs full of cold water. She fished the heavy, steaming shirts and sheets and trousers from the boiling water of the kettle with her paddle, dipped them into the first of the two washtubs of cold water, swirled them about for a moment, then lifted them out, hanging from the paddle blade, and dropped them into the second rinsing tub. She splashed them about in the clear cold water with her hands, then drew them out and wrung them, foot by foot, handing the wrung-out, twisted end of the cloth to her daughter, who backed away with it slowly while her mother twisted the garment to its end. The splashing water stuccoed the yellow sand and dripped onto her feet, making her bare ankles shine like wet chestnut hulls. She carried the damp lumpy coils of wrung-out clothing to the line and tossed them over it, spreading and uncrumpling them carefully until they hung straight, fastening their edges to the line with clothespins from the pocket of her skirt. The sheets and pillowcases she tugged flat until the wrinkles were diminished to pale lines in the wet cloth, her strong, slender wrists and fingers moving with the swiftness of swallows darting over the surface of a pond. She was, I realized slowly, a beautiful woman. I raised my hands and looked at them, unnerved by this discovery.

"Did you fall, when the wasp stung you?" I asked.

"No, suh."

"Did you ever fall, when you were building a house?" He frowned, whether from the effort to remember or from the oddness of the question, I couldn't tell. "I noticed, in your X-rays, that there was some joint irregularity in your right shoulder. As if it might have been injured at some time."

"No, suh. Never did fall." We sat silently for a moment. "Come close," he said.

"You must have good balance."

"You git to, do you do that sort of work long enough. I didn't use to like workin' on a ladder or a scaffold when I was young. No, suh. Look up, you git dizzy."

"How many houses have you built?"

"Lord, I don't know. Built the Kindreds', and the Corks', and the Clays'. Let's see, now. The Telchers', Johnsons', Mr. Lacy, up to Broadwater. Lord,

I coulden say 'em all. Twenty-five, thirty houses, I reckon. Worked on 'em, leastways; I ain't sayin' I built 'em all. Done repairs to a good many, too. Fixed 'em up, you know." He turned his head to me. "How many people you worked on?"

"I don't know." I went on looking at my hands for a time. "How is your head?"

"She hurt some."

"I'll give you some more aspirin," I said. "I have some here." I realized instantly that I should not have used the word, and felt my face burn with chagrin at my stupidity. I leaned over the bag and dug about for the bottle I had brought for him. "I'd better get you some water."

"They be a jug by the sink, in the kitchen," he said. "I be mighty obliged."

I set the bottle on the orange crate and got up and went back into the cabin. The kitchen was partitioned from the main room by a curtain hung on rings from a wooden rod. Against the back wall there was a metal sink, hammered by hand out of a steel drum. The drainpipe ran out through a hole in the floor; the joint of the drainpipe with the sink was fitted with a piece of metal flashing cut with tin snips into square petals, flattened out, and cemented to the bottom of the sink with solder. It had a primitive and very permanent look. Beside the sink there was a hand pump, its base bolted to a wooden shelf. On the shelf there was a tin priming cup and a jug of water. I poured the cup full of water from the jug and primed the pump, pouring the water slowly into the neck of the cylinder while I worked the handle. There was a deep sucking sound for a moment and then the piston caught and the water gushed smoothly from the spout and splashed into the sink. I held the cup under the pulsing flow of water until it ran over the brim and then raised it to my mouth and drank. The water was very cold and clear and tasted of stone. It was a long time since I had tasted fresh well water. I carried the full cup back across the cabin to the porch and handed it to him.

"You have good water," I said.

He nodded. "It's a good well. Deep. My daddy sunk that well. Hired a rig from Tuskegee. Cost him three months' wages and took him six weeks, but he was bound he'd have good water."

"The town water is bad. It tastes of sulfur."

"Town well ain't deep enough. You got to git down below the sulfur, where the water's sweet. Them folks was in a hurry."

I shook two aspirin tablets out of the neck of the bottle and handed them to him. He picked them from his palm with the tips of his thumb and forefinger and placed them carefully in his mouth, then raised the cup and drank. "They built that town in a hurry," he said. "I worked on houses where the studs was set on eighteen-inch—sometime two-foot—centers, so's the floor would bob up and down when you walked on it and the walls would wobble when the wind blowed. I seen rafter joints cut so's you could stick your thumb in the bottom of 'em. Kiln-dried lumber, so green it would warp 'fore you could nail it down. You cain't build like that." He nodded toward the river. "Looky yonder. That river is built right. She'll run for a million years, do they not dam it up. This here world is built right. The Lord weren't in no hurry when he built it." He turned his head to me. "He knowed he had time. All they was of it."

"Yet the Bible says it took him only seven days," I said.

"But do you know how long a day is, with the Lord?"

"No."

He turned to face me fully, raising his hand with the forefinger loosely upheld in a benedictory way. " 'Do not ignore this one fact, beloved, that with the Lord one day is as a thousand years, and a thousand years as one day.' "

I did not understand at first that he was quoting, and the words startled and so strangely abashed me that I felt my face go pale.

"What do you mean?" I said confusedly; and then, realizing that the words were not his own, "What does that mean?"

"I don't rightly know. But they always did sound to me like the sweetest words I ever did hear."

"It's Scripture?"

" 'Deed it is. Second Letter of St. Peter. Chapter 3, Verse 8. I wished I had a dollar for every time I has heard my wife read them words to me."

We fell into silence, staring through the screen at the river. The kingfisher flew suddenly from the end of the log and plunged into the water. It reappeared instantly with a slender, foot-long fish clasped in its beak. The fish flittered stiffly, its scales glittering, as the bird flew off with it into the willow branches of the shore. He watched for a moment the mass of foliage into which the bird had disappeared.

"Needlefish," Walter Lubby said. "His time was up."

"I wonder if he saw the bird at all?" I said.

"Oh, yeah. He seen the shadow on the water. But they weren't nothing he could do." Staring at the river, he spoke again after a moment, "Them kill-birds has got a certain kind of shadow. They got a short neck, short body, wide wing. Kingfisher, hawk, thorn bird. Every one of 'em."

In the yard the little girl had begun to sing in her hoarse, possessed voice:

> *"Steal away,*
> *Steal away,*
> *Steal away to Je-sus.*
> *Steal away,*

Steal away home.
I ain't got long to stay here.''

"She has a very true voice," I said.

"She don't never forget a tune, or the words," he said. "Don't never forget a holy song. Hear it once, kin rimemble it. Sing it perfect. She don't rimemble much else."

I sat listening to the harsh, perfectly tuned, weirdly innocent and ancient voice. When she had finished the verse, I raised my hands again and looked into their palms. "I wanted to talk to you about your leg," I said. There was a considerable silence.

"It ain't no use talkin' about it," he said. "I don't reckon they nobody kin do it much good."

"It's my business to see—" He waited for me to finish the sentence, which had trailed away into a vast silence.

"I reckon you doin' your business," he said after a moment. "I ain't got no call to fuss with it." I did not reply. "It don't hurt too much. Long as I git the pills."

"Well, we have plenty of those."

"Yeah, that's right."

"I should be going," I said.

"Yeah. I reckon you a busy man."

But I made no move to do so for several moments, beyond lifting my bag from the floor and setting it on my lap. I sat fingering the latch, staring through the screen at the slowly sliding yellow water of the river, the ragged patches of sunlight on the surface, the dense clumps of reeds on the far shore, and the shadowed green of the swamp beyond. There was a rapt and vital obscurity about the place, like the cool, ecstatic dusk of a cathedral, in which I felt enfolded and sequestered. I hated the thought of the white sunlight outside the shadow of the willow grove, the hot roads wandering interminably to shabby, sweltering towns and cities blazing with banalities.

"Well, I have to be going," I repeated; and stood up, holding my bag by its handle and looking down at him for a moment. "I'll check on you again in a day or two. If you have any problems, send your son by the clinic."

"Yes, suh. I'm obliged."

I went across the porch to the screen door, and after I had opened it and gone through, I pulled the string and set the latch carefully.

"Goodbye, Mr. Lubby," I said to him through the screen.

"Goodbye, Doctah."

I went down the steps and across the yard to the car. When I had got in, I called goodbye to his daughter, who stood pinning clothes to the line, watching me silently. The little girl stood beside her with a basket of clothes-pins, the livid, rapturous syllables of her song flickering in the shadow of the willows like candle flames:

> *"Shall we gather at the river,*
> *The beautiful, the beautiful river.*
> *Shall we gather at the river*
> *That flows by the throne of God."*

Paula's parties, I learned, were highlights of the Tallacoochee social scene. They began at five, and evolved slowly through a long and growingly animated aperitif session into a gourmandistic frenzy that erupted when the elaborate buffet was placed on the dining-room table at nine. This was followed by a murmurous, euphoric calm, punctuated by the tinkling of coffee cups and teaspoons, that prevailed for half an hour or more, during which the infirm, intemperate, punctilious, and apolitical gradually and gratefully dispersed. By twelve, the ranks were thinned to a core of intimates, the incorrigibly convivial, and what seemed to be a cabal made up of many of the most powerful people in the community: councilmen, lawyers, members of the Board of Censors, and some of the wealthiest planters and merchants in the county. There was evidently no fixed protocol about this schedule of festivities, but people seemed to understand by instinct or long custom their place in the community hierar-chy and in Paula's private social order, and to time their departures accordingly, with no damage to anyone's dignity, expectations, or the general harmony. There was almost always, I gathered, a visiting celebrity or dignitary, around whom was formed a center of energy, volubility, and éclat: a university profes-sor, a regional poetess, an old-time local football star, or a land developer from out of state, rumored to have vast sums of money at his disposal. The final phase of the revels had the informal and fraternal air of a legislative caucus, which in fact it was, since many political decisions affecting the town and county were made or framed, municipal policies regarding land use, zoning, education, public health, and other community matters advanced, discussed, and sometimes tacitly disposed of, and even the destinies of public officials often clandestinely determined. There was, however, nothing conspiratorial or sinister about the atmosphere of these sessions; all this was transacted in the jovial, casual, offhanded manner of gentlefolk commendably concerned with civic matters, and was beguilingly interspersed with accounts of fishing expedi-tions, the prowess of hunting dogs, and the eccentricities of the town librarian (only recently and unsteadily departed).

I learned this because at most of Paula's parties I was accorded the distinction of Visiting Dignitary, and since my field of activity fell within the realm of public affairs, encouraged to attend the select symposia into which the evenings resolved. I was uneasy with the honor, but I appreciated the opportunity to explicate the study and to solicit the favor of the community's patriarchal, powerful elite. Until I was present at my first such function, I had no idea of Paula's influence, energy, and social and political intelligence; although in reconsidering my one previous meeting with her, I realized that I had had plentiful intimations of them. In spite of the immediate dislike I had taken to the woman, I found myself unwillingly admiring her virtuosity, especially since she chose to make me its beneficiary. Seeing in me a legate of the power and glory of the government of the United States, she was an instinctual advocate of my cause, and her word carried weight among the gentry, because she came from one of the oldest and most eminent families in the county, with a lineage that included a land-grant cotton planter, a federal judge, a lieutenant governor, and several state legislators. I'm not sure she understood entirely the nature of the project, or that she had any concern whatever with its moral complexities or ambiguities; for her, it represented the majesty of institution, tradition, and authority embodied in a single enterprise, and brooked no question. Although, this may not have been the single or even the salient motive for her support. I had the impression that there were other, much more personal ones; chief among them, Liam's by now entirely obvious disillusion with the project, which seemed to produce in her the perverse desire to champion it. I don't know that he ever expressed to her his distress at being required to participate in it; but she must have sensed it, and that it should be based on moral grounds she evidently considered, in itself, a highly ironic moral incongruity which she was prepared fully and publicly to explore. She seemed sometimes to challenge him to express his reservations before an assembly of his peers, with the sardonic implication that he was the man among them least well equipped to defend such moral niceties. It was a challenge he always gracefully declined; although generally very drunk by that time of the evening, he was steadfastly noncommittal when the subject came up, or disarmingly discursive, or distractingly effusive about my capacities as physician, administrator, and visionary. Some profound and apparently imperishable sense of dignity, discretion, or perhaps an unexpectedly robust instinct for survival managed to maintain its function in his fuddled, harrowed brain and prevent the possibility of the evening's degenerating into a vulgar, acrimonious private quarrel or inquisition, one which would almost certainly have included a set of insidious references, however subtly or disingenuously fashioned, to Janet Thurmond. Janet herself was never, in my experience, present at the late-hour convocations, and all the more vulnerable in her absence; she would long ago have made her departure, along with the rest of the uninitiated, incapacitated, and ineligible.

We arrived at seven with Elizabeth bundled up in a cotton blanket and great-eyed with silent remonstration. The front door stood open and the tinkling hubbub of the party came floating out into the evening air in a haze of candlelight, cologne, cigar smoke, and the fumes of mint and bourbon. We advanced into this heady atmosphere and stood uncertainly for a moment until Paula, her alertness to all events unimpaired by her apparent absorption in the conversation of her present guests, detached herself from a group of them and glided to us in a shimmer of turquoise silk, her arms outstretched ecstatically, her face radiant with welcome.

"Y'all *made* it!" she cried. "I was so afraid you were goin' to back out on me. And you brought this little darlin' with you. Well, now everything is *perfect.*" She took Molly gently by the waist and regarded her at arm's length for a moment. "You're *Molly,*" she murmured tenderly. "I'm Paula Proctor. It's *so* nice to have you with us. Welcome to Alabama, honey." She drew Molly to her and kissed her lingeringly, pressing her cheek to Molly's own. Molly accepted this homage stiffly but appreciatively, flushed a little by its unexpected fervor. "First thing we got to do is get this *coat* off you," Paula said. She reached out to assist in the process, laying Molly's plain black cotton raincoat across her arm with an appreciative glance. "I'n't that pretty!" She turned to summon Liam from the seething throng behind her with a happy cry: "Liam! Just look who's here!" Then she turned back to us and peered into the folds of the blanket in which I held Elizabeth, plucking fondly at her bangs for a moment with her fingertips and pursing her lips to murmur, "Shh-shh-shh-shh-shh," since the child had begun to whimper. "Now you just cheer up, you cunnin' little thing. Why, you're goin' to have a *wonderful* time. Just wait till you see that cozy little bed we got ready for you!" A faint, enchanted smile crept over Molly's face, allaying my worst fears for the evening; she was captivated.

Liam appeared, a quaint, chivalrous smile fastened to his lips as if with clothespins, and was introduced to Molly. He stood whispering deferentially, closing his eyes slowly several times as if struggling to maintain consciousness, before we were led brusquely away and up the stairs by Paula to what had been her own daughter's nursery: a snug, dormer-windowed room with wallpaper printed with gaily colored figures from nursery rhymes. She put Elizabeth lovingly to bed in an old-fashioned rocker crib, and she stood and rocked it with her fingertips until the child fell asleep, with miraculous promptness and content, evidently as captivated as her mother by Paula's hospitality. We tiptoed out of the room and were led back down the stairs to the dining-room sideboard, where we were fortified—Molly with a glass of mint julep and I with a Coca-Cola garnished with a slice of lemon—for a ceremonial round of introductions. It was far less painful than I had anticipated; Paula's skill as a hostess reached almost into the realm of art. One could see that she delighted in choreographing social situations, arranging personalities into fertile, some-times amusingly combustible combinations, reanimating languishing conversa-tions with vivid, skillfully interpolated themes and resonant allusions, artfully restraining the obstreperous and encouraging the timid, dispensing everywhere a sense of ease and ardor that wove a spell across the party as palpable as the scent of the gardenia blossoms that floated in a great blue bowl on the dining table.

It astonished me to see that under the combined influence of her charisma and Liam's julep, Molly was mysteriously transformed into an independent social being, able to engage the conversational groups to which Paula escorted us with an unprecedented, steadily growing confidence, offer her opinions with an assurance sometimes bordering on temerity, and occasionally express her appreciation of one of Paula's sallies with a startling, spasmodic whinny. I wasn't sure how to account for this. Perhaps she sensed in Paula a soul sister, and under her aegis felt secure enough and bold enough to renounce the pent-up petulance and taciturnity of years in order to satisfy some long-frus-trated hunger for conviviality, approval, and admiration. Perhaps she intuited their common domestic plight, and found in Paula's style and self-possession an unexpectedly appealing avatar of it. Whatever the reasons for her brief, nightlong metamorphosis, it had remarkable results: by the time the buffet was placed on the table she was enthusiastically reciting her grandmother's wisdom to a heavy, deeply nodding insurance salesman and now and then enigmatically applying mint julep to her eyebrows with a fingertip. Paula herself was visibly neither amused, patronizing, nor malicious in promoting this strange behavior. She managed to seem genuinely absorbed by Molly's longueurs, undismayed by her inadvertencies, and undaunted in her mission to sponsor Molly's debut into Tallacoochee society. Or perhaps, like Molly, she sensed a kindred sufferer, sympathizer, and potential ally in whatever adversity time might ordain. (That was my earliest opinion; later in the evening, I revised it sharply.)

She was equally solicitous of me, and as she had promised, engineered some advantageous accords with local men of substance. One of these was a lumber-man who I gathered owned hundreds of acres of pineland in the county and employed a hundred or more Negro laborers. He was a very large, square-shouldered, raspberry-colored man of fifty in a very damp seersucker suit and a shoestring necktie who restlessly shifted his feet and tossed the ice cubes in one of Liam's juleps while he expressed, in a voice like a pipe organ, his opposition to all welfare programs, housing measures, and public health pro-jects to aid "the shiftless nigras" at taxpayers' expense.

"It don't do one bit of permanent good," he said. "It's a waste of taxpayers' money. Hell, you pay 'em off one day, they just as soon buy a bottle of booze and get liquored up instead of coming back to work the next. I spend half my time running 'em down. There isn't a one in ten of 'em will work a steady week. Come back a couple of days later and claim they were sick. Had a headache, back misery, any damn thing they can think of. You ask us to put out money for some project like this one you talking about, you just asking us to throw it down the drain."

"Well, Buck, don't you reckon they *are* sick, sure enough, sometimes?" Paula said. "If thirty-five percent of them have got syphilis, like Dr. Ransome says, they're going to be laid up an awful lot of the time. I'n't that so, Carl?"

"Yes, it is," I said. "They'll have bone problems, heart problems, skin eruptions, fits of mental vagueness, all kinds of things that will make them unfit for work. Even if they show up, you won't get a full day's work for your wages."

"Hell, you talk about mental vagueness: they were *born* vague, most of 'em. There's nothing you can do about *that.*"

"Well, I know, honey, but it's not going to *improve* 'em any, having a disease like that. You might put out an extra twenty-five dollars a year right now, financing a study like this, but unless something is done to improve their health, you're going to lose ten or twenty times that much in trying to get a decent day's work out of 'em, rounding 'em up, trying to keep your field crews together, paying for their mistakes. My goodness, it just seems sensible to me to have good workers."

He frowned and tossed his ice cubes and took a thoughtful drink of julep. "I reckon there's something in *that,*" he said.

"Well, you *know* there is. You're too smart not to realize *that.*" She slapped him impishly on the wrist, jiggling the glass precariously in his hand.

"Hey, look out there, ladybug!" he said. "You're paying for this julep, you know."

"Well, don't you worry about that. I got ten gallons of Jack Daniel's back there in the kitchen; I heard you coming!"

He grinned at me delightedly. "I'n't she something? You let your women talk to you like that up North? You know what we are? We a bunch of damn fools when it comes to women."

"No, you're not, either," Paula said. "You just listen to me once in a while, you'll be all right. And you know another thing that's bad? Letting these people wander around all over the place just running over with all these disease germs. I mean, that's a menace to *everybody's* health. Because it's *contagious.* Just any *kind* of contact with 'em, almost, and you can get it yourself. Just drinking out of the same *glass,* even."

The timber merchant's smile waned. He lowered his eyes to his glass and uneasily examined its rim. Even greater perils seemed to swarm into his mind. "Yeah, that's something you got to think about," he murmured.

Paula turned to me, laying her fingertips on my forearm. "What do you reckon it's going to cost for a study like this, Carl? I mean, for the average taxpayer? What would a one-year per capita expense be?"

"We estimate something like ten dollars per annum, for every citizen of the state," I said.

"Well, my land, that's *nothing!* That's one bottle of hooch, Buck. At least the kind *you* buy."

"Not me," he said. "I drink Old Overshoe, you know that. Sixty-nine cents a fifth. Hell, that'd keep me in liquor for a year."

"Yeah, for just about ten minutes, you mean," Paula said. "Anyway, that's not what you gave *me* the last time I was over at Shadowlawn."

"Oh, well, I get out the good stuff when you come over," the mill owner said. He winked at me gravely. "Get out the fast-acting stuff. Guaranteed results."

She slapped him on the wrist again, crying merrily, "I swear, you're getting worse every *day!* Now you listen to me, Buck Kindred. I want you to go to that meeting next Friday night and throw some weight around. And I mean in the right direction. You know people *listen* to you. You've got a responsibility to this community."

"I'm going to think it over," he said with a sudden gravity, appropriate to this appeal. "You're making a lot of sense to me. For once. They might be something to this study of yours, Doctor. I tell you what, Paula: you rustle me up another one of these juleps, I'm liable to do any damned thing you tell me. Might even do it without one, if you got the right idea."

"I wish you'd *hush,* " Paula said. "Carl's liable to get the wrong idea about what goes *on* down here in Tallacoochee. I'll get you another one if you promise to *behave* yourself."

"I'm not promising anything," Buck said. "Last time I promised a woman anything, I got myself in trouble. I'm not out of it yet."

"Now, I'm going to *tell* Amy that!" Paula cried. "You just see if I don't. You going to regret saying that, Buck Kindred."

I met others—planters, merchants, teachers, lawyers, physicians—each of whose degree of importance was subtly communicated to me by the relative effusiveness of Paula's introduction, the intensity of her attention to his remarks, and the amount of time she allowed him to appropriate in my calendar before gently disengaging me and moving on. The most memorable of these was Dr. Prescott, the chairman of the Board of Censors, a white-haired, quiet-mannered, fine-eyed man of seventy who was semiretired from his private surgeon's practice, but still contributed three hours a week of service without remuneration to Liam's clinic. He had of course heard of the study, and evidently given it a good deal of thoughtful consideration, but after a few courteous, congratulatory remarks about the work of the Public Health Service in general, he went on to talk about orchids, which he raised as a hobby in an enclosed veranda of his home. He addressed a generous proportion of his conversation to Molly—who had joined us at this point—although she had slipped into a nearly speechless stage of felicity and stood with glazed eyes, her lips fixed in a febrile smile.

"Do you know why I am such a great admirer of orchids?" he asked her at one point. Molly shook her head in a rigid, long-vibrating way, like a plucked reed. "Because they made a surgeon out of me," he said. "They taught me how to use my hands. I know that sounds extraordinary, but it's quite true. I was very clumsy with my hands at one time. When I was younger, I once made a very bad mistake at surgery, and it undermined my confidence for years. As a matter of fact, it had gotten to the point where I dreaded to perform an operation. And then I took to raising orchids, on the advice of a friend who saw that I had gotten very nervous, very unsure of myself. He said that there was nothing else in the world that could create such tranquillity in a person. He was quite right. They're so delicate, you know. The blossoms are so tender that you can blight them by a single touch, unless you handle them with great care, great gentleness. By tending those flowers and being around them constantly, I regained confidence in my hands. I learned to have faith in my capacity for gentleness. That is a peculiar truth."

He left very early, and I remember him for the circumstances of his departure as much as for that story he told. He was wearing an old-fashioned gold vest-pocket watch which at ten o'clock chimed distinctly, with ten clear, tiny peals, so startling and pure a sound that it suspended our conversation entirely while we stood and listened, enchanted, and having no idea—none of us but Paula, I suppose—of its origin. There was a momentary hush which fell about us like a nimbus of serenity in the din of the party, and then he plucked the watch from his pocket by the gold chain to which it was attached and held it at arm's length to confirm the message of the bells.

"Well, I've got to go, my dear," he said to Paula, tucking it back into his vest pocket. "I'm a very old man, and all this festivity has taxed my strength."

"Oh, you're not, either!" Paula said. "You're the youngest one here. Anyway, it's *early*. We haven't had time to learn *anything* from you yet."

He took and patted the hand that she stretched out to him in remonstrance; then shook mine and Molly's in turn, declining his head in a courtly way and saying to her gently as he did so, "I'm sorry I haven't had more time to spend with you, my dear."

"Thank you," Molly said in a soft and stately way that astonished me. "I'll think of you whenever the clock strikes ten." I've often wondered if she did.

Occasionally, in the course of the evening, Liam's path crossed ours; he would come wobbling into our purlieu like a planet in a perilously erratic orbit and stand teetering amiably before us for a moment or two, expressing vaguely congratulatory remarks about our capacity to endure bad weather, barbarous customs, a tragic transportation system, and assorted obsolescences and outrages which only the julep, he implied, could redeem. Invariably he would offer to replenish our supply of it, a courtesy that Molly never declined. With growing consternation, I would watch him bear her empty glass off to the bar to make his way back, several minutes later, with a fresh one, grandly and precariously upheld, generally in both hands, as if delivering the Eucharist.

"Now, honey, that's going to be the last one," Paula said finally, with a prudent, plaintive twinkle, "because Viola's going to set out that buffet in a minute, and these folks aren't going to be able to eat a *thing*. And I didn't work on that jambalaya all day just to throw it away. I want 'em to appreciate it."

"You're right," Liam said. "It's time Carl had a decent meal. He's been living on Bayou chili for weeks now. Can't keep him away from the place, he's become an addict."

"Lord, I hope not," Paula said. "The poor man won't get his digestion straightened out for years. You see what happens to 'em, Molly, when they haven't got a woman to take care of 'em?"

"Oh, it's just easier than cooking for yourself," I murmured. "It's not too bad. Liam, did you see the lab report on the Hubbard girl?"

He did not answer, and I saw that there was no need for my hasty diversion of the subject, because his eyes had wandered beyond me to the door, where, following his gaze, I saw that Janet had entered and stood uncertainly, glancing about the room. Paula was even more promptly aware of his distraction than I—so promptly that I had the impression she had been anticipating it all evening. Her instant recognition of it did nothing to diminish her composure. "Why, there's *Janet!*" she cried happily. "I was just wonderin' when that girl was going to get here. I was beginnin' to think you didn't even remember to invite her, Liam."

"I think I did, yes. I must have," Liam murmured.

Paula turned and sped across the room to the entrance foyer, where I saw her greet Janet effusively, reaching out to adjust and finger admiringly the collar of her blouse. She took her by the arm and guided her to us through the close-pressed bodies of her guests, pausing once or twice to present her briefly to others before she arrived before us.

"Carl, I think you remember this little lady," she said.

"Yes, I do. Good evening, Janet."

"Hello, Dr. Ransome."

"Molly, this is Janet Thurmond," Paula said. "Janet's Liam's laboratory

technician. I *think* that's her official position. I'm just so dumb about everything that goes on down there that I'm not real sure. I'n't that right, Janet?"
She turned to Janet with a look of helpless innocence for confirmation. Janet
smiled noncommittally. "Anyway, she's the person that makes everything *work*
down there. That's what everybody tells me, anyway."

"Hello," Janet said. "It's nice to know you."

"It's nice to know you, too," Molly said. "Carl told me how you got
everything ready for him when he came down. How you put things in the
icebox and everything. That was nice of you." The curious, courtly compliment
she had won from Dr. Prescott seemed to have filled her with an unaccustomed
grace.

"Well, it didn't take much effort. It's awful, trying to get settled in a new
place. I wonder if you'd like me to come over next weekend and go downtown
with you? You'll need to know where the grocery store is, and the cleaners, and
the ten-cent store, and all that kind of thing. I have a little car, so we wouldn't
have to bother Carl. Maybe we could have lunch together."

"Oh, that would be nice," Molly said. "Thank you."

"Well now, I was just goin' to suggest the very same thing," Paula said.
"Maybe we could all get together one day."

"Why don't I come over next Saturday morning, around ten o'clock,"
Janet said. "Would that be convenient?"

"Yes, that would be wonderful. I don't know about Mrs. Proctor." She
looked hesitantly at Paula. "About Paula."

"Well, let me see, now. Oh, my goodness, I'm goin' to be *busy* on Saturday
mornin'," Paula cried, her face crumpling with disappointment. "I promised
Mary Beth Davis I'd come to her brunch on Saturday. I forgot all about it!
And I been away so long I don't *dare* miss it. But you girls go on and have
a nice time; we'll get together one day real soon."

There was a considerable pause, during which Janet studiously avoided
Liam's eyes.

"I want to thank you for doing the Lubby test," I said. "I'm sorry to dump
that on you without warning, but I was anxious to get a reading."

"That's all right. It wasn't very good news, I'm afraid."

"It was what I expected."

Buck Kindred heaved out of the crowd that surrounded us, considerably
redder than before, his suit more damp, and the momentum of his heavy
movements less accurately restrained. He caught sight of Paula and leaned
close to her, whispering into her ear. While he did so, I saw that the hand he
had placed on her shoulder disappeared, evidently sliding down her back to
some indeterminate point of her anatomy. I don't think anyone was aware of
this but me; certainly not Liam, whose painted smile never lost its fixity. Paula

gave a merry cry of indignation and said, "Buck Kindred, you *know* better than to say a thing like that! You fool, you go on and tend your business!" The tone was gaily reproachful, but the indignation, I thought, was not completely feigned; there was a nervous earnestness about it that matched the sudden darkening of her eyes.

Buck raised his head and apparently became aware of Liam's presence for the first time, breaking into an extravagantly genial smile.

"You know what I just said to this little lady of yours, Liam?"

"No," Liam said, his smile unchanged.

"I told her I'd give her five hundred dollars if she'd slip me the recipe for this julep of yours. And you know what she told me?"

"No."

"She told me to go on and tend my business! Now i'n't that somethin'? You got yourself one loyal little woman here, Liam; and that is the truth."

"She has many virtues," Liam said.

"You can say that again, old friend." He swung his head back to Paula and raised his lightly clenched fist to tap her gently on the cheek. "Now, you think it over, ladybug. 'Cause if you come up with the right answer, I might just help you out with that request you made a little while ago." He nodded in a heavy, confidential way and heaved back into the crowd like a walrus plunging into the sea.

"What request was that?" Liam said.

"Why, I asked him to throw some weight back of this program of yours and Carl's," Paula said. "And he said he was thinkin' very seriously about it. He said he might even put some money into the program, to help pay expenses. You better be nice to that man, honey. He can help you out." She turned quickly to include me in her confidence. "You know, Carl, ten thousand dollars isn't nothin' more to him than a bag of jelly beans."

"I think I'd rather have the jelly beans," Liam said. "I don't know how you feel about it, Carl, but I wouldn't want the man's money."

"You don't like him?" I said.

"He's a goddamned oaf. His family owns the lumber mill and he pays his hands in company scrip, so they're tied to him for life. The only place they can spend the stuff is in the company store, and they're all six months or more in debt to him for clothes and food and kerosene. Some of them are still paying off their fathers' debts. And he charges them twice what the A & P would, at that. His goddamn money smells of blood. I think I'd rather have Capone's."

"Well, now that's a *very* fastidious attitude," Paula said. "My, my, *my*. I can remember when you weren't quite so squeamish about acceptin' money from people."

"*I* can remember when he believed in people's generosity," Janet said in a voice strained suddenly with indignation. "When he believed that gifts came from the heart. When he believed—" Liam touched her quickly on the wrist with his fingertips, dropping his head. Janet closed her eyes momentarily and licked her lips, which apparently had gone dry. "I'm sorry," she said. "I feel the way Liam does about him. I can't stand the man."

Paula smiled at her steadily, her eyes gone visibly paler, to the gray of winter sky. "Honey, I think maybe you need a little drink," she said. "We been standing here jabberin' away and there you are just dyin' of thirst. I just don't know what's the *matter* with me. Liam, why don't you get this girl a julep?"

"That's all right, I'll get it," Janet said. "Don't let me take you away from your guests. Thanks, Paula." She turned away, then turned back quickly and said to Molly, "I'll see you next Saturday morning, then, Mrs. Ransome; if I don't see you before."

"Yes," Molly murmured. "Yes, thank you."

Janet turned to weave her way through the crowd toward the bar and buffet. I found my eyes following her course through the bodies toward the arch of the dining room with a compulsive interest in her progress and whereabouts, one that was hardly conscious, and yet irrepressible. As the evening went on I would find my attention wandering from the sea of conversation in which I was submerged and my eyes stealthily detaching themselves from the faces that confronted me to search her out among the seething mass of bodies, her tangerine-colored blouse and tan skirt flowing and fluctuating in the subtle currents and ebullitions of the party like a swimmer being swept through the channels and eddies of a swollen river. I saw that her own eyes often drifted, in very much the same way as mine, toward whatever sector of the room Liam was situated in at the moment, and that they sometimes closed or clenched briefly in consternation or frustration, or softened in a moment of eloquent silent intercourse if they happened to meet his. Paula, I saw, was equally aware of this, and far more concerned than I with Janet's whereabouts, with the nuances of her every glance and gesture and expression. Once, so dramatically so that it had a considerable effect on my existence.

She had introduced Molly and me to a small rapacious woman with a very thick throat, very red lips, and very brilliant eyes who expressed a passion for one of Paula's canapés, a sort of liquid dip composed of tomato sauce and minced mussels, a delicacy which she had only just exhausted. "Let me get you some more," Paula said, and went out into the kitchen, to reappear momentarily with a silver bowl of the concoction and a little stack of wafers on a tray. While she held it for the woman to serve herself, her eyes drifted to the arch that divided the dining room from the central hall of the house, where Janet stood beside the glass vitrine that housed Liam's collection of seashells. I watched with Paula as Janet, who had stood looking at the shells for a moment, set her glass on top of the vitrine, opened the door of the cabinet, and lifted one of the specimens out, a small white sand dollar, which she gazed at gently for a moment before raising her hand and pressing it to her cheek. The tray which Paula held tilted in her hand and the serving fork slid off onto the floor. Just as it slipped from the edge she snatched at it with a swift, ferocious movement, catching it by the tip with such force that she plunged a tine into her finger. She dropped it instantly and flapped her hand in pain, raising it to her mouth to suck a blood drop from the fingertip. While she did this, the tray, held carelessly in her other hand, tilted even further, upsetting the dish of mussel dip, from which a stream of tomato-colored sauce splashed down the front of her turquoise gown.

"Oh, my heavens!" Molly cried in horror. "Your beautiful gown. Oh, what a shame!"

"Oh, my lord, now that's *my* fault!" the thick-throated lady cried, throwing up her hands in grief.

"No, it's not," Paula said with a tight, heroic little smile. "It's my own fault, for bein' so blasted clumsy. Anyway, it's nothin' very serious."

I stooped to retrieve the fork and set it on the tray.

"Thank you, Carl. If you-all will excuse me for a minute, I'm goin' to see what I can do about this." She bore the tray off quickly through the crowd, touching backs and shoulders lightly and with a frozen smile as she wedged her way between them to the dining room. She set the tray on the buffet table, then turned and swept up the stairs, holding up her gown to clear the hem of it.

"She might have hurt herself," Molly said. "Carl, you think you better have a look at it?"

"I'll see if it needs bandaging," I said.

"You better check on Elizabeth, too, while you're up there."

"I will."

"You go right ahead," the red-throated lady said. "Molly and me will get along just fine."

I nodded to her and made my way across the room, pausing to set my plate of hors d'oeuvres on top of the vitrine. Janet, who had slipped the sand dollar into the pocket of her skirt and shut the cabinet door, smiled at me civilly. I went up the stairs to the second floor and down the carpeted hall to the nursery where we had left Elizabeth. She seemed to be asleep, one small plump hand strengthlessly adrift among the bedclothes as if in search of something lost or dreamt of. The Raggedy Ann doll had fallen to the floor between the bars of the crib. I stooped and picked it up and set it in the bend of her elbow. When I did so I saw that her eyes were clenched tensely closed as if in fright. She opened them instantly, recoiling from my touch.

"What's the matter?" I said.

"Am I home yet?"

"No, not yet. But we'll be going home soon. What's the matter?"

"I woke up," she said. "There was something out there. It scared me."

"Out where?"

"Out there. Outside the window. There's something bad out there."

I went to the window and raised it slightly, looking out into the silent yard. An animal—Liam's dog, I suppose—sitting beneath the window, started at the sound and slipped away into the shadows of a wisteria arbor that roofed a small flagstone patio at the far end of the lawn. The light of the living-room windows fell in yellow squares on the dark grass and the shadows of the guests roved through them like restless specters. "There's nothing there at all," I said. "Now go to sleep, and when you wake up again, you'll be in your own bed, and it'll be morning." She did not answer. I stood looking down at the pale nebulous oval of her face, like the reflection of the moon in a dim pond, and had the disturbing impression that if I touched it, it would shatter into rippling, aqueous fragments. I said, "Good night," and backed across the room to the door, from where I watched for a moment her face glowing in the dark with its pale, lunar loneliness.

In the hall, I saw the light lying across the carpet from the open door of the bathroom beyond the nursery and heard the splashing of water. I walked to the door and saw Paula standing at the sink rinsing her hand in the flow of running water. I tapped lightly at the open door with my knuckles.

"Yes?" she said, without turning.

"It's Carl. Have you hurt yourself badly?"

"No. It's all right."

"I wonder if I ought to have a look at it. Can I come in?"

"If you like. It's really nothing at all."

I stepped inside and saw that she had evidently stabbed herself quite deeply; there was a steady pulse of blood in the current of water against the white porcelain.

"A puncture wound can be dangerous," I said.

She raised her head to me and said lightly, "I don't think I'm in any very grave danger, but I appreciate your *concern*. You're a very cautious man."

"I'd make it bleed as much as possible."

"Would you? Is that a general principle of yours?" She switched off the faucet and opened the door of the medicine cabinet. "Well, I think I've bled quite enough for one night." She fished about for a moment, removing a bottle of Mercurochrome and a tin of Band-Aids. She set the tin on the sink and turned to hand me the bottle, smiling easily. "I wonder if you'd open that for me?"

"Yes." I started to add, "It's not very effective," but decided the statement had a fatuous ring to it. The bottle was a new one and the cap was sealed with a strip of celluloid which I had difficulty breaking. I pried at it for a moment with my fingernail while she stood silently, holding her hand elevated above the sink. There was time for five blood drops to splash on the white enamel. I looked up suddenly, conscious of the studious gaze with which she watched me. It transposed instantly into a limpid smile that illumined her pale violet eyes.

"I wonder to what I owe this very great concern?" she said.

"To the fact that I'm a doctor, I suppose."

"I see. And therefore interested in pathological conditions? Well, I'm not sure this one is worthy of your attention."

"It could easily become infected," I said. "Have you had a tetanus shot recently?"

"My *Lord!* You mean there's danger of me goin' *mad?* You mean I might start frothin' at the *mouth?*"

"No, I don't think that's very likely. But it's a good thing to take them periodically."

"You mean this sort of thing is apt to happen *again?* You can't have very much respect for my intelligence, Doctor."

"You seem determined to misunderstand me," I said.

"Now what could I possibly misunderstand? I think we understand each other very well."

"You do?"

"As a matter of fact, if it's of any interest at all to you, I think I'd make you the best wife you could possibly have."

I was stunned for a moment by the audacity of the remark, and decided the only possible response was to accept it as lightly as it had been said. I forced myself to chuckle appreciatively.

"Well, it's nice to know you think so."

"Would you like a taste?"

"I'm sorry? Would I . . . ?" She held her dripping finger toward me invitingly. I chuckled again, uneasily. "Oh, I don't think that will be necessary."

"You mean you can judge without even a *taste?* Are you sure that's *wise?* You might be makin' an awful mistake."

I withdrew the glass-rod applicator, which I had finally managed to free, and took the hand which she held out to me, dabbing the puncture in her fingertip lightly.

"Or maybe you think I have a noxious disease of some kind," she said, watching with amusement my methodical application of the Mercurochrome.

"I suppose that's one of the hazards of dealing with diseased folks all the time. You suspect *everyone* of being diseased, eventually."

"No, I don't think so."

"Well, I'm *not.* Just a little wounded, that's all. But I heal very rapidly. With the proper attention."

I put the rod back into the bottle and screwed the cap down carefully. "I think we'll put one of those Band-Aids on now." I took the tin from the sink, took out and peeled a bandage, and wrapped it gently around her fingertip.

"Oh, that feels *so* much better!" she said. "Just what the doctor ordered! Now, there's one more thing you can do for me that will make me your slave forever. I wonder if you *can?"*

I smiled uncertainly, feeling a sudden desperation in her presence, as if I had been trapped by a cunning far beyond my capacity to deal with. "I don't understand," I murmured.

"Well, you must make the *effort.* What does a woman hold dearest to her heart?"

"I really don't know."

"Her *clothes,* dummy! If you can do something about this *dress,* I'll worship you forever. Just *look* at this mess!" She clasped her hand delicately over her left breast, depressing it gently to present for better inspection the blotched bodice of her gown. She had evidently already scrubbed it, perfunctorily, with a washcloth, because there was a water mark surrounding the faint scarlet stain that discolored the light blue silk, "I am a stained woman," she said in a gaily abandoned tone. "Now, if there's anything you can do about *that,* you'll be working miracles. Or maybe you prefer your women slightly stained."

"I'm afraid I don't know how to deal with that," I murmured.

"You *don't?* Well now, that is a very useful piece of information."

"I understand cold water is the best thing."

"Well, it doesn't sound very inviting, but you may be right." She picked up the damp washrag, gave it a mild squeeze above the sink, and handed it to me. "I wonder if you'd oblige me just once more? I can't see what I'm doing, from up here." She leaned back against the sink, thrusting her hips tensely forward and again clasping her breasts protectively while I dabbled at the stain, with growing discretion as I approached the part of it that spread down over the firm swell of her belly. "Oh, that's a hundred per*cent* better," she said. "You know, I'm not really such a terribly self-sufficient woman, Carl. Maybe I've just had to become that way, bein' married to a man who's—well, very romantic—in his nature. But I have a poetic side to my soul, too, believe it or not. Why, when I was a girl, I could just quote Shelley for *hours.* They still i'n't anything in the world I love as much as nature. Would you believe that?"

"I don't know why I shouldn't," I said.

"Well, it's the truth. They i'n't anything I love more than just to sit and watch the sunset. You know that place down there at Broadwater? Where the watchtower is?"

"I think I've passed by it."

"Well, I go down there sometimes in the evenin' and just sit there by the river and watch the sun go down behind the pine trees. Sometimes I stop by there on a Thursday evenin', after my bridge group breaks up, and sit there till it gets dark, just dreamin' like a schoolgirl. I think that's the thing I enjoy most in the whole world."

"It must be a very pleasant experience."

"Yes, it is." She folded the washrag and set it on the edge of the sink. "Well. With a little bit of help from the hair dryer, I think I'll be ready to rejoin society in a minute. Thank you so much, Carl. Why don't you go on down? I'll be with you in a minute."

"I'll tell them you'll be down."

"Now don't you worry about that. They won't miss me one little bit. *You* know *that.*"

I went downstairs, retrieved my plate from the top of the vitrine, and rejoined Molly and her friends, explaining that Paula had cut her finger quite deeply and that I had been attending to it. There were expressions of dismay and concern, which I reassured. In a moment we saw Paula descending the stairs and making her way toward us with complete composure, perhaps even with an added élan.

"Well, you know what your husband has *done?*" she said to Molly. "He has saved my life, that's all! I would almost certainly have died, either from blood poisoning or humiliation—I don't know which—if he hadn't come to my rescue. I hope you appreciate that man. He's goin' to restore the South, single-handed, before he's through."

Shortly after, the buffet was set out: a shrimp jambalaya, a spicy ratatouille, baked ham, hush puppies, corn bread, dishes of water melon pickle, chutney, stuffed mushrooms, and other of Paula's specialties, a delicious and profuse array. Yet I found I had little appetite. I picked at my plateful of delicacies desultorily, occasionally nibbling a morsel from the tip of my fork with a poor pretense of relish, suffering from a rapidly growing disgust with the food, the flushed, frantically mobile faces, the tide of strident, fatuous clamor that swept over me in gusts that reeked of garlic, chives, and Camembert, the restless, wolfish rapacity and posturing.

We stayed for a short time after the ritualistic thinning of the ranks— "Honey, it's just startin' to warm up!" Paula said—and I was able to observe the subtly legislative process that evolved among the elect; even to participate in it briefly, since the syphilis study was evidently on the unwritten agenda for the evening. Liam performed remarkably. For a man who had had so much to drink and who had so little enthusiasm for the project, he managed to give an impression of deep interest and involvement. I saw that Paula was as much bemused by his performance as I; once, after a long, critical surveillance of her husband, she turned her eyes to me slowly, meditatively, her face drawn by a look of serious appraisal, as if making a relative evaluation of our natures for the purpose of determining their approximate market values. Seeing that I was watching her, she allowed a slow smile to straighten out the studious depression of the corners of her mouth, as if she had come to a mildly ironic conclusion, one that I would perhaps enjoy. I tried to discredit this possibility by hastily averting my eyes.

I left not long after, guiding Molly out to the car with ostentatious care, then returning for Elizabeth, whom I carried downstairs bundled up peacefully in her blanket and deposited on Molly's lap—with some misgivings, since her welfare in that situation seemed considerably in doubt. Paula stood beside the car expressing lavish appreciation of our having come. "And I want to see a whole lot more of you two," she said when I had gotten in. "Now you *hear* me?" She reached in through the window to bestow a kiss on Elizabeth's forehead with her fingertips and a pat on Molly's shoulder, and then withdrew and stood with folded arms watching our departure with an air of huge benignity.

When we had turned into our street and were approaching the house, I felt a strong desire to drive past it, to postpone as long as possible the experience of lying sleeplessly for hours beside Molly in that repugnant bed in that still and cheerless house. A restlessness had been ignited in me that could not be allayed by any such grimly passive conclusion to the evening. I wanted to drive or walk for hours, until it had burned out in me and something far more truly conclusive had scattered its bitter embers into extinction. I glanced at Molly and saw that she was as nearly oblivious as it is possible for anyone in a conscious state to be of her whereabouts, course, or destination; she sat with Elizabeth held loosely in her arms, staring through the windshield with the same bemused, mildly beatific gaze that had possessed her features for the last half hour. I drove past the house without a pause and out the street to the end of the town where the brick pavement gave way to the shabby asphalt of the county road and the ceiling of live oak branches suddenly fell away and we were under the unobscured, occultly clear, and glittering sky. We passed the tin signs of the town's fraternal orders, Kiwanis, Rotary, Elks, Civitan; dented, bullet-pocked, and desecrated in the starlight. Beyond them were hardier 666 and Burma Shave signs and, occasionally, nailed to a solitary pine trunk, a splintered board lettered with the straggling, hand-printed message: JESUS

SAVES. On both sides of the road the walls of the pine barrens rose in a dark tall stubble against the paler sky. I stopped the car and rolled the window down and sat smelling their resinous fragrance in the night air. It was like the smell of Christmas in my boyhood, the sharp, sacred perfume of pine sap, a holy ichor stored in golden bullion through the winter silence. I was a boy again, or the ghost of one, staring down between the banisters in the middle of the night at the Christmas tree that stood in glistening majesty in the dark living room, towering over the mysterious trove that was the revelation of grace and the gift of its witnesses. How have I come so far from that place? I thought. Is there any way back? I had stopped beside a sand road that led back between the trees toward the river; peering along the glimmering lane into the forest, I saw that there was something loping up it in the dark toward the highway: a very large dog, perhaps; or even a panther or small bear. It stopped and stood alertly, watching the automobile at the end of the road in a patient, vigilant way, as if summoned out of the shadows by my elegy, like a jackal by the scent of death. I felt suddenly bitterly ashamed of having yielded to that moment of bathos, and grunted, almost in disbelief, at my effeminacy.

"What happened? Did you get lost?" Molly said. Her voice had the muddled sound of someone awakening from sleep.

"No, not really; I just thought a little fresh air would do us good before we went to bed."

"Well, my goodness, it's awfully late for that. I wish you'd take us home."

The animal had disappeared; at the sound of our voices, it had evidently slunk back into the shadows of the pines.

"What's the matter?" Molly said. "What do you see?"

"Nothing," I said; no more certainly than I had said it to Elizabeth a little while before. "There's nothing there." I started the engine and swung the car around in the road in a U-turn toward the house.

"You ought to think about other people once in a while," she mumbled. "Elizabeth could catch her death of cold."

C arl, Assateague is one of the most beautiful places in America; in the world, I think. It's a great long, narrow sandbank that stretches for fifty miles from southern Maryland into northern Virginia along the Atlantic shore. On the east, there's the ocean, and on the west, a wide, limpid sound with warm shallow water that ripples in the lee of the dunes, and great salt marshes where herons wade and wild ponies splash among the reeds and ospreys soar over the blue water like kites swept away in the wind. The dunes are thirty feet high in places, and the dune grass and sea oats bend shining in the sun and rustling in the soft north wind that blows down the beach in autumn. The only sounds are that whispering of the dune grass and the boom of surf and the craking of gulls above you in the blue air and sometimes the cry of a bittern in the marshes, like a sob echoing in a cistern.

It's even more beautiful than the bay. If you grow up here, as I did, you love water and sun and silence; and there are more of those things at Assateague than anywhere I know. There isn't any huddle of houses along its rim, or beer halls or filling stations or hamburger stands; you don't get that feeling that you get here, more and more, when you're driving up Route 2 to Washington, of being on the scabby edge of civilization, like the scabby, seeping edge of a sore that's leaking its purulence into the bay. It's absolutely uncontaminated; on the day Nils and I went there, it lay in the same blazing purity it has lain in for a million years. The vastness of the place dilutes and consumes utterly the rubble and toxin of society, like a gigantic incinerator; all the offal of human life is rendered into cleanly, glittering scoria by the flames of its light and silence and solitude. It was already a National Seashore then, but it was still almost undiscovered in those days; you could pitch a tent anyplace you chose on the fifty miles of wild shoreline, and wander there for hours without seeing another soul. You can go there in three hours from Washington, and walk there for an hour, and be cleansed of the pollution of that city—which is something like a miracle, because of all pollutions, that must be the very worst.

We found one of the most beautiful places on the island for our camp, only a mile beyond the ranger's booth that marks the boundary of the preserve: a wide, flat stretch of beach that sloped down gently to the surf fifty yards or more from the feet of the sand hills and that was laved over, even by the gentlest waves, which came rippling up over the hard white sand in a running shallow flood of bright water that broke glittering over the shells and splashed your ankles and flushed out little scurrying gray sand fleas that went burrowing back frantically into the bubbling sand like tiny armadillos. The dunes were high and softly fluted by the wind, with little warm, still, sunny dells wandering among them floored with a frail, brittle rubble of brown shells and tiny, gleaming nuggets of white-and-lavender mother-of-pearl, worn smooth as pebbles by the tide. We pitched our tent in one of them, out of the wind, in a warm cup of silence where we could lie naked in the sun and hear the distant, muted roar of the surf and the thin, far shrieking of the gulls sprinkling the air like silver, and the vibrant rustling of the dune grass like an Orphic music running in the wind. I think I could find that place today; it was a secret hollow of peace and absolution in the world, just as those two days were a secret hollow of peace and absolution in my life. I would lie there with the man I had loved most, ever, watching the flutter of his lids in the sun, as if the current of dreams ran under them, and the pulse that billowed gently in his throat and in the long veins of his arms, as if he were bound in smooth convulsive cords of blue corundum, and the tawny luster of his body, so subtly contoured that it seemed to have been shaped by wind, or breath, as the dunes were, and his hair spilled onto the sand like a pool of mead, and his sleeping genitals, couched in their golden lair like a clutch of biding wolverines. I would kiss the length of his golden body, from his molded ankles to his lips and temples, so lightly that he would not awaken, but only stir and shiver as if I had bred a dream in him. Then I would lie and look at him, for an hour or an instant, my mind drowsing and drenching in his opulence like a peach in brandy. The weather was so calm and mild that only in the evening did we need to wear our slacks and sweaters when we sat on the dunes to look out over the dark sea pounding softly at the shore, addled with broken moonlight that spilled over it like mercury; and in the morning, when we cooked our eggs and coffee on a driftwood fire in the silver chill of dawn with rivers of red light running through the sky like lava. All through the middle of the day we went naked, splashing in the surf with cool, hard bodies that looked as if they were carved out of the palest amethyst, or basking in our sunny dell beside the tent, or running on the high dunes through the blades of grass that scarified our flying ankles sweetly, until desire overcame us and we would sink down in the hot sand and entwine ourselves like otters in a flashing, lissome lark of love, sometimes rolling down the dunes together like a pair of tangled comets tumbling down the sky. When the sperm burst out of him it was a shower of light out of his loins, as his poetry was a shower of light out of his mind; I drank them like elixirs and felt the white libation swell my veins and run through me like radium until I shone.

After our lovemaking we would be full of the sweet gravity of satiety, and would nestle together, murmuring, in the sun, and sleep until a reawakening mirthful desire sparkled in our blood like diamond dust. Then we would go racing up the beach through the streaming shingle that sprayed up from our flying feet like scattered crystal arrows, until we collapsed, staggering and exhausted and hilarious in the surf. We would chase fiddler crabs that skittered away from us across the sand with astonishing sidewise speed and disappeared into their holes, where they crouched and waved their eyes at us on the ends of little shiny stalks, like wands, casting a sea spell over us. And we ran along the hard wet sand at the water's edge chasing sandpipers that went pattering ahead of us in patient consternation, their heads bobbing methodically. We followed wild ponies for hours while they drifted across the dunes, their tails flowing in the wind, on indolent, meandering quests; and gathered the polished chips of white-and-lavender nacre for me to make a necklace of, and strings of brittle, amber disks of kelp seed threaded together like pale golden coins; and we rescued stranded horseshoe crabs, hauling them by their stiff, spiky, wriggling tails down to the surf and watching them scuttle off into the sea, carrying back into its blue depths in brown, lustrous bucketfuls the knowledge of the earth's enormities.

Once I climbed the highest dune and stood there in the sun and wind, holding my face in my two hands as if the weight of the joy in my mind were almost insupportable, and looking out into the sea and sky, I said to the spirit who reigned over that magnificence: Lord of all vastness, who resides in all atoms and all instants, I can stand before your blue infinities without shame, because I have loved your earth truly and well, and have not defiled it with lies or acts of greed or vanity or malice. I have not sold one grain of its sand, which no man can possess, with false titles scribbled in the dark, nor have I sold an instant of the holy time I was allotted here to the vendors of the spirit who buy and sell the golden moments of our lives as they would buy grist to grind in their dark, satanic mills. I have given what I had to give freely, without thought of profit, and for all I have received I have felt a true and seemly gratitude. I have been a humble witness of your beauty and mystery, and have known anger only toward those who profane these things, which is my duty as your servant. If I could ask you for one special grace, I would ask for the temperance of trees, which grow only to their appointed height into the light, and then rest in the fullness of their being. If that does not please your will, let a red flower take root in my heart, to add the flame of its excess to the beauty of the world. Great silent father of my being, I have served no god but you, and will not ever.

I felt so cleansed of all heresy and so consecrated by my vow that I sank down to where Nils sat beside me on the sand and hid my face against his throat in a shy and shriven peace.

We splashed through the marshes on the shores of the sound and caught soft-shelled crabs in our shirts to fry over our driftwood fire, and dug clams out of the yellow sand and split their shells and ate them raw, our fingers dripping with cool brine, in glorious, undismayed avidity, knowing our deed was hallowed by our hunger, and that the life we took was not dishonored, but apotheosized, transmuted into the rhapsody with which our brains and bodies rang like carillons.

At night it was warm enough to lie in our sleeping bags outside the tent and look up into the black immensity above us, clear as a vault of obsidian that resonated with its arcana of livid, plangent stars flung across the darkness, vibrating ceaselessly like the verbs of an interminable fiat, endlessly intoned. I cringed beneath them, scathed and naked, and felt my nipples harden in the rain of cold, sidereal music; and I turned to press myself to Nils, driven in awe to the mercy of his body's warmth.

On Sunday evening we sat on the dunes above our tent and watched the sun set across the sound; such a glory of red and lavender shoals of riven cloud and towering folds of purple drapery and vast, mullioned panes of rose-bright, lambent air—the whole firmament one measureless cathedral window—that in spite of the knowledge of our leaving, we were stricken into silent surfeit, and went down, when the sky had darkened into layers of gray shale, to strike our tent in speechless, solemn gravity, folding the canvas and bundling up the stakes and cords with patient, stupefied movements of our hands and arms and wandering, inane eyes. Then we lay down on the sand together for the last time, and I clutched Nils's hand and watched the sky turn black, feeling the darkness seep into my hollow breast and heart and head until I was filled with it, and could support the weight of the inky fathoms that lay over me, and not be crushed.

But I woke up in the night with a cool wind fluttering across my skin, and rose and drew a blanket over us and lay listening for something that had disturbed my sleep: a liquid plummeting, as of a stone into a well, or an animal plunging into still water in whose depths I lay; a stealthy, ghastly splash.

"Did you hear it?" I said to Nils.

"No. What was it?"

"I don't know. A sound. Like that rat plunging into the quarry, the day you made me swim through the blood."

"What quarry?" he said. "What rat? I don't know what you're talking about." He rose up on his elbow to look at me, his face wan in the moonlight.

"Don't you remember the quarry? The day you brought the rifle?"

"You must be dreaming," he said. "You're only half awake." He stroked my hair and drew my head down to his breast, so that I heard only the drumming of his heart, like the booming of a bittern in the marsh.

"Who do you think I am?" he said in a moment.

"I know who you are. Don't be silly."

"I don't know. Sometimes I think you mistake me for someone else. Someone you've invented."

"That's idiotic," I whispered fearfully.

"No. There are times when I feel almost imaginary. As if I wouldn't exist any longer if you stopped thinking about me."

"I'll never stop, then."

"But if you do, I won't know," he said, with a quaint, earnest anxiety. "I won't know anything."

Then I heard the sound again, a brutal, fleshy thump and then an empty, quivering pause, like a bird flying into a windowpane and dropping lifelessly. I didn't tell him I heard it, but I shivered, so that I felt his arm tighten about me for an instant and then slacken, as if to let me go.

"I think we have to go," he said. "It must be nine o'clock. We won't get back till after twelve, and you have a class in the morning."

"Yes."

When I tried to carry the bedrolls to the car, such a sorrowful, stony lethargy came over me that I could hardly move my legs; they were numb and wooden, and the weight of the bundles was like boulders. We packed the tent and blankets and the cooking gear into the trunk, murmuring quietly to each other like people at a wake. He went to throw sand on the coals of our campfire, but I said, "No, you always have to leave a little fire burning. That's what they say on the bay."

He stared at me gravely for a moment. "It's not good campcraft."

"I guess not, in the woods. But people do it on the bay. And in the desert, too, I think. I read in books that the Bedouins do that, too."

I looked back from the car at our little starlit dell, with the embers glowing like a heap of garnets in the moonlight and the shadows of the dunes lying on the pale sand. I could not speak for sorrow, and when we drove up the sand road from the island and across the causeway that joins the sandbanks to the mainland, I looked out at the great silent sound, plated with its weird, astral glow, with herons standing in the mist and the silvery marshes stretching off into the darkness until they wore the lowest stars tangled in their reeds like fox fire, and I could almost have gone blind without regret, because I thought I would never see such beauty again, or have a heart whole enough to bear it if I did.

We crossed the causeway and drove along a narrow black-top road through the shadowy pine barrens of the coastal flats, and I dropped my head against Nils's shoulder and let it jostle there in an empty, mindless sopor, staring out at the country stores that passed the car window in the moonlight, and the milky fields and stark farmhouses, in front of each of them an automobile tire hanging stilly from a silent oak in the sandy front yard. There was a bitter electric glare on the horizon that marked the route of the four-lane highway that runs from Ocean City to the bay, and in a little while we joined it, swishing with traffic and blazing with the lights of filling stations and motels and fast-food stands. I sat up and sighed, feeling the memory of those two days at Assateague slide down like a bright stone into dark water.

"Were you asleep?" he said.

"No. Now I am."

I watched his face for a while as we drove, flashed over by the garish play of lights from the roadside stands: yellow and scarlet and blue and green, transforming it into the soulless, gaudy glamour of a chorus boy in the grand finale of a musical comedy.

"Can't you go any faster?" I said.

"No. This wreck'll fly apart if I do." He nodded ahead of us through the windshield. "Look up there. It looks like somebody had the same idea."

Even while he was saying it, I could hear a siren wailing behind us, rising in pitch with the speed of the approaching ambulance. A hundred yards ahead of us there was a cluster of parked cars at the edge of the highway and a police cruiser standing on the shoulder, its turret beacon flashing red and blue as it revolved with a curious, slow, stately punctuality. On the highway, a state trooper in a wide-brimmed hat was bending to set a row of flares on the pavement; they gushed showers of scarlet sparks, like Fourth of July sparklers. The bilious, artificial light flickered over the figures of a crowd of twelve or fifteen people—extras in the show—as if our attention had been drawn to another part of the stage in the same elaborate final number of the musical. That's just what I thought, Carl: It's like a musical comedy, and I seem to be in it, too; but I don't know my lines, or the score, or what I'm doing up here, anyway. I don't know how to act. The people in the crowd were like a chorus, massed in the grand production number between the slowly oscillating lights of the police car, and the flares, and the steady, infernal glare of a gigantic neon sign supported by a steel pole in front of a fast-food stand. The pole had been struck by a very fast-moving automobile and bent into a forty-five-degree angle, so that the sign it bore dangled out over the highway, brandishing its huge scarlet letters in a kind of gruesomely enticing way: ALL YOU CAN EAT—RAW OR COOKED. There was something else written on it, but the glass tubes that formed the letters had been smashed by the impact, and buzzed darkly. Twenty yards beyond the sign the car that had struck the pole lay upside down and crumpled against the bole of an oak tree like a tin can smashed with a mallet. All the windows were broken and it was sprinkled with little granules of broken glass that twinkled in the garish light like artificial ice on a stage set or under a Christmas tree. A state trooper was sitting on an upturned empty wheel well with a hacksaw, trying to cut through the hinge of the crumpled passenger door. It was a faded blue Volkswagen with a University of Maryland parking sticker on the bumper, and the minute I saw it, I knew it was Ron's. When we went past, I saw his arm dangling out of the broken window of the door.

"Stop," I said shrilly.

"Why, for God's sake? You don't want to see this."

"*Stop!*" I shrieked at him. "It's Ron!"

"Jesus Christ. *Ron?* Why? What's he doing here? How do you know?"

"It's his *car*," I screamed. "Stop, Nils! *Stop!*"

He braked the car and pulled off onto the shoulder, twenty yards beyond the smashed car and the string of flares on the pavement. I don't remember getting out of it at all; I just remember the scene expanding in front of me like a zoom shot on a motion-picture screen as I ran toward it: the stage-lit, mumbling crowd with the livid lights flickering over them, and that grotesquely arrant sign skewed across the highway, and a trooper standing in the middle of the pavement waving a flare to block the traffic and direct the ambulance that came howling up the highway, weaving between the cars and thumping over the median strip, and the gang of men tugging at the door of the crumpled, upside-down Volkswagen that was sprinkled with tinsel like a Christmas present. They had got the door off by the time I got to it, and two of them were lifting it carefully away while the trooper with the hacksaw and a fourth man raised Ron's dangling arm and passed it through the window. With the door gone, I could see him crushed back against the seat with the steering wheel pushed through his chest. His head was hanging to one side, and although he was dead, his eyes were wide open in a look of astonishment, as if amazed and perhaps secretly delighted to discover that he was no longer merely a bystander of drama, but a protagonist in it, as I had wanted him to be. Someone grabbed me by the arm and tried to stop me, but I tore my arm away and hit him across the face and screamed, "Let go of me! Let *go* of me! He's my *husband!*"

"Jesus, I'm sorry, lady," the man muttered, and dropped my arm, and I ran up to the open door and fell onto my knees in front of it, and reached inside and tried to put my arms around him. He was soaked in blood and his right hand was pressed against his groin with the fingers clenched around a sheet of paper he had ripped out of my notebook. I pried his fingers apart and took the crumpled page out of his hand and then fell forward over him into the blear of slick, warm, slowly welling blood, oil, engine smoke, metal, plastic, rubber, fabric, all brayed together in an incoherent, vile pottage in that stinking mortar, for the medication, or nourishment, or delectation of no one, nothing, God or beast or man. I fainted with the outrage of it.

Although I knew Walter Lubby for less than a year, my relationship with him was the most compelling of my life. An intimacy grew between us that I'd never known with any other human being. I thought of him constantly, and never was truly at ease or felt contentment or repose except when I was with him. I came to prefer his company to that of any other person I knew —that I've ever known, I think—and felt better accepted, understood, and appreciated by him than by my wife, my child, my colleagues, my parents, the few friends of my school and college days—by anyone, but you.

This is an odd thing, too: I never felt remorse or guilt when I was with him —or apart from him, for that matter; I never regretted the duplicity of my relationship with him. Quite the opposite, in fact. It seemed to me that with him I was more truly myself, less concealed, less cunning and constricted than I'd ever been before; and this was in spite of the constant deception that I had to practice in order for the relationship to exist; on which, in fact, it was founded. That's the strangest thing of all: that he seemed to understand and accept the necessity of that duplicity in me, and thus to dignify it, to exonerate me of it. I believe he did, actually. I'm sure he felt no resentment, hatred, contempt, or even suspicion toward me. In fact, I often had the feeling that he felt far more compassion for me than I for him, that in his judgment of things, it was I who was suffering, I whose ordeal we were undergoing. There was something that could almost have been called charitable in the profound and clement calm in which he sat beside me, bearing my scrutiny of his ravaged face, of the broken buttons of his faded shirt, of his frail hands lying in his lap like dead birds, as if in the knowledge that only that attitude of poverty and consummate reconciliation could ease or edify my starveling gaze.

I must have gone to see him at least fifty times in the ten months before he died, our visits becoming more familiar and comfortable, and yet progressively more ceremonial, more courtly, even. Perhaps we both sensed there would not be many more of them and this made both of us more decorous in the knowledge that our relationship was drawing to its close. In the last days of that sweltering summer, and on autumn afternoons to whose radiance his own ebbing life seemed to contribute a fluttering brilliance like a falling scarlet leaf or a dying flame, and through the hours of a black and rainy winter that besieged the cabin like the loup-garou whose eyes he had looked into, we sat together in our cane-backed chairs as if sharing the same pew of a church, celebrating some silent liturgy that had called us there to be observed.

I developed a desire to touch him physically. As a regular ritual of my visits, I began to give him alcohol rubs. While there was little medical justification for this, I had a pretext for it: the paresthesia had become acute, particularly in his legs, and he had a constant burning and prickling sensation on the surface of both his thighs that caused him distress. With the help of his daughter I would get him into bed and rub his legs and arms and back with alcohol for half an hour or more. By the middle of winter there was considerable atrophy of his muscles, but although his skin was slack and progressively wrinkled over his rapidly wasting body, I felt no aversion at touching it. On the contrary, there was something deeply satisfying to me in stroking the long, black, spare limbs slowly, feeling the loose, sleek, sable skin ripple ahead of my hands and yield to my palms with a moist suavity, like fine and supple suede beneath which I could finger his bones and joints like treasured curios. When I was a boy I used to keep chunks of bright quartz and dried wishbones and walnut hulls and snail shells in a chamois bag beside my bed and finger them dreamily while I fell asleep; when I massaged the old man that sense of nameless, lyric comfort crept over me that I had felt in fondling those shapely souvenirs of the earth while I slowly drifted away from it. I think he shared the feeling, or something like it. He would close his eyes and murmur luxuriously while I rubbed his gaunt, lean legs; and in some way it served to consummate the bond between us. "You is sho' good to my daddy," his daughter said to me once. "They ain't many a doctah would taken such kindly care of a poor old black man. You a good man, Doctah Ransome, suh."

"I do what I must," I mumbled, not with conscious deceit, but in embarrassment at her misconception of the nature of my attention to him. I myself had no illusions about its "goodness," as I had none about its malice, or "evil"; it was simply a part of experimental procedure, and if I was unusually zealous in my discharge of it, it was because his case was of unusual interest. But that other people might find my attachment to the man extraordinary must have made me uneasy to some degree, because I made a conscious attempt to justify it as professional fascination with a particularly complex clinical syndrome. Liam and Dr. Kidd may have been deceived by this (I think they were prepared to be by their conception of me as a coldly objective investigator), and so may other members of my staff, with the exception of Mrs. Farris. Her estimate of me was innocently generous from the first, and my interest in Walter Lubby perfectly in keeping with it; to her, such uncommon concern with the welfare of a patient could only have been interpreted as goodness, and served to confirm her faith in the integrity of the project and the benevolence of our intentions in general. That I almost invariably excused her from accompanying me on my visits to the old man, that I went so often to examine him, kept such a scrupulous account of his condition, and was so accommodating in taking over her traditional nurse's duties of bathing, massaging, grooming, and comforting him, were all evidence of virtue, her appreciation of which she would often express in murmurs of baffled admiration when we spoke of him.

The nearer he drew to death, the more intense my obsession with him grew. I suppose it depended on the inevitability of that event, and the closer it approached, the more I felt the imminence of my release from the obsession, and of some enlightenment that would come with my liberation. I don't know just what. As much as I detested the idea of revelation, I suppose I expected something of the sort. If anyone else had used the term, I would have snorted with contempt.

He lived through the winter and died on the thirteenth of May, on a hot, harrowingly still and clear spring day, ten months after I'd met him at the country church. In all that time I allowed nothing to interfere with my regular visits to him, even in the winter days, when the road through the pine barrens was a slippery quagmire of red mud from which I sometimes had to dig out the wheels of my automobile or along which, the car hopelessly mired and abandoned, I would plod in a leaky raincoat, my boots caked like the hooves of a monster, the desire to be in his presence burning in me like the glow of a coal in an ashpit. On such days there would be a fire burning in the cast-iron stove in the main room of the cabin, and if he felt well enough, he would be sitting in front of it in his rocking chair with a cotton blanket around his shoulders and a poker in his hand, reaching out occasionally to tap the grill of the glowing iron door. There would be a saucepan full of the dark red wine simmering on the stove top—placed there while I had sat on the front porch to remove my muddy shoes and put on the dry socks and the pair of her husband's shoes that his daughter had brought me—and we would sip at it from thick tumblers that warmed our hands, listening to the muted popping of the pine knots in the stove and the rain on the tin roof and the incessant gentle grinding of the rockers on the wooden floor. When he discovered my passion for tea, he had his son buy a box of it in Tallacoochee, and he would brew it for me in an old teapot with a broken spout and brown cracks spraying over it like spiderwebs. He would sprinkle a pinch of crumbled herb leaves in the pot, basil or thyme, which gave the tea a pungent, eerie fragrance, something like the odor of geranium, that would linger on my taste for hours, sometimes into the middle of the night. His daughter became so accustomed to my presence that she scarcely took notice of me; she would work in the kitchen, preparing the evening meal for the family, or set up an ironing board and press the shirts and sheets which she had laundered earlier, the little girl pushing a rag doll around the floor at her feet and humming endlessly. We were left to our colloquies or silences like a pair of cronies by a fireplace. As he grew weaker, he was confined to his bed in the rear room of the cabin, where he spent the last six weeks of his life, his head propped up on pillows to give him a view of the river through the window between the black, leafless branches of the willows. The winter light through the pane cast a pale, astringent haze across his features like a rime; it gave his face the lustrous, austere transparency of a giant gem, a carved obsidian cameo of a mogul or a magus. He knew that he was dying, as I've said, and in so exact a way that I think he knew the very day and hour of his death; but the closer that hour approached, the less often he spoke of death and the less somber his thoughts were. Often he talked about his youth, about fairs and carnivals and the oak-splitting contests at which he had won renown, and berry picking and hunting trips and summer camp meetings. What he seemed to remember most vividly were simple physical sensations, odors and colors and the feel of objects in the hand, their weight and temperature and texture, patterns of bird flight and clouds, the taste of hot fruit and the drone of bees in clover. It was as if his life were in a condition of such perfect order and serenity that he could recall at will scenes out of his past and examine their minutiae with a tranquillity and delight that in the anxiety and fatigue and nerve-dulling labor of daily existence he had never been able to experience, as if he could retrace his way across a meadow that thirty years ago he had crossed wearily or impatiently or hungrily on his way from work, and pause now to stoop and touch the petals of flowers that had once brushed unnoticed against his trouser legs. He seemed able to summon such scenes back in a cool, pale bouquet of memory that he savored like the fumes of a fine, dry wine, almost as a child sees the world when it is first presented to him, free of the obscurities of work and worry and ambition and responsibility, or of the knowledge of treachery or disaster, or the death of friends, or the rebuke of parents, or the indifference of the world. All those obscurities were lifted now; the deaths had been died, the disasters had befallen, the blows had congealed to shining welts across the black skin of his forearms and his knuckles, and he saw the world as one sees it in a painting or a novel, clearly and painlessly, shiningly liberated from the stains of grief and guilt. Sometimes he would fall into a trance of memory and sit humming tunelessly with a kind of frail and plangent gaiety, his voice thrumming with the secret felicities it bore, like the humming of a telephone wire in the wind. These interludes were not departures, really, and they didn't make me impatient or patronizing, as one feels at the ramblings and reminiscences of dotage or senility; they seemed to me something much more like pilgrimages back into his past, to shrines he had not known or recognized as such, or ever paused to fill with his devotions. There was a radiance about him at such moments that did not allow feelings of pity or impatience; it was like watching a man at prayer, or a child transported by the glittering levitation of a hummingbird. I would sit watching his face and feel sometimes as if I were very nearly able to identify, to name at last, something in me that I had never been able to describe except as inconsolable. And then in a dry, clear, almost disembodied voice that seemed to come out of the glimmering air above the river where his gaze was buried, he would tell me about the smell of sawdust and hot canvas in a revival tent on a summer Sunday afternoon, or the stain of blueberry juice on the pale skin of his palms that would last sometimes throughout the summer, or the writhing, glittering, tangled, golden splendor of a seething mass of new-hatched copperheads in a rock pool by the river that he had stepped into. There was no fear in his description of the snakes, although they must certainly have terrified him at the time; they had no power to poison him now, and he could see their beauty with the impunity that art and memory give us with which to see the beauty of the world; and for a moment I could share that impunity with him, and that delight, because he described them as an artist would, a luminous clarity welling out of them with the painless poignancy of a peach on a tablecloth or a bottle of wine sparkling in the sunlight in a Renoir canvas. He didn't speak about abstractly beautiful things, grace or patience or virtue; and then it occurred to me—I think for the first time—that these were all human qualities, all aspects of love, about which he didn't speak either. His love of things was implicit in his recollections of them, in his descriptions of their forms and colors and moving singularities. And that he seldom included people in these luminous litanies troubled me. When he spoke of them at all it was of events in which they had played a part with him, or of sensations they had shared—picking strawberries with his wife on a spring morning, drenched in the hot sweet scent of the sun-warmed berry beds; or fishing with his son for silent hours from a scow moored in the river with the current rippling against the bottom boards like the flutter of a pulse and damselflies dipping and twinkling over the water. It seemed as if the experience in itself were the principal delight, not that it served as a means of communion with another person. I felt in some way disparaged by this, as if he were withholding the most secret and essential part of his nature and sensibility from me, as if his confidence in me were not yet absolute.

Only once, when I questioned him insistently about his wife, did he speak at any length about her.

"She did die birthin' Becky," he said. "She was borned crossways, you see, Becky was. Lord, that was a long night. The midwife didn't know what to do, and it went on all night. I was some kind of a scared man."

"You were scared?"

" 'Deed I was. Some kind of a scared, disconsolated man. And then I seen the loogaroo. I seen the eyes."

"When did you see the eyes?"

"That very night. I went out yonder in the swamp with a gun."

"You went hunting on that night?"

"No, suh. I went out there to shoot myself. I didn't see no hope. My wife dead, and a brand-new baby girl and two boys to take care of, and nobody to he'p me raise 'em up, and work scarce, and the money most gone. I was some kind of a disconsolated man. I set down on a log and cocked the gun, and right then I seen the loogaroo. He come outa the bush and looked me dead in the eye, and I seen the swamp fire burnin' in his eyes. Burned the fear right outa me, and then I knowed to come on back."

After some time I said, "You must have loved your wife very much."

" 'Deed I did. I did love the woman. I do love the woman still. She had a pretty face. Had a little mole up side of her mouth. And always did smell good. Smell like strawberry ice cream. She had the longest legs I ever did see."

"She was a very virtuous woman, I suppose; she loved the Bible."

" 'Deed she was. A very virtuous woman. And a quiet woman. And she never speak nothin' but the truth, from the day she was borned."

"What is it you remember most about her? What is it that you miss most?"

He thought for a moment, and a delicate, merry smile lifted his lips from his dark teeth. "I reckon I miss them long legs." He chuckled faintly, a sound like the stirring of dry corn leaves in an autumn breeze. "Oh, my Lord."

"You don't remember her virtue most? Her truth, her quietness? You don't miss those things?"

"Well, you see, you don't have to try too hard to remember them things, 'cause you don't have to leave holt of 'em. Them things is all goin' to keep right on. They ain't goin' to change. What you got to remember is the things you ain't goin' to see no more; you know, like a mole up side a woman's mouth. Like blueberry pie, and bees buzzin' in the butterfly bush, and them little bitty snakes shinin' in the sun like a potful of hot broth. A good tool in the hand, spare ribs, all like that. You got to remember them things, 'cause you ain't goin' to see them no more." He stared for a moment through the window, the willow branches casting the faint shadow of a seine across his face and breast. He lifted his hands gropingly, as if to disentangle its cords. "I figure they is like a radio, them things. You kin hear the music through 'em, just like through a radio. Them other things you was talkin' about, virtue, you know; truth; all like that: them things is the music. They all the time there, they don't change. That there is the music, floatin' around in the air, comin' right through the wall. But you cain't hear it if you ain't got no radio." He clasped his hands together and drew them in against his chest, sitting huddled for a moment. "They is times when you think it done stopped. But you don't need to worry about it stoppin', 'cause it don't never stop." He gasped suddenly and pressed his clasped hands against his belly in a throe of agony whose obscenity I could see in the convulsion of his face, crumpled like that of a man repulsed by something vile. He turned it up to the ceiling in a withered gaze of pain, the lips drawn back in the absolute, tense retraction of a mummy's, baring his black teeth in a sordid, desiccated snarl, his eyes gone bleak and mucid, rotten with pain, like those of a dead fish on a beach, a thin, long, silver thread of drool descending slowly from one corner of his mouth as if a spider slowly descended on a single thread from its lair. I stood up from my chair and reached out to take him by the shoulders, but they hardened against my grasp like stone. I stood bent over him without speaking, humbled by his austerity, holding him until his muscles relaxed slowly to their lean flaccidity and his eyes withdrew from the white obscurity into which they had journeyed, light and identity flowing back into them as slowly as water seeping through the rift of a rock. He drew a long tremulous breath that sounded like a hoarsely whispered vow and lowered his head until his eyes were level with the window, through which he stared for several moments, idly and hungrily, with the avid languor of a lover dreaming of his lady's face. I released his shoulders and straightened up, standing to look down at him.

"Are you all right?"

"Oh, yeah. Yeah. Just a little quinch. It taken me like that sometime, in the stomach." He looked into the hard, pale winter sky, grained and hued like marble through the trees. "Yeah, them things is like a radio, and you need 'em, long as you down here. But when you git to Glory, you ain't goin' to need no radio. You ain't even goin' to need no ears. Praise God, 'cause mine is near wore out."

"I think you'd better have some medicine," I said.

"Yeah, I reckon I better. It's in there by the bed."

I went into his room and found the bottle beside the kerosene lamp that stood on the box beside his bed. I shook three of the aspirin tablets into my hand and stared at them for a moment in my palm, their passionless, compliant, utterly inert, utterly inanimate capacity for palliation tormenting me for a moment like the soulless charm of a whore to a man long at sea. For a moment I was tempted—I can't tell you how greatly—to open the window of the bare little room and fling them out, together with the bottle, into the wet sand of the yard, and go back to Tallacoochee and bring arsphenamine to treat his sickness properly. This temptation raged in me for a very long, chaotic moment, and then I thought: No; my faith is no stranger than his; neither of them can be understood, but they are what make us worthy of each other's respect. Without my faith, he would despise me, as, without his, I would despise him. Pain is what defines us. Pain gives us the little holiness we have. Without pain we should be nothing; we should not deserve salvation. And the greater pain has precedence.

I took the aspirins in to him and stood looking down at his shriveled mummy's mask of suffering. I will not yield, I thought. It is you who must yield. It is you who must renounce; or complete your ministry. I called to his daughter, who stood inside the kitchen at the stove, "Your father doesn't feel well. Will you bring him a glass of wine?"

"Yes, suh."

She brought the wine and stood beside his chair adjusting the blanket gently around his shoulders while I placed the aspirin tablets one by one into his lips and, when he had swallowed them, raised the glass of wine to his mouth to let him sip from it. When he had finished, he parted his lips weakly several times with a dry smacking sound and sat staring bleakly through the window.

"Are you feeling better?"

"Yes, suh; yes, suh. I'm obliged."

"You'd better get to bed for a while and rest."

"Yes, suh. I reckon I will."

I stooped and gathered him up in my arms and carried him to the bedroom, laying him on the bed and covering him with the blanket that his daughter carried behind me. Then I stood and looked down at him.

"Do you have a radio?" I asked.

"No, suh, I don't. One thing I always did want, but it seem like I never could git the money together, you know."

"Yes, they're expensive."

" 'Deed they is."

The next day I brought him an old table radio that I had seen in the attic of the house a week or two before. I had gone up there one day to search for the source of a leak that was slowly permeating the bathroom ceiling with an insidious brown stain, and while I bandaged a dripping pipe with metal tape, I had seen the radio sitting, covered with dust, on an ancient treadle sewing machine in the shadows of the eaves. It was an old Atwater-Kent with a square metal battery case and a huge, lilylike brass speaker horn, green with corrosion. I spent an hour polishing it, and stopped on my way to his house at the hardware store on Main Street to buy a battery and, with the assistance of the clerk, install it in the case and clean and connect the terminals. It worked very well, considering its age. We switched it on and turned the tuning dial through a succession of rural stations playing country and Western music and of local evangelists waxing eloquent on the subject of damnation. I left it tuned to a program called the Flaxman Gospel Hour.

His daughter came to the screen door of the cabin when I carried it from the car, and held the door for me while I hauled it up the steps, shaking her head in a kind of helpless, delighted wonder, her magnificent teeth gleaming like porcelain in her great soft brown lips.

"Well, my land! My *land!*" she murmured. "Won't he be purely proud!"

"How is he feeling?" I asked.

"He's some better. He ate a little breakfast. I think he's asleep right now. You want me to go see?"

"Yes."

She went across the cabin to the door of his room and looked inside, turning to nod to me.

"I'll tell you what I'd like to do," I said. "Do you think we could put it by his bed and turn it on, so he can wake up hearing the music?"

"Yes, indeed we kin. I'll just clear off the box. Won't that man be surprised!"

I brought the radio into the room, and when she had quietly and carefully cleared the box beside the bed of his pipe, ashtray, and glasses, I set the radio beside the lamp and switched it on. The voice of the Reverend Tommy Flaxman suddenly cleft the silence of the room like the shriek of the disk saw from the mill rupturing the silence of the town after the noon lunch hour. *How can you go to bed tonight and sleep,* he cried, *when you know that you have given your money to Satan instead of to the Lord? How can you lie there and sleep like a filthy hound when you have spent your money on liquor, and women, and poker, and fine clothes, instead of giving it to Jesus to heal the wounds you have inflicted on his heart with your wickedness and your refusal to recognize him as your Savior? I want you to sit there and ask yourself that question while you listen to this song we are about to hear. Look deep into your heart while you listen to this beautiful hymn in praise of the Savior whose suffering you are causing with your sin!*

I watched the old man's face. His eyelids trembled with the stir of awakening consciousness beneath them, as delicate as the stir of leaves at dawn when birds awaken in the trees. The voice of a gospel singer, a rich, soft mezzo, clothing the notes like moss enfolding stone, began to flow from the ancient loudspeaker, ringing with exaltation:

> *I walk in the garden alone*
> *When the dew is still on the roses*
> *And the voice I hear falling on my ear*
> *The Son of God discloses.*

The old man's eyes opened very slowly and a look of beatitude such as I had never seen filled them with a glow like iron heated to lambency, his face falling into the beautiful proud passivity of a girl's hearing the declaration of a lover. As he listened, his eyes drifted from the ceiling to my face, and the glow in them paled momentarily, and then deepened as he turned them to his daughter, and then to the windowpane shot with winter light, and then to the radio beside him on the box, his eyes dusking and waning like molten metal in a crucible. When the music had finished, he murmured softly, "Lord, Lord. I thought I had done crossed over."

I had an uneasy, indignant, and contemptuous feeling; a combination of shame at my deception of him and disillusion at the ease with which I had accomplished it, as well as a bitter sense of triumph. You are a foolish, fond old man, I thought, looking down at his serene and wasted face. This radio has brought you the voice of a false prophet. You have heard false promises of paradise. How little it takes to produce this faith of yours: a little wire and a battery and a wax disk spinning on a wheel is all that is needed to produce the illusion of divinity. But my scorn could not withstand the luster of his eyes; watching them, I thought almost immediately: No, this shabby little hoax has only served to confirm the faith that was already there, that has taken a lifetime to grow out of labor and suffering and joy, out of many deaths and embraces and departures, out of the flow of river water and the glitter of serpents in the sun. Everything confirms that faith, even the sly spite of vandals. This piece of trickery is not very different from the subterfuge I practice with him daily, which has not altered his faith in me. He put out his hand slowly and laid it on the cabinet.

"Ain't that purely beautiful," he murmured. " 'Deed I got to thank you, Doctah."

"I thought you might enjoy it, while you're lying there. It will pass the time."

" 'Deed it will. Lord, I didn't think ever to have such a thing."

After that, the radio was always playing softly in the bedroom when I came to visit him, whether he lay beside it in the bed or sat out by the stove in his rocking chair. His gratitude for it was profound beyond further mention, but the radio was always playing as testimony of it. So far as I know, the station was never changed, and what was extraordinary was that in spite of her passion for religious music, the little girl was totally oblivious of it. For her, the sound of the hymns and spirituals issuing constantly from the bedroom door did not seem to exist. She would often hum or sing different tunes from those it was playing, in bewildering dissonance to them. I had expected her to be fascinated, and her indifference discomfited me. There was something almost disdainful about it, as there was something almost sardonic in her silences at times, when I would find her staring at me from her eyrie beneath the ironing board at her mother's feet, her eyes somber, unflinching, and vaguely condemnatory, vaguely wary and suspicious, as if enfolding some primitive, ironic knowledge about my origins and intentions. She made me increasingly uneasy.

"Doesn't she ever speak?" I asked the old man once.

"No, she don't. Not like regular talk."

"But she speaks to you."

"Yeah, she ast me somethin' once in a while. And she tell me things, you know. Like if it goin' to rain, or if they is a dog in the yard worryin' the ducks, somethin' like that. But she don't use no regular words. She kindly make little noises; like the rain is 'pit-pit-pit,' dog is 'boof,' like that. But she don't do a lot of talkin'."

"Do you think she knows what we say?"

"I reckon so. But she all the time listenin' to the music, you know. She don't hear much else."

"Has she been to school at all?"

"Yeah, she went up to the school last year for a while. But she didn't do much good. Seem like they couldn't teach her to read noways."

"It might be that she simply has a speech defect," I said. "Or a visual problem of some kind. Dyslexia, or something of that sort. Or perhaps a slight hearing impairment. Perhaps something could be done for her. Has she ever been examined by a doctor?"

"Yeah, it seem to me the visitin' nurse done looked at her when she was up to the school. But she didn't figure they could do nothin' for her."

"Well, of course, a nurse doesn't have the training that a doctor has. I'd be happy to have a look at her myself, if you'd like. I might be able to suggest some kind of treatment."

"Well, I do appreciate that a whole lot, Doctah. But I tell you, I don't know how *she'd* feel about it. I tell you the truth, I don't think they is nothin' or nobody goin' to change that little girl. I reckon she just one of the quiet folks, you know. They different from other folks. They is more like the Lord."

"How are they like the Lord?"

"Well, I reckon they got a little bit of the Lord's quietness in 'em. The Lord is a mighty quiet man."

"He certainly is that."

"And you know, I figure they understand a lot more than folks think. Seem like the more a man understand, the less he got to say."

"You think she understands?"

"I reckon she do. All she need to."

"You're sure you wouldn't like me to examine her? I could look at her throat and larynx very easily while I'm here. And give her some basic eye and ear examinations."

"No, suh. I'm mighty obliged, but I reckon she just as well off like she is. I don't reckon they is nobody suppose to mess with her."

We were sitting by the stove. It had rained earlier, but now the sun was out brightly, although it was very cold. He learned forward to rattle the grate with the poker and said, "Your wife, now. I wonder, would she be a quiet woman?"

"I suppose she is. She's very thoughtful sometimes."

"Yeah. That is a fine thing in a woman."

I thought for a moment, and added, as if in defense of Molly or amendment of the modesty of my praise of her, "She likes music very much."

"Do she, though? My wife did, too. Sung in the church choir till the week she died. I reckon the little girl git her knack from her."

"I have a daughter," I said after some time, "about the age of your granddaughter."

"Now I did not know that. Do she sing?"

"No. I don't think she has any definite talents, like your granddaughter's. Not that I'm aware of." I swirled the tea in my cup restlessly and set it on the floor between my feet, leaning forward to peer between the slats of the grill into the seething red interior of the stove. "As a matter of fact, I don't think I understand either of them very well." I said this suddenly, swept by a startling, spontaneous impulse to make the confession; it was in fact more like a momentary debility than an impulse; it came over me like a sudden laxity of muscle and thought, the yielding of body and mind to a wave of fatigue or despair. "I've never been very close to my family. I'm afraid I've always put my work first."

"Yes, suh."

"It seems to me that a man's work has the first claim on him. Before anything else. Don't you feel the great importance of a man's work?"

"Yes, suh, I do," he said. " 'Deed I do. But it do depend on how you look at it. Some ways the work ain't nothin'. Some ways it's a shame to a man, and a burden on him. Do he not see it right."

"How does he learn to see it right?"

"Well, I reckon a man find out different ways. I tell you how I found out." He leaned forward again and tapped further open the grill of the stove door. "They was a man I worked for one time, worked on this house up to Bibb. A real mean man. Bad to colored folks. I worked two days on his house, he cussed me out like I was dirt. I spilt a bag of nails, you see, did rile him up. I say to myself, I ain't goin' to work no mo' for this man, this is a real mean man. I ain't goin' to build no house for no bad man to live in. So I come on home and git my wife to read me from the Bible, see kin I find out what to do. I want to git the word of the Lord. She say, 'Where you want me to read?' I say, 'Start right from the beginnin', I don't want to miss nothin'.' So she start readin' right from the beginnin'. Well, she ain't read but a few pages when she git to the part about Noah and the Flood. And you know what I found out?" He turned his eyes on me, great and hazy as burnished brown quartz.

"No."

"I find out that all mens is bad, just like that man up to Bibb. All mens is corrupt; it says so, right there in the Bible. They ain't no man on the earth that is free of corruption." He thrust his face toward me, leaning forward with his elbows resting on his thighs. "Did you know that the Lord got so disgusted with people one time that he decided to blot 'em off the face of the earth? Now, that is the truth. I done got it by heart." He leaned back in the rocking chair and turned his face to look out of the window at the pale thin sunlight silvering the charcoal black of the willow branches. He began to quote slowly in his harsh, frail voice, " 'Now the earth was corrupt in God's sight, and the earth was filled with violence. And God saw the earth, and behold, it was corrupt; for all flesh had corrupted their way upon the earth. And God said to Noah, "I have determined to make an end of all flesh; for the earth is filled with violence through them; behold, I will destroy them with the earth." ' " The air between us seemed to vibrate with the malediction. I turned my eyes from his, back to the holocaust that seethed inside the stove. "That was one time he said what was on his mind. Seem like he had more to say back in them days then he do now."

"Yes."

"Ain't that a terrible thing. That the Lord would be so disgusted with man that he would be sorry he ever made him. But that's how he felt. He say, 'I has done made a mistake.' It tell you that, right there in the Bible." He closed his eyes and began to quote again, effortlessly, with the fluency of great familiarity. " 'The Lord saw that the wickedness of man was great in the earth, and that every imagination of the thoughts of his heart was only evil continually. And the Lord was sorry that he had made man on the earth, and it grieved him to his heart. So the Lord said, "I will blot out man whom I have created from the face of the ground, man and beast and creeping things and birds of the air, for I am sorry that I have made them." ' " Again the awesome silence fell between us. "You know what it say next?"

"No," I murmured.

"It say, 'But Noah found favor in the eyes of the Lord.' Now, ain't that a peculiar thing. I always did think that was a most peculiar thing. Because you know Noah was a drinkin' man, and a wild man, wild in his ways. He was the first man that ever plowed the ground and planted crops, and the first thing he planted was grapevines, so's he could make hisse'f some wine. Now that's the truth. Then one time he got so drunk he fell down in his tent and passed out, naked as a jaybird. That's what the Good Book say. I always did wonder how come a man like that would be the only one what found favor in the eyes of the Lord. Why do you reckon that was?"

"I don't know," I said.

"No, I don't neither. It is a kindly mysterious thing. But the Lord taken a shine to him for some reason, and he told Noah to make hisse'f an ark, because he was going to bring on the Flood and drown everythin' in the world. Everythin' but Noah and his sons, and they wives. And then, 'cause he taken a likin' to Noah, he made a bargain with him. He promised him he wouldn't never do it no mo'—wouldn't never kill off the creatures again. Just leave 'em be; let 'em do what they liked. Maybe he figured he'd git another Noah, every two, three thousand years."

"It's not very often," I said.

"No, it ain't. Might be less than that. And you know, that's what come to me, listenin' to my wife read the Scripture. I say, 'Why, looky here. Mens ain't no better now than they was then. Not even with Noah for they grand-daddy. Maybe they even worse. They ain't no man in this world is free of corruption. But they all got to live somewhere. Now, all them creatures Noah took in the Ark was corrupt, too. He known that, and the Lord known it. But he told Noah to build an ark and give 'em some place to git in outa the rain, give 'em one more chance. Might be, he figured if they was to start all over again they might turn out some 'count next time.' And then it come to me that I was doin' just like Noah: makin' 'em some place to live."

"You were giving them another chance?"

"No, no. That weren't up to me. All I was doin' was givin' 'em some place to live. The rest of it was up to the Lord."

I picked up my teacup from the floor. The tea was cold. I got up from the chair and went to the window and stood looking out, sipping the cold tea. With the winter rain, the river was rising. The yellow water ran swiftly, level with the top of the bank, tugging at the tips of drooping grass stems that jiggled in the current.

"So you went back to work for this man?" I said.

" 'Deed I did. You see, I known right then I couldn't quit workin' for him just 'cause he weren't no 'count. I had to work for him 'cause he weren't no 'count. 'Cause he was *bad;* he'p make him better. Just like you does. You don't need to work on no man that is in good health. Only call you got to work on a man is 'cause he is in bad health; he'p make him better. You see what I mean?"

"Yes." I came back to my chair and sat beside him, setting my empty cup on the floor. "Do you think the Lord still despises men?"

"I don't know nothing about how he feels about 'em. He don't say. Might be he do. But he done promised Noah he wouldn't mess with 'em no mo', wouldn't kill 'em off no othah time. Maybe he reckon he don't have to; they take care of that theyselves."

"Then you don't love the people that you build houses for?"

"I don't know nothin' about most of 'em. Don't 'change the time of day with 'em. I build they houses, but I don't set down to dinner with 'em. You got to build one house for the peoples that you love. This here is the house I built for them. Built it right and set it up high on poles so's it would stand steady when the water rose. And it did rise. Twenty-three and twenty-seven. Come right up to the floor. Cleaned out many a house from here. Carried 'em down the river like they was kindlin' wood. But this one here stood steady."

We stared through the grill into the fiery lapping of the flames. After a long silence, he said, "I taken a lot of comfort in the fact that Noah found favor in the eyes of the Lord. That do seem to me like a kindly mysterious thing. I reckon them is the mostest mysterious words in the Book." Through the window I saw the gray moss hanging in the winter sunlight like garlands of spun steel. After a while he said, "You know, Noah, he didn't understand his family too good, neither. He had a lot of trouble with his kin. His chirren come to hate him."

"Yes, I seem to remember that."

"I don't reckon it matter too much if you don't love all the peoples what you save. They ain't many a man you save what is any 'count, but that don't matter. Someday they might turn out some kinda good. You got to see 'em how they'd be if you *did* love 'em. You cain't do no better than that."

"You're not a sentimental man," I said after some time. "I admire that."

His lips spread into a long smile over his brown, broken teeth. "I don't know about that. I do love a sweet tune."

"Do you sing, yourself?"

"No, indeed, I don't. I used to try to sing. Would like to have sang in the choir, you know? But always did sound just like a old crow. No, it weren't give me to sing. What I could do was work with my hands. Was real powerful when I was young. I could split a cord of green oak in a hour. Folks come from all over the county to see me do it. I use to win the contists at the county fair. That's how I met my wife."

"She saw you splitting wood?"

"Yes, suh. She come to the contist, and I see her standin' there in a green dress, high-heel shoes. Eatin' a ice-cream cone. Dabbin' at her mouth with a little white handkerchief. Very delicate woman, very quiet. Lord, I did cut some wood that day! They weren't nobody about to beat me! Won a Shakespeare fishin' reel and a Bible with gold letters on the cover. I walked right up to that woman and say, 'Lady, I like you to have this Bible, 'cause I think you brought me luck. We go halves, what you say?' She say, 'Any man don't have no use for the Bible, I don't have no use for him.' 'Well, you see, ma'am, I don't know how to read,' I say, 'so it ain't no use to me.' 'Well, I know how to read,' she say. 'My name is Melissa Peters and I live in Emory Bottom. You come round there next Sunday afternoon, I read it to you.' So I go round there every Sunday afternoon for six weeks, listen to her read the Bible, settin' on the front porch with a pitcher full of ice tea. Then we got married. That's just how it was."

"You must miss hearing her read," I said.

" 'Deed I do. Course, Becky read it to me now, but it was a long time I didn't hear the Word in this house. But I could rimemble it. Just about every word I ever heard."

"Would you like me to read it to you?"

"Indeed, I would admire that. Thank you kindly."

So, often, I would read to him on the winter afternoons, sitting beside his bed and turning the worn, finger-stained pages of the Bible to the light of the window or the lamp while he whispered along with me the words of favorite passages. He never tired of hearing them, although he had learned them by heart years ago. I think he had memorized almost the entire book of Genesis, and made an exegesis of it, full of grave, childlike, wildly magnanimous interpolations to account for its most glaring hiatuses and inconsistencies. The problem of the wives of Adam's sons, and of his grandsons, he solved by making them inhabitants of "this other little place, way back in the woods, where the colored folks lived. Some place like Black Willow, you know, like you don't hear too much about. They was the ones that picked the peas, and fed the sheep and the goats, and all. I reckon they always had to be somebody to do the work, but you don't never hear too much about 'em." The great age of the characters he accepted with perfect equanimity, saying only, "That's how it suppose to be, you see." The profane passions of Sodom and Gomorrah and the teeming accounts of incest, such as that between Lot and his daughters and Abraham and Sarah, he took as solemn confirmations of the unchanging concupiscence of man. "They was real people, you know," he said simply. "That's how you know it's true." A passage that fascinated him particularly—being a carpenter, I suppose—was God's specifications to Noah for construction of the ark. He asked me to repeat it several times, and then would repeat it himself, like a shipwright mulling over the scantlings presented to him by the designer of a yacht. " 'Make yourself an ark of gopher wood; make rooms in the ark, and cover it inside and out with pitch. This is how you are to make it: the length of the ark three hundred cubits, its breadth fifty cubits, and its height thirty cubits. Make a roof for the ark, and finish it to a cubit above; and set the door of the ark in its side; make it with lower, second, and third decks.' " He would scowl with concentration, and sometimes question me about its terms. "How long you reckon that is, a cubit?" he asked once.

"I don't know. I can look it up for you, and let you know the next time I come."

I did so, and reported to him a few days later that it was the length of the forearm, from the elbow to the end of the middle finger; in English measure, eighteen inches.

"That is a foot and a half," he said. He made some rapid mental calculations, moving his lips soundlessly. "That would make that boat four hundred and fifty foot long. Seventy-five foot wide. Forty-five foot high. That is a big boat."

"Yes, it is. Longer than a football field. It would have been bigger than many modern ocean liners."

"Lord, Lord, that was a job of work. How long you reckon it would taken him?"

"I don't know. We're not told."

"What do you reckon gopher wood would be? I has worked with all kinds of wood, but I never did hear of no gopher wood. What do you reckon that would be?"

"I don't think it's been identified. I believe 'gopher' is a Hebrew word, for which there isn't any English translation."

"Gopher wood. I reckon it'd be like cypress, somehow. You know, kindly light and spongy-like; take water real good."

"It may have been."

"Man take on a job like that, he got to believe in what he's doin'."

"Yes."

His eyes hung in the light beyond the window, as if calculating the faith it would demand.

"You must miss carpentry," I said. "I think that must be the hardest thing a man has to do: give up practicing his trade."

"Oh, I ain't through yet," he said. "I got one more house to build. Finest one I ever did build." I watched him for a moment, marveling at his face; it seemed so stern in its absorption, as if dedicated to some transcendent task.

"I hope you live to build it," I murmured, almost involuntarily.

"Oh, I reckon I will. I reckon you git the time you need. I been workin' on it right hard."

"Oh, you mean in your mind," I said in a moment.

"Yeah. She comin' along real good. I git tired sometimes, but I take it easy."

After that, the house became a standing topic of our conversation. I would regularly greet him with a question about its progress: "How is the house coming? Have you got the roof on yet?" His face would be wreathed happily in success or crumpled in preoccupation when he replied, "Yeah, yeah. I done worked out about them shingles, but I tell you it taken some figurin'," or "Well, she goin' slow right now. I got a problem with them pilasters."·I would offer my congratulations or sympathy, as the case required, and he would accept them gravely, nodding to acknowledge my interest as soberly as if I had inquired about the very literal activities of his past few days. Once, after struggling for several days with what was evidently a very difficult construction problem, he replied to my inquiry by saying, with a long and luminous smile of achievement, "Yeah. It come to me how she going to look now. Garden in the middle and a breezeway runnin' all around, between the floors. Keep her cool and let the light in. Flowers growin' down there, an' a well. Oh, it's goin' to be fine." His eyes kindled with the vision of the house.

"I hope someone uses it someday," I said.

"Oh, I reckon they will. Somebody needs some place to live."

He grew rapidly weaker through the last weeks of the winter, and by the first of April I could see that he did not have many days to live. Often he was too feeble to speak and could only nod or murmur to my questions or blink his eyes in gratitude if I raised him in the bed to hold a glass of water to his lips. He died on a very clear, warm day in the second week of May. The windows were open in the room and there was a smell of moist earth from the soft, bulging soil of the hyacinth beds underneath the window and a faint, clean astringence, like that of new wine, from the freshly opened blossoms. When I sat down beside his bed his eyes were closed, but at the stirring of the chair legs on the floor they opened and he gazed at me in silence for several moments as if gathering his strength to speak.

"I glad you got here," he said, each word like the rustle of a dry leaf falling through bare branches.

I nodded. "Would you like to see the river?"

" 'Deed I would."

I put my arm around his shoulders and raised him upright, doubling the pillows behind his back so that he could sit and look out of the window at the flow of yellow water sparkling in the sunlight between the willows.

"Real fine day," he whispered.

"Yes. You have a fine day."

Without taking his eyes from the river he groped for my hand, his fingers tightening about my own in a grip of astonishing force, the tips of the thick blue nails piercing my palm until the blood welled out of it. When I saw that his gaze had lengthened illimitably I disengaged my hand and laid him back gently in the bed, taking out my handkerchief to wipe the blood from his fingernails and crumpling it in my palm.

"Is he gone, Doctah?" Becky said.

"Yes."

"I just as soon not cover up his face. I kindly like to look at him."

"Yes."

She leaned over the old man's body and drew down his eyelids with her fingertips, then she placed his hands together on his breast. He lay like the effigy of a knight on a medieval brass. We stood for a moment looking down at him.

"I make you a cup of tea, suh."

"Thank you."

I followed her into the kitchen and watched while she prepared the tea, which I drank standing up, looking through the window at the light on the river.

"Did he mention to you that he'd agreed to let us perform an autopsy on his body? We can learn a great deal about his illness in that way."

"Yes, suh, he did."

"There's a fee of a hundred dollars in connection. It should be enough to give him a very respectable funeral."

"Yes, suh, he told me that. He said he's real glad you could learn somethin' from him."

"I've learned a great deal from him already." I set my teacup down on the table. "He was a fine man. A fine and decent man."

"Yes, suh, he was. You goin' to miss him, too."

"I am."

I went with the ambulance from Cardozo to bring his body to the hospital for autopsy and assisted Dr. Blakemore, the pathologist, with the postmortem, watching while he removed and dissected the principal organs and prepared tissue for shipment to Bethesda. The heart was very large, exceeding a normal heart by a considerable amount in measurement and weight. When he had removed it from the chest cavity, Dr. Blakemore held it out to me. I took it from him and weighed it in my hand, an experience of a strangeness I shall not forget.

"It's extraordinary."

"Yes."

I watched while he dissected the heart and examined the chambers, valves, and coronary arteries and sliced and stained tissue for his slides. When he had sawed through the skull and removed the brain, I looked down at the body lying on the table like a carcass in a butcher shop, empty of brain, heart, bowels, blood, and those inaudible tidings of eternity with which they had once been articulate. I felt almost equally void as the lean, eviscerated body.

"I'm going home," I said. "I'm a little tired. Will you send me your report in the morning?"

"Yes. You don't want to see the brain? The ependyma should be interesting."

"No. I think I may be catching cold. I'll have a look at your slides tomorrow."

I drove home through the spring night with the windows open and the warm air blowing on my face and throat. There were many stars and a smell of new grass from the fields and torrents running in the dark like streams of melted snow, sparkling with bright lore in the starlight, flowing back joyfully and impatiently to the sea.

I never really knew what happened," Sylvie said. "Why Ron drove all the way to Assateague, I mean; or just when; or why he drove back again, so recklessly, only a little while before we left. Whether he found our campsite on the dunes, or overheard us. Whether he intended only to spy on us, to confirm what he had learned from reading my novel; or to confront us; even to kill us. I suppose that's not impossible. You read every day in the paper about quiet, gentle men running amok one afternoon and slaughtering their families or mistresses or faithless wives with axes or tire irons. It isn't impossible, but it certainly isn't very probable; I can't imagine Ron in anything like a murderous rage; but I can imagine him all too well in the sickening realization of having been mocked and humiliated, betrayed in the most shameless manner conceivable. It's awful to realize that whatever his last thoughts of me were, they were anything but tender; I doubt that there was time for them even to have included a wisp of charity toward me. Do you know what that's like? To realize that someone who loved you, and to whom you owed more, probably, than to anyone else in the world, died thinking you a monster? Died in the belief that you had mocked and betrayed his love? And with good reason for that belief." She stood up from the table suddenly. "I want you to read the page of my novel that he'd torn out of my notebook. The page I pried out of his hand when he was dead."

"I don't know whether I should," I said.

"Yes. You gave me your book to read."

She went out of the kitchen. I sat for several minutes watching the purple clematis blossoms swing softly in the May breeze outside the window, listening to the sound of her footsteps ascend the stairs and then, after a minute or two, descend them, deliberately; rather briskly, as if she had gone to fetch me a road map for a journey I was about to make. She came back into the kitchen and sat down across from me, laying on the table a sheet of lined notebook paper. It was frayed and badly crinkled from having once been crumpled in his clenched fist, and blotched across its center and down one side with a stain that had darkened to the color of Worcestershire sauce.

"Are you sure you want me to read this?" I said.

"Yes. You may have trouble making it out, because of the blood."

I took my glasses out of the pocket of my woolen shirt and leaned forward, resting my forearms on the table, to read the page:

Maybe I had agreed to go with him too hastily, but I didn't think so. I had decided to rely on my impulses for the rest of my life. It was either my impulses or my reason, and in my case there didn't seem to be any doubt at all about which was the most reliable.

Still, I didn't know why I had such an unpleasant, breathless sense of gathering excitement about the trip. I felt as if I were saying to Neil— and to Gavin, too, for some reason—"I'm going as far as I can with you, my love. To the very edge of the sea." All the time I was putting my things in my bag—toothpaste and pajamas and an extra sweater—little instantaneous tableaux kept flashing in my mind like those old-fashioned silhouette cards: scenes of Neil standing there at the edge of the sand at Assateague staring out to where I had disappeared into the blue water. Sometimes it was Neil and sometimes it was Gavin, and sometimes both of them. They stood there with their faces bowed into their hands, and I pitied them so that I thought my heart would break. But there has to be a limit to pity, I thought; and there can't be any limit to what I feel for a man.

When I had packed the bag, I opened the dresser drawer and dug my notebook out from under my underwear and sat down on the edge of the bed and reread the last chapter I had written, slowly, with growing sorrow, with a sense, at last, almost of desperation. Then I flipped through the whole book, from beginning to end, reading passages at random, a paragraph, a page, an entire episode, with a feeling, finally, of absolute despair. *It isn't beautiful,* I thought. *In spite of everything I have vowed and tried so terribly to achieve, my book is not beautiful.* I sat with my head bowed over it, my back slumped in despair. When I closed the book I looked up and saw my face in the mirror of the dresser opposite me, and here is a very odd thing: for the first time in my life my face looked truly beautiful to me.

I got up and went back to the dresser and returned the notebook to the drawer. Then something—what was it? what name could such an impulse have?—made me open the drawer again and lift it out from under the folded linen and lay it on top of the dresser beside the framed photograph that Gavin kept there of his father and mother. He could not fail to see it when he undressed for bed.

And although I would not be able to see his face when he discovered it, and sat down on the bed—as I had just done—to read it, although I could not watch the settling of his features as he turned the pages and read the lines, I had the absolute conviction that his face would be as beautiful in its sorrow, its outrage, its despair, as mine had been. So we are made equal, at last, I thought.

I read the passage twice, and when I had finished, I looked up from the page in confusion. Sylvie had risen and gone to the window, where she stood watching me.

"Is that the end of it?" I said.

"Yes."

"I don't understand. When did you write it?"

"I wrote it sitting there on the bed, when I had packed my bag."

I took off my glasses and began to polish them abstractedly with the hem of my woolen shirt. It was more than I could comprehend at the moment.

"I still don't understand," I said. "You wrote this passage and then left it on the bureau, just as it says? As it predicts, you might say?"

"Yes." She pried a flake of dried paint from the windowsill and began to crumble it between her fingers. "Of course, I don't know how much of it he read, but I have an idea he read the whole book, from beginning to end. The way he ripped out that last page and carried it all the way to Assateague, like that, crumpled up in his fist."

"What happened to the rest of it?" I asked. "Did you destroy it?"

"No. I don't know what happened to it. The first thing I did when I went back to the apartment was to look for that notebook. I felt sure I would find it on the floor somewhere, where he had flung it after ripping out that last page. I searched and searched; but, you know, I never found it. I went all over the apartment, and then I went downstairs and looked along the path to the parking lot and in the shrubbery that bordered it, but I didn't find it anywhere. Maybe he hurled it out the window while he was driving down to Assateague. Maybe it's lying somewhere in a ditch along a country road, turned into a sodden lump of wet, swollen paper, made illegible by the rain. I think something in nature would be indignant enough to expunge it somehow. Or maybe he burned it. Maybe the ashes of that vain apocrypha of mine are still fluttering through the world like ghastly moths." She came back to the table and sat down, drawing the crumpled sheet toward her with her fingertips and glancing down at it in a coldly fastidious way, as if it were an unpleasant laboratory specimen of some kind, a fetus in a bottle or a pickled frog. "That's a typical passage. I mean the tone of it. It's representative of the whole book. Do you think it could even remotely be considered beautiful prose?"

"I really don't know. I'm no judge of literature."

"What did you want your book to be when you wrote it?"

"Well, that was very different, of course. It wasn't literature, and I didn't intend it to be. It was a scientific treatise. I suppose I wanted it to be true."

"Yes. And I wanted mine to be beautiful. Well, I failed. Evidently Ron thought so, too. You know, I really believe that if he'd found it beautiful he would have rejoiced at it, no matter how much it wounded him. I have to believe that, and I do." She looked up at me and frowned. "He loved books, he really did. He could recognize what made them beautiful, almost unfailingly." She began to fold the sheet of paper carefully, pressing the folded edges flat against the table with the back of her fingernail. When she had folded it twice she returned it to the pocket of her skirt and said harshly, "Well, I can tell you this. It's true." I didn't reply. "How would you like to read such a passage, written by the woman you loved?"

I shook my head without speaking.

"You have no idea what I went through with his parents. They came down to College Park to take his body home to Massachusetts. They lived in a little place called Duxbury. His mother hated me, I think. She was a really dreadful woman. I never saw such a parade of passion in my life. I had the impression that it was at least partially intended as a rebuke for what she considered my own indifference. She might well have. It's curious, but after he was dead, I simply didn't know what to do. Whether I should weep, or scream, or sort out his clothes, or write letters. Even about disposing of his body. It suddenly seemed such an awful inconvenience and embarrassment to everybody, that dead body of his. Even Ron would have thought so, I think. I'm sure he would have apologized for all the fuss. I had to keep calling up people and making arrangements in a kind of phony, level voice. Insurance companies, ambulance companies, funeral establishments. I didn't even know his parents' names or address; I had to look them up on letters he had in the desk drawer. Then I had to call them and break the news, and try to explain what had happened. Which was impossible, because I didn't really know what had happened. What could I possibly tell them? 'Your son was killed tonight in an automobile accident on Route 50, a little way outside of Ocean City, Maryland. I wasn't with him at the time. I was in another car, a little way behind him, with another man, a man I spent the weekend with on the beach. I don't really know what Ron was doing there. Maybe it was because he read a novel I was writing.' Well, of course, it wouldn't have made sense at all, it sounded absolutely grotesque, so I didn't even try to explain it. I made up a lie; not so much to spare myself the shame of having to confess what I had done as to save her the distress of knowing that her son had died in a state of mental agony and mortification, and of becoming suddenly aware of all the weird turmoil and conflict of our lives, of the wretchedness I had rewarded his kindness with, and in which he had spent the last hours of his life. What was the point of it? It was so much simpler and more comforting for her to believe that he had died in a state of contentment and harmony, with me and the world. So I told her that I had gone to spend a week at the beach with my girlfriend, and that while we were away Ron had received a phone call saying that her mother had been taken ill, quite seriously ill; could she come at once? And since there was no way he could get in touch with her except by driving to the beach, he had done so. He had found our campsite on the dunes and had given her the message; then we had followed him back immediately, and there had been the accident. I think she was gratified by the story. It gave a faintly heroic cast to his mission and the manner of his death; not the feverish, or distraught, or frenziedly jealous, or simply foolish quality with which the truth would have been tainted. 'That's so like him,' she said. 'Always doing things for others, no matter what it cost him.' 'Yes,' I said, 'it was typical of him.' 'And of course, it needn't have happened at all. This horrible thing needn't have happened at all.' She went on like that for hours; it was awful. But her husband was very nice to me. Such a kind man he was. He said once, when his wife had been going on for quite a while about how her life was over, all her dreams dashed, everything she had worked and hoped for shattered, 'I think we're forgetting how Sylvie must feel about this. I think we're forgetting how much happiness she gave him.' I started to cry then, for the first time, it was such a kind thing to say, and yet the most terrible thing he could possibly have said. When I cried, he came and put his arms around me and patted my shoulders; and I suddenly remembered for the first time in twenty years what it felt like to have a father you could run to when you were miserable or frightened, whose arms you could hide in from the world. I must have cried a gallon of tears, not just for Ron, or for the whole horrible affair, but for everything, all my life, it seemed to me; and suddenly it was Poppa holding me, stroking my hair, telling me it didn't matter, everything was all right, he'd take me up to Offutt's and get me an ice-cream cone."

She stopped speaking suddenly. Her face had gone cold and absolutely immobile. She started shivering in short shrill spasms, freezing into immobility between them. I put out my hand and laid it on hers.

"Let me make you some tea."

She nodded rigidly. I got up and went to the sink and turned on the faucet to fill the kettle.

"Then I had to go up there to Duxbury to the funeral. All these were things I'd never even dreamed of having to do. There's all that ritual and rigamarole when people die. They ought to just blow away like a puff of dust, or disappear into the air or the ocean. Poppa did. You don't realize that you're still responsible for their dignity, even after they're dead."

I brought cups and saucers to the table and set them down.

"He gave me all the furniture, Ron's father did. He said there was no point in sending it up to Duxbury; the shipping charges would be more than it was worth. He imagined that I'd be staying on at the apartment, at least for a while, although the lease was in Ron's name. Why didn't I keep the furniture and just dispose of it when I found I didn't need it any longer? And if there were any personal things of Ron's that I'd like to keep—any of his books, things we had bought together, perhaps a present or something that I'd given him—I shouldn't feel any hesitation at all about asking for them. Everything he said made me cry. I wanted to hug him, I wanted to keep them there. He smelled so nice, a real man-smell. Not the way boys smell at all, but a real man-smell; do you know what I mean? A meaty, dusty, bitter, bullocky man-smell."

I stood at the stove waiting for the water to boil, looking across the kitchen to where she sat with her hands, the fingers laced together, resting primly on the table, like a child reciting at a school desk.

"Well, I did. Stay there, I mean. I stayed there for six months, with all his furniture, all his things. Except what they took back, of course: his clothes, some of his pictures, his chess set, things like that. His father said I was welcome to visit them anytime I wanted. He regarded me as his daughter, he said. That's one of the nicest things anyone ever said to me."

I poured the steaming water into the kettle and brought it to the table.

"I can't find any loose tea."

"No, I've run out of it. I only have those bags. I'm sorry; you hate them, don't you?"

"No, it's fine." I put four tea bags in the kettle, letting the tagged strings hang out below the lid, and sat down again across from her.

"His lease ran just through the end of the term, through May, so I stayed there until it expired. You would have thought I'd have compunctions about it, but I didn't. None at all. It didn't bother me in the slightest, not even when I started having the men. I mean, you'd think making love to a strange man in the bed where he and I had slept together all that time would have made me very uneasy, wouldn't you? Made me feel that I was violating his memory or something—however they put it. But it was simply gone—all of it. I felt absolutely indifferent to the demands of—delicacy, sentiment, whatever they call it. I felt absolutely indifferent to almost everything, in fact, except sex. That was all that kept me going. It's like alcohol for some people, I suppose. Of course, it couldn't be that simple. Maybe that was what I had wanted all along. That opportunity for abandon. Like a kid who's run away from home. Maybe I'm schizophrenic or something. I've often suspected it. Do you think so?"

"No. No more than anyone else. Whatever the word means."

"I don't know. I mean, two or three different men a week. Some of them real ruffians. Some of them even stole things. One of them had pierced ears. I woke up one morning and saw him standing in front of the mirror trying on a pair of my hoop earrings. I just lay there, pretending to be asleep, until he'd gathered up everything he wanted and gone out."

I poured tea into our cups, then added milk and sugar to them and sat stirring. She began to stir her own, staring down into the pale brown, spinning tea.

"And yet there was something about every one of them that I found lovable. Something I could admire or desire. Some of them, of course, were very nice, very sweet. The students from my classes especially. They were generally astonished and terribly grateful and sometimes impotent with bewilderment. One of them even cried. I liked him best of all. He said he had been in love with me from the first day of class, and showed me secret poems he had written to me, about my 'flyaway hair' and 'billowing breasts.' I inspire some very bad poetry."

I sipped at my tea and watched little nebulous coins of sunlight shifting on the table through the leaves of the clematis vine outside the window.

"What happened to Nils?" I asked after some time.

"Oh, Nils, yes. I was getting to Nils." She stared into her cup, spooning beads of froth from the surface of the spinning tea. "He went out to Denver, or somewhere. No, Boulder, I guess; that's where the university is, isn't it? I think he's better now. I heard from someone not long ago who said he was beginning to attend classes again, in the evenings. I think he worked in a garage for a while, as a mechanic. I don't know how he could do that, with his finger missing."

"His finger missing?"

"Yes, he chopped it off, a couple of months after the accident. The index finger of his right hand. He came around to the apartment one night with his hand wrapped up in a piece of bloody cloth and stood there at the door with the blood dripping down onto the hall carpet. 'I just wanted you to know that I chopped it off,' he said. 'My trigger finger. The one I kill people with. So you don't have to worry.' I think he wanted to reassure me that he wouldn't do anything foolish, that he wasn't going to harm me or anything. Because, you see, I'd started having the men by that time, and I was perfectly candid with him about it. He'd been going to pieces ever since the accident. He seemed to think he was responsible for it in some way. He'd gotten to the point where he thought he was responsible for almost everything unpleasant that he heard about; every death, or act of violence, or epidemic, or disaster. He couldn't pick up a newspaper without going into agonies of remorse: an account of a murder or suicide, or the deaths of guerrilla fighters in Latin America somewhere, or a fire in an apartment house or an accident on the beltway; he was convinced that he was responsible, that he had engineered it in some way.

"Maybe it would have helped if I'd let him move in with me. He wanted to, of course, and he couldn't understand why that was impossible. 'We have to,' he kept saying. 'We have to make something out of this, don't you understand that? We have to make something out of nothing, or we have no right to be here. We're only adding to the madness of the universe.' But I wouldn't let him. I knew it had to end somehow, and if he couldn't be persuaded by reason, then it would have to be by reality, by being made witness to the truth. I told him, over and over, 'I can't see you anymore. It's finished; you have to understand that. I'll never devote myself to any man again, not for more than one night at a time, or a week maybe; no more. You have to believe that, Nils. If you want me, you'll have to share me with all of them, thieves, murderers, choirboys, idiots, whatever they may be.' But he wouldn't listen, he couldn't make himself believe it. So finally, one night when he called, I asked him to come up to the apartment. I had another man there, a musician I'd invited home from a live-rock bar on Georgia Avenue. This man played lead guitar, in a way that made me ache. When Nils rang from downstairs I pushed the button to let him in and then went to the door in my dressing gown to wait for him. 'Come in,' I said. 'I want you to meet somebody.' Then I led him across the living room and down the hall to the bedroom, where this gigantic black man was lying on the bed stark naked, except for a scarlet silk rose that I had wrapped by its wire stem around his penis. He was about seven feet tall, I think, and he had a great, glossy, purple razor scar running across his chest. When he saw Nils he grinned at him and held up the bottle of gin he was drinking and said, 'Hey, dude, come on in and have a drink. We having quite a party in here.' Nils sat down very slowly—I remember how his back slid down the doorsill as if his spine were liquefying—and put his forehead on his knees like a little boy who's been scolded, or caught in a lie or something, and didn't move; not for five minutes or so. I went over to where he was sitting and ran my fingers through his hair and said, 'You see, that's the way I am. I kept telling you. Do you believe me now?' He kept mumbling, 'Why? Why, Sylvie?' 'I don't know,' I said. 'That's just the way I am. I don't understand it any more than you do.' He wouldn't say anything else, and every time I touched him he cringed as if he were scalded. After a while he got up and went out down the hall, and I could hear the front door open. I didn't follow him; I didn't even go out and shut the front door. That's the last time I ever saw him."

"You didn't see him at school again?"

"No. I think he stopped going to classes; or if he did go, he was very careful to avoid me. After a month or so, someone told me he'd gone out to Colorado. And you know, I didn't care, really. Of course, I thought about him, and I worried, I suppose, in a kind of dispassionate way, as if he were a character in a novel I was reading, but I didn't really grieve. I was just incapable of any more grief or guilt. I felt as if I'd been cauterized, all my nerve ends burnt and glazed over with scar tissue so I couldn't feel anything else. Not of that kind. The only thing I could feel was sex, adventure. I liked to go into bars and sit there

smoking cigarettes and drinking until I got picked up. There was a little
swingers' bar downtown, on Fifteenth Street, where I liked to go in the late
afternoons when they opened up, around four o'clock. It was the oddest place
in the world for a swingers' bar. It had been converted from one of those old
Victorian townhouses, and there were twelve-foot-high embossed tin ceilings
and a big bay window that looked out onto the street. It had a kind of shabby,
ruined elegance, and you could see the dust everywhere in that strange afternoon sunlight that came in through the old single-paned sash windows. I used
to sit at a table in the bay window and look out at the people hurrying home
from work along the sidewalks and wonder about their lives and pretend that
I was involved in them. I didn't seem to have any life of my own anymore,
and I didn't want any. But the lives of those people out in the street became
very brilliant and beautiful to me, and I would actually weep over them. I
invented histories for them; I must have written the equivalent of a hundred
novels, sitting there with my fingers wrapped around a glass of tequila in that
sunny old bay window with the jukebox pounding out disco music so loud that
the glasses rattled on the bar. After a while someone would come over and sit
down and start a conversation with me, usually of stupefying banality—that
awful, fraudulent urbanity that people affect in a place like that. It was one
of the first swingers' bars in Washington, and usually had a lot of first-timer
trade: young executives out to confirm their grand passion for life, or enlightenment, or just to get a rather shy, surreptitious sip of the new, unfettered
life-style, or whatever particular delusion they were suffering from. A few of
them were really hard, vicious. Professionals. I learned to avoid them, but I
liked most of the couples; they were usually timid, rapturous young married
people, 'giving their lives a new dimension,' or some such simpleminded idea.
Maybe they did, I don't know. I certainly don't want to patronize them,
because I was no better, or wiser, than anybody else. That was the thing I liked
most about the place: you knew that you were all equals in some fervent, maybe
foolish, but genuinely humble way, and in spite of all the artless sophistication,
and bravura, and sometimes quite embarrassingly earnest air of idealism, there
was no pretension, really. It would have been impossible, because we met there
in a kind of fraternal ignominy that both shamed and sheltered us. And some
of them were quite interesting. Really quite sensitive and inventive people. The
girls, particularly. You'd be amazed. Very few butch types or hardened syba-
rites. Mostly sensitive, amorous girls who were out to satisfy some gauzy,
unfulfilled fantasy that had been plaguing them for years like a constant
low-grade fever. They were often very sweet to love."

She took a tremendous gulp of air, like someone emerging from underwa-
ter, straightening up in her chair, her chest swelling; then expelled it in a long,
devastatedly impatient sigh, her mouth open, so that the spicy, tea-scented

fragrance of her breath ruffled over my face like a zephyr from a tropic isle. "I'd be lying," she said, "if I told you that I loathed it, that I was ever consciously disgusted with myself or my life. In fact, I had a more vivid, rabid kind of pleasure in those few months than I'd ever known was possible. I felt no remorse at all, and I didn't regret it, then or ever. I suppose it was something I needed to do, at least once, and for quite a while. Then I was simply through with it, that was all. There was no more pleasure in it. I just stopped feeling it, entirely. I could almost predict what would happen, on every possible occasion, with every possible combination of partners, and I began to be bored, and then exasperated. The only thing I missed, when I stopped going there, the only thing I remember with real delight and nostalgia was that old-fashioned bay window, and that winter afternoon sunlight coming through the dusty pane, the strange sense of solitude and tranquillity that I felt, sitting there with my glass of cold tequila waiting to be picked up. I think about it still sometimes." She sipped her tea, frowning with the odd look of grief into which her face contracted when she reminisced. "I didn't hurt anybody, I don't think. At least nobody fell in love with me. I made damned sure of that. I'll tell you something, though. I fell in love with *them,* some of them, anyway. I mean it. I never went to bed with anybody who didn't have something lovable about him; or her. That I wasn't capable of feeling affection for. That's true, Carl. And some of them I loved very hard, for just that moment, that hour, that weekend. Why *couldn't* it be love? People love cats, or bacon, or automobiles, or Beethoven. At least that's what they call it. Why can't I call that love?"

"I didn't forbid you to."

"Why is it, if you love people, it's either got to be agape or eros. That's all the choice they give you. Well, I simply don't believe it. I think there are a thousand forms of love that are neither of those things, or somewhere in between. How can you limit the love of people to those two categories? It's ridiculous. In fact, I don't think it's possible to love any two people in exactly the same way, or for any two people to love in exactly the same way; any more than it's possible for two people to have exactly the same fingerprint patterns." She looked up at me with a glare of urgency in her eyes. "That's why I wanted to write, you see. That's what I wanted to explore, and understand. That's all that has ever really interested me. Do you understand that? Do you believe it?"

"Yes."

"I love you, for example, in a way I've never loved anyone else. In a way I don't think I could love anyone else. And I don't know what to call it but love. Perhaps we need more words; perhaps we haven't finished Adam's task of naming things."

"I don't think you'd get much thanks, if you did."

"And I don't know if my love for you is nobler, or less noble. Or more spiritual, or less. Or more moral. Maybe it will last longer, but I don't know if you can judge the value of an emotion by that. I think some of the very rarest, noblest feelings I've ever had have been some of the very briefest. Only an instant, they last. Only a glimmer, so bright and intense that it changes you forever, the way heat turns sand into glass or lead into crystal. And you can never be happy again, except in memory." I can't explain why I smiled at that moment, looking into her eyes. "I don't know what I wanted to do, at that time of my life; but I'm not going to make any amateur moralists happy by calling it ignoble. Or sit still and listen to them call it ignoble. While they're dabbing the grease from their lips with a napkin."

"The dinner table isn't the best place in the world to discuss morality."

"It might be the only suitable place. But, anyway, we're only having tea." She gazed at me with her mercilessly blue eyes. "You, now. Did you love that man? That man you killed? Mr. Lubby?"

"No. My God. I wouldn't dare to call it love. No one could. It would make a mockery of the word."

"And yet, suppose you hadn't told me that you killed him. Suppose you'd told me only that you knew a man, once, whose company you enjoyed more than that of any other person you'd ever met. Whom you thought of constantly. Whom you could not be away from and be happy or contented. Who had qualities that you found fascinating, and magnificent, and perhaps terrible. What could I believe, except that you loved him?"

"Then we do need more words," I said. "Because that would be a monstrously promiscuous use of the word 'love.'"

"Do you think Abraham loved Isaac when he raised the knife to kill him?"

"He must have. If he hadn't, the story would have no significance."

"Exactly. And a whole faith has been erected on the fact that he did raise the knife. That he was willing to slay his son."

I shook my head, feeling vaguely nauseated. "That was different. That's a terrible sophistry, Sylvie."

"If it's possible to erect a faith upon one murder, why not upon another? Do you mean to say you had no faith in what you were doing? That you didn't believe in its awful necessity, in the truth it would help you to discover?"

I shook my head, in a deepening sense of nausea, then got up suddenly from the table, knocking over my teacup in my haste. The pale brown liquid splashed across the tabletop, leaving a swollen, liver-colored pool on the blue checkered oilcloth like a glistening, freshly excised organ lying in a basin. Neither of us moved to mop it up. I went to the window and fingered the crocheted circlet of the shade cord. Outside the window a flight of gulls wheeled in wild, avid excitement above a school of fish in the center of the estuary. The water was flurried and glittering with the swarming of the thousands of silver bodies, into which the gulls plunged and then struggled skyward, the bright fish flickering and writhing in their beaks like flames.

"You have at least a shred of genuine comfort," I said after a moment. "Because all Ron asked of you was that you tell him the truth. And it seems to me that that's what you were doing. You were telling him—in the only way you could, apparently. He must have understood that."

"I don't think so. I don't think that's what I was doing, or that that's what he believed. I think he believed that I left the book there by mistake. That I was deceiving him, using him, basely and cunningly."

I stood by the window, watching the candid havoc of the gulls.

"I don't understand," I said in a moment. "I thought that's what you wanted him to believe. Consciously, at any rate. I thought you'd resolved never to let him know deliberately about your affair with Nils. You said you felt that would put him in an ignominious position—that he'd have to consent to it, even at the cost of his dignity. I understood that you wanted him to think he'd been the victim of a—'genuine, old-fashioned betrayal'—I think that's the way you put it. A genuine life situation—not some subtle, sordid demand for his submission that would dishonor him."

She listened quietly, her head bowed. "Yes," she said, when I had finished. "That's what I'd decided."

"And yet, eventually, you did let him know deliberately. By leaving your book there for him to read. And now you blame yourself for that."

"Yes. Because it seems to me equally wicked. Or more so. I think I must have realized that all along. I must have known what it would do to him." She closed her eyes and shook her head wearily. "Good God, how can we ever understand the things we do? Do we ever do anything but wickedness? Is all our moral posturing only a disguise for the desires of our filthy hearts?"

"I don't know. Sometimes I'm afraid so." I came back to the table and sat down across from her. "Let me tell you something that happened to me after Walter Lubby died. Something I did, rather—it didn't 'happen to me.' A series of things—two things—in fact. I didn't know whether I could ever tell anyone about them, but I see now that I have to tell you."

He died in the spring of '41, in May. A month later Paula gave another of her parties. She'd given others during the winter, and we'd been to those, and seen a good deal of her on other occasions. Sometimes she would drive Molly home from a shopping expedition they'd made together, or run by to deliver one of her sponge cakes or a box of her divinity, and would stop for half an hour to have a drink with us or a cup of coffee in the kitchen. At Christmas she came over with a jug of eggnog and a toy for Elizabeth, paused to admire the tree, and delivered a glittering, rueful reminiscence of a Christmas she had spent in the governor's mansion in Birmingham when her grandfather reigned there. On New Year's Eve she held an open house to which town's select drifted in from ten o'clock until two in the morning. At midnight we linked arms, drank a toast in Liam's julep, and sang "Auld Lang Syne" in ominous cacophony. All of these occasions were hugely embarrassing to me, but it would have been improvident to avoid them. I couldn't risk her disaffection—any more than Liam could, evidently. Yet I must say I admired her savoir-faire, her discretion, and her magnanimity, which appeared to be inexhaustible. In spite of the mortification she must have felt at the fact that I had not once, in the year since it had been issued, taken advantage of her delicate invitation to share the splendor of a Tallacoochee sunset with her, she was scrupulously hospitable to me, solicitous of our company, and continuingly enthusiastic in her support of the study. To Molly, who had become almost dotingly infatuated with her, she persisted in her apparent cordiality; she picked her up, unfailingly, on Monday mornings and took her to the weekly coffee klatches she held at her house, and was endlessly convivial and attentive. I couldn't understand her motives for any of this, but I appreciated her undiminished advocacy of the project. I expressed this as judiciously as possible by regular attendance at her parties; solicitation of her advice on political, social, and psychological matters affecting the experiment; a conspicuous respect for her opinions on art, interior decoration, gardening, and cuisine; and an effusive air of gratitude for her patronage—one that stopped short, however, of any possible interpretation as romantic zeal. I think my reputation for sobriety may have come to my assistance in this; it didn't require much virtuosity on my part to foster the impression of a man immune to carnal passion, or indisposed to amorous adventures, or simply exceptionally obtuse about the subtleties of extramarital intrigue. It was an impression I was pleased to let account for the inanity of my behavior during our tête-à-tête in her bathroom and for my apparent churlishness in failing to seize the opportunity to sample her largesse. Paula either was satisfied with this balm to her vanity or, for inscrutable reasons, let me believe that she was. She was impeccably discreet in avoiding any reference to the evening in her bathroom, or any further private encounters or interludes with me. Sometimes there was a fleetingly sardonic flavor to her comments, like the hint of curry in the pilafs she prepared, but it was of a kind that only a far subtler man than I could have interpreted, and she generally managed to make them sound amusingly ambiguous. Until this party I speak of, a month after Walter Lubby's death.

After his death, something very odd occurred to me. It wasn't permanent —I knew that, even while I was experiencing it—and it wasn't depression, exactly; but, for a little while, and without feeling either apathy or fatigue, I had no desire at all to work. As a matter of fact, I had no immediate desire to do anything: work, plan, actively enjoy myself in any way I could imagine, even to think. I don't know quite how to describe the condition. It was an idle, haunted feeling—haunted by strains of both the past and the future—like a prolonged caesura in a line of verse or a double rest in music. I suppose it could be compared to the moment after an orgasm, if there had been anything of that sense of consummation or slowly expiring delight. But there wasn't; I had no emotions at all that I can remember. Once, about a year later, a hurricane swept directly over Tallacoochee, and when the eye of it passed over us there was almost that same sense of momentary timelessness and stasis; a strange, silent, sunlit vacuum at the heart of all the fury that swirled and roared around us, and you could hear both the dying uproar of the storm that had swept over us and the rumor of the tumult yet to come. After Lubby died, I felt very much like that: although I seemed to be at the center of all energy, motion, and velocity, there was a vast immobility in me of will or passion, almost a suspension of life and of the sensations and desires of life, as if all that were left of me were my consciousness and memory, hanging in the air like the reverberation of a chord of organ music in an empty cathedral; the echo of my deed, pealing in an empty firmament.

This is not the best possible state of mind in which to attend a party, especially one called the Vernal Vanities, which was how Paula archly designated her annual spring festival. It was given on the night of the solstice, in late June, and took place outdoors, in celebration of the advent of the summer. On this occasion the buffet was placed on tables set up in the wisteria arbor, where there was also installed a portable rattan bar and a piano. Since there was a great deal of fetching and carrying to be done between the arbor and the kitchen, Paula hired an auxiliary staff to help Viola: her two teen-aged daughters and a Negro barkeeper in white livery. There were paper lanterns strung across the lawn from the chinaberry and mimosa trees, and scented candlelight, and the tinsel din of wind chimes. She had hired also a professional jazz pianist from Birmingham, a stately old black man in a bottle-green frock coat who filled the exquisitely ornamented summer night, imperviously and endlessly, with the dauntless, jocose ribaldry of Basin Street. My sense of the occasion was not at all improved by the fact that he reminded me very much of Walter Lubby; so much so that I found myself lingering around the piano for a large part of the evening sipping at a glass of mint tea while, as surreptitiously as possible, I studied his face, which in the candlelight took on more and more disturbingly the semblance of the man whose heart I had held in my hand a month ago. He looked up at me once and smiled enigmatically.

"You like de jazz, suh?"

"Yes. You play extremely well."

"It come from de heart."

"I can see that."

For the rest, the lavishness of the party was lost on me. I found myself increasingly impatient with the mindless chatter, the restless, wolfish voracity, and vulgar posturing. As the evening progressed, my disgust grew into something very close to hysteria. Absolutely nothing of any significance is going on here, I thought. Absolutely nothing of any excellence, or permanent value, or even interest. What claim has that woman on my attention, with her thick red throat, her painted, bobbling lips, her cruel eyes? (This awful woman was always present at Paula's parties.) I have nothing to learn from her, from any of these people. I closed my mind to their noisy babble in a kind of panic, one which Paula must have recognized, because at one point, when I was almost submerged in a tide of strident sycophancy, I felt her touch my arm, and when I turned toward her, she whispered into my ear, "I don't think you're enjoyin' yourself very much."

"Oh, yes," I murmured. "Perhaps I'm just a little tired tonight."

"Well, my land, that's something I never thought I'd hear you confess. Why don't you come over here and look at my tuberous begonias? If they don't do your heart good, nothin' will." She raised her voice to the faces that surrounded us. "Will you-all excuse us for a minute? I've got something I want to show this man."

I followed gratefully while she led me by an elbow across the yard to a circular flower bed that enclosed a birdbath upheld by a plaster cherub. We stood and looked down at the clusters of vivid white blossoms eerily discolored by the light of the Japanese lanterns that hung over them.

"You know, Dr. Ransome, sir," Paula said in a briskly solicitous tone, "in spite of your *eminence*, and your *intelligence*, and your devotion to your *profession*, I think in some ways you're a very dissatisfied man."

"You do?"

"Yes. Now don't you make fun of me. I'm bein' really serious, for once."

"I see."

"A very *lonely* man. That might sound impertinent of me, but I say it because I think I can recognize your situation. It's one that I believe is similar to my own."

"I hope not," I said.

She allowed herself the faintest of ironic smiles. "My husband, as you must realize by now, is a very brilliant man. I thought at one time that he would be a very important one as well. I believed that to the extent that I invested a great deal in him. Not only of affection, and trust, and faith, but of money, too. A very considerable amount of money. It was me that put him through medical school. Through Vanderbilt. One of the best and most expensive medical schools in the country, as I'm sure you know." She stooped to pick a jonquil from the bed, and after clipping it short with her fingernail, turned to me to slide its stem into my buttonhole. "I don't mean Liam isn't grateful for that—he certainly is; and the last thing he would do would be to default on the obligation he feels to me. He is, I have to admit, a man of great integrity."

"Yes, he is," I said.

"In some respects, yes. But what I've discovered about him, after twenty-five years of marriage, is that he's a very weak man, too. A very—romantic—one, in every sense of the word. He simply does not understand the real world. He is a prey to his emotions, and has been all his life. I was very young when we married, and I failed to recognize that."

"I suppose you hadn't had a great deal of experience of life," I said.

"That's it, exactly. I thought I was investing in a man who would go on to accomplish great things in his profession. Who would make all kinds of discoveries and advances in medicine, and who would win a position in the world that I could respect, and help him to fulfill. But he's a man who has failed, all his life, to seize the opportunities that were presented to him."

"That's too bad," I said.

"This study of yours, for example. He could easily have taken a position of leadership in it. He could have distinguished himself by his contribution to it. But I understand, now, that he never will." I did not reply to this. She went on sadly, "He is saddled with all these wild, liberal—'humanitarian'—impulses that just blind him to reality. That's a terrible failing in a man. It's a generous one, I suppose, but it's also very limiting. And it's also very exhausting, very *exasperating,* if you want to know the truth, to a woman who happens to be married to him. Who expects a man to realize his potentialities." She paused and adjusted the flower in my buttonhole, giving it a delicate pat with her fingertips. "Now does that sound at all familiar to you? Does that sound like a reasonable complaint?"

"I suppose it's quite a common situation," I said.

"Yes, it is. Much more common than most people would admit. But if there's one thing I am, it's honest. I simply don't have time for hypocrisy or pretense. And I will not pretend to be interested in failure." I could not think of a suitable reply. In a moment she went on, in a somewhat more lyrical tone of voice. "There are lots of things I would not demand from a man. I wouldn't demand that he be particularly articulate, or gallant, or amorous—although the Lord knows no woman would *object* to that in a man!—but I do demand that he make the fullest use of the faculties that he was born into this world with. That he achieve a station in life commensurate with his talents. Now I don't think that's too much to ask, do you?"

"I don't like judging people," I said. "But I understand your feeling. A wasted life is a pitiable thing."

"Indeed it *is!*" she said fervently. "And you just put it *perfectly*. A wasted life is a *pitiable* thing. But not necessarily *lovable*. A man simply cannot act on impulse all his life. He must have a philosophy to guide him; a sense of dedication to which he sacrifices everything—even the desire to be regarded by his fellow men as a generous and compassionate man. Even the desire to regard *himself* in that way. Don't you agree?"

"Yes."

"I thought you would, Carl." She raised her head and looked up into the heavens as if enjoining God to take note of this evidence of grace on my part. Apparently not fully assured of his appreciation of the point, she went on. "Of course, it takes a very strong nature, a very *noble* nature, to have such an *austere* faith. It can make a man very much misunderstood. Very lonely, sometimes. And those are the people who deserve our *true* sympathy, our *true* compassion." She lowered her head and turned her face to me with a look compounded of that emotion, of rue, and of moving recognition in me of some subtle common dilemma whose agony we shared. "I wonder if you have such a philosophy, Carl? I wonder if you could put it into words? I'd very much like to hear them."

I think my strong desire to strangle the woman must have been evident in the deliberate curtness of my answer. "If I've ever held a doctrine of any kind about human ethics," I said, "it's simply that one should never do anything that isn't of some practical benefit to someone." This was true, literally; and yet I couldn't help reflecting, even as I said it, that the asperity of the tone belied the doctrine. The softness of her expression faded momentarily to one of mild consternation, succeeded rapidly by a gentle, wistful smile.

"I can understand that," she said. "And I *respect* it. It's what a *man* would say." At that moment a guest bore down upon us, mercifully, out of the lantern-lit dusk of the lawn, a stout lady wearing a slightly skewed gray silk hat and bearing a wineglass unsteadily before her.

"Paula!" she cried. "So *that's* where you got to! Listen, honey, I want you to settle something for me. I bet Jason you raised vegetables, and he denied it. I bet him five dollars you raised that okra we're eatin', right over there in that pot, and he took me on. Now am I right?"

"Yes, you are, Louella," Paula said with a tinkling, modest laugh. "And those string beans, too. I put them up last summer. Do you know Dr. Ransome?"

"Well, sure I do. How're you this evenin', Doctah?"

"Very well, thanks," I murmured. Paula turned her face to me with an expression of humorous regret.

"Carl, excuse me for just a minute, will you? I can't let Louella lose five
dollars."

"Of course. I've got to go up and check on Elizabeth, anyway."

The lady bore Paula triumphantly away toward the arbor, her voice ringing
through the scented air: "That man is just too smart for his britches!"

I went across the lawn toward the house. From the front door, open to the
summer night, a wide bath of light fell on the red bricks of the path. Between
them, tiny blades of fresh grass sprouted, casting frail individual shadows, as
fine as hairs. I went into the house and across the empty, lamplit living room,
pausing to set my plate of hors d'oeuvres on a lampstand in the hall. I went
upstairs and along the carpeted hall to the nursery, where, as had become the
custom, Elizabeth had been put to bed in the old-fashioned rocker crib. She
was asleep, her face pressed into the pillow, her hair splashed like a stain on
the white slip in the darkness. I laid my hand on her forehead and could feel
that it was damp with sweat. The room was very warm, although the curtains
were stirring gently in the breeze from the partially opened window. I went
across to it and raised the sash, afterwards placing my hands flat on the sill and
leaning out into the cool night air. Above the glow of the lanterns on the lawn,
the sky was very dark in spite of its clarity. The moon was down, and only
starlight glittered in the black void above the mimosa branches. I stared up into
the darkness above the shadowy figures and the sea of voices and the tinkle
of the piano from the arbor, and found myself thinking of Walter Lubby. I
thought of his spare, far-focused gaze, his long black slender fingers plucking
at a shirt button while he stared through the winter sunlight with his hooded
eyes. I wanted to be sitting with him on the porch beside the river, hearing
the measured slow pauciloquence of his words, smelling the dry herbal scent
of his worn clothes. I think I recognized at that moment that my solitude was
hopeless, that it was irremediable, ever; perhaps even a dispensation of a kind,
an immunity from any claim of love or pity or loyalty or the ache of any future
loneliness. A numbness came over me like a wave of anesthesia, an emptiness
that I seemed to breathe in from the black leagues of ether that billowed
through the stars.

Immediately beneath me, I heard Liam's voice, slurred slightly and carelessly unlowered. "There's a point," he said, "at which delirium becomes the
only order. That may be the single thing I've learned from him."

Janet's voice, hushed cautiously, replied, "I hope to God I'm not going to
become the beneficiary of anything you've ever learned from him."

I looked down and saw them standing in the shadow of a small outbuilding
immediately beneath the window, a tool or garden shed that stood beside the
wire gate of Paula's kitchen garden. Beyond it there were rows of bean poles
and what looked like the fabric of a low canopy for strawberry beds, stretched

pale in the darkness. Janet stood leaning with her back against the wall of the shed, holding a wineglass in her hands; she bowed her head to it and sipped, a thread of starlight shifting on her hair. Liam put out his hand and touched her face.

"My God, you're lovely," he said. "You lovely, gentle creature."

"Liam, please. It's so dangerous."

"I want to see your breasts, more than anything in the world right now."

She stooped to set the wineglass on the ground and when she stood up he reached his hands toward her and unbuttoned her blouse, lifting it off over her shoulders and turning to lay it across the gate. She twisted her arms behind her and unhooked her brassiere, then slipped the straps over her shoulders and dropped it to the ground. Her naked breasts and shoulders had the pale diffuse glow of milk in the shadow of the shed. "Oh, God, you're lovely," he said. "You seem made out of mist." She took his face between her hands and drew his head down between her breasts, folding it tightly in her arms and pressing her cheek down to his hair.

I drew my head in from the window and went across the room to the door, pausing to look back at Elizabeth. She had not moved since I had entered the room. I closed the door and went down the hall to the stairs. At the bottom, I took my plate from the lampstand in the hall and removed a cigarette stub that had been crushed out in a mound of spinach soufflé. I went out the front door and stood on the path for a moment, drawing a breath of the fragrant, cool night air before I walked back under the Japanese lanterns into the din and fumes of the party. I found Molly and Paula sitting in cast-iron lawn chairs with plates of food and napkins in their laps, part of a circle of busily masticating guests.

"Well, *there* you are," Paula said. "Was she all right?"

"Yes. Sleeping like a log."

"Like an angel, you mean. I think she just loves that little room. And I love to know there's a little girl sleepin' up there. It reminds me of when Lucy was a child. I think children are so sensitive to atmospheres, don't you?"

"Sometimes," I said. "Not invariably."

She raised her head and watched me steadily for a moment. "Carl, you haven't seen Liam anywhere, have you? I need him to mix some more julep, and I can't find him anywhere."

"I think I saw him going down toward the backyard," I said. "With a plate. I had the idea he was going to feed his dog."

"Now, you know, I just bet that's what he's goin' to *do*," Paula said. "Feed my jambalaya to that *hound.* Honest, that man."

"Would you like me to get him?"

"No, that's all right. I've got to go down there anyway: I think I left the hose running this afternoon." She stood up and set her plate down on her chair.

"He was going down toward that little tool shed, or whatever it is, beside the gate."

"Thank you, honey. Excuse me, you-all, I'll be right back."

She swept away toward the rear of the house, her figure dissolving into the dusky haze beyond the lantern light. I sat down beside Molly, nibbling at the shrimp from my plate, nodding vacuous agreement with the occasional mumbled testimonials to its excellence from its busy circle of consumers, keeping a surreptitious vigil for Paula's reappearance. After something like five minutes, I saw her figure emerge swiftly from the darkness of the distant stretch of lawn, the indistinct pale oval of her face assuming identity and then recognizable expression as she advanced into the soft illumination of the lanterns. I saw that her mouth was fixed in the grim, crumpled cicatrice it resembled in her less animated, unguarded moments; this altered visibly as she approached us, and when she had reached the circle of lawn chairs and leaned down to retrieve her plate, it had become again the gay and mobile and invitingly responsive organ that her interlocutors beheld.

"Did you find him?" I asked.

"Yes." She sat down and took up the fork from her plate, thrusting the point of it delicately toward me. "And you were right! That man was feeding my jambalaya to that hound! I swear, he just worships that little bitch." Her eyes clung to mine for a moment as if to confirm some subtle, shadowy entente between us. "It's just what you were sayin' to me, Carl, about promiscuously sentimental behavior. It just leads to *waste!*"

"Is that what I was saying?" I said. "I don't remember that."

"He doesn't remember what he says from one minute to the next," Molly said. "He's always thinking about his work."

"Well, honey, there's worse things than *that* to complain about in a man," Paula said; and reached out and patted Molly's wrist with a condescension that made me burn.

A few minutes later I saw Janet's hasty, ignominious departure. She must have entered the house by the back door to retrieve her coat, gone out by it again, and then fled, not through the front door, where her exit would have been conspicuous, but along the far side of the house in the shadow of the chinaberry trees that marked the boundary of the lot. She walked so quickly, her head covered by a scarf, that I would not have recognized her if I had not known the circumstances. A moment later I heard the unmistakable coughing of her engine at the end of the block as she started it, and then the clatter of her ancient automobile receding distantly. Only Paula shared this knowledge with me, I'm sure; as the sound of the departing car faded into the night, she turned her face to me and allowed her eyes to brush mine fleetingly with a look of intimately candid resolution from which I retreated hastily.

I did not see Liam again until the coffee and dessert had been served, when he reappeared at the bar, where he spent the balance of the evening swaying unsteadily before the expostulations of a big-bellied man with huge convulsive hands in whose gesticulations Liam seemed lost. After the dessert and coffee, the party began to resolve itself into its usual late-hour conclave of the town's elite and Paula's intimates. These dozen or so of the privileged were invited to withdraw into the sitting room and served cigars and cigarettes and Bénédictine while through the open windows we heard the distant clatter and tinkle from the arbor as Viola and her daughters cleaned up the debris of the party. For Liam, it must have been an agony. In the much-reduced company, he was doubly conspicuous; he could not find refuge in obscurity; as host, he could not renege on his responsibilities; and as a principal in the project, he could not avoid participation in the discussion of it that arose, at least to a pro forma degree. He met these demands with a dignity that moved me very oddly. As drunk as he was, and in however great distress, he dispensed the Bénédictine with punctuality and prodigious steadiness of hand, listened with a beguiling air of absorption, nodded a great deal, murmured appreciatively, and managed to produce an occasional inspired periphrasis when pressed for an opinion or advice. But in those few moments when he was able to stand apart, unengaged and unobserved—by anyone but Paula and me—wrapped in his own excruciating reality, his face fell into the haggard stricture of a death mask and his eyes had the blasted look of that of a man without quarter, hope, or even the solace of an undefiled memory. Paula watched him like a jackal watching the death throes of an antelope. My own feelings, as I say, were confused, and so intense that they could almost be called voluptuous. What I felt could hardly have been called affection, and I'm sure it wasn't pity, but it was something as exquisite as either, that simmered in my veins like warm alcohol. Perhaps it was the Bénédictine; I certainly wasn't used to it.

"You drank Bénédictine?" Sylvie said.

"Yes. Several glasses of it, in fact. Something else that violated my criterion for human action. It certainly had no practical benefit; for the first time in my life, I had difficulty driving home."

"What happened to Janet?" Sylvie asked after a long silence.

"She resigned almost immediately. Within three days. She moved away to Montgomery and got a job as a secretary, I think, or an office clerk. I guess it was the only kind of work she could find."

"Did you see her again?"

"No. I didn't have the courage, I suppose. I didn't go down to Liam's office again until I heard she'd gone. I kept myself busy in the laboratory at Cardozo.

Most of our fieldwork had been done, but there were plenty of routine examinations and paperwork."

"And Liam stayed on?"

"Yes. That's extraordinary, isn't it?"

For a while Liam fell into a state of mind that was pretty close to pathological.
His late-night sessions at the laboratory became later, and more frequent. He
drank more than ever, and sometimes I worried, unfeignedly, about his being
on the road in that condition. His wit degenerated into a kind of habitual,
crapulous quizzicality that was undignified and often frivolous. His hands
shook almost constantly and he dropped things, flasks and test tubes, in the
middle of critical experiments. But then he'd manage to pull himself together
and keep going for a day or two. I couldn't for the life of me understand why
he didn't pack his bags and take the train for Montgomery and Janet—why
he hadn't gone with her, in fact.

Then, one night in early July, when I drove to his office after spending an
evening working at Cardozo with Kidd, I found the downstairs door to the
clinic locked, although the light was on in the upstairs windows that fronted
on the street. I knew Liam was there, because his car was parked along the curb
in front of the clinic door. I knocked several times, and after a moment the
light went off in the windows overhead. I walked back to my car, which I had
parked across the street, drove it once around the block, and parked again, at
the far end of the street in the shadow of the oaks. I turned off my headlights
and sat watching the clinic door for something like ten minutes. I was about
to leave when it opened, and Liam and Janet emerged and walked hurriedly
down the street away from me, turning the corner at the far end of the block.
A few minutes later, Liam reappeared, walked back quickly to his car, got in,
and started the motor. He made a clumsily negotiated U-turn in the middle
of the block and then drove past me to the corner of Main Street, where he
turned to the right and disappeared toward his house. As his headlights swept
past me, I slunk down on the seat with my head behind the instrument panel,
cursing as I struck my chin against the steering wheel. I hated having to make
that shabby gesture of concealment, and for some reason I held Janet responsible for my loss of dignity. "Damn the bitch": that's what I muttered to myself.

I think he saw her frequently. In fact, I'm sure it was the only thing that
kept him sane. He began to go more often than usual on his daylong missions
into the far reaches of the county, and since Montgomery was only a two-hour
drive away, I suspected that some of them were in fact excursions to that city,
or to Patkoola, a midway trysting point, where they could spend a few hours
together. I didn't object to this, or question him about the purpose of these
expeditions—not so much out of magnanimity as because it would have

seemed too transparently a reference to his delinquencies, and I didn't want to create any suspicion in him about the stealth of my interest in his private life.

I don't think he had any, ever. He didn't behave any differently toward me, and there was never any intimation that he knew I had betrayed him. He couldn't have known, of course. Paula wouldn't have told him, I know. In the first place, she couldn't be sure of it—I'd directed her steps toward the arbor too artfully for that—and even if she had been, it wouldn't have been of any advantage to her to disclose the fact to Liam. Maybe she was ironically applying my own precept about the practical benefits of any human action, but I don't think she needed any instruction from me on that score. She was naturally far too pragmatic a woman to indulge in what I might well have considered a gratuitous calumny against me—especially since I seemed to figure in her plans for the future. That was the only thing I really regretted about my act—aside from the fact that it was an absolutely senseless violation of my own maxim about human conduct—that it might have encouraged her in making any such idiotic plans. She was making them, I'm sure; with even more than her usual degree of sangfroid and probably in the belief that I was secretly rejoicing in the knowledge of the fact. She quixotically gave another party, about three weeks later, which I think was actually a clandestine celebration of Janet's departure and perhaps the inaugural ceremonies of some new epoch in her own personal affairs that I would just as soon have seen go uncelebrated. Janet, of course, was dramatically and resoundingly absent, and Paula as voluble, self-possessed, and animated as the first time I had met her. I expected no less from her than tact, but the kind of oblivious verve and enthusiasm with which she orchestrated and reigned over the affair—while Liam sank into a more and more laconic stupor or reckless, desperate conviviality—had a cruelty and deliberateness about it that made me cringe. I had little right to such scruples, God knows. Being the co-author of his grief, I had very poor grounds for regretting her indifference to it. But I was, at least, better situated from the point of view of appearances. Whether or not she was entirely convinced of my complicity in his undoing, I wasn't sure, but I was careful to foster the impression of my innocence by an extravagant pretense of concern for his condition. I frowned a good deal when he was conspicuously indiscreet or garrulous, studied the floor with an air of deep regret, and pursed my lips and averted my eyes when—as happened once—he stood on the sofa and declaimed passages from *The Marriage of Heaven and Hell* while slopping julep on the velvet upholstery. Once, in the course of that evening, I suggested to Paula, with becoming anxiety, that he had been working much too hard, that she really must get him away for a holiday or all of us would suffer.

"I know that," she said. "That poor man. I think his work has just about doubled since Janet decided to quit. What could have got into that girl I just don't know. Running out on him at a time like this, right in the middle of the most important piece of work he ever did." I realized, with a start of admiration, that she was trumping my own pretense of generous concern, and perhaps parodying it into the bargain.

"I understand she had some—family problems," I murmured (this was the public explanation of Janet's resignation).

"Uh-huh. I just reckon she did. Well, I hope they're pretty serious ones. Leavin' Liam in the lurch like this, after all he's done for her. I don't think it shows a whole lot of *gratitude,* myself."

"No. He doesn't deserve it. You know, he told me once that he loved sailing. A week or two of that might be just what he needs. Things are slack right now, and it would be a good time for him to get away."

"It might. He's got a little sailboat, down at the beach."

"I know. I think that's almost the first thing he ever told me. He promised to teach me how to sail one day."

"He *did?*" She dwelt silently on this idea for a moment, with growing appreciation. "Well, you know, Carl, you're a *very* intelligent man. That is a *very* intelligent suggestion. I don't suppose you've mentioned it to him yourself?"

"Oh, no. I don't think *I* could persuade him. But I think you have much more influence over him than I do."

There was no doubt about that. The most astonishing evidence of her influence being the fact that they had remained together after the debacle that must have taken place behind the garden shed. Although Liam's dauntless integrity may have helped to account for it. I'm sure she cultivated relentlessly in him the sense of obligation and guilt he felt at her having subsidized his education and provided him, for years, with a comfortable way of life, the house, and travel, and books, and all the indulgences—perhaps, eventually, even the liquor—with which she had guaranteed his conformity and his submission to her own improprieties, which I growingly suspected to be inveterate. All this I attempted to imply in my pronunciation of the word "influence." To no avail. A few days after her party she called me at the laboratory in Cardozo.

"Carl, I been thinkin' about that suggestion you made the other night at my party. You know, about gettin' Liam down to the beach for a while, to do some sailin'?"

"Oh, yes. I think it would do him good."

"I do, too. He doesn't usually come down till September, and not for more'n a week at that. Just a weekend sometimes. Well, the way he's actin' right now, I don't know if he'd come down at all if it was just the two of us.

I don't think I have to conceal the fact from you that we're not gettin' along real well. But I was thinkin': if you and Molly was to come down and stay with us, he might just do it. After all, he *did* invite you, you said. I'd like that, too. I'd like it very much."

"Oh, that's kind of you, Paula. I'd love to come down, and I know Molly would. But actually I'm pretty busy at the moment."

"Now listen, *you!* You told me that things were *slack* right now. Now you know very well you did. I'm just not takin' *that* for an excuse!"

"Well, I suppose I could get away, if Molly wants to. Let me talk to her about it, Paula, will you? I'd rather make it in September, if that's possible."

"I don't think Liam's goin' to make it through September. You said yourself he needed to get away right now. And after all, he promised to teach you sailin', so if you come down there, he's got no excuse in the world for not comin'."

"I suppose not. I'll talk to Molly about it and have her call you."

"I'm goin' to talk to her myself," Paula said. "I'm goin' to ring her right this minute."

"All right. Thanks very much, Paula. I appreciate it."

Whether I had been disastrously misunderstood, or my own piece of journeyman hypocrisy masterfully finessed, I wasn't sure.

That evening at dinner Molly said, "Paula called me this afternoon and invited us to come down to Gulf Shores for a couple of weeks."

"Oh, that was nice of her."

"Yes, it was. She asked us to come down on the fifteenth. That would be wonderful, because it'll be unbearable here in the middle of August."

"Yes. You'd like to go, then?"

"Well, of course I would. We don't ever go anywhere. I get so sick of this house. I don't suppose we'll have a vacation at all this summer if we don't. Don't *you* want to?"

I had many reasons for not wanting to. The necessity of having to make myself unremittingly sociable for that amount of time exhausted me even to imagine, and the prospect of being confined under the same roof with Paula in that intimate a situation, and of being held a fortnight-long hostage witness to the raveled, ruinous relationship between her and Liam, was not far short of appalling. To contemplate his disintegration at that close quarters and in the knowledge of having precipitated it did not strike me as a festive occasion. I had another reason, which would have been equally embarrassing to have revealed: I had an agonizing, lifelong self-consciousness about exposing my body in public. I have probably the least attractive body in the world; it always dismayed me, even as a boy. I could never swim naked with other boys, or take a shower after gym classes, without suffering a feverish, paralyzing embarrassment. Consequently, I had never learned to swim well, since one must learn to swim in the presence and with the assistance of others. In Maine, as a boy and in the company only of my parents, I had learned to do a flailing, old-fashioned sidestroke, but I never enjoyed it. I had come to detest beaches, public pools, and all forms of aquatic recreation, and avoided them rigorously. By the time I was thirty and had begun to put on weight, my flesh had developed an unhealthy, puffy, sallow look; that dimpled, quilted look of adipose tissue around the thighs and belly and underarms that, in men, is unpleasantly epicene, and which doubled my aversion to having to reveal it to the eyes of men—or even to the sun or sky, because I disliked intensely even the feeling of being naked out of doors; it made me shiver with shame, with a scalding sense of vulnerability. All this made the prospect of spending two weeks at a beach resort, in the company of people with whom I had such an equivocal relationship, seem more like perdition than a holiday.

"I don't know, Molly," I said. "I'm awfully busy. I've got an awful lot to do, you know."

"Oh, *you* have. I know that." I stiffened myself for the assault; she seemed, however, to feel it prudent for the moment to relinquish the opportunity to point out, for the hundredth time, my indifference to *her* welfare. She swallowed a piece of veal and sipped from her water glass. "When we were in Washington," she said, "we only went to the shore once. Just once, and it was only an hour away. That time we went down to the bay, and you wanted to leave almost as soon as we got there. As soon as we finished the sandwiches."

"Well, you know how much I dislike the beach," I said. "You know the sun bothers me. I get those hives." I could sense the torrent of protest gathering in her. "Still, it would be a change. I know you get bored here sometimes. I'll admit there's not a lot to do. And of course, Elizabeth's never seen the water. She might like that."

"Of course she would. All children love the beach. There's nothing they like better than to sit and dig in the sand." She turned to Elizabeth, who, with her spoon clenched in her fist like a pestle, was grinding a mound of peas on her plate. "Would you like to go to the beach, Elizabeth?" Molly said. She took Elizabeth's hand, scooped up a dab of the macerated peas, and guided the spoon toward her daughter's mouth. "All that beautiful white sand to dig in. You could make *castles*. *Sand* castles. You could have a little bucket and a nice red shovel. That's something *every* little girl likes to do." The child stared at her with great, pale blue, vacant eyes in which no vision of castles had been engendered, no delectable conglomeration of images of bright red buckets and tin shovels, of the smell of hot rubber and suntan lotion, of deviled eggs and thermos jugs of cold lemonade and waxed-paper cups and blue-and-yellow beach balls, and all the tacky, gimcrack, redolent paraphernalia of the holidays of existence on this globe. They were orphan's eyes; only more terrible, because their penury was not that of the forsaken but almost of the unborn.

I realized suddenly that it was madness to offer even the semblance of resistance. Not only would it have seemed indefensibly, arbitrarily cruel to refuse the invitation; it would have made our domestic life intolerable for as far as I could see into the future.

Well, we went down there, in the middle of August. It was very hot, brutally hot, a hundred degrees or more, and we drove for three hours through that suffocating, interminable stillness that reigns over the Gulf coastal regions in midsummer. It reigned over us as well. On that occasion, we were not only silent, we were virtually inanimate. Nothing approaching the happy converse of a family on holiday relieved the sultry density of the air, the ruthlessly blue and silent sky, the mournful, measureless wastes of pine barrens, the occasional dusty, sweltering towns with their ramshackle general stores and ragged cabbage palms and gaunt, craven dogs. I had been afraid Elizabeth would be fretful, or plaintive, or carsick, but she wasn't; she seemed smitten by the vast inanity of the earth and sky and almost oblivious of the heat, although her little cotton sunsuit was soaked with sweat and her neck and arms ran with it. Twice we stopped and bought her huge, vitriolic-looking bottles of orange Nehi, at which she sucked and slobbered mindlessly, jouncing against Molly's breast with the motion of the car like an overturned mechanical toy twitching against a wall.

The cottage was one of a score or so that made up an old-fashioned resort community bordering the Gulf between Pensacola and Mobile Bay. It was a lonely and, although only a quarter of a century old, already dilapidated place. Behind it there was a jungle of palmetto scrub and tortured-looking water oaks draped in tattered strands of Spanish moss like the rags of rotting clothes. The house was more than a cottage, really; a shambling old twenties-style beach house, with a pair of upstairs bedrooms that had dormer windows looking out across the Gulf. Liam and Paula had rented it every summer for the past five years from a man who lived in Mobile, never used it himself, and took very little interest in the place. Whatever was undertaken in the way of maintenance was left to Liam and the other seasonal tenants; it was very little. The sun and wind had blistered the paint and split the clapboards of the walls and riven the masonry of the chimney. Inside, it was musty-smelling, the carpets were worn to the cord, and the cheap, painted furniture was falling apart. Yet, for some reason, I liked the place. From the first moment I saw it, it seemed profoundly inviting in its lonely, weather-beaten solitude, and I felt in it the promise of consummation of the strange nullity that clamored at me silently. I imagined myself walking along the great empty stretch of beach by myself on successive dawns, away from the sleeping household and into the morning mist above the sand, growing more and more remote as I retreated into the heart of its obscurity.

Whatever her motives may have been, Paula, from the moment she and Liam met us at the end of the clay road that wound into their sandy backyard, was beguilingly hospitable. She hugged Molly, led her by the hand into our quarters, and gaily and fussily helped her to unpack. She was tenderly attentive to Elizabeth and presented her with the Raggedy Ann doll, which she had thoughtfully brought down for her to sleep with. She had perfected a silvery laugh with which she embellished every action and rewarded almost every comment anyone made. With me she was impeccably judicious in her manner; as affectionate as our acquaintance and the occasion demanded, but never inappropriately confidential or attentive. There is this to be said for heartless women: they often make up in sagacity what they lack in feeling. By the morning of our second day I felt reassured enough about her intentions that I was able to get up at five o'clock, find myself a glass of orange juice in the huge, old, uncannily purring refrigerator, and set out from the dark kitchen and the still, gaunt house into the even more ancient, stranger hush that enclosed it. I wandered for two hours or more along the beach, most of the time at the very edge of the water, where the gentle, silent ripplets lapped at the cool, smooth sand. The earth and sky were dark, and I watched pale, rose-colored shoals of light deepen and spread among the banks of cloud in the east. The dawn rose, and cast a soft broad glint across the water from the horizon. I saw shadows begin to form in the depressions of the sand, and mounds of freshly excavated sand, like wet cement, at the holes of crab burrows. I watched fiddler crabs go scurrying away across the beach as I approached them, sometimes pausing to raise and wave one claw at me like a tiny violin. Occasionally I stooped to pick up a shell or chunk of driftwood, which I would examine vacantly for a moment before I tossed it away. After some time I sat down and stared out at the sea, watching the light possess the earth and water. I tried very consciously to think of nothing, to feel nothing, to invoke anew that huge obliterating senselessness, that absolute remission of myself that seemed to call to me like silent music blown across the water from ghostly island paradises. I wanted to become a part of the pale, worn, glamorous rubble that surrounded me: the frail husk of a dead crab, a chalk-white seashell, a strand of blackened kelp, a spiral of bleached vine; nothing more than a speck of refuse on an infinite span of silent, lifeless shore. But I could not renew or consummate that longing. What was renewed in me, on the contrary, was the intensity of my perceptions, my own raging identity. I grew more conscious momentarily; more aware of the magnificence of the nameless, delicate detritus that lay about me on the sand, and this began to produce in me a subtle, sullen despair. I didn't know why, then; now, I think it was because that desire in me to enter into the anonymity of the place was a passion in itself—an immoderate, estranging passion that only served to animate me more. I was all the more bitterly enlivened by it, made all the more peculiarly, miserably sentient among those earnest, shapely ruins of the life of this earth. Because, as I looked at them and picked them up and turned them in my fingers, I saw that there was a comeliness and simplicity and conformity about them that chastened me, that was the product, not of pride or perversity, but of the seemly modesty of their existences. The beautiful decrepitude they dwelt in was true death, not nothingness. They were not unmade or recreant, they had not abdicated or reviled life, but were splendidly exhausted by it, and seemed to wage still, in their marvelous colors and obstinate, exquisite shapes, a contest with oblivion. The longer I studied them, the less like ruins they seemed, the more like artifacts, delicate and stirring sculptures carved by the knives of danger and vicissitude out of the very bodies of creatures whose fidelity and vitality they commemorated. They were as voluble, and as elegant and impassioned in their attitudes, as the seabirds that soared against the sky; they seemed to participate in the guileless ribaldry and rapacity of the gulls and the cleanly swoop and keening of the terns that swept above the water in a rapture of predation. As prey or carrion, they were not extinct; they lent a measure of their energy and vivacity to the daintiness and alacrity of the little scurrying crabs and debonair sandpipers, and of their ebullience to the earth itself, which at the water's edge bubbled with the breath of burrowing sand fleas and coquinas; they were forever involved in the sincerity and zeal and innocent ferocity of that world, which they perpetuated with their death and whose inextinguishability I began to recognize. This was no place of destitution or obscurity, I saw; no desert island wafting phantom balms. It was a thriving commonwealth of life and death, where the quick and dead carried on exuberant commerce with each other and fervent congress with the sun and stars. There was no poverty there except my ignorant, dissolute desire to discover it, nothing wanton or ignoble except my baleful recognition of its grace; nothing unsociable but my willful solitude. Something like contempt for me seemed to be expressed in the eloquent, scattered relics and the resolute, disdainful gulls. I felt desolate and alien. I am familiar with neither the living nor the dead, I thought. My only helpmeet is my virtuosity.

I stood up and went down to the water's edge and found a shard of the shell of a horseshoe crab. It was a broken, shining fragment from the rear edge of the carapace from which three small spikes projected, like hawthorn barbs. I stooped and picked it up and walked back toward the cottage, holding it so tightly in my hand that the tips of the small thorns pierced my palm. They were like the nails of Walter Lubby's hand, clenching my own in death.

· · ·

"I don't know if you can understand such feelings. I doubt it. I began to tell you this because just now, when you were describing the way you felt after Ron's death, sitting in the bay window of that bar in Washington, I suddenly remembered the way I felt that morning on the beach after Walter Lubby died. Not because it was identical, or even similar, but because it was an almost obverse experience, I think. Even though the circumstances were very much alike."

She didn't reply immediately, but raised her eyes to watch the flutter of shadow on the windowpane.

"And what you felt in the desert, in Mexico. I felt no such ecstasy in that place."

"We're different," she said. "But maybe that's why we're able to converse. I think we're equally improvident, at least. And when you talked about the eye of the hurricane—about feeling haunted by the future—I understood that."

"You felt that, too?"

"I feel it still."

She raised her hands and unlaced the fingers. Curling the tips of them into her palms, she pressed them against her open mouth and breathed on them, as if they were very cold.

"I made some watercress sandwiches," I said uncertainly. "I don't know if you'd like one."

She stared at me across her knuckles, her eyes hugely insensible, like those of a freshly awakened child still tangled in its dreams.

"I couldn't eat," she murmured in a moment. "Go on."

On the second morning I got up at five again. I thought there was no one else awake in the house, but as I went out of the bedroom I stopped beside the cot against the wall where Elizabeth slept in the same room with us. I don't know why I did; she had not stirred or made any sound. But I paused and bent down over the cot—because the room was still too dark to see clearly—and after a moment, when my eyes had adjusted to the darkness, I saw that she was awake, her eyes wide open, watching me. We stared at each other silently for a moment, and then I straightened my back and went out of the room.

I walked along the beach again for an hour or more, but this time briskly, almost haughtily in fact, in obdurate possession of myself, as if refusing to allow myself to be dismayed by the inhospitality of the place. I did not pause to stare out at the sea with any further thought of fading into the absolving emptiness that I had found not to exist; and I did not have the humility to sit and contemplate the impervious, sempiternal beauty that ranged across the dunes and dappled water in the morning light. But in spite of my resolutely averted eyes, I saw marvelous shells and sand-dollar skeletons like plaques of bisque pottery and glittering iridescent jewels of mother-of-pearl, but I did not stoop to pick up or admire any of them. I think I feared that in a year, or ten, or twenty, they would serve only as souvenirs of the execration I had suffered there; they would cast their censure at me silently, still, from a bookshelf in my study or the top of a cabinet in my laboratory. I could not have described that fear, but I felt it; I'm sure of that. It was expressed in the defiant vigor of my stride, in my assumed indifference to the sanity and temperance that I found, of all things in the wilderness, most bewildering. Nothing there killed or scavenged out of ambition or desire for distinction, or greed, or rabid ingenuity, but only out of honest hunger. What was slain was eaten, and its slaughter so redeemed. Nothing was not devout in its voracity or magnanimous in its death. In all that festive tumult, I was the only profligate thing, the only creature unconstrained by the grave proprieties of which the world was both the text and the celebration. I was mortified by this discovery; profoundly, inconsolably mortified. What I had all my life despised or deplored as the lawless beauty of the world I saw was nothing else but law. Law was everywhere about me. It rang like anthems in the throats of cormorants and lit their eyes with lustrous, licit hunger and poured in civil torrents through the bright flumes of their veins. That world was in perfect and perpetual order; it had prospered for a billion years without one written statute. It was born and bathed in law, and utterly unconscious of it; imperturbably, unerringly observant of the covenant it recited with its deeds, the dazzling canons it spelled out with its every gesture across the pale parchment of the universe.

As I walked back to the cottage I stepped on the hollow, desiccate carcass of a crab, and felt a faint, pernicious satisfaction at the crunch of the delicate shell beneath my shoe.

When I returned, the house was astir. In the kitchen, Paula was at the stove mixing pancake batter in a bowl. There was the smell of coffee and bacon and the bubbling of the percolator. At the big old wooden table Liam sat with Elizabeth in his lap, jiggling her on his knees and mischievously misguiding her hand while she tried to spoon down mouthfuls of hot Cream of Wheat from a bowl. Occasionally he would lean forward and press his lips against the back of her neck and blow mightily, making a cheerfully vulgar sound. Her eyes would widen with a vast, rapturous, unknown hilarity, an expression so foreign to her face that for a moment it seemed almost as much a convulsion of grief as the evidence of delight. Her expression was intolerable to me, a caricature. I started to say, "What's wrong? What's happened?" and then I realized that I had never before seen my daughter laugh with joy. In a moment Molly came into the kitchen from the hall carrying the yellow bib which Elizabeth wore while she ate. When she saw the child sitting on Liam's lap merrily splattering him with Cream of Wheat, she stopped as if she had been struck and stood stock-still at the door, raising her eyes to mine slowly. I don't know what I saw most in her look: shame, pity, indignation, grief. I realized that for her, as for me, joy had become an embarrassment, almost an indecency.

Our days at the cottage fell into a pattern: When I returned from my morning walk, we would eat breakfast. There would be talk, of an idle, improvisational kind: vagrant observations about the weather, local customs or phenomena, perhaps a discussion of some possible special event for the afternoon—surf fishing, a game of volleyball, or a trip to the village. After breakfast, Liam would go out for his morning sail. He had a little ten-foot dinghy that lay beached on the sand in front of the house. If the wind was fair he would drag it down the beach to the water and sail for an hour or two. It was the thing he loved to do most. He took me out with him the first two mornings, but I didn't enjoy it. I was clumsy, uncomfortable, and I disliked intensely the blaze of the sun on the open water. I wore a hat, long trousers and a long-sleeved shirt, to his great amusement and despair. After those two vain efforts to awaken my enthusiasm, he would go out with his dog, whose company I'm sure he preferred in any case. From the screened front porch I would watch him cruising across the blue, sun-streaked water, lying back flat in the stern, so that only his head was visible, while the dog, standing in the bow with her head thrust forward to scent the breeze, resembled a comical, barbaric figurehead. There was something offensively ridiculous about the sight.

Every morning I sat there on the porch after breakfast with my briefcase, going over data and making out my six months' period report to send to Dr. Turner in Washington. Paula and Molly, when they had cleared away and washed the breakfast dishes and straightened up the kitchen, would go for a morning stroll along the beach with Elizabeth. Paula had an elaborate and quite beautiful shell collection, to which she added at least one specimen every day. When they returned, their morning's discoveries would be exhibited, exclaimed upon, and sorted out for preservation or rejection; then preparations for lunch would begin. When Liam returned from his sail, we would eat on the screened porch, looking out over the beach and the vast blue glittering expanse of the Gulf of Mexico. Elizabeth would be "put down," as Paula called it, for a nap, and a somnolence would descend upon the house, during which people were left to their own devices: letter writing, leafing through the pages of months-old magazines, sewing, doing crossword puzzles. In the early afternoon, at two or three, Elizabeth would be awakened and there would be a general descent to the beach with blankets, towels, toys, thermos jugs, and a pair of bright-colored beach umbrellas. We would stay until four or five o'clock, wading, sunbathing, beachcombing, going for an occasional swim in the remarkably clear and gentle water, reading, or simply staring at the sea. My own activities were restricted almost entirely to the latter two. I did occasionally roll up my trouser legs and wade out cautiously, knee-deep, into the limpid water, but I never overcame my inhibitions enough to remove my long-sleeved shirt, or swim, or stretch out in the sun. Most of the time I sat on a folding chair in the shade of a beach umbrella reading a copy of Kampmeier's *Essentials of Syphilology* which I had brought with me. In order to escape invitations to such diversions as volleyball or water polo, I would, at the slightest opportunity, volunteer to go up to the house to fetch a bucket of ice, a bottle of lemonade, or a tattered paperback mystery novel.

The resort, as I say, was composed of only fifteen or twenty cottages, so that, besides ourselves, there were never many people on the beach; perhaps a dozen or so, strung out in little family enclaves separated from each other by a hundred yards or more of sand. Only with those who occupied the next cottage did Liam and Paula appear to have any sort of close social acquaintance; these were a family named Torrance, who were also from Tallacoochee; it was they, in fact, who had introduced Liam and Paula to the place. Tom Torrance ran an electrical supply company almost directly across the street from the clinic, and had been a boyhood friend of Liam's. I had met him and his wife briefly at one of Paula's parties, and I remembered Mary Torrance and Molly chatting for a moment about their daughters as we had been about to leave. "Liam says he's tryin' to get you-all down to the beach sometime next summer," she had said. "I just hope he does, because they aren't many children come down there anymore, and Doreen doesn't have anybody to play with. She'd just love to have a little girl stayin' next door. It would be real nice for us if you-all could come down." The merciless, premonitory irony of those words are burned into my brain forever.

The daughter she had spoken of, Doreen, was a little girl of nine or ten, a strange child, unnaturally mature, assertive, inquisitive, and astonishingly beautiful. The first time I saw her my breath caught at the perfection of her porcelain-pink features, her unnaturally vivid, coral-colored lips, and her calm, cool, sapphire-blue eyes in which the light shifted like tiny, four-pointed stars, as distinctly as in gems. She had been led across to our beach site by her mother to meet Elizabeth, and after she had been introduced to her and then to Molly and me, she took Elizabeth by the hand and, swinging it gently in her own, raised her eyes directly to mine for the first time.

"Is it all right if I play with Elizabeth?" she asked.

"Yes, of course. As long as you don't take her in the water."

"What sort of things does she like to play? What do *you* play with her?"

"Oh, she likes to make sand castles. And play dolls. All the things that little girls like to do."

"I'll bet she knows a lot of things that I don't know how to do. You think I ought to ask her?"

"Yes, if you like," I said, and felt oddly confounded by the question and by the persistence of her gaze.

"Why don't you start by making a castle?" Mary Torrance said. "Look what a lovely shovel and pail Elizabeth has! See if you can make a castle like the one in your book you like so much." She put the handle of the little bucket into her daughter's hand and patted both the children on the head. "They'll have a lovely time, I know. Thank you for having Doreen over. You let me know when you get tired of her."

I watched them play together with a growing sense of apprehension—then and on subsequent days—as Doreen developed what was to me an oddly unpleasant maternal relationship with our daughter. She played with Elizabeth, not as with a companion, but almost as if she were playing with a child of her own, an imposture with which Elizabeth fell into immediate and enchanted compliance. She was utterly passive and dumb in Doreen's company; she would sit in silent submission while the assured and subtle little mime combed her hair or scrubbed her hands with sandy water from her bucket or painted her fingernails with imaginary lacquer, chattering to her scoldingly or indulgently, as one would to an infant. Elizabeth was awed and delighted by the fancy. Doreen would sometimes take her by the hand and lead her up and down the beach on imaginary errands—"to school," or "shopping," or "to the hairdresser"—urging her to hurry when she dawdled, tugging her upright by the arm when she stumbled and fell, brushing the sand from her bathing suit reproachfully, issuing endless admonitions, instructions, and advice. Liam and Paula, and even Molly, seemed to find this amusing, but it made me extremely uncomfortable. The child was never quite aggressive or domineering enough to justify overt disapproval or intervention, but it seemed to me that there was something deliberately provocative in her behavior that I came to feel was directed insidiously toward me; as if, in her role of mother to Elizabeth, there were a very subtle presumption of equality—and even of conjugality—with me. I know that sounds absurd. I know it's possible that she was simply "playing house," as little girls do, and that along with the appropriation of Elizabeth, as her child, there went the appropriation of myself, as her spouse, to complete the ménage. It's more than possible; it is no doubt the case; but I will never, ever, be convinced of her innocence. What disturbed me most was that there was implicit in her manner an assumption of the prerogatives of a wife as well; a clever and demeaning impersonation of Molly, an almost ironic mummery of Molly's relationship to me and to Elizabeth; a kind of disingenuous travesty of our lives. Sometimes she would borrow an exact phrase or epithet of Molly's with which to chide or exhort Elizabeth, imitating Molly's tone of voice or petulant emphasis of a word or syllable so perfectly that the effect was of an uncanny echo out of our own life: "Now, *Elizabeth!* You *know* you're not supposed to do that! Suppose I let your *father* know you did a thing like that!" It was done with such skill and nonchalance that it was, as I say, beyond reproach; and yet if I turned to look at her in unwilling admiration, I had the impression that she was very much aware of its effect on me, and of a carefully disguised satisfaction at my discomfiture. This air of mimicry was present even in her gestures and the movements of her body, particularly of her hands, which were extraordinary for a child's. Her fingers were very long and slender, attenuated like a woman's, and nimble and artfully fastidious in their movements, like those of a certain type of female guest I had often seen at Paula's parties selecting an especially appealing item from a tray of canapés, the fingers poised above the tray, the knuckles daintily elevated, as if by the conscious delicacy of their attitudes they could disguise or compensate for the avidity that animated them. There was that devious elegance—doubly devious, for its precocity, in Doreen's case—in the way she would flick grains of sand from beneath her fingernails, or run a fingertip languidly along a gleaming blond eyebrow, or pluck an exquisite amber curl from her forehead, her head beguilingly inclined, her eyes brushing for an instant across mine as if to calculate the effectiveness of the gesture. She called us all by our first names, and used them with a casualness and assurance that I found close to impudence. There was something preternaturally sedate and yet alert and boldly inquisitive about her that growingly dismayed me. She would often ask sudden, unsettling questions, or make requests to me to join in her play with Elizabeth which, while innocent enough, she always managed to make seem border on impropriety.

"Elizabeth and I are going downtown and buy some dresses for her. Will you come with us, Carl?"

"I don't think so, thank you."

"Well, it would be very nice if you did. I really think she ought to have your advice."

"Not just now. You run along."

"Well, then, will you help us bury some treasure? We want to make a treasure map."

"No. I have to read."

"Oh, you never want to do *anything!* Honestly!"

Occasionally, aware that her chatter to Elizabeth had ceased for a moment, I would turn my head to find her gazing at me with a curious, canny look whose intentness was almost intimidating. Once, when that happened and my eyes had returned uneasily to my book, she said to me, "Why don't you ever take your clothes off, Carl?"

"I don't—like the sun," I said, faltering before the temerity of the question.

"Why not?"

"Because it gives me hives."

"Hives? What are *hives?"*

"It's a skin rash. It makes me itch and burn."

I returned my attention to my book, annoyed as much with myself as with her, because I seemed unable to make a sufficiently peremptory reply. I also seemed unable to find my place in the text. I read one extraordinarily obtuse sentence twice: *Interstitial keratitis usually appears near puberty and eventually becomes bilateral, the cornea developing a ground-glass appearance with vascularization of the adjacent sclera.*

"I'll bet you're afraid!" Doreen said.

I returned my eyes to her, intending to reprove her with a look of unmistakable reprimand, but I found myself subdued by the poise and persistence of her sapphire-colored eyes and the tauntingly attentive posture of her head.

"Afraid of what?"

"Afraid to take your clothes off. I'll bet you are!"

"You go and take Elizabeth shopping," I said. "I'm busy now. See if you can find a sand dollar. I'll give you a real dollar for it if you do."

"Then will you take your clothes off and put your bathing suit on?"

"Doreen, don't bother Carl, dear," Paula said. "He wants to read."

"What is he reading? He never does anything but read."

"He has to study, dear. Because he's a doctor. Doctors have to study all the time. How could he make you well if you got sick, if he didn't study?"

"You mean he takes care of little *girls?"* Doreen said. There was an insolently expostulatory sound in the question. It hung implacably for a moment in the air.

"Sometimes," I murmured.

"Would you take care of *me* if I got sick?"

"Of course he would," Paula said. "He loves little girls. Now you run on and find a sand dollar with Elizabeth, and then Carl will give you a real dollar, and you can buy some bubble gum. Think how much bubble gum you can buy for a dollar."

"I don't want any *bubble* gum," Doreen said disdainfully. "That's just for little tiny *children.* I want to buy some jewelry!"

"Oh, my goodness, jewelry!" Paula said. "What sort of jewelry?"

"What I want most in the whole world is a pair of gold hoop earrings. Will you buy me a pair of earrings, Carl, if I find a sand dollar?"

"I don't know," I said. I attempted a patronizing laugh, which became oddly strangulated by my impatience. "That's pretty expensive. I'll give you a dollar and you can start saving up for them."

"Do you promise?"

"We'll see."

"You *better* now!" she said. "Because if you don't I'll be mad! You don't want me to be mad, do you?"

"My goodness!" Paula exclaimed. "She doesn't sound like a woman to be trifled with! You go on now, honey, and Carl'll give you a dollar. I'll see to it."

"All right," Doreen said. "But he *better*. You remember now, Carl."

She took Elizabeth by the hand and marched her off across the sand, sternly cautioning her to keep her sunbonnet on, "because if you don't you're liable to get sunstroke!"

On the eighth day that we were there, Mary's parents arrived to spend a week with the family. Like Tom and Mary, they were infatuated with Doreen and cravenly indulgent of her. They considered her posturing, her mannerisms, her use of their given names endearingly imaginative and winsome, and were unable to resist her most capricious request. They brought a gift for her, a new bathing suit, in which she presented herself at our compound on the beach and displayed herself all morning with the flagrant narcissism of a fashion model. At that time women had begun to wear rubber bathing suits; I don't know why —I always thought them abominable: clammy, synthetic-looking, deformingly tight, they enclosed a woman's body like a sausage skin, giving it the look of an overinflated balloon that might burst at any moment. This was the type of garment which they had evidently been cozened by Doreen into selecting for her; and yet, on her girlish body, it was undeniably provocative. The sheath of tight, turquoise elastic gave a startling look of nubility to her slender hips and hard little buttocks and the nascent mounds of her breasts with their clearly distinguishable, newly swollen areolas.

"Oh, my, what a pretty new bathing suit!" Molly exclaimed idiotically when Doreen approached from across the sand, taking the tiny, mincing steps of a belle *en promenade*.

"Thank you," Doreen said. "I think it's pretty, too. My grandparents bought it for me. They let me pick it out. Do you like it, Carl?"

"Yes," I murmured, making a determinedly brief, casual survey of the suit. "It's very nice. Your grandparents are here?"

"Yes, they're going to stay with us for a week. They come down every summer, and they always bring me something. They're just the nicest grandparents in the world."

"I'n't that awful hot, honey? That rubber?" Paula asked.

"No. It just feels wonderful. It's almost like wearing nothing at all."

"It *is?* Well, my goodness! I was thinkin' about gettin' one of those things, but I don't know whether I better. Liam might just have a fit." She turned her eyes to Liam with a coy, ironic look. "Would you, honey, if I did?"

"I don't think so," Liam said. "I can't speak for anyone else, of course."

"No, I reckon not. What do you say, Molly? Shall we get us some rubber bathing suits?"

"Oh, I don't think so," Molly murmured, lowering her eyes to the picnic basket on the sand in front of her. She took her camera out of it and began to adjust the lens. "Can I get a picture of you, Doreen, in that lovely new suit? I'll bet your mother and daddy would like to have one."

"All right. I'd like to have one, too. I'll pay you for it."

"Oh, that's all right. I'll be glad to give you one, if they turn out."

There was picture taking for several minutes, for me an indescribably embarrassing event which called forth equally Molly's passion for preserving such awful occasions and the little girl's serene, strange, somehow sinister vanity. She posed for her photograph like a soubrette, smiling silkily into the camera with the fingers of one delicate hand clasping a hipbone in an arrantly voluptuous way, which, if it had been merely artless or inept, I might have smiled at, but which, as it was, I found less comical than scandalous. In another, she assumed a sylphlike arabesque, her arms held arched above her head, the fingers flung lyrically abroad in such a parody of rapture, grace, and spontaneity—of innocence itself—that it gave the weirdly meretricious effect of a child imitating a very bad mime imitating a child. Other pictures followed: of the two children together, of Liam bearing both of them askew and giggling on his shoulders, of Paula kneeling with her arms around their waists, and, inexorably, of one of Molly's most ignominious inventions: the dog, Enitharmom, with Elizabeth's sunbonnet tied on its head, blinking dolefully in Liam's arms.

I abstained, as long as it was possible to do so without appearing conspicuously dour, from any part in the event, waving aside invitations to be photographed with a crooked smile and magnanimous evasions: "Oh, you don't want me. Take one of the children and the dog," or "No, let me get one of you now, Molly, with Liam and Paula and the children," hoping to God she would run out of film before I ran out of plausible objections to having my acquaintance with that mischievous child indelibly recorded. Doreen, I saw, was exquisitely aware of these deceptions and perversely determined to outwit them. She insisted shrilly, several times, that "there ought to be one of me and Carl and Elizabeth," suggestions which I managed to divert until at last she dragged Elizabeth by the hand to my beach chair and arranged an invidious little domestic tableau, with Elizabeth in my lap and herself standing behind my chair with one hand resting on Elizabeth's shoulder and the other looped around my neck with casual intimacy. I could only smile inanely and submit, trying—not very successfully—to discredit the travesty by a look of agonized facetiousness. Molly, full of pathetic admiration for it nonetheless, stood in front of us bowed over her infernal little camera and with a click like a hammer driving a stake into the sand dutifully entered it into the shabby archives of our life.

On the next afternoon Doreen came across the sand from her family's beach plot to invite Elizabeth to pop corn with her. "We have a grill down here," she said, "and we're going to make a whole big pan of popcorn. Can she come?"

"I don't know," I said. "You'll have to ask her mother."

"Can she, Molly?"

"Well, I guess so," Molly said, "if your mother and father don't mind. I think it would be all right, don't you, Carl?"

"I guess so," I said. "Now don't be a nuisance, Elizabeth."

Elizabeth shook her head in dumb obedience.

"Oh, good!" Doreen cried. "I'll see she doesn't eat too much, or get in any trouble or anything." She took Elizabeth by the wrist and hauled her to her feet with the admonition: "Come on now, Elizabeth; and you've got to promise to be very good, or you won't get any popcorn!"

They went galloping off hand in hand across the sand to where the Torrances had spread their blankets and set up their parasol and a little portable charcoal burner, twenty-five yards or so away from us across the beach. Molly stood up and watched the children race hopping and cringing through the hot sand until they had reached the Torrances' enclave, where they were greeted with outstretched arms and laughingly embraced by Doreen's mother. Molly waved to her and called out, "Do you mind having Elizabeth for a little while, Mary? Doreen invited her to make some popcorn with you."

"Oh, of course not!" Mary Torrance called back. "You had Doreen all morning. We'd be delighted."

"Don't let her eat too much."

"No, we won't. Don't worry."

Liam all this while had been on an expedition of his own along the stretch of beach that ran south of us beyond the last of the cottages. I had glanced in that direction occasionally and seen his figure, growing larger and more distinct, approaching us along the landward ridge of dunes, the dog shambling along beside him, pattering off occasionally on diversions of its own. A hundred yards away, he paused now, and called out, waving to us from a clump of sea oats on a sandy hillock, "Hey! I've found something interesting up here. Why don't you come and look?"

"What is it?" Paula shouted.

"A shipwreck. It's an old one. It's fabulous! There's some fine planks, in good condition."

"Oh, let's go and see!" Paula cried. She stood up eagerly, snatching her sunglasses from the blanket. "We been wantin' to find a piece of timber for a coffee table. Come on, you-all. This'll be *fun!*" Molly rose obediently and began to brush the sand from the backs of her legs.

"I don't know," I said. "Maybe I'd better stay here and keep an eye on Elizabeth."

"Oh, now come on, Carl! You got to see this. And anyway, we might need some help diggin' out a piece of plank. Elizabeth's all right with Tom and Mary."

"It ought to be interesting," Molly said. "I don't know why you never want to do anything."

I closed my book and stood up reluctantly. "All right. Maybe I should bring a crowbar or something."

"No, we might not need it. We can always come back." She waved to Liam and called out, "We're comin', honey. Hold your horses."

Molly turned and shouted across the beach to the Torrances, "We'll be back in a minute. We're just going up the beach a little way!"

Tom Torrance raised his hand and shouted back, "Take your time. Don't worry about a thing. She'll be fine."

We set out, slogging through the hot sand to where Liam stood among the sea oats grinning like a boy. "It's amazing that I found this," he said as we approached him. "I haven't been back here in the dunes for ages. This thing must have been lying exposed for months."

"How much further is it?" Paula said. "I'm just about pooped already."

"Not far. Twenty yards or so. Come on, you can make it."

He led us in a panting single file across the crest of the dunes and then plowing down them through the soft sand into a little valley on the landward side. It appeared to have been newly excavated by the wind funneling through a cleft in the dunes, because at its far perimeter the sea oats were bent over and half buried with the weight of fresh-drifted sand piled against their stalks. On the floor of the little vale the remains of a buried ship were clearly and dramatically visible: a five-foot-long span of hull rising at a sharp, insurgent angle from the sand in a startling and mythic way. There was a section of three planks, fastened to a pair of curved ribs whose broken tips jutted up into the sky like the tips of fingers groping irrepressibly from a grave. The wood was a beautiful, pale, weathered gray, furrowed with rambling longitudinal grooves and broken at its ends into sprays of silvery splinters. There was something faintly harrowing about it, like a skeleton disinterred by the inexorable weather of the world. We stood and looked at it in a kind of humbled astonishment; I did, anyway; I'm not sure what the others felt; although Liam was evidently similarly moved, because he stood with a bemused, soft smile for several seconds without making any move to approach the bared timbers.

"Oh, that's marvelous!" Paula said. "That's just beautiful wood! You reckon we can find a piece big enough for a table?"

"I don't know," Liam said. "It seems a pity to disturb it, somehow."

"How old do you suppose it is?" Molly asked.

"It's probably one of the old coastal schooners. They used to bring down ice from New England, right up through the turn of the century. Not many of them came into the Gulf, though. That's a real find."

"What I want is a hatch cover," Paula said. "I saw one up in Washington the last time I was there. But, my goodness, they cost a *fortune* in those shops. You reckon we can find one, Liam?"

"We might. It'll take some digging, though. What we ought to do is bring shovels down and work on it a little bit at a time, day by day."

"Well, now you've got your work cut *out* for you! I'm just not goin' to be *happy* till we find a hatch cover!"

Liam dropped down the last stretch of duneside to the wreck and squatted over the exposed timbers to run his palms along the smooth, pale surfaces. We followed him. "It's a very old ship," he said. "You see, these planks are doweled, not riven." He looked up at Molly and smiled. "I never found a wreck before. And I've been walking this beach for years."

"Well, come on, let's dig!" Paula said. She crouched down and plunged her fingers into the soft sand beside the planks.

"I don't think we'll find much, like that," Liam said. "This is a section of the stern, from the look of it. I'd say the hull ran out that way, about forty-five degrees from the beach, at least a hundred feet. Those were big boats. And it'll be deep. What I'll do is bring some stakes and line down tomorrow and mark out a plat."

"But, Liam, this thing might be all covered up again by tomorrow."

"I don't think so. The wind has been boring through that breach for months. It'll help us, if anything." He stood up and raked his fingers through his hair. "I think we ought to go and have a julep, to celebrate."

"Well, I'll go along with that," Paula said. "It's just about happy time, anyway."

We started back toward our little encampment on the beach. I trotted down to the water's edge and walked along the cool, damp shingle because the soles of my feet were scalded by the hot sand of the dunes. The women, who wore canvas sandals, and Liam, who seemed inured or impervious to the heat, trudged through the wide, dry stretch of beach above. He stopped occasionally to pick up a chunk of driftwood and hurl it out into the water for the dog to fetch. She went galloping frenziedly after it and plunged in to the gentle, pale green swell of surf, swimming out in a determined and enraptured pursuit of it. The women stood laughing and applauding. I turned away impatiently and went on toward the spot where our bright blue-and-yellow umbrella was planted above our blankets and canvas deck chairs on the sand. In the distance, I saw the children come running back to it from the Torrances' site, Elizabeth carrying a waxed-paper bag of what I supposed was popcorn. She tumbled down onto the blankets and began to scrape together the kernels that had spilled out of the bag. Doreen stood watching her, her hands on her hips, then turned to glance down at the sand; and in slowly dawning horror I saw her bend down to pick up from beside my beach chair the book that I had set there when I went to view the wreck. This book was profusely illustrated with full-page color photographs of syphilitic patients, all of them entirely naked and with their genitals and breasts and skin blighted with lesions of the disease. I was something like thirty yards away, near enough to see with paralyzing clarity the avid yet oddly indolent engrossment with which she turned and studied the pages, but not nearly close enough to have intervened, to have prohibited or interrupted that weirdly composed, languidly protracted act. I had no idea of what to do. I was afraid to shout at her; Liam and the women were still gazing seaward, absorbed in Enitharmom's exploits; I didn't want to call their attention to what was happening, and for some reason, I didn't want the child to know that I had seen. I stood there for an awful moment, until, with a kind of poised, ironically exaggerated care, as if she were returning to its casket some exquisite and very fragile treasure—a decorated eggshell or a delicate porcelain curio—that I had allowed her to fondle for a moment, she closed the book, bent down and replaced it on the sand, and then sat down demurely beside Elizabeth, taking the bag of popcorn from her and daintily extracting one kernel at a time with her fingertips and putting it in her mouth. I turned my back to her hastily and crouched down on the sand, as if I had for some time been examining an interesting piece of flotsam, so that if she glanced in our direction she would not be aware that I had seen her.

Evidently, she wasn't. When we got back to the site she was chatting to Elizabeth in her casual, animated, faintly theatrical way, chiding her for getting butter on the blanket, rapping her reprovingly on the wrist.

"Where have you *been?*" she said, raising her face to us with pretended petulance. "We brought you some popcorn, but then you weren't here, so we started eating it ourselves."

"Well, that wasn't very nice of you," Paula said. "And here I was just dyin' for some popcorn."

"Well, there's a little bit left. But it might have some sand in it. Elizabeth spilled it and then put it back in the bag. She's such a problem."

"Well, never mind, honey. We're goin' up to the house, anyway, and have a little drink before dinner. Would you like to come and have a Coke with us?"

"Thank you. I'll help you carry the things up, but I won't have any Coke. It will spoil my dinner."

We began to gather up and pack our paraphernalia. I picked up one of the blankets and held it by one edge, waving it aloft and flapping the sand out of it. Doreen stood watching me in a disturbing, ruminative way.

"Can I help you, Carl?" she said. "I'm a good folder."

"All right. You take that end."

She took hold of the opposite end of it and walked toward me, holding it carefully aloft and pleating and patting it fussily, fastidious as a housewife. When we had finished, she stood holding it while I plucked the umbrellas from the sand, dismantled and collapsed them and bound the ribs together with tie cords that dangled from their shafts. I saw that she was lingering, waiting to accompany me, and so I took unnecessarily long at the task. Liam and the women had folded the deck chairs and packed the baskets, towels, blankets, thermos jugs, and beach balls, and had set out for the house before I finished tying up the umbrellas. We followed after them, slogging ankle-deep through the soft sand. I don't know why I obliged the child by lingering behind. I think there was something subtly imperative in her manner that demanded my compliance, that suggested she had something to say to me in private. Judging by her equanimity, however, it was nothing unduly dramatic or unsettling. She trudged along beside me in such an imperturbable and apparently congenial silence that I began to imagine, with a kind of frantic self-deception, that the incident had not occurred. Perhaps, at that distance, I had mistaken her action. Or, if not, perhaps she hadn't seen any of the illustrations; perhaps it was only the text she had been poring over, bemused by the clinical vocabulary. Perhaps she wanted to ask me the meaning of some piece of abstruse terminology that had piqued her curiosity. She let me wonder about it for twenty yards or more. Then, when the others had reached the steps and gone up them to the front porch, where Molly stood holding the screen door open for us, she murmured in a serenely taunting, confidential tone, her eyes still fixed on the sand, "I know what it is you look at all the time. I know the kind of stuff you like."

Out of the depths of my devastation I heard myself muttering to that terrible child, "That's an awful thing to say. Don't you know I'm a doctor? I have to look at things like that." I don't know which was more horrifying: the imputation or the brazen, appallingly unchildlike air of venality, and of familiarity, with which she made it. My startled reply was muttered not as if to a malicious child but as if to some presumptuous queen, some Medea who had dared to vilify her lord. "You ought to be ashamed," I said more firmly, trying to assume a tone of stern piety subdued enough to keep my words from being overheard by Molly, fifty yards away on the porch steps.

"I don't see why," Doreen said in a calm, satirical voice elevated just sufficiently, and expertly, to cause me alarm. "I don't see why *I'm* the one that ought to be ashamed."

"What do you mean by that?"

"You know what I mean. You pretend you're so—*dignified*—and high and mighty and everything, but you're not. I know what you're really like. You don't ever take your clothes off because you like to act so terribly *modest* all the time; but you're not. You don't care whether people see you, *sometimes.*"

I stopped and turned toward her, feeling my face grow pale and my body cold with a ghastly welling up of dread, like icy water, in my breast. She went on a step or two ahead of me and then turned back and looked at me like a malignant fairy, a gloating, elfin smile twisting slowly upward the corners of her coral lips. "You even *let* people, sometimes." A fey, fierce giggle simmered in her throat, rising into a crystal burst of laughter that spurted from her lips across the sunny air between us like a splash of glittering vitriol. I don't know what mindless obtusity had prevented me from recognizing or suspecting her before, but until that moment I had never had the slightest intimation that it was *she*—that the peal of scalding laughter I had heard from among the leaves of the catalpa tree outside the rest room of the Bayou Restaurant had welled, unmistakably, from that same slender throat; that for the past ten days I had unknowingly been subjected to the mockery and contumely of this dreadful little charlatan. I could have been forgiven, perhaps, for not recognizing her by sight, since, ensconced at that hellish urinal in my base pretense of being unaware of her, I had never dared to meet her eyes; I had never looked up at her directly through the window or held my gaze long enough in her direction to see more than a blur of golden hair and pale limbs and bright-colored cotton fabric among the branches—but that insidious coquetry, those insinuations of a secret, indecent intimacy between us, that cruel derision of my marriage, of Molly's devotion to me, of my pretensions as a husband and a father, that satirical disparagement of my learning, my decorum, my famed sobriety—by what monstrous lapse of insight or acumen or simple intelligence had I failed to interpret those all too eloquent allusions to my disgrace? All this time, all these days and hours, with every word and action and gesture, she had been reviling me, holding me in secret, insolent contempt. But had it indeed been secret? Had she thought I was truly unaware of her identity, or had she supposed that I had recognized her and, even more perniciously, been conducting what she believed to be our concerted, vile deception of Molly and the others? Had she supposed us to be partners in a lewd, covert intrigue conceived in cynical collusion and carried on before the very eyes of its victims with shameless delight? Looking into those cerulean eyes embedded like the dawn sky with pale silver stars, I shuddered to think them capable of such a vicious hoax. Perfidy of those dimensions and that peculiar virulence seemed to defile not only me, not only my wife, and child, and friends, and profession, but in some terrible, all-subversive way, the whole society of men. Had I been a party to such a deed, even unconsciously? I loathed and feared this child.

"I don't know what you mean, Doreen," I mumbled, and lowered my head in such abject humiliation that I could not muster the energy or resolution for even the pretense of indignation, or to demand—cautiously; I dared not provoke her rashly—an explanation. The chaos of my feelings was mercifully diverted by the sight of Molly waving to me from the cottage steps.

"Carl!" she called out. "Yoo-hoo! Come on now! We're going to have drinks, and Paula wants you to bring a case of Coke in from the shed. Liam's gone to Oglethorpe for some ice."

I raised my head and nodded, smiling and waving to her like a lost soul signaling to a loved one from the fumes of hell.

"I'm coming," I called. She went into the cottage, letting the screen door slam closed behind her. Doreen turned her head at the sound, watching Molly disappear onto the porch; then she turned back to face me with the same lewd, elfin smile.

"You go for a walk every morning up the beach, don't you? I see you when I get up. I get up early, too."

I grunted wretchedly.

"Where do you go?"

"I don't know. Nowhere special. Just up the beach."

"Why don't you take me with you sometime? I know some places we could go."

"I like to walk alone."

"Well, I don't see why I can't go with you. I'll bet we could have fun."

"I have to go, Doreen," I said. "I'll take that umbrella now. They're waiting for me."

"That's all right, I can carry it." She clutched the umbrella possessively to her chest and followed beside me as I turned and resumed my walk toward the cottage, trying to slow my steps so that it would not so obviously resemble flight. The hot sand sprayed up from our toes with a sound of whispering. "You could show me how to be a doctor," she said. "You could show me how to examine people and everything." I closed my eyes and felt the plummeting of my heart into an abyss. "Did you know my daddy has a store on Main Street, right beside the Bayou Restaurant?" Her voice pattered on in a composed, conversational way—such a perfect imitation of the artless chattering of a little girl that I felt a kind of insane admiration for her virtuosity.

I shook my head spastically and croaked, "No."

"Well, he does. And I go by there almost every day after school, because I like to play in the backyard. There's a tree there that I like to climb up in. I can see all over the roofs for *miles*. And I can see right in that *window!*" She paused for an excruciating moment. "Did you ever see me there?"

"No," I said in a hoarse whisper. "I don't know what you mean. What window? I never saw you anywhere before."

"Well, I've seen *you*. And I know what you *do*."

"I have no idea what you're talking about," I said in my quaking whisper, like the voice of a man on his deathbed. "If you think you saw me—anywhere —before, you must be mistaken. I never go near that restaurant. You must have seen somebody else."

"Oh, no, I didn't. It was *you*. And I can *prove* it. Because Millie is the waitress in there, and she knows me, and all I've got to do is *ask* her." She gave an infantile, derisive snicker: "So *hah!* I'll bet *Molly* would be surprised if she knew what you did. And Liam, and Paula! My *parents* certainly would be." I plunged on through the hot sand in hopeless, wordless, nauseous despair. She came trotting a step or two behind me, deliberately and scornfully kicking up sand with her toes against my trouser legs. At the cottage steps I stood the shaft of the umbrella against the wall and stared at her. She set her umbrella beside mine and returned my stare with a contemptuous assurance before which my gaze began to crumble.

"Are you sure you don't want a Coke?" I murmured.

"No, thank you. My mother doesn't like me to have anything right before suppertime."

"Oh. Well, then, I guess I'll say goodbye." I smiled at her in a sickly way and started up the steps.

"I hope I see you tomorrow," Doreen called as I opened the screen door. "I'll be watching for you in the morning."

I felt like weeping. Whether for the profligate child who stood watching me from the bottom of the steps, or for myself, I don't know; or for the innocence from which we both were orphaned, from whose ashes my gray eminence had arisen like a specter to walk the earth in bewilderment and loss.

I did not sleep that night. I lay awake beside Molly in the big old iron bed in a kind of conscious nightmare, staring for hours at the faint, viscous moon-light that clung to the pale walls of the room clotted with lumps of shadow in the curdled darkness. It was stiflingly hot. Although the windows were open at the front and back of the house, there was no stir of air whatever. Through the seaside window I could hear the distant mournful clapping of the waves, but no breeze blew off the water; and from the landward window there was a wandering bitter scent of vetch and the endless shrilling of cicadas in the swamp, a merciless, faint shriek like the creak of ceaselessly revolving mill wheels: those of the gods, I thought; which grind slowly but exceeding fine. It is a very strange thing to know that the night in which one has consciousness divides one's life in two; that before one lies only ruin, nights of sickening shame as interminable and agonized as this one, a sordid obscurity stretching to the grave. Something like the pale, consuming nullity I had experienced after Lubby's death and which I had invoked again in my first morning on the beach seemed to yawn before me, to lap at my feet and ankles, and devour them, as I stepped into it, like an infinite, cool, colorless sea of soothing acid. Behind me lay everything I had ever made or acquired or striven to impose upon the world: the model airplanes I had built so patiently as a boy, the rock collection on the shelf above my bed, the scholarships I had won, my marriage, my career, my years of ceaseless work and study, the monographs I had published and which already had received auspicious attention, all those auguries of the brilliant career for which I longed and which they seemed to promise —and before me that pale, boundless ocean of oblivion from whose waters an odorless, chilling gust blew across my face and throat as I stood ankle-deep in it and stared out across its infinite, exotic wastes. I don't know what I dreaded most: that she would expose me, or that I would yield to her—that I would take her with me in the morning and postpone that ignominy by a day, a week, a year, perhaps forever, by compounding it, by committing ever more and fouler acts to seal my degradation. Perhaps she was right, I thought. Perhaps she knew me better than anyone. Perhaps it would be less infamous than just if she should lure me into the only true intimacy I could ever hope to attain with anyone, one profane and perilous enough to meet the measure of my desolation. After all, the child was already corrupt; what could be added to her depravity? There was something almost augustly absolute about it, like the falling of a star. I watched the moonlight creep motionlessly, hour after hour, across the floor as the great spheres of the cosmos wheeled and turned in their relentless precision toward another dawn, the one that would unmake me. Occasionally Molly stirred restlessly beside me and murmured something in her sleep, some habitual complaint, some shriveled scrap of censure which she seemed to offer in feverish testimony of my guilt. Toward dawn Elizabeth began to turn and whimper in her cot against the wall, as if already she felt and were harrowed by the squalid legacy I left her, the knowledge of her father's degradation. I got up and went across the room to see if I could ease her discomfort, reaching down to free her arms and legs from the damp, tangled sheets with such extravagant, tender solicitude that I myself broke into a cynical, tortured smile, standing above her in the dark.

I went into the kitchen and made tea, sitting at the table by the window that faced the Torrances' cottage and watching, as it began to emerge out of the dissipating darkness, to see if Doreen was abroad. But the stretch of

beach below the cottage was empty, and on a wire clothesline in the backyard her blue bathing suit hung limply in the dim light like the skin of a
flayed animal. I thought of her watching from a window of the cottage opposite as I watched from this one, the two of us staring across the sandy field
of dune grass that separated us in such a fulsome parody of a lovers' vigil that
I would not have been surprised if the boards of the two old stately, weather-
beaten houses had groaned in humiliation at being made a party to it. Nature, I thought, should accommodate art, or piety, by remonstrating in some
audible, explicit way. But, even more eloquently perhaps, with an impassive
irony, she accommodated me instead. It began to rain; a heavy, absolutely
vertical, tropical downpour that fell from the dour heavens with the theatrical suddenness of a movie thunderstorm, bending the field of dune grass
almost flat beneath it, filling the hollows of the beaten sand with stippled
pools, and drumming on the roof like the hoofbeats of a herd. It lasted no
more than fifteen minutes and then abated to a fitful drizzle, one that served
me very well, however, as a pretext for not venturing out to take my customary walk. Instead, I took my briefcase out onto the front porch and began to
compose my monthly report to send to Dr. Turner in Bethesda. I worked for
half an hour on the résumé, marshaling my statistics and composing my
sentences with a scrupulousness and diligence almost consciously designed to
refute the watchful, silent opprobrium with which the world seemed to teem
like the silence of a courtroom.

At around eight o'clock, the others began to appear in their bathrobes and
pajamas, water began to splash in the bathroom and the kitchen sink; there
was the smell of percolating coffee and the sizzle of frying eggs and bacon; the
tinkle of cutlery and china; the earnest, jocular sounds of life resuming, impervious, vigorous, sane. I sat on the front porch listening with the envy of a
reprobate standing with his ear cupped at the gate of heaven. Molly came to
the door of the porch in her bathrobe and said, "Oh, you're still here. I guess
you didn't go for your walk."

"Not in the rain. I wouldn't have gone this morning, anyway. I've got to
get this report off to Dr. Turner."

"Oh. It's awful the way you have to work, even on vacation."

"Well, that's the way it is with doctors. You know that by now."

"I know. I've got you a nice breakfast, anyway. Liam can't go sailing either,
so we thought we'd have an early breakfast. I got some of that Canadian bacon
you like."

"Thank you," I said, and smiled at her, feeling a surge of startling affection,
as if my heart had tumbled over unexpectedly in my breast. An anticipation
of her undeserved humiliation, I thought miserably; certainly not love, from
me. A kind of sentimental, precursory plea for clemency. And yet I felt so truly

humbled at that moment by her simple, unassailable devotion that my voice became unsteady as I spoke. "You're very good to me, Molly."

"Well, I just wish I could give you all you deserve. I try to."

I smiled at her gently. Liam appeared behind her in the doorway and laid his hands on her shoulders.

"Going to clear up," he said cheerfully. "We'll be able to go up to the wreck and do some digging."

I looked up through the screen and saw that it was true. The clouds had broken and there were great shafts of sunlight spraying down on the earth and water from patches of clear sky as blue as mountain lakes.

After breakfast, the excavation of the wreck began. The women forfeited their morning stroll along the beach with Elizabeth, and Liam his daily sail. While Paula and Molly washed the dishes and straightened up the kitchen he went out to the tool shed in the backyard and found a bundle of tent stakes, a reel of heavy fishing line, a shovel, and some garden trowels. He and the women carried them up across the dunes, with Elizabeth staggering after them, to the shipwreck site. I did not go with them. I excused myself temporarily by explaining that I had nearly finished my report and was anxious to get it mailed off to Bethesda that afternoon. I would join them when I had finished it, I said; within half an hour or so. I went back onto the front porch and sat down in the rocking chair to check my figures and make my final assessment of the project's accomplishments to date. It was a still, bright, lucid morning, one of those days of almost haunted clarity that sometimes occur along the sea after a thunderstorm. The air was washed to a cool transparency and sounds carried through it with a fragile distinctness, as if under the dome of a bell jar. My concentration on my work was fitful; I glanced up constantly at the stretch of sand in front of the Torrance cottage and then, alternately, at my wristwatch, watching the minutes advance from ten o'clock to ten-fifteen. I had become familiar with the daily schedule of the family's activities; I knew that by eleven they would be on the beach to set up their umbrella and spread their blankets on the sand. At five minutes before the hour they appeared, Mary and her parents carrying blankets and picnic baskets and their striped umbrella, Tom following them with Doreen astride his shoulders, clutching a thermos bottle and a bright red rubber beach ball. I watched them set up their encampment, feeling secure in the shadow of the porch. I knew that at that distance, and behind the semi-opacity of the old screens, rusted and billowing loosely in their panels, it was impossible for them to distinguish anyone sitting there. In a cold, nauseous anxiety I watched to see if I could detect any evidence of the child's betrayal of me: an arm extended and a finger pointed toward our cottage; a lengthy consultation with her parents, punctuated with frequent glances directed toward the porch, and followed, perhaps, by Tom breaking away to stride determinedly across the sand in my direction. No such dismaying set of events occurred; they went about their usual daily routine in apparent, blessed unconcern; there were no furtive or indignant glances cast in my direction; they chattered happily while they unpacked their baggage and spread out their blankets and smeared each other with suntan oil and stretched out in the sun. Tom and Doreen and her grandfather entered into a lively game of soccer with the beach ball, the men's shouts ringing across the stretch of sand between us, apparently oblivious of me and of her sordid testimony. I am safe, I thought, for a while longer, at least. She will keep her secret for another day, or several, perhaps until we are about to leave. The little devil is delighting in my torment; but she hasn't finished with me.

After a quarter of an hour or so I felt reassured enough to resume my work with a sense of comparative security, distracted only by the sound of Doreen's voice tinkling through the fresh, pellucid air with an intermittent, delicate, derisive sound like the tittering of goblins. It was enough to prevent me from summoning up any genuine enthusiasm or energy for my subject. I stared at my table of notes and data without being able to discover in them anything of sufficient importance, or urgency, or dignity to inspire my usual spate of robust, stately prose. When I did finally compose and inscribe a phrase—in an unpleasantly vivid blue ink—it had an inflated, florid look of ostentation, even of fraudulence, that seemed to violate the purity of the white paper it was written on: *All this I consider to be a body of scientific data of inestimable value which justifies everything that has gone into it in the way of money, labor, sacrifice, and skill. We do not fear to be judged—* It had a distinctly hollow, meretricious sound. I scratched it out and began again: *I cannot sufficiently extol your enlightened stewardship—* This equally unlovely piece of rhetoric was interrupted by a scream; a sound of hopeless, devastated protest against the perversity of life. It reminded me in an agonizing way of the look in Molly's eyes when she had seen Elizabeth sitting happily at the kitchen table in Liam's lap, as if that expression had been translated into sound. It rose to an unbearably piercing vibrancy, trembling in the air until something in me seemed to shatter like crystal shattering at a sound of intolerable pitch. I raised my eyes, starting so violently that the briefcase slid from my knees onto the floor scattering papers everywhere. I clutched my fountain pen convulsively, snapping the barrel in my hand. Down below the Torrances' umbrella on the mirror-bright flat sand at the water's edge, Tom Torrance stood holding Doreen's limp body in his arms, her legs and one arm dangling strengthlessly, her head hanging back across his wrist, her wet hair swinging like a sheath of golden dripping seaweed as he rocked her slowly back and forth in a perverse, strangely peaceful caricature of contentment, as if he were trying to lull her into sleep. In the bleak bright instant in which I saw the scene, the figures of the other members of the family were frozen into immobile, frenziedly suspended attitudes like figures frozen in the flickering illumination of a strobe light. Her mother's hands were outstretched toward the little girl's limp body in a grotesquely theatrical way, like a nineteenth-century illustration of a melodrama; the grandmother had half arisen from the sand, her outspread fingers clasped to her ears in an almost comical excess of horror; the grandfather, incongruously rising from the water like an implacable Poseidon, stretched out one hand, open-palmed, toward the scene, as if offering it in illustration of the disastrous negligence of mortals. I heard the confused uproar of their shouts, the long, tormented shriek sinking to a sob of agony, a wolfish howl of despair from the stricken father, who still stood swinging the child in his arms, almost indignantly now, as if demanding her to awaken, to stir, to be alive. Watching the lifeless swinging of her limbs, I was swept by a sudden vicious exultation. A feeling of such miraculous reprieve, of amnesty, flooded through me that, like air gulped by a suffocating man, it made me light-headed for a moment, dizzily confounded by my fortune. I suppose the best that can be said for me is that I never for an instant regarded it as an act of divine intervention—less from humility than out of my relentless pragmatism. I recognized, even while I sat and marveled at them, that the circumstances of this strange dispensation were too equivocal for it to be attributed to God— although I suppose that if I had expressed the burst of ruthless jubilation in my breast in words, I would have murmured, impenitently, "Thank God. I am saved." My thanks were due, more likely, to the devil, whose protégé it was more reasonable to assume I was; a child's life for my undamaged reputation was certainly a diabolical exchange. But I had no sense of blessing by either god or fiend; the nearest thing to reverence I felt was a kind of licentious awe at the magnificent impartiality of chance. Lazarus had been miraculously granted life; and Faust, delight and power; but at the price of the submission of the spirit. I owed no such tribute. Pride, honor, dignity, the untroubled tenor of my life, all were restored by one prodigious stroke of fortune, freely, without the demand for humility or piety or faith; only the intelligence to turn its largesse to account.

One of the women screamed, *"Go get the doctor!"* with a sound more of fury than of grief, as if to challenge my title to this unblest salvation. I got up swiftly and went into the parlor, bumping into the edge of a little display table and knocking over the bud vase with a sprig of larkspur in it that Paula had placed there the afternoon before. By the time I had set it upright, wiped up the water with my shirt sleeve, and replaced the stem of the flower in the vase, I heard the pound of running feet on the sand outside the screen porch. I stepped into the bedroom. There was no closet, but there was an old-fashioned walnut wardrobe with a mirrored door at the far end of the room. I went and stood behind it, pressing my back against the wall so that I was out of sight to anyone entering the room. I heard the pounding of a fist on the frame of the screen door and the voice of an elderly man, rough with age, exertion, and panic, shouting, "Doctor! Dr. Proctor! Dr. Ransome! Someone, help! Help, please! I think Doreen has drowned!" While I stood there I recited with silent precision in my mind the complete Heart-Lung Resuscitation Method, Modified after Safar. Step by step, the table of procedures ran through my mind as exactly as if I were rehearsing them for an examination: *If a spontaneous effective heartbeat is not restored after 1–2 minutes of cardiac compression, have qualified assistant give epinephrine 0.5 mg (0.5–1 ml of 1:1000 aqueous solution) diluted to 10 ml I.V. every 3–5 minutes as indicated. Epinephrine may be given by the intracardiac route if necessary. Promote intravenous fluids, vasoactive drugs. The use of tourniquets on the extremities may be of value.* While I recited the phrases silently I saw myself, with equal clarity, performing the technic, bending to press my lips to that small, moist, coral-colored mouth, and as I breathed my life into it, watching the black-lashed, sapphire-colored eyes open slowly to gaze up at me with what would become their lifelong mockery. Outside the house I heard the man's voice crying hopelessly, "They're not here! They must have gone out! Tom, they're not here! What shall I do?" I stood motionless behind the wardrobe, and in a moment heard the creak of the screen door opening and then the hasty, distracted blundering of footsteps across the porch, through the living room, into the kitchen, back across the parlor to the door of the bedroom where I stood behind the wardrobe, then to the foot of the stairs and halfway up them, where they paused in exhaustion or resignation. The silence that followed was profound and endless. For a moment I had the impression that time had stopped, that there was nothing any longer to divide or measure it. But in the next instant it resumed, and I heard again my pulse pounding in my temples with a remorseless, metrical persistence, like the throbbing of a locust in the dark. The man's voice called out again, in hoarse, anguished desperation, "Dr. Proctor! Paula! Dr. Ransome! My God, where are they?" Then the footsteps retreated swiftly through the living room, across the porch, and down the front steps. An instant later I heard the screen door, flung open in the man's flight, snap shut with a crack like a rifle shot against the sill. I waited another minute or two, then went quickly out of the bedroom, through the parlor to the kitchen, and down the back steps at the rear of the house to the sandy backyard. I stood for a moment looking back toward the beach, which was out of sight behind the dunes, then I turned and ran across the garden through Paula's dusty beds of larkspur to a sandy glade that stretched between the dunes and the palmetto scrub and live oak of the hammock. In the shelter of the dunes, I could no longer hear the cries from the beach or the clap of water on sand. It was sunny and still, and a mild, warm, idyllic calm lay on the earth. I heard the gentle droning of a bee blundering among the purple blossoms of the railroad vines that grew along the sandy slopes. It moved from flower to flower with tranquil diligence, blowsy with pollen and nectar. I sat down on the slope of a dune to regain my breath, my elbows on my knees and my shoulders drooping loosely. My hands hung limply earthward and I studied them with an inordinate curiosity. I saw that they were beautiful in a way and to a degree that I had never before appreciated: the fingers so prodigally slender, shapely, complex, and articulate. There were twenty-seven bones in each hand, as delicately and intricately conjoined as the web of stars on summer nights above the sea. I moved the fingers one by one, experimentally, astonished at their skill and responsiveness. As if to test their dexterity, I plucked one of the blossoms from a vine and attempted to furl back the edges of its petal without tearing or crushing it, as if I were performing a very delicate operation on a vital organ. The soft, moist membrane resembled the pericardium of a heart, and I was reminded suddenly of the operation I had helped to perform on a Malayan girl who had been brought into the emergency room at George Washington University Hospital when I was a resident and who had died while my hands were struggling to repair her heart. A sense of sickening fulmination took place in me like an abscess swelling to the point of bursting, and I recognized that I was committing a sacrilege that I dared not complete.

I lunged up to my feet and began to run back to the cottage, plowing desperately through the deep sand, scattering the stakes as I raced through Paula's garden, plunging around the corner of the house and up across the ridge of dunes that sloped down to the flat expanse of beach before the water. When I reached the crest of it, I sank down to my knees, panting with exhaustion and staring out across the empty sand in front of the cottages. The Torrances' umbrella was tilted slightly askew as if someone had bumped into it, the wicker basket beneath it was tumbled over and a bright red apple had spilled out and rolled across the blanket to the sand. There was no one in sight, anywhere, neither on the beach nor at the cottage, and the old blue automobile which always stood parked beside the picket fence of their backyard was gone. Otherwise, the sunny calm serenity of the beach was undisturbed; there was the gentle clap of rollers on the strand, a gull flew languidly above the line of breakers, a single cloud, as white and soft as snow, hung in the faultless blue; far out on the glinting water a tiny steamer trailed a plume of smoke across the calm horizon.

I knelt there, groveling in panic, gasping with exertion, trying to compose my celebrated reason, to arrange the facts toward some logical conclusion. What must I do? Where had they gone? In which direction? What in the name of God must I do? The nearest town was Oglethorpe, ten miles away, but it was no more than a crossroads: a country store, a filling station, a lunchroom, a feed-and-grain store—certainly there was no doctor or hospital; not even a drugstore or a pharmacist. I tried to remember the succession of towns we had driven through before it; they were far apart and equally primitive, equally unlikely to have medical facilities. There might, however, be other towns that did, whose locations were unknown to me, any one of which might have been their destination. I could have driven forever without finding it. And in any case, even if I had known where they were going, and had found them, how in the name of heaven could I explain why, having failed to hear their cries for help, I had decided, sometime later, to come hurtling after them? And in any case, I saw, lowering my eyes to my wristwatch, it was too late. Nothing could save her now.

I knelt there, plucking up handfuls of sand and letting it trickle through my fingers helplessly, imbecilically absorbed in the procedure, watching idly while a chip of bright red glass slipped through my fingers in the stream of sand. It seemed to me like my own shining reputation, so miraculously, inexorably salvaged, exposed with equally ruthless caprice as a gaud, a bauble, a bit of shiny rubble plucked out of infinity by the hand of chance and let slide into the light between its fingers. Not only that bright trinket of my fame, but the whole world of phenomena had been cast up by the aimless groping of that phantom hand. It was a heap of worthless, quaint, or vile rummage: this sunny beach, the gulls, the glinting water, the idyllic sea, the gaudy sun itself had been ransomed out of oblivion, as I had, by utter, wanton hazard, by a soulless, blind indifference that only a few minutes before I had exalted as a splendid prodigality, the author and savior of my eminence. It was the author as well, I thought, staring about at it, of this world of gilded dross, of rabid vanity and dire, perverted lust and treachery and self-betrayal, this glittering, jingling, incoherent farrago that reflected nothing but the insensate anarchy of the hand that had fashioned it, as devoid of purpose, principle, or glory as my own inane renown. What might be cast up in the next handful? A severed, delicate ear, a single sapphire eye twinkling like a lost jewel, some appalling scrap of a whole and lovely form or perfect nature that could never be known, never consummated or restored. I closed my eyes and wiped my hands convulsively against my breast, feeling a horror I had not felt since I was a boy, when the knowledge of syphilis had awakened it in me—a horror I had sworn to refute by my profession! I lurched up to my feet and stared out at the sea. A kind of primordial fusion took place in me as I looked out at the blue water in the calm, voluptuous light, a congealing of my horror into an adamant, cold matrix. All that was inchoate in me—the confusion, the panic, the revulsion—slowed in its swirling, molten turmoil and resolved itself into a cool, infrangible core as I prepared myself to accept the sovereignty of the equivalence that wrought the fields of blown, exquisite jade in front of me and sent the gulls abroad in search of carrion and the distant ship on its senseless, picturesque errand. I stood for several minutes, shivering, as I cast my eyes about in an odd, joylessly licentious way at the world in which I had condemned myself to live, and to survive. Then I bent down and brushed the sand from my trouser legs, carefully, fastidiously, as if about to enter a room where I had been engaged to speak; and then stood up and resumed my gaze out into the blue depths of the sky above the sea.

It seemed that I was destined to go about for the rest of my life with my pockets bulging and jangling with the treasure I now discovered to be counterfeit. The child's death was irrevocable; to acquiesce in my own farcical salvation was therefore exigent; it was all that could be done to redeem this absurd disaster from futility. It would require resolution, intelligence, a spurious and yet curiously valiant self-composure, the exercise of my most famous faculties. There was something if not heroic in it, at least eloquent. I would find, in this meaningless event, a challenge, and an occupation; one that would defer the awful indigence I dared not ever allow myself, through which the knowledge of the void would pour like water through a ruptured dike. In the world to which I was condemned the only virtue, indeed the only possible activity, was to survive. What purpose would it serve now to confess my complicity in the child's death? To add a second victim to the totally gratuitous calamity? To reveal that in my desire to profit by it I had delayed until it was irreversible? To protest the sincerity of my having, finally, relented? The world had chosen to distinguish me; it had presented me with opportunities and honors; it had made me a model of achievement, industry, integrity; what purpose would it serve to disappoint that faith or bankrupt those illusions and investments? It would not restore the child, nor would it truly punish me; it might, on the contrary, furnish me with a comforting sense of expiation which I assuredly did not deserve. Far from a service, it would be a cruel betrayal of that trust and honor. One even worse, perhaps, than the tragedy for which I was not, after all, initially or entirely responsible, which I had only very uncertainly abetted by a moment of weakness, of very human panic. Perhaps I was not responsible at all; perhaps the child was dead beyond recall even before I had fled the scene. Perhaps the greatest service I could do the world, or my profession, or myself was to leave the thing in charitable obscurity. Perhaps to bear the truth in silent sorrow was nobler than to publish it. Perhaps that was the greatest penance I could set myself.

The first step in my survival had been taken: I had begun to justify it. To glorify it, even, I thought, smiling at the intractability of my intelligence. Then, immediately after, I sighed; a vastly sincere sigh of forfeiture, renouncing not only truth but with it every hope of joy or contentment in my work, of simple pleasure, peace, or self-respect, forever. I looked down at the little false gem sparkling at my feet, and decided after a moment that I would leave it there, exposed and flagrantly afire in the light, to divert a passing eye, whether of innocence or of ineffable indulgence. After all, I thought, it is no less precious to a child—or a god—than a chip of stone known as alumina rubeus.

I began to walk quickly along the crest of the dunes, setting my feet toward the wreckage of other men's temerity that my wife and friends were excavating from the heedless sand.

When I came into sight of it around the shoulder of a sand hill, I saw that Liam had marked out with the tent stakes and fishing line a probable outline of the hull, and was heaving damp brown sand, with flagging enthusiasm, with his shovel. Paula was on her knees beside the planks, which were now considerably more exposed, digging industriously along their length with a garden trowel. A little apart from them, on a spread-out towel, Molly was bending over Elizabeth to tie beneath her chin the straps of the yellow sunbonnet that had slipped down across her eyes. As I approached, Liam plunged his shovel blade into the sand and straightened up for a moment to arch his aching back. He caught sight of me and waved, calling out ironically, "Don't hurry, Carl! You'll get your turn!"

"How's it going?" I said as I came closer. "Have you found your hatch cover yet?"

"No, we *haven't!*" Paula said. "Not that I think you give one tiny little *hoot!* You ol' goldbricker."

"After you get down a couple of feet, this sand gets hard," Liam said. "It's like shoveling wet concrete. An hour of this every morning will get you in shape fast." He raised his arm and wiped his forehead with the back of his wrist.

"I'll take over for a while," I said. "Sit down and take it easy."

"He just couldn't wait to get here and start diggin'," Paula said. "Well, I don't know if we'll *let* you now."

"I'll let him," Liam said. "I have a heart of gold." He handed me the shovel and sat down on the slope of a dune, expelling an enormous sigh. "You finish the report?"

"Yes. I'll take it in this afternoon."

"These intellectuals," Paula said. "They don't have any time for us poor workin' folks."

We worked for perhaps another forty minutes in the strange, unnerving, sunny silence fraught with the unseen frenzied actions and agonies transpiring somewhere beyond the crests of the huge, soft-shouldered dunes. The sound of the women's chatter and Liam's occasional laconic comments and Elizabeth's contented crooning as she spooned sand into her bucket, and the regular, pacific grinding of the shovel blade into the damp earth, had a startling, almost profane serenity about them. We seemed to dwell in a little space of illicit and unholy peace, a peace of which we were not permitted to partake, which subsumed even our own miseries, all of them; our complaints and perjuries and aberrations. That sunny silence, the earth's vast, arcane forbearance, appalled me. Or if it was a god's, he understood that man was vile, and would not intervene again. He had sworn it, and the old man had attested to it. All that was required was industry and caution; the only sins were sloth and lack of vigilance. What was it that indicted us? Only silence? Only this awful speechless lenity? For a moment I felt addled in my immunity, like the survivor of a shipwreck, a castaway on a raft in mid-ocean, beset by the limitless clemency of the sea. I set my foot on the shovel blade and leaned on the handle for a moment, nauseated by the confounding impassivity of things.

"You'd better take a breather," Liam said. "Let me have that for a while."

"I think we all better take a breather," Paula said. She stood up and glanced at her wristwatch. "My Lord, it's almost eleven-thirty. We better go back and get some lunch together, Molly. You-all can stay and kill yourselves if you like."

"No, I'm coming, too," Liam said. "I could use a glass of iced tea myself. What do you say, Carl?"

"All right. I am getting a little hot."

We gathered the tools together and walked back toward the cottage. As we approached it, and the tips of the crumbling chimneys came in sight, and then the old gray gables, and then the picket fences and the morning glories, I felt a brightening and clarifying of my blood, a bitter brilliance running through my nerves and mind that I welcomed, knowing it was caution and that so long as it was alive in me my survival was assured.

We went in through the backyard in order to return the tools to the shed. As we filed between the larkspur beds, Paula, who was just ahead of me, paused and looked down with dismay at the trampled flowers. "My Lord, just look at that," she said. "Somebody's been trompin' all over my larkspurs." She clicked her tongue disgustedly.

"Elizabeth, you didn't walk in the flower bed, did you?" Molly asked. Elizabeth shook her head mutely.

"I reckon it was that boy that brought the Pargas yesterday. He's just the *dumbest* thing." She bent down and plucked one of the blossoms from its broken stem. "Well, I was goin' to pick the rest of 'em, anyway, this evenin'."

We put the tools away and went up the back steps into the kitchen. Liam let us pass ahead of him, and when we had done so, reached up to reattach the dangling door spring to the metal hook-eye in the jamb. I realized suddenly that I had heard it spring loose when I had flung the door open in my flight. I watched him warily, rebuking myself silently for my negligence. You won't survive if you're not more vigilant than that, I thought. All that can save you in this world is your intelligence. Elizabeth had to go to the bathroom immediately. Molly hurried her out of the kitchen, plucking impatiently at the buttons of her sunsuit. I heard her voice fading plaintively across the parlor: "I'll bet you *Doreen* doesn't have to have her mother unbutton her buttons for her." It wasn't until that moment that I remembered, with a thrill of dread and of indignation at my own stupidity, that I had left my overturned briefcase and my broken fountain pen on the floor of the front porch when I had leapt up from the rocking chair. Paula handed me an ice tray before I could concoct a plausible excuse to make for the front porch to retrieve them.

"Carl, will you and Liam get the ice out of these things for me? They're just the *damnedest* things to get loose."

"Yes."

The levers on the tray did not work properly, and the cubes either failed to budge at all or splintered. I ran it under hot water and pounded it impatiently with my fist. When the cubes finally came rattling out into the pitcher, I refilled the tray hurriedly and replaced it in the refrigerator.

"If there isn't anything else I can do here," I said, "I think I'll go in and put a dry shirt on."

I had barely started through the kitchen door when Paula said, "There is one more thing you could do for me, Carl, before you get changed. Would you get me a couple of lemons out of the icebox on the stoop?"

"Yes." On the back stoop of the cottage there was a huge old refrigerator that was used to store overflow provisions for guests and weekend parties: melons, buckets of crabs, the spoils of a fishing party. I went out onto the stoop and dug around in the vegetable bin until I found a pair of lemons. As I came back through the screen door, I saw Paula leave the kitchen and go across the parlor to the front porch.

"I have your lemons," I called loudly.

"Thank you. Just set 'em by the sink, will you, Carl?"

"What do you need out there?"

"I can't find one of my good glasses. I think I must have left it out here last night."

She went out onto the porch. Liam was still hammering ice out of a tray with his fist and cursing breathily. "These damn things," he muttered. "We had an icebox up until a couple of years ago, and a good old-fashioned pick. Those were the days." I set the lemons on the shelf beside the sink and went out across the parlor to the door of the front porch. Paula was standing at the waist-high ledge that divided the screen from the wooden paneling below. In one hand she was holding my briefcase, which she had tidied up and latched, and in the other, the two pieces of the shattered fountain pen. She turned her head toward me when she heard me enter the porch, and then back to the screen, to look out across the sand to the Torrances' abandoned beach site.

"I wonder where the Torrances went to," she said. "Looks like they left in an awful hurry."

"They're up at the house, I suppose."

"No. The car's not there. Were they here when you left?"

"Yes, I think so. I'm not really sure; I was working."

"Well, I don't know why they'd leave all that stuff right there on the beach. Looks like somebody kicked over the basket or somethin'. And they left their cooler an' everythin'. I hope they're all right."

There was a strained and teeming moment of silence. "Did you find your glass?" I said.

"No, I didn't." She turned to me, her frown transposing to a vapid smile. "But I found this. I reckon it's yours." She held out the briefcase to me.

"Yes. Yes, I forgot it." I moved to her across the porch and took it from her awkwardly.

"There was papers all over the *floor*. I got 'em together and put 'em inside. Looks like you had a little bit of trouble composin' your report. Looks like *somebody* got a little bit *annoyed.*"

"I did, as a matter of fact." I smiled sheepishly. "I did a draft of it, but I wasn't satisfied. I'll have to do some editing before I send it off."

"Uh-huh. Well, I put it back in there. I don't know if it's in order or not." She held out her open hand, with the broken fountain pen. "I reckon this is yours, too."

"Yes, it is."

"My goodness, you're just goin' to have to learn to control that temper, Dr. Ransome. Just *look* what you did to this thing."

"I'm sorry. I threw it down. It was stupid." I plucked it out of her palm, my smile spreading fatuously. "I went in to get a glass of water before I left, and just forgot about it."

"Well, you were just in a *state*, weren't you? You just had yourself a *tantrum!*" She glanced beyond my shoulder to assure herself that there was no one in the parlor, and then tilted her chin at me, her eyebrows twitching mischievously and her voice falling to a beguiling murmur. "I wonder, could it be that you found it hard to *concentrate? I* hope you didn't have anything on your *mind.*" It wasn't until that moment that I understood her implication, and the nature of the woman's idiotic misconception; and I realized instantly, with a kind of revolted but icy resolution, that it might be profitable, eventually, to confirm it. I put the briefcase under my arm and laid my free hand gently and tentatively on her hip.

"I did, as a matter of fact," I murmured.

"Well, Carl *Ransome!*" Her tone of coquettish reproof seemed more odious to me than anything I had ever before witnessed in a woman. "What in the *world* has gotten into you today! I just don't know what to *do* with you!" I felt my disgraceful smile clinging to my lips like a lizard. She removed my hand gently from her hip and placed it on my own, giving it a reproachful pat with her fingertips. "Now you just go and get yourself together, while I make you some lunch. I think a cold shower is what you need!"

She swept past me lightly into the living room, turning to give me a gracefully admonishing glance before she disappeared into the kitchen.

The rest of that day I spent in a constant vigil, one that accelerated in suspense and anxiety and in the determination with which I maintained my charade of self-composure. This self-composure I allowed to be tinctured with a respectable degree of concern about the Torrances. All during lunch we glanced through the screen to their abandoned picnic site, and there were frequent references made to the oddity of their disappearance. When we had finished and gone down to the beach for our afternoon session, they had still not returned, and their empty encampment now had about it an unmistakably ominous air. Liam walked across to it and straightened up the skewed umbrella shaft and put the spilled fruit and sandwiches back into the overturned wicker basket and shook out the scattered towels and spread them neatly on the sand. Our beach party was subdued; there was less chatter and laughter, fewer improvised diversions; and Elizabeth, in her dumb, querulous way, was visibly distressed at the absence of her friend. I could not read the Kampmeier. It fell open, when I parted the pages, to a photograph of a black woman with a papulosquamous rash strung across her breasts and belly in a vilely festive way, like livid beads. I turned to a page of text and stared at it uncomprehendingly, shifting my eyes surreptitiously from time to time to the portion of the Torrances' backyard that I could see from my position on the beach. I turned page after page, each of them crawling with words as if with lice.

The heat was unbearable. We went up to the cottage earlier than usual and sat on the screen porch with our afternoon drinks in the breezeless, suffocating afternoon. An electric fan set on the floor at our feet oscillated slowly back and forth with an endless, wracked, squealing sound, like the squeaking of a mouse being tormented to death by a playful cat. Occasionally a cool caress of fan breeze touched my hot, damp throat and temples like a vagrant, tender memory out of childhood. There were green flies gathered on the screen as if in the knowledge of an approaching storm or drawn by the spoor of carrion. Elizabeth sat on the floor at our feet playing fitfully with the rag doll that Paula had given her. She handled it in such an unmotherly, clumsy, and what seemed to me intentionally pernicious way that it made me savagely impatient to watch. She seemed to be trying, in a dull, perverse way, to twist its arms and legs off or to decapitate it. I don't remember what was said, by anyone; almost nothing, it seems to me, for hot, wretched, silent hours. As I remember it, we sat watching Elizabeth, all of us, in a kind of distracted, anxious forbearance, as patients in a doctor's office, awaiting the diagnosis of some mortal affliction, sit watching the misbehavior of a child.

It was after dinner when the Torrances returned. Elizabeth had been put to bed and the women were washing the dishes in the kitchen. I sat on the front porch looking through the screen to where Liam, in front of the cottage, was puttering with the rigging of his sailboat in the long summer twilight. I heard a car door slam distantly, and the sound startled me like a gunshot. When I raised my head to look across the hundred yards of sandy scrub to the Torrances' backyard, I could see Tom Torrance and Mary's parents going up the back steps of his cottage. He walked behind them, a hand laid gently against each of their backs, as if for guidance or support. They moved very slowly, raising their feet with effort to the level of each tread.

I became aware that Liam had climbed out of the sailboat in front of me and was walking up across the sand to the cottage. When he had come up the steps and onto the front porch, he said, "Did I hear a car?"

"Yes. The Torrances just came back."

"Oh, they did?" He turned and stood looking through the screen. "I wonder if I ought to go over."

I think he was about to do so, but at that moment we saw Paula making her way across the sandy scrub between the two houses, a blue china platter clutched in one hand. She went up the back steps to the Torrances' stoop and knocked against the side of the screen door. After a moment it opened and she went into the house.

Molly came out from the living-room door onto the front porch and sat down in one of the wicker rocking chairs.

"Well, we finished the dishes," she said. I nodded. "The Torrances got back. Paula's gone over to see if they're all right."

"We saw them. Have you checked on Elizabeth?"

"Yes, I just went in. She's not asleep yet, but she doesn't seem to be fussing, anyway."

"Good." We sat rocking distractedly, our eyes wandering to the screen. Liam perched on the ledge, rattling the chips of seashell in his pockets. After ten minutes or so, Paula came out of the Torrances' cottage, down the back steps, and across the empty lot toward us. She walked hastily, snatching the stems of the sea oats impatiently aside from her path and stumbling sometimes in the sand. We heard her feet on the back steps and the slap of the screen door against the sill when she came into the kitchen. In a moment she came out through the door onto the porch. She sat down in the chair beside Molly's and leaned forward, bowing her face into her hands and giving several long, shuddering sighs.

"What is it?" Liam said.

"The little girl is dead. That sweet little girl. That sweet little Doreen." She took her hands from her face and sat up straight in the chair, lacing her fingers together and pressing her hands tightly against her chest between her breasts. "She drowned this morning. While we were up there at the wreck."

"Oh, Jesus," Liam murmured.

Molly lowered her head and began to sob softly.

"How did it happen?" I asked.

"I guess she went down in the water with her granddaddy, and Tom and Mary weren't watchin' real good. And you know, he's not real strong, the old gentleman, and it seems like they stepped into a hole and got carried off by a current or something. By the time Tom found out what was happening, it was just too late. Oh, Lord, it's just too awful to think about."

"Oh, no," Molly murmured between her sobs. "Oh, no, no, no, no." She shook her head helplessly from side to side as if to deny the truth of it.

"I'd better go over and say something to Tom," Liam said.

"I don't think I would right now, honey. He's pretty bad. I told him to let us know if there was anything in the *world* we could do. They're just goin' to pack up their things and go right on back into town. Mary's still up there at the hospital."

"They went in to Laverne?" Liam said. "My God, that's an hour and a half away. She didn't have a chance. Didn't they try to find us?"

"Well, of course they did, honey. They looked everywhere for us. They just shouted and *shouted,* Tom said; but of course we couldn't hear 'em, way up there in the dunes."

"Oh, Jesus," Liam said. He shoved his hands into his pockets and stood rattling the shell chips angrily. "We picked a great time to go on that damned expedition. We might have saved her if we'd been here."

"It couldn't have been long after I left," I said after a moment of silence.

"After any of us left," Liam said. "I don't know. It just seems so god-damned *malevolent.*" He walked rapidly across the porch and laid his hands on the ledge, staring out bitterly at the sea. No one said anything more for some time; there was only the gasping, strangulated sound of Molly's sobbing. After several moments I became aware of the almost palpable weight of Paula's gaze and, turning toward her, I saw that she was watching me with that attentive, ruminative look with which a child scrutinizes a visiting stranger in its household.

· · ·

I stopped speaking and raised my head to the window, closing my eyes and turning my face in the bath of warm light as if to erase the stain of the woman's gaze. Sylvie sat with her head bowed across the table from me, gently nudging a salt cellar with her fingertips in a compassionate silence, one that she did not allow to outlive its mercy and begin to resemble censure or dismay.

"Did you see her again?" she asked gently.

"Yes. Once or twice. Just once alone."

"What did the awful woman do? Did she betray you?"

"No. She wasn't sure enough of the facts to do that. And she had too little to gain, I suppose. And of course, she was too vulnerable, herself, to risk exposing me, although I think she would have liked to. I've found that's generally the case, in relationships between immoral people. And then, of course, I'd regained my composure to the point where I was able to deal with her. With anyone, I think." Our cups were empty. I refilled them from the pot, studying the stream of amber fluid in the light. "You see, I was committed now to defending my honor. My honor—that pocketful of counterfeit coins that chance had threatened to confiscate and then, just as whimsically, decided to let me keep. *Required* me to keep, in fact, after I'd learned the value of them. I didn't really have any further choice in the matter." I passed the sugar bowl to Sylvie and watched her stir her tea.

"Did she suspect you, do you think?"

"Oh, I think so. I'm not really sure. In some ways it was an interesting conversation. Not of any real significance, but interesting. Like the balance of my life. They were both exercises in virtuosity, in simple skill: skill in the practice of medicine and of deception—deception of other people—certainly not any longer of myself."

"You went on with the study, then?"

"Oh, yes. Imperturbably, you would have said if you'd witnessed it. Not with any real passion or zeal, of course; but I was the only one who knew that. It was the same with the experiment as with my life—I had to go on, even past honor, defending the honor of it. What good would it have done at that point to proclaim the immorality of the project? 'You're a bit late in becoming aware of it,' people would have said. And of course, I was; just as I was in Doreen's case. But I told myself that the world would profit no more by knowing the facts of Walter Lubby's death than it would by knowing the facts of hers. It would have been an equally useless—and perhaps an equally self-indulgent—show of conscience to publish them. In either case, it would have produced a general dismay far more pernicious, in the long run, than the event itself. So I went on in exactly the same way as before, both with my life and my profession. Perhaps I was even a bit more proficient, at both of them, because there was less involved. People made certain moves—or nature did—and I replied to them in the most effective and intelligent way I could think of, without being muddled by conviction or passion or illusions of grandeur. There was very little joy in the process, as I say, but occasionally there was a certain amount of—technical gratification—I suppose you could call it, in the skill of the performance. And oddly enough, I often felt something I never expected to feel after such an experience; something really quite strange: a kind of lost, bitter fraternity, at all sorts of times and places, with all sorts of unexpected people, including some of the doctors who were most active and enthusiastic in the project. It was a kind of wretched and extravagant cordiality; something, I think, as close to amity as I had ever known. I even felt it with Paula the last time I talked to her, as much as I despised the woman. A curious sort of feeling. I suppose it's one that must exist among the inhabitants of hell. Maybe it was pity."

"You don't have to name it," Sylvie murmured.

"Oh, I still got furious at her, of course—I was still capable of fury at outright ignorant malice or undisguised envy or the kind of transparent hypocrisy that Paula was capable of; and others. It was her—inelegance—that bothered me, I suppose. Incompetence of any kind, even at duplicity, still disgusted me. Sometimes, at first, I would be outraged by the thought that I myself was not performing well; that I might be failing to deceive someone expertly or entirely; that I'd been detected as an impostor, and judged accordingly. Especially if the person concerned, the person who dared to criticize or judge me, was as demoralized as I. That seemed to me to be especially outrageous, a violation of our code of scoundrels, a failure of respect for the mutual fragility of our façades, our mutual culpability. There is honor, even among thieves. Paula was aware of that rather comic scruple on my part." I chuckled miserably. "I made sure of it."

"How long after—the beach—was it when you saw her again?" Sylvie said.

"Oh, about six weeks, after we'd all come back to Tallacoochee."

I stopped by Liam's house one evening to pick up the report on a clinic examination of a batch of ten or twelve control patients. He'd promised to deliver it to me the day before, but hadn't done so. When I got out of the car I saw Paula sitting in the arbor at the side of the house with a watering can at her feet, smoking a cigarette and staring at a flower cart full of dripping geranium pots in front of her. I went up the front path and across the stepping-stones to the arbor. Paula raised her head when she heard my steps and watched the last ten yards or so of my approach. I said, "Good evening."

"Hello, Carl." She lifted a glass of iced tea from the bench at her side and sipped at it, lowering her eyes from mine.

"I just stopped by to pick up an examination report from Liam. Is he in?"

"No, he's not."

"Oh. Well, I guess he's still down at the lab. I'll drop by there."

"I think you'll be wastin' your time." She sipped at her glass again and set it down.

"You're quite a gardener," I said. "The geraniums look beautiful."

"Well, they don't need much care. Just a little water now and then."

A sharp, suffocating herbal scent hung in the air. "What is that smell?" I asked. "What flower is that?"

"Verbena. You don't like it?"

"Yes. It's very—voluptuous."

She examined me in a leisurely, judicious way and said in a tone of the faintest irony, "Oh, really? Do you think so?"

I was suddenly infuriated by the derogatory distance of her manner; I wasn't quite sure yet of just how deeply she suspected me, and that unaccustomed, undisguised reserve of hers made me uneasy. It seemed to confirm my fear that her suspicions were very deep indeed. It was a fear that had gnawed at me ever since the morning after Doreen's death, when she'd bade goodbye to Molly and me with studied, wary coolness from the backyard of her cottage. I saw that now as a rebuke, and I was filled with a quite untenable outrage of the kind I've described to you. How dare this woman suspect me? I thought. How dare anyone of her kind presume to understand me, or to judge me? A creature as inferior to me as this. To patronize me, even! I stood there quaking with fury, feeling something like a married man who's gone to visit a whore and been insulted by her. After a considerable pause she said, "I'd offer you a glass of iced tea, but I know you're in a hurry. At least you usually are."

"Oh, I have a minute or two. Can I sit down?"

She closed her eyes with a look of weary apprehension that seemed to say she had dreaded this very thing. "I reckon so. If you don't have anything better to do."

"I can't think of anything better to do than to spend a few minutes in an arbor with a lovely lady."

"My goodness, how gallant you've gotten, all of a sudden." She bit her lower lip lightly as if to suppress an imprudent smile. "It must be Liam's influence. He has very much the same impulses. Or weren't you aware of that?"

"Not in this case," I said. "But I wouldn't regret a certain amount of Liam's influence."

"I'll have to tell him that. He'll be very pleased."

I sat down, without invitation, in one of the cast-iron chairs facing her. She was sitting with her legs crossed, so that her brown knees and a considerable portion of one sleek, tanned thigh were visible below the edge of her green cotton skirt. As I sat down opposite her she leaned forward and in a quick, involuntary movement took the edge of her skirt in her fingers and tugged it forward to cover her legs. The gesture dismayed me. I sat sweltering with humiliation, dropping my eyes to the stone floor of the arbor. Staring at the veined gray slate, I thought: You insolent bitch. How modest you've become.

"You seem very thoughtful this evening, Dr. Ransome."

"I was admiring the stone. I haven't seen anything like that around here."

"No, they isn't anything like it in Alabama. Liam drove all the way to Pennsylvania and brought it back in the trunk of the car, a few pieces at a time. I reckon it took him ten trips."

"Oh, yes. I thought it must come from the North." I raised my eyes to hers in a deliberately casual way. "I was wondering about the Torrances. Have you seen them recently?" There was a visible stiffening of her body, as if she were shocked by the temerity of the question.

"No. They're not here right now. Mary was just so destroyed by it that she had to get away, so Tom took her out to California for a few months, till she gets herself together a little better. I don't blame her. I'd like to forget about it myself if I could. I don't know if I can ever go back to that cottage again."

"I know. It was a nightmare."

She glanced at me quickly, then raised the glass of iced tea to the level of her eyes, supported the elbow of her laden arm with the opposite hand, and with an air of evolving resolution studied the beads of moisture that slid slowly down the cold glass. "The fact is, I was never very fond of the little girl," she said. "She was a forward little creature, I thought. But that doesn't excuse her having to die like that. That doesn't excuse the grief her parents were made to feel."

"Excuse it?"

"Yes. There's so much that has to be excused in this world, if one is going to stay sane, and survive."

"I've never thought of it like that," I said. "It would seem an impertinence to me to excuse an act of God."

She considered this remark, then said, "An act of God? Like somebody catchin' syphilis, for example?"

"Yes."

"And yet you do your very best to obstruct that act of God."

"If I have the will and means, I suppose that's part of his design, too; that I should try to, anyway."

"Well, isn't that interestin'. I didn't know you were such a religious man."

"Not a practicing one, I'm afraid. As far as ceremony goes, I mean. I don't think I've been inside a church for years. To pray, at least."

"Well, of course you pray by workin', don't you? Your work is your religion. How does that Latin thing go? 'Laborare est orare.' Isn't that it?"

"I believe so." I watched her sip her tea unsmilingly, her eyes hooded by their lids in obvious and candid disdain. I felt a sudden savage desire to crush the woman, to force her to acknowledge her dalliance with me, to confess the shameless frivolity and venality of her nature. Not long ago she had offered me her body, had celebrated me at her parties, had invited the world to share her homage to me. And yet, how was I changed? I was the same man now that I was then. My eminence then, no less than now, depended upon murder; yet she had not protested. No one had protested; but Liam—whom the world well knew to be a reprobate. What was least forgivable was the irony by which she'd stumbled on the evidence of my crime. Of all the people on earth, only this wretched woman had the power to bear witness to it. She had desecrated my privacy, the dark and precious privacy in which, unnamed, unknown, unborn to the world, I had dwelt as if in an amniotic sea; where I had rocked and bathed and dreamt sweet infantile dreams of destiny, of glory, of some distant, perfect love. I had a very strong impulse to kill the woman at that moment, one that was evidently becoming habitual with me. I think I would have, if I could have conceived of any practical plan for doing it.

I sat there staring at her, trying to think of possible alternatives, the only one of which that seemed to be remotely realistic was to arrive at some sort of scoundrels' bargain, to impose some kind of sordid détente on her, one that would add her subjugation to her silence. At first, her tone had been faintly ironical, even insinuating, as if she were perfectly willing to let her suspicions be known to me; as if in fact she enjoyed my dismay at the possibility that she was aware of what I'd done. Perhaps she even wanted to plague me with the fear that she might reveal it to others. I had the distinct impression that she might. I'm not sure why; it may have been in reparation for the fact that she'd been foolish enough to make those very indiscreet proposals to me, and in revenge for my having spurned them. In fact, I had the impression that she was congratulating herself, openly, for my having done so, and having thus spared her the even greater embarrassment of finding herself the mistress of a monster. I think she was also probing me to some degree, testing my reaction to her insinuations, in order to confirm them. She couldn't have been absolutely sure of the truth of them, of course; the evidence was circumstantial at best, however conclusive it may have seemed to her. But if she did believe that I'd knowingly and viciously allowed the child to die, she may have been so mystified as to what my motives were that she couldn't refrain from making a cautious, morbidly fascinated investigation into them. There was something in her manner that suggested that: a tentative, reluctant sufferance of my presence compounded of that unpleasant interest, of the twin desires to repay my humiliation of her and to affirm her moral superiority to me, of repugnance and of contempt. To be despised by even this vile, treacherous woman seemed to me the ultimate opprobrium I could suffer of my race. I couldn't endure it.

I leaned forward and laid my hand on her knee, clasping it deliberately in a coarse affirmation of our intimacy, the common baseness of our natures. "I'm afraid my religious instincts have deserted me entirely this evening," I said. "Maybe it's the smell of that verbena. Or the sunset. Or maybe that green dress you're wearing has something to do with it."

I could hear her breath sucked in through her nostrils and feel the tensing of her muscles beneath my hand. Her lips tightened in a vindictive smile. "What surprises me, Carl," she said, "is how romantic you've become, all of a sudden."

"Oh, not all of a sudden. You underestimate yourself."

"Well, perhaps not. Perhaps I should say ever since—ever since that day at the beach."

"Yes, I was very moved that day."

I loosened my grasp on her knee and slid my hand gently along her thigh. She recoiled as if it had been a scorpion, withdrawing her knees swiftly and leaning forward to tug her skirt down more securely. Her face had gone grim. "Carl, please. I find that very distasteful. Very. I hope you understand that."

"It surprises you. What I find equally surprising is how fastidious *you've* become, all of a sudden."

"Fastidious? I hope I never seemed any less than that to you."

"I'm afraid you did. As I remember, you suggested that you would be the perfect mate for me. Could I have been mistaken?"

"I think you were. I'm sorry to disappoint you, if that's the impression you had. I suppose I should apologize." She buttoned the topmost button of her blouse and clasped her collar together with her fingertips. I sat back in my chair and tucked my hands into my trouser pockets, regarding her for a moment with an air of ominous serenity.

"You're a strange woman, Paula. A very capricious one. Dangerously capricious. I think I'd do something about that if I were you. You're apt to be disastrously misunderstood someday."

A calculated change came over her in response to this remark. She closed her eyes for a moment and a contrite smile rippled across her lips. She shrugged in a gentle, conciliatory way. A tone of mild indulgence came into her voice. "Well, perhaps we were both mistaken. Lord knows, people are just *always* misunderstandin' each other. I guess that's what makes the world so interestin'!"

"Or tragic, sometimes."

"*Tragic?* Well, I hope not. My goodness, you sound gloomy. I don't know what I could have done to give you that impression, Carl. I don't even *remember* what I said. Maybe it *was* a little bit—imprudent, or something. But— I don't know whether you realize this or not—I was very upset at the time. I had just made a very bitter discovery. One that I'd rather not go into. And I *suppose* I just got a little bit hysterical for a minute or two. I *hope* I wasn't imprudent, but if I was, well, it seems to me that imprudence is forgivable, if *any* of our sins are." She flashed her eyes at me with a look of merry rue.

I saw now that she was certain enough of what I'd done to be afraid of me, at least. The realization had come visibly over her that a man who was capable of willfully letting a child die was equally capable of disposing of the only person who could possibly bear testimony to the fact. I don't think it concerned her very greatly that I was an immoral man—that she'd proposed an adulterous affair with me seemed proof enough of that—but that I might be a dangerous one was a very different matter. She had no intention of contracting a liaison with a homicidal maniac, far less of marrying one. It was evident that all she wanted now was to get out of the situation as quickly and totally as possible, to disavow any previous designs on me, or any future ones, and to avoid provoking me unnecessarily, arousing any murderous intention in me to silence her suspicions. The blithe matter-of-factness of her manner implied that no intimations or invitations of any improper sort had been made—certainly not by her—and therefore could not possibly have been rejected. Consequently no ill will could exist—certainly not on her part— that might lead her to reveal any suspicions she might have on any subject whatever to anyone at all. I could rest assured of that. "I guess we just have to expect a *little* bit of craziness from each other once in a while, in this kind of a world," she concluded whimsically.

"I guess we do," I said. "And I suppose a certain amount of imprudence is the privilege of a beautiful woman." I smiled with an indulgence equal to her own. She laughed with labored gaiety.

"And a certain amount of charity is a gentleman's obligation, after all."

"Yes. My mother used to say it was the mark of gentlefolk."

"She was a very wise woman. She would have got along very well in the South."

"I hope I'll do the same."

"Well, of course you will. And do you know why? Because you're a gentleman. A *born gentleman.* And that's the rarest quality a man can have." She leaned forward and gave me a congratulatory pat on the knee. "And just to show you that I appreciate that fact, I'm going to offer you a little glass of Southern Comfort. Now don't you tell me you've got to go."

"I'm afraid so. Liam may have left that report for me, and I want to look it over this evening."

"My goodness, you're goin' to work yourself to death, you men. Well, I'm sorry to hear it, but I guess you know best. We'll be seein' y'all soon, anyway. I'm goin' to have my Harvest Home in a couple of weeks, and you and Molly just better be here. I'll call her about it tomorrow."

"We'll look forward to it," I said. "Tell Liam I came by, will you?"

"I certainly will. I'm sorry you missed him. Good night, Carl."

"Good night." She stood up with me and smiled in a strenuously gracious way. I went quickly down the walk to the car. When I had reached the row of shrubbery that divided her lawn from the sidewalk, Liam's dog came hobbling toward me from the post behind the hedge where, every evening, it lay to await the approach of his car. It stretched its head toward me, its tail flopping and its mouth happily agape.

"Get away from me, you stinking creature," I muttered. "You ugly, crippled, fawning, stupid bitch." If I hadn't known that Paula was standing in the arbor ceremonially watching my departure, I would have kicked it in the ribs.

"What happened to Liam?" Sylvie said. "Finally, I mean. Did he continue with the study?"

"Liam was a man on whom life never stopped showering ironies," I said. "For a while he was actually in charge of it, when I was temporarily reassigned."

At the end of that year, the Japanese bombed Pearl Harbor and we were at war. Liam tried to enlist in the Army Medical Corps immediately and was refused. He was forty-seven then; that in itself wouldn't have prohibited his enlistment; but he was in very poor health generally. He had an old wound, an injury to his spine from a hunting accident, that made him unfit for any active service, and he was also drinking so heavily that I think he realized himself that he would have been of very little use in the kind of war-wound surgery that he wanted to do. His specialty was syphilis, and the management and control of that disease had very high medical priority in the war years. There was an intensive campaign begun in serologic tests and treatment of draft registrants almost immediately. Among the first 15 million men examined there were something like 750,000 seropositive results discovered, a finding that startled everyone. The armed service testing and treatment program was the first large-scale attempt to reduce the reservoir of 3 million infected persons in the country. A very large part of the work of follow-up and further examination and treatment was done by state and local health units; it would have been impossible for the Medical Corps and the P.H.S. to handle this work by themselves. For that reason, state and county health officials with experience in syphilis control were requested, urgently, to continue in their work, which was indispensable to the war effort. Liam understood this and agreed to it, as perhaps the greatest contribution he could make to the cause of defeating fascism. I suppose he assumed that for the first time in over a year he would be concerned primarily with curing people, rather than watching them die. What he didn't foresee was that later, when I was called back to Washington and temporarily reassigned, he would be required to take over the study in my absence and, as far as treatment went, to make a special exception of the four hundred men who were the subjects of our study. I think that helped to kill him, eventually.

Immediately after the declaration of war a chain of Rapid Treatment Centers began to be set up across the country, a project that proceeded unabated for the next two years. In December 1943, I was assigned to assist in that campaign. From then until the end of the war it occupied more of my time than did the study. It was arduous and almost ceaseless work. By June 1944 there were fifty-eight of these centers, in thirty-three states and three territories, with a bed capacity of over six thousand. I worked in many of these places, and also in our key clinics and research laboratories at Hot Springs, Staten Island, and Johns Hopkins. Thousands of infected men were treated and subsequently inducted, and meticulous records kept of their cure and mortality rates. In 1944 I was working at the Postgraduate Center at Johns Hopkins, where we evaluated records submitted by cooperating clinics using the Eagle-Horton method of arsenotherapy for ambulatory patients, and I remember that for that single treatment schedule we examined almost five thousand records. We were experimenting with five principal treatment technics in those days: an eight-day slow intravenous drip technic, several multiple-injection methods ranging from a six-week schedule to a one-day mapharsen treatment combined with vaccine-induced fever. But scores of other methods were experimented with as well, including sulfonamides and, for the first time, penicillin, which had only recently been discovered by Fleming in England.

That was the most significant discovery, of course, in the entire history of syphilis research. It changed the status of that disease, and our attitude toward it, forever. I would like to say that it put an end to the Tallacoochee study, but it didn't. The use of penicillin on the study subjects was never even discussed or debated. On the contrary, its availability only seemed to increase the anxiety of the Service officials for the study to be continued. Even Parran wanted it to go on. I think the general feeling was that now that a strong possibility existed that the disease would be wiped out forever, the study could never again be duplicated. The new drug had practically eliminated the chance of ever finding again a large number of syphilitic patients for observation or experiment. An inimitable opportunity for learning the pathogenesis of the disease was being threatened, and might be lost forever. The feeling was very common—in fact, it was almost universal among the Service personnel. I don't remember ever hearing a word of criticism of the study among our ranks— moral criticism, that is. It was sometimes criticized for its inefficiencies or technical or procedural inadequacies—in fact, there were methods discussed for increasing the pool of infected subjects while there was still a chance to do so, before the promiscuous use of penicillin and the other new "wonder drugs" had "contaminated" them. But I never heard it criticized for its indignity or inhumanity. No one ever spoke of the suffering it caused, the deformity and despair and shortening of life. Not even Parran. And later, when it began to be written about and condemned as indefensible by the press, by many private physicians, and eventually by a congressional investigating committee, there was a sense of indignation among us, of resentment at this interference in our work by the uninformed, the pusillanimous, and the self-righteous. There were bitter, wrathful articles written in its defense by some of the most eminent physicians among us. By myself, especially. I suppose they felt as I did, that we had to go on defending it, even past honor. We had poured too much imagination and energy and skill into it to be able to disown it now as unethical or misconceived. I felt that more than most of them, of course, because for me it was in a very real sense my lifework, my credo; I could not renounce it without renouncing myself, my whole career, the most genuine evidence of my existence on the earth. (That Elizabeth deserved that definition didn't occur to me.) I remember protesting once, in a letter to Dr. Turner when articles condemning the study began to appear in the press:

> There is no way to penetrate the obtusity of these armchair moralists.
> They simply don't understand the demands of dedication in the real
> world. How many of them will ever demonstrate the work, the
> sacrifice, the faith that has to be exercised if men are ever going to
> escape the darkness they dwell in? They would happily send a million
> men off to die in some outrageous war—they are doing so at the
> moment—and yet they lament the conscription of four hundred in an
> infinitely more practical and equally noble cause. It can't even be called
> conscription, because no one fighting in Europe at the moment is more
> truly a volunteer than these men, in the cause of human
> enlightenment. And yet the comfortable philosophers who criticize us
> affect this hypocritical revulsion at a work that is not only the exercise
> of man's highest faculty, but which will help to liberate them—as
> powder and shot will never liberate them—from the bonds of

ignorance and superstition, suffering and fear. *They* are the vandals, masquerading, as vandals so often do, in the garb of virtue. I really can't stand that kind of fraudulent compassion that procures political advantage for some of them and the guise of righteousness for others.

The guise of righteousness! God save the man who has more skill than sincerity. And yet he wrote back to congratulate me on that fulsome piece of rhetoric. He said that I'd expressed very well the position of the Corps in general, that I'd spoken for all of them and for the institution. And he was right. That's the terrible thing about a crime that's hidden, in the life of an individual or an institution—one has to go on lying about it, rationalizing it, falsifying its details, glorifying it, until the truth is lost forever, until history itself is willfully distorted at last; the history of one's life or of one's nation; and man becomes a patriot of an illustrious Gehenna whose annals he devises with his shame. A deed like mine simply can't be hidden; it has to be confessed, extinguished by exposure to the light or expelled out of the psyche. There's something in the spirit that rejects it, just as the body rejects foreign tissue; and if it fails to do so, it sickens and dies, just as the body sickens if it's contaminated by something inimical to it that it fails to extinguish or expel. There's an integrity to life that can't be violated without resulting in morbidity, of body or of spirit. I came to understand that eventually, not as a religious man, I told myself, but as a doctor, and not as a piece of theological dogma, but as a simple scientific fact. That there was as much of religion as of science in the revelation was something I failed to perceive at the time; but although I had come to accept a definition of disease that included evil, it was less of an embarrassment to me than an auspice. I think I watched the symptoms of the devastation of my spirit with something of the desolated wonder with which Hunter, two hundred years before, had watched the gradual eruption of a chancre in his flesh, rejoicing in his own damnation as the confirmation of an awesome truth he had surmised.

I came to love obscurity; shadows and suffering and stealth and the sonority of death with which the world resounded like a great, bright, empty shell. All the time I was working in Rapid Treatment Centers, in management and control, and in the theory, technic, and interpretation of serologic tests, I had a gathering sense of dislocation and unrest; almost of bereavement at times. I missed Tallacoochee and my patients—my subjects—and their humble, deferential faces, and the slow and stately ritual in which we were united. I missed the hot, long dusks and shadows of the town, the taste of sulfur water from the cracked spigots, the iron benches under the live oaks, and the muttering of sparrows and old men in a dark euphony. I came to long for the scent of magnolia in the night and the pallor of the moon above the streets and the distant shriek of the mill saws tearing the white silence of the noon like a cry of agony.

All the time I was away, Molly remained there, and for the first time I can remember, I looked forward to her letters because they brought me news of the place, even though the tone of them was increasingly lugubrious. She was lonely, she complained. Paula's attentiveness to her had unaccountably dwindled, and eventually lapsed almost entirely. She could not explain this and was confused and hurt by it. I thought I could explain it, but limited myself to the sardonic satisfaction of believing so. I advised her to get out more, now that she had the car at her disposal, go in to Birmingham occasionally for dinner or a movie, take Elizabeth to a carnival. She wrote back that the car was not working well, that there was also something the matter with the plumbing, the tool-shed roof had caved in, and there was an invasion of ants:

I finally got the man from the Sinclair station to come over and look at the car and he says the starter motor needs fixing. It will cost $55.00. Should I tell him to go ahead on it? I really have to have a car because I can't count on Paula anymore. She used to take me downtown shopping twice a week but now she always seems to have some sort of excuse. I just don't understand that woman. I suppose part of the reason she acts so strange is because she and Liam have split up, or at least that's what people say. I don't know whether I told you that in my last letter. He's moved out of the house now and is living in a rented room on Jackson Avenue. I called her up the other day and tried to offer her some comfort but she didn't want to talk about it at all. She acted kind of huffy, in fact. You'd think a woman would want her friends to comfort her at a time like that, but Paula keeps everything to herself and seems to resent anybody's sympathy. I just can't understand a person like that. In fact, I'm not sure it's all Liam's fault that he walked out on her like that, no matter what people say. I met him downtown last week when I went to the drugstore and he stopped and talked to me for quite a while. I must say he was very nice. He seemed to be really surprised Paula had stopped calling me up, and when I told him I was so lonely he said he knew just how I felt. He sounded like he meant it, too. I had Elizabeth with me and she was so glad to see him she just yelped. He picked her up and put her on his shoulders, you know the way he used to do down at the beach, and she just loved it.

Carl, I've just got to get the bathroom fixed. The toilet runs over all the time and I can't deal with it much longer. It just seems to me that everything is going to pieces. I can't understand why God lets all these terrible things happen in the world. And now those terrible Japanese, landing on all those islands. Do you think they might win, Carl? What will we do if we have to live under the Japanese? It's enough to put anybody in fear and trembling. I wake up and think about it all night sometimes. Do you still think you will get back in June? I certainly hope so because there's so much that has to be done around here and a woman by herself can't get anything done in this world. I wish we'd never left Washington. It was so nice there. I keep thinking about those afternoons when we used to walk down to the Cathedral and sit on the stones in the sun. Oh, I wish we could be back there. Everything was so lovely then.

I was very much surprised to hear of Liam's defection. He had said nothing about it in his letters to me, which, although they were very brief, formal, and except for an occasional quixotic, alcoholic digression, confined entirely to business matters, I would have expected to include—one of them, at least—some reference to such a dramatic alteration in his life. They did not, however. They were growingly remote and caustic. In the spring of 1944 I received a particularly ironic one from him at Hot Springs, where I was conducting a ten-week course in Management and Control: it failed to mention even his encounter with Molly:

Worshipful Professor:
    I got a letter last week from D. G. Gill, M.D., who is Director of the Bureau of Preventable Diseases of this state. He is evidently suffering from the misconception that I make administrative decisions regarding our celebrated investigation into the Truth. Although it's addressed to me, I'm passing it along to you, in the happy knowledge that you will relieve me of any such responsibility. That is, I intended to pass it along to you, but I seem to have lost the damned thing. Possibly I burned it, I can't remember. Anyway, he seems to expect an answer, so I suppose I can paraphrase it accurately enough for you to act on. He says he is calling my attention (or yours) to the fact that in their program of getting all draft selectees who are rejected for syphilis under treatment, he feels he may be encroaching on some of your study material. He says that in conjunction with the draft boards he's required to see that all these men take treatment so they will qualify for induction, but he's wondering if he should make an exception of these few individuals whom we have singled out for sacrifice. (The phrase "singled out for sacrifice" is my own. Dr. Gill isn't a man who

would allow himself such a colorful locution.) So there it is, old man, right in your lap. I know you will do the right thing.

As you know, time for the Big Roundup is approaching, and I'm wondering if you're going to send anybody down here to supervise the annual herding in of all the sheep who have been entrusted to our care. I hope so, because I've got too damned much to do trying to cure some of the ones who managed to escape our net. The best I can do is examine a few of them and try to organize the statistical review to some extent. Could you, for God's sake, send us a statistician by any chance? I'm so goddamned swamped with work that I'm liable to include the figures for my dentist's bill in there somewhere.

Summer is icumen in, lhude sing cuccu!

Your obedient servant

A week later I received another letter from Molly, whose change in tone was astonishing. It was very nearly ecstatic:

Dear Carl:

I hope you are well and that your work is going well too. I know you're making a wonderful contribution to our country in its fight for freedom and I want you to know that Elizabeth and I are proud of you.

This has been the nicest week I've had in ages. So many nice things have happened it's hard to believe. You know I told you in my last letter that I met Liam downtown one day? Well, a couple of days later he called up and invited Elizabeth and me to go on a picnic. He said I would get a big surprise because somebody else was going to go with us that I hadn't seen in a long time, and you know who it turned out to be? Janet Thurmond! Wasn't that a surprise? She came back to Tallacoochee recently and has gone to work for Liam again as a statistician (I think that's how you spell it!). She doesn't get paid or anything, she's doing it as a volunteer because the Health Dept. doesn't have enough money to put her back on the payroll, but she wants to help Liam out. I think she's just the nicest person. It was a lovely day and we drove over to Lake Tonawanda and spread some blankets on the grass and had our lunch. We just had a marvelous time. Liam and Janet and Elizabeth went swimming and then Liam rented a canoe and paddled us all around the lake and showed Elizabeth those big golden carp in the water. She calls him Uncle Leem. Those two have the best time together. Janet made a big German chocolate cake and it was delicious. I ate three pieces! Janet said it was a little bit too sweet but I said there wasn't a thing in the world wrong with it except its *name!* I said she ought to call it something besides *German* chocolate and she thought that was the funniest thing she'd ever heard. We had a wonderful time.

Then just two days later Dr. Prescott called up, you remember that nice man we met at Paula's the first time we went there, that had the watch that chimed? Well, he invited us to come over and have dinner with him and his wife. Wasn't that a coincidence, getting two nice invitations like that in the same week? He came over and drove us to his house for dinner and then drove us back afterwards. He and his wife are just the nicest couple in the world. He showed me his orchids and you wouldn't believe how beautiful they are. He must have about thirty different kinds. His house is just like a garden in Taheety or one of those tropical countries. You never saw such beautiful flowers. He picked one of them and pinned it on my dress before I left, and I felt just like a fairy princess. I'm going to press it in my Bible to remember him by. He's one of the nicest people I've ever met. He said they look forward to having us over again very soon.

Another good thing that happened was that I got the car fixed this week, so now I can drive in to get the groceries, and also the plumber finally came and fixed the toilet, so I don't have that to deal with anymore. It was just making me sick. Liam said he knew a man that did odd jobs, one of the darkies that he takes care of, and he said he'd ask him to come around and fix the tool-shed roof. He said the man would be glad to do it for nothing but I think I ought to pay him something. What do you think?

Elizabeth says to send you her love and she can't wait to see her Daddy again. It's hard to believe she'll be starting school next fall. It would be nice if you could get home in June but I know how busy you are, so don't worry about it if you can't. We are getting along just fine and I'm sure the good Lord will take care of us. Other people have a lot worse to go through these days and we will make out all right. I tell myself I have to keep this home together one way or another so you'll have some place to come back to after this terrible war is over.

Love from your loving wife,
Molly

I managed to get home in June within a few days of Elizabeth's birthday. I had forgotten that fact until I got off the plane in Birmingham, took a taxi into town, and was waiting in the Greyhound bus station for a bus to take me on the last leg of my journey to Tallacoochee. As I sat in the waiting room with a copy of the *Journal of Venereal Disease Information,* in which I had an article published about recent developments in the use of penicillin therapy in gonorrhea and syphilis, a little girl and her mother sat down on the wooden waiting bench beside me. The child was almost the same age as Elizabeth and had the same solemn, expressionless air of melancholy. She sat staring at me from my shoes to the insignia on my cap and back again, relentlessly, until I became uncomfortable. Her mother tugged her gently by the wrist and said, "Don't bother the gentleman, Julie," in a tone of voice so like that of Molly's bleak remonstrances to Elizabeth that I remembered, with a little throe of shame, that my daughter's sixth birthday was the day after tomorrow and that I had bought her nothing as a gift; neither had I brought anything for Molly. There was a small booth in the station that sold newspapers, candy, cigarettes, and souvenirs; their stock of novelties was as meager and vulgar as is common to such places, but I found a small celluloid doll dressed in a cheerleader's outfit, holding a pom-pom in one hand and in the other a pennant inscribed with the words YAY, CRIMSON TIDE! I bought the doll for Elizabeth and a dusty box of Whitman's Sampler chocolates for Molly. The stick bearing the pennant was glued very firmly into the doll's celluloid fist, but after a minute or two of strenuous tugging I managed to pull it out. Two of her fingers came with it and her blond curls were badly disarranged in the process, but she seemed to be the only possible solution to my dilemma. I put her and the chocolates into my suitcase barely in time to board the bus for Tallacoochee.

Molly met me at the station with Elizabeth, both of them overcome with a kind of wary, conciliatory intentness, like someone armed only with a biscuit watching the approach of a large bear in a national park. In the six months since I had seen her, Elizabeth had emerged from infancy into childhood. She now had what was recognizable to me as a discrete personality. She was no longer an inchoate bundle of sensations and impressions and mindless, anonymous protest at the nameless discomforts of the world, but a small, thoughtful, exceptionally taciturn human being with an identity and history, capable of valid if elemental judgments about human nature and, I was led to suppose, of disturbingly acute predictions about the course of it. I thought the welcome in the eyes that watched me with such measured apprehension as I approached her on the station platform, and that disengaged themselves from mine with the delicate fugacity of butterflies when I held her up in front of me at arm's length, was tempered by something more than childish shyness or confusion: by conscious meditation, by counsel taken mysteriously with herself or with the angels of her destiny.

Molly's momentary lack of certainty resolved itself into something more predictable and less formidable: a faintly complacent air of fortitude and the subtly inveighed suggestion that the months of separation which to her had been such a cruel ordeal had been a kind of truancy on my part, perhaps arranged in inscrutable collusion with the same dark powers responsible for the war itself, the failure of the plumbing, the invasion of ants, the fact that when it rains it pours, that the good die young, that stolen waters are sweet and bread eaten in secret, pleasant. I assured her, less subtly, that I had drunk no stolen waters nor eaten secret bread; that I had dined for the most part on Salisbury steak, cold mashed potatoes, and peas of the consistency of grapeshot, that the work was hard and endless and largely unappreciated, and that I had dwelt in a succession of hotel rooms of unvarying gloom. I was pleased to hear, however, that she had been enjoying herself.

"Well, not really enjoying myself. I wouldn't say I'd been *enjoying* myself."

"Oh. I understood you'd been seeing a good deal of the Prescotts. And Liam."

"I do see them occasionally. Thank heavens. I don't know what I'd do otherwise. And they're very, very kind people. They understand what it's like for a woman trying to keep a home together in times like these. Not everyone does."

"Liam has been helpful, too, you say."

"Yes, he has. He sent a darky around last week to fix the tool shed. He spent the whole day working on it."

"That was thoughtful of him."

"It certainly was. I think he's really a very nice man. In spite of what people say."

"What do people say?"

"Well, you know. That business about Janet."

"About Janet?"

She flashed her eyes toward the rear seat and raised her forefinger warningly to indicate that, in Elizabeth's presence, it was not prudent to pursue the subject. This confirmation by Molly that our daughter was capable of making moral distinctions produced a very strange sensation in me, something like that sudden sense of fading light and of phantasmal coolness that sweeps over one when a cloud shadow passes across one's body on a summer afternoon.

I found myself watching her at the dinner table with the strangely novel desire to conceal my observation of her. She was silent for the most part and placidly unobtrusive, yet very conspicuously present and alert, although her eyes were generally fixed with conscious prudence upon her plate. She had been promoted from her high chair to one of the huge old dining chairs, where she sat perched on an encyclopedia and a sofa cushion with a curious self-composure, almost a daintiness, as if aware of the greater necessity for dignity which almost hourly was imposed upon her. She cut her own meat and fed herself and was, for the first time, included in the conversation. She was also for the first time in my experience addressed as "dear" by Molly.

"We usually eat in the kitchen," Molly said, "but tonight we're having a special treat, aren't we, Elizabeth? Because Daddy's home."

"Yes," Elizabeth said. "But I like it better in the kitchen."

"Why is that, dear?"

"Because it's not so big. When a room is real big, there are too many places."

"Places for what?"

"Well, for other people, that aren't there. Or for *things.*"

"What kind of things?" I asked.

"Things that ought to *be* there. But you don't know what they are, if they're not there."

"Oh, you mean like furniture. Or maybe a plant or something. Is that what you mean?" Molly said.

"No," Elizabeth said. "I don't know what I mean, because it isn't here. I just think there's too much *space.*"

"Well, that's a strange thought," Molly said. "But I suppose you're right. There do seem to be quite a few things missing sometimes in this world. Would you like me to cut that meat, dear?"

"No, thanks," Elizabeth said. "I can do it myself. You don't make them the right size. I have a special *size.*"

"She certainly does," Molly said. "And *I* don't know what it is. I don't think anybody does."

"Uncle Leem does," Elizabeth said. "He cuts everything just exactly the right size."

After dinner she was put immediately to bed, and while Molly was undressing her and supervising the brushing of her teeth, I went into our bedroom and unpacked my bag. The wan, disheveled doll I regarded unhappily for a moment, then put her back into the suitcase and shoved her under the bed. I took the box of chocolates downstairs and set it on the kitchen table. When Molly finished putting Elizabeth to bed I cleared the dining table and rinsed and stacked the dishes in the sink. When she came down into the kitchen she picked up the chocolate box and said, "Oh, my, is this for me? Well, isn't that nice."

"It's just a small thought," I said. "But I didn't want to come home empty-handed. I remembered that you liked them."

"Yes, that's very nice. Thank you. I didn't expect anything like this."

"It was just a thought. Molly, I don't know where to put these things."

"Oh, just leave them. I'll finish them later, when it gets a little cooler. Let's sit out on the porch for a while. It's so hot in this house."

We went out and sat in the wicker rocking chairs on the front porch in the early-summer dusk. Molly fanned herself with a cardboard fan, one of those with religious scenes printed on them that are set in the hymnal racks of church pews. She leaned forward once to pluck dead leaves from the potted geraniums that stood along the rail, crumpling them in her hand and stuffing them into the pocket of her skirt.

"These are not doing well," she said. "It's just been too dry. But that awful creeper thing is getting out of hand. I think it grows a foot a day. I wish you'd cut it back for me, Carl, while you're here."

"All right."

In the next yard the white blossoms of the magnolia tree glowed like a galaxy of small moons in the darkening air. Their dense sweet fragrance eddied between the porch columns like a flagrant attar.

"I've missed this place," I said.

"Well, I'm getting a little more used to it myself," Molly said. "I guess you get used to hanging if you hang long enough. It must be a great relief to get away from here for a while, though. I certainly would like to get back to Washington someday."

"It hasn't been easy for you. I realize that."

"Well, heaven knows I don't like to complain. I just try to keep a home together, the way so many women are doing." She fanned herself silently for a moment. "How long do you think you'll have to be away, Carl?"

"I don't really know. The study has been given second priority for a while, because there's so much to be done with the military. I guess as long as the war goes on."

"But you expect to come back here when it's over?"

"Oh, yes. It isn't nearly complete. We've only just begun, really."

"I don't suppose there's any chance of you being reassigned to Bethesda?"

"Not permanently, no." I turned to look at her. "I thought you were getting to like it here."

"Well, I suppose I am, more than at first. Of course, I don't really have any choice, I realize that. I have to like it here. But there's really so little here for anybody. Elizabeth will be going to school soon, and I'm so afraid she's going to grow up with that terrible accent."

"I think it's a very attractive accent."

"You do? Well, I never knew *that.* I think it's awful. They sound like they had a hot potato in their mouths."

"Tell me about the Prescotts," I said after a moment.

"Well, they've just been very nice. Suzanne invited me to her church bazaar last week, and I made a cake. I got that German chocolate recipe from Janet, and it was quite a hit. They made fifty-seven dollars, I think. They're going to send it to the U.S.O. in Birmingham. They do a lot for the soldiers."

"That was nice."

"Yes. They're an awfully nice group of women. I wasn't sure about going, because they're Baptist, and that scared me a little. But I had quite a nice time. At least, she's Baptist. Clarence doesn't go at all. He says he's as holy as he's ever going to get. And that's a whole lot holier than most people ever get, believe me. Holy is as holy does. You know what that man gave me last week? He gave me three orchid bulbs from his own hothouse, and told me how to plant them. I've started them on the back porch already. Oh, I hope they come up. They're a beautiful pale gold color with sort of bronze spots on them." She paused, as if her momentary enthusiasm had faded as suddenly as the light from an expiring ember. "Of course, I know perfectly well why they're all so kind to me. And I have to be grateful. I *am* grateful."

She lowered the fan into her lap and stared for a moment at the scene lithographed on it in the soft, romantic colors of the icing on a birthday cake. It was of Jesus standing on the shore of Galilee holding out his arms in an invitation to take and eat to a multitude of roughly clad people who bowed, knelt, wept, and held out their hands in reverence before him. At his feet lay wicker baskets filled with shining fishes and piled high with loaves of bread, and from the parted clouds above, a broad, vast ray of light descended, illuminating the scene like a spotlight from a theater balcony. "Gratitude is the hardest thing of all to learn," she said.

"I suppose I ought to go up and say good night to Elizabeth before she goes to sleep. I told her I'd be up."

"Yes. I don't suppose you brought anything for her?"

"No. I thought I'd better wait and talk to you about it. I thought there might be something special she's been wanting for her birthday."

"Well, there's a little toy range she saw in the Ben Franklin that she was crazy about. It has an oven with a door that opens up and a set of tiny little pots and pans. It's very cute."

"Good. I can pick it up tomorrow."

"Will you have the time?"

"In the afternoon I will, I think. I have to see Liam in the morning."

"I don't suppose we could go downtown for lunch? They have a little table section now in the Ben Franklin, and it's really very good. It would be so nice if we could all three of us go downtown for lunch. We've never done that."

"Well, maybe we can. I'll give you a ring from the clinic and let you know. I'd better go up now."

"Yes. She'll be disappointed if you don't."

"Maybe I'll take her up one of your chocolates."

"Oh, no, Carl. She's just brushed her teeth."

"It won't hurt her for once."

I went into the house, pausing in the kitchen to take a chocolate from the box Molly had left on the table before I went up to Elizabeth. Molly had left the lamp that stood on the chest of drawers lighted for her and she was lying so that the shadow of her face fell across a slat of her crib, tracing her silhouette with her fingertip.

"Well, you're drawing pictures!" I said. "Who is that you're drawing?"

"It's me. Can't you tell that?"

"Oh, I should have known that, because she's so pretty."

"No, she's not. She's ugly."

"Ugly! She's just about the prettiest little girl in the world. I think she's so pretty she deserves a chocolate. And I just happen to have one."

"You don't, either."

"Oh, yes, I do. Look at this!" I drew my hand quickly from behind my back and held the chocolate out to her across the top bar of the crib. She stared at it for a moment without moving.

"I don't think I ought to eat it, because I brushed my teeth. Momma will get mad."

"No, she won't. I'll bring you a glass of water to rinse your mouth out."

She took the chocolate, taking it out of my hand with a look of strange constraint, and began to chew it, slowly and ruminatively, her eyes wandering from mine to the buttons of her pajamas, at which she began to pluck thought-fully with the fingers of one hand.

"Is it good?"

"Uh-huh. It's a chewy one. Thank you."

"You're welcome."

After a moment she raised her eyes to mine and said, "Do you live some-where else now, Daddy?"

"Yes. For a little while. But I'm coming back."

"Do you live in a different house?"

"Yes. I've lived in several of them. I have to move around a lot."

"I thought people were only supposed to have one house."

"Well, sometimes they have to move. They have to go to different places to work, so they have to get another house. Do you remember when we used to live in Washington?"

"Yes. I liked it there. I didn't want to move."

"I guess everybody likes their first house best. It always seems like their real house."

She thought for a little while; then she said, "What was your first house like?"

"It was a lot like this one. It had a front porch, and a swing, just like this one. And an attic. That was what I liked best. I liked to go up there on rainy days and play and read books."

"What's a nattic?"

"It's a room way up at the top of the house, right under the roof. It's a very quiet place. You can hear the rain right over your head. Sometimes I used to get Grandpa's old soldier suit out of a trunk and put it on, and roll up the sleeves, and pretend I was a soldier." She lay silent for a moment. "Grandpa was my father," I explained. "He was your grandpa. It was his house."

"Where is Grandpa now?"

"He's in heaven."

"Does he have a new house now, since he moved to heaven? What kind of a house does he have now?"

"I don't know. I don't know whether people have houses in heaven. I don't think they do. I don't think they need them."

"Why not?"

"Well, they don't need any shelter up there, I don't think, because the weather is very mild. It's always sunny and blue and warm. I don't see why they'd need a house. But maybe they do, just for the sake of privacy."

"What's privacy?"

"Well, that's when you do something that you don't want anyone to see."

"You mean something secret? Like when you hide?"

"Yes."

"What kind of secret things do they do in heaven? Why do they have to hide?"

"I don't know. I can't really think of anything that would require privacy. Maybe they don't have any houses there at all."

"Maybe they live outdoors, like rabbits. Or like those poor people in the park."

"Maybe they do. Maybe they just sit on the park benches in the sun."

"And read the newspaper?"

"No, I don't think so. I don't think there is any newspaper."

"*Maybe* there is. Maybe they read about what's happening on earth."

"I don't think so," I said. "I hope not."

"Maybe they read about what their children are doing. Maybe Grandpa reads about what you and Mommy and me are doing, every morning."

"He might. But I think they just rest, mostly. Which is what you'd better do. You've had a very hard day, and you need some rest."

"Why do I need rest?"

"Because you get all run-down when you stay up a long time, and work hard, and get tired."

"What happens when you get run-down?"

"Well, it's like a clock. It works hard all day, and finally it gets run-down. So then you have to wind it up, so it can go for another day. People are getting wound up again when they're asleep."

"What kind of work does a clock do?"

"It tells time. It measures time, just the way a tape measure measures distance. It divides time up into hours and minutes and seconds, the way a tape measure divides distance up into yards and feet and inches."

"How long is time?"

"Oh, it's very long. Longer than anything. It doesn't have any end."

"It doesn't have any *end?*"

"No. No end and no beginning. It just goes on forever."

"Well, how can you measure it, if it doesn't have any end? What good does that do, if you never find out how long it is? Why do they have clocks, then?"

"Well, they tell us when we have to get up and go to work, and when we have to eat dinner, and when we have to go to bed."

"Didn't people know when to eat or go to sleep until they had clocks?"

"Yes, I guess they did. I guess they made out some way."

"I don't see why they didn't just sleep forever, if they didn't have any clocks. Or just play forever. They wouldn't ever know when to wake up or when to come in for dinner."

"No, they wouldn't, would they? I suppose they must have had clocks inside them that told them when to do things. Like the animals."

"Do animals have clocks inside them?"

"Yes. They have clocks inside them that tell them when to build their nests, and when to fly south, and when to bury nuts. So they don't need any outside clocks."

"Do the animals know how long time is?"

"I think they do. They seem to."

"But we forgot, didn't we?"

"I guess we did. Most of us. Maybe some people remember."

"Who? Do you know anybody that does?"

I looked out of the window and after a moment said, "I knew one man who may have."

"What happened to him? Where is he now?"

"I don't know."

"Was he a nice man? Did you like him?"

"Yes, I liked him very much. I gave him a radio once."

She lay still for several moments and then said, "Did you bring me anything?"

"Well, of course I did. But that's a secret. That's something you can't see till your birthday."

"But I mean something for *now.* You brought Mommy some chocolates. Did you bring me anything for *now?*"

"Well, let me see. Maybe I did, now I come to think of it. Let me go and see if I brought you anything or not." I got up from the chair and went out of the room, down the hall, and into Molly's and my bedroom. I pulled the suitcase out from under the bed, took out the ragged celluloid cheerleader, and after a brief, futile attempt to straighten her curls, carried her back down the hall to Elizabeth. "Just look what I found in my suitcase," I said. "I'd forgotten all about it."

She took the doll from me gravely and held it at arm's length, giving it a long, silent, somberly judicious scrutiny.

"Well, what do you think of her?" I said.

"I don't like her very much. She got hurt, didn't she?"

"Hurt? What do you mean?"

"She got her fingers cut off. And she's all mussed up."

"I don't know. Let me see." I took the doll and examined her hand with feigned surprise. "My goodness, she did, didn't she? Maybe she had an accident."

"I think somebody did it. Somebody that didn't like little girls did it to her."

"Oh, I don't think anybody would do that to a little girl. Maybe she just needs a little rest. Maybe she'd like to sleep in there with you." I laid the doll on the pillow beside her. She turned her head away and looked up steadily at the ceiling.

"I better go to sleep now," she said.

"All right. Shall I put the light out?"

"Yes, please."

I went across to the chest of drawers and switched off the lamp. Outside the window I heard the sound of the ragman's barrow rumbling down the street. The distant grinding clatter of the iron tires on the bricks grew louder as it came abreast of the house. Directly opposite the front porch the wheels stopped suddenly and there was a sound of something breaking: a heavy, dully chiming splintering of something into fragments: a jug of liquid, I thought: cider, or vinegar, or something thicker: molasses or honey. I went to the window and parted the curtains to look down into the street. The old man was bent over in the middle of it, but I saw him only indistinctly in the light from the single streetlamp at the corner. He stooped down to the pavement, plucking up bright, dripping shards which he tossed one by one with poignant tinkling sounds into the barrow that seemed to float among the shadows. I let the curtains fall and sat down again beside the crib.

"It's all right," I said. "It was just a bottle breaking." But I saw that she was asleep, her eyes closed and her lips parted tranquilly. I laid my hand on her heart and felt it throbbing against my palm, each of its delicate convulsions striking like the edge of a fine blade, ceaselessly splitting the infinity of time into past and present while it pronounced the phantasmal moments of our existence with its frail, passionate constancy.

In the morning I drove to the clinic to see Liam. Although it was only nine o'clock there were already old men sitting on the iron benches under the live oak trees beneath the clinic windows, their endless muttered colloquy apparently uninterrupted for the six months I had been away. They nodded and murmured, "Mornin', Doctah," as I got out of the car, following me with their bleak, impassive eyes as if my return, like my absence, had been foretold—as was the last act of my destiny, I thought eerily as I opened the door that led up the flight of wooden stairs to the clinic, feeling the weight of their ancient, prescient gaze upon me.

There were three young black men in the waiting room, dressed in worn and faded overalls and thick-soled, dusty work shoes, all of them nervously, silently upright on the wooden benches, staring at the framed paintings on the walls as if through windows that opened on undreamt-of, fabulous places. Neither their heads nor their eyes moved when I entered the room. They seemed instantly and mysteriously aware that I was white and a person of authority, and that recognition was expressed in the almost imperceptibly increased tension of their bodies and their care not to commit the indiscretion of a candidly judicial glance toward me. But I felt the impact of that silent, servile judgment like the lash of an invisible scourge across my shoulders as I crossed the waiting room and opened the frosted-glass door that led back into the clinic.

The door of Liam's office was open, as it always was. Janet was sitting at his desk with a stack of files and a small mechanical calculator, making entries on a chart. She looked up when I entered the door and watched me cross the room in silence until I came to an uncomfortable halt in the middle of it.

"Hello, Janet," I said.

"Hello, Carl. We expected you last week."

"Yes. I had to put it off for a few days, so many things came up. Man proposes, God disposes."

She smiled in a way that candidly revealed her amusement at the thought of God disposing of any of my affairs.

"We've been rather busy here, too," she said.

"It's good to see you again. When did you get back?"

"About six weeks ago. I'm not *back*, officially. I'm just helping out a little. Liam's so swamped with work."

"That's good of you."

"It's not especially virtuous, if that's what you mean. It's just got to be done."

"I've tried to get help sent down for the survey, but there's not an extra hand to be had. We're understaffed everywhere these days."

"I know." She sat studying my uniform. I took my cap off.

"Is Liam in?"

"He's back there with a patient, giving shots. He'll be in in a minute."

"How has he been? How have you both been?"

She looked at me steadily. "He isn't well. I think he's dying. But he's happier than he's been for a long time. I see to that."

"Oh, you must be mistaken," I said. "He's quite a young man still. I think if he—straightened out his habits a bit—he'd survive for a long time yet. Ages."

"And if the world straightened out its habits, it would survive, too. Perhaps they both would, in that case." She nibbled her lower lip lightly. "There's been a considerable change in our—domestic arrangements," she said. "I'm sure you know about that."

"I—yes."

"Good. Then we won't need to discuss it. Why don't you sit down?"

"Thank you." I sat down in the chair facing the desk, setting my briefcase on the floor and my cap in my lap. She looked down at the sheaf of papers in front of her and shuffled through them for a moment.

"So far, we've got together fifty-seven of the control group for yearly reexamination. Cardozo has done about the same number. There are—let's see —seven we've failed to locate. Most of them moved to places unknown. One died. One reported as admitted to the Insane Hospital at Mount Vernon."

"Was there an autopsy done?"

"Yes. And embalming. But I believe there was some fuss about compensation for it. Liam can give you the details."

"Has there been any dramatic change in morbidity, in the ones you've examined?"

"A certain amount. Cardiac, mostly, I think. I don't have the figures here, but I'll get them out for you."

"It sounds as if you have everything under control."

"Statistics always make things sound as if they were under control."

Outside the window I heard the sudden wail of the mill saws begin in the hot, tawny distances of the morning air. A sparrow cheeped mournfully on the sill of the open window. I looked about the office.

"You've got a new file cabinet."

"They're getting full," she said. "We got that one from the State Farm Administration funds. It took three weeks of negotiating."

"I know. So much time wasted with trivia. I wish to God we could get things better organized." She did not reply to this.

"There's some coffee in the percolator, if you'd like a cup."

"I've just finished breakfast, thanks."

She got up and went across to the file cabinet. "I'll get those files out."

"Thank you. I'd like to take them home and have a look at them."

Mrs. Farris came into the room in her nurse's uniform and paused at the door, her broad, gentle grandmother's face breaking into a sweet smile.

"Dr. Ransome!" she said. "How nice to see you again! My goodness, I didn't know you were coming in this morning."

"Hello, Mrs. Farris. How are you? It's nice to see you, too."

"Thank you, sir. You're looking very well. Are you back with us for good?"

"No, not for a while, I'm afraid. I just have a few days to look in and see how things are going."

"I see. Well, we certainly have missed you around here. I was thinking about you the other day when I went out to see Rebecca. Walter Lubby's daughter, remember? She asked about you."

"Oh, did she? I hope she's not ill."

"No, sir. She's just pregnant again. I went out to get her enrolled in the Maternity Clinic. She's doin' real well."

"I'm glad to hear that. Give her my respects when you see her again."

"Indeed I will. Well, it's real nice to see you, sir. Miss Thurmond, have you seen that file on Lucius Pritchett?"

"You left it on the desk."

"Well, I thought I must have done that. I swear, I'm just losin' my mind." She went to the desk and picked up the file where Janet had set it aside for her.

"I'm not surprised," Janet said. "You must have worked twelve hours yesterday."

"Well, I know, but what would I do if I went home? I wouldn't do nothin' but sit and worry about these people, so I might as well be here." She carried the file to the door, where she turned to smile at me. "I hope I'll see you again, Dr. Ransome, before you leave."

"Yes, I'll be in and out. Goodbye, Mrs. Farris."

When Liam came into the room a moment later, I saw immediately the justice of Janet's opinion. His face had become a strange dull saffron color, as if he were taking Atabrine, or as if it were saturated with tobacco smoke, like the long, faintly tremulous fingers with which he stood plucking the lapels of his laboratory smock. He smiled gently.

"Carl. How very good of you to call on us. I wish I'd known you were arriving. I would have shined my shoes."

I stood up and held out my hand to him. After studying it for a moment as if carefully locating it in space in preparation for some very delicate maneuver, he took and shook it, incessantly, in what seemed to me a parody of cordiality.

"It's good to see you, Liam."

"Oh, it must be. It must be a real delight for you. I'm surprised you're able to contain it so well. Have you had coffee?"

"I don't care for any, thanks. You're really looking very well."

"By God, so are you. New uniform?"

"No." I smiled at him. "I had it pressed."

"Does wonders. I must have mine pressed." He glanced down at the shabby smock he wore. "How often do you have it done? Once a week?"

"No," I said uneasily. "Once a year, at most."

"Not more than that? By God, it makes all the difference, doesn't it? I think we could manage once a year. Janet, will you see to that?" She lowered her head regretfully. "So here you are. We expected you last week."

"Yes, I was telling Janet, things are pretty hectic in Hot Springs."

He grinned at me genially. "Sounds like a musical comedy number, doesn't it? 'Things Are Pretty Hectic in Hot Springs.'" He sang the words to the tune of "They Got an Awful Lot of Coffee in Brazil," brandishing an imaginary straw hat in one hand and breaking into an unsteady soft-shoe dance that carried him across the floor to the desk, where he collapsed into the chair with a look of exhaustion, breathing heavily. "Whew! Lungs are going. Arches, too. Spine. Everything." He looked up at me merrily. "Well, I suppose you want to know the casualty list. How many dead and buried, how many diced and dissected, that sort of thing."

"I'm getting the files together," Janet said.

"Oh, good. Don't forget the Fitzhugh file. We've got a real tidbit for you there, Carl. You remember that case? Jackson Fitzhugh? Osteitis of the lower extremities, with arteritis? Well, it's gone into gangrene in the left foot. Something you won't see once in fifteen years. I think it will give you quite a lift."

"I was wondering if we could have lunch together," I said.

"Oh, I don't go out for lunch. Just have a sandwich sent up from the drugstore, or some chili from the Bayou."

"Maybe dinner this evening would be better, anyway. I'll have had time to go over the files. Could you make that?"

"I don't know," Liam said. "That's up to Janet. She's the chatelaine of our establishment. You knew we had an establishment, by the way?"

"Yes," I said. I lowered my eyes tactfully. "Molly told me. I suppose I should—offer my congratulations."

"Oh, not if it embarrasses you. Not necessary at all, really. By the way, I've seen Molly a couple of times. With Janet, I mean. Nothing clandestine."

"I know. That was kind of you." I turned awkwardly to Janet. "Both of you. I want to thank you for that. It's meant a lot to her."

"She's a very sweet woman," Janet said. "But I suppose you know that." She laid the folders she had been gathering from the drawers on top of the file cabinet. "Carl, here are all the records of the last six months. If you have any questions, you can call me in the morning. Liam, I'm going in the lab."

"Good. If you could possibly get those cases in the rack done, it would be a real blessing. I know it's a job."

"I think so. Don't worry about it." She went out of the office and into the lab across the hall, closing the door behind her.

"You're very lucky to have her," I said.

"Yes. That expresses it very well." He opened a drawer of the desk and rummaged about in it. "There's a letter here I think you ought to see. It's addressed to me, but it's about matters outside my jurisdiction. Money. I hope you'll set these people straight." He fished an envelope out of the drawer and held it across the top of the desk to me. I opened it and unfolded the sheet of official stationery inscribed with the seal of the U.S. Marine Hospital in Mobile, Alabama. It read:

Dear Dr. Proctor:

Some time ago I received notice from Dr. Carl Ransome of the United States Public Health Service that I should visit the Alabama Insane Hospital at Mt. Vernon from time to time to confer with Dr. Partlow, who is Superintendent of that institution, about the condition of any patients hospitalized there who may be in the Tallacoochee study group. Dr. Ransome informed me in his letter that a sum of $50.00 may be utilized in completion of arrangements for and performance of autopsial procedures on any such patient who dies at that institution. I conferred with Dr. Partlow last week and he informed me that he has a patient at the moment whose name appears on the list, a Thomas W. Kincaid, who in his opinion is about to die. I would like to know if you are authorized to make such disbursements, and if so, if you will O.K. the expenditure of $50.00 for transportation of body and postmortem examination in this case.

Yours very truly,

D. J. Prather, Senior Surgeon

"This is dated the thirteenth," I said. "Six days ago. Has the man died yet?"

"Not to my knowledge," Liam said. "If he has, they're keeping it a secret."

"I thought all this was perfectly clear. These autopsies have simply got to be performed. It's the most important part of the whole project."

"Then it would be a good idea to make disbursements directly out of Washington, don't you think?" Liam said. "I have no authority to make them, and I don't want it. I've got a job already. Why don't you authorize Kidd to make them, over at Cardozo? After all, I imagine the majority of the posts will be done there."

"It might be the best thing," I said. "It's got to be cleared up, at any rate. We've got to have a very definite procedure."

"As a matter of fact, it might be better if he took over the whole damn project. I've got quite enough to do, handling the Hackett County Health Department."

"You've been very busy," I said. "I understand that. It's one of the things I wanted to talk to you about." I leaned down to open my briefcase and removed a sheet of his recent correspondence, which I unfolded and scanned briefly. "You say that you've received lab reports on 2,800 registrants, and that you found 360 positives."

"I believe so, if that's what it says. Is that my letter?"

"Yes." I quoted from the typewritten sheet: " 'We are finding that a large majority of these positive cases have never been treated, and have several children, which means they will probably never be called into the Army. Is it—' " I paused over the ironic phrasing. " 'Is it your august desire that we should defer treatment on all married draftees until we receive your final decision?' "

"Yes, I think that's my letter," Liam said. "The style sounds familiar. Not a bad style at all, don't you think? Reminiscent of Swift."

"I haven't read Swift."

"Oh, you should. Wonderful writer. There's a thing of his called *A Modest Proposal* that I think you'd enjoy very much. I've got a copy of it, if you'd like to take it along."

"I don't think I'll have the time," I said. "To answer your question, I think we should withhold treatment, yes. After all, there'll be very little opportunity in the future to add to the study group. Unless they're selected immediately from the list of registrants, we may never again be able to find any significant number of uncontaminated cases."

"Yes, I suppose that's true," Liam said. "At least, I gather it's true, from that article of yours in the current issue of the *V.D. Journal.* Speaking of style, I think you ought to be congratulated on that piece. Really fine piece of rhetoric. I think I've got it here, as a matter of fact. I saved it, especially." He delved into the desk drawer again, and after shuffling about for a moment, came up with a copy of the publication, turned open to the pages of my article. "Yes, here it is. 'A Survey of Recent Drug Therapy Research,' etc. This is a fascinating thing. Just listen to this."

"I've read it," I said.

"Yes, I know, but it's got such a ring to it. One can't hear it too often." He began to read from the article: "'What may well prove to be one of the great therapeutic advances in the history of infectious disease is Alexander Fleming's discovery of penicillin from the fungus *Penicillium notatum.* Reports from the Venereal Disease Research Laboratory at Staten Island cite remarkable results in the treatment of syphilis with this new drug. During the past year Dr. John Friend Mahoney has conducted experiments over a six-month period with one hundred patients in the primary stage of the disease. A dosage of 1,200,000 units of penicillin was administered over a period of eight days, and the healing of lesions was little short of miraculous. At the end of three months of observation, all serologic and clinical evidence was absent in these patients, and continued to be so at the end of the following three-month period. A new schedule of 2,400,000 units administered over the same period of time has since been initiated. There are very strong indications that this research will result in what has so long been anticipated, a specific cure for the disease.'" He lowered the journal and raised his eyes to me, lifting his brows in tribute. "What an extraordinary thing! It sounds like what we've been searching for, for over five hundred years."

"It's very promising," I said. "Of course, these results need a great deal of confirmation. The tone may be a bit effusive."

"Oh, not at all! A very modest tone, I think, considering the magnitude of what you're reporting. Which is virtually an epiphany. Not at all effusive. Is it true?"

"I wouldn't report it if it weren't true," I said stiffly.

"No, of course you wouldn't. Nothing but the truth. You think, then, that we may have an absolutely positive cure for the disease?"

"It begins to look that way."

"Well, then, I wonder if you'd explain to me—in that admirable style of yours—just what the point is in letting four hundred men suffer and die, quite needlessly, from it?"

"The point," I said, "is that there's still a great deal to be learned about the pathogenesis of the disease—"

"A disease from which no one need suffer at all."

"*If* this treatment proves to be as effective as we think. But of course, it may not. There may be all sorts of delayed side effects that make it impractical. It may turn out to be just as dangerous and difficult to manage as mercury. And then, of course, it serves as a control against which we can project the results of the new rapid-schedule treatments. And also relative costs. There are a hundred reasons—" I paused to consider them.

"Why don't we inoculate a few hundred people with smallpox, just to see what happens to them?" Liam said. "Might be all sorts of interesting things turn up. A group of people from Scarsdale, perhaps, or Bucks County. They're very educated and progressive people, I understand. I think they could be counted on to cooperate."

"Don't be so damned cynical," I said. "This study has received worldwide attention. It's become practically a classic observation-in-nature. The greatest authorities in the world in treponemal disease—"

"In other words, it's become an institution," Liam said. "Like the poll tax, and the company store, and segregation. And of course, it has the sanction of the state."

"I don't think that needs to be apologized for. The history of the Public Health Service can compare with that of medical practice in any country in the world."

"Certainly with Germany's. Although they're doing some very interesting things in medicine just now, too, I believe. With Jewish subjects. Hitler's supposed to be very enthusiastic about it."

I stood up and faced him angrily across the desk, clutching the letter in my hand and spilling my cap onto the floor.

"You've got a damned nerve, comparing Roosevelt, or Thomas Parran, to Hitler," I said in a rapid, thin whisper.

"I wasn't comparing them to Hitler."

"Or Moore, or Eagle, or Kampmeier. These are men of conscience."

"Yes, I know," Liam said. His voice dropped to a low, almost ritual tone, like that of a man reciting liturgy. "And so am I. Or so I used to believe, a year ago. That's what really horrifies me, I suppose. That's the really appalling thing." He lowered his head and stared for some time at his knees, then raised his eyes to look at me. His eyes wandered slightly as they stared into mine as if he were struggling to remember something: a name, a telephone number, a message he had promised to deliver. "I'm not a pacifist," he said at last. "I believe there are some things a man has to fight and die for. To kill for, if necessary. I think you know that. God knows you ought to, as often as you've heard me go on about the Spanish war. Or this one. If there was ever that kind of a cause, this is it. But that's a different thing from deliberately inflicting pain or death on people in the name of truth, or virtue, or liberation, or progress. From committing evil in the name of good. I suppose that's the only genuine sacrilege I can conceive of. As you may have gathered, I'm not a very religious man."

I picked up my hat and briefcase from the floor. He watched me vaguely, as if I were a fellow passenger preparing to debark from an airplane. I put on my cap and turned to leave.

"Carl," he said curiously, "do you pity these people at all?"

"No."

"No. That's what makes you so much stronger than me. I do, of course. But that only puts me at the service of their bodies, not their souls. Maybe it's a presumption for a doctor to think he should love his patients at all. Maybe it's the greatest mistake he could make. He ought to be quite content to be simply a mechanic, perhaps. Because a man who does love should be prepared to inflict pain sometimes. Don't you think so?"

"Yes."

"Which leaves you something of a mystery to me. I say that quite sincerely."

"I'll consider it a tribute," I said.

He leaned forward and rested his forearms on the desk, looking up at me wearily. "I helped to found this Health Department, you know. I've been head of it since 1930. Fourteen years. And I intend to remain head of it as long as I'm able to get out of bed in the morning. It was founded for the purpose of easing human suffering, and that's going to remain its purpose—its only purpose—as long as I *am* head of it. You're going to have to find someone else to do your work for you. I've had enough of it."

"You won't reconsider that?"

"No."

"It leaves us in a very difficult position. We're in the middle of locating and reexamining all these people, and it's a very complicated business. Without your experience and personnel it will be very difficult indeed." I paused for a moment, with an uncustomary diffidence. "Besides," I said, "how can we possibly, at this point—" I paused again, as if to let the very silence of the cosmos complete my last appeal to him, my last invitation to give up his picturesque intransigence and join the rest of us in the fallen world below. The appeal itself, I realized as I considered the unspoken portion of it, had not a little of the picturesque about it.

"How can we possibly what?"

"Go on without you. You've become indispensable to us."

"Yes, I suppose I have, God help me. Well, you'll just have to learn to, I'm afraid. I've had enough of it."

I glanced down at my briefcase and tapped it against my thigh. "Will you at least continue to cooperate until we've had time to make alternative arrangements? Say for three months?"

He blinked slowly, turning his hand toward him and opening his fingers to gaze into the palm.

"All right. But that's the end of it. I won't go any further. After that you'll have to get along without me, any way you can."

"Thank you." I went to the file cabinet and took the sheaf of folders that Janet had set on top of it. The laboratory door opened and Janet came across the hall and stood in the office doorway. She looked at Liam, then at me, then back at Liam.

"Are you all right?" she said.

"Yes, fine," Liam said. "I feel better now. Much better."

I went to the door and paused to turn back to him.

"I want to thank you for all the work you've done for us," I said. "You've made a very great contribution—"

He closed his eyes and shook his head, waving his hand in renunciation of my words. "For God's sake, spare me that. If there's one thing I don't want from you, it's thanks."

That was the last time I saw him alive. I've always regretted that I didn't shake his hand. Perhaps I feared that he would decline the offer to do so. At any rate, I abandoned the impulse to make it; and since I had, I couldn't very well offer it to Janet. I said, "Goodbye," hurriedly, in a way that vaguely included both of them, and edged past her into the hall, my leave-taking as graceless and misbegotten as my entire relationship with them had been.

There was no real alternative to his cooperation. It might have been possible to transfer responsibility for the project to Kidd, along with the authority for making disbursements, record-keeping, and conducting examinations, autopsies, and the rest of it—it would, in fact, have been simple from an administrative point of view, since he was familiar with all of these procedures, supervised many of them, and already held a nominal commission in the Corps—but it was a far from satisfactory or permanent solution. All the study subjects were residents of Hackett County, and without the official cooperation of its Health Department, personnel, and clinical facilities it would have been impossible to conduct the study on any longtime basis. I was prepared to secure that cooperation by whatever means necessary, even if they included the dismissal of Liam as head. They almost certainly would have, and it would have been a difficult and bitter business. Pressure would have had to be applied from Washington, and either his intransigence overcome or allegations made and affidavits furnished as to his competence to perform his duties. If there is one article of professional decorum no physician is anxious to violate it is to abstain from offering testimony to the incompetence of a colleague. I certainly did not look forward to doing so, but I considered it, as a contingency, and would have been capable of pursuing it or any other course of action, if it had been required. Fortunately, it wasn't, because he died six weeks later.

I had returned to the clinic circuit and was working in Hot Springs at the time. I did not receive official notice of his death, and would not have known of it in time to attend his funeral if I had not happened to make a long-distance call to Dr. Kidd on the day after he died. We were discussing the transferral of Mrs. Farris to the Public Health Service payroll.

One of the stratagems that had occurred to me was the recruitment of a skeleton staff of workers from the ranks of Liam's Health Department personnel and placing them directly under P.H.S. supervision—with a substantial raise in salary, perhaps, as an incentive—to guarantee their continued participation in the project. With such a core of experienced technicians we would have been able to carry on the work of the reexaminations until some more permanent arrangement was made. The most essential member of his staff in this respect was Mrs. Farris—she had, indeed, become indispensable to us—and I had called Kidd to ask his opinion of the possibility of winning her over to such a proposition. I had not made known to him Liam's secession from the study—I considered it risky to do so, since he had already expressed a shadow of misgivings about the project, and the barest hint of Liam's defection on moral grounds, I was afraid, would have confirmed them and perhaps precipitated his own resignation. I approached him simply on the basis of a proposed reorganization of the study structure for its greater efficiency and the added convenience of everyone concerned. It was Mrs. Farris's reaction I was worried about.

"Of course, I don't know if she'd be willing to separate herself from the County Health Department," I said to him. "She has such a personal loyalty to Liam."

"Well, that won't be a problem any longer," Dr. Kidd said. "He died yesterday." It was some time before I could reply.

"Did you say he died?"

"Yes. About nine o'clock last night. I don't suppose you've heard yet. Cardiac arrest. He was working late, as I understand it, and didn't answer the phone when Miss Thurmond called him at the office, so she went to look for him. She found him on the clinic stairs."

"Good God."

"Yes," Kidd said.

"We had some disagreements, from time to time, but I—well, I wasn't prepared for this."

"I know. I don't think any of us were. It's strange, what a hole a man's death can leave in a community. I suppose this changes the whole picture, really. I mean, if there's a new man in charge of the department, perhaps we ought to wait until we learn something about his policies."

"Yes. Yes, I think I'd better call you again next week, after I've talked to Dr. Parran."

"All right."

"When is he being buried?"

"On Tuesday. There's a service at ten o'clock at the First Baptist Church. I believe it's public—that is, for some. Will you be coming down?"

"I'm going to try to."

"Perhaps we can get together then, if you have the time."

"Yes. I'll be in touch with you."

I arrived on Tuesday morning, barely in time for the funeral. Molly picked me up at the bus station and we drove directly to the church.

It was a very strange funeral. Since Liam was still married to Paula, it was her prerogative to arrange the details, and there was a vindictive and theatrical satisfaction evident in the way she did so. She used the occasion as a combined demonstration of wronged womanhood, unfaltering loyalty, heroic fortitude, and all-redeeming love. She sat dramatically alone in the front row of the pews, veiled, poignant, and solitary, in a black gown of such stunning virtuosity that I was led to the dark suspicion that it had been designed with the occasion in mind. There were a great many flowers, and they had been artfully displayed to emphasize the supremacy of an extravagant tribute, unmistakably her own, of perhaps four dozen red roses, arranged to form a giant heart, which rested stupefyingly on top of the casket. I could picture Liam's crooked smile fixed, eternally, beneath it. The mourners seemed more suitably impressed; indeed, the whole occasion seemed to be addressed far more directly, and transparently, to their sentiments than his. I was astonished at the number of them; I knew he had few close friends with whom he shared real intimacy or affection or, certainly, belief; yet evidently the entire body of the town's hegemony had turned out to praise his memory and the deeds and principles which they had so often found mischievous, embarrassing, or heretical. Perhaps they were celebrating their relief from that vexation as much as anything. I'm sure that if the service had been left to Janet's hands, it would have been extremely modest and performed in a funeral home rather than a church, but nothing could have been clearer than the fact that her opinions had not been solicited. She sat at the very back of the church at the end of a pew, against a wall; yet, as inconspicuous as her position was, there were heads turned occasionally to cast a critical glance at her. I don't think she even noticed; certainly she didn't care; she sat with her face devastatedly downcast throughout the ceremony, and when the mourners rose to pray she was late in getting to her feet, as if lost in her own private obsequies. I could not blame her. The oration was long, lugubrious, and rising occasionally to heights as floral and magniloquent as Paula's tribute on top of the coffin. The pretension of the whole event was dramatized unexpectedly and with a humble, condign clarity when, at the conclusion of the requiem, we followed the casket out of the church and up among the cedar trees to the gravesite in the adjacent cemetery. Standing outside the iron fence that enclosed the churchyard was a group of black people, ten or twelve of them, dressed in their best clothes, the men in ties and carefully pressed suits, holding their hats against their breasts, the women looking astonishingly gracious in their summer hats and freshly ironed dresses and high heels, some of them holding children by the hand whom they bent to quiet occasionally, then standing erect again, motionlessly attentive and decorous as we filed past them among the headstones to the open grave on a little knoll at the far end of the cemetery. The casket was set on a structure of supporting pipes above the carpet of green matting spread over the freshly excavated raw earth of the grave. A pair of attendants stepped forward to set on top of it some of the floral sprays, those of Liam's relatives, I assumed, which they had carried from the church, Paula's centered conspicuously among them. The graveside ceremony was brief and, by contrast with that inside the church, unexpectedly agreeable and natural, with the clear summer light falling through the trees, the clean, sharp scent of cedar in the air, and the piping of a thrush in the fields beyond the cemetery, its idyllic quality unmarred even by Paula's ostentatious grief. She stood at the center of a group of Liam's relatives, her arm linked with that of a slender, strikingly attractive young woman of twenty-two or so, whom I recognized as her daughter from the photographs I had seen of her in Paula's living room. The girl had Liam's slightness of frame and his gentle restlessness of manner, and she seemed to express, in the occasional impatient drowsing of her eyes and shifting of her feet, the aversion which I'm sure he would have shared for the solemnity with which he was being consigned to eternity.

Janet did not attend the graveside service. I suppose she felt that her presence in that small circle of those whose relationships with him were licensed and whose grief was licit would have been a disturbing impropriety, as unnecessary as any further proof of perhaps the greatest constancy that day disclosed. There was one other, whose testimony I hope he was aware of: when we left the gravesite and drifted back among the headstones toward the churchyard gate, strung out in a curiously desultory way, I saw Rebecca standing behind the iron fence that enclosed the cemetery. She was wearing the same white dress and flowered hat that she had worn to her father's—Walter Lubby's—funeral, and was holding her daughter by the hand. The little girl

was crooning a hymn softly, uninterrupted in her devotionals since the last time
I had seen her. I paused to speak to her mother through the black cast-iron
railings of the fence.

"Hello, Rebecca."

"Hello, Dr. Ransome."

"You look very well. I hope your family are well, too."

"Yes, suh, they're real well, thank you."

"This is my wife. I don't think you know her."

"No, I don't. How do you do, Mrs. Ransome, ma'am."

"How do you do, Rebecca."

She was holding a small bouquet of wildflowers, yellow daisies and gentians
and foxglove, their stems bound with a strip of blue ribbon.

"Dr. Ransome, suh, I wonder if you'd do me a favor?" She held the flowers
to me between the railings of the fence. "Would you put these on Dr. Proctor's
grave fo' me?"

"Yes, of course," I said. I took the bouquet from her. "They're very pretty."

"I'd just like him to know we're goin' to miss him very much."

"He'd be very pleased," I said.

"Thank you, suh."

I took the spray of flowers back to the grave and leaned across the matting-
covered chasm to place it on the casket, setting it carefully on top of Paula's
huge rose heart, at the apex of the many elaborate wreaths.

We sat in silence for several moments, listening to the strange asthmatic
purring of the electric clock. Sylvie rested her elbows on the table, clasped her
hands together, and turning her wrists aside, laid her cheek against the uppermost, staring down at the glisten of light on the blue oilcloth. After a time she
closed her eyes and appeared to dream; a sad dream that drew her face into
a sorrowful, unguarded repose.

"I've upset you," I said. "I'm not surprised."

"No. I just wish I were better to you. Kinder. Wiser. I wish I could be
everything you need." She detached her right hand and with her eyes still
closed reached out to me across the table, groping for me in the air like a child
playing blindman's bluff. I took her hand and brought it down to rest on the
table, pressed between both of my own. Looking at her lustrous hair, her bent,
magnificent head, I said, "Tell me something, will you? Truly."

"Yes."

"Have you ever been afraid of me?"

"No. You're the kindest man I know. The gentlest. Except for Aaron."

"That's the thing I fear most in the world—having people fear me. It's
truly horrifying. You know, for a long time I couldn't even take a public

conveyance of any kind, a streetcar or a bus or train, because I was afraid a child or an old black man might sit down facing me across the aisle, and I'd have to sit there for the next quarter of an hour, or half an hour, or more, staring at her face, or his face, unable to avoid their eyes, seeing their fear of me. It happened several times. They seemed almost occultly to be guided to some seat directly facing me, and to sense my guilt unerringly, and be afraid. Once I sat all the way from Washington to Chester, Pennsylvania, in a club car across the aisle from an old black man in a minister's garb, and I don't think he took his eyes from mine the whole way. Every time I looked up I saw them staring at me with that look of fear, almost as if he were about to bless himself. And once, much later, I took a subway in New York and a little girl sat down across from me with her mother and looked at me for a full ten minutes or so with a kind of weird, gathering terror in her eyes; and then turned and whispered something to her mother, who bent her head and listened, it seemed to me, with a look of equal horror and repugnance, and then raised her eyes to mine in such a stony, condemnatory way that I had to get up and leave hurriedly at the next stop, shoving my way through people standing in the aisle. That was a long time later, as I say, after the war. It was on a summer day in 1955, just three months before I was eligible to retire from the Corps and had to decide whether or not I would reenlist. I was on my way to Brooklyn College to deliver an address, but I got out of the subway miles from my destination, in my flight from that child's gaze, at the West Fourth Street station in Greenwich Village. It was a lovely day, so bright and cool and almost supernaturally clear that it reminded me of that day on the Gulf of Mexico. When I came up the subway steps I stood there in the sunlight feeling utterly dislocated for a moment or two, not knowing where I was, or how I'd gotten there, or just where I was going, or how much time I had left to get there. A few yards from the subway exit there was a sidewalk vendor selling ice cream from a pushcart, so I bought an ice-cream cone and began to walk along the sidewalk licking it, and even more remarkably, holding it so carelessly that it dripped on my dress uniform. Across the avenue there was one of those street art exhibitions going on; there were scores of bright paintings fastened to a chain link fence that separated the sidewalk from a public schoolyard on Sixth Avenue. There were artists sitting on canvas stools in front of their creations, hawking their wares to passersby or chatting with potential patrons in the sunlight, everyone in summer clothes and sandals, hot and leisurely and good-humored, nibbling pretzels or licking ice-cream cones, as I was; it was like a fair. I went across the street and joined them, strolling in front of the exhibit, still licking my ice-cream cone. I hadn't done that sort of thing in a quarter of a century; it was as if I'd stolen an hour out of my life for absolute, mindless, idle truancy. I actually forgot, for half an hour or so, that in an auditorium somewhere across the city people were assembling to hear my observations on the pathogenesis of syphilis with a gravity that might very well go unrewarded because of my sudden vagrant passion for the arts. Not that it was a triumph, at last, for aesthetics; most of the paintings were pretty awful, even to my unpracticed eye. There were a great many square-rigged sailing ships and rose-covered cottages and puppies tumbling out of baskets, and a number of boldly experimental works full of fearless discordancies of color and line and lofty liberation from the strictures of descriptive art. There were also several representatives of that genre whose principal themes are Elvis Presley and tigers with blazing neon-orange stripes, painted on black velvet and strangely amiable-looking in spite of their formidable snarls. But all of them were oddly beguiling, full of earnestness and charm and unquestioning acceptance of the primacy of feeling that even when it was sentimental or outrageous was inno-cent of malice or cruelty or vanity, a dauntless, energetic celebration of all that was bright and generous and temperate, like the sweet light of the afternoon. A light that seemed to bless their earnestness, rather than to expose their imperfections, to deal gently with their vagaries of form and color, to alleviate their extravagances and dignify their banalities; to accept them as an uncouth homage to itself. Even the neon-striped tigers, glowering at me from their black velvet fastnesses, reminded me in a brave, implausible way of the tiger in that poem of Blake's that I had heard Liam recite when he got drunk at parties and stood on the sofa to declaim; or of Molly, playing Mozart.

I decided in those few minutes, walking along that outdoor gallery in the summer sunlight, that I couldn't go on with the experiment any longer; that I would retire from the Corps and go into private practice. It was a decision that was quietly, almost matter-of-factly made, the way one decides one doesn't really want, after all, to turn back and slip into the pornographic movie house one has just passed on the street; and with just as modest but profound a sense of reclamation and relief. And just as absolutely; because after I had finished eating my ice-cream cone I took out my handkerchief and wiped my fingers and then went into a phone booth in a drugstore on the corner and dialed the number of the professor in charge of the lecture I was scheduled to deliver.

"I'm awfully sorry," I told him, "but I won't be able to make it. Something very tragic has happened."

"Good heavens. What?"

"A child has died," I said, "who was very close to me, and I have to attend her services. It's something that can't be neglected."

"Oh, I'm terribly sorry. What an awful thing. Of course, it puts us in a rather unfortunate position, but I realize it can't be helped."

"No. I believe you have a copy of the manuscript I'm preparing for the V.D. Journal."

"Yes. It was good of you to send it."

"Perhaps you could read from the section on the Tallacoochee mortality and morbidity statistics. It was to have been the substance of my lecture, as you know."

"Oh, that's a very good suggestion. Yes, I could do that."

"And please express my regrets for not delivering it in person."

"I will, of course."

"You might just add that in all such experiments the investigator should be animated by the hope that his work will receive the blessing of the light."

"I'll do that, certainly. Maybe I'd better just write it down, so that I don't forget."

I suppose it was an unconscionable thing to do, certainly the most unprofessional act of my career; but the thought of standing at a lectern for an hour or more in front of that assembly of solemnly respectful men of science who would be hanging on my every judiciously phrased sentence—sentences I could not bear to hear pronounced in public—was too chastening for me to contemplate.

In September I resigned my commission in the Corps and went into private practice in Bethesda. It did not necessitate a change of residence, as we had been living there for the past five years. Over that time my work had expanded to include far more than the Tallacoochee experiment and had been centered at the N.I.H. From there I had carried on the administrative work of the study and made periodic excursions to Tallacoochee to oversee the annual reexaminations, arrange for alternative autopsial procedures—Cardozo had by this time relinquished its role in the experiment entirely—and coordinate the work of local authorities. Much of my work was now concerned with the National Communicable Diseases Center in Atlanta and with our clinics in Hot Springs and Staten Island, where I spent frequent tours of duty. In fact, so little of my time was by then devoted exclusively to the Tallacoochee project that it would have been impractical to keep up residence there, as much as I had grown attached to the place. In 1950 we bought a house in Bethesda, not many blocks from my office at the N.I.H., and drove up from Alabama with a trailer attached to the car which contained most of our belongings from the musty old white wooden house on Choctaw Street with its moaning woodwork and mulberry-spattered walk and the volcanic fumes that issued from its heating vents. Molly did not share my regret at leaving it forever; I think it was the happiest day of her life. With the exception of the one in which we had spent the last ten years, I had never had much interest in houses; to me the modest suburban colonial into which we moved in Bethesda was indistinguishable from its neighbors, but Molly seemed consoled for every privation of her life by its modern, gleaming kitchen, its brick fireplace, its recreation room, its stone-paved patio, and its conventional allotment of redbud trees and cut-leaf maples and arborvitae hedges. She bit her lips and wept when she first got out of the car and stood looking at it. What consoled her truly was the life of comfortable respectability that went with it, almost as an accessory, and into which she entered with a quiet liturgical passion, immersing herself in the rituals of driving Elizabeth to school on snowy days, attending P.T.A. meetings, sewing fairy costumes—and then Pitti-Sing costumes—for Elizabeth, organizing summer outings for the Brownies and then concert tours to Constitution Hall for the Music Club. She thrived on her sorority with the women whose lives were composed of those rituals and on the deference she was accorded as the wife of a physician. I was very pleased; it was all that I could recognizably contribute any longer to her happiness. That we would ever fall into a passionate, or freely affectionate, or even quietly intimate devotion was too much to hope for; we had grown used to an austere civility from which we could depart now only by an effort of conversion too intense and agonizing to contemplate. I was too inexpert at the expression of affection and too often exhausted or preoccupied to offer any more than that respectful, somewhat chastened civility; but I think she was aware that she enjoyed a new understanding, on my part, of the depths of deprivation that no suburban home or set of social liturgies could ever truly compensate; and a new and humble indulgence of her gaucheries and benign pretensions and the gallant fantasy she promulgated, on anniversaries and holidays, and birthdays, of an immutable domestic paradise. I was so often away that I missed a good many of those debilitating occasions, although I scrupulously observed them with a card, a bottle of cologne, or a spray of flowers telegraphed from Atlanta, Staten Island, or Hot Springs. In fact, I had no sense at all of the flowing, congruent passage of our lives, of time that is spent in genuine intercourse—that gracious confluence of events by which one truly embraced by his life is made blessedly oblivious of its expiration and devoutly conscious of its essence. For me, it lurched and jolted onward with no real coherence or continuity or destiny, in a series of unnerving epiphanies, disconnected, exclamatory episodes enacted not by kinsmen but by barely recognizable intruders or predators or victims with strange, stern faces and cryptic speech and hostile, haunted eyes. When I came home after an absence of a month or six weeks I would be startled at how my wife had aged, how her eyes had suddenly developed the milky opacity of cataracts or how her knuckles had thickened with arthritis, or at how my daughter had graduated pitilessly into miniskirts or pendant earrings; and mortified by her sardonic rejection of the teddy bear I had brought her or my footless attempts at jocular paternal banter. The truth was, I was terrified to be with her. Her presence was a constant reproach to me, a constant conjuration of Doreen in her present, aborted, never-to-be-attained young womanhood; and of the two of them as little girls chattering on the sand in the sunlight of a lost and dreadful morning, in an instant of still-undesecrated time to which I longed to restore her from the silent controversion I felt when she passed through the room without a word to me or set the table for dinner with scarcely a glance in my direction. She could not have known of my longing to turn back the whole process of eternity to that moment of the innocent opportunity for love, but I think she was aware in some mysterious, terrible way of my having forsaken it. Whether or not she knew of my responsibility for its subversion, I think that, like all children who are bred in the wake of evil, she was unable to forgive a crime she could not have conceived of, but in whose fetor she was suffocating.

When I retired from the Corps she was seventeen, a grave, unapproachable, forbiddingly composed teenager, a bit too fat and formidably unembarrassed by the fact, amendable to the fashions of her peers in clothes and slang and pastimes, but less from submission or conformity or an appeal for acceptance than out of a calm independence that saw no need to demonstrate itself. She was not particularly brilliant or talented, but the firm intelligence and aptitude she had were marshaled by a sober sense of purpose toward some end that even when she was a teenager I felt was far more certain of accomplishment, and worthier, than those of her more facile, gifted, or gregarious companions. She was never very popular, and was neither indifferent to the fact nor discomposed by it, but accepted it or fended off whatever occasional abuse or humiliation it cast at her with the same stoic equanimity that protected her from all things, like a rude shield forged with much patient, determined hammering in the modest fires of her heart. The one or two girlfriends she had, however, were inalienably loyal to her, and the fact that they were generally as sober, industrious, and unsought as herself seemed to reassure her rather than to trouble her. What was remarkable was that from the age of fifteen on she "went steady" with a boy who was as far as I could make out the only one to apply for her affections in the whole course of her adolescence. He was a rather odd young man, as reserved and resolute as she, and apparently aware of the same verities that had mysteriously revealed themselves to her from infancy. Molly seemed pleased with the relationship and indulged her in it, as she did in everything from the time Elizabeth was obviously and undeterrably the mistress of her own destiny, which was approximately the age of ten. As the boy was of an Orthodox Jewish family, I saw it as something of a dilemma, but I did not question it, or the discretion that I was absolutely certain governed it, any more than I would have dared to question the origins of that discretion. Indeed I would happily have left any dilemma in the world to the disposition of my daughter's scruples, with the exception of my own.

When I retired and went into private practice I saw more of her, of course;

but not a great deal more, because I worked hard and long, often so late that I did not get home till after dinner, when Elizabeth had retired to her room to do her homework, or had gone out with Jerry or her girlfriends to a movie. Bethesda was a prosperous community, and I was able to earn a sufficient income to maintain Molly in the privileges of conventional gentility so dear to her and still to devote a good half of my time to free clinic work, which I did. I kept myself relentlessly busy, less out of virtue than the fear of idleness, the hour or half hour in bed before sleep blotted out my thoughts, or the moment of incorrigible mind-wandering when I would drop the newspaper to the floor or stare with sudden sightless woe beyond the parade of carnage on the television screen to the faces of the victims of that other holocaust that I was author of. It was a state of mind that did not improve my relations with either Elizabeth or Molly; we grew more and more remote from one another until our intercourse was reduced to a kind of spare decorum and our conversation to occasional subdued murmurs like the dialogue exchanged by fellow mourners at a wake. I think we all understood that we were merely biding time until Elizabeth would graduate from high school and depart. She left when she was eighteen, three weeks after her graduation, for a school she had chosen largely for the fact that it was as far as it was possible to get from Washington —the University of California at Berkeley—thus eliminating the possibility of weekend visits home or family birthday celebrations or frequent reunions of any kind. In fact, she never came back home at all, until Molly died. At Christmas she would write to say that she had been invited to spend the holidays with friends, or touring with classmates, or on ski trips to the Rockies, and when the regular semester was over she invariably attended summer school to avoid spending the holidays with us.

After she left, Molly's fantasy of happy suburban motherhood dissolved. For a time she lapsed into an almost unrelieved abstraction and depression. I encouraged her to go out to California to visit Elizabeth, which she began to do and which became the sole sustaining activity of her life. She would return home in the glow of their adventures and with a store of reminiscences and snapshots that were frayed by their endless exhibition, in matched red leather albums, or by their endless recitations to which I nodded and murmured restlessly at the dinner table. She lived from one to another of her visits, which were of increasing frequency and duration. In effect, she changed dwelling places; her stays at home were merely interludes, during which she basked in the memory of her last visit and her anticipation of the next. She went out to California when Elizabeth received her bachelor's degree and again for her master's ceremonies, sometimes staying for as long as two weeks or a month. Elizabeth took a master's degree in social work and went into the California prison system almost immediately after she received it. In 1965 she married a young man named Eric who was an Air Force pilot, and Molly went out to attend the wedding. A year later our first grandson was born and Molly was invited to his christening, as she was to that of our second, in 1968. In the autumn Eric was sent to Vietnam, and for the two years of his absence Molly stayed almost entirely in California, living in the apartment with Elizabeth and taking care of the children while Elizabeth went daily to her job as a parole officer. Once they took a summer tour together to Europe, which I protested that the pressure of my work made it impossible for me to join, a protest that was very amicably received. When Eric returned from Vietnam, Molly's trips became less frequent; she complained that she had been abandoned by her daughter, and her old malaise began to reassert itself. But in the fall of 1972 they invited her to take an automobile tour with them and the children to the Grand Canyon, a trip from which Molly returned in a state of strange luminous tranquillity, as if its joys had been greater than any she had ever hoped to experience on this earth. It was her last. Ten days after she came back I received a call at my office from the Mexican woman who had come to work as a maid for us. She had made lunch for Molly and gone up to her bedroom to call her down, and had found her slumped across the desk beside the window where she sat to write her letters to Elizabeth. She had begun one a moment or two before she collapsed, and I found it lying there when I returned from the hospital where she died of a massive stroke without regaining consciousness. She had had time only for a final proverb—this one from Psalms—which although it was addressed to Elizabeth and unprecedented in its clemency, I felt certain was cited for my benefit, as all that she had ever uttered had been, but in this case as a final blessing to me:

Dear Elizabeth:
    The Bible says that the Lord shall deliver us from fear of the pestilence that walketh in the darkness and the sickness that destroyeth in the noonday.
    I think that must be true, because even though lately I haven't been feeling

I've often wondered whether she had been ill for some time and had concealed the fact, hoping that by renouncing treatment she would hasten the relief of death.

May was a restless, cold, irresolute month; there were blue days and bitter ones, tantalizing soft, calm hours and then sudden harsh spring gales that set the black branches of the locusts rattling and hawthorn petals streaming in the wind. I kept a fire burning in the hearth mornings and evenings to take the raw chill from the house and by the middle of the month my woodpile was depleted to a dozen sodden black logs. I was very pleased one morning when I sat at the kitchen table with my tea and muffins to hear the thump of fresh logs being tossed onto the pile. I watched through the window as Virgil Bishop replenished my supply of firewood. He was unloading a wheelbarrow, stacking the logs along the backyard fence. When it was empty, he trundled it across the yard and through the gate to the pickup truck parked in the lane behind my garden fence, where he reloaded it with logs from the truck bed. I put on my jacket and went out to help him. He wheeled the barrow back across the yard to the woodpile and we stacked the logs together.

"I appreciate this," I said. "I was almost out."

"Yeah, it's been a cold spring. You're gettin' low. This'll do you till the fall."

"It's good-looking wood."

"Been down a year. Good and dry; it'll burn hot. It's mostly oak, but there's some applewood in there. I been cuttin' down that old orchard back of Barnett's. Makes a pretty fire."

"It smells good, too."

"Yes, it does."

"You shook off that infection," I said.

"Yeah, feelin' good again. I'm obliged to you for that."

When we had stacked the last of the wood, I said, "I'd like to pay you something for this. There's a lot of wood here."

"No indeed. It's worth a lot of wood knowin' we got a doctor here will take care of us like you do. More than I could cut in a lifetime." He nodded and tossed his work gloves into the barrow. "Good mornin', Dr. Ransome. Take care of yourself."

"I'm off to the market," I said. "There's a pot of hot tea on the table if you'd like a cup."

"I might do that," he said. "I'm a coffee man, as a regular thing, but I ain't too choosy right now."

"Help yourself. The cups are over the stove."

I went out of the gate and up the path toward the village, turning to watch him enter the kitchen door.

Two days later, when I came back from a morning walk with Sylvie, there were a middle-aged woman and a young boy sitting in the kitchen waiting for me. They sat very erect on the straight-backed chairs at the table, the woman with her hands folded in her lap, the boy turning his cap restlessly in his hands. There was a crutch propped against the edge of the table beside him and one of his feet, stretched out in front of him, was bound in a thick bandage of torn bloodstained sheeting. The woman was Drusilla Hance; her husband ran the ice-and-bait shack at the end of the small-boat pier on the village waterfront. She stood up when I entered the kitchen.

"Good morning, Mrs. Hance," I said.

"Good morning, Doctor. We took the liberty of waiting in here. I see your car was in, I figured you was up to the store."

"I'm glad you did. I hope you haven't been waiting long."

"No, sir, not more than ten minutes. This is my boy Tim."

"Hello, Tim," I said. "It looks like you've had some bad luck." The boy grinned and nodded shyly. "What have you done to yourself?"

"Jumped on a anchor," he said.

"Jumped right down off the top of the cabin," his mother said. "I reckon he's been told a thousand times not to go barefoot on a boat."

"Well, those things happen," I said. "I'd better have a look at it." I took off my overcoat and went to the pot shelf under the sink, where I knelt down to dig out an enamel basin. "Set your foot in this and take that bandage off. I'll just get my bag." When I came back from the hall closet with my bag he had the foot unwrapped, his heel resting in the basin, holding the bloody bandage in his hand. I took it from him and tossed it in the wastebasket, going to the sink to wash my hands.

"That looks pretty deep," I said. "Was it rusty?"

"No, sir."

"We might have to take a couple of stitches in that." I went back to the table and knelt down to examine the foot. The cut was a dark blue puncture wound that ran from the center of his sole halfway up his instep. It had stopped bleeding, but there were bright-red hemorrhagic rays spraying up across the pale skin of his instep. The ankle was badly swollen and discolored.

"Looks like you twisted your ankle, too," I said.

"Yes, sir. It's real sore."

I felt the ankle gently and he winced. It was not broken, but it was badly sprained. I washed and swabbed out the cut, sprinkled it with sulfanilamide, and put three stitches in it. Then I gave him an anti-tetanus shot and wrapped his ankle lightly in an Ace bandage. "When you get home I want you to take this off and put ice on it," I said. "I guess you've got plenty of ice, Mrs. Hance."

"Indeed we've got plenty of that."

"Have you got an ice bag?"

"I believe we do."

"Keep applying it for a couple of days, and in between, keep it bandaged up just like this. It's not broken, but it's going to be good and sore."

"When kin I walk?" the boy said.

"Well, we'll see. You just test it out, day by day, and see how much weight you can put on it. Where did you get the crutch?"

"It was my daddy's," Mrs. Hance said. "We cut it off."

"Well, that comes in handy. I'll drop around in a day or two and take those stitches out. If that starts getting sore, or you get any pus in it, you let me know. How did you get here, anyway?"

"Lester drove us up," Mrs. Hance said. "He had to get back to the store."

"Well, you'd better let me drive you back. It'll be hard going, on that foot."

"That would be a kindness." She stood up and helped the boy to his feet while I put on my jacket. "They say you don't take money, Doctor."

"No, ma'am, I don't. I've got all the money I need."

"Do you fish?"

"Yes, I do, occasionally. I enjoy it."

"Well, we rent out small boats, you know. Day sailers and rowboats, with outboards. Anytime you'd like to use one, I hope you'll feel free to take one out."

"I certainly will. I'd appreciate that."

"You just come by the office. If you want to take an outboard, we'll give you a can of gas."

"That's kind of you."

I went out to the gate with them, steadying the boy while he hobbled with his crutch across the yard. They waited while I drove the car up the lane behind the fence, and after I had got him into it, I drove them down to the pier on the village waterfront, where a dozen small boats tugged gently at their lines in the river current. The boy's father came out of the office shack at the end of the pier when I stopped the car.

"Dr. Ransome's got him fixed up," his wife called through the window. "There isn't nothing broke. We're taking him on home."

The man nodded and saluted me, calling out, "We're obliged; Doctor."

"That's all right. He'll be fine."

I drove them home, and when I had come back and parked the car beside the cottage I stood for a few minutes looking down over the tumbled roofs of the old weather-beaten cottages to the flat, lead-gray water of the bay that was lost in the morning mist under the sunless, cloud-sealed sky. I felt a peace descend on me too great even to allow a smile. I felt myself to be a part of the timeless, quiet prospering of the small, sea-lapped island with its mists and whispering salt marshes and tides and good, eternal gulls.

June came in a sudden burst of soft commotion and fragrance and wanton music everywhere, like the arrival of a band of gypsies. The air thrummed with it, as if bows were being touched to the shivering strings of the marsh grass and the slender spires of green quince in the hedges. It seemed to call us out of our stern white houses to the fair, to sun-warm wine and dancing under the green pavilions of the trees and dalliance in their dappled shadow. The tiny delicate new leaves were stirred by the soft wind like a girl's hair by a lover's whispering and trembled under sprinkles of warm rain as quick and startling as the flash of finches in a thicket or a silver shower of minnows in a stream. I wandered around the island in a crazed, fond delirium, smiling at birdsong, sniffing the scented air, touching everything, like a child in a toy shop.

It brought no calm to Sylvie. She grew more restless and distracted with every hour of the summer weather. A kind of brilliant, bone-deep distemper seemed to possess her as the days advanced toward her birthday. It almost visibly increased the luster of her hair and eyes and set her porcelain-white flesh aglow with a hectic glimmer, like magnolia petals in sunlight. When we talked, she was impatient, inattentive, and often oddly forgetful. She would fall into long, impenetrable silences or spells of unaccountable gaiety or agitation that made our dialogues fitful or desultory or disrupted them entirely. She would sit broodingly plaiting the split stem of a dune reed into a shining cable, plucking apart a globe of dandelion seed into a diaphanous litter, or tearing into tiny pieces the peel of an orange she had eaten, then suddenly scattering it across the tabletop with her fingertips, either in vexation at some remark of mine that wearied or oppressed her or recoiling at some wayward thought of her own that appeared to have crept into her mind and stung her like a hornet. Or she might simply sit and stare while her tea grew cold in front of her and my vain attempts to keep the conversation alive withered like wildflowers in a tumbler. She came less often to see me and was less often at home when I stopped at her cottage. Often her kitchen was a shambles, littered with empty cereal boxes or syrup tins and unwashed plates and cutlery, left on the table amid a rubble of biscuit crumbs or piled in a jumble under the dripping faucet in her sink. Her plants began to wither and die, unwatered, on her windowsills and wall shelves. Their dry brown leaves fell onto the linoleum floor in the strange autumnal silence that seemed to possess her cottage. I watered them, and wound the huge old Westclox alarm on the shelf above her stove that had stopped at twelve o'clock; and periodically I washed the pots and dishes and swept the kitchen floor that was gritty with spilled sugar and toast crumbs. When I saw her next, she would make no mention of these ministrations. I think she was hardly aware of them, or had forgotten.

She did no washing for weeks. One of the secret joys of my life was to go out into my garden on a Monday morning and while I stood watering my flower beds with a hose, discreetly ensconced behind a leafy tumulus of snowball bushes, to look down the lane and across her picket fences to watch her hang out her washing on the wire clothesline in her backyard. There was something incongruous with her nature and yet infinitely graceful, feminine, and serene —something somehow expressive of eternity—in the sight of her standing with the wicker basket of clothes at her feet in the cool grass, slender and absorbed, her delicate, white, long-wristed, nimbly moving hands lifting, unfolding, carefully arranging, and then pinning to the line the damp, fragrant sheets and blouses, her hair brazed and softly addled by the sunny breeze. In the last days of May this ritual was abandoned; I don't think she changed her bed linen— or her clothes, to any great extent—for weeks. She would wear the same ragged pair of jeans and rumpled blue blouse for days, until she looked like a derelict; I think she may have slept in them.

I didn't know where she was most of the time. I would scour the island looking for her, but I saw her only rarely, wandering along the sand of the river beach gnawing a carrot or an apple, or straying up through the dune grass like a wraith, plucking idly at the bright stems. As the year moved to its summer solstice she seemed to be swept in its pale currents toward some apotheosis of her own for which she had been preparing herself for weeks, for years perhaps —for her whole lifetime possibly—with her rituals of solitude, of fasting, of alternating, almost ceremonial excess and impassioned sobriety, as one would scourge and purge himself in preparation to confront a god.

But in spite of her indifference to her own appearance or condition, she would sometimes express a wistful anxiety about herself that seemed to reveal a vestigial feminine vanity or perhaps a sense of remorse about her self-neglect that was touching and startling. And although our conversations were often reduced to ruin by her vagaries, she would occasionally seek me out to talk with a strange, feverish urgency that seemed to paralyze or strangulate her gift for conversation, as if driven to me by some burning exigency beyond her capacity to discuss modestly or sociably or even to define except by a kind of fervid periphrasis. I could never make out what the subject of these dialogues, or inquests, or importunities was, often because they were accompanied by an air of odd, shy penitence on her part, as if she were apologizing for the intemperance of her manner or the immodesty of her self-concern. Sometimes I would find her sitting at my kitchen table when I came back from one of my spring rambles, or, more likely, standing outside my back door, plucking impatiently at the buds of my gladiolas as she watched me coming down the lane, unable to muster the composure to sit and wait for me calmly in the kitchen; and when I had ushered her inside and was preparing our ritual pot of tea, she would plunge into an abrupt, excited, and often maddeningly elliptical discourse that could baffle and sting and stir me to dark misgivings almost simultaneously:

"Carl, there's something Shakespeare says: 'There's no art to find the mind's construction in the face.' Do you believe that?"

"I don't know. It isn't always true, obviously. I mean, if you have a pathological condition, like mongolism—"

"I'm not talking about pathological conditions. Or maybe I am. I don't know. I mean, take Bertrand Russell, for example. Would you say he had a look of vast intelligence, or wisdom, or greatness of nature?"

"Not really. I've always thought he was rather a weak-looking man, at least according to the popular conception. Receding chin, small cranium, an unimposing, kind of simian-looking face. He certainly doesn't look like one of the intellectual giants of his time."

"That's what I mean. We have such misconceptions about people, such stereotyped ideas about physical appearance."

"As we have about everything."

"Yes." She prowled restlessly about the kitchen for a moment, pausing at the window to tap with her knuckles at the pane. "It would be awful to think people could look at your face and tell what you were like. What kind of thoughts you had, whether you were good or evil."

"Oh, that I don't believe at all. That's nonsense."

"But what's that thing called where people judge character by skull shape? Something -ology."

"Phrenology?"

"Yes. You don't believe that, do you?"

"No. It's nonsense."

"I can't understand why men like me at all. I was looking at myself in the mirror this morning, and I looked awful. I wouldn't like anyone with a face like mine. Do I look mad to you at all?"

"No," I said, and turned to look at her critically. "You look beautiful to me. The only thing wrong with you is that you don't eat enough, and you don't sleep enough. You're getting haggard-looking. And you've got dark circles under your eyes. If you keep it up, you'll ruin your looks, for good."

"Oh, God, you sound like my mother. That's not what I mean. I'm talking about basic appearances."

"If we can judge anything about people by their appearance, it's by what they do to it themselves. People make their own faces, I think, just as they make their own characters."

"You're an existentialist."

"I don't know what that means."

"It's what you just said. That people make their own natures. I can't understand why Americans have always hated Sartre so much. Because he's an atheist, I suppose. And because he scorns the world's prizes. Another weak-looking, myopic-looking little man. Maybe all philosophers look like that."

"Socrates was very ugly, I understand."

"Yes." She turned suddenly. "Have I ever shown you pictures of my family?"

"No."

"I'll go and get them. I'd like to know what you think of these faces."

"Your tea will get cold. You can do it another time."

"No. It won't take a minute."

She left me alone in the kitchen for fifteen minutes or so while she went down the lane to her cottage. When she returned she was carrying a shabby envelope bulging with photographs, which she spilled out onto the table. Most of them were old, faded to pale sepia and frayed with handling.

She shifted them apart on the table until she uncovered one of three children sitting in an apple tree, half hidden by the leaves, their legs dangling down from the branches, dappled in light and shadow. It must have been taken twenty-five years before; Sylvie looked about eleven in the picture. Aaron perhaps a year older, and Jamed six or seven. Their mother stood beneath them on the ground, reaching up to clutch the ankle of one of Sylvie's dangling bare feet in her blunt, work-roughened fingers. It was impossible to tell the woman's age; she had the worn, solemnly expressionless look of fortitude that country women seem to wear from marriage to the grave, staring out at the camera, not with defiance, but something closer to forbearance, as if she were enduring this moment of truancy from her duties, this concession to vanity, to the rituals of family mythology, as gravely as she endured all other mortal effusions and frivolities. And yet it wasn't a bitter or plaintive look; no irony disfigured or diminished the pride with which she presented her progeny to the witness of time, or the stern and speechless love with which she clasped her daughter's ankle.

The faces of the children were shy, rapt, fugitive, and in their innocence and their appearance of being afloat among the leaves and lustrous apples, unearthly. I was fascinated to see Sylvie as a child. Her face was thin and dark, far darker than now—no doubt from endless days of sunburn and the wind on the water—and the skin clove so tightly to the bones of her cheeks and jaw and fierce, shapely little brow that it seemed carved out of brown quartz and polished with a jeweler's emery cloth. The acute, fine eyebrows were drawn together slightly and the delicate lips compressed, even then, with a look of startled sensitivity or dawning disbelief that she was there at all, in that place, with those people, at that moment of eternity, shackled by the clutch of that coarse, ruthlessly mortal, ruthlessly devoted hand on her frail ankle.

Jamed seemed in danger of slipping from his perch, reaching up with one hand to pluck an apple or to point to something, his mouth open and his eyes upraised, blithely and eternally confounded by a cloud, or a bird that soared above the tree, or some mirage among the branches.

Of the children, Aaron was the only one who seemed to be at all aware of the camera, or the occasion, or the fact that it was being commemorated, and enough embarrassed by the fact to produce a shy, uncertain grin that made a deep dimple in his left cheek and set a spray of winsome wrinkles at the corner of each eye.

"That's Momma," Sylvie said.

"Yes."

"Do you think she's beautiful?"

"Yes, very."

"You can see that, can't you? There isn't any mistake about that."

"No."

"I think she was thirty-five then. As old as I am now. God."

"Who took the picture?" I asked.

"Poppa. It's the only one he ever took. We used to sit up in that apple tree and he'd sing chanteys to us. It was the happiest we ever were. I think he wanted to remember how we looked. He took it just before we went to the oyster roast, on the day the house burned down."

"The house burned down?"

"Yes. He burned it down."

"Your father?"

"Yes. He needed the insurance money to keep his shop going."

"That's very hard to believe."

"For you, it is. You didn't know him." She shuffled the rest of the pictures together suddenly in a discouraged way and shoved them back into the envelope.

"Can't I see the rest of them?" I asked.

"Oh, it doesn't matter. I just wanted you to see Momma and the rest of us, when we were little. I don't know what it proves." She shoved the envelope into her pocket and sat down, slumping with a kind of weary exasperation.

"I'm afraid your tea's cold. I'll pour it out and make you some fresh."

"No, it doesn't matter." She picked up her cup and sipped the cold tea, her eyes staring sightlessly across the room. I moved my eyes from her face to the image of the small, dark child in the photograph I still held in my fingers.

"*You* were beautiful, too," I said.

"I look like a gypsy," she said. "A little thief or something. Cunning little devil."

"No, you don't. You look like a very tender little girl."

"Do you think so? Really? I don't look vicious to you?"

"I love the way you looked. I wish—" I could not finish the sentence, realizing suddenly that I had no idea what I had intended to say. She turned her eyes to mine and regarded me gently for a moment.

"Do you like Aaron's face?"

"Yes. Somehow it looks just as I imagined it. He looks like a gentle, happy, very good-hearted little boy."

She took the envelope back out of her pocket, removed the photographs, and after sorting through them for a moment, handed me another, a much more recent picture, a square Polaroid color print. "That's what he looks like now. I took that last summer when he came down."

It was a full-length snapshot of a man with scattered hair and a generally disheveled look standing up to his ankles in the bay, one leg of his rolled-up trousers drooping limply in the water while he held at arm's length a dripping, pale, long-tentacled jellyfish which he was regarding with a grin recognizable as that of his boyhood. There was a distinct impression of his having been stung by the jellyfish a moment or two before, and yet in spite of its tincture of pain, the grin now seemed inured, complaisant, very nearly hearty, reconciled without complaint to this latest in an apparently endless chain of unpleasant disclosures from the deep. It was a humble, ruthful, philosophic face, and yet bereft; somehow consciously defrauded, as if aware that in exchange for wisdom it had traded something dearer.

"He's still smiling," I said.

"It's his least attractive expression," she said. "That idiotic, pusillanimous grin. He'll stop it, one day. He'll have to stop that endless grinning and go back."

"What do you mean?"

"You can't grin your life away like that. You can't go on peddling hemorrhoid ointment and DDT forever and pretending this is the best of all possible worlds, when there's nothing inside of you but stale air and rotten dreams and fear. Fear of truth, of being what you are. He's got to stop that awful grinning."

There was something so imperative and nearly terrible in the way she said this—and something so oblivious of me, as if she had forgotten entirely that I was the author of the question that had inspired it—that I was awed to silence. She took the snapshot out of my fingers and slid it back into her pocket bitterly. I didn't say anything. She seemed to sense the dumbfound quality of my silence and to be chastened by it, because she glanced at me in a quaint, conciliatory way and said more gently in a moment, "What were your parents like? You've never told me."

"Very different from yours. My father was a government attorney in the Patent Office. I never really knew him at all. He was a very methodical and very intelligent man, who never had a genuine passion of any kind. Although he had a hobby—repairing antique clocks—that he worked at with a kind of dogged diligence. We lived in Takoma Park, an old-fashioned community outside of Washington that had gradually become absorbed as a suburb of the city. Every morning at eight o'clock he drove to work in a huge old Studebaker touring car that he owned for twenty years; and every evening at six-thirty he returned, parked the car on the pair of concrete tire tracks that crossed our front lawn, and covered it with a tarpaulin that he lashed to the wheel spokes with carefully measured rope, exactly the same way, every evening. His whole life was conducted with that kind of self-congratulatory precision. Whatever he did—or we did, as a family—was governed by his sense of prudence, order, and respectability. For example, we had a cottage in Maine—the one I've told you about—that we went to every summer, not because any of us was particularly enthusiastic about it, but because it was a regular and theoretically salutary practice that he considered a part of every orderly existence. It was almost a duty to enjoy ourselves for two weeks every year—to ensure our psychological health, I suppose—just as it was a duty to ensure salvation by attending church every Sunday, whether there was any bliss or exaltation involved in the experience or not. I think he would have been embarrassed by bliss, if he'd ever known it. Even my conception, I think, must have taken place in a moment of strict attention to responsibility." I smiled at Sylvie. "He was very different from your father, I believe."

She smiled back grimly. "*My* conception probably took place between two good stiff belts of Jack Daniel's, or a quart of oysters and a chantey tune." She lowered her eyes into a dusk of memory, out of which she seemed to struggle like someone breaking free of shadows. "What was your mother like? Was she demoralized by him?"

"I don't think so. They came from very much the same kind of people. I think it was part of her view of life that a woman should be decently obscured by her husband, or should decently extol his attitudes and ideals. I think she always shared them, really. She seemed contented enough. They never quarreled or contended with each other. Or with me. She reared me with a kind of calm proficiency, as if she were following a recipe, intent on producing a cake or a roast of beef of known digestibility and palatability. I think she would have liked to have other children, but she had some physical problem that made that impossible. It was her only real lifelong occupation. There was altogether too much expectation and concern for my success invested in me by both of them—by all my relatives, in fact. Both my father and mother came from very large families, so that I had a host of aunts and uncles, some of them unmarried or widowed early, and I received too much attention, and advice, and supervision from all of them; and too much celebration for my exploits—as long as they demonstrated prudence and order and respectability, of course. Which they did. I was an obedient, industrious child."

"And you had bad dreams."

"Some very bad ones, yes."

Her eyes dusked over again with the floating wisps of memory that darkened them fitfully, like clouds across the moon.

"It's a funny thing," she said. "—I never cease marveling at it—that the only one of us who never has bad dreams is Jamed. He's the only one who goes to sleep at night entirely contented, entirely at peace. And he can't tie his own shoelaces." When I didn't answer, she went on. "When he was a little boy —a real little boy, I mean—he was afraid of everything. Of storms, and jellyfish, and fire, and darkness; everything. And now there's no fear in him at all. Not of anything. Certainly not of truth, as there is in Aaron."

"Perhaps he's already learned it," I suggested.

"Oh, don't say that. For God's sake, don't say that." Her lips began to quiver very slightly, like the twitching of a dying mouse, and for the first time since I'd known her, she began to cry, silently and without constraint or self-consciousness, the tears running down her cheeks in sparkling rivulets while she sat stilly, wrapped in some ungovernable sorrow. Then suddenly, without wiping away her tears or adjusting her attitude at all, she said, "I won't have his life confiscated like that, by terror and subservience. Or mine. One of us has to survive, at least. Someone has to know what the Linthicums were like, someday. If he can't stand it, he shouldn't have begotten us." She turned to me with a savagely judicial glare. "What did you expect your daughter to be?" The question seemed as nearly cruel as anything I had ever heard her say.

"I don't know," I murmured. "I don't think I had any expectations for her. I suppose I simply wanted her to be as—inconspicuous—as possible."

Seeing my dismay, she put out her hand and laid it on my arm. "That was a stupid thing to say." I didn't reply, and she added gently, "You don't know where she is now?"

"Still in San Francisco, I think. At least that's where her card came from last Christmas. Although she said her husband might be reassigned shortly. Perhaps they've moved by now."

"How long is it since you've seen her?"

"Two years ago, when Molly died. She came back to the funeral. That was the first time I'd seen her in almost fifteen years. I hardly recognized her."

"And it wasn't any different, when she came back?"

"No. We hardly spoke at all. She only stayed two days. She wouldn't go back upstairs to her old room to sleep, not even to look at it. She slept on the sofa in the recreation room, and then left very early in the morning, without saying goodbye. I could hear her making coffee downstairs in the kitchen, and then I heard the door close when she went out." It seemed very quiet in the kitchen when I stopped speaking; as much to relieve the silence as anything, I went on. "She did give me a kind of curriculum vitae the first night she was home; very quickly, as if she were reading it off to a personnel manager. She told me she was happily married and that they had a pleasant apartment overlooking the bay. The children were four and six now, and the eldest, Arthur, had just entered the first grade. I said that I'd like very much to see them, and asked if I came out, if it would be possible. She said that if I came, of course, I'd be—'free to do so'—I think that's the way she put it, but she did feel they'd be confused by my sudden appearance and that it might be difficult to explain 'my part in their existence.' "

"Oh, that's awful," Sylvie murmured.

"Well, of course I didn't go. But I'd like very much to see them. I have I guess a hundred photographs of them that Molly took. They're handsome little boys. Fortunately, they don't look anything like me." Sylvie lowered her eyes to the table.

"When I sold the house, I wrote and asked her if there was anything she wanted. She wrote back and said no. When she'd been home for the funeral, she'd taken a few things back with her, personal things of Molly's, I think a couple of snapshots and a few pieces of jewelry. She said that was all she wanted."

"They're terrible creatures, daughters," Sylvie said.

"Oh. No. I can't call anyone terrible." I felt suddenly very old and weary. I began to pour fresh tea for us in a restless agitation, but my hand was so feeble and tremulous that it sank with the weight of the teapot and I was obliged to set it down. I stared at its unmanageable bulk with an awful, docile futility. "What I fear most," I said, "is becoming simply a frightened old fool. A craven, sentimental wreck of a man, rotten with guilt and terrified of life. Cowed by a teapot or a thunderstorm. Unable to perform a useful action or make a valid judgment. Afraid to go to the post office or open the newspaper, for fear of bad news. Chuckling and nodding and fawning my life away in a parody of virtue, like a department store Santa Claus. A man would be better off dead."

"That won't happen," Sylvie said. "These people need you. You're their doctor. I need you."

I bowed my head to that beatitude with the joy of a miscreant mysteriously called to knighthood.

In the second week of June she caught a terrible cold that accentuated the pallor of her face and wracked her with a harsh, rattling cough that I could hear from inside my kitchen when she passed by in the lane. Looking out of my window one morning, I saw her halt and stand tottering, bent double, in the oyster-shell path while she raised her hand to cough into her fist. I went to the door and called out to her across the yard, "Sylvie, come in here, for God's sake. I want to give you a prescription for that cough."

She turned to look at me in a brief, fugitive way and shook her head.

"It's nothing. It's almost gone."

Before I could detain her she had gone on swiftly toward the shore. I went across the yard and through the gate, following her a few steps down the lane. She turned to face me and called out angrily, "Stop following me. There's nothing you can do. I'm all right."

"You're going to be sick," I said. "You'll have pneumonia the first thing you know."

"It isn't any of your business. What do you think you have to do? Cure the whole world?"

The ferocity of that remark left me standing dumbly while I watched her plunge on down the path toward the beach.

Two days later she came humbly to my back door in the late morning, her face and throat flushed with fever and her voice reduced to a hoarse, croaking whisper.

"I'm sorry I was cross, Carl," she said. "You were right, as usual. I feel awful. You've got to make me well. Will you?"

"I'll do the best I can," I said. "You'd better come in here and let me listen to your chest."

"Yes."

She sat patiently in a kitchen chair while I examined her, staring at her laced fingers in her lap like an anxious child. She had an upper respiratory infection and a deep bronchitis. Her temperature was 100.1.

"I'm going up to Prince Frederick and get you some penicillin," I said. "You've got to go to bed, for a week at least."

"I can't go to bed for a week. Aaron's coming next Tuesday."

"He'll be just in time to bury you if you don't do as I say."

"I'll stay in bed till Sunday. That's four days. With the penicillin, I'll be well by then. Honestly."

"We'll see. Go get to bed now. And drink two glasses of water."

"All right. I'm sorry to cause you all this trouble."

I drove up to Prince Frederick for the penicillin, a box of Kleenex, a bottle of decongestant spray, orange juice, oatmeal, eggs, and a loaf of raisin bread.

When I came back, she was lying in bed in her upstairs bedroom, staring out through the open window at the blue water of the bay.

"It's so still out there," she said in her hoarse whisper. "It's the stillest, bluest place in the whole world."

"Yes. I think it is."

"I don't want it ever to change. I don't want anyone to build new brick houses or hamburger stands or shopping centers. I hate progress. I really hate it."

"Well, penicillin is a part of it," I said. "Take two of these, and then another every four hours. I'm going to come back in an hour and make you some lunch."

She sat up, and while she took the pills and sipped at the glass of water from her bedside table, I fluffed her pillows and stacked them against the head of the bed behind her. When she had swallowed the pills, she sat with her back against the pillows and stared out of the window in a mute, mournful trance, plucking stray strands of hair away from her forehead with her fingertips.

"Shall I bring you up a book?" I asked.

"No, thank you. They're going to build a bridge across the Patuxent, did you know that?"

"My God. Where did you hear that?"

"At the store. Everywhere. And then there'll be a McDonald's and a Peoples Drugstore. And brick ramblers all over the river meadow."

"Good God, I hope not. Is that true?"

"Yes. They've been talking about it for years. The world is being stolen from me. The world I was given for a present on my first birthday. They've snatched it away from me before I even finished unwrapping it, before I ever had time to learn how beautiful it was."

"I hope you're mistaken," I said. "I suppose that'll mean widening the highway, too."

"Oh, yes. A four-lane highway, and a couple of banks with drive-up windows and an air-conditioned supermarket. There won't be any more country stores with wooden front porches on them, and bushel baskets full of string beans sitting out front, and sand in the street, and a dusty old post office with spiderwebs on the ceiling."

"It's a very depressing thought," I said.

"People say you're a wild romantic when you talk like that. They smile and say you're just in love with the picturesque. Well, that's false and chic and glib. It isn't the picturesque that I love; it's old things, true things; and I need them, the way I need Sophocles and Shakespeare and the Bible. The way Poppa needed wood, real wood, genuine weather-seasoned Burma teak, not the kiln-dried junk they throw in boats these days, not fiberglass. And I need the memory of his face when he was planing a piece of it, and of Momma bent over a washtub with the sweat dripping off the tip of her nose, standing there in a faded old blue dress washed so thin you could see her elbows through the sleeves. I'll never forget the sound of her knuckles scrubbing over that washboard, like rain drumming on a tin roof or water rippling over lapstrakes on a wooden hull. That's the music of the world to me, and I need it. I don't need the sound of their goddamned jackhammers all day long, or eighteen-wheeler trucks roaring by, and I don't need their Corvettes or recreation rooms or family therapy, or their cheap, tinfoil skyscrapers or sculpture or poetry that look like they were put together out of Erector sets. What the hell is the matter with these people? Why can't they tell profundity from complexity?"

"I don't know," I murmured.

"Nothing in this country is ever finished. As soon as a building is fifty years old, they tear it down and build a new one. It's 'obsolete,' they say. Well, I want to live in some place that's obsolete. Some place where they're not forever ripping up the streets to put in new electric cables or whatever the hell it is they do down there all the time. I want to live in a town that was finished four hundred years ago and has stood and ripened in the sun and rain like wine in a cask. And I want people like that around me; obsolete people, like the people on this island. People with ancient thoughts and ancient feelings and an ancient sense of the solemnity of life; people who've soaked up every element of reality their roots and leaves could ever stretch to touch, the way a wild rose soaks up rain and sunlight and dark liquor from the soil, until it becomes a rose at last. I want my life to be finished before it ends. I'm not going to trade it away before it's finished, swap it off for some brand-new, chrome-plated piece of spiritual gimcrackery or some shameful, trained-monkey kind of life like Aaron's. My God, watching him peddle patent medicine on the TV is just like watching a chimpanzee in a pair of pants riding a tricycle. I'm not sure of very much, but I'm sure that's not what human life is supposed to be. But that's what it's turned into, after five billion years of evolution on this planet— hustling Little Liver Pills for forty years." Her eyes roamed smoldering through the light above the bay. "That's one reason I respect you, Carl. You have old thoughts, like mine; you've committed old crimes, as I have. We're terrible people, both of us; truly terrible. But we're real."

"Oh, my dear, I'm much less real than most people," I said. "And I've never finished anything. Not my childhood, nor my husbandhood, nor my parenthood, nor my profession. And not my manhood, certainly."

She turned her head from the window to look at me, and the focus of her eyes withdrew slowly from the blue expanse of sea and sky, contracting on my face in a white, blazing nimbus, like light refracted through a lens. She seemed to see me in that moment with such a searing clarity and mercy that I thought my flesh would smoke under her gaze. I was sitting on the edge of her bed, and I was so compelled by the tender comprehension of her eyes that I was drawn bodily toward her, my arms outstretched, as she leaned forward from the headboard and reached out to me, our arms enfolding one another with a soft, ravening desperation. In the clasp of her embrace I felt drenched by a peace that fell as sweetly as summer rain. We clung together for what seemed like an endless crystal instant; worlds evolved, and flowered, and were peopled; cities grew up by quiet waters and light teemed over them; heroes were born and went forth in their exaltation to confirm the tranquil splendor of the land. An ordained, vast, luminous constancy was consummated. Then she stirred in my arms and we released each other and sat apart for a moment, rather demurely, rather shyly, like two people newly plighted to each other, or like a father and child reconciled after an endless, intolerable estrangement.

"Now, I've put some things in the icebox for you," I said. "But I don't think you ought to eat on top of the penicillin. You go to sleep for an hour or two, and then I'll come back and make you some lunch."

"Yes."

"Sleep is what you need most. And then some decent food."

"Yes."

She lay back against the pillows and turned her face to the window, watching the curtains billow gently in the breeze from the bay. Her hair stirred about her temples and the long blue artery in her throat pulsed with the steady, peaceful rhythm of a river current. I sat watching her until she closed her eyes and her face had softened gradually to an exquisite, childlike calm, like a freshly opened flower bated in the expectation of dewfall.

By Sunday, as she had predicted, she was much better. Her fever had gone, and although she still had a harsh, dry cough, it was looser and less insistent. She ate everything I prepared for her, if not enthusiastically, at least with graceful obedience. She grew strangely peaceable, even docile. Her restlessness and agitation had abated with her fever and been replaced by a kind of visionary calm and gratitude that I've often seen in convalescent patients, as if their restoration from suffering or the shadow of death had gentled them, lengthened their thoughts, deepened and softened their gaze. There was that kind of quiet devoutness in her perception of things, the way she turned her head to birdsong, the slow, studious absorption with which she traced the meandering of grain in driftwood or ran her fingertips along the suavity of its curves, the astonished, swift parting of her lips, almost like a gasp, when she saw a bunting streak through the sunlight above the dahlia beds and dip down to perch glittering on a picket; the engrossment begotten in her by the peram-bulation of a tiny ant across her tabletop. I suppose I would have been unequivocally cheered by this development if I had not also seen something of the same demeanor in patients who were dying: a sort of valedictory gravity, like that of a person departing forever from his childhood home who pauses to look at every object of the scenes he has been raised among with an appreciation and a poignancy unknown to him before. She certainly was not dying, but there was a pensiveness and intentness almost of piety in her manner that was as disquieting as it was reassuring.

I came every day and spent the entire day with her. In many ways, it was the happiest time we ever spent together. She seemed entirely contented and almost loath for our comfortable domestic idyll to end. We played chess, sitting on her bed—an unruly, burlesque kind of chess, with the pieces often tumbling among the covers as she shifted the position of her legs—and I read poetry to her, Yeats and Emily Dickinson and John Skelton, laboriously, stumbling over the syntax and getting the meter all awry—which she impassively forgave—and we did crossword puzzles from back issues of the Sunday *Post* that were stacked up to the rafters in her closet. She decided suddenly that it was imperative for her to learn to recognize by sight every tree, wildflower, bird, and insect of North America; and along with this resolution there was reborn some of her old intensity and urgency; but it was of a different kind: something much more like the cool zeal of a postulant than the heretical fever that had burned in her before. She would sit by her window with a tattered old encyclopedia and a pair of binoculars, through which she pored over every plant and shrub and tree she could see from her bedroom and every living creature that visited her backyard, bee or butterfly or vireo or chipmunk, flurrying through the pages of the encyclopedia and chirruping with delight if she was able to discover its identity or muttering with chagrin if she was not. In my profound ignorance of the natural world, I was very little help to her, and the encyclopedia was so sparsely illustrated and poorly organized for her purposes that she was more often frustrated than rewarded for her efforts. On Monday morning after I had made her breakfast, I drove up to Annapolis and in a bookstore by the harbor found a set of pocket field guides to birds, trees, flowers, mammals, insects, and seashells, handsomely and profusely illustrated and arranged for the purpose of field identification. I bought it as a birthday present for her and was back by one o'clock, when I brought it up on her lunch tray and was rewarded with a look of gratitude as artless and endearing as a child's on a Christmas morning.

"You are the kindest man in the world," she said.

"Only the most methodical. When you've had lunch, put on a robe and slippers, and you can come downstairs."

"Oh, can I, Carl!"

I set up a pair of canvas deck chairs in the shade of the mimosa tree in her backyard and for the rest of the afternoon she sat beside me with her binoculars and the field guides, making an ardent inventory of the world. When she grew tired, she laid her book and glasses in the grass and lay back in the chair, the latticed sunlight falling through the branches of the mimosa on her pale, uplifted face and closed eyelids. Once again, watching her face restored to its original, immaculate simplicity in the innocence of sleep, I felt an odd, indignant pity; it seemed unfair and incongruous that such a delicate vessel should be made to hold such corrosive, bitter wine.

I fell asleep watching her sleeping face, and was awakened in the long-shadowed silence of evening by the murmur of her voice beside me:

". . . because I can recognize, from as far away as I can see its shape clearly on the water, one of my father's hulls. I can tell you, by looking at his face, the surname of almost anyone on this island, or in this county. Or if you tell me his name, I can tell you by looking at his face whether he's a bastard, or if there's incest in his family. I can tell from the way a man moves and uses his hands and looks at things whether he's a tobacco farmer or a waterman or a merchant. Once a boy went away for a long time and then came back to the county; I met him three years later at a fish fry at the firehouse in St. Leonard, and I could tell by looking at his eyes that he'd been in jail. I can tell instantly whether a man from this county is lying, and if so, whether he's lying out of concern for my feelings, or for profit, or advantage, or out of shame. I couldn't tell that about a stranger. In just the way that I know what time of day it is by looking at the tide line, I know if men are in debt, or have secret illnesses, or expect to die soon; and I know if women have been unfaithful by the way they speak to their husbands, or sit stroking their hounds, or watch their children eating at the table. These are the most profound things that I know, and I've learned them all in this place, and about this place and these people. When I was a little girl, I couldn't wait to get away from here, because I thought it was stupid and provincial, and that the world outside was full of wonders. Now I know I'll never get away, because my life here was never finished, so I couldn't ever understand or appreciate the wonders that lay outside. Poppa used to say, 'A boat is made to sail, but it won't sail right if it ain't made in a good yard.' My God, he should have known. Of all the people in the world, he should have known.

"I'm still afraid of strangers. When I look at their faces, I can't tell anything about them. All I can see in them is craziness. I look at their bright, ingenious, rabid eyes and all I can see is their crazy vanity and love of luxury and their crazy virtue and religiosity and patriotism, in which the world is drowning. The only people in that world outside this county I can understand at all are its derelicts, the people who couldn't be cozened by prosperity or progress or success into a denial of their youth or a forfeiture of all the things that were never consummated in it. I know the look of mourning in those people's eyes. They're the only ones who don't look crazy to me, who seem sane in their destitution.

"And now they're building the bridge, and all those strangers will come across it with their inscrutable faces that I don't understand at all; all those virtuous, religious, prosperous, patriotic people; and they'll tear down the old stone church and build a new one, with a crazy A-frame steeple and one of those ski-jump roofs, and put a bank on every corner, and build a nuclear power plant at Plum Point, and there'll be jet fighters roaring all day long out of that bloody naval station at St. Marys. They'll kill the oysters and menhaden and the crabs and rockfish with their pollution and contamination, and when Momma dies, I suppose, they'll buy her property and tear down the house and Poppa's boatyard and build a condominium there, and then sit on their balconies and congratulate themselves on their success and amuse each other with stories about the local characters who still hang around the place, like the crazy old woman who lives in a cave on the cliffs and sits there all day counting the shark's teeth in a cigar box; and that will be me."

I sat silently, not knowing how to comment on her sorrowful, rambling soliloquy. After a few moments she compressed more tightly the lids of her closed eyes and said, "How can I know all those things about these people and not know whether or not my father loved me?"

I knew she expected no reply, but after a moment of silence I was moved to mutter, "I think you know he did."

"No. Jamed was the only one who knew. And he sacrificed his manhood to that knowledge."

"Oh, I don't think so."

"Yes, you do. You said so yourself, the other day." She opened her eyes slowly and stared up into the mimosa leaves. "How could I understand and love the beauty of the things he made, and not him? It's almost obscenely mysterious. That's why I couldn't make a truly beautiful thing myself, no matter how I tried. There was too much sorrow in it. My book was too sad to be beautiful. His boats were works of joy. Ferocious and consuming joy. Maybe unholy joy, I don't know. It only terrified us; it bred sorrow in us, Momma and Aaron and me. We weren't equal to it; we couldn't bear it."

"Maybe he wanted you to share it," I said, "and didn't know any better way to give it to you than in the things he made."

"I wanted to believe that, for such a long time. But I couldn't accept it. I can't stand believing that he was no better than we are."

After a time, studying the curious composure of her face in the falling light, I said, "I think you should have been a nun."

"I would have been, I suppose, in another time. Now, I only have my craziness."

"You're not crazy, Sylvie. What you do matters. What you feel must be considered. It matters to Aaron, I know."

"How do you know that?"

"I read his letter. It was written to the person whose acts and feelings matter more to him than anyone's on earth." She didn't reply to this. "I think you'd better have some supper now. You're tired and hungry. There's some cold salmon in the box. I'll make you a salad."

"No, I'm not hungry. I don't think I'll have anything to eat tonight, Carl. But I am tired. I think I'll go in now and sleep. Do you mind?"

"No. You need to rest, if you're going to a birthday party tomorrow."

She turned her head to look at me. "You're so kind to me. You love me, don't you?"

"Yes. More than anything."

"I depend on that. I think I'll go in now."

She gathered up her books and binoculars and I walked with her to the door, where she turned and smiled at me.

"Good night," I said. "Sleep well."

"Good night. Do I look pretty, Carl?"

"Very pretty. Very fresh and young and well."

"I'm happy right now, do you know that? As happy as I've ever been since I was a girl."

"Good. You're supposed to be happy, I think. You could be a very merry creature, really. I've always felt that."

"I know. I want to laugh and laugh, someday."

In the morning she left very early. I had gone out into the garden before dawn and sat on the back steps to watch the sun rise across the river. As it breasted the trees on the St. Marys shore it cast a crimson sheen across the estuary, a lane of rosy, dancing, liquid petals of light on the great broad bosom of the quiet river. I sat smoking my pipe and watching until the crimson light had dissolved into the silver mist of morning, then I knocked out my pipe on the side of the steps and went into the kitchen to rescue a muffin I had left under the broiler. It was burned almost black, but as it was my last, I scraped it resolutely with a knife blade over the sink. It made a particularly harsh and rasping sound that I think must have obscured the sound of Sylvie's motor departing from Port Federation, because I never heard her leave. Half an hour later, when I had finished my tea and muffin, I went back into the garden with a pair of scissors and cut three scarlet peonies for her. I carried them down the lane to her backyard, and when I went in through her gate, I was surprised to see that the shed beside the cottage where she housed her battered little car was empty. It can't be much after six, I thought; this is the longest day of the year. When I went up the path to her door I saw that she had been abroad as early as I, evidently called out into the morning mist by her new obsession of world-watching, because the field guides I had given her lay on the grass beside the deck chair under the mimosa tree. The bird guide was open and a sprig of the mimosa lay along the open page for a marker. Between the delicate, paired leaves I could see the brilliant cinnamon-and-yellow plumage of a cedar waxwing in the illustration it had been laid across. She must have seen a waxwing, I thought. I'm glad of that. She said she'd never seen one.

I took the peonies into the kitchen and put them in a pottery pitcher I found in her dish closet, then tidied up the kitchen, washing a cup and saucer in which she had had her morning coffee and putting away the bread and marmalade she had left on the table. The stillness of the house was somehow faintly appalling; I had an oddly poignant feeling, as if I were straightening up the room of a child who has just left for her first summer at camp or her first year at a university.

It was indeed the longest day of the year; it seemed interminable. It was also the hottest—equatorially, unnervingly hot. I had not felt such heat since I left Alabama. The sun blazed all day in a cloudless burning sky of hard cyanic blue. Nothing moved. The world was seized in a hushed, white, cataleptic trance, its life suspended as in the depths of a great glittering gem. In the late morning I walked to the post office and was soaked with sweat when I returned, my shirt dripping, the waistband of my trousers soggy, and a tea-colored stain crept halfway up the crown of my Panama hat. I took off everything but my underwear and lay on the sofa with a pitcher of iced tea in the breeze of a huge square area fan I set up in the middle of the parlor floor. Outside the open windows the trees stood petrified against the almost glacial blue brilliance of the sky. I tried to read, but found my mind endlessly iterating the eerily apposite words of a paragraph from Ruskin's *The Storm-Cloud of the Nineteenth Century*:

> Blanched sun,—blighted grass,—blinded man.—If, in conclusion, you ask me for any conceivable cause or meaning of these things—I can tell you none, according to your modern beliefs; but I can tell you what meaning it would have borne to the men of old time.

I dropped the book on the floor and lay looking out the window at the light-soaked earth, falling at last into a restless sleep from which I awoke every five minutes or so, recalled by an urgent sense of vigil, and would listen for the sound of Sylvie's motor above the ceaseless whirring of the electric fan. Once,

I was awakened by a terrifying dream; someone was burning in a pyre, her hair ablaze, reaching out to me and screaming, like Iphigenia, in the flames. I got up trembling and drenched with sweat and went into the kitchen to read the time from the wall clock above the stove. It was two-fifteen. I slept through noon, I thought; and felt a curious, dismal sense of delinquency.

I took a cold shower, put on a pair of dry undershorts, and carried the floor fan into my study. I sat down at my desk in front of it and with a cup of cold consommé at my elbow occupied myself for two hours or more with my journal. For the past five days, while I had been nursing Sylvie, I had fallen behind in my daily additions to it, and I decided that the task of bringing it up to date would help to speed the passage of the interminable day. It was of little avail; my irrational but relentless anxiety about Sylvie made it impossible for me to concentrate; I spent most of the afternoon rereading old passages and adding my gloom at their inadequacy to my unease.

By four o'clock I was so oppressed by the still, hot, humid emptiness of the house, the constant sibilant droning of the fan, and the ponderousness of my prose that I closed the ledger and went up to the bedroom, where I put on a sports shirt and a pair of linen trousers. I went downstairs, plucked my still-damp Panama hat from the hat tree in the hall and wandered out into the white, infernal afternoon. When I closed the garden gate behind me, I looked down the lane and saw that Sylvie had returned and that, evidently, she had a visitor. Her car was parked again inside the shed beside her cottage, and behind it, on the hard-packed oyster-shell driveway that traversed the far side of her lot, a second car stood, a dark blue two-door sedan. Aaron has come back with her, I thought. He had wanted to see where she was living, I supposed; perhaps they would have dinner together. She had told me that he had promised to celebrate her birthday with her in any way she chose. I was pleased, of course; nothing could have made her happier than to have a birthday dinner with her brother, and yet my anxiety was not entirely relieved. Her secrecy about his visit disconcerted me. She must have known that I would have liked very much to meet him, if only for a moment, and for her to conceal from me the fact that she had invited him, or intended to do so, was grossly out of keeping with the candor and affection that existed between us. The last thing I would ever have called her was surreptitious. Perhaps her invitation had been entirely spontaneous. Perhaps she intended to bring him up to meet me before he left; it was very probable. I consoled myself with the thought, wandering down to the harbor, where I sat on the rocks of the breakwater for half an hour or so, staring out at the writhing sheet of foil of the estuary. I had better go back to the house, I thought. I must be there when she brings him to meet me.

I walked back to the cottage and put a record on the phonograph, one that

Sylvie had lent me and that I had not yet played: Sibelius's *The Swan of Tuonela.* It was a piece of music that she loved because, she said, it was free of the bombast of symphony. I took off my damp shirt and sat down on the sofa to listen to it. The almost intolerably sad and mythic music crept like fumes into the bare, whitewashed room, coiling up the walls and sinking in lavender pools along the wainscoting. Once, I would have despised it as disreputably romantic, voluptuous in its sorrow, but now the music seemed almost an attar of the natural world, as indigenous to earth as the smoke of faggot fires drifting up from the depths of vast, boreal pine forests in the cold dawn of the world. To conceive of this was an experience of strange prosperity. I felt an aboriginal innocence and sensitivity in my appreciation of the music that redeemed its darkness, that seemed even truer, more unique, than its ancient, orient sorrow. Now I see with your eyes, I thought. I feel with the nerves of your body. I have made me another self for love of thee.

When the music stopped I got up from the sofa and switched off the phonograph. I went to the window and stood looking out between the backs of the neighboring cottages and across the shimmering black asphalt of the road to the distant surface of the bay, flaring like a bowl of mercury in the blank and pitiless light. A kind of mineral ecstasy, not animal, not sanguine, earlier even than the canticles of earth, rang out in the shrieking of the sun. I stood and felt my heart wither. The dire brilliance burned away the frail webs of felicity, of delicate, natal sensibility that I had felt listening to the music, until I was shorn of them, and stood in their smoking rags, naked of everything but dread.

I know nothing, I thought. I see nothing. I move in an excess of light, with outstretched hands, stumbling on the stones of truth.

I went back across the room to the sofa and put on the damp shirt I had dropped across its arm. A fearful urgency called me out into that world of raving brilliance. I went quickly across the parlor and through the kitchen, thrusting my arms into the shirt and buttoning it clumsily as I went out the kitchen door into the backyard garden. Halfway across the yard, I could see that the dark blue sedan was gone from Sylvie's driveway. Inside the shed, the rusty, dented curves of her VW slept in the shadow. He's gone, I thought; and felt an irrational mixture of alarm and consolation at the thought. I strode down the lane to the gate of her backyard and up the path to her kitchen door. I knocked twice with my knuckles and then opened it and went inside. The house was silent. Standing with my hand on the doorknob, I called out, *"Sylvie!"* and was startled at the sound of my voice ringing through the empty rooms. On the kitchen table there was an empty champagne bottle, a pair of tumblers, and a small leatherbound book. I went to the table and picked it up. It was custom-bound in soft brown suede, with shining, gold-edged leaves. I opened it to the title page and saw that it was the *Complete Poems* of T. S. Eliot. Written on the verso in blue ink in a hand I recognized as Aaron's were the words:

Happy Birthday, Sylvie. The one I like best is the one where I've put the marker. I think you'll know why. Listen, don't ever change, will you? Love from Aaron.

I parted the book to where the red silk marker ribbon lay between the pages. The verse was the concluding movement of "Little Gidding," the final lines of which were bracketed in the same blue ink:

> *And the end of all our exploring*
> *Will be to arrive where we started*
> *And know the place for the first time.*
> *Through the unknown, remembered gate*
> *When the last of earth left to discover*
> *Is that which was the beginning;*
> *At the source of the longest river*
> *The voice of the hidden waterfall*
> *And the children in the apple tree*
> *Not known, because not looked for*
> *But heard, half-heard, in the stillness*
> *Between two waves of the sea.*
> *Quick now, here, now, always—*
> *A condition of complete simplicity*
> *(Costing not less than everything)*
> *And all shall be well and*
> *All manner of thing shall be well*
> *When the tongues of flame are in-folded*
> *Into the crowned knot of fire*
> *And the fire and the rose are one.*

I read the passage, then laid the book on the table and standing with my fingertips on the open page I read it again, aloud, my voice engraving the words upon the silence like an epigraph. I closed the book and stood quite still for several minutes, looking idly about the kitchen while a monolithic calm enveloped me slowly from my feet to my head, as if I were turning, inch by inch, to stone. My eyes wandered eventually to the clock above her stove, not now in haste or any clear desire to regulate events, to initiate some course of action, but in the vaguely ceremonial impulse to mark the hour. That can't be right,

I thought, before I realized that in its incorrigible idiosyncrasy the clock had stopped again at twelve. Perhaps he's still here, I thought. Perhaps they've gone to dinner at the Pier. Briefly I entertained the fantasy of walking down to the restaurant and joining them for after-dinner coffee or with the offer of a glass of liqueur to celebrate her birthday; then, almost in shame, I let the thought dissolve, knowing it to be a puerile self-deception. No, he's gone, I thought. And she'll need me. I have to find her. I have to bring her home. I no longer felt urgency or alarm or dread, however; something incontrovertible had transposed those things into a patient, granitic gravity, a composure like that of earth at twilight, a kind of mountainous calm.

I went out of the house and stood for a moment in the yard, looking about almost with the bemusement of a visitor to some illustrious site at the immobile, fabulously illuminated rose of Sharon bushes, the jade-bright, candelabraed mimosa tree, and the stone urn in the center of her yard, its wanton festival suspended forever in the paralyzing light. I saw that the bird book I had given her still lay beside the deck chair underneath the tree. I went to the chair and stooped down to pick it up and carried it back into the kitchen, where I stood in confusion for a moment with the book in my hand, not knowing what to do with it. I should put it where it will be safe, I thought; until she needs it again. Finally I took it out into the parlor and put it on the shelf beside the mantel where she stored the bounty of her walks along the shore: a rusty ship's bolt, a pot buoy veiled with dried, pale green slime, a piece of driftwood shaped like a dove, and a chipped bowl into which she emptied her pockets when she came in, damp with winter sea mist, of pebbles and chips of bright-colored glass and pink-and-blue coquina shells. These were the daily offerings of the earth to her on her morning expeditions, and I thought it meet to set my own beside them, as a handsel for the second half of her existence.

I went back out into the yard and through the gate, turning to latch it carefully, with oddly formal movements of my fingers, and then began to walk around the island at an unhurried, steadfast pace, in solemn certainty that I would find her, and solemnly resigned to her misfortune. I went down to the shore at Embarkation Point and circled the island by the beaches, searching the bluffs and hedgerows with my eyes as I trudged through the sand, climbing the highest dunes to stand and peer out through the shimmering bright air across the church-field meadow—vacant except for a pair of chestnut ponies standing with lowered heads in the shade of the hawthorn tree—and the willow grove below the stone church, where she sometimes lay all afternoon, and the salt marsh that stretched away to Crab Creek, the bronze velvet cattails and the marsh grass silent in the sun. I searched the patch of sedge above the sand hills, wading through the shoulder-high, dry, brass-bright stalks and calling out her name ahead of me into the soft, reticulated, golden light among the rushes.

I did not find her, but I found a trail through the sedge where the tall reeds had been trampled aside by the passage of a body in aimless, stumbling flight up from the river beach toward the field below the church. I followed it through the rushes to where it broke out into the open field. The meadow grass was cropped close by the horses that grazed there in summer, and bordered now at its upper edge by long violet shadows from the sycamores along the road, lying like scissored silhouettes on the gentle ground. I don't know how long I had searched for her by then, but I saw that the sun had fallen low out of its blazing zenith, and that in the long soft light of evening the earth had been enfolded by a tranquillity that was excruciating, that for a moment seemed to me brutal in its indifference. I thought of her plunging through the bright hot field panting with some unknown despair or mad with grief, her wild footsteps no more disturbing its senseless placid splendor than the fluttering of a dying bird among the bracken, and for an instant the amnesty I had been given by that world seemed to me contemptible and I had the impulse to renounce it with a cry of indignation in her name. But the sound died in my throat, because I knew that such a sound, even in her name or in the name of love, would be a calumny that she herself had taught me to despise. I whispered to her through the unfilled silence of that moment that I took as her legacy: This world is too beautiful almost for your bearing, and of all things here your sorrow is most beautiful. Friend, child, bride, beloved stranger, whoever you are, come into this asylum of my ruth, my shadowy, uncouth love.

I stood for some time in the darkling field until I understood in some occult way that I would never find her there, abroad on the island, that she would find her way, eventually, and when her desperation had abated, to my door. I went up across the church-field meadow and down the long, quiet village street, then up the oyster-shell lane behind the cottages to the gate of my yard, where I stood waiting in the growing dusk till she returned. It was almost dark when I saw her, lurching up between the trunks of the black locust trees that line the shore end of the lane. She came through the twilight air with her arms outstretched, stumbling on the stones, thumping against the tree trunks with her shoulders, falling sometimes to her knees, where she would crouch for a moment, her hair hanging tangled across the torn sleeves of her blouse, raising herself with an agonized perseverance and staggering forward for a few steps until she stumbled again or paused to wrench her skirt from the toils of a thistle or to take her hair in both hands and tear it free from the thorns of a low-hanging hawthorn branch. For several moments I couldn't move to help her; I don't know why. I felt consigned to behold and memorize that pageant of her destitution, as if it were my ordained duty to give, one day, the testimony of it which I write now, in this quiet room where she sits beside me touching the warm pane with her fingertips. When I was able to move at last, free of that sense of being a conscripted witness of the scene, I went, stumbling also, in my haste, across the lane and down through the ragged stand of chokecherry thicket to where she leaned panting against a locust tree, clasping the trunk with both hands, her cheek pressed to the coarsely furrowed bark, her face turned to the ground.

"Sylvie!" I called. "Oh, my dear, what's happened to you?"

"Carl?"

She shook her head slightly as if in puzzled inability to recognize my voice; then she breathed deeply and raised her face, and I saw that she was blind. Her eyes were burned out, the irises seared to the opaque white of alabaster, set in bloody, garnet-red pupils that blazed like ghastly gems.

"What have you done?" I whispered.

She shook her head again, as if shaking off the clinging vapor of a dream, and staring sightlessly beyond me into unimaginable distances, she said with a terrible, infantile simplicity, "I've done what I always longed to do. I've looked into the heart of light. And it is black. Black. Black."

I led her home, her arms wrapped around me, stumbling beside me like a child, and sat her down in the kitchen and bathed her eyes with boric acid to lessen the inflammation of the corneas, but the eyes were destroyed, as I had known at once. There was nothing I could do. My knowledge of ophthalmology, which had never been profound, was too long forgotten and vague to be of any use.

"Is there any pain?" I asked.

"No."

"I'll give you morphine if there's any pain."

"No. I don't feel anything."

"I'm going to take you up to Marlboro, to the hospital."

"It isn't any use."

"We don't know that. *I* don't know it. There may be pressure building up from the edema. There may be hemorrhage. All kinds of complications. There may be a great deal we can do."

"You don't have to say comforting things. It isn't any use."

I stood with tears running down my face while I bathed her eyes, praying that by some miracle I could exchange them for my own, that I could revoke the weird and awful inversion we had mysteriously invoked, of her vision for my blindness, her clarity for my obscurity. The unholy irony of that thought stung me like a centipede and made me sigh with pain; and even in that first hour of her blindness her insight seemed to burn more faithfully and mercifully than ever; I am sure she knew my thoughts, because while I laved her ruined eyes she raised her hand and took my wrist and pressed it gently, as if to comfort me, as if to let me know that the thing that had befallen was beyond all appeal, all restitution, all reproach, as inexorable and just as the summer darkness that now enclosed the cottage.

I bathed her face and cleansed and disinfected with hydrogen peroxide the scratches on her arms and legs and throat. She would not go to the hospital.

"I don't want anyone but you to touch me," she said. "I want you to take care of me."

"But I don't know what to do."

"You can do whatever is supposed to be done."

When I had dressed her wounds, she asked to lie down.

"Let me get you some fresh clothes first," I said. "Your clothes are torn and dirty."

"It doesn't matter. I'm very tired. I have to rest now."

I took her arm and led her through the parlor, pausing to flick the light switch beside the door. She clutched my arm convulsively.

"Is it dark?" she asked.

"Yes."

"Did you turn on the light?"

"Yes."

She stood rigid for a moment, and then murmured, "Oh, my God, my God."

"Come up and rest."

She kept her fingers clenched about my arm while I led her up the stairs, lifting and setting her feet down hesitantly on the treads, her hand sliding cautiously along the banister, her face upraised in a strangely reverential, timorous way, like a pilgrim ascending the steps of a shrine. In the guest bedroom she stood with downcast head, listening intently while I switched on the bedside light and drew back the counterpane and sheets.

"Don't bother turning it down. I'll get your sheets all dirty."

"That doesn't matter. Here."

I took her hand and led her to the bed, crouching down in front of her to untie the laces of the walking shoes she wore. They were encrusted with beggar-lice, which I had to pluck off with my fingertips, scolding her inanely while I did so.

"Well, you've gotten yourself into a fine mess. I'll have to clean these for you tomorrow. And we'll have to get you a new blouse. I don't think this one can be mended."

She sat patiently till I had finished, then lay back on the bed and sighed with a strange, afflicted sound of utter satiation and exhaustion, like a bride turning from her bridegroom in pain and ravishment to the deliverance of sleep.

I switched off the lamp and drew the chair from the little writing desk up beside the bed and sat watching her for hours in the moonlight through the window. Occasionally she started and cried out in her sleep, turning restlessly on the twisted sheets, and I would reach out to free her hand from a fold of the tangled linen or to draw her hair back from her face. The moon rose steadily, and westered, the luminous flood of light it cast through the window creeping down the length of her body until her feet were silver-plated, exquisite as a pair of sleeping doves. In the night there were soft, distant flashes of sheet lightning far out over the bay, and then the curtains began to stir and billow gently in the rush of cool night air and in a little while there was the sound of rain falling on the leaves of the dogwood tree outside the window. It rained steadily and softly for an hour, and afterwards the air was very fresh and smelled of earth and wet grass, and then the moon came out again and the tiny, ceaseless creaking of the hot-bugs resumed among the dripping trees. Toward dawn she woke and murmured, "Carl?"

"Yes?" I laid my hand on her shoulder.

"Is it still dark?"

"Yes."

She lay still for a long time, her eyes roaming sightlessly about the darkness, and then began to speak: "I have to tell you this now, before I lose the courage or will, or before I go mad, or die somehow. Listen, will you?"

"Yes."

"I got home very early this morning, almost at dawn, because I wanted to watch the sun come up from the beach below the house. I used to do that every morning when I was a little girl. It was a beautiful sunrise for my birthday. Did you see it?"

"Yes."

"It was perfect, wasn't it?"

There was that lovely rose and purple blush across the water, like the color of persimmons. There are wild persimmons up on the cliff, and the ground is always covered with them. I used to love to walk on them when they were hot and soft in the sun. So I did that again, too, when I came up from the beach; I took off my shoes and socks and walked back and forth through the old rotten persimmons from I don't know how many summers. They squished all up between my toes and felt so good I never wanted to stop. Momma was baking and saw me through the kitchen window and shouted at me, "Miss Sylvie, just what do you think you're doing out there, wading around in all that muck? I must have told you about that a hundred times!" She brought a bowl of water and a towel out of the kitchen and made me sit down on the back steps and wash my feet before she'd let me in the house. "Nobody in this world would ever know you were a Doctor of *Philosophy*," she said. Jamed sat there on the steps with me while I was washing my feet and he kept hugging me so hard I thought he'd break my ribs. I went out on the porch afterwards and played dominoes with him. He's very good at that. He doesn't really know what the numbers are, but he can recognize the patterns and fit them together. I think I'll still be able to do that with him, because you can feel the little depressions of the dots with your fingertips. Jamed is the one who'll have to lead *me* around now. He'll be proud of that. He always did lead us, anyway, but we didn't have the sense to know it.

Aaron promised me he'd get there before noon, and he did. You don't know how good that was of him, because it's hard for Aaron to get anywhere on time, and he must have had to leave New York by five or six; so I knew he realized how much it meant to me; how much he wanted my birthday to be perfect. I went down on the pier with Jamed to wait for him. We sat there with our feet dangling down, dropping sticks and straws into the water and watching them drift out with the tide, and after a while I heard his feet thumping on the pier behind us, and I didn't dare look around. It's such a long pier—I guess fifty yards, at least—and I sat there counting the thumps of his shoes on the wooden planks, and thought it would go on to infinity, that I'd be sitting there forever, listening to his footsteps come up behind me. Jamed started to look around, but I whispered, "No, don't look, because we have to be surprised. If you look, you'll break the spell, and we won't get anything." We used to do that when we were little: sit there and listen to Aaron coming up behind us, and we'd pretend that there was a spell, and if we looked, he might disappear or turn into somebody else. So we sat there and listened, with Jamed giggling and Aaron's footsteps getting louder and louder, till I could hardly tell them from the thumping of my heart. Then they stopped, right behind us, and he crouched down, the way he always used to do, and whispered in our ears, "Hey, what would you guys like most in the world?" He'd always have something for us: a piece of bubble gum or a handful of wineberries or an oatmeal cookie, and we'd have to close our eyes and guess until we got it right, and then he'd hold his hand out and give us whatever it was, and Jamed would go wild, screaming out, "Hey, I guessed it, Sylvie! I got just what I wanted!" So he did that, this morning, and Jamed sat there with his eyes scrunched tight, and when Aaron asked him what he wanted, he said, "A piece of bubble gum!" Aaron put his hand out over our shoulders, and there it was in his palm, a bright red bubble-gum ball, and Jamed grabbed it and yelled, "Hey, I got it, Sylvie! Just what I wanted! Boy, that's magic!" Then Aaron said, "What about you, Miss Sylvie?" and I said, "I want today to last forever." "O.K," he said. "Here's a magic book for you. Maybe you can make it."

"Oh, boy, a magic book!" Jamed screamed. "You got a magic book! Aren't you going to open it, Sylvie?"

"Not yet," I said. "I'll open it a little later. We have to have some ice cream first."

We went up to the house then, and I had my birthday party. Momma had actually put thirty-five candles on the cake, and it blazed like a chandelier. I waited till it was exactly twelve o'clock before I blew them out and cut the cake, and we had ice cream and nuts and candy and paper hats, for Jamed.

Aaron brought a shawl for Momma—I think he's given her about ten of them by now—and she smoothed out the wool with her hand and said, "Oh, my, that's just too nice to use," and put it away in her drawer with all the rest of them. And he had a boat for Jamed, a little tin boat with an electric motor, and we put it in a washtub and Jamed sat there watching it go around and around, giggling and thumping his feet on the floor until the house shook.

Then he had to take a nap, because he was worn out, and Momma said she'd wash up the dishes—she wouldn't let me help, because it was my birthday —so I went out on the screen porch with Aaron. Inside the house we could hear Jamed kneeling down and saying his prayers with Momma prompting him; he does that every time he goes to bed. Out in front of us the bay was so still and blue it seemed to be painted there. There was a sailboat way out beyond the channel, like one of Poppa's ketches in the distance, and it didn't seem to move at all; it was just as if he was out there watching us. I think that's what Aaron thought, too, because he was very quiet, we hardly talked at all, and I could see how different he was, how much gentler and more thoughtful than the last time I'd seen him; and I thought that, for the first time, he understood everything. I could tell he wanted to talk to me, truthfully, and without being evasive or glib or comical or New Yorkerish, the way he usually is, for the first time in his life. Something had ripened in him that had been growing to maturity for years and years, something that he needed to confess to me, to be delivered of. He didn't want to go back to New York at all; I could tell that. I think he'd admitted to himself, at last, that his life up there was meaningless and mercenary, and that he didn't really know where he was going, or why, or even who he was. I knew he wanted to tell me all that, and more, but he didn't know how to begin; he was afraid. He sat there looking out at the bay and the shadows of the persimmon trees on the beach down below and the butterflies above the cliffs, and after a while he took a deep breath and said, "How does it end, Syl, that poem that starts off: 'The world is too much with us; late and soon, getting and spending, we lay waste our powers'?"

" 'Have sight of Proteus rising from the sea,' " I said, " 'or hear old Triton blow his wreathéd horn.' "

"That's it. Who wrote that?"

"Wordsworth."

"Wordsworth. I don't think he will, do you?"

"Will what?"

"Rise from the sea, or blow his wreathéd horn. I thought he might, for a long time. Still, you never can tell. Maybe if we waited here long enough."

"You don't have the time," I said. "You have to get back to New York."

"That's right, I do. I've got to do a *Time* commercial first thing in the morning. And then I've got a voice-over for a Tide spot. And *Time* and Tide wait for no man."

"Don't do that," I said. "You don't have to wisecrack all the time."

"O.K., O.K. I wouldn't see him, anyway, if I waited here forever. Because you've got to be a pagan, suckled in a creed outworn. Isn't that what it says?"

"Yes." We sat still for a few minutes. "Why don't you come down to Solomons?" I said. "I'll cook you dinner."

"I thought I was going to take you out to dinner."

"I'd rather cook for you. We could pick up some soft-shell crabs at Lou's. She had her sign out when I drove by this morning."

"No kidding? You wouldn't like to add some of your homemade bread to that, would you?"

"Sure, I'll make you some. I can make an unleavened bread that doesn't have to rise. It doesn't take long, and it's good. And you could see my house. You've never seen it."

"That's right, I haven't. Listen, what are you going to do, anyway, Sylvie? Stay there forever? I mean, is that where you're going to live, or what? Don't you get lonely?"

"No. I have a friend down there. There's a man there I can talk to. He's very kind to me."

"This doctor guy? How old is he?"

"I don't know. What does it matter?"

"Well, it doesn't, I guess. I guess you have to have somebody. I mean, you can't go on mourning about Ron forever."

"That isn't who I mourn for," I said. "At least, that's only part of it. That didn't even need to happen. It shouldn't have happened."

"What do you mean?"

"I mean it was a mistake. Like most of my life. It was just—an accident."

"I know. But I have the idea that you think you were responsible for it, and that's not true, Sylvie. You weren't responsible for it, any more than I was."

"Oh, I was responsible for it," I said. "But it was still an accident. It wasn't supposed to happen."

He didn't say anything to that; he turned back to the bay and I sat looking at him. I love Aaron's face. I could look at it for hours. It isn't handsome or definite at all, but it's such a hacked-out, baffled, sweetly modest face, full of such wonderful possibilities, and so recklessly, enthusiastically made. It's like a working model for a piece of sculpture that's been dashed off by a very gifted artist for a masterpiece he intends to finish later. A great sculptor, not a fashionable one. A fashionable one would have cropped his ears by an inch at least, all around, and trimmed his eyebrows, and done something about his nose, and couldn't possibly have made eyes like that, of such a crazed, inconsolable gentleness, like a hound that's been ordered to sit and be silent by its master, when he's leaving it behind. And you see, I know everything that ever happened to make his eyes that way, and everything that's going on behind them, because I'm a part of it all; and that's something that no other man can have in his eyes, ever: my whole life, my first high heels, my first lipstick, playing Hudson Bay underneath the blanket on stormy nights while we listened to the apples bang against the house, and the taste of the first cigarette we ever smoked still curling around in both our mouths, and of watermelons we shared, and milk from the same breasts, that has become our teeth and bones, and the same sorrow in our hearts. I thought how much I loved him, and only him, and always would; and when I'd accepted that at last, utterly and unchangeably, all the ire and pride that has stood between me and all the men I've ever tried to love was gone out of my heart, and I felt a meekness so great and sweet flow into me that I was breathless with it—a fresh clear amity for everyone and everything. It poured into my breast as if a spring had opened and cool, pure water had begun to gush into an arid cavern. It was something I've never felt before, or ever known that I could feel until the last few days, when I was sick and you took care of me. Even then, I think I'd begun to understand what was going to happen, what I had conjured with my lifelong rage; and the rage was dying out in me already, because that cool water had begun to well up in me and slake the hot stone of my heart. Oh, such a fabulous docility I felt! I was appeased at last. I was a lamb, a dove, and as mythical in my mildness as those creatures are. I felt ancient, renowned, in my humility. I thought: How am I made so venerable by this outrageous love? How strangely I have earned this rude fame. But I have; and this is who I am. This is my true, immemorial self. I am not the angry creature who has gone raging through the world; I am this abject girl, offering bread to her brother's hunger.

"Will you come and eat with me, then?" I said; it wasn't much more than a whisper.

"I don't know how a man could refuse an offer like that." He turned to smile at me with a look of such bewildering consentience that I was strengthless. I bowed my head as if ashamed of my delight.

"Well, we'd better go in and say goodbye to Jamed before he goes to sleep," I said. "And tell Momma we're going to have dinner together. I already told her we might, so she won't mind."

We went in and said goodbye to them. Jamed was already asleep, which was a blessing because he always hates it so much when we leave; he puts his arms around your neck and hangs on so you have to pry his fingers loose. But he was lying there asleep with his new boat hugged up to his chest, so we didn't have to go through that, at least. We both leaned down and kissed him on the forehead, and he just stirred and mumbled a little bit, off there among his sand castles on that sunny beach of his where it's always half an hour till suppertime and he can hear the whine of Poppa's drill from the shop. Aaron stood looking down at him for a minute and said, "So long, buddy boy. I hope you pray for me sometimes."

Momma came out to the yard with us and stood there with her hands clasped on her stomach the way she always does when we drive away, looking mortally indignant about the whole course of our lives—all that endless rushing around and helter-skelter nonsense—and yet resigned by now to the fact that, like most lives, they were one long series of arrivals and departures from and to nowhere of any great importance, and consoled by having Jamed, anyway; he knew enough to stay where he belonged; he was home for good.

"Now, you children have a nice time," she said. "But if you go to the Pier, you smell them crabs before you eat them. I heard Pauline Wirtz got on some bad crabs there last summer."

"We will, Momma."

"And, Aaron, you start getting some sleep. A man shouldn't look that haggard in the morning."

"Yes, ma'am."

She didn't wave when we drove off; she just stood there watching, waiting for the dust to settle.

Aaron followed me down to St. Leonard in the rental car he'd picked up at the airport, and we stopped at Lou's and bought a half dozen peelers, and Aaron got a bottle of cold champagne out of the ice chest. He held it up and waved it at me and grinned, looking happier than he'd been all day.

"Hey, just like the old days, Syl!" he said. "You and me out on a spree. Remember when you graduated, and we went up to Marlboro to the races?"

I did, because that was the first time I ever got drunk, on Rolling Rock, and he had to bring me home and sit me in the bay and splash me good before he took me up the hill to bed, and I could feel again the blazing chill that ran through me when he stood me up to put my blouse on and his fingers touched my naked breasts.

I don't know what time it was when we got back here, but I've never seen it so bright. The whole island was throbbing with light, like the white-hot chamber of a crucible. When we got out of the cars we stood there for a few minutes looking around while I pointed out things to him, because he hasn't been down here in years—the sandbar in the harbor, and the osprey's nest on top of the beacon tower, and the new Navy buildings over in St. Marys—and the light was so intense we couldn't look at them directly; we had to hold our hands over our eyes and peek through the slits between our fingers.

"Wow, I'd forgotten how bright it gets down here," he said. "Up there in New York the light is sort of like beef bouillon. You need a flashlight most of the time."

He was very shy and curious and delighted about everything; it seemed to be like a childhood adventure for him, like a visit to a museum in Washington or Baltimore when we were kids. He plucked a berry off the pyracantha and reached up to brush his fingers with the whisk of a mimosa blossom and when we got to the center of the yard he stopped suddenly and stood grinning at the urn.

"My gosh, what's this? It looks like a Grecian urn."

"That's what it is."

"Where did you get it, Sylvie?"

"One of the girls in the Art Department made it for me. I showed her a photograph of an amphora from Mykonos, and then helped her design the figures and she modeled it in plaster and then cast it in cement."

"My gosh, that's great." He ran his hands over the hot stone bodies of the fleeting lovers on the frieze. "I know why you have this here. You told me once that poem by Keats was the most beautiful thing anybody ever made out of words; or out of anything, maybe. You said it alone redeemed the whole nineteenth century. Even the Napoleonic Wars." I laughed, because I had; and because he'd remembered it exactly. "You still believe that?"

"Yes."

He looked at me in a kind of gruff, askance way, as if I'd bumped him in an elevator, and said, "You never change, do you? Jesus."

He loved the house. He walked all over it by himself, and looked at everything, upstairs and down, and picked things up and chuckled at them, and sat down in all the chairs.

"Jesus, this place is a wreck," he said. He ran his hands wonderingly over the arms of his chair. "Where do you suppose they get furniture like this? At the bottom of a cliff, I guess."

"They're all priceless antiques."

"They sure are. How much do you pay for it?"

"Sixty-five a month."

"Really? How much do you think a place like this would cost?"

"Mrs. Potter said she'd sell it for eight thousand. And apply the rent I've paid."

"No kidding. You think she'd throw in the furniture?" He got up and prowled around the parlor, rattling the doorknobs and poking his fingers in the cracks. "I guess you'd have to put a couple of thousand into it, to plug up all the holes."

"I guess so. It needs a new furnace, too. But a couple of thousand would make it very livable."

"Jesus, wouldn't it be great to have a place like this." He went over to the window and stood with his hands deep in his pockets, looking out at the bay glittering in the sun. "Are you going to buy it, or what?"

"I don't have the money. Maybe if somebody went in with me."

"Oh, God—" he said, and stopped suddenly, frowning at the floor. "You wouldn't want to do that. I mean, Christ, that would ruin it." I didn't say anything. He wandered back into the kitchen and stood beside the table, looking at that big Toby mug on the shelf that's shaped like Richard Nixon, shaking his head in wonder. I brought two tumblers to the table from the cupboard and took the champagne out of the paper bag.

"Well, how about some champagne?" I said. "Am I going to get a toast or not?"

"You bet." He peeled the foil off the neck of the champagne bottle and began to pry the cork out with his thumbs. When it was almost loose he held it up and tilted it at the Toby mug and fired it off with a pop. "Right between the eyes. This place is a shooting gallery." The champagne gushed out over his fingers, and he poured it quickly into the tumblers, handing me one of them and holding the other out level with his eyes. "O.K.," he said, "let's see. This is to the girl I owe everything to. That use to bite splinters out of my toes with her teeth, and do my quadratic equations, and told Poppa she did it when I broke the compass, and showed me where Momma hid the watermelon pickles, and where the shad bite best, and where the wild strawberries grow. Who showed me where it's at, in fact. And who is one of the very few people in the world who still know. Happy Birthday, Syl."

I didn't know what to say, and I don't think I could have spoken if I had. I took a sip of my champagne and stood holding it in both my hands with my head lowered.

"That's pretty powerful stuff," Aaron said. I nodded. We stood without speaking until he said abruptly, as if relieved it had occurred to him, "Aren't you ever going to open that present?" I nodded again and set my glass down and took the package out of my shirt pocket. It was wrapped in stiff, very weird black paper with little gold fleurs-de-lis all over it. "That's wallpaper," he said. "It was left over from when they did my john." I nodded again—I seemed to have gone dumb—and peeled the paper off the little book he'd wrapped in it. It was a copy of T. S. Eliot's poems that he'd had hand-bound for me, a beautiful little book. Inside, he'd written a message for me that said he'd marked the poem that he liked best. I opened the book to where he'd placed the self-marker ribbon between the pages and handed it to him.

"Will you read it to me?"

He held the book for a minute and then set it down on the table and said, "Not right now, I will later, O.K.?"

"You promise?"

"Sure. I will, no kidding. Let me get my throat oiled with a little bit of this stuff first. Right now it's kind of creaky." And that was true, because he'd said the toast in a quaint, hoarse voice, as if his throat hurt, and everything else in him.

"Have you got a sore throat?" I said.

"Oh, it's nothing serious. I guess I smoke too much."

"Momma's right," I said. "You do look haggard. What's the matter, Aaron? Don't you feel well?"

"I don't know," he said. "To tell the truth, I haven't been sleeping too well. I'm kind of bushed."

"Why can't you sleep?"

"I don't know. I just lie there and think about things. I can't help worrying about you, for one thing. Down here all by yourself. Suppose you fell off a ladder or got sick or something."

"There's a doctor next door."

"Well, I know, but I mean there's nothing for you to do. No theaters, or libraries or anything. Nobody to talk to. What kind of a life is that for a person like you?"

"I have someone to talk to. And there's a library in Prince Frederick, if I wanted to read. I love this little house. I love this place."

He took a drink from his glass and turned it around in his fingers once or twice. "You ought to be married," he said after a minute.

"I was married. It didn't work out at all. I killed him."

"Oh, for God's sake, you didn't kill the man. It was an accident. You said so. And you weren't married to him, anyway."

"I was married as much as I'll ever be. I don't want to get married."

"Why not?"

"Why don't you get married?"

He looked at me in a startled way and then lowered his eyes to the glass. "I never fall in love," he said. "I guess I can't."

"Well, I can't either."

He turned his head toward the window and looked out at the locust trees across the lane. "I guess we're both pretty lonely people," he said. "I guess we're not cut out for it."

"I guess not. Why don't you sit down and finish your drink? You look like you're about to leave or something."

"O.K." He pulled out a chair. "What about you?"

"I'm going to start the dinner, but I'll sit down for a minute." I sat down across from him and picked up the book and stroked the smooth suede of the binding. "This is a beautiful book. I love it. Thanks, Aaron."

"You're welcome." He watched me turn the book in my hands, admiring it. "It is beautiful, isn't it? There's a guy that has a little shop in the Village, on West Fourth Street, where he does that, by hand. A nice old guy with a beard and some kind of an accent. I go in there sometimes, when I'm downtown, and just sit and watch. I like that place. It's sort of like watching Poppa work a piece of wood."

"You get pretty lonely up there, don't you?"

He stared at the tablecloth and nodded. "You know what I do, Sylvie? I get up in the morning and go down to a sound studio, and they hand me a script that says, 'Remember, TUMS spelled backwards is SMUT,' or something like that. So I sit there and watch a monitor while they roll off the commercial and read that crap, about twenty-five or thirty times, until they've got a good take. I do that all day, and then I go down to a bar and have a drink. You know how much I get paid for that? You wouldn't believe it. Nobody deserves to get that much money for doing a thing like that. If I shoveled coal all day I wouldn't deserve it. I've got so much money I don't know what to do with it. There's a bank up there bulging with my money. You know how much this shirt cost I've got on? Sixty-five dollars. I've got to spend the damned stuff somehow, so I buy things. What else can you do with money? I try and send it home to Momma and she sends it back to me. She doesn't need more than a hundred dollars a month, she says. A hundred dollars a month; Christ, that wouldn't pay my bar bill for a week. So then I have a few more drinks, and maybe go to a movie or something, if there's an English movie showing, because sometimes my old classmates from G.L.A.D. are in it, and it's kind of nice to see them again, see how they're doing. And then I go home and try and read a book or do a crossword puzzle or something, or just sit there looking around the apartment. You ought to see that place, Syl—" He looked around the kitchen again and nodded deeply and ironically. "Boy, you'd love it. I got it decorated by some guy that wears leather pants and Aztec jewelry. It was just a way to get rid of some money. Fifty thousand bucks, in fact. There's a coffee table in there alone that cost five thousand dollars. I think it's made out of alabaster. That black wallpaper came out of the john. There's also a statue in there of Actaeon turning into a stag. The bottom half of him is stag and the top half of him is Arnold Schwarzenegger trying to tug off a wet tee shirt.

Then maybe after a while some goofy girl will call up, and be having an identity crisis or something, and want to know if she can come over and talk about it, or if I can go down to some bar and bail her out, or if I'll come over and coach her for an audition, read lines with her or something. Sometimes if I get a day off we'll have a picnic; go out to Long Island, Far Rockaway, or somewhere; and that's nice, that's the only really nice thing I do. But even then I'm not really with her, I'm not really listening to her, whoever she is. I just sit there and look out at the ocean, and think about this place. Wonder what you and Jamed and Momma are doing, and whether they've torn down the hotel yet, and whether they ever found Poppa's boat. And that's the best thing I do: try and keep some goofy girl or other from flying apart. Give her first aid, or enough money to pay her room rent, or get her teeth straightened, or take a plane back to Texas; until she just disappears somewhere, the way people do up there, or I finally figure out there's nothing more I can do for her. That's the only worthwhile thing I do. That's the way I justify my existence."

"What about all those foster kids you've got?" I said. "That sounds pretty worthwhile."

"Oh, well, I do that, yeah; but that's not really work. I've got about a dozen of them by now, as a matter of fact. Vietnam orphans, Down's syndrome kids, child abuse cases, every damn thing. I saw this ad in the paper for one of those organizations one day, and the little kid in the picture looked so much like Jamed used to look that I had to do something. It was like doing it for Jamed, you know? But I mean, hell, that's not really work. There isn't any sweat involved. You don't have to try and shove oatmeal into their mouths all day, like Momma does, or wrap up the stumps of their legs or anything. You just drop a check in the mailbox every six months and then congratulate yourself on your humanity. It's sort of like conscience money, really." He finished his champagne and then poured our glasses full again. "And that's about it. That's what I do for the world."

"You do more than that," I said.

"Oh, well, I feed the pigeons, and every once in a while send a check to some nutty outfit called Anarchists, Arise! They're big on polyandry or something."

"You're going to get yourself investigated."

"I hope to God I do; maybe they'll find out who I am. I hope they tell me." He put out his hand and laid it on mine. "I sound like Job. I'm sorry, Syl. I'm really the life of the party!"

"I like you when you're honest," I said. "And it's a great party. It's the best one I ever had."

He sat looking down at my hand, touching my knuckles with his fingertips. "Jesus, you're such a sweet girl, Sylvie. Jesus, if I didn't know you were alive, if I didn't know you were in the world, and I could come down here and see you sometimes, I don't know what I'd do. I really don't."

"Why don't you come down here and stay with me?"

"Stay with you? What do you mean, live with you? For good?"

"Yes."

"You mean here? In this place?"

"Yes. We could have fun fixing it up. We'd have everything we really need, everything we really want. And we'd be close to Momma and Jamed. We'd be happy, Aaron. Don't you know that?"

"How in the hell could I do that? What would I do? How could I make a living?"

"It's only an hour and a half to Washington. There must be at least ten dinner theaters running in Washington now, or right around it, in Maryland and Virginia. And there's Arena, and the Kreeger, and the Washington Theater Club. There's lots of theater work in Washington now."

"*Dinner* theaters? You know what they pay? They're not even Equity, most of them. Those actors have to scrounge out a living waiting on tables."

"Well, what's wrong with that? I thought you wanted to sweat a little. I thought you were sick of easy money."

"Well, sure, but I'd have to earn *something*. My God, there'd be all kinds of expenses. The mortgage, food, gas. We'd probably have to buy another car—"

"It wouldn't matter what you made. I get a pretty good salary now, and I'll probably make associate next year. I'll be earning fourteen or fifteen thousand."

"You think I'd let you pay my way? My God, Sylvie. And anyway—"

"Anyway what?"

"Well, I mean, what would people say? A guy and his sister living here all alone."

"I don't care what people say. Do you?" He didn't answer me. "You seem to think Wordsworth knew something about life. Well, did you know he and his sister lived together, for years, in a little place like this, in the Lake Country? You know what it was called?"

"No."

"Dove Cottage."

"Dove Cottage," Aaron said. "Isn't that something."

"And they'd go for long walks through the fields and woods and along the shore. With cold pork in their pockets sometimes. And stand under holly trees when storms broke, and watch the rain dripping from the crags and the cloud shadow sweeping over the moors. And then they'd come back, and Dorothy would make tea—"

"My God," he said. "How do you know all that, Sylvie? How do you know what happened?"

"Because she wrote it down. She kept journals. I could tell you them by heart, parts of them."

"No kidding. I'd like to hear that. Say one."

So I closed my eyes and quoted a passage from the Grasmere Journals that I had read so often I knew it word for word. It was the account of an entire and perfect day, one that had taken place on the earth in 1802: " 'March 23. A mild morning. William worked at the Cuckow poem. I sewed beside him. After dinner he slept. I read German, and at the closing in of day went to sit in the orchard. He came to me, and walked backwards and forwards. We talked about Coleridge. William repeated the poem to me. I left him there and in twenty minutes he came in, rather tired with attempting to write. He is now reading Ben Jonson, I am going to read German. It is about ten o'clock, a quiet night. The fire flutters and the watch ticks. I hear nothing else save the Breathing of my Beloved, and he now and then pushes his book forward and turns over a leaf.' "

"My gosh, that's beautiful, isn't it?" Aaron said. "It sounds like a poem."

"It is a poem."

"It's almost like they were still sitting there in front of the fire, reading. Like nothing else had ever happened in the world. Or ever would."

"Yes."

We sat for several minutes with our eyes lowered, not daring to look at each other. He started to say something, but his voice was ragged, and it caught in his throat.

"Is your throat still sore?"

"Oh, it's not bad. Nothing a little homemade bread won't cure."

"I'll get it started." I stood up and pushed the chair in to the table.

"Listen, it's a crime to make you cook dinner on your own birthday," Aaron said. "Why don't we go out?"

"No, I want to. You said you wanted some of my bread."

"Well, sure, but I mean, it's your birthday. What would Gloria Steinem say if she found out?"

"I don't think she'd understand. But she won't find out."

I went to the stove and lit the oven and began to take things from the cupboard shelves to make the bread: honey and flour and salt. These were the only ingredients, because it's a very simple unleavened bread that doesn't need to rise, only to be kneaded briefly and then shaped into flat loaves and baked for less than a quarter of an hour. I got the recipe from a book called *Foods from Bible Days*, and I like to make it because it's old, it's the first bread; it is in Genesis. While I worked the dough he sat and watched me silently, raising his glass occasionally to drink the wine. Once I went back to the table and took up my own glass to sip from it. When I set it down I laid my hand on his head and he sat without moving. The white mark of my hand was left, in flour, on his dark hair.

Then I made a batter of honey and milk and cornmeal for the crabs and while I stirred it Aaron sat listening to the circular, soft thumping of the wooden spoon against the china bowl. The smell of the bread baking in the oven was clean and fragrant in the room.

"It smells wonderful," he said.

"It won't be long. Do you want to put on some music? The records are in that box under the table."

"O.K. Do you have that thing you used to play all the time? Those songs from Wagner? You played it one time when I came home."

"It's on the phonograph."

"No kidding." He looked at me and smiled and then got up and went into the parlor. I could hear him fiddling with the phonograph, and after a minute the rapturous aria of love and springtime began to flood out of the room. He came to the parlor door and said, "My God, that's beautiful. What is it, Sylvie?"

" 'Winterstürme wichen dem Wonnemond,' " I said. " 'The Storms of Winter Yield to Gentle May.' It's from *Die Walküre.* "

"Jesus, it's beautiful. Then she answers him or something, doesn't she?"

"Yes. 'Du bist der Lenz.' 'You are the spring.' "

"You mind if I just lie down on the sofa in here for a few minutes, Syl, and listen to this? I feel kind of bushed. I got up pretty early this morning."

"No. Lie down. I'll let you know when it's ready."

He went back into the parlor and I finished preparing the meal, dipping the crabs in the batter, and when the bread was done, taking the hot loaves out of the oven with a dishcloth and setting them on a wooden cutting board. They were a pale, soft brown, round and smooth and subtly contoured as flesh. I cut a slice from one of the loaves, and when it had cooled for a minute, I carried it in to Aaron in my hands. He was lying on the sofa with his eyes closed, one arm raised behind him and his head resting on the bend of his elbow, turned to the side, and smiling a little, as he used to sleep on the glider on the front porch when he was a boy. I sat down beside him on the edge of the sofa and watched him for a moment.

"Hey, little sister," he said without opening his eyes.

"Are you asleep?"

"No. I'm just sort of daydreaming."

"Taste this."

I held the slice of bread to his mouth and he bit into it gently, opening his eyes in wonder as he ate.

"Oh, that's good, Sylvie. It's still hot. God, that's good bread."

He took the slice out of my hand and finished it, his jaws working with a slow, earnest voracity. When he had finished, there were crumbs on his palms and fingers, which he nibbled off with his lips.

"Shall I put the crabs in the pan?" I said. He didn't say anything, but there was the faintest movement of his head from side to side, which might have meant "No," or might have been a random, wretched gesture of entreaty. He lay looking up into my eyes and in a minute put his hand up and laid it against my face. I covered it with my own and pressed it to my cheek and closed my eyes. "You won't do it, will you?" I said.

"I don't know, Sylvie. I just don't know what to say. I want to."

"Is there anybody else you want to live with?"

"No. God, no. I've thought about it before. I've thought how perfect it would be, but I guess I'm just afraid. You've always been like a sealed well to me, of the sweetest water in the world. I've never been as brave as you." He pressed his hand against my temple, rubbing my cheekbone with his thumb. "You know what's the happiest I've ever been? The most peaceful I ever felt in my life? When we used to lie out in the glider on the front porch and shoot rice through a straw at that spider on the ceiling. He had a web over in the corner, remember?"

I nodded; and then I took his hand and brought it down and pressed it to my breast.

"Sylvie, don't. Please. Please don't."

I let go of his hand and began to unbutton my blouse, my fingers moving down from button to button with a slow, stately audacity that seemed to dwell in them like the memory of a ritual. My breasts ached to be naked to his eyes; all of me ached for nudity as if for air, as if I were suffocating in my flesh. He lay and watched me with a look of strengthless, sorrowful enchantment. I parted the front of my blouse and he raised his hands and held my bared breasts so lightly, in so reverent, intangible a clasp that they seemed to rest in the cupped hands of a ghost.

"Sylvie, please. Don't let me do this."

"I won't stop you," I said. "I'd never stop you. I've been waiting all my life."

He drew me down to him and held his face between my breasts and I stroked his hair. He made a low sound in his throat like the moaning of a nightjar, and then he plucked his hands away from me with a shuddering movement and struggled up from the couch and went across the parlor to the kitchen in long reckless strides, banging into the phonograph and sending the needle shrieking across the disc.

"Aaron, wait. Don't go," I cried out, but he had fled through the kitchen and out into the sunlight of the garden. I rose up from the couch and stood for a minute with my eyes closed in despair, too weak to move until I heard the screen door slam with a sound of agonizing finality like the snapping of a spine, and I knew that it must be finished. I clutched the front of my blouse together and went after him, through the strangely still kitchen, where my birthday dinner stood waiting to be served, and out into the sunlight past the lovers locked in their eternal embrace on the stone urn, and across the garden where he had gone plunging ahead of me through the rose of Sharon bushes, trampling the lily of the valley beds in the shadow of the crab tree, and out the skewed, still lightly swinging gate that he had flung open ahead of him. I followed him down through the locust grove toward the water, and through the chokecherry thicket where the sedge begins. He wasn't running, but striding with long, stricken steps like a man lunging barefoot through a desert of hot sand. He seemed not to notice when he startled and sent volleying up out of the bright dry grass ahead of him a covey of brown quail whose wings whistled in the air with a sound of pandemonium. I came after him, implacably, imploringly, with twigs lashing my face and throat and catching in my hair, calling out, "Aaron, Aaron!" until I stumbled on a stone and fell. He heard my body thud against the ground and my cry of pain when my head struck an outcropping of white flint there on the hillside, and he turned and stood for a moment, staring, before he came to me and knelt down to raise me to my knees and touch my bleeding temple with his fingertips. He took my face in his hands and looked into my eyes as if he were looking through the gate of a locked garden, and then he drew my head toward him and kissed me on the mouth, saying, "You taste of milk and honey." I lay back on the earth and he came to me like a comet falling to the sun; we were drawn together by an awful conjugal gravity that seemed to bend the air above us, crumpling the fields of space in which we lay, convulsing time itself; for one bright, cataclysmic moment distorting the whole fabric of the universe, twisting the clear shield of infinity awry.

I stared beyond his shoulder into the sun that burned above us, holding my eyes open with an inhuman effort until the white sublimity had flooded them and washed out of my sight forever all that was not pure, all that was not the inimitable, aneling light that I at last beheld and that reigned in my sight for an instant of immeasurable brevity before it sank to a scarlet deeper than a fathom's depth of blood, and then to an unhallowed blackness blacker than the leagues before conception.

Then he rose and I heard his breathing like the sigh of surf on sand as he stood above me, and the halting shuffle of his feet among the reeds as he turned to go.

"Where are you going?" I cried softly. "Aaron, don't leave me. You can't leave me now."

"I have to," he said. "I can't stay here. Forgive me, Sylvie."

"If you leave me now," I said, "it will be a greater wrong than you have done already."

"I have to go," he said. "I can't stay with you now. Forgive me, Sylvie."

"If you asked Poppa, he would let you stay with me."

"What do you mean?" he said. "Why do you say that?"

"I don't know. But it's true. Believe me, Aaron."

But he would not stay. I heard his feet go plunging off among the rushes, fainter and fainter, until there was only the soft whisper of the summer breeze among the reeds and the distant murmur of the river and far away the inconsolable cry of a bird.

I am not a man who prays without embarrassment, but I prayed, for days, that her eyes would be restored, that their exposure to the sun had been brief enough to cause only a temporary blindness that could be treated or would in time spontaneously improve. But within a very few days I could see there was no improvement; on the contrary, there was visible deterioration. She developed an intense conjunctivitis, her irises became bloodshot, and there was a marked dilation of the pupils. I thought also that I could detect corneal lesions of some kind, but she refused to go to a hospital, to see a specialist, or even to let me use an ophthalmoscope to make any kind of accurate diagnosis. "It isn't any use," she said, repeatedly.

"But, my God, Sylvie, I think you may be getting ulcers on the corneas. They've got to be treated. It must be painful."

"No. There isn't any pain." I knew she was lying. She would clench her eyes closed constantly and spasmodically and sometimes raise her hand involuntarily to them in obvious distress.

I took down my Pritkin and turned to his passage "The Pathologic action of Light":

Injuries from sunlight result from the effect of the sun's rays on the rods and cones of the retina with resulting atrophy. Bright electric lights have the same effect. Visual defects caused by intense glare may vary depending on the intensity and duration. Blurred spots may be formed, which are usually temporary. Once permanent damage has been done to the retina, a scotoma may result.

In electric welding, a few minutes without protection is sufficient to produce the so-called flash burn, characterized by minute corneal lesions, conjunctivitis, and chemosis of the lids. The same is basically true of snow and solar blindness.

Rays which are absorbed by the eye exert either a photochemical (abiotic) effect or a thermal effect. There is also a fluorescent effect, produced by the emission of light of a different wavelength than the incident radiation.

Abiotic lesions occur with the absorption of rays below 3,000 Angstrom units. Repeated exposure within intervals of less than 25 hours is equivalent to one long exposure. The reaction comes on in a latent period, depending on the intensity of the exposure. The photochemical change seems to affect the proteins of the nuclei of the cells. This produces histologically an acidophilic degeneration, nuclear chromatolysis, with formation of red granules coalescing into inclusion bodies which replace the whole nucleus of the cell. In the surrounding tissues there is a vascular reaction with an eosinophilic infiltration.

In the cornea, the reactions are seen clinically as a keratitis with an associated conjunctivitis. The reactions are seen chiefly in the epithelium. Severe exposures may cause corneal ulcers.

In the iris, the pigment absorbs all the radiant energy and converts it into heat, thus an eosinophilic reaction occurs only in the albino. There is a marked contraction of the pupil due to the direct action of the actinic rays, which liberate histamine, affecting the muscle cells.

In the lens, the capsule becomes swollen and the subcapsular epithelium responds with an eosinophilic reaction and proliferates to form an epithelial wall around the pupillary margin. Cataracts are not formed, but the lens efficiency is impaired, rendering it more prone to develop cataracts.

In the retina, long exposures cause pathologic changes.

Thermal effects are caused by infrared rays. In the cornea they produce coagulation and opacities. In the iris, the pigment absorbs much of the heat, which may cause severe hemorrhagic congestion, pupillary dilation, depigmentation, and iritic atrophy.

In the lens, there is an exfoliation of the zonular lamella and in severe cases, coagulation of the proteins of the lens and formation of a cataract.

In the retina, the pigment layer absorbs the heat so that in severe exposures to infrared rays necrosis will occur, affecting the rods and cones. This may also be transmitted to the choroid.

I called an ophthalmologist at the N.I.H. in Bethesda who had worked with me in the fifties on the Tallacoochee study. He gave me little cause for hope.

"Who is this patient?" he asked.

"A friend of mine. She isn't really a patient."

"Why don't you bring her down to see me?"

"I don't think she'd come, Clarence. She seems totally resigned to her condition. She's a rather unusual woman."

"What is her condition exactly?"

"Well, as far as I can tell, she's totally blind. There's no vision, and no light response whatever. There's marked dilation of the pupils, in the left eye especially, and I can see opacities in the corneas, and what look to me like ulcerous lesions. The irises are badly inflamed."

"How long ago did this occur?"

"A week."

"You say she looked into the sun? How long, for God's sake?"

"I don't know. She's rather vague about it."

"It must have been for one hell of a time. You might expect a discrete scotoma, but my God, it sounds to me like the whole retina is gone. Which doesn't make much sense; no one would stare into the sun that long. Have you used an ophthalmoscope?"

"No. She won't let me."

"You've got a very odd duck there. It doesn't sound as if the woman wants to be treated. I can't really tell you anything without looking at it. It sounds to me like she's burned out the retina, but that's only a wild guess. If you've got massive necrosis, of course, nothing can be done. What can I tell you, Carl?"

"Not much, I guess. What would you use to treat the ulcers topically?"

"I don't know; Neodecadron, I suppose. It can't do her any harm, unless the thing is due to an acute infection of some kind, which isn't the case, apparently."

"No. That I'm sure of."

"If you can talk her into coming in, I'll be glad to take a look."

"I'll try. Thanks, Clarence."

I drove up to Prince Frederick, bought the ointment he had recommended, and after a fierce argument, persuaded Sylvie to let me apply it regularly. After ten days or so, the conjunctivitis appeared to be controlled and the corneal lesions reduced in severity.

She no longer blinked constantly in the painful way she had, or raised her hand to her eyes in obvious distress. But there was no improvement in her sight. She asked me to buy her a pair of dark glasses, which I did, and she wore them constantly until a week or so ago. Now, looking at her eyes, no one who had not known her before would be aware of any obvious disfigurement; the rusty-brown eosinophilic stain that discolored the corneas has diminished, and they are almost clear. The only marked change is that her eyes are now a very pale and ghostly blue; there is a visible depigmentation of the irises, which, if anything, makes them more beautiful than before.

In the weeks after she went blind there were days when I doubted whether she would survive her catastrophe. She would wander about her bedroom all day in the dark with the blinds drawn, dressed in a stained and crumpled dressing gown, clutching at the curtains, opening drawers and raking restlessly through their contents, sitting at her dressing table for hours, staring sightlessly into the mirror, clenching a handful of hairpins or the handle of a brush, pawing at her tangled hair, and whining like an animal. On some days she would not get out of bed at all, but lie bleakly in the matted covers kneading her forearms and her wrists and elbows as if they ached, staring motionless, for hours, at the ceiling with her blind eyes. She seemed almost unaware of my presence at those times, or, if at all, in a cowed, submissive way. If I brought her up a cup of bouillon or opened the blinds and windows to let the air into the room or stooped to straighten her bedclothes and plump her pillows, she would slink back against the walls or into a corner of the room, wary and craven, like an animal whose cage is being cleaned by its keeper, barely exchanging a word with me. Once, heating a can of soup for her downstairs in the kitchen, I was horrified to hear her voice rising in a wail through the walls above me, a demented, long-drawn, throbbing howl of torment, like the cry of a wolf with its leg crushed in a trap. When I came into the room she sat on the edge of the bed swaying from side to side in an abandoned, quivering lassitude like a marionette whose strings are being jerked wildly by a mad or mischievous puppeteer, her arms dangling, her head snapping convulsively. I set the bowl down, trembling, on the dressing table and went to the bed to take her in my arms. She pressed her head against me and moaned in a sickening, guttural way, raising her hands to hook her fingers into my belt, clutching me against her.

I would have to feed her like a sick child, lifting the cup or spoon to her lips until she parted them listlessly and swallowed a mouthful of the soup or bouillon. "Thank you," she would murmur. "No more, Carl."

"Just another three spoonfuls. You're going to be sick if you don't."

"All right. Then no more, please."

Then I would brush her hair, sometimes for half an hour or more, while she sat with bowed head, sunken in her speechless solitude, until perhaps the curtains rustled in the breeze, or a curlew called outside the window from the river shore in a long, hollow note, clear as a flute; and she would stir and raise her hand to clasp my own, listening with a bewildered, nostalgic attentiveness.

And yet she recovered from those moments or days of despair with a force of will that was truly awful to see, a relentlessly self-imposed, almost inhumanly calm submission to her state—I thought, sometimes, of dedication to it—that I began to understand nothing could obstruct or compromise. She refused, quite literally, to succumb to her grief and guilt, as if she regarded it as an ignobility to do so, a mean default on her destiny; as if she had sworn to honor them with her suffering, out of some consummate pride, in observance of some covenant she had made which she held inviolable. Gradually, witnessing that strange and stately thing, my fear that she would find refuge in madness or suicide, as a lesser spirit might, was dispelled. She seemed to clutch the worldwide darkness in which she walked about her like a mantle, as if it alone befitted her, as if it alone were sumptuous enough to clothe her agony.

For a long time she did not smile. If I brought her a brace of tomatoes from my garden or a pair of scaled and gutted spot I had caught that morning or a bunch of chrysanthemums, she would accept them with a brief low murmur of thanks and lay her hand on my arm in gratitude; but she did not smile. Not until I brought her one morning a yellow kitten that had followed me along the road. "Hold out your hands," I said; and when she had done so, her brow wrinkled with perplexity, and I had placed the weightless, fluffy creature in them, wriggling and mewling, she caught it against her throat in such a spasm of tenderness that it made my heart surge to see her, bending and swaying with it pressed to her cheek, her face for a moment as radiant as a child's.

She began occasionally to listen to music again, although her mind would often wander off into its corridors of tortured thought before a piece was finished. Sometimes I would come into the house and find her sitting with her face turned to the light of the window while the needle ground and crackled in the last groove of a completed record.

She developed a passion for words even greater than that she had before. She would listen to them, and speak them, and consider them as if she were sorting jewels with her fingertips. On Sunday mornings I would walk up to Dorsey's and buy the Washington *Post,* and we would sit in the sun on the back steps with a cup of tea and a plate of buttered muffins and work the crossword puzzle. For a long time these seemed to be the only moments of genuine reprieve she had from her suffering. She would sit bent forward over her knees, her hair ablaze in the sun, reaching down to tickle the head of the kitten—which she has adopted—while it tumbled about her ankles, searching in her mind for the word whose definition I had read to her until it issued from her lips like a gem polished by the slow, aching peristalsis of her memory. There is hardly a word that she does not know. There are some that she hasn't used, I'm sure, for ten or fifteen years that she finds stored in some corner of her memory like a dahlia tuber stored in a cool cellar, waiting to be brought to fresh life in a new season.

In the second week of July, there was a letter from her mother, which she asked me to read to her and to which she listened with a blanched, resolute impassivity, her face as taut and still as if coated with a transparent varnish.

Dear Sylvia:

I surely did enjoy talking with you on the telephone last week. You are a good daughter to remember your mother so kindly and regular. I thank God I have got good children. There are so many that are just a tribulation in these times.

My girl, I pray that your eyes are some better. You must take care and do just what the doctor tells you, so they will get well soon. You must not despair, because the Good Lord always has you in his sight. That is a truth that nobody can deny.

I am sorry you couldent get up for the 4th. Aaron was not able to get here either, but he did call and talked to Jamed, which tickled him. He sent some fine fireworks, which I believe is an infraction of the postal rules, but my they were fine. Bud Offut set them off for us. There was a couple of rockets that went up I guess a mile or more into the air and sent off such a shower of lights it was like a fountain. Oh my, did that make Jamed just dance! I wish you could of seen that poor boy. Well we missed you both a bushel.

Aaron says he is thinking about giving up his work in N.Y. This will be a great surprise to me if it comes to pass, although I don't think he has ever been truly happy in that place. It was my heart's wish that he would take over your poppa's boatyard, but I do not speak of it. I don't care what the boy does as long as he is happy.

We had a bad blow on Wensday, I guess you got it down there too. We lost most of the tomatoes although I had them staked good. I guess I will be spared putting them up this year, there is some blessing in every loss.

Mrs. Cryer got a Heart Condition and will have to go to Calvert General for some tests. I sat with her on Tuesday and she was poor. She said to send you her love. Paisley's husband in the marines was made a corporal and she is some proud.

You take care young lady and mind you eat right. I would send you some of my fruit soup if I knew how. The next time Bud Offut goes down to Solomons I will try to send you some by him.

Love from your loving Mother

When I had finished reading it, she said, "Thank you, Carl," and held out her hand to me, taking the letter and refolding it with careful precision into its bulky quartered square.

"She seems well," I said.

"Yes. Is her handwriting firm? It gets very shaky when she's not feeling well."

"Yes, very firm."

She slid the letter into its envelope and tucked it into the pocket of her skirt.

"I haven't told her yet, you see. I want to get her used to the idea, little by little."

"I suppose that's best."

"Not that she won't be able to stand it. Better than I. She can stand anything, I think."

"I would say so, from looking at her photograph."

"It's Aaron I'm worried about."

I didn't answer, and after a moment she dropped her head with a look of sudden, strengthless despair. I laid my hand on her hair. She shook her head as if to deny her own weakness and raised her face to me with an expression of fierce, wracked resolution.

"My God, why are you so good to me? Why do you give me so much? What can I give you in return?"

"Give me a little of your grief," I said. "I'd be proud to bear it for you."

"Oh, love, as if you hadn't enough of your own."

"Not now. You've taken mine from me."

Now, in the autumn, the days are like steel; fine-edged, cool, glinting with October light, tempered to an austerity that clips the crab apples from the trees and crumples the iris and impatiens in my garden and splashes the sumac and the gum tree at the end of the lane with gouts of glittering red. Only the dauntless asters and marigolds thrive, adding their astringence to the thin, bright air. It is the saddest and most beautiful of seasons; almost spectral in its sad, livid silence. But it is not the sadness of despondency; there is a fine, tranquil exaltation in the air, as if the earth were not falling into decrepitude or death, but stilled by a throe of transformation. Things seem translucent; leaves, buildings, even brick, have an eerie, luminous insubstantiality. The light seems to shine through them like the flames guttering behind the rind of the hollowed jack-o'-lantern melons on the front steps of the houses. One has the feeling that he could plunge his hand through objects and touch the cool flame glimmering within that illuminates them. The hot summer finiteness of things is beaten out into a transparency as bodiless and indestructible as the furniture of dreams. These autumn flowers are almost imaginary, these woods and waters painted on a fabric as diaphanous as air, these gaunt white houses that stand so strange and pale along the lanes seem to be standing shapes of ash, leached, lixiviated by the light, the weightless clapboards cleft in place by nails of wrought delirium, the windows welling with phantasmal firelight.

Sylvie is marvelously aware of this, and marvelously a part of it. She walks beside me with her head lifted in that awed, attentive look of recognition, herself aglimmer with a soft, wraithlike effulgence, as if the summer light were buried in her as deeply as in the subtly incandescent world around her, were buried in her bones, and cast up from the cool ebullient marrow the faint glow that shines through her pale skin.

We walk the island together almost every day by the same routes, morning and evening, and it seems to me she has never been more aware of its beauty or its nuances of light and shadow, temperature and odor, and its delicate, metabolical stirrings and pulsations—the faint tremble of leaves that comes with the rising of the breeze under cloud shadow; the cooling of stone and sand as the light begins to slant into the long rays of evening; the waxing of odors into the spice-sharp potpourri of scent brewed from herbs and flowers in the shrill noon light, and the waning of their fragrance into the dim bouquet of afternoon. She will pause to press her foot to a shell that she has trod upon, absorbing its temperature and texture through her sole, or reach up to pluck a leaf or plume of blossom from a tree and brush her lips and throat with it to sense and share its frail attenuation, or stand with lifted head and listen to the passing soft furor of geese's wings across the sky. She has learned with an uncanny exactitude the physical disposition of the entire island, the length and breadth of lanes and roads, the density of thickets, the distances between buildings and fence posts, I think the location of every tree and stone and dune and wire fence within two miles of her house, so that now she can walk abroad almost with the confidence of a person who can see. At first she would venture out only if she held my hand, hesitantly and for short distances; but now she walks beside me without fear or hesitation for an hour at a time, matching her steps to mine along the lane or across the sand or through a field of rushes, her fists doubled in the pockets of her cardigan, her head lifted in that serene, intrepid way, as if enchanted by the freshness of the world she was discovering. Often she goes out alone. I've seen her climb up the rocks of the breakwater with her old agility and speed, and run splashing through the shallow water at the shore's edge with her sandals dangling by their straps from her hand,

and build a fire of driftwood on the beach, patiently gathering the sticks and bleached white branches and weaving them together with the same dexterity she had last spring. She goes down to the docks sometimes and sits for hours in the sun with her knees clasped in her arms, listening to the suckle of water under the hulls, the slap of halyards and the mewling of the gulls. She loves to be with children, and the island children have grown to consider her almost one of them. In the evening after school and on Saturdays and Sundays, if she is sitting on the pier, they will come and join her in groups of twos and threes, or walk with her along the beach or harbor, chattering stories of their day's adventures, tugging at her dress to gain her attention, running to her with bits of curious debris from the tide line, which she will finger admiringly and store in the pockets of her cardigan. Sometimes she tells them stories, to which they sit and listen cross-legged, tugging at their shoelaces and grinning with excitement or solemn-faced with suspense. When the pokeweed berries were ripe she would pluck them from the bushes along the lanes and crush them in her hands and paint the children's faces, holding their chins cupped in her palm and running a streak of purple juice along their noses with her fingertip, painting a bright circle on each cheek and the tip of the chin while they stood and giggled under her transforming hands. Then, in a fit of wild mischief, they would snatch handfuls of the glittering berries and smear her with their juice as well, smudging her face and arms and clothing until she was dabbled with motley patches of royal purple like themselves, and then run capering and shouting beside her in the sunlight in an elfin, jubilant harlequinade. She can be very gay, with a childish, heedless gaiety; and sometimes impenetrably somber. I have come to her gate after supper if we have dined alone—as often she insists on doing—and seen her sitting on the steps outside her kitchen door, still and cool as stone, her face lifted to the last light of evening, gone almost lifeless with solemnity. But it is not any longer the solemnity of despair—no more than the solemnity of this autumn is that of death or dissolution. It is as if she were engulfed by the same vast tide of quietude that transforms the earth, and as lambently submissive to it as the scarlet plum tree in the lane. I think there are moments when she requires herself to bear again—and often, daily—the realization of what she has done; and in those moments she seems to be deaf as well as blind; senseless of anything but the knowledge of those enormities. And yet I no longer fear for her sanity, because I think her spirit has been tempered to a diamond fortitude equal to the contemplation of them. Yet they must be awful moments; as awful as my own, which I would not have thought it possible to bear a year ago, before I knew her. One day last week, when I came through the gate at evening, she was standing at the urn in the garden, pale as a phantom in the dusk, her fingers laid lightly on the stone, her head bowed as if in grief. But when I halted on the path and was about to turn and go, feeling suddenly ashamed of my intrusion, I heard her murmur in a voice I scarcely recognized, a voice as clear, as denuded of profanity as light itself, " 'Oh, thou who lovest me, set thou this love in order.' "

The next evening I cooked dinner in her kitchen and she ate almost silently, murmuring to me only if she needed salt, or butter, or a slice of bread. She was not sad, exactly, but withdrawn into a fragile, voluminous reverie, like the soft, aspirate tumult that stirs the fresh leaves in an April breeze. I did not try to make conversation; speech would have seemed almost an impropriety in such a delicate silence. Afterwards, she dried the dishes as I washed them and put them one by one into her hands, reaching up to set them carefully on the shelves, abstracted and yet very diligent, as if grateful for the discipline the task required. When I said good night to her she came and put her arms around me and laid her head against my shoulder for a moment. I walked home through the cold clear air of the early-fall night, stopping at my gate to look up at the sky above the bay. Orion was rising, and the low stars cast a glittering, undulating pattern in the black water, like the evolution of some bright, inextinguishable thought there in the darkness. When I went in, I lit the first fire of the autumn in the hearth, setting a match to the stack of kindling and dry applewood logs that had stood ready since the spring. I lay down on the sofa to watch the flames, which were of such beautiful shapes that I became lost in them; even the agonies of the last weeks dissolved into insignificance before the lovely, constantly changing fluid forms of the firelight. I don't know how long I had lain there—perhaps an hour—when I heard the kitchen door open and close gently, and Sylvie's footsteps coming cautiously across the kitchen floor, around the table, and to the parlor door. She stood there for a moment before she said softly, "Carl?"

"Yes?"

"I was afraid you were asleep."

"No, I was just lying here looking at the fire."

"Can I come in?"

"Yes. Please."

"Don't get up." She came slowly to the sofa, reaching out to touch the backs of the furniture with her fingertips, and stood listening to the crackle of the flames.

"It sounds lovely. What are you burning?"

"Applewood, from the old orchard. Virgil gave me a cord of it."

"I thought so. I could smell it in the air." She held her hands out to the fire. "It's cold outside."

"Yes. There may be frost tonight. Why don't you sit down?"

"I'm lonely," she said. "I need to be with you."

"I'm glad you came."

"Do you ever sleep there, on the sofa? In front of the fire?"

"Sometimes. At least until it burns out. Then I wake up, if it's very cold."

"Can I stay with you tonight?"

"Of course."

"I'd like to sleep in someone's arms tonight."

"There's an afghan over there on the back of the rocker," I said. "Bring it over."

She felt her way to the chair with an outstretched hand and then back to the sofa with the afghan. She tossed the knitted robe across my body and then lay down beside me on the sofa, holding up the outer edge of the cover while she wriggled under it. I put my arm around her, and she laid her head against my shoulder and stretched one arm out to encircle my chest, giving the great contented sigh of an exhausted child.

"Were the stars out?" she asked.

"Yes. Orion is just rising. It's just above the water."

"If there's frost tonight, maybe I ought to bring my plants in from the porch."

"I think they'll be all right; they're under a roof. I'll help you with them in the morning."

After a moment she said, "Listen. Do you hear that bird singing?"

"Yes. Isn't that beautiful? What kind of a bird is it?"

"A mockingbird, I guess. They sing at night, like nightingales."

"How beautiful."

We listened for several minutes to the clear notes caroling outside the cold panes of the windows.

"I'm going to learn to type," Sylvie said. "I've got to be able to write without bothering you. Will you help me?"

"Yes."

"I have to learn so many things."

"I think you ought to have an electric typewriter. People say they're much easier to operate. Let's go in to Annapolis next week, and you can try them out."

"I think I'd be afraid to go in to a city yet. With all the traffic and the crowds."

"No. You'll just hold on to my hand, and there won't be anything to be afraid of. Shall we go in on Monday?"

She didn't answer, and I realized that she had fallen asleep. Her breathing lengthened into the deep, pacific whisper of untroubled rest and continued like that for hours. If I grew cramped or uncomfortable and shifted my body slightly, she would murmur sleepily and adjust herself to my altered position, and then her breathing would resume as evenly and serenely as the distant wash of waves. Once in the night, when the fire had burned down to a heap of coals, I got up carefully, trying not to disturb her, and put fresh logs on the grate and then lay down again beside her.

"Is it morning?" she murmured.

"No. Go back to sleep."

"All right. You won't leave me, Carl?"

"No. I won't ever leave you."

I find it hard to keep this journal any longer. My enthusiasm for it and its own few, feeble felicities are extinguished by the brilliance of the things I have recorded in it, as if I had tried, with candlelight, to contemplate the sun. There is an essential impropriety in trying to describe a life one reveres or a woman whom one loves. She was, and is now more than ever, ineffable. Words—these words, at any rate—betray her mystery; before the shining face of grace, all testimony is travesty; even praise is gratuitous; prayer itself, at last, seems parlous or promiscuous. Only the silent salience of love can play upon the beloved scene and reveal it, like light refined to utter volatility. Only the silent eloquence of love can render it. Who is Sylvia, what is she, that all the swains adore her? These pages, even if they were written by a Donne or Dickinson, could not tell. One would have to see her with my eyes, standing on a dune above the river shore in the morning light, as pale and sovereign as the moon in a dawn sky, to understand her beauty.

And yet Sylvia herself, sightless, sees grace in everything. Often, in the evenings after dinner, I read to her, and she listens with a look of devout attention, as if the words, like the transfigured world, have some new meaning for her, some new place of origin; as if they were not printed on a page where they reside, in a book that can be stored on a shelf, and taken down and recited, but are proceeding, even as I speak them, out of some inexhaustible source of concept in the darkness that swarms about her with a traffic of ideas like swarming, speaking souls; as if they were deathless, dateless, eternally contemporary, eternally intoning their separate asseverations of a single, indivisible excellence that makes them all mysteriously synonymous. "I never read before," she said once, wonderingly. She has no particular preference as to what I read to her; all texts are of equal worth and fascination to her. If I ask what she would like to hear that evening, she says, "It doesn't matter. Whatever is there. Close your eyes and choose." So we have Dickinson one night, Dickens the next, then Ruskin perhaps, or Thoreau, or a cookbook, or the description of a songbird from the manual I gave her; whatever I find on her shelves, in whatever order—and for her there seems always to *be* order; she finds nothing boring, random, or irrelevant. One book or poem or passage is conjoined to another by her burning recognition of its necessity and consonance, and takes its place in those ceaselessly exfoliating tidings that she hears in every text, the intelligence that arranges the spectrum of all utterance into the white syntax of light. In that integrity a recipe for bread is as essential as a Shakespearean sonnet or a linnet's song.

Only once has she expressed a preference. One night last week, when I had lighted the kerosene lantern—which she prefers to electric light because she can hear the faint flutter of the flame and sense the heat of the glowing chimney—and had sat down across from her with a book I had plucked from the shelf, she said suddenly, "What have you got, Carl?"

"*A Sentimental Journey*."

"No. Not that. Do you know what I'd like to hear this evening?"

"No."

"Your book. I never finished reading it. I want to hear it now."

"Oh, Lord. It's not in a class with Laurence Sterne."

"I'm not sure there are any classes. Anyway, I want to hear it. You asked me once what I thought about it, and I promised to tell you."

"That was vanity. It doesn't matter to me now. And it's such an awful book. It can't do anything but depress you."

"You mustn't argue with me. You gave it to me to read. You wanted me to hear it."

I got up very reluctantly and went across to the bookshelf, replacing *A Sentimental Journey* and searching along the spines with my fingertip for the slender fiberboard volume of my thesis.

"I don't see it here," I said.

"It's in the drawer of the desk where I keep the clippings."

I went to the desk and opened the drawer and found the book under a stack of faded clippings. I carried it back to the chair beside the lamp and saw that there was the tip of a stem of sea oats projecting from the pages.

"I marked it with a piece of dune grass where I stopped reading," she said. "Start reading there."

I opened the thesis to the marked page and began reading from the top:

"'The microorganism *Treponema pallidum*—the Pale Worm—is well named; it is the palest of all living things. Its transparency is so absolute that it is characteristically invisible in ordinary light. Conventional methods by which bacteria are studied, culture examination, hanging-drop preparations, impression films, or fluorescence microscopy—reveal little or no evidence of its presence. Even when dead it is extremely elusive to sight; in smears prepared in the ordinary manner and colored with the usual bacterial stains, it remains invisible. To be seen at all in a living motile state, it must be viewed by means of a process known as the Dark Field Method, in which it appears as the single illuminated object in a surrounding field of darkness. The process is an exotic one, requiring the use of a uniquely constructed microscope and considerable necromancy with light. A special condenser fits into the substage of the instrument, and the center of its top lens is opaque, so that none of the central rays of light can pass through it, the organism being illuminated only with very oblique rays. None of the light goes directly up the objective as in the ordinary way; the rays pass through the object almost at right angles to the objective and nearly parallel to the stage. Through the microscope the field appears dark, and against it the *Treponema pallidum* individuals will be seen to stand out as bright refractile objects, like particles of radiant dust in a beam of light across a dark cellar.

" 'They are quite beautiful. Their form is that of extremely delicate filaments, eight- to fourteen-thousandths of a millimeter in length and with anywhere from six to fourteen sharp, closely set, regular spirals. The ends taper to an incalculable fineness, as if merging imperceptibly into nothingness. In the bath of light the nearer half of each coil is brightly illuminated, like an arc of translucent metal of startling rarity. In their movement they show a kind of serene languor, in contrast to the active, often frenzied motility of the *Borrelia refringens, Leptospira,* and other organisms of their family. When they move at all, this regal, unhurried motion is characteristic. Sometimes they exhibit a musical, accordionlike compression or extension of the coils. Often they remain virtually stationary in their field, revolving in a slow, dreamlike gyration around their axes.

" 'These creatures are not only extremely difficult to see but almost impossible to grow. Because of their delicacy and fragility and, apparently, their fastidiousness as to environment, they are not cultivable by any of the ordinary methods or in any of the ordinary mediums in which other microbes are reproduced for study. They are killed by cold, moderate heat, drying, weak disinfectants, even soap and water. They cannot live in the presence of air. Schereschewsky reported cultivation of them in 1909, but his cultures appear to have been contaminated by other microorganisms. Noguchi later reported the growth of several strains in a serum water medium containing a piece of sterile fresh rabbit kidney or testicle, but his reports remain unconfirmed or disputed, and there is serious doubt whether they have ever been isolated in pure culture. I have myself experimented with the maintenance of the Reiter, Nichols, Kroo, and Kazan strains in a heart infusion broth containing glycose, cysteine, and filtrate of coagulated plasma, but my results have been highly inconclusive. One would have doubts as to the actual existence of these creatures if they were not equaled in their ghostly, evanescent beauty by their virulence; almost the only method of obtaining them is by extraction from the serum of a syphilitic chancre, or from the secondary lesions of that disease, which they produce in man.' "

I paused and looked up from the book. She was listening intently, her head downcast in concentration, her throat clasped lightly in her fingers. I laid the book in my lap and went on, as if I were continuing to read, inventing the text as fluently as if I saw the words upon a page:

"I will never forget the astonishment I felt when I saw these tiny animals for the first time through a Dark Field microscope. I don't know what I had expected to see. Something hideous, I suppose. Some tiny, obscene monster with the face of an ogre or a devil, magnified to the point of horror. And yet here was nothing but grace and radiance. Here was the most exquisite and insubstantial of living things, almost immaterial in its rarity, spinning in its spellbound pirouette like a dancer in a dream, bright as quicksilver against the blackness that surrounded it. When I think of that moment now it seems to me a moment of such privilege that in itself it would redeem a lifetime of obscurity or tedium or pain. If I close my eyes I can see it still, that luminous thread of life, that shining virus, possessed, devouring, breeding, whirling in its rapture, in the utter animation for which I know no word but love. Why did I not see it then? Why did I not have the vision to understand that what I saw there in the heart of darkness was light, pure and everlasting?"

When I had stopped speaking she raised her head and looked at me through the lamplight with her dazzled eyes.

"You asked me once if I thought there was any good in it," she said. "You were afraid it was ugly or perverse. It's beautiful, Carl. I think it's as beautiful as Keats, or apple trees, or that lamplight that I feel on my face. And as true. You have nothing to fear."

Now she is studying Braille and learning to type correctly. She has used a typewriter for years, of course, but only with a hunt-and-peck system—one of peculiar ferocity which used to make the floor of the parlor tremble and her ancient L. C. Smith-Corona creep gradually across the table as if in flight. But two months ago I bought her a typing manual and since then she has been learning to touch-type in the standard way. At first she was very dependent on me. I would place her fingers on the keyboard in accordance with the chart, moving them, one by one, to the keys they were required to cover, then reading her the exercises, beginning with the most elementary and proceeding to business correspondence and technical charts, which she is now able to transcribe from dictation with very few errors. She does this in conjunction with her study of the Braille system, and in the two months since she began has made phenomenal progress in both. Already she can read Braille with astonishing rapidity and accuracy—a full page of text in perhaps ten minutes—and can type at a rate of something like thirty words a minute.

Every morning, after we have had breakfast and gone for an early walk, if the weather is pleasant, she sits at a little gate-legged table by the open window of the parlor and practices for an hour or more. This is where she was sitting, two days ago, when I brought her the letter from Aaron. I had been on a shopping expedition to the market and on the way back had stopped at the post office, where it was set before me on the letter booth by Mr. Becker's ghostly hand. I put her groceries away when I got back to her kitchen and went into the parlor with the letter in my hand. The cool morning air flowed through the open windows, scenting the room with the faint salt fragrance of the bay.

"They had some fine Valencia oranges," I said. "I got you half a dozen. They're in the vegetable bin, so don't forget them."

"I won't. Thank you, Carl. Will you stay for lunch?"

"If you let me make it."

"All right. You spoil me. Come and see if I've made any mistakes."

I went across the room and stood behind her, looking at the sheet of paper in the typewriter. She had written:

The quick brown fox jumped over the lazy dog. The quick brown fox jumped over the lazy dog. I think there is a cricket in this room. I hear it all night from my bedroom, singing down here. The quick brown fox jumped over the lazy dog. In 1555 or thereabouts, St. Teresa of Avila wrote, "Nada te turbe, nada te espante. Todo se pasa." The quick brown fox jumped over the lazy dog. Carl Ransom, you are a saintly man to bear witness to all my errors and help me to correct them. The quick brown fox jumped over the lazy dog. Now the shadow of the dogwood has moved from my shoulder and I am in light again. The quick brown fox jumped over the lazy dog.

"Are there any mistakes?" she asked.

"Two. My name is spelled with an 'e,' and I am not a saintly man. Otherwise, it's flawless."

"You're sure?"

"Yes."

"What's the matter?"

"I have a letter for you." She became very still. After a moment of sitting motionless, she held out her hand. I put the envelope in it and she brought it to her breast and held it there in both hands, staring stilly at the wall in front of her. "I thought I'd make a tuna fish salad," I said. "Is that all right?"

"Yes."

I went out into the kitchen and began to make the salad, washing a stalk of celery under the faucet and chopping it on a cutting board. After a few minutes she came into the kitchen and sat down at the table.

"Would you like some chives in it?" I asked.

"Yes, that would be good."

"Did your father build a boat called *The Ark and the Dove?*"

"Yes. How did you know?"

"It was in the dock this morning, taking fuel."

"How did you know it was his?"

"Because it was so beautiful, I suppose. You said he made the most beautiful boats on the bay, and this was the most beautiful I've ever seen. Is it a schooner?"

"No. A two-masted skipjack. I think it's the finest boat he ever made. It's made of white oak and applewood and Norway spruce. It will sail forever."

"It looks it. Why did he give it that name?"

"Because those were the boats that the first settlers to Maryland came in, the *Ark* and the *Dove.* They landed here in 1634, right across the river in St. Marys City. They were led by Leonard Calvert, the man this county is named for."

"I didn't know that. How very interesting."

"I'll tell you something else that's interesting. They weren't Protestants, either. They came here to escape Protestant persecution, and they were the first people in America to pass a law that guaranteed freedom of conscience, the Toleration Act, in 1649. It didn't do them much good, though. The Puritans swept it aside, five years later, and seized the government from Lord Baltimore and put them all under disabilities as severe as any ever imposed in this country. Poppa used to tell us about all that, even before we could read. He was still indignant about it because he said the spirit of the original settlers had been stamped out long ago."

"It wasn't stamped out in him, evidently."

"Oh, no, not in Poppa. He loved those names they gave their ships. And he loved Noah, because he was the first boatwright and the first man to make wine." She raised her hand and laid the fingertips against her forehead as if it ached. "He wanted Aaron to follow that trade more than anything on earth. I told him not to."

I scraped the chopped chives into the salad from the cutting board and laid down the knife. "I thought I'd crumble in some feta cheese. How does that sound?"

"Very good. There's some bread there, in the box. I made it yesterday. It's the first I've baked."

"Oh, that's fine," I said. "And I've brought a bottle of very good white wine. Would you like some?"

"I think I would, today. Carl—"

"Yes?"

"Where was it sent from? New York?"

"No. England. It has a Stratford on Avon postmark."

"Is there a return address?"

"Yes."

I stared out of the window for a moment at the mimosa tree, pale gold in the throbbing clarity of the autumn light.

"I don't know whether I have the right to make a suggestion," I said at last, "but perhaps you could explain that you couldn't read it, because—of what has happened. But that you wanted him to know that you'd received it. Of course, I don't know if you're ready to tell him yet." She sat silently. "Or how it happened," I added in a moment. "It might be merciful to say you'd had an accident of some sort. Something that wasn't related in any way—something that wouldn't add to his guilt. I suppose you'll have to let him know sooner or later."

She did not answer. I went on preparing the salad while she sat at the table with the letter in her hands, listening gently to the delicate, intermittent sounds I made at my task: the clicking of a spoon against a glass bowl, the chopping of a knife against a wooden board, the opening of a cupboard door, the dainty rattle of china being taken from a shelf and set upon the table, the rustle of serving spoons through lettuce. When I sat down across from her, she put the letter into the pocket of her skirt and smiled at me steadily.

"Thank you, Carl," she said. She lifted her fork and, finding the edge of her plate with her fingertips, began to eat, her head turned thoughtfully and peacefully aside. "Maybe it's just as well that I don't know what he says. The words aren't so important. What matters is that he found the words to say. That he wants to speak to me again, and can."

"Yes."

"And it doesn't really matter whether he's in England, or Africa, or Elysium. As long as there isn't silence anymore. It's really only silence that appalls me."

"I know."

"When you were making the salad just now, you made such lovely, gentle sounds. They seemed to bless me." We went on eating quietly, and I rejoiced with her in the music of our meal together: the muted clink of cutlery and china, the hushed effusion of decanted wine, the ancient whispered syllables of broken bread, a gracious plainsong welling up from that inhabited instant of the universe of time.

On these mornings, when Sylvie is practicing her typing and studying her Braille, I go down to the shore and launch the rowboat that I rent from Captain Jack and row out into the estuary to troll for spot or rockfish for an hour or two in the early dawn. Often it is before sunrise when I go out, with only a great soft blush pervading the calm immensity of morning from the long, steel-gray line of the bay's horizon. The clouds are still obscure, scattered motionless across the cool, dark sky, their lower edges rouged faintly, peopling the vast unconscious vault with the soft persistence of a dream. It is cold on the water, and I like that; I like the smooth, hard substantiality of the oar handles through my mittens, the tingle of my cheeks and ears in the sweep of moist air across the water, the creak of the oarlocks pivoting in the gunwales, and the chortle of the glassy water spinning away behind the paddle blades. Occasionally I hear the whir of the locked reel of my troll rig, and ship the oars to take up the pole and yank it gently to set the hook, then reel in the rock and lift it aboard, the flittering bright fish breaking the smooth surface of the water like a shattered pane and flopping about in the bottom of the boat in a frantic, glittering spray of splintered glass. If I am made at all uneasy—as Sylvie tells me Thoreau was—by the thought that "it would have been better if I had not fished," I have, to assuage it, the vision of her bending above her plate to pry the white flesh from its bones and raise it to her lips with an innocent, august avidity that would absolve a man of any crime committed in its service.

The sun has risen above the low banks of cloud when I come in from the estuary, and I see the town rise out of the glinting shoals of light to landward. I ship my oars and sit to watch the blazing of its windowpanes, its rooftops shingled in resplendent crystal shale, the coruscations that flash and ripple over the wet hulls like runes scrawled in quicksilver, the tender limpid air that veils the town in the mist of a mirage. It is my home, this island of the wise and passionate king where I have been naturalized; whose language I now speak; whose fairest daughter sits at her window listening for the sound of my footsteps in the lane.

Sometimes she tires of her studying and comes down to the water's edge to wait for me, and while I row in to the shore I can see her walking there, stirring the pools of mist with her white feet, the light glancing on her chestnut hair as she stoops to pluck a seashell from the sand, like the coppery brilliance that slips along the stems of rushes when they bend to the wind across the marshes. She stands and listens for the sound of my oars across the quiet water and reaches to fumble for the line I toss in from the bow. When I have stepped ashore she helps me tug the boat up onto the sand and we walk together across the pebbles of the beach and along the white lane under the plum tree whose branches toss in the spring breeze like carillons. They shake down a shower of light as clear and cool as witch hazel that sprinkles our skin and seems to tinkle on the stones—shillings of jingling light, basins of bright alms flung down from a minstrel gallery by a munificent seigneur. We walk in through the garden and I stand and watch while Sylvie kneels to touch the flowers, the tulips reeling before her wandering hands, knocked awry by her ardent groping like small bright goblets brimming with the mead of sunlight that splashes on her wrists. She closes her fingers around the petals of a Canterbury bell as if she could feel its merry pealing in her palm.

Sometimes in the middle of the day we pack a picnic basket and walk out across the meadow to the church to eat our lunch in the shadow of its weather-pitted wall. She will run ahead of me and crouch down beside the creek that threads its way across the field and dabble her hands in the swift, clear rill of running water and fondle the cool, moss-slick stones, giving a quick gasp of delight if she feels a crayfish scuttle across her fingers as lightly as a leaf. We spread a tablecloth in the shadow of the church wall and eat our cheese and apples and drink a bottle of wine, staring out at the haze above the clover and the palpitating light above the river. When we have finished we pack the basket and walk up through the graveyard among the gray stones under the cedar trees and follow a line of telephone posts across the meadow to the harbor. In the white-hot distillery of the sky the sap is rendered out of them in amber droplets that bead their length like gems, like the little golden nuggets of delight rendered out of the throats of ravished doves that line the wires overhead. Along the lane hummingbirds dart and hang trembling over masses of honeysuckle that seethe like pools of simmering magma, then plunge down, crazed with light, to immolate themselves. Inside the wire fence of Mrs. Cryer's yard, a cock, in ruins, sheds showers of iridescent rubble from its plumes. We walk out onto the pier above the harbor water where schools of slender fingerlings twist and flicker, tossing up fresh-minted coins, handfuls of shimmering medals that spangle Sylvie's breast and face while she stands and spreads her hands above that coolly boiling cauldron, dressed in her regalia of light, bemused, bizarre.

In the summer evenings it is light long after dinner, and often we leave the dishes on the table and walk down along the river through the warm air until the dusk has fallen on the island and twilight has begun to flood up from the end of the broad, scarlet-lacquered road of the Patuxent that divides the darkening masses of oak forest on the St. Marys and the Calvert County shores. As the light fades, a velvet, saffron-colored robe is cast across the low hills, and in among the cattails of the creek, herons stand raving softly in the dusk like candle flames. High above them the first of the pylons of the new bridge juts into the sky, rising insolently into the sweet, rose-tinted air. At its feet and in its monstrous shadow a flock of gulls stand motionless on the wet, mirror-bright sand flat, their heads turned east, all at identical angles, arranged in ranks as if aligned by some invisible wind or some faultless natural rectitude in which they flow. They are shabby-feathered, oil-stained, uncouth, some of them maimed, with the stump of one leg dangling above the sand. They look like a defeated army standing at last post or taps; some ceremony of mourning to mark the conquest of their homeland, the devastation of the beauty which they serve. But they are not defeated; they are an army of invincible canaille, and in their humility and patience and obscurity I recognize the bearing of the only genuine aristocracy of this world, and its only true supremacy. I pray they will prevail against the vanity that has arisen on the earth like a profane mutation, a travesty of their own temperate pride; if they do not, their decorum is all that will redeem the desecrated world or lend its ruins a measure of renown. So long as they survive, it has dignity and beauty. They will survive me, I am sure; and beyond the knowledge of that blessing no man's hope can reach.

I am glad Sylvie cannot see the pylon; or its shadow, falling across the shores where she wandered as a child; although she can hear, well enough, all day long, the distant brutal thump of the huge hydraulic pumps sucking the sand out of the cofferdams on the far bank for the laying of the caissons. They are like the footsteps of some invading vandal horde. Sometimes when she is standing at her sink in front of the window, she will pause and listen for a moment and her face will fall into a still, attentive look, as grave and vigilant as that of the ranked gulls on the sand flats down below us. But then she will hear the whistling of plover in the marsh or a flurry of halyards from the docks in a sudden gust of air or the cry of a gull across the harbor sky, and her face will soften in a reassured slow smile and her hands resume their task, the flashing of her fingers as she dries the dishes weaving into that same simple pattern of perpetuity. She is like the gulls; grave, maimed, wild, dauntlessly besieged. I think she understands their language, almost literally, she will stand in such a sisterly affinity among them on the dunes and lift her head to listen to their calls: their languid mewling, their bursts of ire or peaceable dissension, their sudden scalding cries of indignation or ecstasy that spill across the blue air like streams of molten silver. Often she will fill a paper bag with kitchen scraps, crusts of bread and potato peelings and chicken bones, and take it to the beach and stand and fling the bits of refuse up into the air above her head, where a flock of gulls assembles instantly and magically, shrieking and circling and soaring triumphantly aloft as they snatch the morsels from the sky. In her penitence, she seems to have joined them in their lowly, consecrated calling of cleansing the earth of offal, and yet she is as regal in that task as when I see her wading through the mist along the shore like a madonna of the morning, rapt, elite, slender as a scepter. With the eyes she has bequeathed me I see a world made out of light, spun from the spume of stars, stuff without substance, without shadow, the wild flax of the sun, of which are woven her bewildering hair and numinous white flesh and the lustrous sinews of her soul. At dawn I will rise again to bring her its bounty from the silver waters and see again the spires of the village ring with the eternal reveille of light as the island rises streaming in the splendor of its renascence, wrapped in a blinding caul, a shining birth slime, writhing in the throes of its delivery, emerging out of gulfs of light, depthless, radiant wombs.

A Note on the Type

The text of this book was set in a digitized version of Electra, a Linotype face designed by W. A. Dwiggins (1880–1956). This face cannot be classified as either modern or old style. It is not based on any historical model; nor does it echo any particular period or style. It avoids the extreme contrasts between thick and thin elements that mark most modern faces and attempts to give a feeling of fluidity, power, and speed.

Composed by The Haddon Craftsmen, Inc.,
Scranton, Pennsylvania

Display typography by Graphic Technology Inc.,
New York, New York

Printed and bound by Fairfield Graphics,
Fairfield, Pennsylvania

Designed by Cecily Dunham